ZERCY
THE NIRA CHRONICLES
BOOK 2

KORA KNIGHT

ISBN: 9781980488538
Independently published

Edited by Lucas Cornelius

Cover art by LAS-T
www.artstation.com/las-t
https://las-t.deviantart.com/

Text design by Jay Aheer of Simply Defined Art

Titles available from Kora Knight:

The Nira Chronicles
Kríe Captivity (Book 1)
Zercy (Book 2)

Upending Tad: A Journey of Erotic Discovery
Loser Takes All (Book 1)
Test of Endurance (Book 2)
Sideline Submission (Book 3)
Prized Possession (Book 4)
Bringing It Home (Book 5)
Afterglow (Book 6)

THE DUNGEON BLACK DUOLOGY
(An Upending Tad Spin-off: Max and Sean)
Unearthed (Book 1)
Revived (Book 2)

Anthology
This Beautiful Escape (Volume 2)
The short story, "Closing Time,"
featuring a cameo with Tad and Scott.

For my beloved beta team and editor who helped make Zercy possible.

Love you to infinity and beyond.

CHAPTER ONE

* * *

Astrum Industries Search & Rescue
Location: Planet Nira of the Siri Star System
Heart of the Niran rainforests

"Man, this place is wild. I feel like I'm in the Amazon, but in an alternate dimension... tripping balls."

Garret Scott, first captain of the search and rescue team, lifted his brows as he tromped through knee-high foliage. "You've been to the rainforest, Kegan? And done LSD?"

"Yup and yup," his ginger-haired co-pilot chuckled. "Best and worst days of my life."

"Worst? How come?" Eli piped up a few yards back, the former marine's electro-pulse rifle slung over his shoulder. "You almost get eaten by a three-headed anaconda? No wait, by a kaleidoscope-eyed jaguar."

Kegan chuckled again and looked at their six-foot-three escort. "Nope. Those you can shoot. It was the bugs, man. The bugs. The ants and the spiders. Mosquitos the size of your hand."

"Jesus," Helix grunted, blazing a trail up ahead. He'd never admit it, but he was having a blast. Slashing through gargantuan, low-hanging tree leaves with his machete. Hacking through unruly vegetation.

Like Eli, the dark-skinned ex-marine was one of their unit's two large escorts, there to provide safe passage as they searched. Specifically, for the previous team who'd arrived there one year prior. Six Astrum Industries employees just like themselves, sent in the name of exploration.

Unfortunately, the space station lost contact with said team as soon as their ship entered the planet's stratosphere. Many suspected they'd crashed, with damage explaining the lack in communication. Others suspected magnetic interference.

Of course, Garret was inclined to put his money on the former, considering how his own landing went. The crash left his team with only a distress beacon to call for help—just like the first team's beacon that Garret's men were hunting down now.

Paris, their tracker, glanced over his shoulder, his piercing blue eyes half-hidden by loose, black bangs. "I've been to the Amazon twice. Why were you there?"

"My volleyball buddies talked me into it," Kegan answered, stepping over a log. "Learned all kinds of shit. To keep snakes away, we poured salt circles around our tents."

Paris nodded, using a gloved hand to tuck a lock behind his ear. "Tobacco water gets rid of leeches, too. They hate that stuff."

Garret grimaced and glanced around, scratching his dirty-blond scruff. His teammates' exchange of fun facts was making him wary. "Monster mosquitos. Snakes. Leeches. Fucking hell. This 'alternate dimension' better not have *any* of that crap."

Sasha coughed a small laugh.

Garret glanced back at their medic. Traipsing along beside ink-covered Eli, the guy's expression did *not* provide comfort. "Please tell me you were laughing at something unrelated."

Sasha smirked and gave a shrug, his light blond mane brushing his shoulders. "I'm just saying, don't get your hopes up. I hosed you down with that repellent for a reason."

"Great," Garret muttered, reaching down to scratch his shin. Suddenly, he felt itchy all over.

Eli chuckled, shifting his firearm on his shoulder. "Don't worry, Chief. If I see anything crawling up your leg, I'll light that fucker up with my rifle."

Garret laughed. "Soldier, if you relieve me of one of my limbs, you are *fired*."

The escort's wolfish snicker rose up but faded just as fast, lost in the cacophony of the forest; mostly insects, but also a plethora of tree creatures, chirping and squawking and clicking and trilling and chattering their noisy little asses off.

One sound in particular, though, became more apparent than the others. Louder, closer, with an incessant staccato that was disturbingly similar to that of pit vipers. Specifically, the rattlesnake, with its telltale warning rattle. Except, where rattlers gave off a rapid, reedy noise, these jangles were slower—and sounded *heavier*—as if its owners were a more substantial size.

Garret frowned and glanced around. "You guys hearing that?"

Beside him, Kegan nodded, looking just as unsettled.

Up ahead, their tracker stopped. "Yeah. Been keeping tabs on it, actually." Paris peered toward some brush. "I think we're being followed."

"Or hunted." Helix chilled from his hack fest to turn in a circle, his dark eyes keenly searching the vicinity. The rattles grew closer. The marine's gaze narrowed. "Yeah, man. I'm counting at least five."

Paris shook his head. "I hear seven." No one contested. The tracker's wicked hearing was one of his trademarks. That and his uncanny sense of direction.

"Fuck," Garret bit out, reaching for his gun. "So, what you're saying is we got a pack of hungry somethings on our ass?"

"Think so, Chief." Paris nodded.

Awesome. "Alright, guys. Weapon up."

Already clutching his rifle, Eli eagerly scanned their surroundings. "Time to raze some jungle to the ground."

Kegan cursed and pulled his hand-held Ruger blaster from his chest holster. "I hate being prey."

Sasha drew his pistol, too. "How 'bout we fire some warning shots. Scare them away if we can." He frowned and peered around. "No need to kill the wildlife unnecessarily."

The ominous sounds came closer. The tree chatter quieted.

Helix glanced up and glowered at their hidden audience. "It ain't unnecessary if they're trying to eat us."

"They're just following their instincts."

Helix shot Sasha a look. "So am I, Doc. The instinct to survive."

3

The rattles grew louder, more agitated—or maybe excited. Then a few menacing rumbles chimed in, too.

Garret stiffened. "Eli. How 'bout that warning shot, soldier?"

"Alright, but if that doesn't deter 'em, I'm gonna have to move straight to introductions."

"Introductions?" Kegan questioned, raising his pistol with both hands.

"Yeah, *me* introducing *them* to the new top of the food chain."

"Fine. Whatever. Just do it," Garret grated. "Before they beat you to the punch."

Eli loosed a volley of electro-pulses into the canopy above, the bodiless bullets sending the tree life to instant turmoil. Winged creatures scattered from their tall, leafy hiding places, others dove to branches in every direction. Even entities in the groundcover up and took off, rustling the dense foliage all around them. Tense moments later, everything went quiet. Garret and his team warily glanced around.

"I don't hear 'em anymore. Think they're gone?" Kegan murmured.

Paris slowly shook his head. "No. I don't think so. Pretty sure I can still hear their—"

A braying roar tore through the silence as a black beast emerged, launching from the brush straight ahead.

"Shit!" Eli barked, spraying the creature with more heat.

It bellowed, rearing abruptly, then dropped back on all fours, appearing somewhat stunned, but mostly just pissed. It bared its fangs, its position no more than a dozen yards away. Garret gaped at its appearance. Alarming, yet striking, its face like a giant king cobra. Its hide looked like a lizard too, but its body looked like a panther—a panther three times bigger than the norm. Yellow slashes covered its scales. Matching spikes ran down its spine. And at the tip of its tail jutted three ten-inch barbs.

Sasha stumbled back as Helix raced over, his monster knife fully sheathed, a rifle like Eli's clutched in his hands. He arrived just in time as two more lunged from the left. With a shout, he blasted the closest with sizzling slugs.

"Fuck!" Garret shouted, unloading on them, too.

Kegan did the same, hollering wildly as he fired.

But more just kept coming, and while the team's barrage threw them off balance, it definitely didn't stop them from advancing. Hell, some were moving too fast to hit at all. Juking and cutting turns faster than any animal Garret had ever seen, which made predicting their next position all but impossible.

Paris darted to Sasha's side, the pair quickly teaming up, firing their blasters as they stood back-to-back.

The skirmish was deafening; six guns rapidly discharging, their attackers' angry bellows just as loud. Adrenaline slammed Garret's system. His heart pounded riotously. The monsters weren't relenting, barely affected by their firepower, like all their piercing electro-pulses were little BB's. What's more, now the creatures had started tweaking their strategy, making their movements more erratic and harder to track.

"E-mag's empty!" Kegan scrambled to grab another.

It snapped into place just as Garret's ran out. Paris and Sasha quickly fumbled to reload, too. Helix and Eli just kept blitzing with a vengeance, spraying their foes with a stream of asomatous bullets.

"Goddamnit! How many are there?" Garret kicked back into the fray, firing blast after blast as fast as he could.

"Eight—I think!" Paris shouted.

The beasts lunged, jaws snapping. Some took hits. Some dodged. Some jerked backward or sideways, while as others sprang from multiple directions. Their advance was too fast, their erratic movements disorienting. Even Garret's military escorts were getting rattled.

"Motherfucker!" Eli leapt back, barely avoiding the barbs of a tail. "Their hides are too thick! Our ammo's not piercing 'em! Aim for their eyes!"

The team quickly homed in on their faces.

But then one tore out of the brush, slamming Helix hard in the shoulder. Garret watched him go stumbling as the beast chomped down on his rifle and viciously yanked it out of his hands. The firearm went flying.

Helix snarled and quickly righted himself. "Okay, you son of a bitch. *Now* I'm mad."

Manifesting a pistol in the blink of an eye, he unloaded it with a fury into the beast's skull. The creature went down, but right on its heels, another pack mate lunged for Helix's throat. Way too close to fire upon, he slammed its head with the butt of his gun. It staggered to the side, and that was all the time he needed to juice its brain with raw current at point-blank range.

Garret's second e-mag expired. So did the others', but there wasn't any time left to reload. The pack was too close.

"Run!" Eli bellowed, spraying electro-bullets left and right. "They're not backing down! Go! I'll cover you!"

"*What?* No way!" Garret shouted. They couldn't separate.

"I'll catch up in a minute! Now *RUN!*"

Garret hesitated, brutally torn. Goddamnit, they had to stick together.

"*GO!*" Helix roared, yanking a second gun from its holster. With both arms extended, he promptly went to town, pulling his pistols' triggers in quick succession. Eli was his partner, his right hand, his friend. No surprise that he was staying behind to help.

BLAMBLAMBLAMBLAM!

The ex-marines fired furiously, as Garret and the others took off running.

"This way!" Paris shouted. "Up ahead. I see a path!"

They cut slightly left, tearing through the brush, leaping over downed logs, hurdling bushes. Garret's pulse raced chaotically. He could hear Eli's shouts. The two men were already retreating. Not a good sign. Either they were nearly out of ammo, or they'd quickly become overrun by those creatures. God knew, the pair were viciously outnumbered. Last Garret counted, the black beasts' numbers were more than eight.

A few yards to his right, Kegan wove between trees, while to his left, Sasha dashed like a cat. All graceful and shit, but that was just how he moved. Nearly soundless, while Garret and Kegan crashed like rhinos. Up ahead, with a speed and agility that always floored him, Paris led the way like he knew the place by heart.

The soldiers' shouts got louder.

"Move it! *Move it!*" Eli boomed.

Unfortunately, the four's speed was already maxed out. Those rucksacks they were toting were frickin' *heavy*. Just like Garret's, Kegan and Sasha's bounced on their backs, visibly jarring their balance as they ran.

"Faster!" Helix bellowed.

They'd nearly caught up with them. But how? *How in the fuck?* Garret glanced over his shoulder.

Damn it. *That* was how. Both men had straight-up ditched their packs, and the reason why was alarmingly apparent. The creatures were hot on their asses. If the things weren't injured, they would've already taken the guys out.

"Lose your gear!" Garret shouted, shucking his backpack as he sprinted.

It was an order he hated to give, but what was the alternative? Their stuff wasn't going to do them any good anyway if they wound up inside the bellies of those predators.

The team obeyed immediately, rucksacks dropping fast, everyone instantly picking up speed. As Helix and Eli caught up with them, their unit pulled away, steadily growing the distance between their pursuers.

The beasts' heavy paws pounded in the distance, their angry brays echoing into the treetops. Garret glanced over his shoulder. They'd slowed some but were still coming. Hadn't given up. Goddamnit, they must be *really* hungry. Which was disconcerting as fuck, because how long could his team evade them? They only had so much ammo left on their persons.

The sound of rushing water resounded up ahead, followed by Paris' very unhappy curse. Seconds later, the team caught up to him—but only because he'd stopped.

"What's wrong, Paris?" Garret panted. "Why are you stopping? They're still—*Oh, shit.*" Just past Paris' position, between the trunks of countless trees, he spotted a huge drop off... to a river. AKA a cliff. AKA a dead end.

"Fuck!" Eli barked. "Well, come on, let's go left!"

Paris shook his head anxiously. "We can't. The river curves that way. It'd force us back in the direction of those creatures."

"Then to the right!" Garret ordered. "Come on! We gotta go!"

Again, the team took off running, moving parallel to the river. A heartbeat later, though, two of the beasts intercepted their path. Up in the distance, maybe forty yards away. They bared their cobra fangs. Their yellow lizard eyes glowed.

The men slammed on the brakes and did a rapid one-eighty, then beat feet in the opposite direction. But before they could ever even reach top speed, more predators materialized to block that route as well.

The team pulled up short.

"Son of a bitch!" Garret shouted.

With the river behind them, they stared back into the forest, at the only remaining option left to take. It wasn't as if they could dive off the freaking cliff. The water below could be toxic at best. At worst, teeming with creatures worse than these.

But just as they readied to make a dash for it, a third batch emerged in their final option's path. Pushing through the jungle's dense foliage in the distance, their yellow eyes locked like missiles on the team.

"Shit," Helix bit out. "How much ammo you guys got left?"

"Half an e-mag in each pistol," Garret gritted, watching the creatures.

Kegan nodded. "Same."

Paris and Sasha weren't any better.

Eli glared at the beasts, each batch now thirty yards away, licking their chops as they intently stalked their prey. "One e-mag left, and my pulse-rifle's out. Gotta couple boom dogs, though, itchin' to be used."

Helix nodded. "Me, too." He looked at Garret. "I advise we form a semicircle with guns at the ready. Eli and I'll try one more time to deter 'em."

8

Simple translation? This was their Hail Mary, and if it didn't work, they'd be fighting with fists and knives.

Garret's heart thumped wildly as he motioned to the others. "Backs to the river, men. Be ready to fire on my mark."

The team fell into position as, on either side, Eli and Helix lobbed their first couple grenades. Unlike the frags of their militant forefathers, these puppies blew in only half of the time. They hit the ground with heavy thumps just a few feet from their targets. The beasts brayed angrily, but just as Garret had hoped, a few of them couldn't resist taking a sniff.

BOOM!—BOOM!—BOOM!

A mushroom of energy exploded, lancing blade-like shards into their hides.

Howls rent the trees. Some dropped. Others scrambled. Ultimately, only three went down and stayed down. The rest just shook it off as if their bells had been rung, then turned their murderous eyes back on the team. Great, now they looked more pissed than ever. Planting their front paws, they threw their heads forward and roared louder than shit. Leaves everywhere trembled. Garret's ears rang.

"Goddamnit," he bit out.

This was not going well.

Kegan resituated his grip on his guns. "They're like tanks."

"Yeah," Paris chimed in. "With Kevlar skin."

Simultaneously, the beasts charged.

"Again!" Helix shouted. He and Eli chucked two more. Another round of howls erupted as the frag grenades detonated. But the majority kept coming, even as they bled.

"Fuck me," Eli snarled. "After these, I'm frickin' out."

"So am I," Helix grated. "Make 'em count."

The creatures closed in, only twenty yards away, as the very last boom dogs went airborne. But shit, at the rate those ruggedized bastards were suddenly moving, they were going to gallop past before they blew.

"Fire!" Garret shouted. They needed to slow them down.

All around him, guns unloaded, bullet pulses flying furiously.

The creatures reared back—

BOOM!—BOOM!—BOOM!

More prehistoric bellows. Now they sounding angrier than ever.

A few more dropped, leaving five to contend with. Five vicious monstrosities and—no ammo. Garret cursed and dropped his pistols as the others did the same, each man tugging free his last-ditch hunting knives.

The beasts snarled menacingly, teeth bared, eyes blazing, and commenced again, barely ten feet away.

Eli widened his stance and leaned forward, glaring. "Protect your throat and head. They're most likely gonna go for one or the other."

Helix nodded and brandished his machete. "Aim for the same. If you lose your knife, punch their snouts as hard as you can, or gouge their eyes. Whatever you do, just *don't* play dead."

"Jesus," Garret muttered, heart thundering in his chest.

"*Hate* being prey," Kegan repeated.

Sasha muttered a bleak curse.

Paris shook his head. "Under most circumstances, I'm a pretty solid optimist. But, yeah, it was really nice knowing you guys."

"Fuck that," Helix grated. "We're not dead yet."

"Damn straight," Eli bit out. He shot his friend a look. "If I'm going down, I'm taking those motherfuckers with me."

The creatures stalked closer, finally caging them in.

Pausing, they crouched as if readying to pounce, their yellow-barbed tails slashing back and forth.

Garret braced, gripping his knife. Time to do or die. To greet his maker or find a way to deny him. Whatever ultimately happened, he just hoped it happened fast, because getting eaten alive did *not* sound like fun.

But right as the creatures lunged forward with flashing eyes, another set of bellows tore through the treetops. A different kind of roar though, from a clearly different species. Instantly, dark blurs dropped from branches above, landing with keen precision atop the beasts.

10

Instantly distracted, the creatures went ballistic, furiously trying to buck their attackers off.

Garret gaped, utterly shocked, and watched the crazy scene unfold. Huge, dark purple aborigines had just descended out of nowhere and were now flat-out slicing those creatures apart. Snarling with their knees dug into the animals' backs as they gripped their spikes and rode the things like broncos. With one hand, they held on as, with the other, they slashed throats, their jagged blades already glistening with blood. Again and again, the beasts reared back as thick spurts of blood shot from their jugulars.

The team looked on, each face a mask of awe, until several moments later, the slaughter ended. At the feet of the newcomers, all five creatures laid dead, some of their heads nearly severed from their bodies.

Garret swallowed and took his first good look at their rescuers. A half dozen males packed with outrageous muscle, wearing flaps of long, black hide like tribal loincloths. Black dreads draped their shoulders. Small claws tipped their fingers. Gold-pierced horns curved backward from their temples. Pierced horns, just like their nipples and nasal septums, as well as along their big pointed ears.

Chests heaving, bodies splattered in the blood of their prey, they looked at Garret's team and grinned smugly.

Shit. They had fangs, too. Short but *sharp*.

"Beesha," the largest rumbled.

Co-pilot Kegan chuckled warily. "I really hope that means *hi* and not *you're next*."

CHAPTER TWO

* * *

"Keensay tay?" the huge native asked, looking them over.

Garret paused. Damn, the guy's *eyes*. Big and gold like a cat's. Striking didn't even *begin* to describe them.

Eli rubbed the top of his head and made a face. "Come again?"

The other males approached, flanking the speaker's sides.

Their spokesman tried again. "Tay." He gestured to Garret's men, then showed his blood-covered hands. "Keensay tay?"

Paris pursed his brows and glanced at Garret. "I think he's asking if we're hurt."

They cared if they were injured? That had to be a positive.

Garret glanced at his comrades, heart still hammering. "You guys good?"

"Just scrapes and bruises, Chief," Eli answered, eyeing the natives. "Thanks to these big, purple bad asses."

The rest of the team nodded.

Thank God. No one was hurt. Garret looked back at their rescuers. "We're all right." Not that he expected them to understand.

The dark giant smiled as some of his buddies wiped their blades. "Bellah," he murmured. "Genji may."

"Right. Okay." Garret scratched his chin. He had absolutely no idea what he was saying. Oh, well. Why not add some one-way speak of his own? Rubbing his shoulder, he offered a smile. "Thank you… by the way… for the save."

The large male looked down at the beast he'd just slayed, then casually nudged its side with his foot. Like taking down the fucker had been no big deal. Like maybe he hunted their kind all the time. "*Tachi*," he stated.

Garret glanced at the thing. Was he telling him the name of that species?

The other five dropped to their haunches and manned their kills.

He watched as they gripped the beasts' jaws and wrenched them open. Geez. What were they doing? But then the males grabbed their knives and got to work removing the creatures' fangs.

Garret grimaced at the sound of blade grinding against bone, until another noise abruptly stole his attention. A heavy thump at his team's back, only a couple feet away. Evidently, another pack mate had arrived. But before he could do more than turn his head, the large male clutched Sasha's shoulders from behind.

"Meesha," he growled softly, burrowing his face in the medic's blond hair.

Sasha froze like a statue, his blue eyes wide.

"Hey!" Helix barked, shoving forward to grab the male's wrist.

Eli, however, merely did a quarter turn. No doubt, to keep one eye on the rest of the pack while his buddy, Helix, took care of business. Garret moved to assist though, and Kegan came as well. Something the male at Sasha's back didn't seem to like.

Snarling in warning, he bared his fangs, then spun Sasha around and—stopped dead. His expression immediately fell as he raked the medic's face. Clearly, he was disappointed. He hid that shit fast, though. Curling his lip, he let go and glowered at Helix—which Helix took as a clear sign to step off. Smart, that soldier. After all, these guys were huge.

The spokesman smirked at his angry friend. "Mah, Gesh. Mahn meesha."

The male shot him a glare. "Tah, Roni. Deletta et."

Sasha backpedaled fast, bumping into Paris. Helix, on the other hand, stayed put, undaunted.

Garret eyed the newcomer suspiciously. He'd thought Sasha was someone else. As in, another *human*. Which meant, at some point he'd been in contact with the others.

Quickly, Garret ran the first team's file through his brain. He stopped on one man's image in particular. A younger guy. With hair very similar to their medic. Noah, he believed his name was. One of the scientists.

Determined to get some answers, he faced the male directly. "You thought you knew him." He pointed to Sasha. "You've seen others that look like him. That look like us."

The dusky giant clenched his jaw and leveled him with knowing eyes. "Tah," he murmured darkly. "Ocha *hewmens*."

Kegan stilled at Garret's side. "Did he just say 'humans'?"

"Think so." Garret studied the guy, then lifted his chin. "You speak English?"

The male's lips curved. He pinched his fingers. "A *leetle*."

His spokesman friend beamed and nodded. "Bitch."

Garret's brows rose. Bitch? He swapped looks with Kegan.

"Yeaaaah, I don't know about you, Chief," Eli drawled. "But if bitch is the only word this big fucker knows? Doesn't sound like the chitchat between species was all that pleasant."

"Yeah," Helix grunted, narrowing his gaze. "I don't trust them. At all. Something's off."

Sasha frowned and rubbed his nape. "I dunno. He felt pretty friendly just a second ago."

"Right." Paris nodded. "Meaning he was probably friendly with the other team, too."

Eli crossed his arms. "God, I hope not, 'cause that did *not* look like 'friendly' to me. More like 'I'm about to fucking mount you'."

Garret stiffened at the thought and shot the male a look. "Where are they now? The humans. We need to find them."

The newcomer eyed him broodingly. Opened his mouth, then shut it. As if he too knew the language barrier made speaking pointless. Looking to his pack mates, he pointed into the jungle. "Filli. Fin. Miros. Aussa tuga gai."

Three males stood up, two looking identical, and obediently tromped off to God knew where. Guess the newest arrival was this formidable pack's leader. Garret watched the trio leave, then looked back at their boss, still waiting for an answer to his question. What he found though, was the dark male curiously eyeing the team's medic. Must still be thinking about his lookalike.

Garret gestured to Sasha. "You thought he was someone else. Who? What was his name?"

The leader averted his gaze, clearly fighting back a frown. Long moments later, he muttered, "Noah."

14

* * *

The three males returned not too long after, each carrying a load of orange, pear-shaped objects. Kind of looked like fruit, or maybe they were vegetables, although for all Garret knew, they were some kind of freaky eggs.

As they drew to a stop, boss man rumbled off fresh orders, gesturing once again to Garret's team. The trio ambled over and offered each man a share. Then the non-twin, Miros, tossed one to their leader.

The big fucker caught it and turned back to Garret, making a pointed show of taking a bite. "*Gewd*." He motioned for Garret to eat his, too.

"Did he just say 'good'?" Kegan asked, eyeing his gift.

"Think so," Eli answered, studying his, too.

Helix scowled and looked at Garret. "He doesn't seriously expect us to eat this."

"I think he does," Garret muttered, giving his 'pear' a brief sniff. Smelled okay. He turned to Sasha. "Looks safe, but you'd better check it."

The medic nodded, then stilled. "Shit. I can't. The instruments were in my pack."

Fuck. Didn't take long to feel the bite of ditching their stuff. Garret exhaled and dragged a hand down his face. "Right. We should probably go back and look for our gear."

The pack leader shot him an incredulous look. "Mah. Mahneenta kai. Moyos besh dedók tay tacha."

Garret stared at him in utter frustration. He could tell from the male's tone that his message was important, but still had no clue what he was saying. He looked at Paris. "Did you catch any of *that*, by chance?"

Paris frowned. "Sorry, Chief."

Garret turned back to the seven-foot giant. "Look, man," he extended his arms out to his sides, "I can't understand a word you're saying. And we really need our stuff to survive."

He gestured with his chin for his team to head out. This exchange was getting them nowhere, and now that the coast was clear, they needed to find their stuff while there was still light. If any luck whatsoever remained on their side, the scientists would be somewhere near their beacon.

"Mah." The leader threw out his hand to stop them. Features tight, he prompted them again to eat their food. "Eat. Help talk." He ordered his pack to do the same, as if trying to assure Garret the stuff was safe. The natives all but rolled their eyes, but nevertheless took big bites.

"Mmm. Bellah kai," they rumbled, nodding encouragingly.

Their boss grinned at Garret. "Tah. *Gewd.*"

"Oh, my God." Helix grimaced at the males in disgust. "These big, purple bad asses are fucking idiots. Like we can't see through their stupid charade."

The leader shot him one seriously scathing glare, looking as though he'd understood Helix's remark. Jaw clenched, nostrils flaring, he turned back to Garret, clearly discerning him as the human in charge. "*Eat,*" he insisted, sounding frustrated now, too. He pointed to Garret's forehead. "Help talk."

Garret frowned and looked at his fruit again. The male acted as if the stuff would somehow allow them to communicate—which made no sense at all.

Eli eyed the orange pear he'd been given too, then offered up his own brief two cents. "I doubt they're trying to poison us, if that's what you're worried about. I mean, if they wanted us dead," he glanced at the beasts on the ground, "I think they'd've used quicker methods."

"They might not think it's poison," Sasha countered, expression nervous. "It might *not* be poison to them."

The big leader growled in aggravation. "Mah, mahn besh. Bellah. *Gewd. Noah* eat." He pointed to Garret's brow again, a tick forming in his jaw. "Eat. Now. Talk *gewd.*"

"You know what? I say fuck it," Paris chimed in impatiently. "These guys saved our asses. They're not the enemy. And what if we aren't able to find our shit? Eventually we'll have to eat this planet's food anyway. If we can't trust the guys that literally wrenched us from the *jaws of death*, then who in the fuck *can* we trust? Besides, he's *obviously* saying this stuff'll help us communicate. If that's true, that's one serious advantage. Lemme try it, Chief. I won't eat the whole thing. And we've got anti-poison pills in our belt's first aid kits, remember?"

Garret cursed under his breath, but reluctantly gave a nod. Discovering what these natives knew about the scientists *was* important. They might prove helpful in other ways, too.

Sasha frowned.

Helix scowled.

Kegan muttered and crossed his arms.

But as Paris lifted the whatever-it-was up to his mouth, Garret stilled, because his veggie-fruit was different. Not a fat, orange pear, but what looked like an eggplant. Which the native leader did not seem happy about, either.

Bristling, the male stalked over and snatched it away, then shot a venomous glare at the twins. *"Senna`sohnsay?* Mahneeta tay?" he snarled, whapping them upside the head.

The two males grinned wolfishly and rubbed their skulls. "Tah," one murmured quietly. "Senna`sohnsay *gewd.*"

Their leader growled and yanked a pear from one's hand, then turned and irritably handed it to Paris. Paris took it, looking— understandably—a bit warier than before, but nevertheless took a decent-size bite.

Munch—munch—munch—

A smile curved his lips. "Tastes great. Like a strawberry-flavored apple."

Eli quirked a brow and eyed his own. "Yeah? I *love* strawberries."

"Wait till Paris is finished," Garret muttered. "We don't need more than one of you barfing."

The tracker continued cautiously until half of it was gone. Ten minutes passed. He shrugged. "I still feel fine."

Sasha's tense expression eased. "If it was poisonous, it'd've kicked in by now."

The pack's boss smiled and crossed his arms. "Denza?" he rumbled smoothly. "Gai bellah. Reesa tay."

Paris' eyes flared wide as he looked at the male. Then his mouth fell open, too. "Holy shit."

Garret glanced between them. "What?"

"I totally understood him. He said, 'See? The fruit's good. It won't harm you'."

"Shut the front door." A grin spanned Kegan's face.

"No fucking way," Helix muttered.

"That's it. I'm eatin' it," Eli announced. He looked at Garret. "Right, Chief? So we can talk to them? Find out about our boys?"

Garret couldn't believe it. It didn't seem possible. And yet it was exactly the outcome he'd hoped for. "Uh, yeah." He nodded, scratching his head in amazement. Cutting the natives a look, he brought the fruit to his lips and took a tentative bite with his team.

* * *

Twenty minutes later and all kinds of stuff had been sorted, including proper name introductions. Not just of those present though, but of things like the planet—which it turned out was Nira, their sacred 'mother.'

When that concluded, Gesh, their 'Kríe' leader, went on to explain the language barrier—or rather, its disappearance thanks to the fruit. Evidently, its nutrients triggered a kind of awakening, unlocking a portion of the brain humans didn't use. One that involved a type of telepathic communication. Which wasn't to say they could read minds now or anything, just somehow decode the language of other species.

Now, as they sat around on big fallen logs, they finally addressed the specifics about the scientists.

"So you spoke to them?" Garret clarified. "Gave them food like us, and interacted?"

"Tah." *Yes.* Gesh inclined his head. "We fed them and interacted."

"Extensively," the twin, Filli, piped in, grinning.

His brother, Fin, chuffed a laugh and nodded. "Tah, extensively. We helped them do research. It was fun."

Garret frowned at their tone. It sounded suspicious.

The big Kríe named Miros spoke up. "Their leader was strong. Protective." He pointed to Garret. "Had eyes like you."

Alec Hamlin. Ex-combat pilot. Garret remembered him, too. Although, according to his file, Alec's eyes were blue-green, where Garret's, incidentally, were blue-gray.

Garret nodded. "That'd be Alec."

Miros smiled fondly. "Tah." *Yes.*

Roni, the spokesman, chimed in next. "The big one liked to wrestle. He challenged me. I beat him." He shrugged a beefy shoulder. "Still called me bitch."

Eli swapped looks with Helix. "I think he's talking about Chet. The military escort in the file."

Kegan coughed a chuckle, eyeing Roni. "One of their team took on *this* guy?"

The male rumbled, grinning. "He had fire in his veins. I enjoyed our time together very much."

Garret narrowed his gaze, getting a strange vibe off him, too. Like he and his pack were enjoying some inside joke. Sitting straighter atop the log, he looked back at Gesh. "So where are they now?"

The Kríe shuttered his expression. "We went separate ways just two days after meeting. Many moons have passed since."

"Do you know where they went?" Sasha asked, a few seats down.

Gesh slid his eyes to the medic, his gaze lingering on his face, then smiled sadly and shook his head. "Mah." *No.*

"Well, damn," Eli muttered. "That sucks."

"Yeah, it does." Garret exhaled, then looked at Paris. "Their beacon still on your radar?"

The tracker tapped his wristband. "Yup. Still blinking."

Garret nodded. "Alright, men. We should probably get moving."

Across the way, Gesh stiffened. "Mah. You cannot leave."

"We have to." Garret stood. "Gotta find our stuff, and then our people."

Gesh rose to his feet too, and gestured to some of his pack. "Naydo. Miros. Beng. Go find their things." He turned back to Garret. "You stay."

Garret frowned as the three Kríe traded looks, then trudged off.

Kegan sidled up beside him. "That wasn't weird."

"No," Garret muttered. "Not weird at all." Back to suspicious, he crossed his arms. "Why's it so important that we stay?"

Gesh met his eyes and held them. "Because otherwise you will die. And that cannot happen. You are far too important."

Garret stilled, Gesh's sentiment hitting his brain all wrong. It should be comforting, after all, to know the Kríe wanted them safe. That he planned on taking measures to protect them. Instead, all it did was make him feel apprehensive. Like Gesh wanted them alive for his own benefit.

Garret narrowed his gaze again. "Important to whom?"

Gesh's eyes flared hot. Pressing his lips tight, he lifted his chin. "To those you came for. They need you, do they not?"

"Yeah, but why do *you* care? They mean nothing to you. You haven't even seen the guys in ages."

A gravelly growl rumbled in the big Kríe's throat, as if Garret's words had inadvertently struck a nerve. But instead of baring his fangs, or angrily lashing out, he reeled in his ire and stiffly shrugged. "They would want us to help you. And we are kindly creatures."

Roni grinned a few yards away. "*Very* kindly."

Garret cut him a dubious look.

Helix grunted, not sounding sold.

Kegan, however, seemed notably less put off. "Don't mean to sound like the devil's advocate here, guys, but what are our other options? There's no guarantee we're gonna find our gear. For all we know, it's in the possession of some spider monkeys now. And if that's the case, then what do we do?" He dragged a hand through his ginger hair and frowned. "These guys might be handy to have around."

Gesh looked at Garret. "We will escort you to their beacon. Keep you safe from predators."

Garret fought back a shudder at the thought of a tachi repeat.

Sasha nodded. "I like that idea. In case more sniff us out before we find our gear."

"Yeah," Eli added. "And our ammo."

Garret held the Kríe's eyes, still sensing ulterior motives. But maybe he was just frazzled from the attack. Paranoid that everything on this planet was out to get them. He didn't want to put his team at unnecessary risk just because his nerves were shot.

He looked at his co-pilot, his second in command, the man he always defaulted to in times of uncertainty. "So that's your vote? To stick with these guys?"

"It is," Kegan answered, eyeing the purple pack. "I think they're our best bet. At least for now."

A sentiment the rest of the team seemed to concur with. Well, except for Helix. Brows furrowed, muscles tense, their military escort remained silent, staring at the Nirans as if he trusted none of them. Which wasn't really surprising. The toffee-skinned, ink-covered ex-marine trusted no one. With the exception of Eli. He trusted him.

Reluctantly, Garret turned back to Gesh and gave a nod. "Okay. We'll stick together. Thanks for your help."

Gesh grinned, eyes glittering. "Wise choice."

Right. They'd let time be the judge of that.

Garret shifted his weight, anxious to get moving. "Do we need to wait for your guys? The ones you just sent off?"

"Mah." *No.* "They will catch up with us soon enough."

"Okay. Cool." Garret motioned to their tracker. "Alright, Paris. Lead the way."

The black-haired, twenty-seven-year-old studied his wristband, then glanced toward the cliff's edge and frowned. "Shit. The beacon's on the other side of that river."

"Do not fret," Gesh rumbled, happily gesturing to their left. "There is a crossing not too far from here. I will show you."

* * *

"Oh, yeah." Eli nodded as they tromped alongside the river. "Definitely better than getting chased down by more cobuars."

"Cobuars?" Kegan chuckled. "Is that what you're calling them?"

"More fitting than 'tachi.' I mean, fuck, did you *see* them? Face like a king cobra on steroids? With the body of a jag big enough to ride?"

"God." Sasha shook his head. "And to think they almost ate us."

"Don't remind me," Paris mumbled. "Nearly shit myself. For real."

"At least you would've died quickly," Helix tossed in gruffly. "I was a prisoner of war once, and let me tell you, humans are way crueler. They keep you alive."

Eli nodded, but didn't reply.

Garret frowned at the thought, but promptly refocused on the present. Specifically, the fact that they'd been following this river for what felt like a couple eternities. He glanced over at Paris. "How far off our path are we getting?"

Paris checked his wrist gear's intel screen. "A half dozen miles. We'll have to backtrack for a while."

"Wonderful," Garret muttered, looking ahead at Gesh's back.

Leading the way beside Roni, with the twins pulling up the rear, the huge male's demeanor seemed noticeably lighter. As if, with each step he took, he was taking them closer to a location he was eager to reach. But why? Surely a bridge wasn't all that interesting. And if he was anxious to see Noah, why hadn't he tracked him down sooner?

Unsettled, Garret called to the oversized Kríe. "How much farther to that crossing?"

Gesh peered over his shoulder, his dreads shifting against his back. "Not far. Almost there." He smiled and flashed his fangs.

Kegan chuckled at Garret's side. "Damn. Can you imagine getting bit by those things?"

"I'd rather not." He forced a smirk and looked at his friend. "I'm not into vampires. How 'bout you?"

"Depends." Kegan wagged his brows and grinned roguishly. "If the vamp was a babe, I might be game."

Garret laughed before he could tamp it. "True. Only live once."

"That's right, my man." Kegan nodded. "Hence, why we're *here*."

True again, Garret thought as he scanned their surroundings. Adventure, after all, was what drove him. Fueled his fire. What kicked him out of bed every morning. That unquenchable thirst to live hard and never stop. It was a yearning he'd had since as far back as he could remember. To push himself. Go far. Explore his boundaries as well as the universe's. And here he was, getting exactly what he'd wanted.

Well, minus those cobuars who'd nearly eaten them for lunch.

They trudged on for what seemed like another eternity, with Paris peering more frequently up through the trees.

"What's wrong?" Garret asked.

The tracker shook his head. "Just watching the sky. The time spans are different here. Not much daylight left. Maybe five hours, tops."

22

Kegan cut Garret an uneasy look. "We can't travel at night. Gonna have to set up camp."

"With what?" Sasha chimed in, glancing back the way they came. "Those Kríe Gesh sent out have yet to show with our gear."

Garret frowned and called ahead to their guide again. "How long till your guys catch up? And how much farther till that crossing?"

"Soon," Gesh answered, not bothering to look back.

Helix glowered. "That's what you said two damn hours ago."

And still, they trekked on, only breaking to pee or rehydrate, which quickly depleted the water in their canteens. After that, the Kríe provided fruit from trees in the vicinity whose produce were like little juice receptacles. Sweet and refreshing, the liquid didn't just quench their thirst, but kept them feeling satisfied and not hungry.

Didn't keep away the tension though, that was steadily building—in Garret's gut, but especially on Helix's face.

As the convoy resumed, Helix irritably addressed Gesh. "How much longer till we cross this river?" he demanded. "We've been traipsing across this jungle all goddamn day."

Gesh chuckled and slid him a patronizing smile. "Be patient. I assure you, I know where I am going."

"Really? You sure?" Helix bit out, halting. "'Cause, honestly, it doesn't fucking seem like it."

Gesh narrowed his eyes and growled. "You know nothing, *hewmen*."

Helix glowered right back. "I know more than you think."

And, yup, that's pretty much when the other shoe dropped.

Helix heatedly turned to Garret. "He's playing us."

Garret cursed and pulled to a stop. He'd been suspecting the same thing. He shot Gesh a glare. "You've been lying?"

Gesh shook his head. "Your companion is confused."

"The fuck I am," Helix snapped.

Eli quickly concurred. "Not Helix."

Garret clenched his jaw. "Where," he gritted. "Are you. Fucking. Taking us?"

Standing at Gesh's side, Roni amicably smiled. "To your friends, of course. Just as we said."

"Bullshit." Helix pulled out his big-ass machete. "They're up to something. I can feel it. They're lying."

Unfortunately, Garret's gut was saying the same.

These Kríe were deceivers, which made them dangerous.

They needed to part ways with them *now*.

Kegan cursed.

Sasha and Paris appeared just as wary.

Garret slid his men a look. "Time to go."

An order the team seemed happy to obey, but nevertheless, would be impossible to fulfill. Without warning, Miros and Naydo dropped from the trees and yanked Eli and Helix into choke holds. Evidently, the fuckers weren't just sneaky, but strategic; they'd just eliminated their largest threats first.

"Fuck!" Garret barked, charging forward with Kegan, but the twins snagged and restrained them before they could help. The final arrival, Beng, faced off with Sasha who, impressively, managed to land a couple shots. Not really a surprise, though. The medic was tougher than he looked. Excelled in Aikido something fierce. Martial arts that typically worked well against larger adversaries since its strategy utilized the motions of its opponents.

Unfortunately, Beng wasn't the average contender. Once he managed to secure a grip on Sasha? Yeah, the end. These Nirans were just too big and too strong.

A species that took down cobuars like it was nothing.

Roni chuffed in amusement, his hand a manacle around Paris' nape. "Moyos ochay." *Funny creatures.* "As if we would let you just leave."

The marines grappled furiously to get free from their detainers, but Naydo and Miros refused to loosen their holds. Holds that, evidently, were pretty fucking tight, going by the men's blue'ing faces.

Garret fought the full nelson Filli had him in too, but the hulking Kríe's cage wouldn't budge. Glowering, he sliced his venomous glare to Gesh. "What the *fuck* is your problem?" he grunted. "Let us go."

Gesh smirked, like the smug prick he was proving to be, and casually sauntered over to Sasha. Like the others, Sasha's dagger had been confiscated in the scuffle, only his empty gun remaining in his possession. "I do not have a problem," Gesh murmured, clutching

Sasha's jaw. His smirk widened. "Not anymore, that is. Thanks to your team."

Garret gritted his teeth. "What the fuck's *that* supposed to mean?"

Gesh's grin ebbed a little as he stared at the blond's face. "It means you are the restitution I have been waiting for."

Garret wrenched his head to the side to trade looks with Kegan. His co-pilot looked equally as baffled.

Gesh moved to Paris next and confiscated his wristband. "Many moons ago, someone was taken from me, and only one thing will get him back. One specific payment that is acceptable."

Garret swallowed. Oh, shit. That did not sound good.

"Us?" he bit darkly. "My team is the payment?"

"It is." Gesh exhaled a small, contented sigh. "So long I have waited for your arrival."

Garret bristled. "We're not currency. Not your property to trade."

Gesh chuckled and leisurely strode over to Kegan. "Mah?" *No?* "You do not think? Because I am very certain that you are—and have been since the moment my pack first rescued you."

Helix coughed a livid curse and tugged harder on Miros' elbow. Eli dished every defensive move to get free, too. But all that did was spur on their handlers to wrench the men's arms into submissive holds as well.

Heart pounding, Garret struggled too, but as he helplessly glanced around, the truth of Gesh's words swiftly sank in. Once the Kríe had come onto the scene, they'd been under the pack's control but hadn't realized it. To the point that they'd just walked *voluntarily* for *hours* toward whatever fate those bastards had in store for them.

Garret seethed as the big fucker waltzed over to him next. "Let us go," he grated, peering angrily up at him, "and we'll help you get what you want. We've got firearms."

Gesh's golden eyes hooded, a soft chuff sounding in his throat. "Your firearms are worthless. Look how they served you thus far. You were nearly eaten by a pit of tachi. And now, detained effortlessly by my pack."

"We were taken off guard by those *things*," Garret snapped. "And you motherfuckers deliberately tricked us. If we had the chance to strategize, we could come up with a plan and—"

"Mah," Gesh cut him off. "I am not interested in your plans. You and your team are my one and only option. I have waited long enough. I will not risk it."

"But—"

"Quiet, *hewmen*," he snarled, his mood snapping to glacial. "Or I will silence you myself with a muzzle." Features tight, he stalked to a liana-covered tree and irritably broke off the vines. "Bind them," he ordered, tossing the tendrils to his pack. "We go to the castle *now*. I want my meesha."

CHAPTER THREE

* * *

"I can't *fucking* believe this," Garret muttered to Kegan, glaring down at his tied wrists as they walked. And he meant that literally, because what were the odds? The chances they'd have this kind of shit-ass luck?

Although, he supposed in the grand scheme of things it did make sense. Crashing, then hunted by cobuars, then straight-up captured? That was three strikes right there. The big, fat universal, *you're out.*

Not that he planned on accepting this crappy hand for long. Just needed some time, a way to outsmart these brutes. Because, clearly, only intellect could save them now.

Kegan exhaled and glanced around. "Well, I guess there *is* a bright side to this whole fucked up mess."

Garret shot him an incredulous look. "A *bright* side? To *this?*"

"Yeah. I mean, think about it. As much as it blows being captives to these jacks, it'll always be way better than being lunch."

Garret supposed he had a point, but their situation still sucked. And who knew what would happen once they got traded. What if their new handlers viewed them as *dinner* like those tachi?

Looking around, he noted Paris eyeing the sky again. He glanced up, too. It was well past midday. How long were Nira's evenings? Hopefully longer than Earth's. The jungle already looked darker—and it'd been naturally dark to begin with.

He frowned and looked back at Kegan. "We need to escape before we get to that castle, while we can still fucking see where we're going."

His friend's expression didn't seem very optimistic. In truth, Garret wasn't so much, either. "I know. I'm keeping my eyes peeled for any opportunity. But if we can't?" Kegan gestured with his chin toward the leader. "Who do you think he's exchanging us for?"

Garret shrugged—then grimaced in pain. Son of a bitch. The vine between his thighs that his bound hands were attached to, the one that connected to his new collar from behind—it just abraded his nuts for the umpteenth time just from barely lifting his shoulders.

He clenched his jaw, "Good question," then called to the Kríe leading the way. "Hey, Gesh. This meesha you want back so badly—who is he and why's he so important?"

Gesh glanced over his shoulder. "That is none of your concern."

"The hell it's not," Helix bit out from the back of the line. Back of the line, meaning the end of the leash that the whole team was tied to. Single file. Like slaves. "We're getting traded for this Joe. I'd say it couldn't concern us *more*."

Gesh slid the marine a slow, superior smile. "Perhaps, but since *your* concern is not a concern of *mine*…"

Helix rumbled deep in his throat, his resentment straight-up spiking. Garret could feel that shit rolling off him from yards away.

"Wow," Eli piped in. "You, my man, are something else. Surely your mama taught you better."

Gesh pulled up short and pivoted around, his big eyes locking hard on Eli's face. "My *mama*?" he muttered menacingly. "Are you referring to *Nira*?"

"I don't know," Eli shot back. "Is Nira your mom? 'Cause if she is, she should be ashamed. She raised one grade-A fucking *cunt*."

All went still, as if the oxygen had been sucked from the jungle. Then, as one, every Kríe let loose a growl. The dark menacing kind. As if they all planned to pounce at once. With claws out and ready to start shredding.

Garret tensed. What, were they all brothers or something? All equally offended by Eli's quip? Kegan cursed under his breath. Paris and Sasha did the same. Helix, however, stepped forward to face-off with whoever. Garret could tell because the gunman's dark face had gone darker, his expression a mask of try-it-asshole-and-die.

Gesh bared his fangs ominously, and stalked his ass over, shoving Helix out of the way like he weighed nothing. Helix stumbled, trying to right himself as Eli shifted to defense mode, but his hands trapped by his crotch made blocking impossible. Gesh seized his throat and drove him backward into a tree, dragging all on the leash along for the ride.

Eli's skull hit the trunk with a hearty whack, but before he could react, Gesh was inches from his face, dark rumbles vibrating from his chest. "You speak her name again and I will rip out your tongue." He tightened his grip. "You provoke the wrong Kríe."

Eli coughed and jerked his head as, in the blink of an eye, Helix rammed his muscular shoulder into Gesh's side. "Fuck you, motherfucker! Get your goddamn hands off him!"

Gesh tottered from the hit, but quickly regained footing, snarling as his pack lunged to engage. Like they'd been biding their time, waiting for the opportunity, eager to get rough for any reason.

"No!" Garret dove in like an armless defensive lineman.

Kegan followed his lead, and just like that, Paris and Sasha were plunging in, too. Probably figured what the hell, they'd be there no matter what, with that leash keeping them all in such close quarters.

A fist met Garret's jaw, then an elbow nailed his ribs, but he was too busy ramming another Kríe to fully register it. Adrenaline slammed his veins, his heart hammered furiously, as again and again, he shouldered snarling males. He had to, though. Had no choice. Those bastards kept going for Eli and Helix, lunging for them with the clear intent to maim. Hell, in truth they'd probably have *ended* them by now had they not needed Garret's team to make that trade.

Angry bellows filled the forest of both human and Kríe alike. Unfortunately, Garret's men were losing the fight. Not that they ever really had a chance, but hey, the instinct to survive was a powerful thing.

Sharp claws slashed Garret's shoulder. And, yeah, *that* one he felt. Belting a curse, he whirled around, ready to line drive a motherfucker into the ground. But what he saw instead had him stopping in confusion—Roni, still as a statue, his expression that of shock, as an angry snarl ripped past his lips.

What the hell?

But then Miros and Beng responded the same, each one hissing as he grasped a bleeding body part. Garret's eyes flared wide. They'd been shot with arrows. Or at least by something that looked really similar. Another pack mate roared, then another after that. Jesus. Their convoy was being fired upon by some foe. Some unforeseen opponent just as shrewd.

"*Tohrí*," Miros snarled.

Others angrily echoed the same.

And then Gesh got hit right beneath his shoulder. Throwing his head back, he roared in fury, ripping the arrow free as he glared up into the trees. The rest of the pack trained their heated eyes upward too, all attention diverted away from the humans.

"Get down!" Garret motioned for his team to seek cover.

The last thing they needed were arrow injuries. Each man's mini first-aid kit was fine for the small stuff, but puncture wounds would require Sasha's supplies—one of the many things that they still didn't have because those motherfuckers never got their gear.

They scrambled as one under a huge nearby bush, haphazardly tripping and stumbling as they dashed.

Once hidden, Garret peered through the branches at the craziness.

Now Kríe were dodging an incessant barrage, each male at one point trying to scale a tree. No doubt, to get ahold of their unwelcome ambushers and rip them apart limb by limb. Regrettably for them, that just made them easier targets against an adversary with one seriously wicked aim. Forced back to ground, bodies bleeding from countless wounds, they furiously bellowed, then retreated.

Gesh was the last to go though, which Garret supposed shouldn't surprise him since the team had seemed to mean the most to him. Holding his breath, he watched from the brush as the Kríe anxiously scanned the vicinity—no doubt for the humans he'd just lost. A couple more arrows connected, and still he searched, his face a mask of rage and desperation.

Back-stepping, he grimaced and pulled a shaft from his side, then snapped it with a roar and took off—out of sight to Garret's team, but evidently not to the ambushers, because they instantly tore off in hot pursuit. Not that Garret could see them. He could only *hear* them leaving. Or rather, just the rustle of branches above swiftly fading in the direction Gesh had bolted.

When it appeared they were alone, Garret turned back and cleared his throat. "You guys okay?" Holy hell, his heart was hammering.

All five men nodded, some eyes wider than others. All sporting at least a couple of bleeding cuts.

"We need to go," Helix muttered. "As soon as they lose those archers they're gonna be hunting us down."

"Agreed," Garret concurred. He looked at their tracker. "Think you can get us close to where we started from?"

Paris rubbed his wrist where his tracking band used to be, then glanced up through the bush. "Yeah. I'll get us there."

Garret was confident of that, too. Had merely asked to prompt a move-on. Paris' sense of direction was always stellar.

Eli grunted as they rose up and exited their cover. "Just make sure to take us back a different route. No need to make it easier for them to find us."

Paris frowned and peered around. "We should cover our scent. Keep your noses alert for pungent plants."

"Awesome," Kegan murmured as they kicked it into gear. "Get to cover our sweaty butts with even stinkier funk."

"If we're lucky," Sasha pointed out, "it'll help us on a couple of fronts. To hide our scent from their pack while deterring other predators, too."

Garret scanned their surroundings. "I'll second that notion. Don't need any more tachi on our asses."

"Cobuars," Eli corrected. He slowed to reach for a leaf— "Shit. My nuts," he grunted. "These goddamn vines. Wish I had my hunting knife."

"And my machete." Helix glared at their binds and shook his head. "We gotta find something to cut these off."

Paris nodded as they picked up the pace again. "True, so keep a lookout for sharp objects, too."

"That's gonna be easier said than done soon," Sasha muttered, peering upward. "Nightfall's coming fast. It's almost dark."

Garret cursed at the ramifications of those sobering words. Because what in the fuck were they going to do then? No way should they be traipsing around with a bunch of nocturnals. With their luck, they'd all be ravenous carnivores. But they couldn't exactly set up camp either, and not just because they didn't have tents. It'd be a sure-fire way to let Gesh's pack catch back up with them.

Beside him, his ginger co-pilot frowned as they jogged. Was Kegan thinking the same thing?

"Once it's night, we're totally screwed."

Yup. *Exactly* the same thing.

"Nah." Eli glanced around. "Just keep your eyes peeled for extra-big trees. If we find one of those, we can hollow the ground beneath it. Hunker down under its roots and cover up."

"Right," Sasha agreed, second in line to climb over a log. "'Cause sleeping up high's definitely out of the question."

Paris peered back up through the trees at the sky—or what could be seen of it, anyway. "An hour or two of light left at the most."

"Outstanding," Helix muttered.

Garret opened his mouth to agree, but paused when he caught a whiff of something. He slowed and looked around, inhaling deeper through his nose. "You guys smell that? Think it's strong enough?"

"Hell, yes." Kegan nodded. A wry grin curved his lips. "Come to think of it, it kinda smells like skunk weed."

"Yeah, it does," Sasha chuckled. "A stink that just won't quit."

Garret pointed to some shrubs. "I think it's coming from those."

"Hurry," Eli bit quietly, glancing over his shoulder. "I suddenly got a feeling we're being followed."

Son of a bitch. They'd been antagonist-free for what, ten minutes?

"Just break off a branch," Garret grated as they hustled. "If they're close enough to sense, then we seriously gotta *move*."

But right as they made it to the big stinky plant, something soared whisper-fast past Garret's head. He sucked in sharply, every muscle locking tight. "Did you see that?"

"No, but I heard it." Kegan peered around.

Another two whizzed by.

"Down!" Helix barked. "They're arrows."

Holy hell. The band of *archers*? *They* were the ones following them?

Three more tore past.

The team dropped in a hurry—but once down in the groundcover, the arrows stopped.

Goddamnit. Heart thundering, Garret lowered his voice. "Anyone hit?"

"No," they rasped in unison.

"Although, *how* makes no sense." Helix shook his head. "Their aim with those Kríe was spot on."

"So they're trying to scare us away?" Garret scowled. "Then why follow us?"

Nobody seemed to have a logical answer to that. As their hushed talking ceased and the eerie silence descended, he wondered if this could get any worse.

Above, subtle rustlings resounded from the trees. And then things went quiet again. Too quiet.

"We see you, little oddlings," came a silky, amused voice. "It is safe to come out now. We are done."

Garret swapped looks with Kegan. "Gesh wasn't lying about the fruit. We really *can* understand other Nirans."

"Understand them, yeah," Helix muttered. "*Trust* them, no."

Paris frowned. "Seems to me we're in their crosshairs no matter what."

"Shit. Something's crawling on me," Eli gritted irritably. "I vote we stand up and say hello."

Cursing under his breath, Garret reluctantly nodded. Because honestly, Paris was right. They didn't have much of a choice.

Yet again, they'd been goddamn cornered.

Tentatively, they rose to their feet and glanced around. Nobody. Anywhere. Garret lifted his gaze—and froze.

"What the *fuck?*" Kegan murmured.

Yeah, what the fuck indeed.

Unmoving amidst the darkening canopy above, small golden entities blazed brightly.

"What are they?" Eli frowned. "Some kind of freaky, alien fireflies?"

Sasha stared at them intently. "They don't look like they're flying. Just hovering or something… with no wings."

In fact, they didn't seem to be *alive* at all. Just clusters of angular shapes, sleek and graceful. All different, with inexplicably sharp edges. They were captivating. Mesmeric. And yet bizarrely intimidating. And, damn, the way they glowed, blackening-out everything around them? It made them stand out that much more.

Helix turned a slow circle. "There's a batch in every direction."

And those batches were staying *suspiciously still.*

Garret narrowed his eyes. Glanced from cluster to cluster. Were these what had talked to them? No way.

Whatever. They didn't have time for games.

"Well?" he called out. "Here we are. Where are you?"

A chuckle that reminded him of a cool, refreshing breeze drifted down from the direction of one of the clusters. "You are looking right at us. Would you prefer we move closer?"

Garret stilled, gaze locked on the cluster that just spoke. "Do you promise not to shoot us?"

"Ah well, now see, that depends. Do *you* promise not to run away again?"

Garret stared at the glowing shapes. They'd moved a little—but as one. As if they all were somehow firmly connected. He glanced at Kegan. His friend looked just as wary. After all, nothing on this planet had proven trustworthy so far. Why would this species be any different?

But again, what were their choices? If they didn't stay put, they'd probably end up pin-cushioned with arrows.

He glanced at Eli and Helix. Eli shrugged. Helix sighed.

Yup, Garret's sentiments exactly.

He looked back up and nodded. "Yeah. We promise."

"Marvelous."

He could hear the male's smile in his tone. Although, unlike the Kríe, it wasn't smug. More like, well, pleasantly satisfied. But before he could put much more thought into that, those strange, glowing shapes abruptly dropped. Not much, but enough to reveal the silhouette of a male, one who'd just sank to his haunches atop a branch.

Crouched, he canted his head and looked at Garret. "See me now, oddling?" His voice dipped a little bit lower. "Or perhaps you would like me even closer."

Garret's lips parted in surprise. Those shapes weren't clusters of an entity. They were actual markings on the male's body. Glowing designs that ran across his chest. And down his arms. And up the center of his abs.

Garret stared. So did his team. "Uh..." He cleared his throat. "Closer... Sure."

The Niran smiled again, and this time Garret saw it. His span of white teeth. And little *fangs.*

"Very well." Like a nimble cat, he dropped from his perch, with the rest of his band following suit.

They touched down damn near soundlessly, despite their size, which appeared slightly shorter than the Kríe. Only by a few inches, though, standing maybe six and a half feet. And their builds were leaner too, like basketball players. All slender and cut, where Kríe, on the other hand, looked much more like big, ripped pro-wrestlers.

Garret watched as the sole speaker straightened from his landing, then watched as his markings went dark. Like he'd hit some kind of internal light-dimming switch in his skin. Some strange source of bioluminescence.

Garret regarded him in a new light—or lack thereof. Because now that those markings weren't glowing anymore, the male in his entirety was much more visible. Not merely the silhouette of a tall, toned body. And truth be told, he was quite a sight.

If Kríe were smoldering demons, these guys were angels.

Minus the halo and innocent vibes.

But they *did* exude *something*, he just couldn't discern what. Maybe because he was too busy staring. Couldn't help it, though. Every aspect of the male's appearance was fascinating.

Like his eyes; larger than a human's, with dark-chocolate irises ringed in gold. Irises, incidentally, that were larger than humans' as well, leaving much less space around them for white. His pupils seemed bigger too, and likewise ringed in gold, making his alien gaze feel downright piercing.

Garret shifted as he took in the rest of his face. Masculine, but not brawny. Deeply tanned. Flawlessly chiseled. As if meticulously sculpted from caramel granite. Each feature, perfectly smooth. A strong, defined jaw. Refined nose. High-molded cheekbones. Well-shaped lips.

The poster boy, in essence, for ethereal virility. Which, okay, sounded like a total oxymoron. Garret just couldn't think of any other way to describe him.

His gaze slid to the Niran's mane of long white-blond hair. Draped over one shoulder, its silky-straight locks looked like liquid sunshine cascading down a cliffside. Not that it glowed or anything. Just lots of warm white, finespun with hints of blond honey.

Some of the males had the sides of their hair braided. Others had the top half pulled back. The one talking to Garret though, had a little of both, with more tucked behind his pointed ears. Pointed ears that had cuffs, but also piercings—three studs from his tragus to his helix. Exotic for sure. The Niran females there must love them.

Garret's gaze dropped to his attire. Goodbye angelic, hello elvish warrior… with one seriously minimalistic version of armor. No joke. All he sported were sleek metal guards—three sets: for his shoulders, shins, and forearms. That was it. The only other stuff he had covering his body? Dark sandals, a belt for weapons, and some kind of mini man-skirt. Oh, and a quiver on his back and thigh—both of which still visibly stocked.

Garret looked him over. Yup, other than that, just bare skin.

That was tan. And visibly firm.

With lots of muscle.

The male took a step, then stopped and leaned forward. "Now, little strangeling? Surely you see me now."

Garret frowned at his tone. He was dealing with a smartass. "My name is *Garret*," he muttered. "And yeah, I can see you… now that you've turned off your light bulbs."

The male's lips curved. Casually, he straightened and looked at his comrade. "What are light bulbs?"

His friend grinned. "A strangeling thing."

Garret slid him a droll look.

Paris coughed a laugh.

Eli and Kegan chuckled.

Helix just grunted.

The first male's smile widened as he turned back and tipped his head. "Seekesáy." *Greetings.* "I am Airis. Of the Tohrí."

Garret nodded once. "Nice to meet you… Airis of the Tohrí." Quickly, he introduced each of his men.

Airis did the same, starting with Kato, the one who'd answered his little light bulb question.

36

Eli frowned and glanced around. "Wait… There's only *four* of you?"

Airis cocked a brow. Canted his head. "You prefer there would be more?"

Eli blinked, then chuckle-snorted. "No. I just—"

"Right," Helix scoffed. "Only *four* of you drove off those Krie."

Airis glanced at his band with a tiny little smirk. "They are not so tough. And so much slower than our arrows. Although, they did manage to elude us. I will give them that."

"So, you're saying they're long gone?" Sasha asked, sounding hopeful.

"I believe so, leí." *Yes.* "But our *dekdónni* are scouting the area."

Paris frowned. "What are 'deck donny'?"

Good question, Garret thought. Hopefully a backup of buddies.

"Our allies and faithful companions." Airis paused and peered past them, toward the river they'd just fled from. His pointed ears twitched. "Ah. Here they come."

Kato smiled with a nod, then right on cue, a faint snapping of twigs sounded in the distance. Garret turned to get a look, but couldn't see much. Just far-off shrubs and trees jostling briefly.

Wait.

He saw something.

Garret narrowed his gaze, then froze ramrod stiff with a curse.

Charging their way were four *really* large animals. Like cobuar-size animals. Moving *fast*.

His teammates went rigid.

Helix went for his machete. Yeah, the one he no longer had.

Likewise, Eli reached for a rifle that wasn't there. "Please tell us those things are your pals."

"Leí." Airis grinned. "And mine is winning."

Garret cocked a brow and watched as the four beasts bound closer, some rocketing from branch to branch, others tearing up the ground. They ran like the tachi, like big predator cats, yet somehow their movements looked more fluid. And where the tachi were black with streaks of mustard yellow, these mugs wore coats of butterscotch fur.

They came up fast and slammed on the brakes, those racing on the ground taking the win. Their rivals yelped crossly, then dropped from the trees, landing with soft, muted thumps.

Garret stared, jaw slack, but he wasn't alone. Every member of his team was doing the same. Why? Because holy ancient mythology, Batman, the things looked like big, modified griffins. The only notable differences? One, true griffins were lion-size, and these… these had the mass of a saber tooth.

And where griffins were said to have the wings and head of an eagle, these only had the massive wings. Or at least he *assumed* they were massive, to carry all that weight, since the things were currently folded against their sides. And the wings looked different, too. It was hard to describe. Like they were covered in soft, suede scales instead of feathers.

And now that the big beasts were close enough to scrutinize, one could see that those same scales covered their bodies. Bodies that reminded him of short-haired lynxes. Big paws. Sharp claws. A small, strong tail. Even their folded-back ears had those tufts. They *did* still have beaks, however, instead of muzzles. But they were subtle beaks. Compact. Like a gyrfalcon.

One trotted over to Airis and nudged his arm, then turned its head and studied Garret's team. Intently. As if sizing them up. Which wasn't surprising. They were clearly these guys' pets, and pets were protective.

Although, that other one *did* just lick its chops.

No. Surely their owners kept them properly fed…

Garret warily cleared his throat. "So… These are… dekdónni?"

"Leí." *Yes.* "And since they have all returned, we can assume the Kríe have fled a great distance."

A chorus of exhales resounded from the team.

"God, that is…" Kegan chuckled and rubbed his nape. "That is so unbelievably freaking awesome."

Paris and Sasha traded smiles.

"Ha!" Eli bumped Helix with his shoulder. "You hear that? We're back on top of the food chain."

His broody, right-hand man smirked and shook his head—then sobered back to serious and peered north. "I want my machete. And we need our stuff."

Too true. And time was wasting.

Garret nodded in agreement and looked at Airis. "So, you're not gonna shoot us, right? We're free to go?"

Airis' friendly smile faded. He flicked his band a look. Casually, the four reached behind their backs, pulled an arrow from their quivers, and drew their bows.

"Hmm. Not exactly." Airis aimed for Garret's head. "I think we should like you to stay."

"Son of a bitch," Helix cursed.

The dekdónni bared their fangs.

Goddamnit, Garret thought.

Not again.

CHAPTER FOUR

* * *

— ONE YEAR EARLIER —
Astrum Industries Science & Exploration Team
Location: Castle Múnrahki, Mighty Realm of the Kríe

"I'm gonna kill 'em. Every last one of 'em. Gonna beat their asses, and then kill 'em."

Alec Hamlin, captain of Astrum Industries' science and exploration team, slid their military escort an irritable look. "Not sure retribution's really part of your job description."

Chet glowered his hard gray eyes at the guards leading them down the castle corridor. After having been sold by Gesh's pack to the Kríe king just moments earlier, the big crew-cut marine was less than happy. "Consider it on the house. I'm feeling generous."

"Good luck with that," their co-pilot muttered, sounding less than optimistic. Peering ahead past Bailey, Jamis, and Noah, then over his shoulder past more guards, Zaden cursed and shook his head of jet black hair. "Gotta escape to catch up with them, but we're not going anywhere. This prison they dumped us in's sealed too tight."

An assessment Alec unfortunately had to agree with. There were guards literally everywhere; patrolling the corridors, stationed at junctions, not to mention all the eyes and ears of loyal servants. And then, of course, there was the biggest obstacle; the six Kríe assigned to them personally. Specifically, the purple mammoths walking with them now, leading them by their group leash to some bath house. Or at least, that's where Alec assumed they were going, since the king had specifically instructed it.

But even if they could somehow pull a slip on their handlers, they couldn't just jump out a window and be free. And not because the drop was too far to handle. They were still on ground level, so that'd be cake.

It was the castle's outer wall that'd be the pisser. Easily thirty feet tall, there was no way to climb it. Unless they had rope, which they didn't.

Alec swore under his breath and scanned their surroundings. After exiting through a door in the main hall's back corner, the guards had ushered them left down a corridor. Long and commodious, it extended forever, offering more of the same décor as the foyer. More whitewashed stone walls. More masculine-carved statues. More wrought-iron chandeliers with pillar candles.

The aroma of prepared foods filled the large expanse, too. The freshly-baked bread, cheese, and meat were easily discernible, as was the fragrance of sweet pastries. Alec's stomach rumbled. A kitchen was somewhere close by, although he sensed it was in the opposite direction. As in, not behind any of the doors they'd just passed, and definitely not behind that exceptionally large set up on the right. Alec eyed the pair curiously, so majestic and ornate. Clearly, they provided entry to somewhere very important. Not that he could see where. The fuckers were closed.

Finally, they reached the end of the hall, at which point they took a right and kept going. Not for much longer, though. A dozen yards down, they came to a stop. Right in front of a set of double doors. Not huge ones like that other pair, but they were still pretty big. Then again, everything felt big in this castle. Which he supposed made sense since it was built for big-ass Kríe.

Alec felt the humidity even before the guards pushed open the doors.

Yup, the bath house.

And, damn, what a bath house it was.

His brows rose as the six Kríe ushered them in, the one in front pulling them unyieldingly by their leash. The place was big—like, *really* big—its 'bath' easily sixty feet long. A walkway circled its perimeter, and down the length of each side stood a half dozen pillars connected by decorative arches. Large sconces lined the walls, while in the water, exotic flowers floated serenely. Red, with pointed petals, they reminded Alec of small lotuses. And wow, he could smell them from yards away. Sweet and inviting, their fragrance like a siren, beckoning him to join them in the water.

Not that he had the option to sit this one out. By the way the guards were pulling his team toward the steps, taking a soak in this bath was clearly non-negotiable.

A couple of the Kríe got busy cutting them free. Their wrist binds, then the collar around their necks.

"Take off your clothes," the largest guard ordered.

The trio tensed uneasily, but Chet just glared. "How about I take off your head instead?"

Zaden rolled his dark brown eyes.

Alec groaned and pulled off his tank top. "C'mon, guys. Let's just do this. Definitely not the battle to pick."

Jamis, one of their astrobiologists, followed his lead. "This place could be worse."

Noah, the other biologist, eyed the water. "Right. If it's good enough for royals..."

Bailey, the third scientist, shucked his clothes and stepped in. "*Ahhhh...* Hell yeah... It's warm."

Alec was first to join him, and as the rest filed in, the guards took up posts around the pool. Arms crossed, stances spread, looking openly bored—and maybe a little irritated to be babysitting.

Alec waded in deeper until water lapped his pecs, then reached for one of those exotic red flowers. Definitely not waterlilies. These weren't attached to anything. Fresh ones were probably tossed in every day. The others drew to a stop a few feet away, Noah looking especially unhappy.

"They're not coming back, are they?" he murmured. "This is it."

"They couldn't even if they wanted to." Bailey frowned and glanced at the guards. "They'd never get past the front gates."

Noah pursed his lips, then shook his head. "If he wanted it bad enough, he'd figure out a way."

And they all knew exactly who he was referring to. Gesh. The pack leader who'd sold them to the king. The same Kríe whom Noah clearly had it bad for. Although, how he'd grown so attached so fast, Alec couldn't quite understand. He sure as hell didn't have feelings for Miros. Then again, unlike Noah, he wasn't gay and didn't have that innate, natural tendency.

"I don't think it's that simple," Zaden told the blond scientist. "There's only a small pack of them, but the king? This castle? Shit, this place is swarming with soldiers."

Noah's angry façade faltered. He glanced down at the water. "How could he do this? He likes me. A lot. I felt it. How could he just up and *sell* me?"

"Because he's not like us," Jamis pointed out, raking his brown hair out of his eyes. "He doesn't think like us. He's not human. Hell, I doubt he even recognizes that he likes you."

That didn't appear to make Noah feel any better.

"No." Alec shook his head. "He'll be back when he's able."

Noah looked at him. "You really believe that?"

"Yeah. I mean, think about the shit we just witnessed. Cool-and-collected Gesh losing his ever-loving mind. Giving the *king's guards* a beat down just for touching you. For fuck's sake, they had to friggin' *drag* him away, Noah." He chuckled darkly. "Yeah, I'd say he's coming back."

"Good," Chet muttered. "Saves me from having to hunt him down." He cracked his wet knuckles and glared at the door. "His big, grape ass had better bring Roni."

The team paused to look at him. So close, Alec could see the Kríe's bite mark perfectly, the one he'd left at the base of Chet's neck. Thing was, the teeth marks weren't an angry, inflamed red, but more like a smoldering, deep purple.

Chet shrugged with a grunt. "What. I told you, I'm gonna beat his ass, then kill 'em. I'm not all forgiving like 'meesha' over here. I hold grudges. Exact justice."

"You mean *revenge*," Bailey corrected.

Noah scowled. "I don't forgive him. That asshole can kiss my ass."

"Good." Jamis nodded. "He doesn't deserve forgiveness."

"Or his front fucking teeth," Chet added darkly.

The guard at his back chuckled. "Moyo ochay."

Chet turned around and glared poison daggers at the guy. "No, you purple kumquat. I'm not a funny creature. I'm a fucking *pissed off human*, ready to murder."

The big Kríe smirked and shrugged a beefy shoulder. "I wish you the best. I hope you succeed. Gesh is a bane we do not need."

"Yeah, a real bane." Chet's eyes went all shrewd. "So how 'bout you let us go so we can off him."

"Mah."

"*Come on.*"

"Mah."

"But—"

"Be quiet, moyo. Take your bath."

Bailey muffled a snort.

Chet looked at him and glared. "You think that's funny?"

"Chet," Alec ground out. "Shut the fuck up for once. I can't frickin' think with all your bitching."

"Fine. Whatever." Chet curtly turned away. Then just like that, was off rocking a perfect front stroke.

Good. Blow off some steam. Alec needed to as well.

Zaden exhaled and dragged a hand back through his stick-straight bangs. "We need a plan, but I got nothing."

Alec glanced toward the door. "Yeah, me neither. But one will present itself eventually. It's got to."

Bailey sank beneath the water, then stood back up and shook out his curly brown hair. "Well, at least we're not in any immediate danger."

Jamis wiped his spattered face. "True. They don't appear to wanna kill us."

"No, they don't." Noah scooped up a flower. "But they *do* want us smelling good. Question is, why?"

"So we don't stink?" Bailey chuckled.

Noah slid him a look. "Yeah. Meaning someone's gonna be sniffing us. But who? Who's gonna be that close?"

Alec tensed. Zercy would be. Somehow, he knew this instinctively. Hell, the king had already been close enough to smell Gesh's pack on Alec earlier. That was the very reason they were taking this bath now. His heart thumped faster. Zercy had called him 'pet.' What if he'd meant that literally?

Abruptly, the big, double doors shoved opened, lending the way to two more Kríe.

The guards playing babysitter acknowledged them but stayed silent, as if the approaching pair held some unspoken authority.

The two came to a stop at the edge of the pool. "It is time," one said, his timbre rich like caramel. "One of you must come with us. Now."

A chill raced up Alec's spine. He had a bad feeling about this. Frowning, he turned and faced them. "To go where?"

"The physician's chambers. To meet with Sirus."

Aw, fuck. That was the Kríe Zercy mentioned earlier. The one he wanted them taken to for 'tests.'

He cleared his throat. "And if we refuse?"

"Then we will forcibly take all of you."

Damn it.

He was the captain, which made this his burden. Time to go down with the ship.

Clenching his jaw, he squared his shoulders. "I'll go."

"What?" Zaden piped up. "Alec. Wait. No."

Alec met his friend's gaze. "You're in charge while I'm gone."

"No, way. I'll go," Chet announced from behind.

Alec turned to him. "No, Chet. I appreciate it, but I'm captain."

"Yeah, and I'm the bodyguard." Chet marched through the water. "I'm to keep all you jacks out of harm's way, remember? Definitely, indisputably, part of the job description."

"Right, which is why I need your ass to stay put. You're to look after the team. *That's* your damn job. And you can't do that if you're gone."

Chet drew to a stop beside him. "No way, Boss. Forget it. I can't—"

"I'm not asking."

Chet pursed his lips.

Alec narrowed his eyes. On this, he wasn't budging. Chet was part of the team so technically Alec was responsible for him, too.

The two guards swapped looks, then chuckled darkly. "Kerra." *Relax.* "Sirus would be happy to take you both."

* * *

45

Alec's hired gun stayed behind—because a direct order was a direct order. Not that Alec believed for one minute that Chet *wanted* to come. Only a crazy person would earnestly want to hand himself over to a sex-driven species' ominous head scientist.

As they exited the bath house, the guards cut a right and led Alec down the long stone corridor. Orange rays spilled in through countless arched windows, spaced evenly down the left side of the passageway.

He peered out one of the openings, a towel wrapped around his waist, his bare feet slapping quietly against the floor. The sky was clear, and damn, check that out—the sunset contained *two* blazing suns. With everything going on, he'd somehow forgotten that Nira was part of a binary star system. Not that multiple suns weren't common, because they were. Even more so than single stars like Earth's.

Come to think of it, he'd forgotten about something else as well. Something that would explain why the past two days had felt so effing long. According to Astrum Industries' calculations, not only was the planet they were stranded on smaller than Earth, but it rotated at only half the speed, too. Meaning, each day had a lot more hours—something he would've noticed had those fuckheads not taken their intel-data wristbands with everything else.

Alec lifted a brow as something else came back to him. The fact that not only were the days there longer, but each revolution around their suns took nearly twice as long as well. Which meant, while to the rescue team it will have taken a year to get here, only half of a year will have passed to those on the ground. Not that, ultimately, it wasn't still the same amount of time, but hopefully the longer days would make it go by faster.

Alec pulled his gaze from the sunset and looked straight ahead. With one guard in front of him and one behind, they headed toward the south side of the castle. It took a few minutes—the place was huge—but eventually they came to a spacious, curving staircase. One that led up, and not *down*. Alec paused and exhaled in relief. Oh, thank fuck. They weren't going to some creepy-ass dungeon.

"Move," the guard at his back grunted. "Sirus waits."

Alec frowned and resumed, glancing over his shoulder. "This Sirus guy. You like him?"

The Kríe shrugged. "He is strange."

Strange. Frickin' awesome. *So* not the answer he was looking for. "Guess that means no," he muttered.

"Just not yes."

Alec lifted his gaze as they ascended the stone steps. The circular stairwell's ceiling was too high above to see. Just a small, distant darkness despite the windows along the way. Which, Alec presumed, meant they were heading up a lookout tower. He wondered how many the castle had.

After a good bit of climbing, his legs started to ache. Fuck, he really hoped their destination wasn't at the top, because if so, they still had a *long* way to go. A few more minutes passed. Sweat bloomed across his brow. His muscles began to burn. His breaths came faster.

He eyed the guard in front of him. He didn't even look winded. Then again, by the size of his thighs, he probably climbed stairs like these all day long.

Finally, they reached, yup, the very top.

"Jesus," Alec groaned breathlessly. "You need to install a fucking elevator."

The guards turned and eyed him.

"Elevator?" the front Kríe asked.

"Yeah. You know... a big box? With a pulley? Takes you up and down without stairs?"

The males traded looks. The one behind Alec poked his shoulder. "You tell this to Sirus. He is strange, but also clever. He will build it. Makes things for the king all the time."

Alec frowned. "I was kidding. He'd need stuff you don't have. Steel ropes... hydraulics... an elevator shaft—"

"Tell him," the front Kríe insisted. "You must. We want to see."

Alec stared at him incredulously.

The male's dark lips curved. "Do this, as a favor to us, and I will suck your little cock."

What?

Alec stiffened, then scowled at the fucker. Miros had made a similar remark about the size of his dick, and just like then, Alec didn't appreciate it. "First of all, asshole, my *cock* isn't *little*. And secondly, keep your fangy mouth away from it."

The guard's brows hiked, as if surprised by Alec's response. What, were blowjobs on this planet some kind of lucky-score deal-sealer? The other male coughed, then threw back his head and laughed, his booming baritone echoing through the stairwell.

The first Kríe just grunted. "You are stranger than Sirus." Turning back around, he faced the door they'd stopped at—but suddenly went still as he eyed it. With a grimace of chagrin, he glanced at his comrade. "It appears we have taken the wrong tower."

Alec froze, his eyes widening. "We did *WHAT?*" he exploded. He'd never survive a second climb.

The Kríe took one look at his horrified face, then exploded into laughter with his friend. "Jesting, moyo. Jesting. My Nira. You are *gullible.*" He opened the door and shoved Alec inside.

Alec stumbled but quickly righted himself, his relief too strong to stay irritated. Blinking, he glanced around, getting a look at the place. It was big, clearly the entire top level of the lookout tower, and easily a good forty feet in diameter. All around its circumference, more arched windows offered openings, which in turn, allowed a subtle breeze to circulate. Supply shelves were everywhere, stocked with jars, bottles, and sacks. Bowls, tools, and writing materials covered the worktables. Which there were many of. This Sirus guy was a busy Kríe.

Alec eyed the floor-length drapery hanging off to the left. Heavy and crimson, they were clearly for privacy, or maybe even to create closed partitions. Alec frowned, diverting his gaze upward to one strange-as-fuck formation embedded between two wood beams in the ceiling. His frown deepened. What in the hell was that freakish thing? It looked like a junk sculpture gone *all wrong*. He shuddered, averting his gaze again, not wanting to know.

He spotted some books on a table—hand-bound with stamped brass and leather fittings stacked into piles. Although, several *did* lay open, exposing vellum insides; their pages packed with intricate little symbols. Their very own written language.

Wall torches and candles added light to the expanse. Strange plants basked in the sunset along each sill. At the far end of the room, next to a crackling stone fireplace, critters the size of gerbils skittered around a cage. They reminded him of bats—but wingless, and blue—all chittering and clinging to the bars.

Maybe he'd get a chance to check them out.

Another Kríe emerged from behind a curtained divider. His keen eyes locked instantly on Alec. "Beautiful Nira…" he rumbled. "Who is this you bring me?"

"Sirus, meet King Zercy's brand-new pet."

"Tah." *Yes.* "Of course…" His golden gaze glittered. "And as I understand it, *my* brand-new project."

Alec tensed, not missing the hint of glee in his tone. Heart thumping anxiously, he studied the approaching Kríe. Leaner than the guards, he wore a snug black tunic, tied with black rope around the waist. His dreads were pulled back, too. Dark sandals hugged his feet. And wrapped around every thick ankle and wrist were countless bands of black, masculine beads.

But there was something else about him, something Alec couldn't exactly see. It was more like an aura, an invisible vibe, whispering that he might be a nut job. A truly crazy scientist. And those gold, fixated eyes were *not* helping.

Alec's pulse spiked faster. He didn't want to do this. What if Sirus gave him a lobotomy? For all he knew, *pet* meant *vegetable zombie* in Kríeland and it was Sirus' job to make him nice and *compliant*. With a spike straight into his freaking cerebellum, so he'd sit nice and quietly on a leash.

Oh, God.

Breathing a curse, he glanced at his escorts by the door. Maybe if he bribed them, they'd help him escape. Evidently, his expression had been pretty transparent, because the bastards just smirked and shook their heads.

Fuck.

Alec turned back around—and froze.

Sirus was less than a foot away… peering down at him way too intently.

"Beesha." *Greetings.* He smiled. "I am Sirus."

"Yeah. I kinda caught that."

"And you," he studied Alec's face, "are exquisite."

Alec cringed and rubbed his nape. Ugh. He needed to get back to his team.

"So, uh, what exactly is the plan here, big guy? You gonna weigh me? Take my temp? Get my blood pressure? Record my height? 'Cause I'd kinda like to get this over with so I can leave."

Sirus chuckled and stepped back. "So eager to begin." He gestured toward the partitions. "Come this way."

Alec swallowed and followed him over, watching nervously as he pulled open a drape. A sectioned-off area, just like he'd suspected. Roughly eight feet by ten, it had a window at the other end, as well as more candles placed about. Three sides were nothing but huge swaths of crimson, with a large disturbing table in the center. Disturbing, because clearly it was designed for examinations, with a fuck ton of metal shackles mounted around it.

Apprehensively, he studied the thing, making note of all its oddities. The surface looked like stone, but smoother, and curiously, *softer*. And though as a whole it was rectangular in shape, there were clearly distinguishable sections for each body part; a narrower, rounded portion on the end for the head, long segmented supports for arms and legs.

"Wait here." Sirus sauntered to a shelf of various flasks, grabbed a small, rectangular empty one, then headed back. "I would like a urine sample." He handed Alec the container.

Alec regarded the thing. Could be worse. "Yeah, uh... okay."

But instead of turning around, the Kríe just stood there. Clearly, these fuckers did not grasp privacy. Scowling, Alec turned around, lifted his towel and did his thing, then dropped the cloth back down and handed it over.

Sirus gave it a sniff and smiled.

Alec watched him. Really? They were sophisticated enough to have their own friggin' language, but couldn't resist smelling piss like it was pizza?

Sirus set the sample aside and strode to another crowded shelf, this one holding decanters of varying shapes. Thoughtfully, he scanned all the colorful choices, then picked one with indigo liquid. Pouring a tiny glassful, he swiftly returned.

"Drink," he commanded, extending it to Alec.

Alec eyed the stuff suspiciously. "Do I have to?"

"Tah." *Yes.*

"Why?" He frowned. "What is it?"

"Not poison, if that is your concern. Just a swallow of good health."

"Riiight. Good health," Alec deadpanned.

"Indeed. Promotes peak performance and virility."

Yeah, okay. That didn't sound sketchy as fuck.

Alec stared at the liquid.

Sirus grinned and took his hand. Pressed the glass against his palm. "Drink. Be *brave.*"

Ugh. Alec scowled and clutched it freely. "Fine. Whatever. But swear to God, this better not be the juice from that damn fire fruit."

"Fire fruit?" Sirus grinned. "Do you mean senna`sohnsay?"

"Yeah," he muttered.

The Kríe chuckled. "Interesting... But no, this is merely *kirah* nectar."

Relieved to hear it, Alec gave a small nod, then downed the dark liquid in one gulp. Sweet, but also tart. Kind of syrupy, too. Not bad, though. Would probably rock mixed with club soda.

He handed the glass back to Sirus, who smiled and set it aside, then motioned for Alec to move to the table.

Aw, fuck. Not *that.*

Alec frowned at it warily. Rubbed his brow. "Uh...Yeah, I don't think so."

Sirus strode to its side where a captain's wheel was mounted—or at least that's what it looked like to Alec. With a couple of turns, the table got moving, rotating from horizontal to perfectly vertical.

"Nenya," Sirus prompted again. *Come.*

Alec eyed the iron restraints. So many.

"Do not be nervous. I will not hurt you. I gave my solemn vow to the king."

Which obviously did nothing to reassure him.

Sirus waited. Crossed his arms. Tapped his big-ass Kríe foot. Moments later, his face turned stern. "For Nira's sake. Time is wasting. Do I need to have the guards come and help?"

Alec bristled. He was playing *that* card? What a dick.

He glanced over his shoulder at the two Kríe guarding the door. The males merely grinned and widened their stance, as if saying, *Yup, we like forceful. That's our jam.*

Damn it.

Alec glowered and turned back around. Whatever. Sirus promised that he wouldn't hurt him. Might as well get this over with.

CHAPTER FIVE

* * *

Forcing himself forward, Alec stepped to the table.

"Good pet." Sirus grinned. "Now stand with your back against it."

"Do you have to restrain me?" Alec asked, complying.

"Tah. Keeps movements minimal. Very helpful."

"For *you*," he muttered. "I happen to like moving freely."

"Tah. As do I. At least one of us will be happy."

Smirking, Sirus positioned Alec's arms by his sides, then locked his wrists and biceps into place. The same was done to his legs, starting with brackets above his knees. Then more unyielding clamps for each ankle. And still the Kríe wasn't done. Alec's heart hammered faster as Sirus reached for his throat. A second later, his freaking neck was pinned down, too.

"Hmm…" Sirus tapped his clawed finger to his chin. "There was something else… *Ah, yes*."

Off went Alec's towel.

Alec stiffened, inhaling sharply. Cool air licked at his junk. Butt naked and wholly immobilized with three behemoths in the room. He'd never felt so defenseless in his life.

Sirus studied him, his gaze lingering longest on Alec's cock. "Modest, but handsome."

Alec groaned and looked at the ceiling.

Sirus lifted his eyes. Slowly, he grinned. "You and me. We are going to have fun."

"We?" Alec grumbled. "Or maybe just you?"

"Well…" The Kríe nodded. "Tah, probably just me." Next thing Alec knew, Sirus was back at that wheel, returning the table to horizontal. Alec shifted atop the molded surface. It wasn't soft per se but definitely not hard. Like rubber-coated memory foam or something.

The sound of a lever releasing met Alec's ears. The table lurched, then started to gently sway, as if suddenly floating in a big tray of water.

What the hell? A reedy, winding noise rose up from where Sirus stood, like a little wheel turning on a spindle. What was he doing?

"You weigh sixty-three *teags*."

Oh. He'd been weighing him. Interesting method. Alec did a bit of division. Last time he checked, he was about one-ninety. So, a teag was roughly three pounds.

Sirus shoved that lever thing back into place and, just like that, the table was back on sturdy ground. The big Kríe disappeared, but returned moments later with what looked like a retractable ruler. Wasting no time, he began his next task; taking and recording Alec's measurements. The circumference of his head. And limbs. And waist. The length of absolutely every conceivable body part.

"Your cock is seven *terahs*. My cock is eighteen. I will measure it again later, though, when you are hard."

Alec glared and bit his tongue.

Sirus gathered more findings. But soon things turned considerably more hands-on. Starting with Alec's throat, he tracked his pulse with two thumbs, but then promptly moved higher to study his hair.

Which Alec supposed made sense. They didn't seem to have that stuff on Nira. None on the body, and certainly none on the head. At least where the Kríe were concerned. They just had those dread things—that didn't look like they should be 'cut'—and some thick, black lashes and brows.

Sirus fingered his light brown hair, tugged it, combed it with his claws. "Like a Tohrí," he mused. "But short. And dark."

Alec didn't reply. Sirus moved to his face, tracing his features, then studying his scruff. "Tiny little bristles on your cheeks and chin…" He turned Alec's head to the side. "What is this?"

"This?" Alec drawled. "Gonna have to be more specific."

"This small, dark brown circle." He grazed it with a thumb. "On your jawline, not so far from your ear."

"Oh. That's a birthmark."

"Ah."

Yup, pretty self-explanatory.

He pried open Alec's mouth and studied his teeth, then moved on to inspect his ears. Ears that, in comparison to Kríe ears, were nearly half the size. And didn't have those subtly-pointed tips.

"So round… and little," Sirus noted, sounding amused.

Alec sighed. To these Kríe, he'd forever look small.

His examiner moved south. "And what is this?" He touched the front of Alec's shoulder.

"A scar. From battle."

He stilled. "You are kensa?" *Warrior.*

"Uh, well, a soldier. And I *was*, but the war ended."

"Hmm." He seemed to ponder that, but instead of asking more, got back to work. Which evidently was now the brand-new task of intently fingering absolutely *everything*. Alec's shoulders and traps, his bicep and forearm, all around his pecs and upper abs. Like he was tracing the muscles beneath Alec's skin, and getting the layout of his bones.

He took a break to scrawl a few notes.

Scratch-scratch-scratch on some parchment.

When finished, he extended Alec's arm supports out from the table. Right, better access to the sides of his ribs, which Sirus swiftly got busy prodding the shit out of.

Oh, no. Aw, fuck.

Alec twitched and squirmed, yelping a curse before he could stop himself.

Sirus paused with a frown. "What? What is wrong?"

Alec clenched his jaw. "I'm ticklish."

"Ticklish?"

"Yeah. As in, don't touch me there."

Sirus grunted and prodded his groin.

"Ah!" Alec yelped again. "Not there, either!"

"So sensitive," he chuckled, moving farther to work his leg. Thigh… knee… shin and calf… foot. Once done, he flashed a smile. "Time for Mina."

Alec exhaled, glad that was over, but—Who was Mina? His assistant? And what's more—a female? This ought to be interesting, not that he relished the idea of more company. One Kríe was plenty, thank you very much.

Sirus stepped from their cubbyhole, but returned just moments later. "Mina," he announced proudly. "Is she not captivating?"

Alec's eyes flared wide, following the line Sirus towed. Holy shit. He'd somehow dislodged that junk-sculpture from between the wood beams and pulled it over via a track in the ceiling.

"Yeah, sure... Real captivating..." In a nightmarish sort of way. But Alec would keep that to himself. No point in hurting the Kríe's feelings.

Sirus beamed as he situated it directly above. "She is my favorite invention, the product of my advancements. I am brilliant, you see. Have made many discoveries. And Mina is the culmination of them all."

Alec stared at "her," trying like hell not to grimace. But she was just *so bizarrely grotesque*. Although, oddly enough, her actual body wasn't the issue—That was just a simple casing made out of wood. Smooth and black, similar in shape to a small blanket chest, with foliage and shit growing out of the top. Fat leaves and skinny leaves, thistles, and grass—no doubt, the reason it'd been wedged into the ceiling. They were plants, after all, and needed sun. And what better way to get it than through a hole in the roof.

But no, what disturbed him was all the other freaky stuff dangling off of it. Like those creepy-ominous gadget things attached to its belly and sides, whose purpose he could only freaking guess. Not that he wanted to know. Although, some *did* appear less intimidating than others. That cluster in the corner, for instance, that looked like a bunch of test tubes. Or that doohickey that resembled headgear with steampunk goggles.

But the gadgets weren't the worst. What concerned him most were those fleshy, gray roots hanging limply from random holes. Or maybe they were vines, just really fat or something. Come to think of it, they kind of looked like—*oh, shit*—tentacles. Alec's body went rigid. Even his lungs locked up tight. Swear to God, if those things started moving up there? He was going to have to scream—really loud.

"So, uh..." He cleared his throat. "What exactly does she *do*?"

"Hmm. I think I shall show you as we go." Sirus cocked his head. Tapped his chin. "Now, what to investigate next... Ah. I know. I love this part."

Oh, hell.

Sirus reached up and unhooked that headgear thingy and carefully slid it onto his head. Alec regarded it curiously. It looked like a helmet framed in some sort of metal, with the rest purely organic, made of roots. Little ones, though, that resembled veins. And they were clearly all from different types of plants. Different sizes and textures, different colors as well. Although, they definitely *did* have one thing in common. The location in which they ultimately converged. At the base of Sirus' skull, against his nape.

He blinked at Alec through his bulky, bronze eye gear, the thick lenses making his eyes look twice as big. Alec swallowed as he stared at him. Mad scientist indeed. The big Kríe grinned, then slid the goggles upward, resting them atop of his helmet. Alec exhaled. Good. Those bug eyes were freaking him out.

Sirus straightened the headgear further, then reached around back, blindly fumbling with the part by his nape. A moment later, his big body twitched. He closed his eyes and dropped his arms, then subtly rolled his head atop his shoulders.

Alec frowned. What the frick?

"I am ready." Sirus lifted his gaze to Mina and unhooked one of her tentacle thingies. "This is a *suki* vine. Sukis harness energy from the plant life around them then channel it through their vines as they hunt. Little zaps to the prey they wish to eat, shocking them into temporary paralysis. Of course, by the time the little critters regain motion, they are wrapped in suki leaves and half digested."

Alec frowned in confusion. "Wait. A *plant* can do that? Electrocute small animals and *eat* them?"

"If they are suki, yes."

"But plants can't move, or think, let alone hunt."

The Kríe's smile faded. "Of course they can... They are from the *dygon* genus. Do you not have sentient plant life on your world?"

"No." The closest thing he could think of would be a Venus flytrap. But they didn't have a central nervous system, just specialized cell systems that responded to stimuli.

"Interesting," Sirus mused. "Well, here we do."

"So, they're *aware*?"

"Tah, but not like you and I, or any other animal. Their brains are more like insects. Very simple."

"Weird," Alec murmured. And a little bit creepy.

"At any rate," Sirus went on, "I have invented a way to manipulate their little minds, to control their actions, bend them to my will." He reached up and stroked his lurid creation. "Every dygon within Mina, I can control."

"How?"

Sirus grinned and tapped his root-woven crown. "Intercept their network of nerve cells and fibers, swap out their nerve impulses for mine."

Alec stared at him blankly.

The big Kríe chuckled. "*My* brain tells *their* bodies what to do."

Holy shit. That was nuts. And admittedly, impressive as hell.

"Wow," Alec mumbled. "That's… really cool."

"Tah." Sirus nodded, pointing to himself. "See? I am brilliant. Brilliant me."

If the situation was different, Alec might've actually laughed.

"So. Now that that is all clarified, let us begin."

Moving in close, between Alec's extended arm and side, Sirus tapped the tip of his suki vine to Alec's pec. Instantly, his muscle contracted in response to the small zap.

Alec sucked in sharply. "Whoa."

Sirus smiled. "Indeed."

He did the same to Alec's other pec. It bunched the same way. Then he touched it to the inside of Alec's bicep. Not a tap this time, though. This time he trailed it down his arm, each muscle group constricting tight in its wake.

"Fuck, that feels weird," Alec breathed.

Sirus smirked—then slid it to the center of Alec's palm. Immediately, his fingers contorted all awkwardly. And yeah, the feeling wasn't fabulous.

"Uh! Cut that out. Geez, Kríe. What the fuck?"

The big Kríe snickered and moved down Alec's body, starting at the arch in his foot. The muscles locked up, his toes quirked all crazy, but before Alec could bitch, he moved higher. Alec's calves proved pretty good entertainment, too, especially when each contraction made his toes point. Before long, though, Sirus continued on, giving the side of his kneecap little taps. His leg tried to kick, like he'd used a reflex hammer. Sirus grinned and kept going, to Alec's thigh.

"Such a nice group of muscles here," he mused as he played, making Alec's upper leg go berserk. Contracting and twitching all across the top, then along his inner thighs, too.

Alec grunted repeatedly, in control of absolutely none of it. Wherever that vine beckoned, his body responded. Alec kept his mouth shut, though, despite all the strangeness, choosing to just deal and get it over with.

Unfortunately, that plan kind of flew out the window when Sirus moved all the fun to Alec's midsection. Not so much initially, as he manipulated Alec's abdomen, making it undulate, then dance like crazy. No, it wasn't until Sirus removed part of the table that Alec found himself turning nice and vocal. A portion beneath his hips, just suddenly gone, giving the Kríe access to his spine. Or more specifically, his *lower* spine, where evidently lots of nerve bundles lived.

Sirus ran his hand under Alec's side and felt around, as if seeking a specific location. His fingers stopped. He'd found it at the small of Alec's back. Donning a mischievous grin, he met Alec's eyes. "Let us see if your nervous system is anything like ours. If it is, you will either love this—or hate it."

Oh, God.

Knowing how Kríe thought, Alec did *not* like the sound of that. But right as he opened to his mouth to object, Sirus touched that vine right above his butt dimple. Current dove instantly into the cradle of his pelvis and lit up his unsuspecting sphincter.

Alec gasped with a jerk. "What the f—Damn, Kríe. Shit."

"You felt that?" Sirus chuckled. "In your—"

"*Yeah*," Alec bit out. "Please don't do that again."

"Fine. I will try somewhere else instead." He moved the vine a smidgen and tapped a second time. That zing shimmied straight to Alec's balls.

He sucked in a breath as his scrotum firmed, then leveled his captor with a glare.

The Kríe beamed wolfishly. "You felt that in your—"

"*Yes!* I felt it in my *nuts*. Cut it out."

"Esh. So testy." Sirus tried a third spot, and yup, this time it surged up Alec's cock. It was a strong one, too. The strongest yet, making his hips do a jig.

"Ah! My dick!"

The rat bastard cackled, holding his sides and everything. Clearly, he'd orchestrated it and knew exactly what he was stimulating. Kríe were such pervs. Swear to God.

Sirus cleared his throat and returned the suki back to Mina. "All right. That was fun. But we must move along."

Alec groaned. "Aw, Jesus. You mean there's more?"

"Tah." Sirus re-donned his goggle contraption, its lenses making him bug-eyed again. He looked at Alec and smiled. Alec sighed and shook his head. The guy looked like a bona fide moron. Again, if things were different, he would've laughed.

Sirus pulled something out from under the table with his foot, then stepped up high on the thing and hiked his knee. Hiked it right over Alec's freaking torso, and just like that, he was straddling Alec's body.

Which was still helplessly pinned.

And wholly naked.

Alec's eyes flared wide, staring up at him in alarm. Good frickin' Lord, what was he doing?

The Kríe chuffed, amused, and scooted back on his knees. "Móonday." *Do not fear.* "I will not sit on you, moyo. Crushing your little body would cost me my head."

Alec exhaled in relief, but then stiffened with a frown. "You saying I'm fragile?"

"Mah, of course not. Not at all..." He glanced down Alec's body. "Actually, tah."

Alec scowled and ground his molars.

Sirus smirked and unhooked one of those glass things from Mina's body. Alec glanced at it. Yup, definitely looked like a test tube, only a little bit shorter, and fatter.

Sirus held it for him to see. "Tree sprites. Very hard to catch."

Alec's lips fell open as he studied the contents—a half-dozen tiny entities, with even tinier translucent wings, flittering around behind the foggy glass.

"Are those like... fairies?"

"Fairies?"

"Little people that fly?"

"Hmm." Sirus eyed them through his thick, bronze goggles. "I do not think so. Although, they *do* have tiny cocks."

Alec cut him a dry look.

Sirus shrugged, "I checked," then gave the receptacle a gentle shake. Instantly, it lit bright. Like really, really bright, the sprites no longer visible amidst their radiance. Naturally, they reminded him of fireflies on Earth, but with a hell of a lot more potency to their punch.

Sirus pulled down a sleeve from the tube's metal rim, but it only appeared to extend along one side. Apparently, he wanted all that bright-ass light shining in just one direction. Carefully, he snapped it into place on his headgear, positioning it horizontally above his goggles.

Huh. A helmet light. How very clever.

Sirus moved to fiddling with his eye gear next, flipping countless lenses up and down. Evidently, there weren't just two thick ones after all, but a whole freaking slew of them back-to-back. Like that thing people looked through at the eye doctor's office that narrowed down their ocular prescription.

Click-click-click—Round discs cranking up and down.

Finally, he found the right combination.

"There. All ready." Sirus smiled broadly. "I will be moving very close now. Just stay still."

Alec frowned. He didn't like the sound of that *at all*. Next thing he knew, Sirus was straddling him on all fours, his massive body suddenly looming ominously. Alec stiffened like a board. This close, the male looked *enormous*, blocking virtually everything else from sight. But right as Alec readied to demand some personal space, Sirus firmly clutched his jaw, rendering it immobile.

Alec inhaled sharply. He could feel the Kríe's claws. Poking his cheek, against his ear, along the hairline of his neck. He swallowed, stomach flipping. Sirus shifted his weight, then brought his other hand to Alec's eye.

"Do not move," he rumbled softly, carefully prying it wide.

Alec's heart went nuts. He was going to lose an eyeball. Sirus slowly leaned closer, till that light had Alec blinded. "Shit, Kríe," he grunted. "This *cannot* be safe. You've got friggin' *claws* for fuck's sake."

"They are short."

"They are *sharp*."

Sirus grinned but didn't reply.

Alec tamped back a growl—but ultimately focused on staying still. He could smell the Kríe's body, feel his heat, and his dreads. Or at least the ones that had slipped over his shoulder. They were soft against his skin. He bet Zercy's would be, too.

Alec inwardly stilled. Where the fuck did *that* come from? But Sirus swiftly distracted him from his thoughts.

"Your eyes are like the ocean," the big Kríe murmured. "Green and blue with little specks of sun."

"Yeah, uh, thanks. That's great. Are we done?"

"Mah. Look to the side."

Alec exhaled, but complied.

"Bellah." *Good.* "Now to the other."

Alec obeyed, officially blinder than a bat.

"Hmm... That is interesting..." He let go of Alec's eye. With a frown, he rose back up. "And unfortunate."

Alec blinked, seeing nothing but a great big spot. "What do you mean, unfortunate?"

"Eh. It is nothing you would miss."

Click-click-click—Back the Kríe went to switching lenses.

Alec blinked some more, that blotch in his eye slowly fading, but not before Sirus re-gripped his jaw. Cranking Alec's head back, he pressed a thumb to Alec's nose, pinning its tip upward to peer inside. Alec grunted, shifting awkwardly as the Kríe leaned back in. Did he really need to—

"Uh!" Alec stiffened in abject shock. Something cool just slid up his nose and—*"UH!"*—wriggled! Instantly, he shot into tugging wildly at his binds.

"Kerra." *Relax.* Sirus held his head fixed. "This will take but a moment. That is all."

"No! Aw, God! What the fuck's up my nose!"

"Just another part of Mina. Now *be still.*"

Fuck him and fuck that!

Alec tried to turn his head as that thing wormed deeper, desperate to dislodge it from his nose. But the Kríe's grip was strong and wouldn't budge, so it just kept slithering its way into his sinuses. His eyes watered. His pulse thundered. Then, all of a sudden, it reemerged in the back of his throat. He coughed and gagged as it tickled his epiglottis.

Sirus pried open his mouth and peered inside. "Ah. As I suspected." He compelled it to withdraw.

As soon as it pulled completely free, Alec shouted, "Oh, my *God!* You're such a *dick!*"

Sirus muffled another snicker and turned Alec's head to the side. "Stop complaining. And stop wiggling. I am trying to work."

Alec inhaled sharply when clawed fingers clutched his ear. "Swear to God," he ground out, on the verge of losing his shit, "if that *thing* touches my ear, I'll—"

"What," Sirus chuckled, sounding wholly unconcerned. "You will hurt me when I release you? That should be interesting."

Oh, God— Oh, God—

Alec broke into a sweat.

Sirus flat-out laughed. "Be calm, moyo ochay." *Funny creature.* "It is only me this time. I give my word."

Alec groaned, pretty sure he'd never been so relieved, but his body stayed braced, nevertheless. It wasn't like he trusted the prick. He could easily be lying.

Fortunately, Sirus *did* stay true to his promise, examining Alec's ear with only his goggles. A few moments later, he released Alec's jaw and sat up, careful not to put weight on Alec's legs. Alec glared at him crossly—that spot in his eye finally gone—but Sirus didn't seem to notice, or even care. He was too busy messing with those lenses again.

Click-click-click—

Click-click-click—

When he finished, Alec tensed. God only knew what was next.

Sirus chuffed, sliding the goggles halfway up his forehead. "Breathe. Just me and my lenses for this." He tapped the side of his eyewear and grinned in earnest excitement. "The lenses in place now are derived from a *ganshee*."

Alec's brows scrunched. "Are you saying some of these plants can *see*?"

"Tah… But not in the way that we do." He paused, as if searching for the words to elucidate. Ultimately, though, he just waved it off. "Too hard to explain. Besides, it is not *how* but *what* they see that matters."

Alec eyed the things warily. "And what do they see?"

"Shades of gray, but more importantly, only the *outline* of organic matter. *All* organic matter, regardless if it is enclosed. Solids, like flesh, simply do not register. So they see right through it as if it was not even there. I believe this is so they can quickly locate life, efficiently discern between inanimate objects and prey. After all, what is more obvious than the outline of a beating heart? Even if an animal is trying to hide. Fascinating, is it not?"

Alec lifted a brow. "Actually, yeah."

In fact, he was pretty sure scientists back home would kill for this. Not that their technology didn't totally kickass. But this? This was cool as freaking shit.

"So now," Sirus beamed, "*I* can see through matter, too." His golden eyes twinkled as he covered them with his goggles. "And right now, that matter is *you*."

Alec shifted beneath him. "Kinda figured that. What, uh, exactly will you be looking at?"

The Kríe leaned in closer—but not as close as last time—and got to work studying Alec's throat. "Your organs. Your blood vessels," he murmured. "All within."

Alec exhaled, so damn grateful for a break from being touched.

Sirus nodded when finished and moved to scan his arms, eyeing them curiously for a moment. He proceeded to Alec's chest next—and stared at it intensely—remaining there for quite a bit of time. Which wasn't really surprising. A lot of important stuff was crammed in there.

But then something occurred to him. He looked at Sirus and frowned. "Why didn't you use this with my head before? Instead of letting that thing crawl up my nose?"

"Cannot see through thick bone. The skull is very dense. Same with the pelvis and thigh."

"Oh." Alec supposed that made logical sense.

A happy little rumble made its way up Sirus' throat. "So pretty inside. With such a busy little heart. It beats so very fast. Is this normal?"

Not really, Alec thought irritably. But, hey, that's what happened when one got captured by alien behemoths, stripped and restrained, then intimately examined on top of a table.

"Yes. Perfectly normal." Although, he suspected Sirus knew the truth. Probably asked Alec the question just to rib him.

Seemingly content with what he'd seen in Alec's chest, he scooted down to study his abdomen. But instead of looking bored with the abundance of nothing but bowels, Sirus paused with a frown and cocked his head.

"How peculiar," he uttered, giving Alec's stomach a couple prods. "I do not understand what I am seeing…" Alec grunted, instinctively tensing his abs. But that only made the Kríe poke harder. A low, perplexed sound emitted. It'd come from deep in Sirus' nose. He nudged Alec some more. "So abnormal."

Alec grunted through each one, scowling up at the guy. "Seriously?" Grunt. "You're seriously saying you've never seen," grunt-grunt, "*intestines*?"

Sirus stilled and met his eyes. "Intestines?" He looked totally baffled.

"Yeah. You know, *bowels*? That path from your stomach to your ass?"

The big Kríe recoiled. "But that implies they are connected."

Alec stared at him, nodding, feeling a bit confused now himself. "Yeah. Because they *are*." How could brilliant boy not know that? Was he messing with him or something? It didn't look like it.

Sirus didn't reply, as if absorbing his words, but eventually looked back down at Alec's stomach. "Intestines," he mused. "Such a foreign concept." He rubbed his chin. His lips slowly curved. "An anomaly that I simply *must* investigate."

CHAPTER SIX

* * *

Alec stilled. Oh, God. What the fuck had he done?

As Sirus removed his goggles and slid off the table, dread surged like icy sludge in Alec's gut. Because, come on, how many ways could there be to investigate bowels? Probably not too many but, from what he knew of Sirus so far, Mina would undoubtedly be involved.

Alec shuddered, swallowing thickly. "Is this really necessary?"

"Tah, of course." Sirus gathered a few tools. "I was tasked to find out *everything*. Not just *some*."

Alec swiveled his wrists anxiously. "But there's really not much to see. Just a tunnel. Very boring. You'd be bored."

Sirus smirked as he spread Alec's legs and stood between them. "I do not think that will be the case."

Alec cursed, his heart back to hammering like mad. "How about a rain check?"

"I do not know what that is."

He gripped Alec's leg supports and bent their middle hinges, then guided Alec's knees toward his chest. The position was strange. Like Alec was sitting in a chair, but a chair that was lying on its back. Curiously, in folding his body like that, it angled a section of the table up, too. The part that his ass had been resting upon. Apparently, the table was just a bunch of separate pieces that could angle in virtually any direction. Or be removed completely, like the portion Sirus had discarded when he wanted a little access to Alec's spine.

Alec shifted warily, starting to sweat, his skin sticking to the table uncomfortably. God, if only he'd kept his mouth shut and just let the Kríe keep on poking.

Sirus locked the different sections into their new positions, then focused on one part in particular. The part that was acting like a seat against Alec's ass, a barrier between his butt and the big Kríe's prying eyes. Not that Sirus would be thwarted. He'd probably just take it off like the other one.

Sure enough, Sirus reached for the segment, curling his fingers around its sides. Alec braced and exhaled nervously. When the time came, he'd be ready. Ready to squeeze his cheeks tight. Like hell would he grant that Kríe entrance without a fight. If he was lucky, Sirus would just give up.

Thing was, Sirus didn't take it off after all. Instead, he revealed something very disheartening. That the portion covering Alec's ass wasn't one piece, but two—and those two goddamn pieces could slide apart. Like motherfucking theater curtains. And in doing so, they just took his sticky-from-sweat ass cheeks with them. Took them and now were holding them *very* spread.

Alec glowered. So much for making Sirus work for his in. He'd just handed him his backdoor *on a plate*. Wholly unobstructed with a friggin' welcome mat. Alec bristled as a flush of heat crawled up his face.

Screw it, he still could clench.

Sirus locked those pieces in place like he had the others, then settled his hands on Alec's knees. "There. I am ready to explore your bowels."

Alec groaned.

Sirus chuffed and reached for Mina.

Alec stiffened like a ramrod.

Sirus noticed.

"Hmm..." He dropped his hand and eyed Alec thoughtfully. "Perhaps I should do one more thing."

Heart racing, Alec watched as he strode out of sight, returning a moment later with something in hand. A thin scrap of fabric, maybe three feet long.

"For your nerves," the Kríe murmured, tying the thing around Alec's head.

He was blindfolding him?

"Wait—Why?" Alec stammered. "Why can't I see?"

"It is better this way. Trust me, moyo. I am smart."

Alec clenched his fists, but truth be told, no visuals of Mina looming above was definitely welcome. Air whispered over his skin as the Kríe stepped away. The smell of candles and sweat met his nose. Alec's sweat, of course, and—were those creature things chittering louder? The crackling fire suddenly sounded louder, too. His other senses, they were stepping up now that his sight had been stripped.

Sirus' footsteps resounded, then he was back between Alec's thighs. Two seconds later, he was lubing up his hole. Alec gritted his teeth and clenched his entrance tight. The Kríe added more. His claw grazed Alec's star. Alec jerked. Fuck, so sensitive. He clenched even more.

Sirus chuckled. "That will not work."

"We'll see."

"So we shall."

The tiny tip of something touched the center of Alec's ring. He twitched, then quickly vised his door even tighter. Which wasn't especially easy with his cheeks pried apart. But whatever. In this moment, he refused to yield. On the plus side, that thing felt like metal or something, so it couldn't be one of Mina's creepy tentacles.

Unfortunately, no matter how hard he squeezed, that thing was just too little— and far too lubed. With slow, steady pressure, it breached his tight ring, then smoothly glided past his sphincter. Alec growled in defeat.

"Bellah," Sirus murmured, sliding it deeper. *Good.* "But now you must relax."

Alec cleared his throat. "What is that thing? And how does it investigate?"

"Investigate? *This* tool? Mah. This tool is purely a preliminary."

Alec shifted with a frown. "What the fuck does that mean?" And was that thing getting bigger?

Yes. It was. It was definitely getting bigger, because his hole was *definitely* stretching to accommodate.

"It means this one's job is to offer unobstructed entry."

Alec froze at his words. A heartbeat later, that thing in his ass started opening. Opening, as in expanding, like a speculum. He winced, then cursed, then winced again as it kept doing its thing.

"Fuck, Kríe," he ground out. "Unobstructed entry for what?"

"Hmm. I do not think you really want that answer."

The tool stopped widening. Alec exhaled in relief. Any larger and his ass would've been seriously protesting. Warm breath brushed against his cheeks.

Alec scowled. "Are you... looking up my ass?"

"I am," Sirus answered. "Your rectum is lovely. And your jewel is coming along very nicely."

Alec groaned and rolled his eyes, but then quickly frowned. Coming along? What did *that* mean? But before he could ask, a rustling sound above stole his focus. That was Sirus fooling with Mina, and the reason was obvious.

Shit. He knew it. This was so not good.

Alec squirmed and shook his head—as much as his neck restraint would let him—but knew that any objections would be futile. The Kríe wouldn't listen. He only took orders from the king. Was seeing out one of his orders right now.

"Ah. Here we are." Sirus' wide smile was palpable. "In you go, beautiful."

Alec's eyes shot wide. Sirus hadn't been talking to him. He cursed urgently, clenching as tight as he could. Although, why he thought it'd do any good, he didn't know. Sirus' gadget was holding his backdoor wide open. But Alec was kind of freaking out, and panic made people stupid, and—

His whole body went rigid the instant he felt it. That foreign entity entering his body. Sliding all slippery past his defenseless sphincter with absolutely zero resistance. Made no difference that he was squeezing like a mad man on crack. It was like he wasn't clenching at all.

"Oh, God." He could feel the thing gliding... gliding along the prongs of that speculum. A thick, undulating muscle, all supple and slick, with countless nubs down its sides. Not huge nubs, but large enough to wreak havoc on his prostate. He could literally track each one as it passed. Which swiftly derailed his focus, diverting his attention more to his G than to the thing actually sliding against it.

He twitched and jerked. Gasped and cursed. So damn sensitive there. But why? He didn't understand. One thing he *did* know? That creepy thing working its way through his channel felt way too good to be okay with. Not that he could do anything about it. As far as he could tell, those nubs ran the length of its body, meaning as long it kept on entering, it'd keep on teasing him. Which he supposed was a positive in a backward sort of way. It'd definitely keep him distracted. Thing was, he was pretty sure that that probe was a tentacle, and to relish a tentacle in his ass was just plain wrong.

Fuck. A tentacle. He couldn't believe this. It was just too surreal.

Shifting his hips futilely, he tried to dislodge it, but it was already *way* beyond that speculum. He groaned. "Kríe... It's going so *deep*."

"Tah," Sirus murmured, palms splayed against Alec's abdomen. "I can see it through my lenses. Can feel it *moving*."

Alec cringed at his words, restlessly swiveling his wrists. Guess Sirus didn't plan on making it stop anytime soon. Farther and farther it pushed into his channel. Louder and louder his prostate sang. Fuck, those nubs. They were making him crazy.

Juicy, slick noises filled the silence, like a lazy, lubed dick, gliding steadily through a hole.

His brain visualized the image before he could stop it, but the 'hole' wasn't that of a *woman*.

Oh, God. He couldn't analyze that right now.

Heart pounded riotously, he fought like hell to focus. For fuck's sake, a creature was roaming his bowels. But for some insane reason, he wasn't panicking. Did he still think this was out-and-out *nuts*? Hell, yes. Thing was, he wasn't scared. Just disconcerted. Probably because it didn't really even hurt. According to his prostate, it felt exactly the opposite.

This was all just so bizarre.

Alec moaned, feeling the probe slow to take a turn, then make its way across the top of his abs. All while, in his rectum down below, it kept mercilessly tagging his G.

Oh, God. Too intense.

"Shit—" he panted. "Fuck—"

"You enjoy this," the Kríe noted.

Alec shook his head, even as his hips fought to thrust.

Sirus chuckled. "Why not admit it? I administer Mina's pleasures to patrons every day. They come to me eagerly. No need for restraints. Although, I insist on them anyway because I love them. In truth, Mina is just one of countless services I provide. And many are *far* more outlandish."

"*More?* Than *this?*" Alec groaned, his prostate blissing. "I find that very—*ungh*—hard to believe."

"It is true," the Kríe murmured. His attention sounded split, half of it no doubt locked on that probe. "Did you see those little critters in that cage by the fire?"

"Yeah—" Alec's breath hitched. He swallowed and licked his lips.

"Those are called *tibbi,* and *many* clients request them."

"*Request* them?"

"Indeed. It is really quite delicious. My customers lie down, much like you are now, and I fill their channels with sticky-sweet syrup. A few moments later, I open them wide, just as I have done with you. As soon as my tibbi smell that warm, scrumptious nectar, they scurry right on in with *much* excitement."

Alec gaped, forgetting instantly about the probe shoving deeper. Sirus' words were just too jarring. He *had* to be hearing wrong.

Sirus snickered. "They are lively feasters, which of course, is the draw. The nectar is like a stimulant to their systems. But when the pickings grow thin, they turn rather feisty. Like little addicts who do not want to share."

Holy shit.

Alec shook his head, panting. "You have *got* to be kidding."

Sirus loosed a husky laugh and just kept on going. "My customers, how they writhe when the tibbi start to grapple—which is where restraints are nice and come in handy. Not that the tibbi could ever hurt them. I remove their claws, and their teeth are not sharp. But for such little creatures, they *do* get aggressive, and wrench very *big* noises from my clients. Ah. The mess. My patrons spill so hard. Shoot their seed absolutely everywhere."

An unbidden visual assailed Alec's brain. "Oh. My. God."

Sirus chuckled, hands still roaming Alec's abs. "It is quite a scene. But the funniest part? All those raucous squeaks echoing inside their channel."

Alec grimaced and shook his head, trying to shake the image, which inadvertently shifted his focus back to that tentacle. It was *still* entering him. Still tormenting his G. To the point that it felt like his ass was going to come.

His toes curled as he braced through a quake, his sphincter clenching as he gritted his teeth and moaned. It ebbed a second later, and that's when it registered. How his entire freaking abdomen was straight-up *moving*. Mina's probe was probably nearing his small intestines. At which point things were going to get really snug. Not that things weren't crammed enough already.

"How much longer?" he strained out. His prostate was pulsing. "How much farther you gonna make that thing go?"

Sirus gently kneaded his belly. "Till it reaches the end."

"What?" Alec balked. His labored breaths quickened. "That's impossible. It's too far. Like twenty feet."

"I do not know your measurement of *feet*."

Alec shuddered, pelvis twitching. "That's like—*ungh*—the length of three of you."

Sirus paused. So did the tentacle. "Three of *me?* That *is* long."

"Right," Alec ground out. "Too long."

The big Kríe quieted, as if internally deliberating, but ultimately came to the same conclusion. "All right then." He lifted his hands. "I have explored the best I can."

Carefully, he slid out the tool in Alec ass, then promptly began removing his pet.

Alec exhaled in relief as the thing withdrew, but then shuddered with an embarrassingly loud groan. Couldn't help it, though, because now those nubs were tagging his sensitized prostate from the opposite direction. Forbidden, taboo pleasure coursed through his channel, making every inch of him quiver.

"Shit," he rasped raggedly. His muscles tensed. Swear to God, if that tentacle made his ass come, he was going to be scarred for life.

Fortunately, Sirus extracted the fucker pretty quickly, but to Alec's dismay, let its tail end remain tucked inside. Flushed and breathless, Alec frowned and moved his hips—then clenched without thinking and nearly gagged. With the speculum gone, his sphincter and all its nerve endings had just inadvertently hugged that probe. And sure enough, the thing felt *exactly* like a tentacle. Of an octopus or something.

Do not freak out. Do not freak out.

He quickly cleared his throat. "Is there a reason that's still in my ass?"

"Tah. Because it needs to be."

"What? Are you shitting me? *Come on.*"

"Be quiet. I am going down the list in my head. Skeletal, muscular, circulatory..." he droned on, "...digestion, central nervous system... Tah. I was right. We are down to the last."

"Great," Alec muttered. "And which is that?"

"Your reproductive functions. So, let us begin, starting with a species compatibility test."

Alec stiffened. Compatibility test? What in the fuck was that?

Without delay, the tail of that tentacle started swelling, growing thicker. Alec shifted against the intrusion, instinctively clenching. Not that it did any good. Thankfully, it didn't hurt—especially where it pressed against his prostate. Which, now that he thought about it, felt suspiciously full. Like when that *senna'sohnsay* had been kicking his ass.

Heady pressure filled his channel and spanned into his junk. A soft moan breached his lips. Behind his blindfold, his eyes rolled closed— until finally, it started stretching him to his max. A dull burn emerged.

He groaned.

"This pains you?"

"It's getting there."

"So just discomfort. An entirely normal sensation during mating."

During mating? So that's what this was all about? To find out which size species his ass could handle?

The tail kept swelling. Alec growled and rocked his hips, his backdoor trying feverishly to adjust. A sharp sting flared to life. He tensed with a hiss, the pain overriding his happy prostate.

Grimacing, he clenched his jaw and balled his hands. "Stop," he strained out. "Make it stop."

"Hmm." All stretching ceased. "The king... He will be disappointed."

Alec scowled, not wanting to think about him, wanting instead to be infuriated by the remark. Hell, if nothing else, he should be gladdened by their incompatibility. But to his consternation, a part of Alec suddenly felt disappointed, too. What the hell? He *must* be losing his mind. For fuck's sake, he was strapped to a freaking exam table with a big ballooned tentacle up his ass. Given those circumstances—on top of everything else—he should *not* be bummed that he and the king wouldn't *fit*.

Although, technically, he supposed they could if they used the venom. Seriously, considering how worldly Sirus was, how could he not know about tachi?

As the tail shrank back down, Alec forced the thought away. He needed his brain as blank as humanly possible. It wasn't like he could escape this shit if he kept on pondering the craziness. Might as well just stop thinking altogether. Besides, Sirus *had* to be almost done anyway. God knew, he'd already prodded every inch of flesh, and probed damn near every freaking hole.

More scratching noises sounded; Sirus adding to his notes. "Ah. Nearly finished. Just one thing left to do."

Alec tried not to tense. Had the worst been saved for last? Surely all the tough stuff had been done. Warily, he shifted as Sirus finally removed the tentacle and returned his legs to their original position.

"This one gonna hurt, too?"

"That is up to you."

He didn't like that answer. Sounded way too much like *probably*.

Without warning, Sirus gathered Alec's junk in his hands, and began firmly stroking his cock.

Alec sucked in a breath. The Kríe wasn't just measuring. Definitely had an endgame in mind. "Hey—What are you doing? Let go of my dick."

"When I am done."

"How 'bout *now*."

Sirus grunted and kept on pumping. "This last task requires you to be hard."

"What task, getting me off?" Alec irritably jerked his hips. "Forget it. You're *not* making me come."

Sirus didn't reply, just continued to stroke, as if uninterested in debating the inevitable. Long moments later, though, when Alec had barely hardened, he loosed a growl of frustration. "Obstinate creature," he grumbled, relinquishing Alec's dick.

Alec blinked behind his blindfold. Just like that, he'd quit?

A rustling sound above made him instantly frown. Definitely *not* the sound of Sirus quitting. More like the sound of him rummaging for more options. Alec balled his hands, determined to stand his ground. But right as Sirus paused with a pleased little rumble, Alec detected the arrival of a new presence.

"My lord," Sirus blurted. He sounded surprised.

Alec froze.

Oh, no.

The *king* was there?

CHAPTER SEVEN

* * *

"Beesha, Sirus. I had meant to stop by sooner. My apologies. Any new developments in the search?"

"I am afraid not, my lord."

Alec's ears perked, distracted from his efforts to stay calm. Developments in a search? That sounded on-going. Clearly, they weren't talking about him.

"I see... Keep looking." The king sounded grim.

"I will, Sire. With every spare moment I have."

Zercy's golden eyes settled on Alec's face. He could feel them. Like a big heated balm roaming his features. "And how are things faring with my new little pet?"

Fuuuuuck. His timbre just dipped a couple octaves, gliding through Alec's eardrums and into his body. Unsettled, he fought back a shiver and swallowed. That Kríe needed to leave. His effect wasn't natural.

And shit, with Alec bound to a table and naked, exposed to his bonfire stare? Who knew how his body would behave around the male. His gut told him it wouldn't be good. In other words, it'd let the cat out of the bag. Reveal the fact that, for some fucked up reason, King Zercy destabilized his dick.

"Things fare well, Sire. I have much to report."

"Indeed?"

"Oh, yes. So many interesting things."

"My curiosity is piqued."

"Come closer. I will show you."

The king strode over and stopped by Alec's side. Immediately, a warm knuckle brushed his cheek. Alec stiffened, not missing the current the contact created. His heart picked up speed. Sirus joined them on the other side of the table.

"As you can see," the Kríe began, "his structure is similar to ours, but it does hold some unique differences, too."

"Expound," Zercy instructed. Alec could feel his gaze wandering.

"Of course." Sirus pulled back Alec's upper lip. "Denza." *Look.* "No fangs, yet sharp teeth—which implies that his species eat meat."

Alec irritably jerked his head away. He was done with Sirus touching him.

Unfortunately, Sirus didn't take the hint. His fingers grazed Alec's temple next. Alec bristled and ground his molars. "They have no horns whatsoever, nor claws, or a tail. No spikes of any sort, not even barbs."

Zercy's hand moved to Alec's collar. "So vulnerable," he murmured.

Vulnerable? Alec scowled. He'd show him vulnerable.

Later.

When he could move.

And wasn't naked.

"Indeed, my lord. Even some of his senses seem subdued." He touched Alec's brow. "When studying his eyes, I discovered they are not equipped to see in the dark. Unlike ours, his rods and cones do not connect. His hearing is not as sharp as ours, either."

Zercy's rumble sounded troubled. "They would not last long on our world."

"Mah, they would not, with such minimal protection. Not even venom or defensive excretions were detected. But he *is* strong for his size, which at least is *something*. Although, he will never be as strong as Krie. Such is physically impossible; his kind have only half the muscles."

"Truly?"

"Tah. Take, for example, his upper arm. Where ours have eight muscle bands, his has only four. And since this was the case for every muscle group in his body, it explains his much leaner physique."

"Interesting." Zercy stroked Alec's clavicle with his thumb.

Alec shifted under his touch, heart thumping faster.

"Internally, his constructs are much like ours, too. His skeletal design... Respiratory and circulatory systems... Two lungs, one heart, an intricate network of blood vessels... His digestive system, however, does seem to differ."

Zercy's thumb paused. "Differ in what way?"

"His kidneys are much smaller, as is his bladder... But the biggest distinction has to do with his stomach. Ours has two chambers, his has only one. And where our broken-down nutrients pass from the second chamber into our bloodstream, his appears to continue into his abdomen."

Zercy's frown was palpable. "I do not understand."

Alec thought back to what Miros said about never having bowel movements. In hindsight, he guessed it made sense considering they didn't have bowels. Evidently, that second half of a Niran's stomach served the same purpose as small intestines.

"His digestive tract," Sirus clarified. "It continues... in the form of a channel. A long, tubular organ that fills his lower cavity, winding around until it connects with his rectum."

Yeah, Alec thought. Awesome subject. Now, if only someone would just untie him.

"Their digestive tract is connected to their... reproductive organs?"

"It seems so, my liege. I have never seen anything like it."

Zercy didn't reply.

"What is curious, however, is that when I explored this strange passage, no real matter was present. It is as if his body has discontinued using the channel, directing all nutrients solely to his bladder."

A soft grunt. "That would be fortunate."

"Tah... Although, I am not quite sure how much it matters."

"Why do you say this?"

"Because according to his test results, he is unable to accommodate our kind. His entry point is just too... well, too small."

Ugh. Alec shifted awkwardly, heat suffusing his cheeks.

Above him, Zercy again didn't reply.

Was he pissed? Consider Alec defective? An inadequate pet?

Alec scowled. Whatever. Because, again, he should be relieved by Sirus' findings. After all, they just bought him an official waiver; sex with the Kríe king was off the table. And a part of him did feel relief on some level, but another part of him definitely did not. That part felt pissed that the king would think less of him. It also felt more of that low-key disappointment. Which he hated. He hated that he felt that way. His jaw ticked angrily. He was sick of these Kríe.

"Tell me more," Zercy muttered. "What else have you found?"

"Aside from those discoveries, in regard to reproduction, his organs are much like ours, except *smaller*. A two-testis scrotum... a barbless cock... his sensitive inner jewel... Although, I am still in the process of examining him. His emotions are somewhat... hindering the process."

Zercy resumed with his thumb. "Are they now."

"Unfortunately, yes, Sire. His restlessness and agitation appear to affect cooperation. I do not understand why, but the last test I attempted seemed to unsettle him greatly. Getting him to full erection has proven arduous."

"I see," Zercy murmured. Was that amusement in his tone? "So, this means you have yet to collect a sample."

"Yes, my lord. I was attempting to do that now."

"Ah. Then proceed. I should like to observe."

Alec tensed. Aw, fuck. He was going to stay and *watch?*

"Yes, Sire. Right away. In fact, I have the instrument right here." Sirus shuffled a few steps over, then promptly returned.

Zercy stilled and clutched Alec's shoulder. "*That* is your tool?"

"Yes, my lord. A *bahka* reed. They are remarkably effective siphons."

"Yes, but surely..." Zercy's voice sounded tight. "Surely that will hurt him. *Greatly.*"

Oh, God. What the fuck was a *bahka* reed? Alec's pulse raced faster. He pulled at his restraints.

"Yes, my lord," Sirus answered. "I am afraid it will. If he was hard it would not, but he resists."

The king grunted darkly. Alec could feel his gaze—scrutinizing Alec's face, and then his dick.

"Perhaps I might have better luck."

Oh, shit. His timbre. It'd gone way too husky. Heat spread through Alec's belly as realization struck—the king would most *definitely* have better luck.

Zercy moved in close. Warm breath kissed Alec's ear. "Hello, my pet. It is I, your mighty king. And as your mighty king, I command you to *harden.*"

Alec's cock gave a twitch, as if saying *okay!* Disloyal bastard.

"Fuck off."

Sirus exhaled. "It is pointless, Sire. He will not comply."

Zercy chuckled, ignoring his servant, his breath tickling Alec's neck. "Oh, come now. Just this once." He settled his hand on Alec's throat. "Please your king like a good little human."

Asshole. And yet ironically, his words were turning Alec on. Anxiously, he swallowed against the Kríe's heavy palm. He could feel his dick thickening, growing bigger.

"No," he bit tersely.

Don't get hard—Don't get hard—

Quickly, he pulled to mind disgusting images.

Rotten cabbage—Chunky milk—

"You deny me?" Zercy murmured.

Shit, his low rumble was making things worse.

"Yes," Alec rasped.

"With all due respect, Sire. Perhaps we should commence."

Zercy chuckled again, still ignoring his physician, and snagged Alec's lobe between his teeth.

Alec sucked in a breath as current zinged through his junk, powering a surge of blood up into his shaft. Motherfucker! He fisted his hands.

"My lord," Sirus groused. "You are not even touching it. I seriously doubt that just talking to him will—" He stopped in mid-sentence. "I... I do not believe it. Your pet... He is *fully erect*."

Fuuuck.

Alec clenched his jaw.

Zercy released his lobe, most likely to get a look for himself. His mouth returned quickly though, and grazed Alec's ear. "Ah... You could not do it. Could not keep your cock soft. Your king stirs your loins. *I arouse you*."

Alec didn't reply, because honestly, what was the point? He couldn't exactly argue the obvious.

Sirus emitted a perplexed sound. "I suppose we should begin."

Zercy straightened back up, or so Alec assumed, since his breath no longer teased Alec's skin. "Tah. By all means."

God, the bastard sounded smug.

"Of course... Tah... Um... Hmm. Perhaps *you* should hold his cock."

This couldn't be happening. Alec gritted his teeth. "How about *no one* holds my cock?"

Zercy ignored him. "It would be my pleasure."

Warm fingers curled around Alec's shaft. Potent zings engulfed his crotch. He tamped back a moan. Oh, God. He was going to come in that smug Krie's hand. Maybe not this second, but definitely soon. Just the king's grip alone was making him crazy.

"Good, Sire... Although, perhaps you could hold it below the head. With just your thumb and finger... Tah, perfect."

"Imagine that," Zercy mused. He was smiling. Alec could hear it. "King of the Krie holding his pet's little crown."

Alec bristled, glaring daggers behind that blindfold.

Sirus chuckled. "Indeed." Two more fingers touched Alec's glans, right on either side of its hole. Firmly, they pulled it open, then warm liquid oozed inside.

Alec tensed from head to toe. "What is that? What are you doing?"

"There," Sirus announced, as though Alec hadn't even spoken. "We are ready to begin. Hold him steady, my lord, while I slip the... reed... inside..."

Whoa, what? Alec tensed even harder than before. Above, the king loosed a sultry growl. All hungry-sounding and dark, and blatantly aroused. But then it hit. That raw burn where something was entering his cock.

He jerked instinctively. "What are you doing?"

Zercy clutched his hip with his free hand and held him secure. "Be still, pet. All is well."

"No. All is not well," he ground out. "That thing stings."

"Not for long," Sirus murmured, sounding utterly focused. Farther he fed that reed into Alec's urethra until, finally, the thing gently bottomed out.

A grunt breached Alec's lips at the foreign sensation, pleasure stirring in the root of his cock. He shifted his hips, wishing like hell he could see. Even though the reed didn't hurt anymore, it still felt weird as shit inside his dick.

A second drizzle of liquid eased its way inside. Sirus moved the reed up a little, then slid it back down, like he was testing the level of lubrication. More drizzle. More testing. Soon resistance was nonexistent.

The Kríe chuffed softly. "Denza, Sire. Watch it now." On the heel of Sirus' words, Alec felt the reed being pulled upward till it lingered just inside his glans. "I let go and, look, gravity does all the work." Right on cue, the reed sank back down, slow and steady, with clearly no one holding on. It softly bottomed out again. More bliss roused in his junk.

Alec bit his cheek. Swallowed. Swiveled his wrists in their restraints.

"Captivating," Zercy rumbled. "I should like to try."

"Of course."

Oh, for fuck's sake. Alec braced as the king took a turn, pulling the reed up... then letting it go. Smoothly, it descended. More zings as it touched down. Alec tamped back a moan—which only seemed to spur the king on.

"He likes this," Zercy purred, repeating the action.

Alec shuddered and restlessly clenched his teeth.

Zercy chuckled, relenting. "You may proceed."

"Yes, Sire. Just allow me to wake the *bahka*."

Alec stiffened, his crotch thrumming. "You mean, that thing's *alive*-alive?"

"Tah," Sirus answered. "*All* of Mina is. Every part."

Alec's heart sped faster. He tried to close his knees. Then, deep inside the base of his cock, that slippery reed started to *shimmy*. Licks of current instantly branched in every direction.

Alec sucked in sharply. "*Ungh*—" That felt unreal.

Zercy growled, all low and heady. "What is it doing?"

"Loosening the soil."

"The *soil*?"

"In theory, yes. As a fundamental root, to extract what it needs, it vibrates the ground to break it up, making it easier to pull in its meal. Water, insects, whatever it requires. What I have discovered, however, is that when manipulated in controlled environments, these vibrations work incredibly well for other purposes... Like stimulating a male's jewel from a different direction."

"Through his cock," Zercy surmised. "Instead of his channel."

"Correct, my lord. The uppermost part of every male's jewel is nestled against the root of his member."

Alec shuddered and jerked as they jabbered the fuck on, the intensity of those currents flat-out rocking him. His eyes rolled back. His heart hammered faster.

"Incredible," Zercy mused. "And this will make him spend?"

"It should, Sire. Tah."

"And his seed, when he does?"

"The *bahka* will siphon it into this holding pod."

Alec bit back a groan. Those fuckers were unbelievable. Talking about his cock, about his orgasm, like he wasn't even there.

"How long will it take?" The king's gaze was on his dick. Alec could feel its heavy weight. Feel its heat.

"Not long. But outside assistance would speed up the process."

"By stroking him," the king presumed.

"Tah. That would help."

The Kríe stopped talking, no doubt to watch the reed working. Teasing Alec's junk with a barrage of bliss as he furiously fought not to thrust. He tried to fight it back, all that intoxicating pleasure, but holy freaking shit, it wasn't easy. Already, he needed to come so bad.

"Please," he panted before he could stop himself. His junk was going nuts. He couldn't take it.

Zercy released Alec's hip and slowly roamed his fingers over his abs. "You wish to spill?" he rumbled smoothly.

"*Yes—*"

"Hmm… By *my* hand?"

Alec bristled, but to his consternation, that was easier to admit than he'd like. "Yes," he gasped breathlessly.

"Ask nicely."

Grr! "Please—"

"As you wish," Zercy conceded. He loosed his hold on Alec's crown and gripped his shaft. "Sirus, I am ready to make him spill."

"Very good, Sire. Just remember not to stop prematurely. I gave him kirah nectar to increase his production. To halt before he is finished might cause him pain."

Wait, *what?* So, *that's* why his prostate felt so full?

Fucking Sirus. He'd said that stuff was for his health. Not to *stockpile cum.*

"Understood," the king murmured, starting a slow, loose stroke. "Do not stop until my pet is fully milked."

Alec shivered at the feel of his hand wrapped around him, at the sound of his rich, decadent voice. He still couldn't believe this. That this crazy shit was happening. That this Kríe, who just purchased his team an hour ago, was about to make him come.

And a part of Alec was going to love it.

With that reed still down his dick, Alec rocked his hips, absently syncing them up with Zercy's hand. God, those fingers, moving so steadily but staying so loose. They were stoking a maelstrom in his junk. Pleasure mounted, pressure surged. Alec helplessly groaned.

Zercy growled again and swiped his thumb across Alec's crown. Alec's whole body shuddered.

He panted roughly. Licking his lips, he fisted his hands. As good as this felt—and it felt like rapture—he needed it to end as soon as possible. Not just so he could finally bust his load, but for another unexpected reason, too. The sinking suspicion that if this went on much longer, he'd end up irrevocably addicted. Or in other words, royally screwed.

Alec twitched as Zercy lazily jacked him. "Yeah—" He nodded restlessly. "Fuck—Don't stop—"

The mighty Kríe purred and palmed Alec's cheek with his free hand, then slid his strong fingers into Alec's hair. His claws grazed Alec's scalp. Alec moaned before he could stop himself, the tantalizing sensation only making him crazier.

Pressure mushroomed in his crotch. Pleasure coursed up his shaft, flicking up his length, teasing his crown. His balls firmed. His toes curled. His muscles locked tight.

"*Ungh, God*— So close—"

"Tah…" Zercy growled. "Right on the verge. Spill for me, pet. Spill for your king."

Like a fuse that reached its end, his command set Alec off.

"*Fuuuck!*" he belted.

Pleasure exploded through his prostate, then detonated his nuts. From the base of his cock to its bulging, rock-hard crown. Ecstasy. Running rampant. Making him quake.

But as his spine fought to arch and his hips went wild thrusting, not one splat of hot cum hit his body. Instead, as his balls and G kicked his massive load free, he could feel that eager *bahka* siphoning it up. Drawing it from the source even faster than he could pump it, creating the most erotic sensation of suction. Powerful and unceasing, heightening his release. A mind-blowing compliment to Zercy's hand.

Out of nowhere, the sensation had him picturing the king. All dark and stunning, with his lips around Alec's glans, sucking Alec's cum straight from his nuts. Oh, God. That visual. Way too stimulating. He launched into a brand-new release.

"Shit—" he croaked loudly. "*Ungh*— I can't stop— coming—"

"Mah, you cannot," Sirus chuckled somewhere distant.

"Moonsah," the king growled. *More*. "Give me *every drop*."

Alec panted as his reeling prostate pulsed. Surely, he'd already given up a *vat*. But just like last time, the stuff kept on coming. And his stupid freaking hips kept on thrusting. Like the king was controlling them, wasn't letting them stop. Not that it felt bad, Alec was orgasming for fuck's sake, but his sanity was getting siphoned up with his cum.

Sometime later—he had absolutely no idea how long—a blissed-out, broken groan crawled up his throat. His lungs burned. His muscles twitched. Sweat covered his body. And as a dull ache formed in his nuts, and his prostate hummed, he shuddered, then slumped like a noodle.

Finished or not, he was out of gas.

"Krye…" Zercy murmured. "You are beautiful."

CHAPTER EIGHT

* * *

"Well done, Sire," Sirus rumbled. "You have wrought much seed." Slowly, he withdrew the reed from Alec's cock.

Alec fought another shiver. Tamped another moan. God, he felt boneless. Unable to move.

Quiet shuffling noises sounded, as if things were being put away, then a low, deep-throated purr met his ears. It was coming from Zercy, blanketing his body from above. Alec stilled as the pumping vibrations sank under his skin. What was Zercy doing?

Beneath the blindfold, Alec peeled open his eyes, instinctively wanting to see the king's face. Nothing but black. Agitated by the blindness, he shifted against his restraints. He wanted off this goddamn table.

As if reading his body language, Zercy's soft thrumming ceased. "You are finished then? No longer need him?"

"Yes, my lord. His exam is complete."

Alec exhaled in happy relief. He'd made it through alive, sane, and still in one piece. Granted, he was a few ounces lighter than before, but he supposed the means-to-an-end there could have been worse.

"Just allow me a moment to quickly unbind him and—"

"Mah," Zercy cut in. "I should like to do that myself."

"As you wish."

Above them, Mina's casing creaked as Sirus' presence left Alec's side. Guess he was taking his 'assistant' with him. Good, and good riddance. Another exhale left Alec's lungs. Until, that is, warm fingers grazed his neck. Then more air sucked back in and refused to budge.

Zercy chuckled low and unlatched the restraint. "You do not like Mina?"

"Not really." Alec twisted his freed head. Ahhh. Movement.

Zercy unlocked his arm next, his claws grazing the inside of Alec's bicep. Alec tensed, nerve endings stirring back to life.

"She is not so bad," the king murmured. "She enables discovery and has helped Sirus save countless lives."

So, Sirus wasn't just a mad scientist/ provider of creepy pleasures? Alec turned his head in Zercy's direction. "You mean, he's also a doctor?"

"Tah. He is many things. His brilliance knows no bounds." He reached across the table, his warmth brushing Alec's chest, and pulled Alec's other arm support back to the table. "I depend on him," he unlatched more brackets, "for very important matters."

And then his scent hit him, and Alec's stupid mouth watered. He couldn't help it, though. The Kríe smelled unexpectedly good. Like golden-brown marshmallows over a campfire.

Zercy freed his second wrist restraint. Two arms officially liberated. At which point, he moved to Alec's legs. Alec tugged off his blindfold and—*oh fuuuuck*, what an eyeful. That big-ass dark king looming over his naked body, his strong hands doing their thing against Alec's thigh. Alec's hamstring twitched as another claw grazed him, then his traitor dick gave a twitch, too.

Zercy paused and lifted a brow, eyeing said traitor dick, then slid Alec a smirk and resumed.

Alec scowled, waiting impatiently for him to open the last shackles. When he did, Alec sat up—and covered his junk. Heat suffused his cheeks. Not that everything hadn't already been fully seen.

The king's full lips twitched. "Sirus, fetch me a garment."

"Yes, Sire," Sirus called from outside the partition. He appeared not long after with something dark clutched in hand. "A youngling-size wrap. I believe it will fit better."

Alec shot him a glare. He wasn't child-size, goddamnit.

Zercy chuffed a little and walked it over. "You still look tired. Would you like for me to help you put this on?" There was teasing in his tone. In his *deep, rich* tone. With its titillating lilt that roused Alec's senses.

"I got it," Alec muttered, quickly taking it from his hand.

The king didn't seem surprised. Crossing his thick arms, his bicep cuffs gleaming, he watched Alec secure it around his hips. "Are you ready, my little pet? Able to walk?" His lips curved.

Alec's jaw ticked. He knew why he'd asked that. After the brain-blitzing orgasm he'd just friggin' given him, he figured Alec's knees might not be steady.

Whatever. Smug bastard.

Alec slid off the table. "Yeah, I'm *able to walk*. You're not *that* good."

The king's dark brows lifted. Then he barked out a laugh. "You will be disciplined for that. I hope it was worth it."

Visions of whipping posts inundated Alec's brain. But before he could even attempt to do damage control, Zercy turned to Sirus. "Bring me a harness."

"Yes, my lord."

"And a leash. Not too long. I want him close."

Alec bristled from head to toe. Another goddamn leash?

He shot the king a look. "I'm not an animal. I have dignity."

Zercy tilted his head and stared at him, his gold piercings glinting. Up his pointed ears. Along his sleek horns. Were his nipples pierced, too? Gesh's pack's definitely were, but then, so were their septums, and the king didn't have anything through his nose.

Distracted by curiosity, he glanced at Zercy's chest, wondering if he could tell through his tunic. After all, the dark green fabric looked notably thin. And smooth. So smooth, in fact, it probably felt and moved like silk. Against his rock-hard pectorals. And his washboard abs. And, shit yeah, those tiny pointed nipples.

He eyed the little peaks, looking for any hint of piercings—until the king gave a rumble and flexed his pecs. "Dignity? Are you sure? You seem to function much on instinct."

Alec froze, aghast, and glanced back up. What had he been doing, all ogling his captor's chest?

Although…

In his defense…

The Kríe's pecs *were* practically eye level.

Clearing his throat, he frowned and looked away. "I don't need a leash. That's degrading as hell."

Sirus returned with Zercy's request and handed it over, then turned on his heel and disappeared again. The king stepped close and clutched Alec's jaw, firmly turning his head to face him. "It is not meant to degrade," he murmured. "But to *emphasize*. That I value you. That you please me. That I do not wish to lose you."

Alec gripped Zercy's wrist and shoved his hand away. "Yeah? Well, to me what that 'emphasizes' is that you see me as a possession that you *own*."

The king's gold eyes blazed. "You are that to me, also." He held up the harness. "Now give me your arms."

Alec chuckled humorlessly. Took a step back. "Bullshit. I am *not* wearing that."

"Tah, you are."

"*No*, I'm *not*."

Zercy's jaw tick-ticked. "Very well." He called to his guards. "Kellim. Setch. I will be needing your assistance."

* * *

Alec glowered indignantly as he descended the stairwell, securely harnessed, and led by King Smug. He hadn't even bothered resisting Zercy's cronies. Encourage a bout of manhandling with two Kríe twice his size? Yeah, he'd pass. He'd been humiliated enough already.

Fortunately, the harness wasn't too big or elaborate. Just hide straps that wrapped around the front of each shoulder, then crisscrossed at his back to bind his elbows. A separate strip was used to tie his wrists together, too, and—surprise, surprise—a collar was wound around his neck. Whatever. Which wasn't to say he'd ever get used to being detained. He was just grateful the getup didn't draw too much attention.

Zercy took the steps beside him as his guards led the way. Namely, the two comedians who'd escorted Alec to Sirus, nearly giving him a heart attack in the stairwell. The same two who'd just strapped him into his harness. In fact, Setch—the one who'd offered him that blowjob earlier—even asked if he'd told Sirus about the elevator. Right in Alec's ear, all hopeful and shit, as he held him against the wall while Kellim buckled him.

"Sorry," Alec had bit out. "I was kinda indisposed."

The Kríe had merely grunted in disappointment.

Alec eyed said Kríe now as they neared the bottom, then glanced over his shoulder at two others. A second pair who'd been posted outside Sirus' door, no doubt having come as Zercy's escorts. All four were probably part of his royal guard. Alec wondered how many there were in total.

They reached ground level and cut a right, heading down the east side of the castle. Nobles milled about with wine-filled goblets, their stately garb giving testament to their status. Servants of various species hustled around. All, however, paused in whatever they were doing to look Alec over with appreciative eyes.

Alec tensed, feeling awkward. And embarrassed. And exposed. For fuck's sake, all he had covering his body was that wrap, which barely covered his goods and upper thighs. He could feel their hungry gazes. It was the marketplace all over again, with every species undressing him with their stares. Something that Zercy clearly noted, too, if his rumbling growl was any indication.

Subtle and low, but its meaning was clear. And, yup, all eyes quickly averted.

Alec eased in relief and diverted his gaze, too, to the east corridor's stretch of large arched windows. The two suns must have dipped beyond the mountainous horizon. Only hints of purple still lingering in the young night sky.

He frowned, wondering how long he'd been gone from the team. Where were they, and how were they faring? He needed to get back to them. Now.

Turning his gaze, he looked at his handler. With Alec's leash wound casually around his large wrist, Zercy strode along like a big, serious cat. He wasn't smiling but wasn't frowning. Just looked kind of pensive—until he turned his head and met Alec's eyes. He smiled a little, but the gesture looked fake. As if their walk through the castle was killing his mood. Something, as it stood, that wasn't Alec's problem. He had enough of his own, thanks to the Kríe.

"I want to see my men."

Zercy inclined his head. "Of course."

They came to the junction of that hallway from earlier, the one they'd walked when headed for the bath house. This time, however, they were at the opposite end, where another staircase happened to be situated. They strode to the thing and started their ascent.

"Where are we going?" Alec muttered.

Zercy smiled wryly. "Up."

Grr. "Up to where?"

"The second floor."

Wow. Just as aggravating as Gesh.

Alec grumbled and looked away.

Zercy chuckled and tugged the leash.

Soon they reached the top of the steps. Alec looked around. More hallways. And doors. And ambling workers. Like maybe a wing of the castle where servants lived. There was also another immediate flight of stairs. Stairs that their convoy promptly turned right and headed for.

He glanced back at Zercy as they started their next ascent. Didn't bother asking this time, though. No doubt, all he'd get was an 'up' again, or 'third floor.'

They reached the next level, which looked similar to the last. But nicer. Cleaner. With décor and better lighting. His guess: the nobles' quarters. In fact, there was one now, exiting his chambers with a male. A young adult, maybe early twenties, who was considerably smaller than the aristocrat. And definitely not a Kríe like the larger male.

Alec regarded his colorful skin. It was purple, too, but lighter and pinker than the Kríe's. With jaguar spots along his lean arms and legs. Had horns too, but they were dark gold. And shorter. And spiraled. Like dainty little unicorn nubs at each temple. His ears were pointed like the Kríe's, and though he had dreads as well, his were dark gold and in a mohawk. He also had two sets of nipples— which looked super erect—and a twitching tail of matching golden dreads.

Alec watched as the huge Kríe pulled the smaller male against him, growling as he palmed his ass and squeezed. His plaything growled back, but it wasn't as robust. His bite to the Kríe's pec, though, certainly was. The Kríe straight-up shuddered with a guttural snarl, then lifted his boy toy and sank his fangs into his neck. The young male shot instantly into writhing. Breathless grunts punched past his lips.

Alec blinked, that bite reminding him of Roni and Chet. The Kríe pinned the male against the wall with his body. In turn, the male snapped his thighs around his hips. Just like that, the noble started grinding against his crotch.

Fuuuck.

Alec swallowed and quickly turned away. Should probably pay attention to where they were going. Because, nope, the guards weren't stopping on this level, either, but turning to yet another set of steps. Again, they repeated the climb, and as they arrived on the fourth floor, Alec happily noted that they'd reached the last of the stairs.

He glanced around. This level was different than the others. No stretches of hallways. No servants wandering about. Just a spacious landing with grand, double doors. Alec's heart thumped warily. Where exactly had they taken him?

Setch and Kellim strode forward and, without preamble, unlocked the bronze panels and went inside. The rest of them remained where they were.

Alec frowned. "Where are we?"

Zercy smiled. "Your king's chambers."

Alec stiffened. Oh, God. They were at his *bedroom*?

He shook his head. "You were supposed to take me to my men."

Zercy quirked a brow. "Was I?"

"Yeah. We discussed this just a minute ago. Remember?"

"Ah. I do remember. You *demanded* to see them instead of asking." Zercy's expression grew dark. He leaned in close. "But I do not take orders. From anyone."

Alec stared at him, frustrated—and now a little intimidated, too. "But… you said, 'of course'."

Zercy chuffed and looked away, straightening back to full height. "Tah. Meaning, 'I am very sure you do'."

Alec blinked, then bristled and opened his mouth just as the two guards reemerged from inside.

"All clear, Your Highness. It is safe to enter."

They turned and led the way, with Zercy pulling Alec along by his leash. Reluctantly, he entered, but stopped the second they breached the doorway. His jaw went slack. Holy shit. Zercy's bedroom... it was effing incredible.

Although, honestly, it was way freaking more than a bedroom. More like his own lavish living space—in a Kríe-esque sort of way— open and spacious, with lots of plants and windows.

He glanced around, eyes rapt. There was cool stuff everywhere. Forgetting momentarily about his ire—and his team—he settled his gaze on the centerpiece. A huge, steaming hot tub, recessed flush with the floor, with a slightly raised border of masculine stone. It kind of looked like granite, with its mottled grays and browns, but its edges weren't sharp, and its finish wasn't polished. Alec eyed the water, noting more of those little floating lotuses, and how the firelight reflected off its surface. Firelight that burned not just from a grand hearth to the right, but also from countless wall sconces around the perimeter.

He eyed said walls, easily fifteen feet tall and textured in a white, coarse-grained stucco. In conjunction with all the potted trees, rounded windows and inset shelves, it gave the space an exotic, cave-like ambiance. Primal, yet strangely inviting.

"Nenya." *Come.* Zercy tugged his leash, having paused by Alec's side. "I will give you a little tour of your new quarters."

Whoa, *what?* Alec shot him a look.

But the king just turned to his guards. "You are dismissed. Setch and Kellim, take first shift." Which presumably meant standing sentry outside the door.

The Kríe gave clipped bows and swiftly departed, shutting Alec in with the king. His heart thudded faster. He didn't want to be alone with him. With the one male on this planet that messed with his head.

God, this wasn't good.

He fisted his bound hands.

Zercy slid him a look, then casually sauntered left. "My slice of secluded peace within a world of anything but." His lips curved a little as he gestured to...

What *was* that?

Alec frowned, trying to decipher what the hell he was seeing. Eight-foot-high wall partitions along the room's whole left side, curiously arranged amidst themselves, creating paths. Or rather, obscure walkways, like a maze of bookshelf aisles gone awry. It sort of reminded him of a little piece of the jungle. Although, that was probably due, in part, to all the plants. Tall, slender flora of dark greens and purples placed flush, here and there, against the walls. Walls, incidentally, that looked like Swiss cheese, riddled with large cut-out shapes you could peer through.

Alec pursed his brows, still clueless as to what all of it was, but decided nevertheless not to ask. It'd probably slow down the tour, and he strongly suspected that he wouldn't be going anywhere until it was done.

Zercy cast him a look. "Would you like to enter?"

Kind of, actually, yeah. But instead, Alec glared. "No. I would *like* to see my men."

The king just smirked gruffly and continued on, pointing to a small, tiled opening in the wall. "Where you take your cock to urinate." Lovely. They kept going toward the far corner. Zercy gestured to a wooden desk facing away from them. "Where I write. Or draw. Or stare out the window."

Alec's brows rose as he followed, surprised that Zercy drew. Not so much that he wrote; he seemed educated.

They turned right and strode along the chamber's back wall, passing more arched openings and tall plants. But right as they came upon the halfway point, Zercy paused at one window in particular. Only this one was noticeably larger, and semicircle shaped—its bottom flat, the rest a generous curve. What was curious though, was how, unlike the others, this window was closed-off by curtains. Well, not really curtains. More like heavy swaths of crimson velvet.

Zercy slid him a smile, then pulled open one side.

Alec stiffened.

It wasn't a window.

It was the entrance to where Zercy slept.

A private cove within his mega-massive cave. Which wasn't to say that the cubby wasn't big, or opulent, because it was definitely both of those. Shaped like a semicircle inside as well, it looked roughly five feet high and eight feet wide. Equally short windows wrapped around its perimeter, boasting of both mountainous views and lay of the land. And yet, the whole enclosure was entirely sleeping space. One wall-to-wall sea of furs flush with the entry. Just climb through and, bam, you're in bed.

Alec eyed the cozy nook, wishing he had one just like it. But all the space station offered were twin-size bunks, that you shared with a roomie in cramped living quarters. No space. No privacy. No room to stretch or think. Yeah, an upgrade like this would be heaven.

Zercy gestured inside, his gilded gaze gleaming. "Would you like to try it out? It is *very* soft."

And just like that, Alec's dick gave a twitch. From just the sound of his voice. But, God, he couldn't help it. It was just so *heady*. Like the rumble of a sex storm on the prowl.

Clearing his throat, he quickly shook his head. "No, thanks," he muttered. "I'll pass."

Zercy released the swath and resumed with the tour, leading Alec by his leash to the other corner. This one had an oversized chaise amidst the windows, covered in luxurious black suede. A spotted fur throw was draped over the arm. A small wooden table sat to its left. And on that small table, Alec happened to notice, was an eclectic dish of glassy-smooth rocks.

Come to think of it... He glanced around... On flat surfaces everywhere, more bowls sat full of similar stones. He studied them from afar. "What are those rocks for?"

"They calm me," Zercy answered.

"*Calm* you?"

"Tah. So smooth. I find them soothing." He didn't expound further. Just tugged Alec along, gesturing half-heartedly to the fireplace.

"My hearth, but I assume you have similar things. Ah, yes. Here we are." He stopped a few steps later, in front of what looked like a bar. A fully stocked bar outcropped from the wall. One that not only displayed countless thick-glassed decanters, but also assorted dishes of peculiar edibles. "Thirsty?" the king asked.

Actually, Alec was—considering the way he'd just been worked over. Strapped to a table, and made to strain and pant? Not to mention that brutal orgasm they wrenched out of him. Problem was, parched or not, he didn't trust whatever Zercy was offering.

Watching as the king poured himself a ruby liquid, Alec licked his dry lips. "No. I'm good."

Zercy took a large swig from his goblet. "Suit yourself."

Alec glanced at the door. "So, are we done now? Can we go?"

Zercy tilted his head. "Go?" Amusement flickered in his gaze.

Alec clenched his jaw. "Yes. To see my team."

"Ah." The king took another swig, then sauntered past. "Not tonight. Perhaps tomorrow... If you are good."

Alec's mouth fell open as he reluctantly followed, that damn leash pulling him along. "Tomorrow? Are you kidding me? No way. I go now."

Zercy slid a dark look over his shoulder.

Shit. No doubt, that had sounded 'demanding.'

Alec pursed his lips. "Please."

The king's features eased. He stopped in front of the hot tub. "I will think on it while I soak. My mind needs to relax."

Alec scowled, stopping, too. "Wouldn't relaxing be easier alone? Your guards could take me to them while you—"

"Mah," Zercy interrupted. "I should like you to stay."

With Alec at his back, he removed his sandals, then dropped the leash on the rock ledge and stepped on it. As if he suspected Alec might try to scurry away or something. But seriously, what would be the point of that? Like he could get past those two hulking guards.

Alec swallowed, staying put, as he watched him unfasten his belt.

Oh, fuck.

He was taking off his clothes.

CHAPTER NINE

* * *

Zercy set his belt aside, along with its dagger, then gripped his midnight green tunic and kept going. Alec's lips parted as he tracked the silken garment's ascent, sliding up over his dark, chiseled ass before climbing the length of his muscular back. And then it pulled over his velvety black locks, taking them along for the ride. A split second later, it was off and on the ground, with those curious dreads tumbling back down over his shoulders.

Of their own volition, Alec's eyes dropped back down to where only a jockstrap-type loincloth remained. His dick gave a nudge. He cursed and closed his eyes.

Keep that thing on, Kríe. Do *not* take it off.

A soft chuff met his ears, then the sound of water sloshing.

"Nenya, pet. Join me." Zercy's voice sounded husky.

What? Get in? Oh, *hell* to the *no*.

Alec opened his eyes, relieved to find Zercy in the tub. He'd left his metal bicep cuffs on, as well the rings on his fingers. Alec's gaze dropped to his pecs. Pecs that boldly displayed—yup, he'd totally called it—dark, little, rock-hard, *pierced* nipples. Not hoops, though, like Gesh's pack. Just tiny horizontal bars, capped on both ends with small, golden gems. In truth, they looked bad ass. He'd love to get a look at them up close...

Fuck. He was staring.

He quickly glanced away to focus on Zercy's pile of clothes instead. Shit. That damn jockstrap was sitting right on top. Which meant that big motherfucker had nothing on. Alec swallowed again and shook his head. "I already bathed."

Zercy settled in across from him, Alec's leash back in his clutches, his drink set on the smooth stone to his left. "That was not a request. And right now it is not a bath. Just a place to relax and converse."

Alec eyed him warily, and then the round tub. If Zercy only wanted to talk, maybe he'd be willing to compromise. Stiffly, he stepped forward and sat down on the ledge, easing his lower legs into the water. He looked at the king. The Kríe's mouth quirked. Then, with a wicked grin, he gave the leash a *yank*.

Alec yelped, falling forward helplessly.

SPLASH!

He went under, then shot back up.

Zercy chuckled.

Alec glowered. "That was so not cool."

"Tah. But it was so very fun."

Alec ground his molars and moved to the farthest spot possible, settling on some kind of underwater seat.

The king just watched him with those mesmerizing eyes, then smiled a little. "Admit it. This feels nice."

Alec looked away, still irked.

"You truly do not like it?"

"No," he snapped. "I truly do not like it. I don't want to be here. Remember?"

"My accommodations do not meet your standards?"

"That's got nothing to do with it."

"Then it is my company you do not like. Do I repulse you?" Zercy murmured.

Alec tamped a humorless laugh. How he *wished* he repulsed him. "That's got nothing to do with it, either."

"Hmm." The king stared at him, an impish look in his eye. "So, you enjoy my company... and like the way I look."

Alec stiffened. "I didn't say that."

"I believe you did."

Alec clenched his jaw again. "Why won't you let me see my men?"

"It is your punishment for earlier."

Alec furrowed his brows. "Punishment?"

"For speaking disrespectfully to your king. I told you I would discipline you. Did you forget?"

Actually, no, he hadn't forgotten. He'd just expected... far worse.

Zercy's lips curved at his expression. "You thought I would have you beaten?"

In truth? Yes, he did.

Alec clenched his fists. "I don't know."

Again, the king chuckled. "Kríe are *civilized*, not *savages*." His grin widened. "Kidding. We are *absolutely* savages."

Alec stared at him, not exactly sure how to respond.

"Do not worry." Zercy's eyes glinted. "You are my favorite. You are safe."

"Great," he muttered.

The Kríe's face sobered. A few moments ticked by. "Tell me about your time with Gesh's pack."

Ah. Subject change. Not that this one was any better.

Alec shrugged a little. "He pretended to be our friend, then tricked us into eating senna`sohnsay."

Zercy's brow lifted. "Senna`sohnsay? How very insidious."

"Yeah, no shit. Then he took us friggin' prisoner."

"Hm. You must have been furious."

"Hell yeah, we were furious. I mean, seriously, what the hell. And then to sell us on top of that? To me, that's even worse. Swear to God, that whole pack's a bag of dicks."

"But he sold you to the king. Not some jungle sadist."

"I don't give a fuck *who* that bastard sold us to. We aren't merchandise. Commodities to be sold. We're human fucking beings with dignity."

"Ah," Zercy murmured, clearly noting his anger. "Your dignity. That means much to you."

"Yes," he grated. "It does."

They both went silent, gazes locked, bodies still.

Eventually though, Zercy resumed with his questions. "So, you were angrier to have been sold than tricked into eating senna`sohnsay. Does that mean you enjoyed how it made you feel?"

Alec glanced away. "Would've been nicer under different circumstances."

The king's voice dipped low. "How did you spill?"

Fuck, he could feel Zercy's timbre in his crotch. Awkwardly, he shifted atop his underwater perch—one that kind of felt like a bike seat—and cleared his throat. "I, uh, yeah... I had sex."

Zercy's brows rose. "Willingly?"

Ugh. Truth time. He nodded.

"But with whom? If your men could not spill as you could not, then—"

"With a Kríe," he answered tersely. "I had sex... with a Kríe."

The king paused at that, looking downright confused. "But our species are not compatible. Your kind is too small."

Alec averted his gaze again, not wanting to go into specifics.

Zercy's frown was palpable. "Did he hurt you?"

Alec looked back at him. Shook his head.

The king studied him intently. "How? Was he deformed?"

Alec coughed a humorless laugh. "Uh, no. He wasn't deformed."

"Then *how* did he not hurt you? Your size cannot accommodate."

Fuck. Alec's stomach clenched. He did *not* want to answer that. And the reasons why ran the gamut. The most obvious being that if he told Zercy how, then the king could easily use that method, too. A prospect that truthfully made Alec restless as hell. Because deep down, a part of him would love for that to happen, which was an utterly FUBAR way to feel.

Problem was, whether he told Zercy how it happened or not, the king would find out. He'd just be pissed at Alec for making him work for it. And since he'd be in the big Kríe's presence for the foreseeable future, it'd probably be wise not to start off on the wrong foot.

"They, um..." He cleared his throat again. "They used tachi venom."

The king's brows wrenched high again. "Tachi venom. How resourceful." His gaze turned probing as he locked eyes with Alec. "Did you enjoy it? Find pleasure in laying with a Kríe?"

Gah. Alec's face heated. "I... I don't know."

"You do not know if you enjoyed it?" Zercy sounded incredulous.

"It was... intense."

"Intense..." Zercy canted his head. "Would you like to do it again?"

"Uh..." Alec's dick nudged his thigh beneath that wrap. Thank God he wasn't naked. Not that the wrap was helping much. Just sort of floating over his junk.

Zercy's features tightened. "You would. With the same Kríe as before."

Alec scowled instantaneously and blurted, "Fuck, no."

Miros and his pack could kiss his ass.

"You are still very angry with him."

"Uh, *yeah*. He helped Gesh sell us. *Sell us*. What kind of scum do that?"

Zercy's brows rose again. "You believe they are evil?"

Alec pressed his lips tight. Then exhaled. "No. Not really. They're just a bunch of... overbearing shits." He shook his head thoughtfully. "But... with the way things ended earlier, down in your hall, I'm thinking they might actually feel bad. Regret their decision." He looked away. "I don't know... Maybe they *do* have consciences."

"I assure you, Kríe have consciences. We just put ourselves first."

"Yeah. I've noticed," Alec deadpanned. "Awesome trait."

Zercy captured a floating flower in the palm of his hand. "Our species is supreme. It is just the way it is. But I do not hold others' inferiority against them."

Alec coughed out a laugh. "How big of you."

His lips quirked. "Tah."

Alec shook his head. "Okay, so, you claim to have a conscience. But if that's true, then how are you okay with holding us prisoner?"

"I am not holding you prisoner. You are my special guests."

Alec's next laugh came harsher. "Who aren't allowed to leave."

Zercy chuffed indignantly and waved off his words. "Semantics. And you are viewing it all wrong."

"Oh, really." Alec shifted again. Water lapped at his chest. "And how exactly am I supposed to be viewing it?"

"As luxurious living. Indefinitely."

"Gee," he ground out, "how hospitable. But guess what. We'd rather be free."

The king shook his head. "To be free would mean death. *I* can ensure your safety in a world you would not survive in."

That one was hard to argue.

"We're smart. We'd adapt. It's better than captivity. That and never knowing what the hell you're gonna do to us."

Zercy paused from toying with the flower and looked at him curiously. "What exactly do you think I have planned for you, pet?"

"You tell me. I mean, what the hell do you need six humans for?"

The big Kríe shrugged. "To delight in. Show off. Entertainment for my guests."

Alec stiffened. Every one of those answers made him wary. "Entertain how?" he muttered.

Zercy lifted a devious brow.

Alec paled.

Oh, God.

"No." He adamantly shook his head. "I heard how Gesh described us. But we're not your playthings. I don't care how much you paid for us. You can't just—"

"Silence," the king barked, his big eyes flashing. Alec stopped and stared at him. Zercy stared right back. "I vow that I will never use your men for sex, nor will I whore them out to others."

Alec eased a little. "Never? To anyone?"

"Not even my royal guard." He smirked a little. "I can already hear them complaining."

Alec exhaled before he could stop himself. That news was just such a relief. Although, now he couldn't help wondering as a result—what would compel the king to promise that?

Shifting again, he eyed the Kríe suspiciously. "Why would you make such a concession for us? I mean, clearly you view us as mere objects of indulgence. Why not just take what you want? You don't owe us anything and I know your species. Sex is like the crux of your existence."

Zercy held his gaze. "I am king. Such would be beneath me. I can fuck countless prospects whenever I want. Have my cock sucked in court should I wish it." He paused, eyelids hooding. His voice dipped again. "Besides," he took the leash and started drawing Alec forward, "I want your adoration, not resentment."

Pulled from his seat, Alec instinctively braced. "As long as you keep us prisoner," he dug in his heels, "we'll *always* resent you, no matter what."

"Hmm." The king slowly drew him closer... and closer... not even remotely fazed by Alec's resistance. "Then I will have to be clever and find a way to compensate."

Alec bit back a curse, struggling harder to stay put. But shit, the Kríe was so strong. And with his arms trapped behind him and only a flat floor to brace his feet on? Goddamnit, he didn't stand a chance.

"Stop," he grunted, resisting regardless. He needed to maintain distance. To keep some space.

Zercy smirked and shook his head, steadily reeling him nearer.

Alec's heart pounded anxiously. He strained against the leash. "I'm serious. Don't. Stop."

Only two feet left between them...

"Are you sure that you want that?" Zercy rumbled. "You look conflicted."

One foot and closing...

"Yes," he grunted. "I'm fucking sure!"

But the king just purred and closed the final gap. His big knee parted Alec's futilely bracing legs. His free hand firmly clutched Alec's hip. Then, with one last unyielding tug, he slid Alec over his thigh until he straddled it.

Alec tensed, stiff as a board as all that muscle made contact. Contact with his ass cheeks and nut sac. But what messed with him most was the feel of Zercy's cock against his leg. All big and thick and heavy and long, casually brushing against him like it was nothing. But it *was* something. Something major. Contact that was simply not okay. Mostly because it was going to give him a boner.

But then anger surged, overriding his trepidation. This Kríe was just as bad as Gesh's pack. Arrogant, domineering. Ridiculously sexual. Exasperating the ever-loving shit out of him.

"Let go of me," he demanded as Zercy's big hands clutched his sides. "I don't want—I don't want you to touch me."

But Zercy just peered down at him, looking unconvinced. "Why? You liked when I touched you in Sirus' chambers."

Alec bristled and glared up at him, their faces inches apart.

Zercy stilled, then frowned. "You are angry about that?"

"Of course, I'm angry," he grated. "You made me *come*."

"You said you wished to spill. Specifically, by *my* hand."

"Well, *yeah*, because you—" Alec stopped himself before he started shouting. What was the point? Kríe didn't get it. Were just flat-out oblivious.

As if backing up his point, Zercy canted his head, looking befuddled. "Why are you upset that you found satisfaction? I brought you to ecstasy. Made your body *sing*. Nira," he rumbled. "The sight was intoxicating. Made *me* wish to spill, too. All over *you*."

Oh, *fuuuck*.

Alec's dick bucked. His blood pumped hotter.

Fighting the urge to picture that, he quickly closed his eyes. "I'm upset," he muttered slowly, "because that kind of thing is personal. It's not like just eating a sandwich."

Zercy was eyeing him oddly. Alec could feel the weight of his stare.

He looked back up at him. "It's intimate. An *intimate act*. You know, like something you do with a lover?"

When the king just stared at him, Alec scowled. "For real? You don't ever think of sex as private?"

Zercy's brows furrowed. He shook his head. "Mah. Not really. Kríe fuck whoever whenever. Often in public."

Yeah, kind of like the freaking sex party at Gesh's.

"In fact," he went on, "there is a chamber in my castle specifically dedicated to public sex."

Whoa, what? Why did a twisted part of Alec want to see that?

"Some say it is different when one finds a mate," Zercy mused, "but, to me, that is hard to believe."

Of course, it was. Because Kríe were wired to fuck indifferently.

To them, sex was *exactly* like eating a sandwich.

Which meant this conversation was moot.

"Whatever," Alec muttered, rubbing his cheek with his shoulder. "I'm done talking about it. Just forget it."

Zercy watched him, then smiled a little and gently stroked said cheek.

Alec pulled his head away and frowned. "Don't. Just… don't touch me."

"I cannot help it. You ceaselessly compel my hands to your body." His fingers slid down Alec's throat and traced his collarbone "You compel other parts of me, too."

Alec shivered. Goddamnit. Zercy's touch. His words. They were giving him a full-fledged boner. "Don't," he rasped, shaking his head, way too focused on that hand. "Fuck— Please— Just— Please just stop touching me."

"Why?" Zercy murmured, watching his fingers roam. "You like this. I can see it on your face. In your eyes." His gaze glittered. "Can feel it heavy on my thigh."

Oh, fuck.

Pissed and mortified, Alec squirmed to get off him. "No. You're wrong. So just let me—"

"Be still," Zercy ordered, clamping a hand around his throat. "You are my *pet*," he growled. "You do not tell me what to do."

Alec clenched his teeth and glowered. "I'm nobody's pet. So stop calling me that. My name is *Alec*."

The king's grip tightened, his gaze churning brighter. Must not have liked Alec giving him another order. But right as he opened his mouth to chastise, he paused, tilted his head, and murmured, "Al-*lick*…"

Oh, *God.*

Alec instantly bit back a moan. Couldn't help it. The way he just uttered his name. Like a honey-drenched purr wickedly manipulating that last syllable, flooding his brain with visions of zealous tongues.

He shifted against Zercy's thigh and cleared his throat. "No. It's *Alec*." He enunciated clearly. "Al-*eck*."

"Tah." Zercy nodded. His gaze dropped to his mouth. "That is what I said… Al-*lllick*…"

Alec's lips parted. *Fuuuck.* Another stroke to his dick. But, God, the way Zercy said it with that titillating lilt, rolling his name like a sex marble off his tongue…

He shook his head, the sound alone making him feel drunk. And, truth be told, really horny. Tamping a restless groan, he tried to lean back, needing to put more distance between them. But either Zercy read his intentions wrong, or was just being deviant, because instead of pulling him close again, he did the opposite. He gripped the back of Alec's harness and slowly pulled back and downward, forcing his upper torso into the water.

Alec grunted, shifting awkwardly atop the king's thigh, suddenly struggling hard to stay upright. Easier said than done though, with his arms bound behind him. Body taut, abs contracting, he fought Zercy's strength, but his own was no match for the Kríe's. The water reached his jaw. Was he going to pull him under? His heart raced urgently. Canting his head back, he sucked in a breath. Zercy halted a second later and held him inclined.

Alec shifted uneasily. Water lapped at his ears. And then the king's free hand palmed his chest. He stilled at the feeling of those warm, splayed fingers, so long they reached both of his nipples. Zercy grazed them lightly with the tips of his small claws. His nubs tightened instantly to hard rocks.

He grazed them again. Current sizzled down Alec's torso, delving into his crotch, stiffening his dick even more. He tamped another moan and peered warily at the king.

"What... are you doing?" he rasped.

Zercy's lips curved a little, but his smile wasn't smug. Oddly, it looked kind of affectionate. "Just enjoying my pet. Mmm... I mean, my *Alick*." He slid his hand lower, to Alec's stomach.

Alec sucked in sharply and tensed his abs, then shuddered when Zercy lazily thumbed his navel. Aw, God. That claw. And the others, too. Every single time they made the slightest contact, his nerve endings went berserk. Which, in turn, made his traitor dick stand at attention, sending that wrap drifting up and off his crotch.

Shit, damn it, fuck.

He shifted his hips, squeezing Zercy's thigh for extra purchase. No way could he let him see his boner.

The king growled huskily and dragged his claws across his belly. At the same time, his cock brushed Alec's leg. Holy hell, it felt like stone, and twice as freaking long as before.

He gasped and twitched, heart hammering like crazy. "Aw, God— You need— You need to stop."

Zercy's rumble turned dark. "Are you giving me more orders?" Blatantly, he grazed those claws down Alec's groin. Again, his steel pole brushed Alec's leg.

Alec jerked, sending that wrap floating upward again. "No— I'm not— I'm— Please— *Please*, will you stop?"

The king chuffed softly. "So sensitive indeed." Lifting Alec back up, he smiled and met his eyes. "Now you see what happens when you try to distance yourself. Perhaps you would like to try it again?"

Arrogant bastard.

Alec scowled, his dick still reeling. "Are we done talking?"

"I suppose." Zercy reached around and deftly unfastened his harness, then pulled it off, leaving only the wrist binds and collar.

Alec moaned at the feeling, his elbows finally free, able to hang in a much more natural position. Zercy slid him off his knee and stood to his full height. Alec stared at the view before he could stop himself. But, damn, in his defense, Zercy hogged up all the space in front of him.

Alec's gaze locked raptly on his dark, glistening torso, then slid to his pecs, and those pierced nipples. He stared at the barbells all over again, wanted to give their beads a nice hard tug. With his fingers. No, his teeth. Would the arrogant king like that? Or would it royally piss the fucker off?

He stopped himself right there. He needed to get a grip. His mother effing boner was making him loopy. It was also the reason he needed to stay in the tub. No need to flash Zercy an eyeful of erection. He'd already encouraged the Kríe way too much. Unintentionally, but still. A boner was a boner, and pretty much meant one universal thing.

Its owner was aroused and wanted to fuck.

Alec groaned and closed his eyes.

What the hell was wrong with him?

Maybe he could use that drink after all.

Abruptly, two clawed fingertips lifted his chin. Alec looked up. The Kríe king was gazing quietly down at him.

"I am tired," he murmured. "I would like to retire. It has been a long day. Nenya." *Come.*

Alec stilled as Zercy dropped his hand and turned to exit the tub. Oh, hell no. No way were they sleeping in the same bed. And for shit's sake, Alec couldn't just 'come' with him anyway. He was still dealing with his flagpole.

Zercy reached what evidently were some steps to the right but paused when he realized Alec wasn't following. His features hardened. "Nenya," he repeated, giving the leash a tug.

Alec cursed under his breath. As soon as he got out, his little wrap was going to get clingy, which would display with great effectiveness his 'current state.'

Frowning, he shook his head.

Zercy's jaw ticked. "What is wrong?"

His cheeks heated. "Nothing. I just... want to... stay here."

The king narrowed his eyes.

Alec awkwardly shifted his weight.

Which evidently was a big frickin' giveaway.

Zercy stilled, then slid his gaze down Alec's torso, down to the where the water obscured his view. His lips curved knowingly.

Alec muttered another curse.

Zercy chuckled and turned back to the steps. "As if I did not already know. Your cock has been eager this whole time."

Alec opened his mouth, shut it, then ground his molars and scowled—until Zercy emerged naked from the tub. Then Alec was back to cursing under his breath while quickly cranking his head in the other direction. He was trying to *lose* his boner, not fan its flames.

Zercy pulled his leash again, unyieldingly this time, forcing Alec to move to the steps. Reluctantly, he climbed them, feeling utterly exposed. Which was ridiculous. Zercy had not only *seen* his rager before, but *worked* it till Alec blew a monster nut. But the circumstances were different then. He'd had an excuse for being aroused. Now he had nothing but stark truth.

Eyes averted from the king's body, he reached the top and stepped onto the ledge, right beside a basket of rolled towels.

A husky little purr curled at the base Zercy's throat. Alec could feel his gaze on his stupid saran-wrapped dick. "So proud for its size," he rumbled. "So proud, like its owner." Moving to Alec's back, Zercy murmured in his ear as he reached around front to untie his wrap. "You cannot sleep in this. You will get my bed wet."

Alec swallowed, then froze. Zercy's cock just brushed his hand. His fingers tingled where it grazed him. Current bee-lined to his crotch. Then that clinging drenched wrap dropped from his body. He stiffened as cool air engulfed his junk—until Zercy wound a towel around his hips from behind.

"There. All better," the king stated softly. "Now no more delays. Come along." Stepping away, he rounded the large tub and sauntered his naked ass toward that cubbyhole. That strange little fancy-schmancy nest in the wall—that he clearly expected Alec to join him in.

Warily, he followed him, but when they reached their destination, Alec hesitated as Zercy pulled back the velvet flap. His heart picked up speed. His breaths came faster, too. Because once he breached that threshold, God only knew what would happen. Last time he got horizontal with a big-ass Kríe, he ended up getting the living shit fucked out of him. Not that it didn't feel mind-blowingly incredible. But it'd all been so intense, like some tumultuous erotic tailspin, his body having stripped his mind of all control.

And that shit couldn't happen again. He needed his head clear. As it was, just being near Zercy drugged him up. What if he tried to seduce him on that bed in there? And what if Alec was unable to resist? He didn't need, and couldn't afford, any connection with this male. But something told him if they got physical that'd be unavoidable. Which would only distract him from getting his team out of there.

Zercy turned and gestured for him to climb in.

Alec quickly peered inside, diverting his gaze from naked cock, and eyed all the flickering sconces. Then he glanced through the windows at the view. Village torches glowed near and far through the realm, with a backdrop of black mountains beyond. And damn, look at all those gazillion stars in the sky…

No. Ugh. He couldn't let himself get distracted.

"I'm not tired," he blurted, turning, but keeping his gaze high. "I want to see my men. You said you'd think about it."

The king's eyes hooded irritably. "Tah. My decision remains."

"But—"

Zercy's growl cut him off as he clutched Alec's hips, then hefted him up and tossed him through the opening. Instantly, he sank into soft, plush warmth. Damn. Zercy hadn't been kidding. It *was* 'very soft.' The king joined him, and man, did he take up some serious space. Alec knew that he was big, but in a small space like this, it felt like he took up every inch.

Zercy dropped onto his stomach with a contented rumble, and nuzzled his exotic face into the fur. Alec watched him, unable to help it. He was just so striking. So inexplicably and savagely handsome. With those thick pierced horns and those masculine pointed ears, and that tantalizing mass of bead-strewn velvety dreads.

Alec gazed at his closed eyes, and their thick fringe of lashes, then regarded his mouth—and his partially exposed fangs. Instantly, he thought again of Roni and Chet, and how the Kríe's bite seemed to drive the guy crazy. Chet fronted like he hated it, but it was pretty obvious he didn't. Most likely just didn't want to admit it.

Which, of course, made Alec wonder what it actually felt like. Clearly really good, something Miros had corroborated. Hell, at one point, he'd almost bitten Alec. But he didn't. Got interrupted. And for some reason, Alec was glad. Had a feeling he'd feel different though, if it'd been Zercy.

As if sensing the weight of his stare, the Kríe lifted his lids and locked his golden eyes on Alec's face. His gaze trapped Alec's instantly.

His heart thumped anxiously. "I'm not tired," he murmured again, still laying where he'd been tossed on his back.

Zercy rolled onto his side and propped his head in his hand. "Mah, you are. You will realize this once you let yourself relax."

He was right. Alec knew he was. He could feel his exhaustion down to his bones. But his men, he had to get back to them. He couldn't go to sleep.

"Esh," Zercy grumbled. "Stop worrying about your team. I vow to you that they are safe and very comfortable."

Alec studied his face. He wanted to believe him so bad. Because, in truth, he *was* tired. And this bed was so damn soft.

The king's lips quirked, and then he was up on all fours, reaching over Alec's body for God knew what. Alec stiffened, staring up at him. Jesus. He was huge. Abruptly, something swayed in his periphery.

Without thought, he glanced over—then cursed and quickly looked away. Right. It was the Kríe's big dangling dick.

Alec groaned as Zercy clutched his leash and secured it to something on the bed's wraparound headboard. Or at least, a headboard is what Alec assumed it was, although, it did look a lot more *involved*. As in, lined with countless small, decorative pegs. Or hell, maybe the things were little levers.

Zercy finished what he was doing and peered down at Alec. "Now you cannot slip away and leave your king as he sleeps."

Yeah, right. Like that shit was even possible. But now Alec felt like a dog tied to a tree. Irritably shifting atop the furs, he glared at his captor. "Will you free my wrists then? Now that I can't go anywhere?"

Zercy eased back and settled down a few feet away, clearly giving Alec some personal space. "You may not be able to leave while I slumber, but your free hands could still do much harm."

Alec blinked at him, surprised, then chuckled incredulously. "What, you think I'd try to kill you in your sleep?"

Zercy held his gaze. "Would you?"

Wow. He'd asked that in all seriousness.

Alec made a face. "No. Because where I come from, that's murder. Something we view as very, very bad. Kind of like kidnapping and human trafficking." He leveled him with a pointed look. "And keeping people prisoner."

A smile tugged at Zercy's lips, even as his eyes hooded drowsily. "You amuse me, *Alick*," he murmured. "I am glad to have found you." His big body eased, his muscles going lax. "Tomorrow I will take you to your team… as I promised…" He settled his hand on Alec's hip and closed his eyes. "Thank you," he exhaled.

Alec frowned. "For what?"

His regal vibe sobered as he drifted toward sleep. "For giving me something to finally be happy about."

CHAPTER TEN

* * *

"Did you hear that fucker? He said he wanted to milk my dick, but would drink straight from the tap if I wanted."

Noah sighed, listening to Chet gripe about one of the guards as he irritably stalked around, scrutinizing their new sleeping quarters. They'd been taken to this location maybe an hour after Alec left, their captain having volunteered to take a big one for the team. 'Big one' being an exam he'd be given by some Kríe named Sirus, whom Noah gleaned was a scientist of the king. Talk about a stand-up guy. Because, yeah, had Alec *not* made that selfless gesture, they *all* would have gone through the same procedure.

Thanks, Cap. Sacrifice very much appreciated.

Noah chewed his lip and glanced at the door. Zaden was eyeing it, too. He looked worried about his friend, hadn't wanted Alec to go. Noah hoped the captain was okay, too. They hadn't seen or heard from him since the bath house.

Across the way, Bailey nodded at Chet. "Yeah, I heard him. Saw him sizing you up, too. Better watch your ass around that one." He smirked. "Like, *literally* your ass."

Chet shot him a peeved look. "I'll break his hand if he tries anything."

Jamis laughed. "Yeah, because you had such great luck fending off Roni."

Their hired gun's jaw ticked. "I was having an off day. Next time, I'm taking his ass down."

"Next time?" Noah tucked a sandy blond lock behind his ear. "I wouldn't hold your breath. They're not coming back."

Chet paused from rapping his knuckles down the side of a wall. "Oh, they better," he muttered. "'Cause if I gotta hunt them down, they're gonna feel the wrath of one irate motherfucker."

Bailey and Jamis swapped looks of skeptical amusement. Noah, however, felt no urge to smile.

Turning his gaze away, he glanced around the room. It was spacious. And clean. Adorned with interesting décor. Wrought-iron sconces of varying designs along walls impressed with artistic, tribal-esque motifs. Lanky, dark-purple trees sat in corners and by arched windows. There was a sitting area with Kríe-size chaises placed in a circle. Beside the loungers, colorful decanters sat atop an outcrop from the wall, accompanied by trays of curious edibles. Striped, oversized fur pillows were stacked by a fireplace. Across the way was a table with matching stools. Stools which, incidentally, the team sat upon now as they watched their angry bodyguard scour the room. The ceiling had wooden beams. The floor looked like slate. And the double doors they first entered through were dark bronze.

His guess was that the enclosure—roughly the size of a small tennis court—was used to accommodate guests of nobility. Definitely nicer than a servant's dwelling. Or even regular guards for that matter. Located on the third floor, down a long elegant hallway, it was the last set of doors on the right.

Their four Kríe escorts had dropped them off there with the promise of fetching them first thing in the morning. Of course, that was also when the guard named Mannix propositioned Chet with that hand job he was pissed about. Noah's lips curved a little as he recalled their little exchange. If looks could kill, that Kríe would've dropped like a brick. But they couldn't, so he'd continued to work Chet's nerve, even though he'd clearly wanted to 'work' something else.

Noah sighed again, looking for the umpteenth time at the last, and most peculiar, element of their lodging—the little sleeping alcoves in the walls. Like, literally, *in the walls*. That you had to climb through an opening to get into. He'd peered inside one earlier, there were six in total; nothing but bedding and windows. Weird for sure, yet oddly inviting. And as fatigue set deep into the marrow of his bones, he suddenly wanted to give one a test drive. Or rather, a test snooze, so he could sleep off his funk and hopefully wake up not giving a shit about Gesh.

That asshole.

Noah still couldn't believe what he'd done.

Raw pain flared in his chest again. He breathed a tired curse, then absently glanced over at all those decanters. Were some equivalent to liquor? How sweet would that be? Would probably help his cause better than sleep.

But as he stared at the rainbow of various thick-glassed bottles, he didn't even have the energy to do some sampling. He was just too drained, both physically and mentally, from all the nonstop craziness since they crashed.

God, he'd hiked more in the past two days than he typically walked in an entire week. And that was saying a lot considering how often he hit the treadmill. Add to that the emotional stress, the unrelenting need to fuck, then ultimately getting plowed by a giant, and yeah, he was definitely running on fumes. The rest of the team had to be feeling similar.

He glanced back at the door. It was getting pretty late. They must have Alec crashing somewhere else. Fuck, he hoped he was okay. When would they see him again?

Frowning, he slid off his stool and looked at the others. "I'm beat. Calling it a night. Gonna go check out my little wall nest."

Jamis nodded.

So did Bailey, his dark curls bouncing subtly. "Yeah. Sounds good. Think I will, too."

Across the table, Zaden stood up, looking ready to help Chet investigate. "Alright, man. Get some sleep." He looked exhausted, too. "God only knows what tomorrow has planned for us."

Chet pulled his head back in through a window, no doubt scoping out their prison's exterior. "Pretty sure we won't be bothered again 'til morning."

Yeah, probably not.

Noah kneaded his neck and scanned his options. Out of the room's four walls, there were cubbies in two of them—the exterior walls, with the windows looking out over the land. Or in other words, the room's back and left side. Noah chose one in back and ambled over. Its opening was a good four feet off the ground. He climbed through and was instantly on a bed of lavish furs. And while his first instinct was to flop down right there with clothes still on, he knew he'd sleep better if he stripped.

Pulling off his hiking boots, then his cargo shorts, tank and socks, he wondered if Alec ever got his clothes back. The guards who'd taken him had only allowed him a towel. Which was unsettling at the time and still was now. Noah frowned, trying hard not to worry about their captain. Alec was nothing if not level-headed. And sensible. And smart. He'd keep himself out of trouble. He would.

Noah pulled his hair tie out and raked a hand through his mane. Long bangs dropped down and brushed his cheek. Absently, he tucked them behind his ear. He was ridiculously tired, and yet his brain was still churning. Drawing his knees close, he used them to prop his forearms, then glanced out one of the alcove's three curved windows.

Of course, the first thing he rested his eyes on was the lake. With only a dozen acres of land between it and the castle, it spanned the entire length of the fortress's rear grounds. In turn, at its farthest shore, it appeared to reach the mountains. The very range, in fact, that circled the kingdom. It wasn't a huge lake, he could make out its entire perimeter, but somehow it still felt majestic. Maybe because its surface glittered like diamonds under the moon. Or maybe because those huge mountains looked like a crown. It was probably some of both, but what captivated him the most was the breathtaking waterfall at its far end. Illuminated by moonlight, he could see it perfectly as its lunar-lit waters cascaded down the mountainside.

His mind eased a little, its distant roar soothing, just far enough away for perfect volume. His gaze slid back down to the shimmering lake. Did Nirans fish in it? Swim in it? Was its temperature warm? He stared at it, his chest feeling strangely unsettled. Like the water was triggering some internal—

A memory surged abruptly to the forefront of his mind. A very specific one from last night. When he and Gesh had been in their own little body of water. The hot spring near the encampment's front entrance. Surrounded by big rocks and thick, lush plants, it'd had more privacy than any two males could ever need.

"Shit," he muttered, not wanting to go there. Not wanting to think about Gesh at all. He closed his eyes. Then covered them with the heels of his palms. But to his dismay, that Kríe stayed put. Talk about ironic. When Noah wanted nothing to do with him, the dickhead wouldn't leave. And yet, just hours ago when he'd desperately needed him ...

Yeah, Gesh had split.

Well, okay, so technically he'd been thrown out—on what Noah hoped was his *actual ass*—but the end result of his actions was still the same.

Noah dropped his hands in resignation and looked back out at the lake. It was futile to fight his feelings. Gesh had burrowed too deep under his skin. Which meant all he could do was just wait it out. Wait for his mind to forgive and forget. Wait for his heart to let him go.

* * *

Alec roused the next morning to the light against his lids, but mostly to the strange sounds infiltrating the alcove's windows. His guess—earlybird critters from the nearby mountain range. Although, the loudest noises sounded more like dolphins on speed than any flying creature he'd ever heard.

Eyes still closed, he shifted on his back, then frowned, remembering his wrists were bound. No wonder his shoulders ached. They'd been in an unnatural position all night long. Muttering a curse, he rolled onto his side, then lifted his drowsy lashes—and froze. For two reasons.

One, because less than a foot away Zercy lay fast asleep, with just a gray pelt over his crotch. The rest of his body? Wholly uncovered. One great big expanse of muscles and sleeping face.

The second reason Alec stilled was for, ironically, the same reason, but regarding *his* state instead of Zercy's. When he'd shifted to his side, the towel Zercy had wound around him the night before had unfastened and come completely undone. Sliding off his hips, leaving him utterly bare, exposing his skin to cool morning air.

Instinctively, he rolled onto his back again, and gripped the wrap with his bound hands. But, of course, that was pointless. It wasn't like he could toss it over his goods. Which really sucked because he was sporting some serious morning wood. A visual he didn't particularly feel like sharing. Zercy might wake up and get the wrong idea. For all he knew, Nirans didn't experience hard-ons when they woke, and Zercy would assume Alec's had arisen for other reasons. He glanced again at that pelt hiding Zercy's junk to see if there was any sign of a—

Oookay, never mind.

Nirans definitely got morning wood, too.

Alec's groggy brain cleared as he considered the situation. Two guys in bed with raging boners—who'd both had sex with males in the past. Well, just *one* male in the past where Alec was concerned, but like that really made any difference. Hell, as far Zercy would be concerned, that'd be the second erection Alec popped around him. *Two*, in the span of how many hours?

Nope. Wrong message. Waaaay wrong message.

Which left him with only one real option to take. Hide the incriminating evidence by repositioning onto his stomach.

Fisting the wrap beneath him, he glanced to his left. Damn it. Not enough room to maneuver in that direction. Evidently, while he slept, he'd scooted as far over as possible. So much so, that if he rolled that way now, he'd wind up with his face pressed to the wall—as he clutched a handful of towel to cover his ass. Yeah, that wouldn't look totally ridiculous at all, and *definitely* wouldn't prompt Zercy to roll him back over again.

Surprise, big guy! Look what I was hiding.

Right. An outcome that'd be far worse than if he just freaking lay there with flagpole standing.

Alec glanced the king's way again, measuring the distance between them. It'd be tight, considering Zercy had scooted all the way over, too. Only a handful of centimeters to spare. But once he got there, he could angle his head in the other direction and pretend he was sleeping when Zercy woke. Which would make the close proximity appear utterly unintentional while hiding the problem jutting from his groin.

Drawing in a breath, he steeled his resolve and slowly began rolling toward the king. But just as he'd barely made it onto his side, Zercy stirred, his big frame shifting atop the furs. Alec froze, not wanting to wake him. Zercy's arm slid his way. Then his face turned in Alec's direction, too.

Alec held his breath. The Kríe's eyes stayed closed. And what do you know, there was some more good news, too. When his purple hand had slid into Alec's personal space, it'd pushed a mound of fur against his junk. He exhaled. Thank you, cosmos. His dick was finally covered. Looked like he didn't need to get too close for comfort after all. He could stay nice and still on his side.

Which he did for a good couple minutes after that, scrutinizing absolutely everything in his line of sight. The white, textured walls. That peculiar headboard. The sconces that'd long since sputtered out. Even outside the windows. From where he lay, he could see the mountaintops, and the early morning's yellow-orange sky. Evidently, that was the color of the sky on Nira because it seemed pretty clear with minimal clouds. But, wow, did those few clouds look wild. Every shade of purple, in wispy spirals, their tapered tips jutting high into the stratosphere. He watched as they slowly swirled their way out of view, past where he could see them from the window.

And then his bored eyes were drifting back down. He'd avoided looking at the king for as long as he could, but in truth, Zercy was the most interesting thing around. Granted, the furs he lay upon were pretty exotic—what with all their rich colors and patterns—but in juxtaposition to the king's incredible body, even they couldn't hold a candle.

Alec frowned and looked away. Slowly rolled his achy shoulder. But before long, his focus was back on Zercy. Only his face, Alec resolved. He'd only look at his face. The rest of his big body would stay off limits.

Alec studied his dark lashes. So thick as they rested atop of his cheekbones, they almost—*almost*—rivalled his masculine brows.

He slid his gaze to one of Zercy's horns. Up close like this, the texture alone was incredible. Like rich, black velvet molded over bone. Matte, yet with a soft, subtle luster. Its curve was subtle as well, its tip was barely sharp. And those polished stones and gold studs that ran along its ridge? Alec had never seen anything so... alluring. Out of nowhere, he had the strongest urge to touch them...

What? Yeah, *no*. No yearnings to touch his *captor*.

That was entirely unacceptable.

Entirely.

He pursed his lips and dropped his gaze to Zercy's ear. Big and slightly pointy with, shit, more of those piercings. Yup, time to move things right along. His eyes dipped lower, to the king's powerful jaw, which in turn, led his focus to Zercy's chin. A chin that, in fairness, was perfectly commendable—good proportions, nicely shaped—but it just couldn't compete. Not with what was above it. *That mouth.*

Absently, Alec swallowed as he studied the king's lips, all full, and firm, and partially parted. Enough to show a hint of his fangs. Just the tips, though. Nothing more. But apparently that was plenty. Alec's stomach tightened as he eyed them. So much sharper than Zercy's horns. Able to pierce flesh like a hot knife through butter. *Yeah.* He bet a clean, swift penetration like that would feel incredi—

His boner kicked so hard, he saw the fur move in his periphery.

Alec blinked and looked away. Jesus. What the hell was wrong with him?

Evidently, Zercy's mouth needed to be off limits, too.

Heart rate bumping up a notch, he inadvertently glanced at Zercy's torso—and was instantly snared by his huge pecs. And those mesmerizing pierced nipples. God, the way their studs glinted every time Zercy drew in breath…

Nope. Not even going to go there, either.

And yet, before he could stop himself, he slid his gaze lower—then stilled in brand-new, rapt fascination. Because there on Zercy's abdomen, circling his navel, was a marking Alec hadn't noticed before. Probably because until now, he'd kept his eyes ever averted, not letting them anywhere near the Kríe's naked dick. Although, now that he could steal a glimpse without Zercy seeing?

He regarded his new discovery, but quickly turned confused. Because not only was it captivating—a blazing sun around his belly button—but set in a rich, *shimmering* gold. Didn't look like a tattoo, though, or *anything* done by hand. No, somehow its appearance looked natural. Which made no sense. Living flesh couldn't be metal, or contain metal in its composition.

Alec stared at the pattern, at its starburst of rays, radiating outward like regal waves. It wasn't big, though. Maybe three inches at its widest point, with its top and bottom beams slightly longer. But damn, the way it glimmered against that canvas of deep plum, emanating stark majesty—and raw sex. Like some innate carnal lure, seducing his eyes. Hypnotizing him. Drawing him in.

His wrists swiveled in their binds. His boner hardened more. Of their own accord, his hips rocked against the fur. Shit, that felt good. He did it again. His lashes fluttered. His dick thrummed, his gaze still glued to that mark.

He frowned. What in the hell?

When had suns become such a turn-on?

A soft, husky rumble resounded in the quiet.

He froze, then glanced at Zercy's face. He was watching him, eyes hooded, still drowsy from sleep. But his lips, yeah, those lips were definitely curved. Fuck. He'd caught Alec staring at his body.

Cheeks heating, he looked away, wanting to roll onto his back and put as much distance between them as possible. Problem was, his stupid dick was still hard. So, instead, he just frowned irritably. "It's not how it looks."

"Hmm. That is a shame." Shit, his voice. So sleepy and gruff. Like a little velvet stroke to Alec's dick. Zercy shifted atop the bedding. "Is it at least how it *feels*?"

Alec frowned and glanced back at him. "*Feels?*"

"Tah." He smiled. "Your hard cock pressed against my knuckles."

Alec stilled, then eyed that mound of fur covering his crotch... realizing in horror that Zercy's arm was still part of the jumble. Earlier, when he'd shoved the covers over in his sleep, he hadn't moved the thing back. It'd stayed put. Good God. That's probably what woke him up; Alec rubbing his boner all up against his hand.

Tamping a groan, he felt his ears heating, too.

Zercy chuffed in amusement and rolled onto his side. "I do not know why it is so important to you that your cock stays hidden, but it is a waste of time. A waste of energy."

Alec met his eyes. Their faces were less than a foot apart now. "I don't know what you're talking about. I'm not hiding my dick, and it's not hard."

Zercy lifted a smug brow. "No? So, I can pull back this fur?"

Alec stiffened. Ground his molars. "I'd rather you didn't."

The groggy king grinned wider. "What a surprise." Without warning, he pushed Alec onto his back, then swiftly moved closer and laid on top of him.

Alec sucked in a breath, their mouths just inches apart, Zercy's morning wood pressing against Alec's stomach. "What the—fuck are you doing?" he grunted anxiously. "Get off. Jesus, Kríe. You weigh a ton."

Another sleepy rumble worked its way up Zercy's throat. Casually kneeing Alec's thighs apart—despite his efforts to keep them closed—he rocked his strong hips against Alec's groin. "Hmm. You say you are not hard. Perhaps our definitions are different." Lids at half mast, he nuzzled Alec's neck.

Alec's jaw went slack, his skin flushing from head to toe. But not just from embarrassment. He was pissed off, too. And aggravated that he was getting so freaking horny. Couldn't help it, though, goddamnit. Those warm lips against his skin? Not to mention Zercy's scent again, assailing his nose. *Mmm, fuck...* Roasted marshmallows, all hickory sweet...

His mouth watered. His eyes rolled back—

Gah. No.

What was he doing?

Fighting to snap out of it, he squirmed beneath Zercy's heft— which, to his distress, just spurred the Kríe to rock his hips again.

Heat coiled in Alec's nuts. "Don't," he rasped. "You're crushing me."

Not really, but it was a valid enough excuse.

Zercy lifted his head and regarded him, his dreads brushing Alec's chest. A few seconds passed. But then he smiled and rose onto his elbows. "There," he murmured, his weight gone from Alec's torso. Lazily, he ground their cocks together. "Taahhh... Much better..."

Alec's dick kicked. His pulse spiked. "Stop," he groaned. "I don't want this."

Or at least, he *shouldn't*. For crying out loud, this male was holding him captive.

Zercy paused and peered down at him. Then frowned. "Are you certain? I do not need to enter you, pet." His gaze dropped to Alec's lips. "Our hands would suffice... as would our mouths."

Fuuuck. Alec's dick bucked even harder that time.

Mortified anew, he glowered. "Yes, I am certain. I don't want hands or mouths, either. *I'm good.*"

Holy hell, his heart was hammering. Could Zercy hear it inside his chest?

Zercy studied him silently, a strange look on his face, as if he didn't understand why Alec was resisting. But right as he opened his mouth to respond, a deep-toned chime reverberated through the chamber. He peered through the alcove's opening toward the room's big double-doors. His smoldering gaze cooled. His expression turned resigned. "Tah," he muttered quietly. "The day begins."

And just like that, he was off Alec's body, grudgingly climbing from the comforts of his warm nest. Alec stayed where he was, heart racing in his chest. That was close. Truth be told, he'd been teetering on the verge, his dick readying to go rounds with his brain. Thank fuck for doorbells, or whatever that thing was.

Closing his eyes, he willed his heart to calm. God knew, his dick was a lost cause.

The sound of the great doors opening stole his focus. He turned his head and peered out the opening. Zercy stood at the entrance, naked as a jaybird, talking with a Kríe Alec recognized. The male at Zercy's side in the great hall yesterday. The one Alec assumed was his advisor.

Another male was present, too. He was clearly a personal servant—who, as it seemed, was tasked to dress the king. Alec watched him, half-smiling, as the male got to work, all but wrestling Zercy's hard-on into a jockstrap. Or maybe it was a loincloth. Or a hybrid of both. Whatever it was, he eventually wrangled it into place.

Not that the king noticed. His focus was on his advisor.

The servant moved on, sliding Zercy's arms into a garment, then closed the two sides and tied it off. Like a sleeveless robe or something, made of a black-suede material, that reached down to the lower half of his thighs. It looked soft. And those gems looked really cool, too. Small and gleaming, in patterns of green and gold, embellishing not only his

123

deep-v neckline, but his arm holes and bottom hem as well. Majestic and masculine all wrapped into one.

And, admittedly, not a bad look.

The male wound a belt around his lean waist next; thick, black leather with a sleek, burnished buckle. Once fastened, he dropped down and gripped his king's ankle, deftly sliding a sandal onto his foot. It reminded Alec of the kind that ancient gladiators wore; dark straps around each foot, horizontals ones up each calf, with a single, vertical strap up each shin.

He wouldn't lie, they were badass. And yet, somehow regal, too.

And still, Zercy didn't acknowledge the guy. Had all focus on the Kríe jabbering away. Not that Alec hadn't noticed the servant enough for all three of them, intently watching as he buckled in Zercy's calves.

His dark, *muscular* calves…

He could probably leg press a house…

Alec's junk thrummed—because clearly, it had yet to relent. He groaned in frustration and rolled onto his back. Glowered down his torso at his dick. He needed a bucket of ice. This shit was ridiculous.

If he could just get the hell out of this castle.

Closing his eyes, he inhaled deep, held it for a while, then let it out. He was going to see his team soon—if Zercy kept his word—so he needed to wipe these thoughts and clear his head.

"Are you ready to get dressed?" the king rumbled to his left.

Alec jerked with a start, then quickly rolled over, instinctively wanting to hide that-which-had-not-yet-gone-down. Not very nonchalant, though. Zercy must think him an idiot.

But instead of confirming his suspicions, the king reached through the opening, clutched Alec's hip, and rolled him back over. Alec stiffened, wholly exposed, but to his surprise, Zercy covered his crotch with fur and made a face. "Your behavior is strange. I assume it is a human thing."

Cheeks hot, Alec peered up at him, but didn't know what to say.

Zercy's eyes hooded. Slowly, he shook his head. "Hide your cock all you like, but it is pointless. Do you know why?"

Alec warily held his gaze. "No," he mumbled. "Why?"

Zercy leaned in through the opening and murmured in his ear. "Because I can *smell* it, *Alick*. From across the room. I do not need sight to know my pet is aroused."

A shiver rolled up Alec's spine, then prickled along his scalp *Fuuuck*.

Zercy's timbre. His proximity. His words.

Alec swallowed, but before he could formulate a reply, Zercy unclipped his leash, straightened, and pulled Alec upright by his collar. And he wasn't done there. Next, he freed Alec's hands, then clutched his legs and tugged them through the opening.

"There." He smiled as Alec sat on the ledge. "Would you like to see what Lotis fashioned for you, bashful human?"

Alec slid him a glare and rubbed his wrists.

He wasn't frickin' bashful.

Zercy loosed a small chuff. "You will love it. He is brilliant."

Alec shrugged. "Fine. Whatever. Then we go see my guys?"

"Tah." The king nodded and stepped to the right, swiping something off a small table against the wall. Looked like a little, folded garment of some kind. Velvety, like Zercy's get up, but it wasn't black. It was purple. Dark purple. Like Zercy's skin. The king snapped it open, then held it for him to see. "Is it not handsome? Just like my *Alick*."

Alec stared at the thing, trying to make out what it was. An outfit of some sort, clearly, but... it looked like half was missing. "I don't know about handsome, but it's definitely small." He frowned up at Zercy. "Where's the rest?"

"There is no 'rest'. This is everything—aside from your loincloth." He gestured for Alec to stand. "Now put it on."

No rest? That was it? Aside from a loincloth?

Alec balked. "I am *not*—"

"Very well. Go naked."

Alec bristled. "I want my own clothes."

Zercy shook his head. "Mah."

"Why not?" he grated.

"Because. They are no more."

Alec stared at him. "No more? What, did you have them burned or something?"

Zercy cast him a look of confirmation.

"Son of a—" Clenching his jaw, Alec vibrated, furious. "Whatever," he bit out, shoving off the ledge. "Just give me the damn thing. I want to go."

"Hmm. On second thought…" Zercy glanced back at the table. "Perhaps you should put that on first."

Alec eyed the slip of material the king was clearly referring to. Right. The loincloth. Didn't want to forget that. Otherwise, his dick would be swaying in the breeze. And going by the length of his 'specially fashioned' getup, it'd be swaying in the breeze *for all to see*.

Lips pursed into a line, he stalked over and grabbed it—then promptly began *trying* to put it on. Around and under, he wound the straps. Nope. Under and around. Even worse. He scowled at it menacingly. Stupid frickin' thing. No matter what order or direction he wrapped it, it still came out all freaking wrong. Damn it, that servant had made it look so easy.

"Fuck it," he muttered. He'd make it a thong. Not because he wanted a wedgie up his ass, but because he just didn't give a shit anymore. Tying up his goods into a very sad package, he turned back to Zercy and glowered. "Next."

Unfortunately, the king didn't hand over the garment. Just crossed his arms and regarded Alec's rig job. "Hmm…" He tapped his chin, then shook his head. "Mah."

Alec gritted his teeth. "Sorry, your Highness. It's the best I can do."

"I will do it for you. Come here."

"No."

"That was not a request."

"Does it look like I care?"

Zercy narrowed his eyes. "Take care how you address me."

Alec opened his mouth, then shut it. The last time he'd said something the guy resented, his plans to see his team got revoked.

The king smiled a little, as if sensing Alec's resignation, but he didn't look smug. Just kind of glad. Like he was mentally tired or something and didn't want to fight.

Stepping close, he turned Alec away, then curled his fingers around Alec's wrists. Alec tensed, instinctively fisting his hands. Zercy lifted them up to Alec's nape. "Link your fingers behind your neck."

Alec's heart pounded as he obeyed.

"Good," Zercy murmured. "Now keep them there."

Alec stared at the wall. The king was standing so close, he could feel him like a barrier of heat against his back.

Zercy released his wrists and moved his hands to Alec's waist, untangling the mess he'd made with the wrap. His claws grazed Alec's groin. Alec sucked in a breath. Then the swath let go, as though conceding to the king's will. Naturally, Alec's boner twitched, always happy to be free, but then jerked again when Zercy nudged his feet apart.

"Widen your stance, pet. I need room to work."

Alec bit his cheek but complied. Swear to God, if Zercy groped him—

He stiffened as warm hands wound the cloth between his thighs. And what do you know, a minute later, the king not only had him wrapped up right, but had done it while never once touching his junk.

Alec exhaled, relieved and grateful, every nerve ending on high alert. That could have gone way worse, and yet, Zercy had surprised him. Had been considerate instead of an asshole.

Alec dropped his hands, ready to handle the rest on his own, but Zercy grasped his wrists and brought them right back up again.

"I *said* to keep them *here*," he chided quietly.

Alec made a face. What could there possibly be left to do?

Zercy stepped to the small table and gathered a few more items; three strips of black, embellished hide. Alec frowned, eyeing the knot of tassels hanging from each end. What was getting put on him now?

The king turned with a smile and held one for Alec to see. "He is a master at his craft. I am his biggest fan. Every item I wear, Lotis designs."

Hands at his nape, Alec eyed the short strap. Zercy wasn't kidding. It was definitely impressive. A work of art in its own right. Sleek, masculine designs, embroidered in gold, green, and purple, masterfully twined around small, regal stones. Stones which, incidentally, looked like the ones in Zercy's dreads. Gleaming opal and onyx, striking tiger-eyes, too. Even a couple equivalent to blood-red rubies. A composition both dramatic and artistically refined.

Yeah, this Lotis guy had some skills.

Alec gave a little nod. "Nice. But what are they for?"

"Decoration." Zercy stepped close and wound it around Alec's wrist, tying it secure with those tassels. "Made specifically for my handsome new pets." He wrapped another around Alec's other wrist.

"Decoration," Alec muttered skeptically.

"Tah." Zercy tapped Alec's hip. "Lower your arms."

Alec dropped them and tentatively peered over his shoulder. He didn't like the Kríe always at his back.

Zercy's claws grazed his neck as he went for Alec's collar. Goosebumps. Everywhere. Alec scowled. He better be taking that thing off. Sure enough, a heartbeat later, the thick band fell to the floor—only to be replaced by a new one. The final strap.

Goddamnit.

Alec glowered at the wall. "Seriously? Do I really have to wear a freaking collar?"

Zercy tightened it at Alec's nape, then gripped his shoulders and leaned in close. "Tah, *Alick*," he rumbled. "You really must. How else will I secure your leash?"

Alec clenched his teeth, even as shivers raced up his spine. "Leashes are overrated. I say we ditch it."

Zercy loosed a soft chuckle. "Soon. If you behave."

Alec exhaled in frustration and looked at the ceiling. But then something occurred to him. "You said these 'decorations' were made specifically for your *pets*. Does that mean my guys are wearing this stuff, too?"

The king turned him around. "Tah." He handed Alec his outfit. "You may put this on now… If you are able."

Alec shot him a droll look.

The Kríe's lips twitched.

Rolling his eyes, Alec shook his head and got busy. At least he wouldn't be the only one wearing this shit. And more importantly, if his teammates were sporting these duds, too, then they couldn't rib his ass for looking stupid. Which, yeah, was a totally dick way to feel. But misery loved company, so sue him.

Stiffly, he shoved his arms through the getup's sleeveless holes, then tied its two halves together beneath his navel. Like Zercy's, it was fashioned like a robe of sorts, but *unlike* Zercy's, it was a hell of a lot shorter. Hell, the stupid thing barely covered his upper thighs.

Scowling, he took the belt Zercy handed over next and secured it with irritable jerks around his hips.

The king's eyes glittered. "Handsome *Alick…*" he murmured.

Alec's dick twitched at the sound. Zercy needed to stop saying his name. Maybe 'pet' would be better after all.

He frowned and looked down at his two-piece attire. Simple and yet not, what with the way it was adorned. Much like Zercy's, although not nearly as elaborate. But the stones, how they gleamed along the edge of each opening. Around his shoulders, across his thighs, down the open-v neckline—the one that offered a generous view from chest to navel. Yeah, didn't leave much to the imagination, but all in all, not a *terrible* look.

He glanced at his bare feet, but Zercy was already on it, moving to grab the last articles from the table. A pair of sandals similar to his own, except not as badass. Meaning simpler in cut, with shorter ties that looked to only reach the base of his calves.

He sighed and moved to take one.

"Mah." The king shook his head. Draping the footwear over his muscular shoulder, he gripped Alec's hips and hoisted him back onto the ledge. "Sit. Do not move. I shall put these on for you."

"I can do that," Alec objected.

"Probably, tah." He smiled a little. "But I should very much like to do the honors."

Alec paused, swearing he'd heard a hint of affection in Zercy's tone. He eyed the king nervously. Affection would not be good.

Ugh. Whatever. Didn't matter either way. To argue would be a total waste of time.

Zercy's smile curved higher as he clutched Alec's ankle and slid on the first of two sandals. It fit to a T. Alec frowned in confusion. How would Lotis know his freaking shoe size? Oh, wait. Almost forgot. Sirus had measured his feet. Must've passed along the info at some point. Zercy straightened it just so, then propped Alec's foot against his chest and wrapped the dark straps up past his ankle.

His grip was strong, his fingers adept, sending tantalizing, warm current up Alec's leg. He swallowed and grasped the ledge, his hard-on giving a nudge.

One sandal done.

On to the second.

Zercy held his foot secure. More teasing heat straight to his crotch.

Alec clutched the sill tighter, then swallowed again, eyes glued to Zercy's fingers as they worked. A claw grazed his skin. Sharper zings tore up his leg. He sucked in a breath, every muscle tensing. Fortunately, the king proved not just capable, but swift.

Dropping Alec's foot, he reached to help him down, but Alec shoved off the ledge before he had the chance.

"I got it," he muttered, regarding his new footwear. Huh. Look at that. He had gladiator feet. A smile tried to form. He fought it back.

Zercy grunted gruffly. He hadn't liked Alec's slight. But instead of chastising, he simply moved past him and reached his hand inside the alcove's opening. Two seconds later, Alec's leash was in his grasp. He smirked. "Time to go, pet. Turn around."

Alec bristled all over again.

The king lifted a brow. "You *do* wish to see your team now, do you not?"

CHAPTER ELEVEN

* * *

They made it to the breakfast hall in just a few minutes, escorted by Setch, Kellim, and two other members of the king's guard. The trek hadn't been too bad, just the four flights of stairs, then a short way down that spacious, central corridor. Not far enough to pass the great hall's entrance up on the left, or those huge, mysterious doors on the right. It was, however, long enough to pass plenty of nobles, and thus garner plenty of looks.

Surprisingly, despite Alec's 'swanky' new garb, the hike hadn't been as awkward as last night's. Maybe because he wasn't harnessed with his arms bound behind his back. Or barefoot, wearing a freaking *kid's* wrap.

Although, in truth, things felt different with those staring at him, too. The looks he'd received from the wandering highborn weren't nearly as smug and leering. Which wasn't to say they hadn't looked just as intrigued, because they had, just in a more respectful way. It was as if his upgrade in attire—and downgrade to just a leash—had somehow boosted his overall status. No longer did they eye him like some morsel the cat dragged in, some lowly creature for Zercy to nibble on in his chambers. Now they seemed to perceive him as the king's prized pet, worthy of higher regard by mere association. Not that being seen as a pet didn't still rankle, but at least the fuckers weren't openly ogling him.

Yeah, so for the most part, Alec hadn't felt too embarrassed. Well, except for that one instance when a statue snagged his attention; a life-size Kríe at the base of the staircase. Wielding nothing but a sword, it emanated an air of primal warrior. It was also completely naked. And totally erect. How he'd missed it the night before was hard to fathom. Then again, he'd been coming from a different direction, so the statue *had* been facing away from him. He definitely hadn't missed it this time, though. Hell, at first glance, he'd thought its big-ass cock was a club.

So naturally, when he finally got a *what the—whoa!* look, he'd kind of done a double-take and slowed his step. Which was when the 'bout of embarrassing' came into play. Not even breaking stride, Zercy had given his leash a tug, causing Alec to stumble after the guy. Man, did that chafe, being treated like a dog. He'd still been low-key bristling when they arrived.

Although, the minute he laid eyes on his team, a lot of that irritation vanished. It was just so good to see them safe and unscathed. As expected, they were decked out in similar attire, with some looking less pleased about it than others. 'Some,' of course, referring mainly to Chet, going by that scowl on his face.

A grin tugged at Alec's lips. Finally, someone more aggrieved than himself.

He headed their way, in step with the king. His men spotted them within just a few seconds. All five pairs of eyes instantly locked on his face, as if trying to discern if he was okay by just his expression. He offered a small smile and an even smaller nod. Their tense shoulders visibly eased.

Zercy came to a stop at the team's raised table, the thing clearly built for Kríe-size diners. Alec grudgingly fell in beside him. Not because he *wanted* to stand next to the guy, but because the damn Kríe still had him leashed. Alec fought not to scowl. Nope, no need to play recipient to a power-play demonstration with his subordinates looking on.

Zercy glanced at the Kríe he'd clearly assigned to Alec's men—four of the six guards who'd escorted them to the bath house. No words were spoken, though, and then his eyes were on Alec's men.

"Greetings." He inclined his head. "Sleep well?"

Chet glared. "Yeah, that hole in the wall was just great."

Zaden eyed the king but said nothing.

The trio just nodded.

Expression cool, Zercy focused entirely on Chet. "Perhaps more furs will make your 'hole' more comfortable."

"The furs weren't the problem. Try the locked goddamn doors."

"Ah." The king's lips curved. "Well, no wonder. Those 'locked goddamn doors' are extremely hard."

Chet bristled, then shoved off his lofty stool. But before he could get out a single retort, the huge guard behind him intercepted. Clamping his big hands atop Chet's shoulders, he yanked him back on his seat, then shoved his head. A clear, wordless warning for Chet to watch himself—which, of course, Chet didn't appreciate.

Cranking his mug around, he glowered at the Kríe. "Touch me again and I'll break your fucking nose."

The guard's eyes flashed, as if Chet's words weren't a threat, but a promise for some unruly fun. Alec shook his head. What was it with Kríe and confrontation? One mention of violence and they were up and ready to party.

The guard looked to Zercy, as if requesting permission to engage.

Zercy smirked. "Mah, Mannix. Perhaps after breakfast."

The male rumbled.

Chet stiffened.

Alec stifled a groan.

It was Chet and Roni all over again.

Wonderful.

Zercy's fingers touched his nape. Started fiddling with his collar. Alec stilled, hope surging. Was he taking off his leash? He looked up at the king.

Zercy smiled a little. "Tah. I must relinquish you for a time. Responsibility calls."

Oh, thank God. Alec exhaled. The king's presence was overwhelming. He could use the time away from him for a while. But right as a tiny spark of happy ignited, Zercy reached for Alec's hands. Alec frowned and looked down, then cursed in disappointment. The bastard was binding his wrists.

"Is this really necessary?" he grated.

Zercy clutched his chin. "Tah. When I can trust you not to leave me, this will change."

Alec ground his teeth. Zercy gestured for him to join his team. Upon doing so, he realized his men were bound, too. Their hands had just been in their laps and out of view.

The trio looked empathetic.

Zaden met his eyes. Clearly, his friend was happy he was back.

Zercy crossed his thick arms and addressed them as a whole. "Once you finish eating, your new life here begins. As you will learn, I do not like 'idle.' I like structure. Routines. Minds active, not stagnant. Bodies moving. Therefore, your time shall adhere to these standards. To please me, yes, but just as much so, for your own good."

Chet's brows furrowed low as the trio's eyes brightened. Even Noah looked happy at the prospect of staying busy.

"Every day," the king went on, "there will be lessons. You will *learn*. About this planet. About its realms. About my people, and our history. As it stands, you are ignorant of far too much. It makes you vulnerable," he glanced at Alec, "in ways I will not allow. Ryze will fix this. Will teach you. Make you smarter than a noble."

He glanced over his shoulder at said nobles milling about. "Not the hardest of feats," he grunted. "I assure you."

Jamis and Bailey's lips quirked. They were already smarter and knew it, but that glint in their eyes said they couldn't wait to broaden their horizons. Total nerds and proud of it. Pretty geeky about science, too. And to top it all off, they were also good-looking. Talk about winning the lottery.

"When your lessons conclude, you will have another meal, then once your stomachs have settled, you will resume." Zercy gestured to one of his guards. "Kellim will head your physical activities. Time in the bath house will follow. Then final meal."

"The remainder of the day's ours after that?" Zaden confirmed.

Zercy inclined his head, but then paused. "Unless there are festivities planned."

Bailey's ears perked. "Festivities?"

"Tah." The king smiled. "Which you are welcome to enjoy—when, that is, you are not the main event."

Every team member stilled, quickly swapping wary looks.

Alec frowned. "Okay, yeah. What exactly does that mean?"

"Sometimes you will share in the arranged entertainment. Other times," he smirked, "you will *be* it."

Chet's mouth fell open, appalled. "Like hell we will."

Zercy slid him a look—one that said, *Human, try me*—then gestured to the stream of approaching servants. "Ah. Your meals. Very good. Eat well." His gaze returned to Alec. His cocky grin ebbed. "I will see you in my chambers after dark."

Shit. Alec's stomach flipped. He scowled and squared his shoulders. "I want to stay with my men."

"Tah. Of course." Right on cue, his aide arrived. Zercy gave the male a nod, then turned to Kellim and Setch. "Stay and help chaperone. My humans are still adjusting. When the suns go down, return my pet to me."

Alec fumed, less than thrilled by that last directive. He was sick of being Zercy's 'pet,' didn't want to go back to his room. What's more, Zercy's dismissal pissed him off. Rude bastard. Not that his behavior surprised Alec much. He was ruler of the Kríe. More than likely the most pompous species on the planet.

The king turned to go but looked one last time at Alec's team. "Relax. Enjoy your new, carefree lives. No longer are you burdened with the weight of the world. Recognize your good fortune and embrace it."

Chet glared in dissention.

Alec clenched his jaw.

But before they could voice a single difference of opinion, Zercy pivoted on his heel and strode off with his assistant.

"Can you believe that shit?" Chet grated. "That dude is totally delusional."

Jamis nodded as servants began loading their table with food. "I overheard Miros say that, as of late, the king's been 'erratic.' Probably safe to say that means 'crazy'."

Alec groaned and scrubbed his face. Not what he wanted to hear. But Jamis was right. Miros *had* said as much about Zercy. Had warned him to tread carefully around the guy.

Pewter plates were set before them, then their goblets were filled. Filled with something that looked like milky lime juice.

"So, we stay off his radar." Bailey reached for one of the serving bowls. The one piled with rolls that smelled like honey. "Lay low until we find a way outta here."

"That might be easier said than done for some of us," Zaden murmured. He looked at Alec. "You're at the *center* of his radar."

Alec shook his head. "Tell me about it. I have no idea what his deal is."

"Seriously?" Jamis chuckled, snagging an object off one of the platters. A big, red flower blossom, with petals the consistency of plump grapes. "I'd say it's pretty obvious. He's smitten with you, Cap. Just like Gesh was with Noah."

Noah's jaw ticked—no doubt from the mention of Gesh's name, or the fact that Jamis had said *was* instead of *is*. He looked at Alec. "Yeah, good luck with that. These Kríe are some real stand-up guys." To his left was a square plate of marbled, yellow globes, each the size of a golf ball and stacked in a pyramid. Noah plucked one off the top and gave the thing a sniff.

"What is it?" Bailey asked.

"Cheese, I think. I dunno. Kinda feels like a waxy banana."

Chet frowned at Alec. "I feel your pain, Boss. No joke. This big, purple man-whore," he thumb-pointed over his shoulder, "propositions me for sex every hour."

Alec's brows rose as he eyed the guard standing at Chet's back. The extra-big fucker named Mannix. The male met his stare and slowly smiled.

Alec glared, then turned his focus back to Chet. "Don't worry. Zercy promised me that no one's allowed to touch us. Not without our permission. Not even his guards."

Chet paused. "No shit?"

Alec nodded. "No shit."

"Well, what do you know." Snickering, he turned on his stool. "Ha. You hear that, Mannix? You giant walking boner. No nooky-nooky for *you*."

* * *

Mealtime wrapped up just a few minutes later. Escorting them from the dining room, their six big-ass guards led them down that big central hallway. This time, they *did* pass the great hall to the left, as well as those mammoth doors on the right.

Again, Alec peered at the giant bronze panels, wondering what could possibly be behind them. The king's court, perhaps? Didn't look very active, though. In fact, activity seemed *discouraged*. Because curiously, instead of standing on either side of the doors, the guards on post stood directly in front of them. As if implying that no one should even *try* to enter.

Alec continued to eye them as their entourage passed.

Interesting...

Soon, they reached the T-junction at the end of the corridor, but instead of going right or left, they strode to a large door straight ahead. Kellim's biceps bulged as he pulled it open, and suddenly they were entering another lookout tower. One built into the side of the castle, though, and not into one of its corners. Alec eyed the circular stairwell. Take a left and they'd go up, take a right and they'd go down. Setch and Kellim promptly headed right.

Looked like class was in the dungeon.

They made their way down the cool stone steps, but soon a faint clanking met Alec's ear. Ceaseless and dissonant, echoing up the tower, implying much activity down below. He frowned, peering around when they reached the bottom. Just a whole bunch of big sconce-lit tunnels.

They took another right and walked for a good twenty yards, passing more corridors as they went. Finally, they stopped at a large, wooden door. Setch gave the thing a knock. Heavy footfalls resounded. The thick slab swung open a moment later.

"Ryze," Setch grunted.

Ryze grunted back. "Greetings." Then his golden eyes slid to Alec's team. "These... are my pupils?" He curiously looked them over.

"Tah. They know nothing. Zercy wants you to fix them."

Alec pursed his lips.

Chet muttered something.

Ryze canted his head, studying them further. "What are they?" he finally asked.

Alec met his gaze. "We're humans."

"Humans," he murmured, testing the name. "I do not know your species."

"Because we're—"

"Aliens," Setch cut in. He grinned wide. "With elevators."

Alec rolled his eyes.

Ryze's brows shot high. "Aliens? With… elevators?"

"Tah."

Bailey laughed. "You were talking to them about *elevators*?"

Alec scowled at his teammate. "Yeah, okay? I was. We'd just finished climbing a mountain of stairs and—Ugh. Just… Never mind."

Jamis stifled a chuckle. Even Zaden's lips twitched.

Ryze grinned and gestured them in. "So much to learn from each other. Nenya." *Come.* "Let us begin."

* * *

Their time with Ryze was interesting, to say the least, and far more enlightening than Alec had expected. After, that is, their big Kríe instructor had finished picking *their* brains first. Ryze hadn't seemed able to help it, though, by the look in his eyes—those gold irises churning brighter with each thing learned.

Tons of things had fascinated him, human technology at the forefront, but he'd also been riveted by the dual-gender dynamic. Evidently, species on Nira didn't reproduce via opposite sexes. So, their world was made up almost entirely of males. Something, truth be told, that Alec had started to suspect, since he'd yet to see a single female anywhere. Talk about wild. No wonder Gesh had looked so friggin' confused whenever there'd been mention of a 'woman.'

Ultimately, Ryze *did* get down to business with his lessons, though, and man, did he teach them a ton. In the span of one morning, he'd covered the entire planet's basics. Its age, its continents, its oceans, and seas. The terrain and atmospheric conditions of said regions. He touched on the main classes of indigenous life forms next, creatures of water and sky, land animals, plants.

By the time Ryze concluded their session for the day, Alec's brain was all but bursting with Niran knowledge. Zaden looked just as maxed out. Chet, however, looked half-asleep. Which wasn't to say he didn't appreciate what Ryze was teaching—if anyone could benefit from that intel, it was him. But knowing Chet and how dutifully protective he was of the team, he'd probably slept with one eye open last night. Alec wondered how long it'd been since he'd gotten some decent rest.

And then there was the science trio who, by the end of Ryze's lessons, were straight-up glowing from all they'd learned. Right off the bat, they'd asked for writing tools and parchment, and after one session, their leather-bound notebooks were damn near full.

A smile tugged at Alec's lips. A silver lining to all their misfortune. After all, that's why their exploration team had come to Nira; to learn as much as possible in the name of science. And for the past couple hours, that's exactly what the threesome did—to the point they'd barely been able to jot it all down. No question, his little trio was on cloud nine.

What they'd be doing after lunch, though, would be a much different kind of stimulation; rigorous exercise under the direction of Kríe guard, Kellim.

As they headed back down the tunnel toward the tower's winding stairwell, Alec again heard those persistent, distant noises. He glanced at Zaden. He looked just as curious, his brows drawn, his dark eyes peering over his shoulder.

Fuck it, Alec thought. He was just going to ask. He looked to one of the Kríe. "Hey, what's that sound?"

The guard met his eyes. "Prisoners. Serving their sentences."

Alec tensed a little. "So… you're saying there's a dungeon down here, too?"

"Tah." He returned his focus forward.

Bailey paled. "Holy shit. Like torture chambers?"

The Kríe didn't answer, just kept on walking. None of the other guards answered, either. Alec frowned, not quite getting why that question was so tough. Or why their chaperones were suddenly throwing such dark vibes. It was like he and Bailey had hit a nerve. Which made no sense. They were *guards* in a *castle*. 'Mighty' *Kríe,* for that matter. Dungeons and torture chambers shouldn't faze them at all.

They made it to the stairwell and climbed back to ground level, then exited the tower and headed back to the meal hall. Right on cue, his stomach rumbled. Alec frowned, surprised. For real? He glanced over his shoulder to one of the arched windows. The suns were high. Damn. They'd been with Ryze longer than he'd realized.

Fortunately, lunch went smoother than their first meal. Chet's little freak out at breakfast—when a bite of food started moving in his mouth—must've sent the message loud and clear, because everything fed to the team this time was wholly inert. And, truthfully, it had all tasted pretty good. Not that Alec had had a clue as to what any of it was. Some he could guess at, but just as many had him stumped. He was starting to suspect that Nirans had more than five food groups.

When they finished eating and their stomachs had settled, their escorts led them back out again and down the same corridor. At the end, they turned and ambled past the bath house. Next thing Alec knew, they were exiting a back door and making their way across a rear courtyard. As they approached the castle's protective wall, Alec eyed its south-side gate. Smaller than the front gate they'd entered through yesterday, but definitely still big by all accounts.

Slowly, the fifteen-foot bronze doors opened, revealing one hell of a view; a giant meadow, easily ten acres wide, with a gorgeous lake and mountains in the distance. Alec regarded the ground cover they walked upon as they left the fortress's protection. Similar to grass, but different. Like little fern fronds. Condensed, and deep plum, with lime-green tips.

He looked straight ahead to the captivating water. Dark teal, but its surface gleamed bright tangerine, reflecting the sky above like panes of glass. The mountain range behind it looked nearly black, the waterfall dividing its peaks, a misty silver. At its base, on the very far left end of the meadow, stood a dense line of trees the color of raisins. Alec eyed them thoughtfully. So did Zaden and Chet. To them, that stretch of cover screamed 'potential escape route.'

Kellim drew things to a stop at center field, then helped his fellow guards untie the men's wrists. Alec frowned. There were suddenly only four Kríe present. He glanced back and found the last two standing by the gate, their eyes still intently locked on the team. Like they were keen for things to start, eagerly awaiting a good show.

Seriously? What was so fascinating about guys working out?

Kellim answered his question a heartbeat later.

"Today you wrestle. Strip down to your loincloths."

CHAPTER TWELVE

* * *

Alec ached all over. From head to toe. The byproduct of being paired up with Chet. And not just periodically. For the whole session. Three hours tackling and tumbling with the guy. A guy who weighed a shit ton more than Alec. And fuck, Chet hadn't gone easy on him either. Which was fine. To be babied on the field would've been worse. But man, Alec was going to be feeling that business for days.

"Bath time is over," Mannix announced brusquely. "You have soaked your little bodies long enough."

The team stifled unhappy groans. All that warm, steaming water just felt so good. To Alec's muscles. To his joints. Hell, in truth, even to his sanity.

Ducking under the surface, he reemerged, then slicked his hair back with bound hands and looked at Mannix. "Where're you taking us now? No way it's time for another meal."

The Kríe shook his head. "Mah. King Zercy sent word. He wants us to give you a tour."

The trio perked up instantly—even *Noah's* eyes brightened—and immediately hobbled their way toward the steps.

Zaden slid Alec a look, letting the waterlily he'd been toying with float away. "Yeah. Absolutely. I'm absolutely down for a tour."

The reason why went without saying. If they ever wanted to blow this joint, they'd need to learn as much of the layout as possible. Alec wondered if Zercy had considered that at all. Or was he really just that confident they couldn't escape?

Chet nodded wholeheartedly, already in route to the ledge. "Hell, yeah. Let's do this. A tour of this penitentiary sounds perfect."

So, for the next hour or so, that's exactly what they got, a room-by-room tour, with a couple exceptions. They started with the castle grounds; outside, but still inside the wall. Four courtyards, two training areas, a guardroom, even a stable. Man, were the creatures in that thing bizarre.

Once back inside, they headed to the castle's main stairwell. They bypassed the second story, aka the servants' quarters, and soon reached the third.

Zaden pointed with tied hands down one of the hallways. "Our place is down there. One big room with six beds."

"You mean, holes in the wall," Chet corrected.

"More like nests," Bailey countered.

Jamis shook his head. "Nope. No way. They're *sleeping cubbies*."

Zaden grinned a little and looked at Alec. "You get the idea."

Yeah. He did. Alec nodded, fighting a frown, remembering how much he hated the current arrangements. He should be with his team, damn it, in that sixth bed. Not holed up under the covers with the king.

But their escorts didn't take them down that corridor, anyway. They led them down a different one instead. "Those rooms are all private. Not for your eyes to see." Setch gestured ahead and grinned. "This way is better."

Warning alarms instantly sounded in Alec's head. He and Zaden swapped looks. The trio, however, were already speculating, guessing what made this other hall so superior.

"Medieval home theatre."

"Pfft. *No.* Game room."

"Screw it. I'm rooting for a decked-out arena, with props and shit for *motherfucking larping!*"

They all sucked in sharply, their optimism palpable.

Chet groaned. "Oh, my *God.* Could you *be* any geekier? Kríe don't *live-action roleplay.*"

"And you know this how?" Bailey countered.

Jamis jutted his chin up. "Yeah, how?"

But before Chet could answer, the guards came to a stop, right in front of two big, gaudy doors. Setch turned to them and grinned. "I do not know of this *larping*, but I assure you, Kríe most definitely like to play."

"Tah, and this is our playroom," Mannix rumbled, opening the way. "Come. See what Kríe consider fun."

Warily, Alec entered, but then froze just inside, smacked with an eyeful of *how* these males played. Holy freaking hell, talk about a den of iniquities. This must be the place Zercy had talked about.

He peered around, assailed by not just sight, but also sound. And smell. His senses bombarded with unadulterated kink. It was like they'd just stepped into a whole different dimension. One that made their fling with Gesh's pack look like a tea party.

The science trio gaped. Even Chet looked floored.

Alec glanced at Zaden. "And we thought *Roni* was twisted."

His co-pilot nodded distractedly. "Yeah," he murmured. "This place is... *Damn.*"

Yup, pretty much.

Just a bunch of horny Kríe and... a boatload more of *that one species*. The kind he'd seen just yesterday in that super-posh corridor, getting all but fucked by a noble against the wall.

Alec eyed one in particular. Lean, not super masculine, but his body was still cut. Almost pretty even—but not in a feminine way. Noah would probably consider them twinks, none looked older than early twenties. Made Alec wonder how fast Nirans aged.

He turned to Setch. "Who are they? And why are there so many?"

The guard grinned, eyeing one appreciatively. "They are *Súrah*."

"Súrah?"

"Tah. Sex nymphs. Very fun. Taste good, too."

Alec stilled, surprised. "Wow." He regarded them. "Are they slaves?"

"Mah," Setch laughed. "They *run* this lair. Relish being used by our kind."

Alec shot him a skeptical look.

Setch chuckled. "It is truth. They liken us to demigods. Consider our touch to be a drug."

"Damn," Alec murmured. His voice dropped to a mutter. "Definitely not how *I'd* describe you people."

Setch's next bout of laughter sounded notably smugger. "You say that now, moyo," he rumbled. "Just you wait."

Alec frowned and looked away, tentatively studying their surroundings. The room was huge and divided into themes. Very *distinguishable* themes.

His heart thumped as he took them all in. One area looked like a spanking center, another, a pen where one could apparently charter 'pets.' There were areas for masochists, others for sadists. Even a corner for fetishes like what Sirus had described.

Alec stiffened.

No. Not *like* them. Try *exactly the same.*

What those two Kríe held in their hands were most definitely tibbi. The mouse-size animals he'd seen caged in Sirus' workshop. The ones that'd looked like miniature wingless batts.

Unable to look away, he stared in shocked captivation. Several nymphs were on a platform, naked and bound, draped over a giant wedge. Ass up, face down, they yowled in rapture. Not because their rectums had been stuffed with big, hollow butt plugs, but because of *what* those hollow plugs lent passage to. A whole bunch of hyperactive critters.

One of the Kríe grabbed a squirming tibbi. Dangling it by its tail above the Súrah's ass, he dropped it into the butt plug's generous opening. Down the tunnel it went. A tunnel, incidentally, that looked drenched in oil. No doubt, so the tibbi couldn't climb back out. Not him, or any of the other ones already inside.

And evidently there were several, going by the urgency of those Súrah's shouts. Or the strength in which they bucked against their restraints. It probably didn't help that those Kríe kept stroking the nymphs' erections—and mercilessly tugging and kneading their laden balls.

The Súrah started quaking, and then one furiously came, blasting the wedge beneath him with thick, white seed. A second Súrah followed, coming so hard that veins popped from his neck, his rectum straight-up firing a tibbi out. Laughing, his handler caught it, patted its head, then dropped the squirming critter right back inside.

Fuck. Just wrong, Alec thought on a shudder, even as his dick gave a nudge. He needed to look at something tamer. Something chill. Turning, he spotted what looked like a lounge area. Well, sort of. In the sense that there were thick, high-back chairs, atop which several nobles sat conversing. What *wasn't* the norm, however, was what 'accompanied' each seat. More crazy-ass Súrah, shackled and suspended by their hands and feet, tailbones lightly resting on little pedestals. Which, essentially, meant they were folded in half, each one in easy reach of their highborn guests.

On top of that, they were also blindfolded, with ball gags stuffed in their mouths. Wait. No, not ball gags. Some kind of mouthpiece filled with blue liquid. An indigo color that reminded Alec of kirah nectar. Whatever it was, those Súrah really seemed to like it, urgently nursing the stuff between muffled moans.

Alec regarded the males further, noticing that their upper legs had been tightly bound together. The reason as to why was obvious: it kept their junk in place. Junk that'd been securely tucked between their tethered thighs, making their goods available from behind. Alec eyed the clever arrangement. Jutting boners and heavy nut sacs positioned just above tight backdoors. Everything all neatly consolidated and utterly accessible.

And they were definitely being accessed—each Kríe stroking his Súrah's cock while idly talking with his friends. And man, were those nymphs loving it, each looking a hair's breadth away from igniting. Their balls had climbed as high as they could go. But there were other signs, too. Like the twitching. The mewling. And how they'd visibly started sucking faster on their 'juice.'

Alec shifted his weight as one highborn paused and eyed his little plaything, then used his free hand to fondle the Súrah's nuts—as if weighing them or gauging their fullness. The Kríe grinned wolfishly, looking satisfied. Letting go, he slid his index finger down the Súrah's taint, then pushed it through his glossy hole. The male gasped, clenching around that big purple digit, only to moan as his handler resumed stroking his cock.

The noble rumbled. "You want to spill." His Súrah nodded urgently. "Bellah. Because I am thirsty for your seed." Licking his chops, he got busy with his buried finger, stroking what was presumably the nymph's prostate. "You feel that, little Súrah? Your master rubbing your swollen jewel?" Another nod, along with an exceptionally anxious mewl. The big Kríe growled. "Tah. I feel it pulsing, desperate to spend."

"*Unngggh*," the Súrah whimpered, his body shuddering, his dark brows pinched.

"Give your seed *now*, pup. It is time." Enclosing his mouth around the male's crown, the highborn flexed his forearm, as if pushing some magic detonation button deep inside. The Súrah went rigid, his eyes clenching tight. Two seconds later, a muffled yowl exploded. His boner started bucking. The big Kríe got busy, squeezing the smaller male's nut sac with every swallow.

Alec's dick thickened fast. No. That was *not* arousing! Wincing, he ground the heel of his palm down his crotch.

Soon, the Súrah was spent, but his handler was anything but. Continuing to milk him, the Kríe leisurely suckled, while lazily kneading his plaything's sac. A sac that curiously looked smaller now, and kind of *deflated*.

Finally, the noble relented and unlatched his lips with a scandalous *pop*. "You are empty." His Súrah shivered. He reached up and tapped on the limp male's mouthpiece. "Mmm. Be a good little pup and drink more of your nectar."

Alec's jaw went slack. That stuff was kirah nectar. And all these nymphs drank it intentionally—so their 'demigods' could literally drink them like cocktails at a dinner party.

Wow.

He shook his head, adjusting his crotch. He needed to get out of there. He was starting to feel drunk—along with a swiftly-growing need, goddamn it, to fuck.

Turning, he looked at Setch and cleared his throat. "I think we get the picture."

"Yeah," Chet rasped. He irritably squeezed his junk. "That all you twisted fuckers are seriously depraved."

Setch's lips curved wryly as he eyed Chet's bulge. "Like minds, I see. I can bring you any time. The Súrah will gladly service you as a favor."

Chet stiffened, then scowled. "You're crazy." Cheeks heating, he angrily stalked toward the door.

Alec looked at the others. Each teammate looked equally floored. And yup, every one of them had boners. Which he supposed made sense where Noah was concerned. But the rest of the team? Him and Chet included? He scrubbed his face. This place was messing with their heads.

The guards led them back out the way they came, but this time *did* head down the teammates' hallway. Sure enough, at the very end, were their large private quarters. They stepped inside briefly so Alec could check the place out, then ducked into another tower stairwell.

They reached ground level and continued on their way.

"Where're we going now?"

"Castle's grand foyer."

Alec frowned. They'd been to that entrance hall before, the day they'd first arrived. To be sold. Terrific memories. The best. They rounded a bend and, just like that, they were there, stopping at the first set of doors.

Kellim pushed the things open. Setch led them inside. Alec peered around, instantly captivated. They'd just entered the throne room where Zercy presumably spent much of his day heeding that call of responsibility he'd mentioned earlier. It was huge, with tiered rows of seats all around, reminding Alec of a scaled-down arena. And at the far end? Yup, a throne atop a dais. Masculine and imposing, black and adorned, its backrest literally built into the wall. Like a raised relief sculpture in the shape of tree trunk, big and ancient, branching skyward into a canopy.

Alec envisioned Zercy there, looking powerful, imperial. And, goddamnit, he got another boner. Clenching his jaw, he turned and stalked out, the first in their entourage to leave the room.

The next set of doors, the middle one, directly across from the grand entrance, was a space with which he was already familiar—the great hall, where asshole Gesh sold them to the king. He frowned, not even bothering to go inside. His men reacted the same. Guess the place had left a nasty taste in their mouths, too.

Fortunately, the foyer's final set of doors brought swift relief. Much smaller overall, but instantly Alec's favorite. A history museum of sorts, from what he could tell, dedicated entirely to Kríe culture. Art pieces, maps, books, items of importance. Everywhere he turned. It was amazing. Naturally, the trio looked just as charmed. Unfortunately, they weren't allowed to stay. Their escorts were being cranky. Wanted to keep things going. Most likely to finish the tour so they could dump them off at dinner—then take turns heading back to that lair.

They exited the vault, then rounded the bend and strode down the castle's east side. Along the way, they paused at a lavish lavatory. No toilets, of course, since Nirans only urinated. Just a bunch of intriguing urinals and swanky washbowls.

Resuming, they soon reached that all-too-familiar T-junction, and headed into the airy central corridor. First door on the right, the castle's giant kitchen, which encompassed other smaller enclosures, too. A pantry. A bakehouse. Hell, even a brewery. Alec loved trying new beers. Maybe sometime he'd give their mead a try.

They continued down the hall. Up ahead, Alec spotted *the doors*. The huge secretive ones that he'd never seen open, that were guarded day and night by two big Kríe. Would he get to see inside? Would it be part of the tour?

Their entourage ambled past them. Alec sighed.

Guess not.

Next thing he knew, they were back inside the tower. Looked like they were dungeon-bound again. Not that they finally got to *see* the prison, though. Apparently, it was forever off-limits. They did, however, get a look at the castle's large wine cellar, as well as its barracks and armory. The king had quite the army at his disposal, that was for sure. Alec wondered why he needed so many soldiers.

"One last stop," Setch announced from up ahead with Kellim.

And man, was that last stop incredible. Just a bit more down the tunnel and around a bend and, bam, holy wow, there it was. A floor-to-ceiling windowpane in a large, open room, displayed just like a mural against the wall. Of course, what was so striking was what was behind that sheet of glass. An underwater, sea-creature's view of the lake, presumably the side closest to the castle.

Alec felt his jaw drop open but was too floored to care. The incredible sight demanded all of his attention. It was stunning, mesmerizing. And for the briefest of seconds, he felt like he was at the

National Aquarium back on Earth. Except, yeah, the wildlife he was currently gaping at was anything but Earthly in nature.

Some had similar traits, though. Like the thing that just swam past. That one reminded him of a manta ray, but with much longer fins, and a face full of feelers like a catfish. Alec eyed a second creature farther back on a boulder. That one looked a little but like an octopus, only, it had more than eight arms. And the front two were much longer than the rest, with what resembled little snapping mouths at the ends.

"Whoa, look at those," Bailey murmured to Alec's left.

Alec followed his line of sight. His lips swiftly curved. A school of small, rainbow-colored bird-fish was getting ready to breeze past the window. They were beautiful, enthralling, but what struck him as peculiar was the unexpected formation they'd assumed—a horizontal cylinder, completely hollow in the middle, maybe four feet long with a three-foot diameter.

He watched them, perplexed. Why would they take such a shape? But when they abruptly dipped down behind a much larger fish, Alec saw *exactly why*. As if scooping their prey into a cup, the second they had it surrounded inside their colorful tube, the whole school converged, constricting around its body.

Jamis sucked in a breath. "They just shrink-wrapped that dude."

Chet chuckled, nodding. "Awesome."

Moments ticked by as the cluster shimmied in place, then just like that, they spread back out and went on their way.

Alec watched a couple of bones float out the rear of the cylinder. Bad day for that fish. He wondered if those schools got any bigger.

A few minutes later, his team was ushered from the room. Although, honestly, he could have stayed there for hours.

Back at ground level, they headed toward the back of the castle, past the bath house and Lotis' *bottega*, AKA the artist's workshop. They didn't get a look inside the latter. Evidently, Lotis was in a 'session' and couldn't be disturbed.

Around another bend, and they were on the south side, striding down a hallway with no doors. Just a whole lot of big, arched windows to the left, offering one hell of a view of the mountain range and lake.

When they reached the end, Setch gestured to a corner-tower stairwell. "To Sirus' workshop, but he is busy now, like Lotis. Busy and also very strange." He made a sour face and motioned them on. "We will go this way instead."

Alec exhaled in relief, his memories of that workshop not the greatest.

But as they ambled past, Setch grinned at him over his shoulder and mouthed, "Tell him of the elevator. Do not forget."

"Oh, for fuck's sake," Alec muttered under his breath.

A minute later, they were back at the big, center corridor.

"Your tour is finished, humans," Setch announced. "Now you eat."

The Kríe ushered them into the main dining room. Alec paused at the entrance and glanced down the hall. Down at those big mysterious doors. He'd really wanted to see what was behind them.

Mannix grunted at his back. "Esh. What do you wait for?"

Alec gestured with his chin. "Down there. Where those guards are posted. You never showed us what was inside."

The Kríe peered that way. His brusque expression faltered. "They guard the central courtyard."

"Can we see it?"

"Mah." He shook his head. "It is no longer open. Off limits to all."

Alec's brows furrowed. "Why?"

Mannix frowned. "The sickness."

The sickness? What was that?

But before he could ask, Mannix pushed him forward. "No more talk. Now you eat."

CHAPTER THIRTEEN

* * *

Dinner lasted longer than both previous meals combined. Probably because they were finally finished with their rigid schedule and, as promised, had the rest of the day to themselves. For well over an hour, they'd chilled at their table, eating one curious course after another. The main dish, Alec and Zaden had guessed was some kind of seafood. Large, steaming platters piled high with pale, pink meat. Only it was lighter than meat, less dense and easier to chew. Just fell the fuck apart when met with teeth. It'd been served with a chartreuse dipping sauce of some sort, and holy hell, did that stuff taste savory.

Alec had eaten way more than he should've, that was for sure. He hadn't realized they'd be bringing out dessert. And just like the course before, it'd seriously rocked. Kind of reminded Alec of dark-chocolate pudding, even though it was red, mixed with nuts that had the consistency of pistachios. It'd been doused with thick cream and sprinkled with yellow fruit chunks, and, man oh man, had each mouthful been like heaven. Regardless of his current opinion of Kríe, this species knew how to eat.

So, yeah, they'd kicked back and made the most of their captivity. Truth be told, the reality had been clear on all of their faces. The unspoken fact that they were faring far better than they would've been had they still been back in the jungle.

Of course, the drawback to their leisurely respite was that when it came time to go, the remainder of their day was pretty much over. In fact, when the guards had ushered them out of the dining room, the suns were both nearly completely set. From there, they'd been led up the main flight of stairs, only to go separate ways when they'd reached the third floor.

Alec had asked to hang out with his team in their room, but Setch and Kellim insisted he needed to get back. That Zercy would have their hides if Alec wasn't there when he returned. Which, evidently, was soon by the way they marched him onward, all the while promising he would see his men in the morning.

Alec hadn't been happy, but knew arguing would be pointless. In this, his chaperones were like talking to a wall. But as he climbed the stairs, each step taking him closer to Zercy's chambers, he couldn't keep his heart rate from accelerating. Or his stomach from flipping. Even his palms got all clammy. They reached the top landing. He swallowed and eyed the doors, then bit the bullet and tried one last time.

"You sure I can't hang out with my team a little longer?" He smiled at Setch. Wagged his brows. "Let me, and Kellim will suck your little dick."

Setch blinked… then broke into boisterous laughter, catching Alec's play on his past offer at Sirus' door. "Moyo ochay." *Funny creature.* "You are certainly crafty." Kellim chuffed and opened the way. Setch jovially slapped Alec's back, inadvertently sending him stumbling through the doors. "Fine idea, though. Fine indeed. Maybe once Zercy is in for the night, I will have Kellim do just that, right here on the landing."

The image assailed Alec's brain before he'd even regained his footing. Setch against the wall with Kellim down on his knees, bobbing his head of dark dreads up and down. Alec had seen a similar sight in the past—Gesh and Roni—and just like then, it made his dick do a jig. Of course, that first time, he'd had senna`sohnsay to blame. God only knew what his deal was now.

Frowning, he watched the brutes pull the doors closed, then turned and glanced around the familiar room. The windows were dark. The sconces flickered brightly. But no one was there. It was quiet. His tense muscles eased. For the first time in days, he was alone, experiencing total, glorious privacy.

He closed his eyes and sighed. A small smile curved his lips. Maybe if he was lucky the mighty king would be delayed. He lifted his lids and glanced at the hot tub, remembering his time inside it the night before. Arms bound behind him as Zercy pulled him closer… until the fucker had Alec straddling his thigh.

Alec shivered and shook off the memory, turning his gaze to the right, his focus quickly locking on the wet bar. All but licking his lips, he eyed the colorful bottles. What he wouldn't give for a Long Island Iced Tea, right down the gullet in seconds flat. That'd certainly take the edge off the last couple of fucked-up days. Unfortunately, he had no idea what any of this stuff was. How it'd taste, but more importantly, how it'd affect him. The last thing in the world he needed was to be all drunk and loopy when Zercy strode in.

Still, he couldn't stop staring at their vibrant colors. Like a rainbow of liquid gems, each one beckoning him equally, to come and have an innocent little sample. Absently, he turned and faced the vast array of bottles. After all, it couldn't hurt to merely look. Next thing he knew, he was moving toward the things, his eyes locked on the decanter of sparkling sapphire. For some reason, it felt less risky, a safer gamble than the others. Not that he was actually going to drink it.

His hand reached out of its own volition.

Fuck it. He'd have one. Just one drink.

But as his bound hand's fingers tentatively curled around its neck, another unbidden vision abruptly nailed him. One from that sex lair, involving a bunch of hanging nymphs. Nymphs who'd been drinking a similar liquid. Only theirs had been indigo blue instead of sapphire, which they consumed from glass ball gags instead of cups. Casually nursing, then urgently sucking as their handlers mercilessly teased them.

Alec clutched the bottle tighter and forced the image away, but not before his stupid dick twitched again.

Scowling, he glared down at it. "Seriously? Are you kidding me?" That crude shit did *not* turn him on. Not *at all...* He groaned and squeezed his bulge.

Shit. Maybe it did just a little.

Time to get his stupid brain onto anything else—fast. Snatching up the decanter, he poured some into a goblet. Wow. It smelled good. Like a piña colada. He turned his back to the memory-provoking bar and took a tentative sip. Nice. Kind of tasted like coladas, too. Not as sweet, though, or syrupy, considering it wasn't frozen.

He took another sip, searching for alcohol-type qualities, or any mind-altering attributes at all. He couldn't detect anything. He took a bigger swig. Then another. Still nothing. A healthy gulp. He waited. Waited some more. Nope, still nada. Looked like the stuff was pretty safe. Although, he doubted Zercy would allow anything harmful to be sitting around anyway.

Of course, the irony—after the day he'd had—was that a part of him wished it *would* get him drunk. Rip-roaring wasted, so he could forget about everything, then pass the fuck out before Zercy got there.

Sighing, he ambled through the large, open space, regarding things he hadn't been able to study yet. Like that big, marble bowl in that cut-out shelf, the green one holding all those tumbled rocks. It was weird. The stones just called to him, enticing him to come closer. To revel in their silky-smooth texture. So, he did. Why not? Had nothing better to do.

Walking over, he set his cup down, then sank his bound hands into the dish, slowly delving his fingers between the stones. Though varying in shape, most were the size of walnuts, in every imaginable color and opacity. Their glossy coats instantly calmed him, in a way he didn't understand. Fortunately, in this moment, he didn't care to understand. To just enjoy the little pleasure was enough. Which he did for several minutes before resuming his private perusal.

Of course, he strode right past Zercy's bed without stopping. To look at it would only stress him out. But when he reached that strange configuration of foliage-strewn walls, he couldn't resist stopping to have a look. Because, honestly, what in the frickin' hell *was* that thing? Zercy had called it his 'slice of secluded peace,' but that told Alec nothing. Did the king go in there to meditate or some shit?

Before he realized what his feet were doing, he stepped through the anomaly's leafy archway. Sconce light reached in through wall cutouts and branches, painting the pathway walls with fragmented shapes. As he inched in deeper, he peered around curiously, peeking around one of the partitions. The place was bizarre, like a mini jungle labyrinth, with no clear indication of which way to go. Left? Right? Straight ahead?

Alec paused in his advance. With his crappy luck, he'd get lost if he kept going. And yeah, how embarrassing would that be? He could see it now, Zercy having to come and rescue his ass. Alec laughed in spite of himself, unable to help it.

And suddenly, in that moment, it was game on. A challenge delivered, the driving desire to conquer this maze. After all, he was a navigator, this was in his blood. He could do it. He knew he could. Piece of cake.

Striding forward, he let go, allowing his subconscious to take control, to steer his feet toward which path to take. Right... Then left... Then another left... Then a right...

Before long, though, another pull joined his instincts at the helm. A whisper of his heart. An inner draw. An intrinsic yearning taking him toward an endgame—and endgame more substantial than just success.

He took his time, then finally, some ten minutes later, emerged in front of an unexpected balcony. Triumph roared through him. He grinned and stepped out, gazing ahead at the range of western mountains. So, this was the grand prize for beating the game?

Not bad. He drew in a lungful, then noticed stairs off to his right. Made of stone, they scaled up the side of the castle, leading to... he didn't really know. He planned to find out, though, because, no doubt, *that* was the true prize—and quite possibly connected to what had been directing him.

Climbing the steep steps, he soon reached the top, exhaling at the sight that greeted him; a rooftop oasis, as large as the sleeping quarters beneath it, decked out with so many plants it looked like a garden. Huge, stuffed lounge chairs took up center stage, and—Alec canted his head and slowly smiled—on one of the end tables sat a bronze, handheld telescope, retracted with a definite steampunk vibe. He wondered if it'd been Sirus who fashioned it.

Unable to resist, he strode over to check it out, marveling along the way at the view. Talk about panoramic. 360 degrees, minus the occasional lookout tower. Up front, the whole realm, as far as the eye could possibly see. Majestic highlands wrapping protectively on both sides. He could even see the lake behind him. Hear the faint, distant roar of the falls.

Alec stopped at the chairs. Looked up at the sky... His heart skipped a beat. God, the stars... He missed them already. Felt homesick for space. For far-off glittering suns and vast abyss. Which didn't really make sense. Why would voids and pricks of light soothe him? He wasn't really sure. He knew it was strange. But ever since his parents died, his only blood family, it was like the emptiness called to him. Mirrored his soul. A kindred spirit of sorts, that he sought out and grew attached to.

In hindsight, it was probably the driving force that made Alec choose to move his future off planet. And now, after all these years amidst the peaceful vacuum, that connection had grown to something more. It wasn't just his mirror; an entity like himself. It was the one and only place he truly belonged. A sentiment that might sound morbid to some, but to him, it was just the way things were. Problem was, their captivity threatened indefinite separation, and just the prospect of staying away made him ache.

He sighed and looked back down, his eyes landing on that telescope. Right off the bat he picked out three kinds of metal. Bronze, black wrought iron, and gold. He reached to pick it up—

"I am impressed," Zercy rumbled.

Alec jumped and whirled around. The king stood just six feet away. "Jesus, Kríe. Don't do that."

Zercy regarded him. "Do not do what?" For some unknown reason, he didn't look happy.

Alec frowned. "Never mind." He met the king's gaze. Shifted his weight. "Why are you impressed?"

Zercy feigned a small smile. "Because my *Alick* found his way. Very few have done so in the past."

Alec paused. Lifted his brows. "Get out. Are you serious?"

"Tah," the king chuckled, but his timbre was tight. "They go in circles, round and round, always ending where they began. Only those that Nira allows can find this refuge."

Alec laughed, not buying it. "Oh, come on. Surely, after a couple tries…"

"Mah." Zercy's eyes glinted. "Nira changes it constantly. The way is never the same. Always different."

Alec paused again. "She *changes* it?"

The king crossed his arms. "Tah. She is mystical. Can do *many* things."

"Uh… okay. But why change your maze?"

Zercy's features softened some. "I think she knows that I enjoy the challenge and takes pleasure in my delight." He averted his gaze. His eyes turned sober. "As of late, I think she does it to try to cheer me."

Cheer him? Alec frowned again, but decided not to pry. "You *like* getting lost?"

"I do not *get lost*." He sounded almost affronted. "But the times when I struggle, she quietly guides me. And then I do not need my eyes to see." He stared into the distance, his expression thoughtful.

Alec watched him. He looked troubled.

Several moments ticked by.

Finally, Alec cleared his throat. "No one led me. I followed a call."

Zercy looked at him. "Who called to you?"

Alec shrugged. "Not who. *What.*" He lifted his gaze to the sky. "Those stars up there... *They* are my beacon. *They* are my god."

Zercy seemed to ponder that. Another stretch of pensive silence. A few moments later, he changed the subject. "How was your day?"

His vibe was strange, subdued.

Alec regarded him. "Interesting... I guess."

Zercy peered toward the mountains. "Did you enjoy your lessons with Ryze?"

"Yeah. He's quite the font."

The king nodded once. "Indeed."

More quiet between them.

Alec's insides turned uneasily. Zercy didn't seem himself. Something was wrong.

The king inhaled deeply. Lifted his chin a little. Met Alec's eyes. "Kellim... He tells me you are a natural at wrestling."

Alec blinked, thoughts diverted to a completely different track. "Did he?" he chuckled. Not the report he would've expected.

"Tah." Zercy's golden gaze flickered again. "He said that because you hold a position of power, he paired you with the largest opponent. He wanted to see if you were worthy of your rank." His lips curved slightly. "He said you ever held your ground. Made your adversary work hard to take you down. Said you managed to prevail a few times."

He was blatantly stroking Alec's ego. But why? Not that it mattered. Already, Alec could feel his insides succumbing, helplessly lighting up from Zercy's praise.

A reluctant smile emerged. "I did okay."

The king smiled a little, too.

But then the silence resumed.

Alec fidgeted. Zercy's strange behavior had him off kilter. He seemed mad or sad, or something, but was holding it in, as if afraid he might bite Alec's head off.

Which Alec wholeheartedly appreciated, if that were the case.

"Did you enjoy your tour?" Zercy finally murmured.

Alec tensed a little. "For the most part."

"There were parts you did not enjoy?"

Alec shifted his weight. "A couple."

Zercy watched him. "Do tell."

Right. Like the fucker didn't know what he was talking about.

Fuck it. Alec would get the worst over with first. Squaring his shoulders, he held Zercy's gaze. "Well, for one, that lair they took us to? *Way* over the top."

"Ah. You did not like that. Why am I not surprised?"

Alec scowled at his tone. "I'm not a prude, if that's what you're implying."

Zercy chuckled humorlessly. "I do not know if I am implying that." He tilted his head. "What is a prude?"

Alec clenched his teeth. "Someone who doesn't like fun sex."

"Hmm. I see." Zercy chuckled again. "Then, tah. That is *exactly* what I am implying."

His goading shouldn't bother Alec, he should be able to let it go, but for some reason that accusation pissed him off. A reaction which, in turn, pissed him off even more. He shouldn't care what the king thought. His opinion shouldn't mean squat. But for some fucked up reason, it didn't. Not that Alec planned to have a debate. Zercy wouldn't just take his word for it. He'd insist Alec prove it.

Yeah, not happening.

Drawing in a lungful, he slowly exhaled, then took a turn changing the subject. "Another part of the tour I didn't enjoy was not being able to see the central courtyard."

Zercy visibly tensed, his arms constricting against his chest. "Visits to the courtyard are not permitted."

"Right. Mannix told me. But I don't understand why."

Mannix had mentioned 'the sickness' but that could mean countless things, *all* of them holding negative connotations. Clearly, nothing good was taking place behind those doors, and since his team was being held beneath the same roof, it was Alec's responsibility to find out more.

"Because I said so, that is why," Zercy muttered darkly.

"Yeah, that's not an answer." Alec held his surly stare. "Correct me if I'm wrong, but a central courtyard's kinda like the focal point of a castle. Its centerpiece. So, to lock it up makes no sense."

The mighty king's jaw ticked. Even his pointed ears flicked. "It does not have to make sense. My decree is my decree."

"Wrong." Alec stood his ground. "No offense, but that's bullshit."

Zercy's eyes flashed angrily. "You demand what is not yours."

"What? You mean the right to know that my men are safe?"

"They are safe. I assure you."

"That's not good enough," Alec grated. "I need information, to know for sure."

Zercy's nostrils flared. Every inch of his big body vibrated. "In this, you will simply have to trust me."

Alec balked incredulously. "No way. I'm responsible for their welfare and I take that seriously. Like hell will I just 'simply trust' our *captor*."

The king dropped his arms, his hands fisting at his sides. "That is unfortunate then, because I will not discuss this with you. I am not obligated to explain *anything* to my *pet*."

Alec's heart rate spiked faster, but not just from anger. Zercy's refusal to divulge even the smallest bit of intel was making him seriously nervous. Why withhold information unless it *did* impact Alec's team— on a life-or-death level, for all he knew. Which meant he *needed* to find out. As their captain, it was his duty.

Steeling his resolve, he stared Zercy down. "Tell me," he bit out.

The king seethed. "*Mah*."

Alec lost it. "Fucking tell me! What's behind those fucking doors!"

"*Death!*" Zercy thundered. "For *my* people, not yours!" Eyes blazing, he stalked forward and gripped Alec's throat, then yanked him off his feet. "Only mine!"

Alec froze. Holy shit. The Kríe was out-and-out shaking. Like a time bomb ready to blow. He shouldn't have pushed him. He'd known the guy wasn't right. He should've at least waited till Zercy looked *stable*.

Struggling in his hold, Alec dug at Zercy's fingers, trying like hell to pry them off his neck. "Please," he rasped. "I can't breathe." Soon his vision would start to spot.

Abruptly, the king released him, stepping back with wild eyes. Breathing heavy, he shook his head. "I..." His tone was ragged. "Apologies."

Alec coughed and rubbed his throat, heart pounding against his ribs. He had a feeling he'd just dodged a monster bullet.

Zercy's face turned distraught, a deep frown etching his features. Glancing around, he looked hesitant, unsure what to do, as if debating whether to just leave or take Alec with him. Ultimately, he re-closed the distance between them, seized Alec's bicep, and strode him toward the staircase. "No more talk of this. Ever. It has stolen my calm."

Alec hustled to keep pace but didn't say a word. God only knew what might happen next time. A one-way flight off the roof, maybe?

They made it down to the balcony in no time. A few minutes more and they were exiting the labyrinth. Zercy's claws bit into Alec's muscle, but it didn't seem intentional. By his expression, the king looked barely coherent. Like he'd shut his shit down, withdrawn inside his head. To keep Alec safe or something? Who knew.

One thing was certain, though. This king had issues. Anger-management issues, to be exact.

Zercy marched them past the hot tub, past his writing desk in the corner, their destination all too clear; Zercy's bed.

Alec's heart raced faster. Under normal circumstances, he'd try to stall, to prolong the inevitable at least a little. But after Zercy's mini meltdown back there, he was pretty sure that wouldn't be wise. So, he bit his tongue and went with it, didn't say a single word. Not when the king stopped and intently gazed down at him, nor when Zercy stripped him to his loincloth. Likewise, he stayed quiet when Zercy re-tied his wrists—behind his back this time—before lifting him onto the furs.

All the while, his brain whirled in conflict with his body, all this contact and close proximity making him crazy. No joke. How the hell could his dick be getting hard when his head was still so stressed out?

Zercy secured Alec's leash to the wraparound headboard, then stripped too, and settled down beside him on the bed.

Sprawled on his back, Alec turned his head and looked at him.

Zercy met his silent gaze. Exhaustion oozed from every pore. "You are angry with me," he murmured. "I am sorry, *Alick*. Forgive me."

Alec's heart tripped in his chest. Zercy sounded so sincere. And genuinely remorseful for his actions. Alec nodded a little but stayed silent.

Zercy frowned and touched his throat. "Did I hurt you?"

"No."

"Bellah." *Good.* "But I frightened you."

Alec didn't respond.

Zercy exhaled. "I did not mean to."

And he meant it. Alec could tell. Could feel him radiating regret.

Alec cleared his throat. "I shouldn't have pushed. It was obvious you weren't... feeling well."

"Tah... I was not..." Zercy's hand moved lower, his fingertips absently following Alec's collarbone. "The day has been long... bringing only bad news."

Alec fought a tiny shiver. What kind of bad news? He wanted to ask but posed a different question instead. A safer one, albeit just as important. "Are you... okay?"

Zercy paused from his toying. Feigned another small smile. "Are you inquiring for your sake... or mine?"

"Both," Alec murmured, a truth he'd yet to acknowledge until now.

The king's smile widened. "You care if I am troubled."

"I wouldn't go *that* far."

Zercy's lips twitched. "Indeed. I am better now. Thank you."

Alec shrugged. "No thanks needed. I was only asking."

The king's touch resumed, moving down to Alec's pec. Slowly, leisurely, he circled his hardened nipple. "I was not thanking you for that."

Current sprang from the site and shot to Alec's groin. His lashes fluttered. "Then... for what?"

Zercy dipped his gaze to watch his fingers play. His warm thumb swiped over Alec's nub. God, so sensitive. "For restoring my calm. It was not you who upset me before. I was already tense. But I am better now, *Alick*, because of you."

Alec shuddered—that thumb felt so good—then stilled as he registered Zercy's words. Wait, what? *He* affected the king that way? Being a toy Zercy found attractive was one thing, yeah, but a source of comfort? That was all around different.

He looked at Zercy's face, fighting to focus, which wasn't easy. That lazy thumb's stroking was making him lightheaded. "I don't get it. How did I do that? I haven't exactly been warm and fuzzy."

Zercy chuffed. "Indeed. But I am Kríe, I do not mind. In fact, I think your ire is what relaxes me."

And now Alec was *really* confused. "That makes no sense."

Zercy exhaled, shook his head, then draped his arm across Alec's stomach. "Perhaps I like you because you do not want this... To be here in this castle. With me."

Alec stared at him blankly. "Yeah, I still don't understand."

The king smiled a little, but quickly sobered. "Those who want inside these walls, to give themselves to me... I do not trust them, *Alick*. Not even a little."

"Why not? Doesn't that kind of devotion imply loyalty?"

Zercy's expression went cold. He stiffly shook his head.

Again, Alec wanted to ask, but managed to refrain. He had the feeling this subject matter was pretty rocky. So instead, he digressed to something else he wanted to know. "None of my men want this, either. To be in this castle, with you. But you picked me specifically. Why?"

Zercy met his gaze, gave a tiny, playful smile. "Because you are pretty?"

Alec eyed him drolly.

He exhaled and looked at Alec's mouth. "Because the moment I saw you, I felt my beast within ease. A peace inside I forgot even existed. Your men did not give me this. Only you."

Alec's heart thumped restlessly, moved in a way he wasn't comfortable with. He didn't want to be glad by that knowledge, but he was. Sure, on some level it gave him an edge over the Kríe, but for some fucked-up reason he didn't care. All he seemed focused on was the fact that he'd helped him. Lifted some of the weight of Zercy's burden. Because he definitely seemed burdened. The plight of a king, Alec supposed.

Softly, he cleared his throat again, not sure what to say. "Huh... Well, that's just... really... unexpected."

Zercy chuckled and pulled him closer. Alec stiffened and looked at the ceiling, unintentionally offering access to his neck. Of course, the king capitalized on that immediately and happily nuzzled his face all up in there. A rumbly growl emerged. Alec reeled from head to toe, his dick hardening, his bound hands balling behind his back.

Zercy murmured against his skin, "Would you like me to touch you?"

Yes... God, yes...

Alec rasped weakly, "No."

Zercy inhaled slow and deep. His nose brushed Alec's lobe. "Are you certain? I can smell your arousal. Your need." He squeezed Alec's hip, then grazed a thumb along his groin. "Let me ease your ache, make you spill."

More warm current coursed straight to Alec's cock. If he said yes, Zercy would have him coming in seconds. A release Alec could really use. His breath quickened. He swallowed. "I'm—I'm good."

Zercy grazed his lips against Alec's ear, then brazenly rolled his hips into Alec's side. *Fuuuck.* He was just as hard as Alec. "Then perhaps you would like to touch me?"

Alec's brows pinched. God help him, he totally would. Wanted to make the king all crazy like he was. But that'd be wrong. For shit's sake, Zercy had *bought* him like a slave and was holding him there against his will. Add to that the fact that the guy was an *alien*. A *male* alien. With fangs.

"No," he rasped, frustrated, both mentally and sexually. "I think I'm gonna pass on that, too."

The king's soft sigh sounded more like a groan. Stilling his thumb, he relaxed against Alec's body. "I would never hurt you," he promised quietly.

But Alec already knew this. Had somehow always known.

Closing his eyes, he pressed his cheek against Zercy's, way too tired to put up a front. "Then let me go."

The king didn't respond, just nestled Alec closer. The silence stretched on. Long moments later, Zercy murmured against his neck. "Tell me about your world, *Alick*. About Earth."

Twenty-four hours ago, Alec probably would've told the guy to go fuck himself. But as he lay there in the arms of this dark, troubled giant—who'd just displayed some very real vulnerabilities—Alec couldn't find it in himself to do so. In truth, the *last* thing he wanted to do was add to the stress plaguing Zercy's mind.

He didn't know the specifics of this crisis the king faced. But one thing he sensed down to the marrow of his bones? Zercy was carrying the weight of the world on his back. And it was starting to take its toll.

Sighing, Alec shifted beneath the king's big, lax arm. "It's the third planet in our solar system."

"*Solar* system?" Zercy mumbled.

God, he sounded exhausted.

"Yeah, um, the name's derived from the Latin world 'sol,' which means sun, another name for star."

"Mm…" His breath tickled Alec's neck. "So, one of your gods is named Sol."

Alec shivered, trying to stay focused. "Uh… Well, we only have one sun, if that's what you mean."

"Only one?"

"Yeah, I know. We're an oddball star system."

"Hmm… Odd indeed…"

His lashes brushed Alec's ear. Alec felt it down to his cock. He shifted his hips. "Um… so anyway… it's a lot like your planet... Oceans, continents… Our sky's blue, though, instead of orange, and—"

"*Blue* skies?" Zercy murmured. He was smiling. Alec could hear it. "I would very much like to see that."

If it wasn't for Gesh's pack stealing their stuff, Alec could actually show him. He had an album on his cell phone loaded with photos. Every single place he'd ever visited on Earth. Every photo he possessed of his parents, too. His chest went heavy at the thought of those two. God, he missed them so much.

Fighting a frown, he cleared his throat again. "The seas are blue, too. But our plant life's green like yours. Well, kinda like yours…"

He talked about home for a good half hour, until the king's soft snores joined the peaceful quiet. Alec's heart thumped steadily to the slow, rhythmic sound, a strange satisfaction washing through his body. He'd helped Zercy find sleep, something he suspected no one else could do. He wished that didn't make him feel so good, but it did.

As he lay there listening to the big Kríe breathing, something else occurred to Alec as well. The fact that, despite all the shit that had happened, in this moment, he felt inexplicably… content.

CHAPTER FOURTEEN

* * *

"Well, that was a colossal waste of fucking energy."

Scowling, Chet inched back toward his hole-for-a-bed's window. After the others had gone to bed, he'd decided to do some investigating. Specifically, that of the castle's perimeter, sidling along the ledge that circled the keep's exterior wall. The guards had untied them when they locked them in for the night, so he'd figured why not make use of his free hands. Do a bit of recon on the fortress' outer structure, in search of any and all potential escape routes.

His efforts had been fruitless, though. All that ledge provided was a precarious, four-inch path to other windows. Granted, had those windows been to anything besides other sleep-holes, his outing wouldn't have been such a fail. But they hadn't, and since every single sleep-hole was occupied, access to them was pretty worthless.

Talk about an interesting expedition though, *fuck*. As he'd shimmied past each opening, he'd had to crouch down, lest the residents spot his ass and turn him in. Problem was, those residents hadn't merely been sitting there, conversing about world affairs over tea. Hell the fuck no, they'd been rutting like mad dogs. Growling and snarling, clawed hands braced on the windows, as their bang buddies slammed them from behind.

He'd spotted some Súrah in a few of those holes, too, as well as some other species he didn't recognize. One had a tail. Another, wings. A third had suspect spikes down his back. Suspect in the sense that each thick, upturned tine looked not only flesh-covered, but veiny.

Admittedly, Chet had paused to watch that specific couple romp, convinced those things were more than just barbs. As luck would have it—for once—the males were facing away, offering up one seriously unobstructed view. And sure enough, as the Kríe gripped those thick spikes like handles—tugging on them roughly as he fucked—the curved tips had straightened, then turned bright red, with those little veins bulging in stark relief. The big Kríe had chuckled. The spiked male quaked. All while Chet peeked in from outside their window, teetering as he struggled to adjust his boner.

Friggin' kinky aliens.

God, he needed to get laid.

Muttering under his breath, Chet climbed back inside and flopped down on his back atop the bed. Discouraged, he stared at the low, stucco ceiling, brooding over the findings of his mission. Specifically, how it confirmed what he'd hoped wasn't true; that a night escape via the windows was totally impossible. Not because there weren't means to climb to the ground, though—no steps or ladders or conveniently protruding bricks. Hell, they could rig makeshift ropes no problem. The issue was how to scale that thirty-foot protective wall with a top patrolled by vigilant guards.

Thing was, even if they *did* manage to get over the huge barrier, a second, even bigger quandary still awaited them. One that had presented itself much more evidently tonight as Chet had peered out at the mountains. Or rather, at the skyline's countless sentry watch points, each post clearly marked by blazing torches. Chet had groaned when he spotted them. There was easily one every fifty yards. God only knew how many more guards were in stealth mode.

The king wasn't playing around. His realm was seriously fortified. Meaning escape was going to be even harder than Chet had anticipated.

He clenched his jaw and glared, all his anger resurfacing. Part of him *still* couldn't believe they were in this mess. His glower deepened. *Fucking Gesh.* This was all his fault. His, and all his dick-for-brains pack mates.

Roni's irritating face pushed to the forefront of his mind. Chet's scowl intensified but then downshifted to a frown. A contemplative one, as he thought about the bastard. Was Roni even *trying* to find a way to get them out? Working with Gesh *at all* to fix their fuck-up? Or were Chet and his team totally on their own, already gone and purged from Roni's thoughts?

Chet's stomach clenched at the prospect of Roni dumping him like trash.

No. That dick still thought about him. Chet knew he did. The way Roni scrapped with those guards in the merchant hall? He'd wanted their sale withdrawn just as badly as Gesh, had looked furious when the king hadn't allowed it.

Man, how Roni had brought it, giving those Kríe one serious beat down, until a triad of them finally took him out. *Three* of those fuckers it'd taken to stop him. And every single one was as big as him.

Truth be told, it'd been beautiful, the way he brawled like a beast. A sight that got Chet all fired up, too. Unfortunately, his efforts hadn't amounted to much. His hands had been tied, for shit's sake, to a rope pulled way too snug between his thighs.

Chet exhaled and scrubbed his face, then palmed his crew cut and closed his eyes. But the visual of Roni fighting still remained.

"Fuck," he muttered. He didn't want to think about him, but the stupid scene kept looping in his brain. Which, in turn, kept things pumping too fast in his chest. A hot, swirling mixing pot of emotions. Anger, frustration, restless apprehension.

He also sensed some residual excitement. Something that irked him since it spawned from images of Roni. But on the flip side, it helped to quell some of his ire. Because all those charged memories of the asshole tearing shit up reminded Chet of the time they faced off. In the woods, after the pack had taken those three flyers down, when Roni had brazenly challenged him, and Chet had accepted.

He growled at the memory. Balled his hands against his head. A part of him wanted to rumble with Roni again. He may be an asshole, a smug son of a bitch, but that Kríe was also one hell of a challenge. And Chet loved his challenges. Craved worthy one-on-ones. Which wasn't to say wrestling with Alec earlier wasn't invigorating. But next to Roni? Yeah, no comparison.

He groaned and dropped his fists, remembering what happened at the end of their scuffle. Specifically, when Roni bit his neck. His pulse quickened just thinking about it. He absently rubbed the site. His body had been so frantic. Frantic to bury his raging boner into something. Preferably something tight. And hot. And slick.

A shudder rolled through him.

"Shit," he breathed, rocking his hips.

His eyes slid closed. Below the waist, his hard-on thrummed. He clutched his junk and tried to squeeze it into submission, but the memory had already spread through his system.

Goddamnit.

Now he was horny and wanted to whack off.

But he wouldn't. Fucking refused.

Not in this state of mind.

Not when all he'd be thinking about was Roni.

* * *

"Would you like me to touch you?"

Alec groaned and looked down. Zercy sat between his knees, his mouth way too close to Alec's cock. He was having that dream again, and the only reason he knew was because he'd had the same one for five nights straight. Ever since the king straight-up lost it on the rooftop, then offered Alec a handjob on his bed. He couldn't explain it, but the phenomenon remained, this dream set on repeat in his head.

With every one, Alec found himself deep in the jungle, alone, with not a single soul in sight. Likewise, in each sequence he'd been tied to a tree, but unlike with Gesh, he wasn't sitting in the dirt. Instead, his ass rested on a big, fat, downed log laying flush against the very trunk detaining him. Acting, for all intents, like the seat of a chair with his toes barely touching the ground.

But then, just like every single episode before, the king would emerge from the brush. Eyes glittering, he'd saunter over and sink to his haunches, positioning his naked body in front of Alec's.

Alec shifted atop the log, wearing nothing but his loincloth, snared like every time before by Zercy's gaze.

The king smiled a little. His husky timbre dipped. "Would you like me to touch you?" he repeated.

Fuuuck. Instant boner. Alec's dick bucked on cue, exactly as it'd done the last five times. Fortunately, in all dreams prior, he'd managed to say no, somehow finding the strength to turn Zercy down.

But with each consecutive invite, it'd grown harder to do, which naturally made Alec really freaking wary. How much longer could he resist before he finally just let go? Before his willpower buckled and he gave in? Already, his hard-on was trying to come out and play, pushing as much as it could against its wrap.

Heart pounding, he swallowed.

Zercy stared at him hungrily. "Tell me," he rumbled. "Would you like me to touch you?" He clutched Alec's knees and pushed them apart.

Alec's nuts tightened. His boner throbbed. God, he wanted this so bad. Zercy's big, hot, clawed hand around his dick. Like it'd been in Sirus' workshop, all making him crazy. Only now he wasn't blindfolded, and if he said yes, he could *watch*.

But shit, he really shouldn't.

Zercy palmed his inner thighs.

Alec's cock shot straight up, harder than steel.

Screw it. This was nothing but a stupid-ass dream. Maybe if he gave in, it'd finally stop.

Aaaand there went the last of his paper-thin restraint.

Quickly, he nodded.

The king grinned. "Say it."

"Yes," Alec rasped. "I want you to."

"Want me to *what*?"

Fuck, he couldn't believe he was saying this. "To touch me."

Zercy loosed a small growl and ran his splayed hands toward Alec's groin. "Where, *Alick*? Tell me."

Alec's pulse shot sky high. "On my dick," he blurted. "Please. I need you to touch my dick."

His tormentor chuckled. "Suddenly so impatient." He reached for Alec's loincloth and parted the strips of fabric, creating an opening right where it counted. Alec tensed, breaths quickening, but didn't say a word. Zercy slid his fingers inside and clutched Alec's package.

"Shit," Alec breathed.

Zercy purred and pulled it free, clutching his balls in one hand, his cock in the other. "Tah," he rumbled. "My pet is so ready. So ready to spill for his king."

Alec's hips bucked against his will. He cursed and fought to steady them, his dick flat-out howling in Zercy's grip. But it wasn't easy;

Zercy's touch was like some high-octane drug. One he needed more of right now.

The king chuffed and subtly tightened his grip. "Like this, pet?" he murmured.

Alec's junk went nuts. He nodded. "Yeah, like that. Oh, fuck. Jack me."

"Jack you?" Zercy's gaze hooded. "What does that mean?"

Alec moaned. Did he really have to frickin' explain? Surely, the Kríe could deduce. Screw it. Whatever. He thrust against Zercy's hand. Pleasure surged down his shaft. "*Ungh...* It means stroke me."

Zercy rumbled. "Hmm, I see." His grip remained still. "And at what speed would you like me to go?"

"Fast," Alec ground out.

"How fast? Show your king."

Shit. For real?

Alec cursed and pulled his knees up, propping his feet on the log for better leverage. He thrust into Zercy's fist again. Bliss exploded, briefly distracting him. He moaned once more, shivering, then forced himself to focus, rolling out a quick demonstration. His pelvis rocked upward in swift repetition, pushing and pulling his dick through Zercy's grip.

"Like that," he gasped. "Fuck..." His hips thrust again.

The king growled heatedly. But then he furrowed his brows. "If I grip you like this... and stroke you like that..." He shook his head. "Too much dry friction."

He squeezed and tugged upward.

"Uh!" Alec jerked. "What the fuck?"

Zercy frowned. "Your hard cock... It gives no lubrication."

"What?" Alec shuddered through a scowl. "Yeah, it does..." He looked at his dick. A drop of precum glistened. "There. Some lube." Case in point.

Zercy grunted incredulously. "You consider *that* lubrication?" He shook his head and reached for his own rigid cock. His bicep and shoulder flexed, then he reclaimed Alec's dick, clutching its crown with five coated fingers. Again, his grip stayed stationary. "Show me now," he commanded.

Without thinking, Alec obeyed with another eager thrust, shoving through a fist of warm lube. Ecstasy assailed him. His eyes briefly closed. "Fuck, yeah," he moaned.

So slick and tight...

Zercy's timbre dropped an octave. "Tah. Now do that many times."

Lost in sensation, Alec complied yet again. Steadily, he pistoned his hips forward and back. His lips parted, his breaths shallowing as he plunged into heaven, watching his glans emerge and disappear. Bursting through the top of Zercy's strong, dark grip, a glossy crown popping in and out of view.

Oh, God. Felt so good.

Zercy watched with smoldering eyes. "Tah, *Alick*. So handsome. Do not stop."

Alec didn't plan to. Hell, his hips were driving themselves.

Pressure mounted. He moaned, helplessly trapped in Zercy's gaze. But then the king loosened his grip. Like he knew Alec was close and wanted to stave off the inevitable.

Alec groaned, shifting his feet atop the log as he thrust. "No—Grip me tighter—C'mon, please—Wanna come—"

Zercy rumbled. "So soon?" He sounded reluctant.

Alec's heart raced. His chest heaved. "Yes—" he panted. "*Please—*"

A low, heady thumping sound filled the jungle's quiet. "Very well." Zercy strengthened his slippery hold. "Would you like to spill on your chest... or in my mouth?"

Alec's hips bucked like a bronco, his brain nailed with both visuals. Zercy lapping his spattered nipples. Zercy sucking his dick. Pleasure roared through his crotch and up his shaft.

"I dunno—" he gasped. His body shook. "Shit—So close—"

"Tah," the king growled, incinerating him with his stare. "I can feel your cock throbbing in my hand."

Alec moaned, fists clenching against the tree at his back. "Almost there—" he panted raggedly, pelvis rocking fast and furious. "Oh my God, Kríe— Feels so good—"

"Del`ahtchay." *Delicious.* "Do not stop, pet. Keep going."

Alec's mind spun, rapture raging through his groin and into his ass. Restlessly, he nodded, his hips kicking like mad. "Yeah—" he grated. "Fuck, yeah—Aw, God—Need to come—"

Zercy's grip abruptly tightened.

Alec gasped, eyes slamming shut. "Shit, Kríe—Shit—" He undulated feverishly. His dick was going to bust so effing hard.

Schlick—schlick—schlick— as he fucked that fixed hand.

Zercy loosed another growl.

Current surged, then ignited, blitzing the living hell out of Alec's junk.

He could feel himself fragmenting—

His heels dug into the log—

A heartbeat later, he arched. *"Ungh! I'm coming!"*

His hips bucked erratically. Tight, wet heat locked onto his glans. And as his nuts furiously unloaded, a muffled snarl resounded. Not that it registered much—Alec was far too distracted, rocketing like a missile toward the stars...

Long, jumbled, incoherent moments later, his brain finally came back online. Except, when he finally opened his eyes, he wasn't in the jungle. Breathless and groggy, he regarded the low ceiling—then froze in realization. He'd been so caught up in that self-imposed handjob that he totally forgot he'd been dreaming. Dick sated and humming, he warily turned his head.

Oh, God.

Zercy.

Quietly watching him. Head resting on his bent elbow. Gold eyes hooded.

Alec's heart skipped, disquieted by the king's expression. All affectionate and low-key possessive. Shifting atop the furs, Alec swallowed, still catching his breath. His post-O haze was making it hard to concentrate.

He cleared his throat. "I..." But his train of thought faltered.

Zercy's lips curved a smidge. "You are welcome."

Huh? Alec frowned. He was welcome? "For what?"

The king's amused chuff sounded morning-groggy, too. "Ochay." *Funny.* His eyes gleamed. "You proved me wrong."

Oh, hell. Should he ask?

"About what?" Alec rasped.

Zercy gave a little smirk. "My *Alick* is not a prude. Likes his fun."

Alec's mouth dropped open.

Oh, crap.

A cool breeze wafted over his junk. He glanced down, then instantly tensed up all over again. Not only was his clockwork morning wood wet and limp, but completely out of its loincloth's confines. Even his nuts were fully exposed as if he'd manually pulled them free.

But he hadn't.

His hands were still tied behind his back.

A shiver of dread rolled up his spine.

No. No way. All that stuff had been a dream. Just a stupid dream. Right?

Right??

His eyes anxiously darted between the king and his dick. Zercy's hand *had* felt exceptionally real in that jungle... And now his gaze *did* look suspiciously pleased.

Alec's body went taut. Had that motherfucker groped him? Fondled his goods while he slept? He frowned, then sighed. No, the king wasn't like that and, truthfully, seemed genuinely oblivious. Not a trace of foul play in those big auric eyes. Not an ounce of dubious intent in his vibe. And while Alec didn't know the specifics of what exactly went down, Zercy clearly thought that Alec had been awake. Thing was, the only reason he'd even get that impression was if Alec had been talking...

"Oh, God," he groaned. The stuff he'd said in his dream... Had he said all that out loud, too?

Son of a bitch. His brain had been hijacked by his traitor-ass dick. Although, he supposed that shouldn't come as much of a surprise. Since they'd gotten there, he hadn't been able to jerk off even once. Something that normally wouldn't be a problem, except that 'normally' he wasn't constantly around Zercy. And in his defense, that big fucking Kríe was proving to be one seriously formidable stimulant.

But for that to drive him to sleepwalking? Or more accurately, sleep-*messing around?* The king must *really* be getting under his skin.

Zercy frowned at Alec's expression. Studied his face. Looked him over. "What has happened? What is wrong with you?" He clearly sensed Alec's stress, which Alec appreciated, but the situation still sucked.

Stomach twisting, he shook his head, hardly ready to speak.

Zercy continued to watch him.

Alec's heart pounded warily. He needed to ask 'the question,' but a part of him didn't want to know the answer. It'd drive him bat-shit crazy if he didn't find out, though. Might as well bite the bullet.

Steeling his resolve, he drew in a breath. "What just... Fuck, what just happened?"

Zercy cocked his head, looking amused, but mostly confused. "You want me to recapitulate?"

Alec shifted awkwardly. "Yeah... But maybe cover me up first."

The king quirked a brow, then shook his head and propped himself higher on his elbow. "Humans. So peculiar. Or perhaps it is just you."

Alec fought back a scowl.

Zercy, in turn, tamped a grin, causally pulling a fur over Alec's crotch. "You woke me with your pleas," he began, meeting Alec's gaze, "imploring me to touch you. To make you spill."

Alec's heart tripped. Every ounce of blood drained from his face.

Zercy must have considered his speechlessness a prompt to continue. "You were breathing so heavily. It quickly aroused me." He ran his hand atop the soft pelt covering Alec's hip. "At first, I did not understand when you said, 'I want you to.' So, I asked, 'Want me to what?'"

Alec groaned, remembering all too well how he'd replied.

"You said you wanted me to touch you. On your *dick*. You said *please*." He dragged his small claws down the fur on Alec's thigh. "You sounded so desperate for me to ease you."

Alec shivered, his brain trying to dive back to dreamland, to plug back into his little jungle fantasy.

The king rumbled softly, as if reliving the moment, too. "So, I freed your eager cock and clutched it in my hand. You were already so hard... So close to spending."

Alec's heart pounded faster. It was true. He *had* been close.

"From there," Zercy went on, "you took what you needed... Eyes closed, skin flushed as you greedily fucked my hand, emitting the most decadent noises..."

Alec groaned in mortification.

Zercy paused with a frown. Must have detected a spike in Alec's anxiety. "You are sending strange signals. What is wrong with you now?"

Hell. Should he even *try* to explain? If he didn't, it would leave Zercy to believe he'd truly wanted it. Which wasn't to say he hadn't, but only in his dream.

Shifting his gaze to the ceiling, Alec swallowed. "I... wasn't awake."

Zercy quieted. Time stood still. Then, abruptly, he laughed, the sound so rich and deep—and utterly genuine. "More jokes... Peculiar human."

"I'm serious," Alec muttered. Heat crawled up his neck. "The stuff I said... I was... talking in my sleep."

Again, the king went silent. Did that mean he finally believed him? Alec turned his head—and frowned. The Kríe was eyeing him wryly, in a way that said he thought Alec was kidding.

Smirking, Zercy leaned in and nuzzled Alec's ear. "In your sleep?" Ugh. He was 'playing along.' Alec could hear it in his tone. "So, this means my *Alick* dreams about me, too?"

"No!" Alec blurted. Total lie, but what could he do? "I was just sleeping. It wasn't real."

"Ah. I see." Zercy still wasn't buying it.

Alec fumed. "You know what? Just forget it."

Zercy's next chuff was laced with a hint of endearment. "I do not understand why you are angry."

Alec exhaled and frowned at his soft, happy dick. "Because you made me come again."

"Tah. I did. You were beautiful."

Alec's insides clenched. He looked at Zercy. "It shouldn't have happened."

The king's small smile vanished. "Why? You enjoyed it."

"Ugh. Really, Kríe? You can't figure it out?"

Zercy stiffened, brows furrowing. He suddenly looked offended. "Mah, I cannot. I cannot *figure it out*. You asked me to touch you, so touch you I did. As a result, you spilled like a sensuous young god. Now you are eased, and I am quenched. I do not understand how that is bad."

Alec blinked, derailed by Zercy's unexpected take. Specifically, his little reference to Alec's orgasm. "You thought I spilled like... a *sensuous young god?*"

"Tah. You were captivating. I could not look away."

Wow. No one had ever given him a compliment like *that*. The way Zercy regarded him... It shouldn't make Alec want to smile. But it did. In a way that made him nervous.

Another of the king's sentiments rebounded in his mind. Alec froze. "Whoa. Wait. How exactly are you *quenched?*"

Zercy's small smirk returned. "How else but with drink?"

Alec's jaw went slack, recalling a certain beverage Kríe liked. He glanced at his chest, then the king's chest, then the furs. Nope. Not one single drop of cum.

Son of a bitch. That tight, wet heat around his glans when he unloaded? That'd been Zercy's mouth, catching every spurt. Alec's gaze dropped to Zercy's lips. He probably should be pissed, but instead all he felt was disappointment. Disappointment that he hadn't gotten to watch.

And how seriously fucked up was that?

Zercy stared at him intently, as if trying to read his mind. Eventually, he just grunted and sat up. "Your actions confuse me. Your words are no better. When I give you what you ask for, it upsets you."

Alec frowned, finally realizing how nonsensical he must seem. If he were Zercy, he'd be exasperated, too.

Again, he tried to explain. "But I wasn't really asking for it. Whether you believe me or not, I was dreaming."

Zercy turned his head and looked at him.

Alec averted his gaze. "I hadn't meant to do that... with you."

Even as he said it, he could taste the blatant lie. He *had* really been asking for it, and he'd *definitely* meant to do it—very fucking specifically *with Zercy*. He just couldn't admit it. Not to the king, and not to himself. He refused to go there. Just wasn't an option.

The silence turned glaring.

He glanced back at Zercy, instantly noting the king's unsettled expression.

He met Alec's gaze. "If what you say is true, I apologize. That is not the way I want things between us."

Alec shifted atop the covers, feeling partially to blame. "Okay," he muttered. "Let's just… not do that again."

Zercy nodded in compliance, but then canted his head and eyed him. "But why? It is obvious you like to spill. Is it because I am Kríe? A species dominant to your own?"

Alec coughed and rolled his eyes. "No. And no."

"Then why?"

Alec averted his gaze. "You're my captor."

"Is that the only reason?"

Alec didn't answer. Didn't want to get into specifics. These days the specifics were too ambiguous. Too blurred around the edges. No longer defined.

"*Alick…*" Zercy gently gripped Alec's chin and turned his head. "Is that the only reason?"

Alec met his gaze, his heart pounding anxiously in his chest. "No," he rasped. "It's not." He struggled for the words, words to an explanation that no longer added up. "I'm not gay," he finally stated. "I have sex with females. Before Miros I'd never had sex with another… male."

Zercy stared at him blankly. "Gay? Females? Male? I do not understand any of these terms."

"Because you only have one gender in your species. Ours has two. Males and females. And most males of my species, the version with dicks, are attracted to and like to fuck females."

Zercy thought on that for a while, clearly trying to understand the concept. "Most," he finally repeated. He looked at Alec. "But not all?"

Alec shifted atop the covers, stomach clenching. "No. Not all. Those who fuck other males are gay. But I… I'm not gay... I like… females."

"Hmm." Zercy pondered again. "So, you do not prefer the version with dicks…"

Last month, Alec would've given him a resounding hell no, but now...

"No," he muttered, hating the convoluted lie in his mouth. He didn't understand. When had things changed?

Zercy nodded, clearly still grappling with the concept. Which Alec got. His behavior with the king was probably misleading. Especially with what just happened a few minutes ago.

Long moments ticked by. Finally, Zercy turned and regarded him, a strange little glint in his gold eyes.

Alec fidgeted. "Is there a problem?"

"Mah, but... who were you speaking to?"

Alec frowned. Speaking to? "When?"

"In your dream. Who was touching you?"

Alec's gut clenched. Uh-oh. "I don't know." More lies on his tongue. "I kept my eyes closed. Never saw them."

Zercy's tone dipped coolly. "Not even a glimpse?"

Alec shook his head.

"But they were definitely *female*?"

"Uh...Yeah." Alec nodded.

Zercy's jaw ticked. He narrowed his eyes. "Then why did I hear you call them *Krie?*"

Aw, shit.

Alec scrambled for a logical explanation. "Uh... Well, because I..."

The king watched him closely. When Alec continued to flounder, Zercy smirked a little and eased. "You are lying. There was no female. You were dreaming of me."

Alec stiffened. "No, I wasn't."

The king's grin widened. "Tah. *You were.*" Dropping back onto the furs, he shoved his hands behind his head. "You were dreaming of me and begging me to touch you."

"What—I didn't *beg!*"

Zercy chuckled. "Tah, you did. I believe your exact words were—"

"Okay! Whatever!"

The king loosed another of those rare, robust laughs.

Alec scowled and looked away, but deep down inside, a part of him savored the happy sound. That, and the fact he'd played a part in eliciting it. Yeah, okay, so it'd happened at his expense, but he still couldn't help enjoying the hearty rumble.

For several long moments, they laid in silence, the atmosphere feeling easier than normal. Because they'd unwittingly connected on an intimate level? Alec really hoped not. That'd bring nothing but problems.

Screw it. He'd blame the feeling on endorphins.

Abruptly, the door chime reverberated through the room, swiftly turning the light air to heavy. Alec felt the change immediately, the king's mental shift palpable, like an oppressive weight just dropped on the guy.

Zercy exhaled and sat back up, all seriousness returning. "It is time, *Alick*, to face another day."

CHAPTER FIFTEEN

* * *

They arrived at the meal hall less than twenty minutes later. As usual, Zercy walked Alec there by his leash after they'd both gotten dressed in their new duds. Alec's getup today? Just like that of every day, a short tunic wrap in some deep jewel tone, this one being the coolest dark, rich ruby. But just as they'd been since the first one Alec donned, each was designed somewhat differently than the last. The stitching, the neckline, the gemstones, and their placement. The same went for Zercy's attire. Nope, never once had they worn the same thing twice. Compliments, as always, of the talented Lotis.

Whom, incidentally, Alec still had yet to meet.

Leading the way, Setch and Kellim pushed through the hall's double doors as two more royal guards pulled up the rear.

Zercy peered down at Alec as they approached the team's table. "Are you glad to nearly be rid of me?"

Alec briefly met his gaze. A strange light gleamed in the king's eyes. Alec looked away. "Absolutely."

Zercy chuffed low in his throat. "You are lying again."

Alec tamped a small chuckle. "And you're delusional."

"Tah. So they say."

Alec looked at him. "Really?"

Zercy kept his eyes forward, his expression hard to read. "Some whisper that I am mad. An unsound king."

Alec supposed that shouldn't surprise him, since Miros had said as much, but for some reason it still did. It also unsettled him. After all, he was forced to be around Zercy continuously. Was the guy a loose cannon waiting to blow? Alec wasn't especially keen on being collateral damage.

Thing was, despite what others thought or said, Zercy didn't seem crazy to him. Sure, he'd initially had his reservations, but aside from that incident on the rooftop last week, Zercy always acted pretty collected.

Super stressed, no question, but not off the rails. And since, unlike others, Alec spent time with him in private, he'd like to think he'd seen the real deal. Yeah, Zercy was a spoiled, haughty, confident ruler. But he was also very honest and straightforward.

What's more—and Alec couldn't believe he was even thinking this—apart from the fact that Zercy was holding them prisoners, he seemed otherwise of pretty good character. He didn't abuse Alec or talk down to him and, unlike Gesh's pack, despite his utterly extreme sexual nature, he'd never acted deviously to get in Alec's pants. So far, the king had been patient, earnestly trying to understand Alec's ways. And again, excluding that time on the roof, he never made Alec feel threatened.

Alec blinked from his musings. Seriously? What the hell.

No more defending the hostage holder.

They reached his team's table a few strides later.

Alec tipped his chin. "What's up, guys."

Zaden returned the gesture. "Hey, man."

Chet grunted and half-heartedly saluted him with his cup.

Jamis swallowed what he'd been chewing. "Morning, Cap."

Noah and Bailey still had mouthfuls though, so those two just gave a couple of nods.

Then all five men's stares turned to the king.

Zercy offered a polite smile and unclipped Alec's leash. "Greetings. I trust my pets are faring well?"

"Don't you mean your *prisoners?*" Chet countered tersely. "And I won't speak for them," he jerked his chin toward the others, "but no, I'm *not faring well.* All this Magic Kingdom captivity shit sucks."

Bailey's eyes flared, undoubtedly thinking the same as Alec—their hired gun loved treading on thin ice.

Noah and Jamis swapped looks.

Zaden sighed and scrubbed his face.

Mannix, however, shoved the back of Chet's head. "Mind your mouth, or I will stuff it into silence."

Chet shot him a glower, having nearly face-planted in a bowl of God-could-only-guess-what, and flipped the Kríe off with both bound hands.

Zercy smirked and looked at the others, dismissing Chet entirely. "You have stayed here many days now and have yet to cause me trouble. I should like to reward your good behavior."

Bailey sat up straight, his head of curls subtly bouncing. "Reward?"

Jamis perked, too.

Noah looked a bit more cautious. If anyone knew not to trust Kríe, it was him.

"What kind of reward?" Alec asked, settling onto a stool.

"One I believe you will like." Zercy turned to their chaperones. "Today, after second meal, take them into town. Let them pick out something nice from the market."

The guards inclined their heads.

Alec's brows rose. Seriously? The last time they'd been to a market in Kríeville was the day Gesh had taken them to the castle. Talk about a crazy-colorful walk. Every kind of species, in every imaginable shade, peddling damn near all things under the sun—er, *suns*. Definitely an eye opener to Nira's spectrum of indigenous life. It'd also been a sinus opener, too. Some of the more pungent aromas wafting around had made him want to snort a vat of bleach.

But then another aspect of their stroll speared his memory. The way so many of those market goers had ogled his team. Like they wanted to skin them. Or eat them. Or fuck them. Or hell, maybe all three at once.

He glanced at his teammates. They looked wary as well. After all, should things go south while they were out there this time, how could a couple of guards protect them from a crowd?

Zercy's pleasant smile faded as he watched their faces. "What is wrong? Why do you frown?" He looked at Alec, confused.

"Uh…" Alec winced and scratched his cheek with bound hands. Fuck, how to explain. Why was everything so awkward?

Chet rubbed his buzz cut and shook his head.

Bailey's knee bounced like crazy on his stool.

Zaden exhaled a curse.

Jamis fidgeted with his goblet.

And at the end of the table, Noah warily chewed his lip.

Zercy's brows knit tighter as he waited for an answer.

Alec shifted on his stool. Balled his hands under the table. "It's just that the last time we were out in your *town*, your town *folk* acted really freaking weird."

Zercy crossed his arms and frowned, his bicep cuffs gleaming. "Weird in what way?"

"Like they wanted to mount us."

Bailey nodded beside him. "Vigorously."

"Then roast us over a fire pit," Chet grated. "For dinner."

Zercy stiffened, glancing quickly from one team member to the next, before cutting his golden gaze back to Alec. Intently, he regarded him, his face, his attire, as if taking him in through a different set of eyes. His expression quickly darkened, his demeanor turning possessive. Then a subtle little tick formed in his jaw.

Inclining his head, he forced a tight smile. "I see. That is unfortunate and will not happen again." He looked at Setch and Kellim. "You will accompany them as well. See to it that each is outfitted with a cloak—one with a hood to hide their faces. If any should try to touch them without your consent, cut off their hand as a warning."

The two Kríe nodded.

Alec's brows hiked. Damn.

Shoulders easing, Zercy turned back. "There. It is done. No one shall mount you, vigorously or otherwise. Nor shall they eat you for dinner."

The team exhaled as one, and despite his efforts, Alec couldn't tamp the smile that started to form. As much as he hated to admit it, Zercy's sense of humor amused him. Especially considering how on most occasions, Alec wasn't sure he was even trying to be funny.

"Awesome," Chet muttered.

Alec nodded a little. "Thanks."

Again, the king inclined his head, but then his aide walked through the door. Zercy eyed him briefly and turned back to Alec's team. "Duty beckons, but I look forward to seeing all of you tonight."

Alec paused at his words. His men looked confused, too. "*All* of us?"

It'd always been just the two of them after dinner. Just Alec and Zercy. Alone. In Zercy's room.

The king's lips curved. "I did not tell you?"

Alec tensed. "Tell us what?"

"I am hosting a summit meeting. Many dignitaries are coming. As is tradition, we must celebrate their arrival."

Bailey's face lit up. "A party? You're throwing a party?"

"I am. And as expected, that requires many things. Capital accommodations. The finest foods." His gaze flashed. "Live entertainment."

Noah eyed him suspiciously. "What kind of entertainment?"

"My very favorite. Rigorous competition."

"Like sports." Jamis grinned.

Chet actually smiled, too. "Hell yes. What type of sports?"

"Full contact, naturally. I like my bouts lively."

Chet grinned with a nod. "As do I."

"Bellah. Kellim vows that you are all most agile. I have every confidence you will give us quite a show."

Alec stiffened. "Whoa, *what?* But we're just spectating… right?"

The king smirked a little. Shook his head. "Not tonight. Tonight, my little pets will entertain."

Jamis' face fell. "Oh, shit."

Bailey paled.

Noah swore.

But right as Alec opened his mouth to object, Chet barked out a laugh. "In your dreams."

Zercy chuckled. "Quite hardly. I will be very much awake. As will all my captivated guests."

Alec shook his head emphatically. "No way. We won't do it."

Zercy cast him a look, one that said, *why be difficult?* "To deny me would not be worth it. I assure you."

Alec clenched his jaw.

"Besides," the king continued, "you love sports, do you not? This is nothing but a glorified competition between athletes. Surely, you have as much on your Earth."

Chet's hard gray eyes glinted. Like he was calling to mind a memory. Of his days playing college football maybe? Back then, he must've competed in front of thousands. To him, tonight's match would be nothing.

Alec frowned and looked at his co-pilot. Zaden definitely wasn't thrilled. In fact, out of everyone, he looked the most apprehensive. Like he suspected there was more to this than just a simple match. And he was probably right. These Kríe were all dubious motherfuckers.

Alec turned back to Zercy.

The king smiled. "It will be fun."

"Define fun," Alec deadpanned.

Zercy all but rolled his eyes. "Enjoy your outing to the market, pets. If something pleases you, it is yours. No price is too high." He turned on his heel, but briefly glanced back. "Tonight, I expect a superlative performance. Do not disappoint me in front of my guests."

* * *

"It is time. You have bathed long enough. Get out."

Alec peered up at Mannix as the guard gestured impatiently. "What's the rush? We were told the *festivities* didn't start 'til dark."

The big Kríe crossed his arms. Gave a nod. "That is true, but first you must be properly prepared."

Zaden frowned, wading next to Alec. "Prepared?"

"Tah. And with so many of you, that will take much time."

A few feet away, the trio traded looks.

"Prepared how?" Noah asked, tucking a wet lock behind his ear.

Setch smirked, chiming in, "You are going to Lotis, so to know is impossible. His creations are different every time."

The other guards nodded, a spark of anticipation in their eyes, like they couldn't wait to see the male's next wonder.

"Outstanding," Chet muttered. "Guess that means a simple jersey's out of the question."

The Kríe chuffed at that, grins lighting their dark features.

"Nothing Lotis does is *ever* simple," Setch explained. "I do not think he understands the concept."

Bailey shrugged, his short, dark ringlets dripping against his face. "He makes our clothes, right? And they're not so bad. Tonight's getups will probably just be fancier."

"Fancier," Chet intoned, his voice beyond flat. "I don't love the sound of that."

"Esh. It is what the *king* will like that matters," Mannix rumbled. "Your opinion makes no difference. Now get out."

Alec exhaled and headed for the large bath's steps. "Come on, people. No point in speculating. Let's just get this shit over with."

Zaden plodded along beside him. "Remind me again why we agreed to this? There's no way this thing's just a sporting event."

Alec met his friend's dark gaze, but then looked away and sighed. "Because according to Kellim, Zercy said he'd separate us. Keep us isolated from each other indefinitely."

Zaden didn't reply to that, nor argue Alec's decision. Not that Alec was surprised. Aside from his total respect for authority, Zaden understood that they needed to stay together. That at the end of the day, that was the most important thing.

Truth be told, if it ever came down to it, each of his men would unquestionably choose physical punishment over being disbanded as a team. But physical punishment hadn't been a choice they'd been given—because Zercy was shrewd and knew Alec's weakness. His deep-seated sense of responsibility to watch over his team, to keep his men close at all times.

Granted, Zaden and Chet would undoubtedly be fine, but the trio? They were younger, and smaller, and less street smart. And Alec had pledged to keep them safe. In a way, he kind of felt like their big brother.

Besides, strength in numbers and all that. As long as they stuck together, they'd be fine.

Exiting the water, Alec briskly dried off, then headed over with the others to grab his clothes. But Mannix blocked their path and shook his head.

"Mah. You do not need your garments. Leave them here."

Great. Déjà vu. The last time Alec departed from the bath house in just a towel, he'd been taken to Sirus for that exam. Unease washed over him at the mere memory.

Still clutching his swath of terry cloth, he tried to tie it around his hips, but discovered that was impossible without free hands. Looked like all he'd be wearing were cuffs and a collar. Frowning, he glanced at his men. They weren't happy either. Which made sense since they were in the same boat.

"Whatever." He brushed it off in an attempt to ease their anxiety. "We'll be putting on different stuff in a minute anyway."

Chet scowled and finished drying but didn't say a word. Probably figured, what was the use at this point. The others followed suit and, just like that, both man and Kríe were filing out the door.

Deep, pulsing, otherworldly music met Alec's ears, coming from the front of the castle. The festivities must've begun while they'd been in the bath house. Guess all the guests had arrived.

Zaden fell in step beside him, swiping black bangs from his eyes. "If memory serves, this guy's *bottega* is just up ahead. One of the places we didn't get to see during the tour."

Alec nodded, his gaze straying toward the windows on their left. The suns were setting, the sky's hues turning harsher. Burnt orange and deep mulberry, not the lemon tangerine that had kept things bright for their journey into town.

And man, what an excursion that turned out to be. Talk about sensory overload. It hadn't taken long for them to reach the place on foot, and the trek itself had definitely been colorful—odd structures, strange faces, exceptionally small Nirans that he ultimately concluded were little tykes. But once they arrived at the bustling market? All five senses, instantly bombarded.

Lord almighty. He'd forgotten how crazy that place was. As stressed as he'd been when they'd first come with Gesh, his brain must've blocked the worst out. Fuck, the smells, the sounds, the sights. All the things the natives were selling. And *doing*.

Yeah. Bizarre behavior. Some were downright disturbing. One dude they came upon was openly giving his pal head by *literally* sucking on his *head*. And not the little head presumably between his legs. The big bald one propped atop his shoulders. Which, yeah, meant the giver had one *really big mouth*. And one seriously double-jointed jaw. No joke, his lips were stretched down over the dude's eyes. Baldie's mouth was still visible though and hanging wide open as he grunted and groaned in shameless bliss.

Fortunately, Zercy's guards were experts at maneuvering and got the team to suitable tents in decent time—suitable, meaning tents selling less-outlandish wares. At that point, their chaperones had given them some space, allowing them to roam freely between stands. After all, their wrists were still securely bound. Their cloak sleeves merely hid them from view.

The hoods of their cloaks hid their faces nicely, too. And thank balls for that. Because while most of the natives looked relatively non-threatening—some, he had to admit, were even attractive—there were others who were hideously intimidating. So, to stay off their grid had been priceless.

Ultimately, every team member tracked down something he liked. The trio grabbed a bunch of potted plants to study, along with more leather-bound journals for their notes. No surprise, really. The ones Ryze had given them were maxed out, and they'd only freaking been there a week.

Chet's final selection had been more of a negotiation. After Mannix had repeatedly thwarted his efforts to buy weapons, Chet irritably settled for some bronze bicep cuffs. Not a bad alternative, in Alec's opinion. The things were badass.

Zaden scored a Niran-style compass and a map of the region, which Setch initially looked hesitant about. Two seconds later though, his Kríe arrogance must have kicked in, because he promptly lifted his chin and gave a nod.

Ultimately, Alec chose a map of sorts, too. A star map, from Nira's perspective. The moment he'd laid eyes on it, it instantly captivated him. Such a different expanse than from Earth's viewpoint. Of course, in all his travels, he'd seen countless regions of stars, but to behold one so artistically depicted on alien parchment? It was beautiful in a way that had called to his soul. He hadn't been able to resist.

Alec pulled himself from his musings. The two Kríe leading them through the castle had come to a stop. They'd arrived at Lotis' studio. He glanced forward and regarded the ornate double doors. Meticulously engraved into the image of an exotic landscape, they were unique from all the others around the palace. Alec wondered if Lotis had carved them himself.

Setch gave the things a rap with his big dark knuckles. A moment later, they swung open wide. Alec eyed the Kríe in the threshold. Looked kind of normal for an artist.

"We have brought Lotis his subjects," Setch informed the male. "Is he ready?"

Ah, okay. So, this guy wasn't him.

The Kríe regarded Alec's team, then gestured with his chin. "Tah. Ready and waiting. Bring them in."

Setch and Kellim led the way into the unfamiliar space. Alec glanced around. The room was spacious, but also kind of dark. Made sense, though. Every wall of the enclosure was internal. Meaning, the light their windows provided was basically second-hand sun filtering in from the corridors. Which explained the abundance of candles in every direction, flickering in wall sconces, burning in candelabras.

And there were a ton, since the room was as big as the bath house. As big but divided into sections. One clearly for painting, another for sculpting. Unsurprisingly, he spotted a sewing corner, too. The place where, no doubt, the king's duds were fashioned—the king's, as well as all of Alec's team's.

They reached the back of the workshop and slowed to a halt, where Alec finally got his first look at their host. Standing with some others beside a row of six small platforms, Lotis gestured as he rattled off instructions.

But Alec knew it was him despite his litany of directives. The giveaway was the Kríe's eccentric air. Alec took the guy in, his presence so different from the others. Not in the sense that he wasn't a ripped, seven-foot giant, because just like every Kríe, he absolutely was. Everything else though, oozed artisan chic. His appearance a work of art in its own right.

Alec regarded his ponytail, captivated by the colors, his velvet dreads painted an array of rich jewel tones. Deep ruby, purple onyx, midnight emerald, burnished gold. His horns were striped in gold, too, and his eyes were painted as well. Outlined, like an Egyptian's, in thick black kohl.

Predictably, his outfit was just as unique. Not the typical tunic or wrap regularly seen around the castle. His looked more like a skimpy little toga. Just a dark, iridescent strip of satin draped over one shoulder, secured by a thick gilded belt. From there, the swath continued to form one hell of a mini man-skirt, showing more leg than even Alec's getups.

His footwear looked like a hybrid of leg-wrap sandals and knee-high boots. Above them, golden bands wrapped around his thighs. A matching set hugged his biceps and, encircling each wrist, was a big badass gem-studded cuff.

Lotis glanced their way, then stilled. Guess he was seeing them for the first time, too. Approval gleamed in his eyes. "Bellah. You are here." He approached with a smile and immediately started circling. Like a big curious shark taking them in. "Tah," he rumbled. "Lovely. The king was right."

"The *king*," Chet muttered, "can kiss my *lovely*—Hey!"

Alec glanced over in time to catch Lotis squeezing Chet's ass.

"Smooth and firm." Lotis nodded. "The perfect canvas."

Chet whirled around and glared. "Keep your purple paws off me."

Lotis cocked a brow, studying him, then glanced at the guards.

Setch chuckled. "We think perhaps he is defective."

Chet shot him a glower. "I'll show you defective."

Mannix shoved his head. "*Esh*. Be quiet."

Chet bristled and got in his grill.

"Leave it alone, Chet," Alec bit out. "I'm not in the mood." Standing naked in that strange room wasn't helping.

Chet grumbled but stepped back.

Lotis resumed his perusal—prodding pecs, inspecting torsos, fingering Bailey's head of curls. A smile curved his lips. He turned to the guards. "Remove their collars and secure them. It is time to begin."

Alec tensed. Secure them? But their hands were already bound.

Setch unlatched his collar and took his arm. "Nenya." He led him to one of the platforms, then ushered him up its three steps to the top.

Alec glanced at his men. They were mounting their stands, too. Setch lifted his tied wrists above his head. Alec peered up and spotted an iron hook.

He instinctively tried to pull away. "Wait. Aren't we just getting dressed? What are you doing?"

"Kerra, moyo." *Relax.* "This is just to keep your arms out of the way." He attached Alec's cuffs, then dropped down off the stand. "And this is to ensure full access to your legs." Gripping Alec's ankles, he spread his feet wide. Alec stiffened as he latched them to the platform.

"This isn't really necessary. I can stand like this on my own."

Setch grinned and looked up at him. "Lotis likes his art contained."

"Great," Alec muttered. Now they were art. He didn't want to know what that entailed.

Lotis joined them a moment later, with five helpers by his side. "Since there are six of you and only one of me, I have recruited some of my pupils to assist." He stepped to a table just a few feet away and picked up what looked like a plasma gun.

Alec froze at the sight of it. All rounded and fat, it had a distinct pistol shape. That and an obvious trigger. What the fuck was it? And more importantly, what was its function? Made of metal, but with an odd organic presence about it too, its steampunk vibe reminded him of Sirus. Alec wondered if he'd made it for Lotis.

Lotis gathered a few more from the table's mess of tools and handed one to each of his aides. Cocking his own, he turned and strode to Alec, the top of his head only reaching Alec's shoulders.

His golden gaze met Alec's. "You are Zercy's chosen, yes?"

Shit, how'd he know? And honestly, why was that even relevant?

Jaw clenched, Alec nodded.

Lotis grinned. "Bellah kai. Zercy asked me to attend to you personally."

"Ah. Lucky me," Alec mumbled under his breath.

Lotis lifted his device. "Now remain very still."

Riiight.

Alec nervously eyed his weird gun.

But when Lotis aimed it at his thigh and readied to squeeze the trigger, Alec panicked, twisting away. "Wait! What are you doing?"

Lotis chuffed in amusement. "Reesha tay." *I will not harm you.* He gestured to his tool. "This is just paint."

"Oh." Alec sighed in relief. But then he stilled. "Paint? Whoa, wait. You're gonna *paint* us?"

"Christ," Chet muttered a couple platforms down. "This shit just gets better and better."

Lotis' big eyes glittered. "We are indeed. The king is going to love you. Now be still."

Alec quieted with a sigh. No point in delaying the inevitable. It wasn't like body paint posed much of a threat.

Before too long, he found himself utterly engrossed, his gradual transformation straight-up fascinating. For all intents and purposes, the Kríe were airbrushing their bodies, covering them with a thin sheen of black. Every single inch, minus their faces, chests, and stomachs. Thankfully, their junk got skipped over, too.

Finished with step one, Lotis switched out his colors, resuming with a warm shade of gray. On the light side, though, like river stones, not too dark. Coating the front of Alec's torso, then his palms and the soles of his feet.

He switched to a deeper shade of gray not long after and began the painstaking task of body contouring. Darkening Alec's nipples. Defining each pectoral. Skillfully accentuating each muscle of his abs. By the time Lotis was done, Alec had to admit, his six pack had never looked so ripped.

Lotis stepped back and regarded him. "You are coming along nicely." He glanced at Alec's team. "As are your men."

Alec shifted against his binds. "Guess that means you're not done." His skin felt tight, but not as much as he'd expected. Like he was wearing a snug body suit more so than paint.

Lotis set down his airbrush gun. "Eetay." *Soon.* He glanced around. "But first you must put on your garments."

Alec's insides lit instantly. He glanced down at his cock, all pale and bare, hanging limp against the black. He'd been hoping its untouched state meant he'd get to wear clothes, why paint it after all, if it'd be covered. But until this moment, he hadn't been sure. He exhaled. Thank God. Because while facing a crowd nude would suck, facing them with only his goods unpainted seemed far worse.

Although, now that he thought about it... Alec peered down over his shoulder. If unpainted parts meant they'd ultimately be covered, then why had Lotis bothered with his ass? And not just with a cursory drive-by spritz. That Kríe had spread his cheeks and airbrushed his crack.

Lotis opened a small chest on the table. "I finished these yesterday, fashioned them carefully from *enyids*." He reached in and smiled, as if touching them brought him pleasure. "Pliant and thick, yet soft like a flower petal. A second skin you will relish." He pulled one out.

Alec eyed the black scrap. It was tiny. He frowned. Surely that wasn't their attire.

Lotis held it up proudly for the whole team to see.

"Aw, fuck," Alec groaned. It looked like a toddler-size jockstrap.

Chet reared back, balking incredulously. "*That's* our garment?"

Jamis squinted and leaned forward. "Can barely see it."

Zaden cursed and closed his eyes.

Bailey grimaced. "That ain't right."

Noah, however, just coughed a tight laugh. Like maybe he wore that kind of stuff already.

"Lotis," Alec finally groused. "That thing's way too small. No way it's gonna cover up our junk."

Lotis' grin turned smug. "You think not? Let us see." He returned to Alec's platform and unlatched his ankle cuffs. Then he held the thing by Alec's feet. "Step inside."

CHAPTER SIXTEEN

* * *

Alec sighed but obeyed for the sake of argument. He could feel his men's eyes on him as Lotis pulled the scrap up his legs, its soft material easily stretching around his thighs. When he reached Alec's ass, Lotis situated its straps, then focused his attention on Alec's package.

"Now I test your theory." His rumbling timbre sounded confident.

Alec held his breath, tensing as Lotis moved things into place. Sure enough, the thin scrap barely covered even half. Like a G-string between his nuts—not very flattering at all—with the rest of it only shielding the base of his dick.

Lotis met his eyes. Alec pursed his lips. This was not going well.

But then the Krie chuffed. "Ah, wait. Foolish me. I positioned it wrong. Let me try again."

Pinching the dense fabric with his clawed thumb and forefinger, he pulled it away from Alec's goods. Alec braced with a frown, watching him stretch it even farther. Swear to God, if he let that thing snap like a rubber band…

But before he could verbalize a single threat, Lotis firmly clutched Alec's cock with his other hand. Alec tensed at the contact. Lotis moved it into position, then loosened his taut hold of the material. Alec watched in fascination as it settled over his length, hugging it like a thick layer of hot wax.

"Holy shit," he breathed. "That feels so weird."

"Tah." Lotis proceeded to cover his balls the same way. "Looks better than I had hoped. I am pleased."

Alec could hear his teammates murmuring, their voices low and wary, but at the moment he just couldn't pay attention. Was too busy staring at his freaking package, which now looked like a black latex dildo. The realistic kind, with a nut sac and everything. On the bright side, at least it finally matched the rest of him.

It was bizarre, though. Because even though he was technically covered, the snug fit made him still feel kind of naked.

Lotis stepped back and studied him. A smug grin emerged. "I do believe I have disproved your theory."

Alec rolled his eyes. "I stand corrected." But then he stilled as something occurred to him. If this business on his dick had sealed around him like wax… Glancing nervously at his new getup, he looked back at Lotis. "This thing won't hurt to get back off again, right?"

"Mah." Lotis handed his apprentices identical garments for the team. "It does not adhere, only clings to the body. And as you witnessed, it will also stretch when necessary." He paused to pointedly eye Alec's crotch. "A convenience you will appreciate when you grow hard."

Alec stared at him. Was he kidding? No way in hell was that going to happen. Getting freaked out and frazzled were definite possibilities, but turned on? Aroused, in front of a crowd of strange indigene? Not in this lifetime. Probably not in the next, either.

Chuckling at the absurdity, he absently tugged at his restraints. "Yeah. There'll be no boners tonight."

Lotis quirked a brow, then smirked, but didn't reply. Just made quick work of re-securing Alec's feet. Stopping back at the table, he grabbed a smaller airbrush, checked its cartridge-looking thingy, and loped back over. "Time for the details." He moved to Alec's back. "Start at the spine and work outward from there."

Swift pulses of paint danced over Alec's skin. He turned his head. "What kind of details?"

"Animal markings."

Alec stilled, then peered down at his two-toned body, regarding it in a whole different light. No way. For real? He glanced at his men. Chet's Kríe was giving him stripes like a primordial tiger. Zaden's guy was giving him leopard spots in wicked patterns. Jamis' marks looked similar to a zebra's, but meaner. Noah's big angular blotches roared 'ferocious.' And damn, down the line, Bailey's Kríe was on fire, decking their astrobiologist out in scales. Like a dragon or sea creature, the marks a blazing silver-gold. The same color used for all their markings.

Evidently, a certain artist liked continuity.

Alec's lips curved in spite of himself.

Lotis was transforming them into fearsome Niran predators.

Zaden peered Alec's way and studied his appearance. His brown eyes flickered imperceptibly. Looked like he was low-key digging their makeovers, too. Alec glanced down as Lotis came around and started on his thighs. After all, he'd been working on Alec's back this whole time so this was the first chance Alec had to see his own markings.

His jaw went slack. Jaguar spots. Lotis was giving him jaguar spots. Or rather, something similar, but way more intense. Edgier, literally, with each blot's border thick and jagged, their centers a blend of gold and silver gradients. Striking. Savage. Expertly grouped to emphasize his muscles. The creation coming to life was downright mesmerizing. Meaning, yup, he continued watching until the very last spot was painted. Fortunately, Lotis and his crew worked pretty fast.

"Tah. Bellah kai." *Very good.* Lotis stepped back, inspecting his work once more with gleaming eyes.

But he wasn't done, and Alec knew this because of one simple fact: every inch of him had been tended to except for his face. Well, minus his jawline, that'd been airbrushed with his neck. Even his short, light-brown hair had been covered. But from his forehead to his mouth? Totally untouched. Glaringly unfinished.

No way was it staying that way. No way.

As if on cue, Lotis set down his tool and grabbed another. This one looked like a wide-bristled paintbrush. Once, twice, he dunked its business end into a bowl. Then, grabbing the step stool he'd used several times already, he planted it in front of Alec and climbed up.

Alec stiffened. Any closer and personal space would be breached.

Lotis studied his face. "Close your eyes."

Alec complied, anxious to be done.

Soft, slick bristles touched the bridge of his nose, then slid down over his right lid to his temple. Alec could feel the thick paint all the way to his eyebrow. Lotis repeated the action on his left side as well. After that, he did the same beneath each eye.

"Open," Lotis commanded.

Alec lifted his lashes.

Lotis studied his work, turning Alec's head left and right. Satisfied, he hopped down. "You are ready."

That was it? Just a black stripe across his eyes? That surprised Alec. But whatever. Who was he to question an artist? Besides, he was sick of being shackled to this perch. He smiled. "Nice. We're done."

Lotis headed to another chest. "Mah. Not done. I said *ready*."

Alec frowned and glanced at his teammates. They were sporting eye stripes, too. He looked back at Lotis. "Ready for what?"

"Your mask. I will show you." Lotis cracked the thing open. A second later, he pulled out a facepiece. "This one is yours."

Alec's brows shot high. Lotis grinned and brought it over. "I finished these yesterday, as well. Yours is the mask of a *koosa*."

Alec eyed the thing. "A koosa…"

Lotis climbed back onto the stool. "Tah," he rumbled. "The king's favorite quarry."

Alec froze and quickly looked at him. "Wait what? We're gonna be prey?"

"Mah." Lotis chuckled. "Tonight, you are predators."

"Then why…?"

"Because," Lotis smiled and touched Alec's jaw, "I wanted to surprise him with something special."

Alec paused and stared at him. There was affection in Lotis' eyes. And in his tone. He liked Zercy. A lot. But in what way, Alec couldn't tell. Although, come to think of it, Zercy seemed fond of Lotis too, all but singing his praises each time he dressed. Were they casual lovers or something? Having a bromance on the side?

Alec's stomach clenched, unsettled, which made no sense at all. He didn't give a shit who Zercy got with. Hell, the more fuck pals he had the better. They'd keep him sated so he'd leave Alec alone.

His gut twisted tighter, suddenly feeling way too anxious. Dropping his gaze, he focused on the mask. Honestly, it *did* look somewhat similar to a jag, but with a small, spiky lion's mane and bigger fangs. Its snout was broader, too. And its ears were rimmed with barbs. The same type of jutting barbs that lined its brow. What's more, since its maw was peeled back into a snarl, a simulation of its three-layer tongue was also visible.

Weird.

Lotis grinned, clearly proud of his creation, and carefully slid it onto Alec's head. "Zercy's koosa," he rumbled softly. "His heart will race for you tonight."

As if triggered by his words, Alec's own heart picked up speed. "I don't want that," he muttered restlessly. The mask felt cool against his face.

Lotis paused and canted his head. Met Alec's eyes through the openings. "You do not want to be wanted by the king of the Kríe?" He looked genuinely perplexed.

Alec shifted his weight. They were talking quietly, but could the others still hear? He lowered his voice. Forced the word out. "No." But even as he said it, it felt untrue. Which didn't sit well with him in the slightest.

Lotis stared at him. "Why do you lie?"

Fuck.

Alec averted his gaze. "I'm not." He cleared his throat. "If I could leave right now I would. But I can't. He won't let us." Which Lotis surely already knew. "I just want tonight to be over with. To be done."

Lotis didn't reply. Alec turned back and looked at him. His dark lips were quirked into a smirk.

Alec frowned. "Something funny?"

Lotis chuffed and crossed his arms. "This night will not be over with for a very long time. You might as well enjoy yourself and have fun."

Right. Have fun.

Alec peered down at his getup. "I'm thinking that might be easier said than done."

Lotis grinned and shoved his shoulder. Alec wobbled in his restraints. "Do not worry. It will be *very* easy to say *and* do. I planned it myself, I should know."

Alec stilled, watching him drop off the step stool again. "*You* planned tonight's activity?"

"Tah. I plan all events." He strode down the line inspecting the others.

Alec checked them out too, every mask distinctly different, each one captivating in its own animalistic way.

"*Dembra*," Lotis offered as he eyed Chet's state, presumably the name of the predator he represented. Lotis studied Zaden next. "*Kygo*." He nodded, then moved to Jamis. "*Tegmai*." His perusal continued to Noah. "*Fekni*," he rumbled. And when he finally stopped at Bailey, Lotis all but freaking purred, admiring his shiny scales. "*Belshay*... Tah."

Alec had to agree as he regarded him, too. Bailey's look was uniquely kickass.

Bailey shifted against his binds, the curls at his nape still wet with paint. "Are we done now?" he asked, his voice muffled by his mask.

"Nearly." Lotis handed his assistants another item. Thick black collars studded with metal spikes.

Everyone knew where those were going.

Alec scowled as Lotis mounted the stool once more and buckled his into place. His neck had been enjoying the reprieve.

The music he'd heard earlier in the corridor grew louder, its boisterous rhythm thumping through the windows.

He swallowed and met Lotis' eyes. "You gonna tell us what you've planned? All they said is that it's some kind of sport."

Lotis chuffed and stepped back down again. "They do not tell you more because they do not know more. As I said before, I want to *surprise* the king." He gestured with mild disgust to Zercy's guards. "They have big mouths. Every one of them. Can keep nothing to themselves. So I tell them nothing... just to be safe."

Setch and Kellim swapped half-hearted looks of offense. Mannix grunted where he stood against the wall. The other three grumbled something under their breaths, but not one of the six bothered to argue.

Lotis headed to a counter housing various containers. "But it is safe now to tell you." He hefted a large tub into his arms, then carried it over and set it on the table. "After all, you must know what is expected of you, yes? In order to deliver a prime performance?"

Alec traded glances with Zaden, frowned and looked back at Lotis. "Yeah, so let's hear it. What're we doing out there?"

"You are competing," Lotis began, fiddling with something in the bin. "A wrestling match of sorts, using your training."

"Our training?" Jamis asked from behind his mask.

"Tah. Your training with Kellim." Lotis looked up and smiled. "He tells us he has taught you rather well."

The trio's chests puffed instantly. They were beaming. Alec could feel it. And honestly, they deserved to feel proud. They busted their asses on that back field every day. What's more, they seemed to relish the newfound knowledge. Evidently, they knew certain types of strategies via their gaming, but not the real-life, physical stuff that Kellim was teaching them.

"We're gonna be wrestling? That's it?" Chet asked. "How underwhelming."

Lotis' grin turned wolfish. "Tonight's match will be special. No ordinary competition."

"Because of our costumes?" Noah asked, his blond hair now black.

"In part, but not for such reasons as you might think."

"Will you just spit it out, for fuck's sake," Alec grated. "What's different?"

Lotis' golden eyes flashed. "I have altered the objective."

The team stilled as one.

Alec's gut filled with dread. "Okay," he muttered. "What's the *new* objective?"

An impish expression flittered over Lotis' features. "I think I should like to explain things using visuals." He casually slid his gaze down the line of Alec's men. "Who will volunteer to be my example?"

Fuck, not again.

Alec bit back a curse. Last time he put his ass out there for the team, he ended up naked, strapped to an exam table. But damn it, nothing had changed. He was still captain, so this still fell on him. "Me. I'll do it."

Lotis inclined his head. "Very well."

"No, I'll do it," Chet spoke up. He looked at Alec. "My turn, Boss. I got this."

Alec shook his head. "Chet, no. You guys are *my* responsibility."

"And *you're* mine," he countered. "My job's to have *your* back, too." He tilted his head to the team. "Not just theirs. Besides," he shrugged, arms restrained above his head, "it's not like he's gonna hurt me. He needs me able to compete. I'm just helping him demonstrate." He looked at Lotis. "Ain't that right?"

Lotis tipped his chin, a glimmer of approval in his gaze. "Tah. This is true."

But Chet wasn't fooling Alec. He could see in his bodyguard's eyes that he knew shit was coming. That he knew what Lotis had planned was dubious at best. Honestly, their whole team would always suspect Kríe intentions. In everything they said and everything they did. They'd never be fully at ease when Kríe were around.

No, this was definitely Chet offering himself as the sacrificial lamb. For his team, but especially for his captain. Which Alec appreciated beyond words, but he still couldn't allow it.

Unfortunately, before he could reject the offer, Lotis motioned to two of his pupils and got things rolling. "Take the big one down and stand him next to this table."

Chet stiffened imperceptibly as the Kríe obeyed, no doubt bracing for whatever was to come.

Lotis turned and pulled something black from that tub. Alec's brows scrunched as he eyed it, utterly clueless to what it was. A plant maybe? Its bottom half kind of resembled a carrot. A long one, glossy and wet, like it'd been kept in some glycerin-type liquid. And yet, its top half looked like a big hunting knife. Easily twelve inches long, not including the dripping handle, curved with a chunky serrated edge. An otherworldly fern frond would be Alec's guess, but with notches only running up one side.

Lotis waited until his helpers had Chet standing in front of the table, then turned and faced the rest of the team. "Naturally," he began, "your goal tonight remains. To find victory. To triumph. And to do so with verve. The difference is what you must *do* in order to achieve this."

"I thought we were just wrestling." Alec glanced at Chet. Those Kríe had set up post on either side of him.

Lotis inclined his head. "Tah. But you must do more than pin your foe. You must conquer him. Dismantle him before the king."

"*Dismantle* him?" Bailey sounded just as confused as Alec felt.

"Tah." Lotis held up that odd-looking plant. "Your goal is to take this from the grips of your opponent before your opponent is able to take yours from you."

Chet eyed the thing. "What is it? A knife or something?"

"Mah." Lotis motioned to his aides at Chet's side. Each Kríe took one of his arms and turned him around. "It is the most important piece of your costume."

Chet tensed as they held him in place. "Paws off," he grated, glaring at their holds. "I'm a big boy. I can stand on my own."

Alec frowned. What were they doing? But before he could ask, they bent Chet over Lotis' work surface. Flanking his hips, each Kríe palmed one of his shoulder blades, then used their other hand to clutch his butt cheeks.

"Fuck," Chet hissed as they spread him wide.

Lotis stepped close and sank that slippery carrot to the hilt.

"Uh!" Chet went rigid, clenching his striped ass like a mother.

Alec gaped. Holy shit. In the span of two seconds, his bodyguard just took eight inches.

Lotis gestured to Chet's new tail. "This beautiful plant is called a *gen*. Its kind grow in Nira's marshlands."

Alec shifted in his restraints, regarding the thing warily. Sure, it looked cool, no argument there, but that didn't mean he wanted one up his rectum.

"Do not worry," Lotis continued, "they are harmless. I use them often. Very hardy. Very versatile. In fact, tonight they play two roles. Your tails," he grinned, "and your rival's sole objective."

Alec did the math. "You mean, like flag football?" he grated. "We gotta remove our opponent's *tail?*"

"Tah." Lotis' smile widened. "But it will not be easy."

"Why not?" Zaden muttered from behind his kygo mask.

Lotis opened his mouth but didn't get to answer before Chet stilled atop the table and stifled a groan.

Alec tensed. "What's wrong with him? You said those things were harmless."

Lotis glanced Chet's way. His lips quirked. "They are. He is merely experiencing one of the reasons *why* it will not be easy."

The team stared at him blankly.

"Denza." *Watch.* "I will show you." He gripped Chet's tail and gave a slow, easy pull. Chet moaned even louder, his hips following Loti's hand. The plant, however, didn't even budge. "You see? Its root swells when enveloped in heat."

"Goddamnit," Chet groused irritably. "Are you people fucking kidding me?"

"Wait. So, it's *stuck* in there?" Bailey blurted, sounding aghast.

"Mah," Lotis chuckled. He palmed Chet's ass to keep it stationary, then gave another unhurried pull. Again, Chet loosed a deep-throated groan, but this time the inflated root *did* ease outward. "You see?" He illustrated. "It is definitely removable. The swelling simply helps keep it secure. The other element involved, however, is what will make things even trickier."

He slid it back into position. Chet grunted a strained breath, his tight ring cinching once more around the root's top. Which was narrower than the root, as well as the blade, reminding Alec of the workings of a butt plug.

Chet shifted atop the table but didn't bother fighting. Probably for several reasons. One, he'd openly volunteered for this shit. Two, he was overpowered so what was the point. And three, because chances were that thing felt kind of good, going by those low noises he kept making.

Alec cleared his throat as unbidden memories filled his mind. Memories of being stuffed deep himself. By Miros. Then Mina... "What other element," he rasped.

That impish light flickered in Lotis' eyes again. "*Kulai.* A slippery-sweet blend of oil and nectar. It will coat every inch of your bodies."

The room went silent, minus the music pulsing in the background.

They were going to be oil wrestling all but naked in front of a crowd?

Alec's skin went tight at the thought.

Lotis went on. "Things will be slick. And sloppy. And delicious. But the ridges in your tails will help aid in their removal. In truth, if you ever were to bear down hard enough, you could probably force your tails out on your own. Of course, I would not advise this. Rebellious behavior is always punished. If any expel their *gen* tails prematurely, a crowd member will be chosen to shove it back—with the rest of the assembly looking on. And I assure you, the chosen will not be gentle nor kind. When excited, Niran nature is always aggressive."

"Awesome," Alec muttered. He glanced over at Zaden. Maybe they could pretend to give it their all during the match, but never ultimately pull the fuckers free. His co-pilot's gaze seemed to flicker with similar sentiment.

As if reading their thoughts, Lotis tacked on more warnings. "Likewise, I would not advise feigning your performance either. Should stage monitors deem that you are intentionally failing to acquire your rival's tail—or allowing them to take yours without genuine effort—you will be penalized with that of a two-fold punishment: the first, an immediate show of reinserting your tail. The second, incarceration after the festivities.

"What? *Incarceration?*" Jamis' wary frown was palpable.

"Tah. So do not play the king a fool."

Chet cursed under his breath.

The rest of the team swapped sober looks.

Finally, Noah exhaled, "Fuck me."

Lotis glanced his way. "That is certainly permitted should you lose. Encouraged even. Our guests would indeed love nothing more."

Noah stiffened.

Jamis and Bailey barked out restless laughs.

Alec scowled. "Don't hold your breath, Kríe. That's not gonna happen."

Lotis slid him an unconvinced look. "You do not think?"

Alec squared his upturned shoulders. "Not a chance."

"Hmm. We shall see." Lotis gestured to Chet's junk. "Your friend is already aroused from just two tugs."

Alec frowned and eyed Chet's goods, then stilled. Sure enough, sheathed in black between his muscular thighs, his dick looked undeniably half erect.

"Fuck," Alec muttered. And yet he couldn't stop staring. Because even though Chet's semi was covered and held contained, it still gave the illusion of being naked. An impression Alec now suspected was intentional.

"Tah. *Fuck,*" Lotis encouraged, repeating Alec's sentiment. "And you can do so without removing your garments. Enyid skins are waterproof and, as I stated before, will stretch around your organ as it grows."

It was certainly doing that to Chet's half-hard cock. Like a super-thick condom that covered both dick *and* nuts. In truth, it kind of reminded him of that PVC fetish clothing.

He looked at Lotis. "What exactly are enyids anyway?"

"Aquatic plants of the dygon genus. Their flexible skins detain their prey."

Dygon. Alec remembered that term. Sirus had called them sentient plants. He stiffened and looked down at the bizarre thing hugging his crotch.

Lotis chuckled. "Do not worry. They no longer have thought. I have also removed their skin's flesh-eating membrane."

"Awesome," Alec muttered.

Chet shifted atop the table, then with a low muffled moan, appeared to bear down. The frond's root began emerging.

Lotis smirked and sank it back in. "You must always hold onto this tightly, no matter how strong the urge to push it out."

Chet groaned another curse and restlessly rocked his hips.

Lotis looked at the team. "If there are no other questions, we need to proceed. Time is wasting."

Crickets.

Alec opened his mouth, but nothing came out. Because, honestly, what could he say? There'd be no getting out of this mess.

"Bellah." Lotis motioned to his helpers. "Attach their tails. It is time to send them off. The king awaits."

And just like that, they were pulled off their individual platforms, and bent over the nearest horizontal surface.

Alec tensed as his feet were shoved apart. "You know," he grunted, his mask pressing against his face, "there are less-intrusive ways to wear a tail—*Ungh!*"

Cool, tapered hardness plunged deep into his channel. A sharp sting flared fast. His stuffed asshole clenched. And yet, at the same time, a strange thrill engulfed his body. Stark horror, fierce excitement, both racing through his blood, volleying his heart into an all-out fiery sprint.

His men loosed similar grunts, taking theirs, too. A heartbeat later, he was back up on his feet. His handler freed his wrists next. He rubbed them, but then grimaced. In this upright position, his tail felt huge. And was starting to crowd his prostate as it swelled.

His teammates shifted awkwardly, looking just as uncomfortable.

Lotis strode down the line, briefly tugging each tail, pausing at times to make sure they curved just right. Soft grunts coincided. No doubt, masks hid some winces.

When finished, he gestured to one of his aides. "Pull back the partition. They are ready to go."

Alec tensed, apprehensive, as the Kríe loped to a curtain. He pulled the thing back. Alec's jaw went slack at the sight. Sitting in wait was a huge iron cage. Not tall, though—no way a guy could stand in that thing—but big enough to hold his team.

"Your transport," Lotis announced.

Chet stiffened. "A fucking *cage?*"

"Tah. You are animals. You must be brought in accordingly."

Sure enough, Alec spotted two long poles at either end. Thick and horizontal for easy carrying. His heart pounded faster. Oh, God. They were doing this.

"Tacha." *Quickly*. Lotis prompted them onto their knees. "Don your new personas and crawl inside. Tonight, you are feral. Hungry, primitive beasts. I expect to see this conveyed through your performance."

CHAPTER SEVENTEEN

* * *

"Well," Bailey sighed, gripping their cage's bars, "this crazy shit is definitely a larper's wet dream."

Jamis clutched the bars beside him as the team bounced along. "Yeah. Talk about some hardcore fucking Cosplay."

Alec glanced their way, then looked back out the front of the cage. Their convoy, now accompanied by several more Kríe with tiki torches, was headed toward the front of the castle. To the great hall maybe? Is that where the fun was taking place? Or should he say, their coming night of raw debauchery?

The music grew louder, relentlessly pulsing along Alec's skin.

Jamis looked at Bailey. "Promise me something?"

Bailey met his gaze. "What?"

Jamis forced a small grin. "If we get paired up tonight and you win the match? Don't stick your dick in my ass, no matter how much you want to. I know I said it felt good after that insane stuff with Gesh's pack, but the next time it happens? I want it to be special. You know, without an audience watching us bang."

Bailey stared at him, then barked out a genuine laugh. "Fine, but you gotta promise the same."

Jamis' grin widened as he and his buddy bumped fists.

"Great," Chet grumbled from the corner, eyes straight ahead. "How 'bout we all make that promise right now. One stick up my ass tonight is plenty."

"Like *you'd* ever lose," Noah asserted dryly. "You outweigh the biggest of us by fifty pounds."

All masks shifted to face the second largest member of their team. Alec frowned under their gazes, anxiously clenching his stupid tail. Which, by the way, felt even bigger than before.

"Don't worry, Boss," Chet assured. "I'll go easy on you if we get paired up."

"Awesome," Alec muttered, peering back down the hall. They'd passed the central corridor and rounded the final bend. In other words, they'd reached the grand foyer. The guards up front slowed, then stopped at the first set of doors. Not those to the great hall, though. Those were farther down the way. These big double panels led to—

"Zercy's throne room," Setch announced as he shoved the things open.

The steady pound of music instantly spiked to twice as loud.

Alec's heart rate spiked just as hard.

He peered inside as their entourage filed through, heading toward the giant room's open center. It looked different than the last time he'd seen it, minus the gyrating Súrah dancers wearing strange, feathered garb. He clutched the bars to steady himself as the team bounced and pitched, and eyed the open area with morbid intrigue. It had changed, but not just because of the new props surrounding it. For some reason it now reminded him of a colosseum.

But why?

They drew closer.

"The floorboards," he finally murmured. They'd been removed, exposing a different surface beneath. A recessed stage of sorts formed into the ground. An effect that made the tiered rows of seats seem even taller—and the ceiling above, a million miles away.

Alec glanced around, his heart a banging drum. Said rows of seats looked packed to the freaking gills. Easily a hundred dignitaries or more. They were decked out in all kinds of attire garb, some wearing head pieces, others masks. He could hear their rumbling chatter, too, intertwining with the music. Music, he realized, that had suddenly changed tempo. Its new thumping cadence made him think of a dance club. With a Niran vibe, of course. All heady and tribal. Relentlessly pumping its energy into his bones.

The cacophony was overwhelming. The sights, the sounds, the smells. Music pounding, torches flickering in every direction, eyes boring, the musk of lust thick in the air.

He looked back at the center of the room as they drew nearer, and noticed its sunken stage was split into sections. Three large circles positioned side by side, with the middle round slightly elevated and overlapping its counterparts.

Alec regarded them, riveted by their naturalistic appearance, each enclosed by smooth oversized rocks. They looked like a triad of shallow pools, nestled close together, but void of any water.

His eyes slid to the slender space between them and the audience. Just a pathway of sorts, wide enough to accommodate musicians around the perimeter. Kríe holding pan flutes and bongos and colorful maracas. Or at least, that's what the things looked like to Alec.

He watched them, then turned back to the dancing Súrah, their movements strange, yet captivatingly rhythmic. They certainly held the attention of the spectators above. Most had yet to even notice the team's arrival.

That wasn't the case for long, though. A moment later, the music ebbed, those wielding instruments turning to regard them. The din of rowdy discourse receded, too.

Their convoy eased to a stop, pausing just outside the stage pit.

"Oh, God. Here we go," Bailey muttered. "I'm gonna puke."

Jamis quickly inched away. "Aim for the guards."

Alec frowned and studied his men. They looked tenser than shit. Chet, however, looked ready to climb the walls.

"The night's main event," Setch announced, his deep voice booming. "A tribute to our guests, and to our king."

Alec stilled, pulse spiking, and quickly glanced around. Zercy was there. But where? Rubbing shoulders with other royalty? And then he saw him. At the far end of the room, up on his dais, staring at their cage from his throne.

Alec's heart tripped and slammed against the wall of his ribs. Zercy rose to his feet, lifted a hand, and crooked his finger. Evidently, he wanted them closer. The team jerked forward as their carriers resumed, descending the handful of steps into the pit. The Súrah took their cue and quickly departed. Then just like that, their cage was set on center stage.

Alec peered up at Zercy, taking him in at closer range. God, he looked huge—and majestic as hell, all garbed in special attire for the occasion. Not that he was wearing much, but he was definitely decorated. Alec wondered if Lotis had a hand in his appearance. That painted band across his eyes certainly looked like Lotis' handiwork. Hell, he'd put one on Alec's face not ten minutes ago.

Zercy's, however, was meant to be seen, his thick black stripe lined with tiny jewels. Along the length of his brow, across his cheekbones below, making his big golden eyes gleam that much brighter. Larger gems adorned his horns. Others rimmed his pointed ears. Even the tips of his velvet dreads had been accentuated.

Alec's gaze dipped. Broad and naked, Zercy's chest subtly shimmered, as if his dark skin had been dusted with glitter. His pecs looked huge, and his nipple piercings new. Bold, inverted triangles lined with gems. Embellished regal cuffs hugged his biceps and wrists. Even his golden navel marking seemed extra shiny.

But what grabbed Alec's attention and held him captive was the exotic chain skirt circling Zercy's waist. He studied it intently, starting with its jewel-encrusted belt. Because not only did it hug the king's strong hips like a lover, but also supported the weight of countless necklaces. Or at least that's what they looked like, draping his thighs instead of his chest. Silver, gold, and black against muscular midnight purple. But that was it. Nothing else, minus his sandals, to clothe his body. Just sleek lengths of chain hiding his goods.

Which made Alec wonder: if Zercy were to suddenly whirl around, would all guests in the vicinity get an eyeful? He imagined the decadent glimpse before he could stop himself. His blood pumped hotter.

Zercy eased back onto his throne, snapping him out of it.

Their cage door started to rise.

Setch gestured for them to exit, his voice low for only their ears to hear. "Tonight you are animals, so stay on all fours. Should you challenge this and stand, you will be punished."

Alec all but fucking balked, but one look at Setch's face and he knew to try to argue would be useless. *Just get this night over with,* he thought, grinding his molars. *Just power fucking through it and be done.*

The team filed out, staying low to the ground, moving on hands and the balls of their feet. No way would they *crawl.* Setch could kiss their painted asses. Besides, they maneuvered easier this way.

Their handlers directed them to form a line facing the king. Alec fought the urge to look at him again, but failed. Couldn't help it. That damn Kríe drew his eyes like a magnet. His gaze rose up, up, and finally stopped on Zercy's face. Behind his mask, Alec watched the king study the team, inspecting their appearance with gleaming eyes.

Alec shifted under his scrutiny, but soon the king's gaze changed. He wasn't just admiring Alec's men anymore. He was searching. Examining each person for something specific. Was he trying to identify them? To discern who was who? Aside from Chet, they probably all looked pretty similar.

His gaze reached Alec. Their eyes instantly locked. Alec stilled. So did Zercy. Then the king slowly smiled. He recognized him. It was obvious. That little smirk was his hello. But Alec's face was hidden, and his whole body covered in paint. How had Zercy distinguished him from the others?

Alec blinked behind his mask as a strange warmth filled his chest. That the king had been able to identify him so easily? That should be scary, but for some fucked up reason, Alec couldn't feel anything but *flattered.*

Inwardly, he groaned. He was losing his mind.

But then Zercy's gaze dropped to his spots. His grin curved higher. A glint formed in his eyes, as if he wasn't merely pleased—but also amused.

Like he was sharing some inside fucking joke with Lotis.

Alec bristled and looked away as the music resumed, noticing that their cage had been removed. Kríe had also begun carting jugs to each of the small stages. He watched them tip the things, splashing liquid all around. No doubt, that kulaí stuff that Lotis had mentioned.

Setch and Kellim ambled off next, but returned with jugs, too. Alec frowned, eyeing the pair—and their pitchers—suspiciously. Why were they headed back to the team, not dousing the ground?

The Kríe drew to a stop on either side of Alec's men and expectantly looked up at the king.

Zercy smirked, eyes flashing, and gave a nod.

Alec tensed. An order had been given. But before he could say *oh shit*, Setch and Kellim tipped their jugs. A hardy drizzle landed on the back of Alec's head, then eased down his neck and over his shoulders.

He grimaced. It felt like warm glycerin against his flesh, slowly, steadily soaking the whole of his frame.

More kulaí. Evidently, getting the floors wet wasn't enough.

But surely the stuff would wash away some of their paint. He looked down at his body. Nope. It hadn't in the slightest. Instead, it made his paint job that much more lustrous.

Wonderful.

He peered down the line of his men. They shifted uncomfortably, too.

He drew in a breath and got a whiff of the stuff. Sweet, hinted with honey, like the jungle they'd once traipsed through. It also held a faint acerbic bite. Would it taste the way it smelled? Like a little sweet tart candy?

"As promised, tonight's main feature," the leader of ceremonies began. "Beginning with three savage bouts."

Instantly, the alien crowd broke into boisterous applause.

"The predators before you," he went on, "will be paired, then unleashed upon each other to do battle."

Jamis coughed a nervous laugh three heads down from Alec. "Wow. You guys hear that? We're gonna be *unleashed*."

Noah choked on a laugh of his own. "To *do battle*."

"Should be interesting," Zaden muttered.

Bailey mumbled to himself. "Larping... We're just larping.... We're just larping..."

The announcer continued. "The beast to dismantle his foe the fastest will be victor and advance to the next round."

An air of restless dread engulfed the team at the reminder. Their objective tonight left lots to be desired.

"Just wrestle hard, guys," Alec encouraged his men.

Chet shifted his hips. "And grip light."

Small nods and anxious chuckles were the gist of their response. Logical. This shit was nerve-wracking as hell.

Kellim loped over to Noah and Jamis and prodded them with a baton. "Fekni, tegmai," he gestured to one of rings. "You will wrestle there. Nenya." *Come.*

The scientists swapped looks, then reluctantly followed, clambering on all fours to stage right.

Setch moved to Zaden and Bailey and gave a couple of prods, too. "Kygo, belshay. Your ring is left. Aussa." *Go.*

Alec frowned, watching them amble off, then turned and looked at Chet. It was just the two of them now. On center stage.

He peered up at Zercy. The king met his gaze and smiled. He looked pleased, and yeah, definitely a little bit smug, but mostly his vibe just emanated excitement. Barely contained, by the way he gripped his armrests. Like he was chomping at the bit for things to start.

"First bout," the announcer boomed, kicking things off. He pointed to Jamis and Noah. "Tegmai, fekni! Dóonda!" *Fight!*

Crouched atop the rocks at opposite ends of their ring, the two men lunged forward with all their might. They touched down dead center, colliding in a tangle, hands clutching each other's biceps in iron grips. Noah threw Jamis onto his side. Jamis took his friend with him, rolling to pin his rival underneath him. Both men grunted stark curses. Hardly a surprise. In their tumble, both had banged their curved black tails.

The bongo beat drummed faster. The maracas went wild. Even the flutes shot to an invigorating clipped staccato.

Alec watched his men tussling. Kellim had trained them well. In truth, they seemed perfectly matched. Damn near equal in size and skill. A seamlessly choreographed fight inside their ring. Tossing and twisting. Shifting and bending. Determined fingers grasping for their target.

For the longest time, the two showed no signs of fatigue as the raucous audience hooted and howled above. But then they seemed to falter—although, they didn't exactly look *tired*. Their movements just seemed different. Not sluggish, per se. More like distracted.

Alec frowned at their behavior. While they still seemed fully functional, something about their performance had definitely *shifted*. He just couldn't place exactly what.

More grunts and breathless curses rose up from the pair. Then moans and groans came fast and furious, too. Which Alec supposed made sense, their asses were being tormented, each slippery tug to their tail no doubt intense. Thing was, those noises coming out of Jamis and Noah? They didn't sound aggressive, they sounded *needy*. Like the two guys weren't fighting *each other* anymore, but instead some powerful urge to stop and fuck.

He glanced at their crotches for confirmation. Sure enough, both of the scientists were erect. And not just with semi boners either. Even Alec had one of those, thanks to Lotis' makeshift tail. No, they were sporting full-fledged flag-pole hard-ons—which made no sense for all kinds of reasons. One, they weren't attracted to each other. At all. Hell, Jamis wasn't even truly gay. But even more pertinent, they were in front of a *crowd*. Their brains just wouldn't let them get *this* horny.

Alec eyed them in confusion, but stilled a second later, when Noah finally shoved Jamis onto his stomach. Scrambling, Noah quickly straddled his hips and dove for his tail. Alec couldn't see his face but determination blazed in his eyes. With one hand firmly planted at the top of Jamis' ass, Noah gripped the strange plant tight and started pulling.

Jamis' whole frame went rigid. He restlessly shook his head, but otherwise made no other sound. The poor guy was probably holding his breath. Chest heaving, Noah slowly, visibly, added more force, until the hilt of that tail finally dislodged.

"Ungh!" Jamis belted. His hips shifted urgently.

Noah dipped his head, clearly trying to talk him through it.

Before too long, though, Jamis cleared the thickest part, and yup, it was all downhill from there.

The tail slid free. Noah held it high victoriously. His teammate slumped in relief. The crowd went wild.

Alec blinked, jaw slack.

That was some kind of show.

"Fekni triumphs!" the announcer exploded. "He will go to round two!" He pointed at Noah, then to the rowdy sea of spectators. "Now pick a Niran to take your place in the ring."

Noah stilled.

So did Alec.

What the fuck did that Kríe say? An audience member would get a go at them, too?

The rowdy rows of onlookers teemed with anticipation.

Noah glanced Alec's way, apprehension in his eyes. He wanted his direction, but what could Alec say? It wasn't like they had much of a choice. Holding Noah's gaze, he relayed his best advice.

Choose cautiously, Noah. And preferably someone small.

Noah gave a slight nod from behind his mask, then turned and carefully scanned the brazen crowd. Tense moments later, he exhaled in visible relief and pointed to the left of Zercy's throne. Alec followed his line of sight. Surprised, he quirked a brow. Noah's pick wasn't someone small, but nevertheless, a Niran the team knew and trusted.

Ryze stood from his seat, turned and bowed to the king, then casually took the steps down to the stage.

Rumbles of disappointment shook the open room.

"Ryze. The king's scholar. A conservative choice." The announcer smirked and pointed Noah toward his circle's rocky border, where a cluster of tire-size stones formed a mound. "Take your place there, Fekni. You will fight again soon."

Noah swapped looks with Jamis, then clambered up the bank and perched on hands and haunches as Ryze arrived. The instructor stepped inside and wryly grinned at his new plaything. Jamis stiffened, lifting his eyes to meet his stare. The Kríe's gaze flickered. He sank down to his haunches. Then, playfully, he stalked his prey on hands and feet.

Jamis braced, eyeing him curiously. Ryze's impish grin widened, the only warning before the big Kríe flat-out pounced. Jamis dove out of the way, but Ryze's reach was huge, and was yanked into his side despite his efforts. They went down in a tumble with Ryze absorbing the impact, and just like that, the two were spiritedly wrestling.

Alec couldn't be sure, but going by Jamis' vibe, the scientist seemed to be almost enjoying himself. As if now that the pressure of protecting his tail was gone, he was letting himself have a little fun.

"Second bout," the leader of ceremonies resumed, redirecting the crowd. He pointed to Zaden and Bailey. Both men looked spring-loaded and ready, crouched at opposite ends of their ring. The stadium thundered. Alec's muscles re-tensed. "Kygo and belshay! Dóonda!" *Fight!*

The teammates sprang forward. Did Bailey just *roar?* Evidently, a certain scientist had switched to larp mode. Alec watched them engage. Zaden moved with raw agility, all decked out in those feral zebra stripes.

Bailey did a bit more ducking and diving in the oil, which incidentally, fit his getup to a T. Belshay were obviously some kind of badass water predators, so what better way to represent? All that ducking and diving merely drove the look home.

A smile tugged at Alec's lips. Good for Bailey for getting into it. Maybe a little of that enthusiasm would rub off on Zaden.

All around, the spectators cheered in rowdy approval. Even Zercy looked riveted by the brawl.

But just like Noah and Jamis, after a good bit of tussling, their little dance-floor scuffle shifted tunes. No longer did they grapple for their rival's tail so fiercely. Now they seemed compelled to just make contact. Slippery limbs needlessly entwining and tangling, even as both men struggled to stay on course. Reaching for their target only to get distracted as their rival's body pressed against their own.

Right on cue, a slew of heated moans rose and mixed with their grunts, the aggression in their movements turning carnal. Alec furrowed his brows, noting their rigid boners, too. He didn't understand. They wrestled the same way every day. All of them did, in Kellim's sessions. Could their butt-plug tails be making that much of a difference? All those grips and slippery tugs derailing their logic?

Either way, just as Alec had contemplated before, they shouldn't be this anxious to fuck. Not in public, but most especially, not with each other. Alec's men just didn't have that kind of chemistry. Yeah, some joked around, but sexual attraction was nonexistent. So, no. This shit did *not* add up at all.

Without warning, Zaden lunged with a raw, husky shout and snapped his muscular arms around Bailey's ribs. Momentum sent them slipping and sliding across the ground. Zaden shifted behind him just as they crashed into the rocks, taking the brunt for both of them with his back.

They grunted on impact, but Zaden didn't let go. Instead he shoved his knee between Bailey's thighs and wrenched sideways, pinning Bailey's leg against the stones. Which not only trapped his teammate's leg, but spread his thighs and cranked up his ass. Bailey squirmed on his side, one arm trapped under his body. Zaden released his hold and trapped Bailey's other arm in a half-nelson.

Just like that, the scientist was rendered immobile.

With his tail wholly accessible to his opponent.

Zaden reached down the front of Bailey's body with his free hand and curled his trembling fingers around the plant. Bailey stiffened. Zaden pulled. Slow and easy. Bailey moaned. Their boners still rock hard against their groins. Zaden pulled a little harder. Bailey hissed and rocked his hips. His tight black ring reluctantly widened. Zaden ground against his backside, then finally tugged it free. Bailey shuddered. Zaden quickly shoved him off and scrambled upright. Eyes wired, he held the tail for all to see.

Again, the stands erupted in rambunctious applause.

"Kygo wins!" the announcer shouted, just as amped.

Zaden visibly exhaled and glanced Alec's way. Alec wished he could see his friend's face. He looked tense, hands still shaking, like he was vibrating out of his skin. Was he pissed? Strung out on a rush of adrenaline? Desperate to fuck?

Hopefully not.

The leader of ceremonies turned to Zaden and grinned. "It is your turn, kygo, to pick a replacement. Perhaps one of ours *guests* this time," he prompted.

Zaden ambled on all fours back to help Bailey sit up, seeming to speak with him briefly before looking around. Intently, his dark eyes scanned the indigenous faces above. He didn't seem to see anything he liked. He scanned the crowd again, periodically glancing at Bailey, as if checking to see if potentials were of similar size. None seemed to satisfy him. The crowd turned impatient, some stomping in discontent, some braying loudly.

Alec cursed in empathy. He didn't envy his co-pilot this task. Zaden was literally putting his teammate in a stranger's hands. The pilot's roaming gaze abruptly stilled on a male straight ahead. The Niran must've pushed his way to the front to be spotted. Zaden was certainly studying him now.

After a long thoughtful moment, Zaden pointed to the male as his choice.

Alec stared in the Niran's direction, waiting to get a better look. From his angle, the guy was hidden behind other males.

"Prince Nen," the announcer introduced. His tone felt curt. "Oonmaiyos delegate and heir to the throne."

Another round of unhappy brays rose from the crowd. Although, unlike with Ryze, Alec swore he detected animosity, too. Toward the prince? But why? Wait. Hold up. The leader of ceremonies had said *Oonmaiyos*, whom—if Alec remembered correctly—Naydo had said Krie didn't get along with.

The dignitary emerged.

Bailey visibly stilled.

Guess he was finally seeing him for the first time, just like Alec.

Alec looked the prince over. He looked younger than the others. And leaner, too. Maybe six-foot-one with an athletic build. He hit the steps and casually made his way toward Bailey's circle, his pale skin gleaming curiously in the fire light. As if infused with some strange luminescence or something. Not that Alec could really see much, only his arms and face were showing. Well, his neck too, and a little of his chest. The rest of him was covered in sleek ocean-chic attire. Snug leggings and a belted tunic that hugged him just as tight, each piece dark blue and iridescent, with glints of color.

Alec watched as the prince stepped into the ring, his sapphire hair in one long braid down his back. He peered down at Bailey with big purple eyes, dark and yet alight with keen intrigue.

Bailey tipped his head back and gazed up at him, too. Nen's lips curved into a small friendly smile. Without breaking his stare, he strode right over and sank down onto his haunches. Tentatively, he reached forward and traced a patch of Bailey's scales. He looked enraptured by the things, as if drawn to their appearance. A shimmering lure for this nautical alien prince.

Nen reached for Bailey's mask next and touched one of its fins. A slender fan of spikes behind his ears. Not that his mask had ears, per se, but in that general location along his head. Bailey didn't move, just let the young prince inspect it. Let him inspect some of his painted gills as

219

well. Nen would never believe them to be real, of course. He may be young, but he exuded stark intelligence—and a very obvious streak of curiosity.

The crowd grew impatient and started to clamor in the stands. Nen paused to peer up at them, and to Alec's great surprise, Bailey swiftly took advantage of the distraction. Shifting his weight, he lunged forward and tackled the prince, driving Nen onto his back. The prince's eyes flared wide, but a split second later, flashed bright with exhilaration.

Like a happy puppy eager to play.

Next thing Alec knew, the two were tangoing to their own beat, seeming utterly oblivious to those around them. Alec shook his head, but again, couldn't help his smile. His boys knew how to roll with the punches.

Setch and Kellim ambled over with their big ole batons and nudged Chet and Alec in the ribs. "Assume attack positions on opposites sides of your ring." Kellim grinned. "Up on the rocks for good spring action."

Alec's heart took off racing. Fuck. It was time. His and Chet's turn in the spotlight. He glanced Zercy's way. The king was watching him. Alec's skin went all tingly under his stare.

"First round's final bout!" the leader of ceremonies recommenced. He gestured to Chet and Alec. "Koosa and dembra! The fiercest of all! Who shall triumph? Who shall fall? It is time for us to see! Dóonda!" the big Kríe boomed. "Dóonda!" *Fight!*

In the blink of an eye, Alec and Chet shoved off their ledges, charging across the circle to engage. Alec met Chet's gray gaze. They looked steely and focused, like a man on a mission to get shit done. To give all those fuckers above a wild show, so he could climb back into his hole in the wall and be done.

Their bodies collided. Both men grasped the other's biceps, fighting to throw their rival to the ground. Teetering his weight on one knee and one foot, Alec struggled to keep his balance under Chet's brawn. But the bastard was *big*—and aggravatingly *strong*.

Alec gritted his teeth and absently glanced back to the throne. Zercy's hot gaze was hooded and—

Chet threw all his bulk to the right without warning, taking Alec's upper body with him. Alec cursed and tried to counter, but then Chet threw his foot forward and shoved Alec's knee out from under him. Alec crashed to the ground. Chet followed him just as hard. And just like that, a full-fledged floor grapple ensued.

The audience went crazy as they slipped and slid and wrestled, that oily nectar on the floor coating them further. And man, was it slippery, leaving traction a thing of the past. It was heady-as-shit sweet too, in such large quantities. Not just a generous drizzling over their frames. The stuff was flat-out everywhere, thick and glistening. He could smell its tang in his nostrils as they tussled, their body heat making its scent rise up between them. Entering his lungs, his bloodstream, with each pant. Making a strange buzz hum all over his skin.

Alec lurched back from Chet's hold and flicked Zercy another look. He couldn't seem to help himself. It was that damn magnet effect. The king's eyes bored into him, his expression intense. Alec's dick bucked from the mere fucking sight.

Crap. He couldn't get distracted.

Spinning around, Alec faced off once more. Chet snarled something and tackled him back to the ground. Not that Alec didn't try to dodge the big brute. Chet's reach was just too great to fucking escape.

Alec gripped Chet's slippery biceps and tried to shove him off. Chet grabbed his wrist and pinned it to the ground.

"Goddam it," Alec grated, jamming his forearm against Chet's throat, before kneeing him hard in the ribs.

Chet grunted, pitching sideways. Alec scrambled up and launched on top of him, but nearly slid right over him completely. Chet's back was so damn slippery from the oil. Alec snapped his arms around him from behind as Chet regrouped. But when Alec tugged him to the ground, he jarred his own tail extra hard. Current tore through his ass like a bullet.

He gasped, going rigid. Again, his eyes shot to Zercy, the jolt of pleasure snapping his focus back on the king. Zercy didn't appear happy. He looked tense and possessive, that air of excitement nowhere in sight. Fuck, that broody expression, it made Alec's ass sing even harder.

Abruptly, Chet twisted lightning fast in his hold, kicking up a spattering of that kulaí. Some flew into Alec's mouth. Panting, he licked his lips. Just like sweet tarts. It made his tongue tingle. Kind of like Zercy's gaze was doing to his dick.

Alec forced himself to focus, scrambling to keep his slippery hold, but the harder he breathed, the more of those sweet fumes entered his body. Fumes that were starting to make him feel dizzy. But not the sloppy drunk kind. His movements weren't hampered. In a weird way, they felt invigorated.

More charged to win this round.

To fucking dominate.

Chet growled, grinding against him as they rolled in a tangle. His slick, contracting muscles felt so firm. Strange heat flooded Alec's system. His head felt all wrong. Chet's next heated growl felt wrong, too.

Determined to shake it off, he shoved an elbow into Chet's ribs.

Chet grunted, then chuckled huskily. "Nice hit, bitch."

Alec's brows scrunched. Did his teammate just call him *bitch?*

But before he could figure out the wtf's of that, Chet juked low, picked him up, and slammed him down face first.

"Uh!" Air burst from Alec's lungs in a rush. Then a torso was pressing atop him from the side.

"How you like *them* apples," a deep voice snarled in his ear. "Paybacks are hell, you purple fuck."

Alec stiffened. Whoa, what? His mind started to reel. Then a strong rigid groin rocked into his hip. His dick responded instantly, his brain filling in the blanks. Melding the sounds, the weight, the words, all into one. Rumbling timbre. Massive body. Purple fuck. They all spelled *Kríe*. And in that moment, the only Kríe Alec knew was Zercy.

More blood rushed in a hurry to his cock as his head swam. Zercy was on top of him. Grinding his body into Alec's. Wait, no. That wasn't right. Yes, it was. Ugh, fuck. This kulaí-thick air was scrambling his head. Is this what happened to the others? Had these vapors affected them, too?

A big hand grabbed his wrist and pinned it high against his back. Pain screamed down his arm.

"Motherfuck!" Alec shouted.

A richer chuckle followed, as did another shameless grind. Alec gaped. One hell of a boner just jammed his ribs. He shifted to alleviate some of the pain in his shoulder. A huge knee shoved between his thighs and wedged them apart. Another jar to his tail sent him vibrating. Someone was grabbing it, sending ecstasy through his channel as they pulled—

No. Gotta stop this!

He tried to focus.

Something told him he shouldn't lose his tail just yet. Had to hold on. Had to keep it.

He clenched his ass hard, but all that did was make shit worse, pressing the plant's root against his prostate. He ground out a curse, back arching as more jolts rocked him.

"No—*Ungh fuck*—" He rammed his elbow up into his opponent.

The male atop him grunted. Then loosed a gravelly laugh. "Not ready to give it up yet? Want me to fuck you with it first?" The voice sounded mumbled. He tugged Alec's tail again. "You're such a dirty bitch, Roni. You know that?"

Alec moaned at the sensation, his face pressed hard against the ground. Why in the fuck was Zercy calling him Roni? No, wait. Not Zercy... Or was it? He couldn't think. His dick bucked in its confines, throbbing as he envisioned the king pinning him. That weight atop him shifted, the hold on his wrist no longer there. But then a big ole knee pressed down on his spine.

"Shit," Alec grunted, palming the ground to try and push up.

His rival pulled his tail again. "Let go," the deep timbre grated. "Stop clenching, so I can fuck you with this right."

"Ungh!" The tugging was going to drive Alec crazy. He canted his ass as more pleasure assailed him, unable to help it, despite his efforts. His eyes shot upward, needing an anchor. Searching for Zercy. His hungry gaze found him. He was still on his throne, leaning forward though, muscles rigid, his neck and shoulder tendons like taut cables. Probably because he was gripping his armrests like a beast, his black claws gouging deep into the wood.

The Kríe looked pissed.

Alec blinked to clear his mind. If Zercy wasn't down there wrestling with him, then who was? His brain churned urgently. Someone was this close to fucking his ass. And if it wasn't Zercy, he didn't want it.

He started to struggle wildly. Angry shouts shot up his throat.

But the heavy weight against him wouldn't budge.

"Not gonna win this time, Roni," the voice grunted breathlessly. "I am. And I'm not cheating, like you did."

All around, thunderous cheers rose to a fevered pitch.

Alec's tail started to slip, his sphincter losing its grip. "No!" he shouted. White hot ecstasy shot straight to his junk. His dick was so hard, he could barely stand it. Not that he wanted to use it at the moment. Not if the guy working him wasn't Zercy. His mind spun like a whirlwind of conflicting sludge. Spiking anger, restless confusion, surging lust.

But right as he buckled down to really lose his shit, something heavy slammed the ground right by his head. The body atop him stiffened. The audience went silent. Then one unholy bellow tore through the throne room. So loud and powerful, it vibrated Alec's bones. He shot ramrod stiff.

Someone *really pissed* had just joined them in the ring.

The male atop him quickly shifted off Alec's back. Heart pounding, Alec turned to look.

Holy fuck.

It was Zercy. And he looked ready to *blow*.

Chest heaving, Zercy pinned Alec's foe with murderous eyes. He was going to kill the guy. There was no doubt about it. Alec shifted to get a look at his opponent and gaped. Realization shot through his haze.

Oh, God. It was Chet.

He'd been wrestling Chet.

And now the king was going to slaughter him.

Chet blinked up at the king, seemingly steeped in his own fog. Face paling, he looked at Alec, clearly struggling in his head, then quickly pinned his focus back on Zercy. His eyes narrowed. He'd just assessed the king as a threat. Clenching his jaw, he lurched protectively in front of Alec.

Good intentions and all, but a very bad idea.

Zercy hit the fucking roof. Shoving his face in Chet's grill, he bared his fangs and unleashed another roar. Alec cringed, the furious bellow back to rattling his bones. Chet braced, too, but before he could do much else, Zercy grabbed his shoulders and tossed him out of the way.

His manic stare turned to Alec. Stalking over, he yanked him up. "Mine," he ground out, voice guttural. "You come with me."

Alec gaped up at the guy like a deer in headlights. Zercy's blazing eyes looked out-and-out unhinged. "I..." he rasped. He should probably stay put. His head was still messed up, but more so than that, Zercy's state of mind right now looked kind of tenuous.

Not that the king gave a damn either way. Emitting a low growl that said *don't test my patience*, he hefted Alec into a fireman's hold and pivoted around.

Alec stiffened atop his shoulders, wholly stunned and utterly mortified. "What the fuck are you doing?" he barked. "Put me down!"

But Zercy just ignored him and stalked toward the exit, his big hands securely gripping Alec's limbs. He wouldn't put him down until he got to where he was going, that much was painfully clear.

Nevertheless, Alec couldn't fight his instinct to resist. "Put me down," he yelled again, struggling to jar himself off Zercy's frame. He could hear the king's guards hustling to catch up. Alec bristled, his ass hiked for all to see. He shoved at Zercy harder. "Let me go!"

Zercy tightened his grip and shoved through the doors. "Silence," he snarled. "You are in much trouble already. It would be very unwise for you to add to it."

CHAPTER EIGHTEEN

* * *

By the time Zercy reached his private chambers, his royal guard had fallen into step. Alec scowled behind his mask, no longer fighting to get free, but rather to figure out why he was in trouble. For fuck's sake, he'd just spent the last ten minutes oil wrestling—with a tail shoved up his ass—for *Zercy's viewing enjoyment*.

Setch and Kellim ambled in first to check the place out. A moment later, they waved the king through.

"All clear, my lord," Setch grunted. His expression looked guarded. Like he was pissed that he'd had to leave in the middle of the show but knew better than to pout in front of the king.

Zercy rumbled something growly and tramped inside. Alec winced, draped over the guy like a fur. Each terse step Zercy took shoved his shoulder into Alec's gut—which in turn, jarred that motherfucking tail.

The doors pulled closed behind them.

Zercy stalked over to his tub, then pulled Alec down the front of his body. Setting him on his feet, he tugged off his mask and tossed it aside. Alec wobbled a little. Even now he still felt off kilter. Not nearly as much as before, though. His head was definitely starting to clear. Evidently, now that he wasn't surrounded by, and rapidly inhaling, all that kulaí, his brain was getting a chance to air out the fumes.

Zercy glared at him accusingly. "You told me you were not *gay*. That your taste was not in *males*. And yet tonight, another male has completely aroused you. Brazenly. Right in front of my face."

Alec frowned and blinked up at him. That black band across his eyes made them look so much bigger. And ten times brighter. Churning like molten lava.

What was he going on about? Alec furrowed his brows. Blinked a couple more times. "Did you say *aroused? In that pit?* No way."

"Do not lie!" Zercy exploded.

Alec jerked back and shook his head. "I'm not lying!" he insisted. "Chet didn't get me hard!"

"Tah, he did!" The king looked like he wanted to throttle something. "I watched your cock rise with my own eyes!"

"Yes! I mean—I know! It's just—" He cursed and rubbed his brow. "Goddamnit. It's not what you think, and—" he squared his shoulders defensively. "You don't get to be mad at me! I should be pissed at you!"

Zercy balked. "For what?"

"For what? Are you kidding me?" Alec pointed to his backside, exasperated. "I have a fucking *root* jammed up my *ass!*"

Zercy grunted. "That was Lotis' idea, not mine."

Alec bristled and glared at him.

Zercy's jaw *tick-tick-ticked*. He opened his mouth, but then closed it. Narrowing his eyes, he scanned Alec's face. Studied him intently. "You seem different. What is wrong with you?"

Good question.

He shot Zercy a glower. "You tell me."

Zercy came back with an even darker glare of his own. "How would I know?"

Alec eyed him. In fairness, the king looked genuinely clueless. Alec cursed. "Are you telling me you didn't notice they were drugging us?"

Zercy stilled, looking surprised. A second later, though, he bristled. "I would *never* condone such a thing."

Alec scowled in confusion. Now Zercy not only looked pissed but wholly offended. "But you watched them pour that kulaí shit all over us. *You* gave the order."

Zercy's face pinched angrily. "Kulaí is harmless. What is your point?"

Alec gaped. "Are you for real? Its fumes alone made me hallucinate. It was messing with my teammates, too." Chet, for one, had thought Alec was Roni and had been seconds away from exacting some serious payback.

Thank God Zercy had lost it when he had.

Zercy furrowed his brows thoughtfully. Finally, he shook his head. "Mah. Kulaí oil has never had that effect."

Alec ground his teeth, staring up at him. "Maybe not on *Nirans*."

Zercy stiffened at his words, then warily scanned Alec's body, no doubt noting how he was still covered in the stuff.

"Ságe's cock," he hissed irritably, hoisting Alec back off his feet.

Son of a bitch. Not again.

And who the hell was Ságe?

Alec scowled in his hold. "Damn it, Kríe, I can—"

Zercy dropped him into the tub.

KERSPLASH!

Alec plummeted under the surface.

What a dick!

He lurched up with a shout. "What the—"

SPLASH!!

More water in the face.

Zercy had chucked something into the bath.

Alec coughed and sputtered, furious, then chopped the surface as hard as he could, hoping he'd drench the asshole's frickin' legs.

"Wash yourself," the king grated, easily sidestepping Alec's efforts. "Your time as koosa is over. I want my *pet*."

Alec clenched his teeth. Haughty bastard. Although, truth be told, he was ready to get this shit off his body. Feeling around with his foot, he located the item Zercy had tossed in, then did a quick dip to retrieve it. A hide-skin sack of soap rocks, going by the way it sudsed in his hand. Normally, he used the lotus petals. Maybe this stuff was for paint.

Muttering irritably, he got busy scouring his arms, then moved to his legs, but the motion of lifting his knee shifted that tail. Licks of current zinged through his channel. Alec stilled, stifling a grunt. Time to ditch that puppy pronto. He and his ass had had enough.

Reaching around back, he curled his fingers around its base, then gave the thing a healthy little pull. A moan shot up his throat as his asshole instantly objected. More pressure surged through his rectum. His boner kicked.

Great. This was going to take some effort.

Alec scowled and glanced at Zercy, hoping like hell he wasn't watching.

Nope. He was busy cleaning his body paint off too, down on his haunches besides the tub soap-scrubbing his face.

Good. If Alec was lucky, he'd lose the tail with dignity intact. But just as he readied to bear down like a mother, Zercy tensed, tersely splashed his face, and shot him a glare.

"Is *he* why you always want to be with your men? Because you always want to be with your Chet?"

Alec quickly let go—then proceeded to blanch. "With *my Chet?* Are you crazy? Not in a million freaking—"

"You do!" the king bellowed, shooting to his feet. "You fuck him each day while I toil!"

Alec's jaw dropped. Fuck *Chet?* Was this Kríe friggin' nuts?

"And then you come to my bed each night *sated!*"

"No!" Alec shouted, flat-out freaking appalled. "I don't want Chet like that. He's my teammate."

Zercy seethed, then gestured to Alec's hard-on beneath the water. "Then tell me, why did your cock turn to rock while you wrestled?"

Alec glanced down at his boner. Closed his eyes and inwardly cursed.

Because you were there, Zercy. My dick was hard because of you.

"I told you," he muttered, "it's not what you think."

Zercy glowered incredulously and crossed his bulky arms. "Then what *is* it?" he grated.

Alec shifted his weight. He really, *really* didn't want to say.

Zercy bristled. "It is. It is *exactly* what I think." Emitting a growl that sounded pissed, but also distraught, he fell into a dark pensive pace. Back and forth, back and forth, like a brooding caged panther, agitation rolling off him in waves.

Alec exhaled, not quite sure if it was worth it to even argue. The king wasn't hearing a word he said.

Tense moments ticked by. Alec quickly finished bathing, watching the king from his periphery. Maybe for now, he'd put the tail extraction on hold.

Zercy seemed to calm a little. Making another lap, he shook his head. "I do not think I want you near that male anymore. You are mine, *Alick*. Mine."

Alec tensed. "No, I'm *not.*"

229

Zercy stopped, still ruminating, and looked at him. "Tah, you are." He nodded once and resumed pacing. "Only mine."

Stubborn ass.

"You can't keep me from my men."

"Of course I can. I am king. But perhaps I will remove your *Chet* instead."

"No!" Alec shouted, getting exasperated all over again. "We're a *team.* We stick together. No matter what."

The king chuckled humorlessly as he stalked back and forth. "Your rules are not mine. You can keep all but Chet. I will not share your affections, *Alick*. Not with anyone."

"Ugh!" Alec chucked his sack of soap rocks. "You're so frustrating!" Stomping up the steps in just his collar, tail, and jockstrap, he glowered at the king, dripping wet. "You say you have eyes, but do you have freaking ears? I told you, *I don't want Chet like that!* I'm not attracted to the guy! At all!"

Zercy screeched to a halt. Fresh ire churned in his eyes. "Then explain your erection, *Alick!* Explain this to me! If your Chet did not arouse you, then *who* did?"

"You!" Alec shouted. "*You* did! I could feel your eyes watching me! Watching my every move! It drove me crazy! I couldn't concentrate! Then that kulaí shit kicked in! Made me think that I was wrestling you—*you* in that ring! That it was *your* hands all over me, not his!"

Zercy stared at him, lips parted. He was clearly in shock. A moment later though, he shook himself out of it. "You are lying again. You do not desire me that way."

Alec shifted his weight. Cleared his throat. "I don't want to… But I do."

A spark flickered in the king's auric eyes. Like a tiny flash of hope. "Prove it. Touch me." He gestured to his chest. "Touch me and I will know if you are truthful."

Alec froze. He had *not* anticipated *that* response. "Uh…" He fidgeted.

Zercy narrowed his eyes.

Fucking hell.

Alec steeled his resolve. "Yeah… Okay." Stepping close, he eyed the king's muscular torso, then noncommittally poked Zercy's sternum.

Zercy frowned down at his finger, an almost sad look on his face, but quickly concealed it and shot Alec a glare. Baring his fangs, he got right up in Alec's face. "You *lie*," he snarled. "The lack of interest in your touch is proof."

Alec shook his head. "I'm not lying."

Zercy straightened and threw up his hands. "And why should I believe you? You lie *always, Alick. Always*. Just this morning you lied to me in this very room. Swore that it was not me in your dream—" Abruptly, Zercy stilled. His big eyes flared wide. "It was *not* me in your dream! It was Chet!"

Alec cringed. Oh, God. This was getting worse fast.

"No," he insisted, shaking his head again. "It wasn't Chet."

"It was!"

"It wasn't!"

"Then who was it?" Zercy roared.

"You! It was you!"

"So, you *did* lie! You *are* a liar! And could very well be lying *now!*"

Alec opened his mouth. Shut it. He was starting to get frustrated. And, honestly, a little bit pissed. Clutching his crotch, he gritted through clenched teeth. "This is hard because of you, Kríe. I swear it. I'm not lying."

Zercy stared at him, nostrils flaring. "I do not believe you."

"Yes, you do. You know it's true. I'm always hard when you're around."

"Tah. And you always deny me as the cause."

"Well, yeah. Of course. You think I *want* you to know?"

Zercy studied his face. "You use logic to deceive me."

"I'm telling the truth."

"Convince me." His meaning was clear.

Alec tensed. "I…" He clenched his fists. "You're just gonna have to take my word for it."

"Tah," Zercy muttered. "I suppose I shall. While your bedmate Chet makes do in his new quarters." Face cold, he turned to walk away.

Shit.

Alec grabbed his arm. "Wait."

Zercy glowered at him over his shoulder.

"I'll prove it," he forced out. "I'll show you I'm not lying."

Zercy's eyes narrowed again. He turned back and faced him. "You think to trick me. Deceive me. Make a fool out of your king."

Alec's heart hammered. He couldn't believe he was going to do this. "No. I'm not… And you'll be able to tell." His glanced at his hand, the one still gripping Zercy's arm. Tentatively, he stroked Zercy's skin with his thumb.

Zercy stilled and looked down at it, watched it graze him again. Then his blazing golden eyes locked hard with Alec's. "I want more proof like this, *Alick*. But not on my arm."

Alec paused in understanding, but before he could object, Zercy hooked a finger in his collar and started walking.

"You will show me more here," he stated, heading for his bed.

Alec's eyes went wide. He dug his heels in, not that it made any difference, and quickly clutched Zercy's hand to pull it off. "Whoa. Uh… Yeah, not there, okay? How 'bout we just stay—"

Zercy halted in his tracks and heatedly pinned Alec with suspicious eyes. "If I arouse you, my bed should hardly be a problem."

Alec's pulse spiked faster. "It's not a problem. I just don't—"

Trust myself with you in there.

"Bellah. If it does not pose a problem, then we go." And just like that, Zercy resumed his determined march.

Alec's traitorous dick bucked.

Oh, God. Oh, fuck.

They reached the wall nest and Zercy tossed him in.

Alec landed on his stomach with a bounce, and thank God. Had he landed the other way? On that big ole tail? Yeah, he'd be hurting something ugly.

Zercy climbed in beside him and flopped down on his back. Shoving his hands behind his head, he grunted, "More."

Alec tensed as he righted himself. His eyes roamed down Zercy's body. Christ, he was muscular, just his freaking arms alone, with those regal bicep cuffs accentuating each bulge. And then there was his chest, all buff to perfection. Bulky in true Kríe form, but not overwhelmingly. His abs and powerful thighs were flawless, too.

Alec's dick firmed harder. He cleared his throat. "Yeah. Okay."

Sitting up, he again couldn't believe he was doing this. But desperate times and all that. This was for Chet, he told himself. He was doing this for his team.

Resolute, he situated himself perpendicular to Zercy's side. Then he eased down onto his heels, leaving room for his tail. He'd love to reach around and finally yank that fucker out, but no way could he do that with Zercy watching. God knew, the last thing he needed right now was the king demanding to help with its removal.

Alec exhaled and peered down at the king's muscular torso. Spellbinding, the way it glittered so subtly beneath the firelight, the sconce's flickering flames making it shimmer. He moved his studious gaze to Zercy's thick, sculpted pecs, then specifically to their dark little nipples. Jesus. Their piercings. Sexy-as-hell. Made him want to give them feisty tugs.

"Touch me," Zercy rumbled. "Put your hand on my body."

Alec swallowed. Nodding a little, he tentatively palmed Zercy's pec. Oh, God. So hot, and smooth, and firm, beneath his hand. He splayed his fingers wider and brushed its nipple with his thumb. Instantly, it hardened, beading into a tight little pebble. Alec held his breath, afraid he might moan from the sensation.

Zercy's lids hooded. "Tah. Touch me there more."

Alec met his eyes and decided what better time than the present to get what he'd wanted after all. Securing Zercy's piercing between his fingers, he gave a pull. Just a little one, but not gentle by any means.

Zercy hissed, arching slightly. His mouth curved. His eyes glinted. "Again," he growled softly. "Both at once."

Alec's lips parted at the command. He'd love nothing more. Adding his other hand, he obeyed without question. This time, however, he tugged a bit harder. He also tacked on a little twist.

Zercy growled and rocked his hips. Alec's groin zinged in reaction, his dick straight-up humming in its sheath.

"My stomach now," Zercy instructed, his voice like abraded velvet. "Touch my stomach now, *Alick*. Use your nails."

Alec all but fucking groaned. Way too hungrily, he eyed Zercy's abs. The king liked some pain mixed with his pleasure. He cleared his throat, gave another imperceptible nod, then slowly dragged his fingertips down Zercy's torso.

Zercy's lids dipped lower. "Harder, *Alick*. I want to feel you score my flesh."

Alec stifled another groan. This Kríe was making him need to fuck. Tamping the urge, he complied and added pressure, dragging five blunt nails down Zercy's abs. Along each dip and clenching swell, until he couldn't help but pause at Zercy's navel. Its golden sunburst was just so captivating.

"Feel it," the king murmured. He slowly rocked his hips. "See what happens."

Why not. Alec had certainly done worse with the king. Tracing it with his index, he raptly watched it *move*. Not away or even into a different shape, more like lava coming to life in its confines. Shifting like thick liquid under the pressure of his finger, while retaining its sleek design as if still solid. As solid as it could be, that is, because again, it was his flesh. Flesh that also looked somehow metallic.

"Damn," Alec breathed. "That is… Wow, that's so cool."

Zercy chuffed low in his throat. "You find it pleasing?"

"Uh, *yeah*. But what exactly *is* it?"

"The birthmark of my royal bloodline."

Alec met his gaze. "Seriously? It wasn't put there by someone?"

Zercy smiled a little. "Mah. Unless by someone you mean Nira."

"Nira," Alec repeated.

"Tah. While she formed me in her womb."

The king's words raised more questions than answers in Alec's head, but he decided to wait for a different time to ask.

Zercy slowly rolled his hips. "Do not stop, *Alick*. Keep touching me."

Alec's blood heated at the feel of Zercy moving against his hand. He cleared his throat, "Um… okay," and resumed tracing Zercy's mark.

"Lower," Zercy rumbled. "You have played there long enough."

Alec's heart rate spiked faster as he eyed Zercy's happy trail, warily following its path with his finger. A path that didn't have hair, incidentally. Just a tantalizing line of darker purple. The king emitted a husky sound. Alec stopped at his belt, grateful that Zercy's chain skirt was still concealing stuff. Didn't do a damn thing to hide the fact that Zercy was hard, though. But at least the chains were heavy enough to hold things down.

Alec exhaled and eased back. "There. I touched you. Gave you proof."

A grin tugged at Zercy's lips. "Your proof thus far is unsubstantial."

Alec balked incredulously. "I played with your nipples."

"I play with my nipples, too," Zercy chuckled, undoing his belt. "But that does not mean I am attracted to myself."

"Totally different," Alec protested, starting to panic in realization. Zercy was going to take that damn thing off.

The king lifted his hips and pulled the chainwear out from under him. "Tah, and yet a valid point all the same." He tossed it through the opening onto the chamber's hard floor.

Alec froze in horror even as his dick bucked in glee.

He glanced down before he could stop himself. Oh, thank God. The king wasn't naked. He was wearing one of his loincloths. Not that his cock wasn't still trying to bust free, straining hard where it was pinned against his hip.

Zercy chuffed low in his throat and slid his thumbs under its waistband. Then, without warning, he sliced a claw through each side. The material fell away as his boner sprang upward, jutting tall and proud for all to see.

"Son of a bitch," Alec cursed, quickly jerking his eyes away.

The Kríe was absolutely naked *now*.

Naked and undoubtedly about to tell Alec to—

"Touch my cock."

Alec clenched his jaw. Totally called it.

An anxious groan rose up his throat. Because deep down—and honestly, right at the surface, too—he knew that touching the king's dick would not be wise. Crazy shit would end up happening that probably shouldn't.

Heart pounding, he shook his head. "That wasn't part of the deal."

Zercy smirked, cocking a brow. "We made a deal?"

"Well, yeah. I mean, we didn't go into specifics, but it was a given, goddamnit. No touching dick."

Zercy canted his head and eyed him, then grinned. "You are scared. My giant cock frightens you. You are afraid."

Alec blinked, brows furrowing. "What the f—*No, I'm not!*"

Zercy laughed. "I was jesting." He grabbed Alec's wrist. "Are all humans so adorably gullible?"

Alec frowned at the insult, but before he could respond, Zercy curled Alec's fingers around his shaft. Alec froze. Slid his gaze down and looked at his hand. His heart crashed like cymbals.

Aw, hells.

He swallowed, but finally allowed himself to have a look. A true look at Zercy's huge, majestic cock. And man, was it that, all regally jutting, easily twelve inches and almost as thick as Alec's forearm. Meaning, nope, his fingertips did *not* touch while wrapped around it. Talk about some seriously impressive girth.

It was gorgeously proportioned, too. Alec eyed its generous glans. Definitely larger in ratio to its length than a human's. Beautifully bulbous, but not fat. Like some perfectly shaped lure, enticing its bedmates to come a little closer. Closer, so they could wrap their lips around its smooth head, then give the thing a long and lazy suck.

Which, in some inexplicable way, Alec wouldn't mind trying, but was far too distracted ogling something else. Exotic bands of gold encircling Zercy's erection, one at its base, one at the top beneath his glans. Holy cosmonaut. They looked sexy as hell. Hypnotically contrasting with his midnight purple flesh, gilded rings against a dark imposing shaft.

Alec inwardly smirked, supposing the top band was fitting, a mini crown for the king's *other* head.

"Tah," Zercy rumbled, interrupting his thoughts. "You like my handsome cock. Want to pet it."

Alec tensed. He'd been staring.

He quickly averted his gaze. "No. I was just—"

"Wanting a taste?"

Alec cut him a scathing look, opening his mouth to deny it, but then froze when something nudged his palm.

Shit. He was still holding Zercy's wood.

The king's lips curved.

Alec scowled and released his hold, but Zercy held his hand firmly in place.

"Kerra," the king murmured. *Relax.* "You are not done."

"Yeah, I am. I touched your dick like you asked, so now I'm finished."

"You think merely touching my cock has convinced me of your claim? Even now you do not hold it voluntarily."

Alec glared. The king could shove his need for proof up his ass. Steeling himself to say as much, Alec absently re-tightened his grip.

Zercy's eyes slid closed. "Tah ..."

Alec froze, distracted instantly. That husky growl was like a shot straight to his groin. There and to his brain, igniting his neurons with lust. Derailing his thoughts until his boner flat-out jumped.

No. He'd been getting ready to do something, but what?

He suddenly couldn't remember.

Screw it, who cared. He wanted to hear that again.

Heart hammering, he looked at Zercy. His eyes were still closed, and his mouth was parted, with the tips of his fangs just barely visible.

Alec licked his lips. Yeah, just one more squeeze and he'd be done. Just one more throaty rumble and he'd be set.

He looked down at his hand—or where he knew it to be—dwarfed inside the clutches of Zercy's fingers. God, he couldn't believe this. He was holding a Kríe's dick. An otherworldly purple alien's ginormous erection.

Whatever, something hot and hungry argued inside his brain. Truth be told, he loved the way it felt. Like a velvety-smooth rod of thick, hot granite against his hand.

He gave the thing a second, heartier squeeze.

Another heated growl curled in the base of Zercy's throat. Alec's dick went wild. This was so frickin' crazy. A heady thrill washed through him. This small power was exhilarating—and something he suddenly didn't want to lose.

Zercy's lashes slowly lifted. He met Alec's stare, then leisurely dragged their two fists up his shaft. Alec held his gaze, trapped in those smoldering auric eyes. Zercy pulled their fists back down again a moment later. More rumbles in his chest.

Oh, fuck. So sexy.

Alec's happy little reward for not resisting.

It made him feel drunk.

And hungry for more.

Zercy kept their eyes locked and did another up-and-down, sliding their fists from one band to the other. On the second trip, however, when they reached the top ring, Zercy wrapped their tangle of fingers around his crown. Alec squeezed it without prompting, then dragged his thumb across its slit.

A moan pushed past Zercy's lips. "Tah," he rasped. "Bellah kai." *Very good.* "Do not stop, *Alick*. Keep going."

CHAPTER NINETEEN

* * *

Alec's heartbeat raced faster. He shouldn't be enjoying this, reveling in the act of stroking Zercy's cock. But God help him, he was—and wanted to keep going. In truth, a part of him wanted to make Zercy come. It'd only be fair. Zercy made him come earlier. Right here on this very same bed.

Alec gave a tentative nod at Zercy's command to keep going, moving their fists together, establishing a pace. Zercy's eyes hooded lower, then a few strokes later, he let go completely of Alec's hand.

Alec slowed, feeling instantly and strangely exposed.

Because without the king's grip wholly covering his own, every action from this point forward was clearly voluntary. What he did to Zercy's dick, the sounds he drew from his throat. All done by choice.

Because Alec wanted to.

His stomach clenched restlessly. This was wrong. He shouldn't be doing this. He was a captive, for shit's sake. He should stop.

But before he could make himself let go and stand down, Zercy reached forward, clutched Alec's hips, and relocated him. Specifically, atop his lap so Alec straddled his thighs. Alec frowned, not understanding why he'd had to suddenly move, but nevertheless eased down gently and got situated. Didn't want to jostle that tail of his. His ass was already way too sensitive.

Zercy peered down his torso and smiled a little. "Continue."

Alec fought a grin and complied.

And just like that, he was back in heaven, enjoying the feast of five senses. The sight of virile Zercy subtly undulating beneath him. The warm savory smell of his arousal. The sound of each low moan as it crawled up his throat. The rigid intoxicating texture of his cock. Alec eyed Zercy's erection. His taste buds salivated. Only one thing left to experience. Zercy's flavor…

Alec frowned, pumping slowly. Something was really wrong with his head. He shouldn't want his *mouth* on Zercy, too. His hand was one thing. Not too overly intimate. But his lips on Zercy's skin? That was different.

He swallowed, his gut tightening, but as his gaze returned to Zercy's, something inside just sort of shut that worry off.

His fist picked up speed again.

Zercy hissed and clutched his knees, his short claws biting into Alec's skin. Alec's hard-on twitched excitedly. Oh yeah, the king was definitely feeling it—that decadent pressure inside his balls that *Alec* was building.

Zercy's eyes turned scorching. "Want to take you," he growled breathlessly. "Want to bury my cock in your heat and make you *writhe*."

Alec froze and warily stared at him. "That is *not* a viable option." Zercy's mega-dick would rip his ass in two.

Zercy's expression turned frustrated. Clenching his jaw, he muttered, "I know."

Alec exhaled, only partially relieved. Because in truth, goddamn, he was really horny, too—and still remembered well how good Krie dick felt. When Miros had stuffed him with his cock and made him come? Alec swore he'd never known such physical ecstasy.

But his ass had been under the influence of tachi—something that, unfortunately, they didn't have now. Which was probably a good thing, if Alec was going to be honest. Because with Miros, there hadn't been any real attraction. No true feelings of connection as they fucked. They'd just been two males working together for one cause. No messy emotions whatsoever to make shit complicated.

Something that Alec couldn't say about Zercy. Despite not understanding the hows or whys, he *was* attracted to Zercy. Always had been. A predicament that, deep down, he knew would cause problems if they ever found a way to have sex. If he gave himself willingly to the king, he'd get attached. He knew he would. And that just couldn't happen. Not under the circumstances he was bound to now.

Wrong fucking time, wrong fucking world.

Zercy growled and rocked his hips. The sight was intoxicating. Alec stifled a curse and got back to pumping. Could he get the king to come? What would it look like? What would it sound like? Time to add five more fingers and find out.

But right as he moved to throw his other fist into the mix, Zercy reached for his collar yet again.

"Need you closer," he rumbled, pulling Alec forward.

Alec tensed, letting go to brace both hands on Zercy's shoulders, his knees advancing to straddle the king's waist. "Shit, Kríe," he rasped, looking down at the guy. "How many more times are you gonna—"

"Do not stop what you were doing," the king demanded, cutting him off.

Alec peered into his eyes. Zercy wanted him back on his dick. Truth be told, Alec wanted back on it, too. He still hadn't made the big bastard come. Wanted to see Zercy lose all control.

Which meant Alec would have to support his weight with one arm.

Relinquishing one of Zercy's shoulders, he reclaimed the king's cock and got back to slow and steady stroking.

Zercy growled, pulling him closer by his collar to nuzzle his cheek. "Your touch… It is starting to convince me."

Alec coughed a wry laugh. "Just *starting* to?"

Zercy chuffed, nuzzling harder, then grazed a fang down Alec's jaw.

The tantalizing sensation dive-bombed straight to Alec's junk. He shuddered, dropping his weight down to his forearm instead, making his ass the highest point of his body. He couldn't help it, though. If he lowered it, he'd be sitting on Zercy's dick with his nut sac all pressed against its shaft. As it were—considering his new position straddling the king's waist—he was already poised halfway up the Kríe's erection. Which demoted him to only partial access of the thing, meaning he could only stroke its length from midpoint on.

Without looking, he envisioned Zercy's cock in his hand. His blood heated instantly. His hand picked up the pace.

Zercy seemed to like that and latched his teeth onto Alec's lobe. Using his free hand, he palmed Alec's nape and started kneading. Alec stifled a moan, muscles loosening fast. But those fingers didn't stay there for long. Soon they were slowly sliding lower down his back, grazing Alec's flesh with their claws. He shivered as heady current pooled in his tailbone, then quickly splintered out to all things sensitive.

Shit, that felt good. Way *too* good, in fact. His lust levels spiked through the roof.

Zercy passed the small of his back, brushing the thin band of his jockstrap. A second later, he eased to a stop at Alec's ass. Splaying his fingers, he gave an unhurried squeeze. "I am king and yet you somehow have me envying a tail."

Alec fought back a smile. Tried to focus on stroking. "Take it up with Lotis. Not my idea."

"Hmm," Zercy rumbled, sliding his hand toward the frond. "I would much rather take it up with you."

His thumb dipped between Alec's cheeks. Alec clenched with a start. It'd just swiped the base of his tail—and grazed his sphincter. Which, incidentally, was now tingling from the contact, needing urgently to swap that tail for something *purple*.

Which was madness. He shouldn't want Kríe dick up his ass.

Making the king come was one thing. Being reamed by him was another.

Alec swallowed a conflicted groan.

Zercy seemed to understand. With a growl, the king relented and move his hand. Not back up again, though. Lower. Down Alec's hamstring, giving subtle squeezes along the way. Alec's dick kicked in bliss, loving the zings each squeeze elicited. Like tantalizing kisses straight to his groin.

Alec shifted, trying to focus. To keep his fist moving on Zercy's cock. Wasn't easy, though. Zercy's touch was driving him wild. His less-than-gentle nuzzles weren't fucking helping, especially now that he'd added nips of teeth.

Zercy's hand reached the back of his knee and lingered briefly, then eased around front and slid back up. Alec sucked in a breath, tracking those fingers as they climbed. They were headed for his junk, he knew they were.

Higher… higher… higher they rose.

His boner bucked eagerly. Zercy's hand breached his groin. Alec opened his mouth—*uh!* The king just cupped his balls from underneath.

Alec froze. Stopped freaking breathing. "Kríe," he rasped. "What are you doing?"

Zercy chuckled against his ear. Gave his nuts a frisky squeeze. "I am fondling your balls. What are *you* doing?"

Uh, currently nothing, Alec thought with a frown. All movement on his part had ceased completely. His mind spun. He should resume. Get back on track with his task. No, hold on. Zercy needed to let go. If he didn't, bad things would surely happen between them. Bad things that would feel *really good.*

Problem was, Alec's brain wasn't firing at the moment, and couldn't send the order to desist. Not that it mattered. If Zercy's groping hadn't short-circuited it, that finger caressing Alec's taint now surely would.

A moan slid up his throat as he tried to close his thighs, but he was straddling Zercy's waist, so that was futile. He rocked his hips restlessly, brows pinched. "Fuck, Kríe..."

"You do not like?" Zercy growled, his timbre like a drug. Clutching Alec's sac, he added another digit and lengthened their strokes. From the base of Alec's nuts back to his uber-sensitive hole, two fingers lazily sliding back and forth.

Alec undulated, eyes closing. "Aw, shit—Please—Not there—"

Zercy doled another nuzzle. They were getting more aggressive. "Then where?" he rumbled, biting the shell of Alec's ear. His two short claws grazed Alec's taint.

"Fuck!" Alec's whole body jerked. He shook his head. "I..." His brows pinched. He couldn't find the words. Because a part of him *did* want his hand right there. His *other* part just didn't want to admit it.

The king withdrew his fingers from between Alec's thighs, his other hand still clutching Alec's collar. "Your silence, it leaves me no choice but to guess." He curled his fingers around Alec's dick.

Alec groaned with a shudder and clenched his molars—which promptly drew Zercy's attention to his jaw. The king bit down loosely on the bone with his teeth, then playfully gnawed along it while starting to stroke.

Pleasure flared through Alec's cock.

Oh, fuck...

His eyes rolled back again. He couldn't think. Gripping tighter, he upped his pace, instantly distracted by Zercy's glans. How its hard ridge teased his palm, yeah, but what he especially found riveting? How it snagged that stretch of skin between his index finger and thumb every time he gave an upward pump.

Zercy growled and squeezed the head of Alec's cock in return.

More bliss shot down his shaft. Alec bit back a moan.

Zercy huskily chuckled and bit his jaw harder. "You like me there."

Yes, yes he did. In fact, he totally loved it.

Zercy kept on with his stroking, clearly not waiting for a reply.

Alec loosed a ragged curse. God, that felt incredible. Earlier, when Lotis said they could fuck with their jockstraps on, his meaning—Alec now realized—had been twofold. The enyid would stay snug enough to not hinder the act, but it also wouldn't lessen the sensation. Something Alec could give testament to. His dick definitely felt naked in Zercy's hand.

Of their own volition, his hips started to rock.

Felt too good. He was going to cave.

Zercy rumbled dark and heated against his skin. "Tah, *Alick*. Your body. It is trying to speak. To tell me what it wants when you will not."

Shit.

The king growled and nudged his nose up underneath Alec's ear. "You want to fuck, *Alick*. Just say it. No one will hear this truth but me."

Alec groaned. Because honestly, why deny the obvious? Besides, a confession wasn't the same as a green light. They couldn't have sex regardless; they didn't fit.

"Yeah," he rasped. "I do, okay? Not that it makes a difference."

Zercy rumbled in approval. Stroked Alec's dick in blatant praise. "Tah, because your star flower is too small."

"No," Alec grunted, back to rocking his hips, "because your mammoth friggin' cock is too big."

Zercy chuffed at that, but then quieted. Even his fist slowed to a crawl. "I wish we were compatible. In all ways, but especially this." He nuzzled Alec's cheek, thrummed warm breath against his ear. "I would sink into your heat and bring you ecstasy."

Alec's whole body sizzled, his hole clenching at the thought.

In this moment, he wished they were compatible, too.

Without warning, Zercy let go and palmed his ass cheek instead. "Whether my cock is too big or your star flower too small, I can still fuck you well in *other* ways."

Alec exhaled at the reprieve, but then stilled at his words. "Other ways? Wait, what?" He tried to rise back up onto his hand.

Zercy held him in place though, via that collar. "Be still," he rumbled. "I will show you." His hand on Alec's ass started to move.

Alec tensed. Oh, God. It was headed for his tail.

The plug shifted subtly.

He'd taken hold.

Alec's heart went berserk. He couldn't let him do this. Couldn't let him use that tail to literally fuck him. It'd be wrong, no matter how good it'd probably feel. He was his captive for fuck's sake. But the problem with that argument? What kind of *captive* would *voluntarily* jack off his captor?

That wicked root lodged in his channel eased in deeper, then pulled back just enough to tug at his sphincter. Raw bliss engulfed Alec's prostate, as sharp pain shot through his ring.

He groaned, "Oh, *fuck*," and pressed his forehead to Zercy's temple. "That thing's too big too, Kríe. Not gonna work. Not for that."

The king growled softly. "Reesha tay." *I will not harm you.* He repeated the same small action, but nothing more. Just that steady push deeper, then that easy retreat, giving his backdoor no more pressure than a nudge.

It felt incredible.

Alec's g-spot sang.

Zercy sank in deep a third time with more of the same.

Alec moaned, unable to help it. His channel was blissing. Hell, even his asshole seemed to like the attention. Evidently, now that it knew it wasn't in danger of getting ripped open, it'd actually relaxed a tiny bit.

Shit yeah, if this was all that Zercy had planned for Alec's ass, then Alec didn't want to resist anymore. He needed it. Maybe it'd ultimately take off the edge.

Plus, he still wanted to make the big Kríe come.

Zercy pushed the tail in deep again.

Alec shuddered and rocked his hips. Then tried like hell to focus on Zercy's cock.

Up and down—up and down—along the top half of his shaft, his grip expanding as he circled the king's broad glans.

Zercy growled low, "Tah, *Alick*," and backtracked with that root. Alec could feel his ring protruding under the pressure.

But just as that elusive burn threatened to flare, Zercy stopped just like always and retreated. Which ricocheted all attention straight to Alec's G.

"Fuuuck," Alec rasped. His ass was in rapture. And his nuts felt like they might start trying to climb. His strokes turned erratic. Concentration was getting harder.

Zercy rumbled low and closed his teeth back down on Alec's lobe. Then he released the tail to grip his own cock. Their hands brushed on Alec's down stroke. But Zercy's kept sliding lower than Alec's could reach. But why? What was he doing? A second later, Alec had his answer. Their fists reconnected, but Zercy's kept on going, pushing Alec's hand straight up his shaft. Next thing Alec knew, his fingers were wet and slippery.

Looked like the king just drew a batch of precum.

Guess he thought Alec needed some lube to work with. Very astute, actually. Lube would definitely make things easier. Alec smoothed it over Zercy's glans, then down thing king's length. And just like that, he was back to doing his thing.

Zercy resumed, too, reaching again for Alec's ass. He didn't grip his tail, though. Instead, he traced its base, slowly running his finger around Alec's ring. Alec's lashes fluttered drunkenly. Felt so warm and slick back there. Which made sense, he supposed. Zercy couldn't've dodged all that precum. For certain, some had gotten on his hand.

That tail pushed in deep again.

"Uh!" Alec pumped faster.

Zercy growled and tugged it back against his entrance.

Alec's heart rate kicked up a notch.

He could feel his asshole straining—never to the point though, that it actually hurt.

The king tugged at his earlobe, then bit back down on his jaw, soft snarls erotically lacing every breath. And Alec loved it. Loved those aggressive front teeth gripping hold. Not breaking skin, just possessively laying claim. Because in this moment, with Zercy handling his 'limitations' so attentively, Alec didn't mind pretending he was his.

The king moved things faster until he'd found a suitable pace, then maintained that pace and got back to nuzzling. Licking and shoving his face into Alec's as he rocked his hips and worked that buried tail.

Alec's mind spun deliriously. His boner kicked, too, his nuts getting desperate to unload. Not thinking, just acting on pure instinct, he spread his knees to get lower and started grinding. Up and down the lower half of the king's massive cock, rubbing their balls together but mostly their dicks.

Screw it. Didn't care. He needed to come so bad.

Just this once. He'd get his freak on just this once.

"Tah..." Zercy thrummed. Oh, God. His voice was like a drug. Tugging harder on Alec's collar, he bit his neck. Again, not hard enough to puncture the flesh, but Alec sure as hell could feel the bastard's fangs.

He stiffened, then undulated, derailed instantly by that tail. It'd just pushed against his G and lit more fireworks.

"F-F-Fuck—" he gasped, gripping Zercy's shoulder with his other hand, pretty sure his blunt nails were leaving marks.

Zercy chuckled and kept going. Just kept fucking his ass, the length of each plunge at most two inches. Pathetic, but whatever. It felt fabulous. To the point that his thighs had started shaking. Goddamn, his prostate. It was making him mindless. Like the thing—no joke—was going to blow.

His heart hammered wilder. His lungs sawed for air. "Sh-Shit," he panted urgently. "You're gonna m-make my ass c-come—"

"Bellah," Zercy growled. "The first is going to be delicious."

The *first?* Alec thought in the whirlwind of his mind. But before he could ask, Zercy accelerated his speed and, yup, threw him over the edge.

Alec's orgasm detonated.

"UNNNGGGFFFUUUCK!!" he shouted. White hot rapture just blasted his G. His spine arched, his body quaked, as his ass furiously clenched.

But the king still didn't stop. Still kept on going.

Which quickly shot Alec's climax to critical.

"Ungh—SHIT!!" he belted, his G exploding again. His channel went wild, stripping the last of his control, forcing his ass to bear down as hard as it could.

"UUHHH!!" he strained out, so loud he'd never be able to forgive himself. No doubt, veins were even protruding from his neck.

Not that Zercy noticed. He was busy freeing part of that root, using Alec's pushes to slide it loose. Alec panted, trembling wildly as his orgasm ebbed, his ass still bearing down against his will. In smaller bursts, though. Like little aftershocks.

Zercy growled and took advantage of that, too. Plunging the tail back and forth through his sphincter, steadily, through the duration of each hard push. And yet, the very second Alec's rectum stopped contracting, Zercy immediately paused to spare him undue pain.

Alec moaned. By the feel of things, the king had halted mid-delve, with the root lodged at perhaps its thickest point. Alec's asshole strained anxiously. It was nearly too much. But under these conditions, with Zercy acclimating him this way, the true pain somehow stayed just out of reach.

Catching his breath, Alec swallowed. "That thing feels huge."

Zercy rumbled dark and wickedly. "Tah, but now you are adjusted. Now I can *properly* fuck your little star."

Alec's heart skipped a beat. "That wasn't proper before?"

Zercy chuffed and bit his jaw. "Mah. That was just to loosen you up. There is no pain now, yes? You just feel very full."

"Um… not at the moment, no, but…"

He was still coming down from that O. He couldn't think. Did he want what Zercy was proposing? Or would he end up unable to walk? All he knew was that that orgasm had drained him like a noodle, and apparently it was just the prelude.

"But?" Zercy murmured. "But what? What is wrong?"

"I…" Alec floundered. *I have no clue.*

Zercy smiled against his cheek. "Ah. Of course. Your cock wants freedom."

Again, he let go of Alec's tail and reached between them. Evidently, releasing Alec's *collar* was out of the question. Fingers grazed Alec's hip, then hooked his jockstrap's waistband. A small tug later and the thing felt noticeably looser—like Zercy had sliced through part of the wrap with his claw.

"Lift your hips," the king commanded.

Alec hesitated, but ultimately complied. In truth, his dick would *love* to finally breathe.

Zercy's fingers moved over and pinched hold of the clingy material, right at the base of Alec's happy trail. Alec tensed, then sucked in a breath as Zercy pulled it from his skin, then peeled it down his length and off his balls. Damn, felt so weird. Not like a condom at all. Although now his dick truly *was* naked.

Alec's pulse pounded restlessly. Zercy eased the scrap lower, then sliced another spot and tugged it free. Two seconds later, it landed by the king's discarded skirt.

Zercy curled his big fingers around Alec's—which, yeah, were still clutching the king's shaft. Up and down, he guided them. A thick moan breached his lips. "Your soft hand on my cock... I never want it to leave."

Alec closed his eyes and cursed. Tightened his grip. Tried not to think. Just focus on Zercy's beautiful dick. Because the thing *was* beautiful. No point in denying that fact. Beautiful just like the rest of him. So perfectly primal.

Zercy's vocals rumbled heatedly. He rocked his powerful hips, the movement causing their erections to make contact. Alec's boner twitched eagerly. Zercy heeded its call, using his thumb to hook Alec's dick and pull it close. The instant their cocks were flush, he wrapped his hand around both, then paused, clearly waiting for Alec to follow.

Right. Group hug. Until now, he hated those. This one however, seemed... yeah, way more appealing.

Uncurling his fingers, he added his own dick to the mix. And just like that, they were back to steadily stroking. Pleasure surged down

Alec's length and re-stimulated his crotch. A break-time's-over shout out to his balls.

He stifled a moan. He'd had a similar exchange with Miros, but it hadn't felt like this. This felt different. Intimate. Not frantic to fuck. To come for the sole purpose of ending an affliction. No, this felt genuine, with not one trace of exploitation. Because this shit he was doing in that alcove with Zercy? He was doing it because he wanted to, with no ulterior motives. He'd long since proved what he'd needed to. Chet was cleared.

Zercy paused, but not for long, and clutched their crowns firmly. "Hold them together," he rasped in Alec's ear. "Do not let them go. Keep them here."

Alec's whole body thrummed. He nodded and held them snug. Zercy let go and reached down lower between their bodies. His fist bumped into Alec's from below a moment later. More silky-thick fluid oozed over Alec's fingers.

Zercy guided Alec's hand down their shafts and out of the way, then did the honors of juicing up their dicks. "Continue now," he ordered. God, his timbre sounded starved.

Alec's whole body tingled in response.

But as he got back to stroking, Zercy didn't resume with him. Instead, he swiped up the rest of the precum still on his stomach. Once his fingertips were loaded, he reached around to Alec's backside and made quick work of lubing things there, too.

Alec bit his lip, fist pumping, as Zercy slicked up his ring, the anticipation of what was to come making him crazy. Zercy's touch disappeared, then the tail subtly moved. No doubt, he'd just taken sturdy hold.

Warm lips brush Alec's jaw. A hot tongue licked his ear. He shivered, exhaling roughly.

Zercy rumbled and bit his lobe. "I am ready to fuck you. To take you apart. Cannot wait to spill my seed all over your body."

"Fuuuck," Alec breathed. He couldn't wait, either.

"Push," Zercy growled. "And do not stop."

Aw, God. No tachi. Here we go.

Heart jackhammering, Alec braced himself and dutifully obeyed.

The second he bore down, the king got to work, making like a piston with that root. Delving it in and out, slowly first, then gradually faster, gliding with little resistance into his channel.

"*Shiiiiiit,*" Alec groaned, as pleasure mushroomed deep inside. So badly, he wanted to clench. To grip that tail and squeeze tight. But somehow, he knew that he shouldn't.

So, he didn't. Just kept pushing as he jacked Zercy's cock, listening to all the scandalously juicy sounds. Of his fist as he sluiced it up and down their glistening cocks, but especially of that lubed tail spearing his hole. The way it *shhhlurped* to the hilt, then *shhhlicked* right back out, again and again, the sounds so succulent, it made him moan.

It made his brain check out too, leaving that root with free rein. Of his asshole and rectum, but also his prostate. Which, incidentally, was on cloud nine, pumping his passage with rapture for each connect.

And there were a lot of connects. Zercy's rhythm was swift, impaling his ass as he would if truly fucking. No, scratch that. His hips would definitely be going faster. Alec wasn't sure how, but he knew this for certain: when Zercy fucked, he fucked like a beast.

Pressure surged in Alec's groin. Tongues of bliss teased his cock, his strokes to their erections were taking their toll. He could feel his balls tightening, climbing higher under the assault. Of all those lashes of euphoria snaking down his shaft, yeah, but also from the blitz around back. All those jarring pulses punching from his G.

He squirmed, trying to take it, all those mind-blowing sensations, but the ecstasy bombarding him was relentless.

"Shit—" he panted, "Fuck—" His abdomen danced furiously.

Zercy snarled and pulled him closer by his collar. His teeth secured hold again, this time on Alec's shoulder. Something Alec was beginning to find *really hot*. Like some primordial instinct the king was succumbing to, to immobilize his prey.

Zercy thrust into Alec's hand, shoving his cock through Alec's fist. Then he bit a little harder and feverishly sucked.

Fuuuuck. Alec was close. Ready to come harder than hell. But by the look of things, Zercy wasn't far behind. Meaning, soon he'd see the mighty king erupt.

Zercy plunged his tail deeper, faster, harder, as Alec bore down. But it was getting harder to concentrate on pushing. Save for a couple split seconds to suck in breath, he'd been damn near bearing down the whole time.

Little snarls started rolling in a steady stream. Alec pumped their shafts faster with a curse. He wanted to set Zercy off like a bomb, but couldn't without lighting his own ass up, too. Zercy wanted their dicks jerked together for the duration.

But the pressure, oh God, he wouldn't last much longer. Hardcore ecstasy was blasting his nether regions from every direction. Urgently, he shifted atop the king's powerful body, grinding his dick, thrusting his hips, as he pumped. But, goddamn, that tail—his ass was about to come again.

His breaths came fast and furious, his mind spinning, his body reeling. The orgasm charging his prostate was almost there. His muscles quaked and shuddered. Still, he pushed against that root, loud moans tumbling hard past his lips.

"Zercy—" he gasped frantically, digging his fingers into Zercy's shoulder. He needed something to ground him so freaking bad.

The king unlatched his teeth and jerked Alec's head up by his collar, looking shocked as he met Alec's eyes.

Now.

Not thinking, Alec lunged for his anchor, attacking Zercy's mouth with zealous need. Zercy froze, exuding surprise, but when Alec shoved in his tongue, he growled and resumed his vigorous fucking. Just kept on going as Alec devoured his lips, gasping and panting and moaning against his mouth.

Not that the Kríe king was kissing him back. He did keep his jaw slack and his lips parted though, with a hot little backdrop of husky rumbles. In truth, Zercy seemed too enthralled to reciprocate, with just enough focus to keep fucking—and, as a result, slam-dunked that climax straight home.

"FUUUCK!!" Alec shouted, his mouth wide against to Zercy's. His body shot rigid, then started to shake. "Zercy—" he croaked. *"Ungh!* Zercy— *Fuck!"*

"*Alick*—" Zercy grunted, hard and breathless against his lips. He ground their cocks together with determined ferocity.

Oh, fuck. He was going to make Alec come on both sides.

He cursed and started to scramble, tangling their dicks, his prostate orgasming. He couldn't handle two. Not at once. Not right now. He was barely keeping his sanity through just the one. But right as he readied to plead for time, Zercy pulled the tail free and tossed it aside.

He snarled and palmed the back of Alec's head. Then he heatedly crushed their lips back together.

Alec's heart derailed instantly, his whole body lighting up, and not just because of the endorphins. Zercy was kissing him back—or at least, he was trying to, seemingly imitating what he'd remembered from Alec's efforts. And it was beautiful. Utterly beautiful. His motivations transparent. Zercy was trying to stabilize him, just as Alec had tried earlier, but he was also trying to give human passion. A gesture Kríe weren't familiar with, going by Zercy's initial response. But he was trying. Trying to reach Alec through Alec's ways.

Alec moaned against his mouth as their hips ground faster and kissed the king with all that he had. After all, though his one O had finally receded, the one in his balls was ready to rip.

Their lips moved feverishly, their tongues a tangled dance, keeping him afloat as their final storm descended. Zercy's fingers clutched tighter on the back of his skull. Alec gripped Zercy's side, abandoning their dicks. Had no choice, their boners were grinding so hard that his hand no longer had any room.

Zercy's fangs knocked Alec's teeth. Alec grinned though wild pants. Because even though his efforts were all awkward and clumsy, Zercy's kiss was still the best Alec ever had.

Pressure surged in Alec's nuts. His brows pinched. "Aw, fuck." His rocking hips turned erratic. "Zercy—*shit*—"

The king growled, low and urgent, as if on the same page, then actually released Alec's collar to palm his ass. "*Tah, Alick,*" he snarled, his voice like honeyed gravel. He ground their dicks even tighter. "So very close."

Alec nodded frantically, the onset of climax welling fast. "Yeah— *Uh*—*Fuck*—I'm talkin' seconds—"

Zercy chuffed against his mouth, the chuckle breathless and tight. But then his eyes rolled back, and his six-pack started clenching. His claws dug into Alec's butt cheeks. His thrusting hips twitched.

"*Alick*," he gasped hoarsely. His dark brows pinched hard. Snarling, he bit Alec's lip. "Spill with me *now*."

His words hit Alec's brain like a freight train, then plummeted into his crotch and lit him up. Orgasm crashed hard. His body went taut. "*Shit!*" he howled, unloading. "Zercy!—*Shit!*"

Not that Zercy heard. He'd just been brutally slammed, too. Head kicked back, he arched on a bellow, both hands clamped on Alec's ass cheeks as he came. And holy hell, Alec could feel every pulse up Zercy's shaft, against his stomach and his own bucking dick. He could also feel Zercy hitting him with huge pelts of hot cum. Which, wow, there was a lot of, and the stuff was still coming, unlike Alec, whose load was quickly puttering out.

He panted, catching his breath, then jerked as more nailed his ear. He chuckled, but the king was wholly oblivious, still pumping small, pearly jets from his cock.

Alec watched him, entranced, Zercy's expression pure rapture. Lips parted, fangs glistening, masculine features tense, knees drawn, feet planted flat on the bed.

Zercy grunted, then groaned raggedly, his head still back, his spine still arched. When his cock finally calmed, he slumped back down. His chest rose and fell. His arms dropped to his sides. "*Alick*..." he moaned, his timbre thick, eyelids closed. "... I have never spilled so hard in all my life."

CHAPTER TWENTY

***

Fuck. Zercy's sated voice. It made Alec's muscles go limp. He sagged in post-fuck bliss atop the king's chest. *Yeah, oh yeah...* That beefy shoulder was like a pillow. All big and warm and firm against Alec's cheek.

Zercy's hand settled onto the small of his back, and for a long comfortable moment, they laid in silence. Alec's body hummed happily. His brain readied for sleep. Until a curious sound cut through his haze.

Brows furrowing, he listened. Something very close was thrumming. He could literally feel the vibrations against his cheek. His frown deepened. But what was it? It sounded oddly familiar....

Then it hit him. What it reminded him of.

He smiled. No way.

Lifting his head, he looked at the king. "Are you..." He quirked a brow. "Are you *purring?*"

Zercy's drowsy eyes darkened. His lips curved. "Perhaps."

Alec's smile spread wider. He couldn't help it. The sentiment was just so bizarrely cool. And while Miros had emanated something similar at the fort, it hadn't sounded nearly as pronounced. Like the emotion that triggered it was stronger in Zercy. And coming from a much deeper place.

Alec's eyes grew heavy. That soft pumping was strangely soothing, lulling him into a state of unexpected peacefulness. He looked away and cleared his throat, trying to shake it off. He shouldn't feel this content, not in Zercy's arms. Nor as utterly okay with what just happened. What he'd willingly done in passion to the king's fantastical body. What he'd allowed the king, in turn, to do to his.

As if sensing his thoughts, Zercy ceased all happy thrumming. Rolling them over, he pressed his waist between Alec's thighs. Alec grunted under his weight until the king lifted his torso, propping his hands on either side of Alec's head. Alec peered up into his eyes.

Zercy smiled and scanned Alec's chest. "You are a mess," he rumbled softly.

Alec blinked, then coughed a laugh. "Yeah, you're not faring so well yourself."

Zercy's eyes straight-up twinkled. "I do not know what you mean." Glancing around, he grabbed a small swath of fur, one of many amidst his sea of cozy bedding. With one arm supporting him, he quickly wiped his chest and cock, then tossed it from their nest and looked at Alec. "See? I am not messy. Only you."

Alec's lips twitched, his head still partially floating on cloud nine. "What, you're not gonna help me out, too? Eighty percent of what's on me is yours."

Zercy chuckled, "Indeed," and sat back on his heels, then spread his knees and tugged Alec's ass between his thighs. "Do not worry," he draped Alec's legs over his, "I would never neglect your delicious little body."

Instinctively, Alec tensed. What was the king up to now?

Zercy grasped Alec's right hand and brought it to his mouth. "I will start with this first." He dragged his tongue up Alec's palm. "It worked very hard for us tonight."

Alec's jaw went slack. Zercy smiled and met his gaze, slipping his tongue between two of Alec's fingers.

"Shit," Alec breathed.

The king's pupils dilated. He sucked on each digit, then gave the tip of one a nip.

Air rushed from Alec's lungs.

Zercy grinned and resumed, unhurriedly lapping clean each sticky crevice.

Alec fought the urge to moan. For crying out loud, Zercy was licking his freaking hand, not sucking his dick.

Zercy paused a moment later and pressed his lips to Alec's palm. "You spoke my name," he murmured quietly.

Alec stilled. "What do you mean?"

Zercy smiled. "My name. You have never spoken it. But you did tonight. As we fucked."

Alec's heart lurched. He didn't remember. But either way, that wasn't good. Already, he'd kissed the guy, which in hindsight wasn't smart. The urge had just been so instinctive, so overpowering. But to have said his name, too? That spoke volumes.

About stuff he didn't want to consider.

He shifted atop the furs, stomach anxious. "Huh… That's… *Huh*."

The king's eyes hooded. Twining their fingers, he nosed Alec's knuckles. "To hear it on your tongue for the very first time… as you writhed in the throes… I was bespelled."

Alec smiled in spite of himself. The things Zercy said sometimes, so *out there*. And often—just like now—oddly flattering.

He cleared his throat. Chuckled awkwardly. "Okay… That's… great."

Zercy eyed him, then chuffed, amused. "Say it now."

Alec's smile faded. "What?"

"Say my name again, *now*."

Ugh. But why? Alec frowned at his predicament. He didn't want to say it but denying Zercy was futile. Screw it. Whatever. It'd be different this time anyway. Wasn't like he'd be orgasming as he said it.

"Zercy."

The king smiled.

Alec's heart clenched.

"Again."

What? *Again?* Alec perused his lips. "Why?"

Zercy's lids eased lower. "Is it so hard to say? Perhaps my name on your lips makes you needy."

Alec stiffened, appalled. "Your name does *not* make me *needy*."

"Then *say it*."

"Fine," he ground out. "Zer—*unnnnngh*—cy."

Goddamnit.

That bastard just squeezed his dick.

"*Tahhh…*" Zercy rumbled with a smirk, letting go. "It sounded just like that. Very pleasing."

Alec scowled half-heartedly and flipped him the bird, fighting off a grin of his own.

Zercy chuckled and leaned forward. "Bayo ochay." *Funny pet.* Then he dipped down and dragged his tongue over Alec's pec. Right up the middle, hitting his nipple along the way.

Alec sucked in a breath, feeling it instantly harden. His other did the same beneath Zercy's dreads. So velvety, with their softly clinking gems and subtle weight, all tickling his nub into a little rigid point.

"Mmm. So messy..." Zercy growled, beginning again, this time laving one side of Alec's collarbone.

Alec stifled a moan. That was sensitive terrain. He shifted atop the bedding, suddenly feeling caged in, the bulk of Zercy's body just inches above him. His pulse shifted gears, running a little bit faster. The king's proximity, *and that tongue*, were going to make his dick hard again.

Palming Zercy's chest, he gave a tentative push. "For real, Krie? You can't seriously plan to clean me off like this."

The king lifted his head. Donned a sassy wolfish grin. "Actually, I can. And I will. I am king." He clutched Alec's wrists and pinned his hands above his head. "This will not hurt. If it does, I will stop."

His smile turned smug as he dipped back down. The Krie knew damn well it'd never hurt. It'd feel something *else* entirely.

But to argue was pointless. Zercy did what he wanted, pushing his boundaries with Alec to the edge. Although, in fairness, Alec knew that were he to truly resist Zercy's advances, the king would ultimately yield and not force him. Problem was, right now, as Zercy lapped and suckled his skin, Alec found it really hard to *want* to resist.

Meaning, yet another standoff that Zercy would win.

Closing his eyes, Alec surrendered to his pampering, relaxing against the king's obstinate hold. A heartbeat later, Zercy focused on his neck. But first he had to lose Alec's collar. It hit the chamber floor not five seconds later, then Zercy was dragging long licks up the side of Alec's throat.

Soft little growls emerged, tickling Alec's skin. Alec twitched and bit his lip. Zercy lapped up under his lobe, sending tendrils of bliss straight to his crotch. Things only got worse, though, when he swiped its sticky shell and realized Alec's ear needed much attention.

Chuffing, as if amused by the firing range of his cock, Zercy delved the tip of his tongue into Alec's canal.

Alec gasped with a start, eyes popping open in alarm.

Zercy chuckled and did it again. Every muscle in Alec's body locked up tight.

Frantically, he squirmed. His ears were sensitive. And one of his most powerful erogenous zones. "Zercy!" he gasped. "No—Please—Too ticklish!"

But Zercy didn't merely ignore his pleas, he plopped his weight on Alec's torso to keep him steady. Steady, while he drew Alec's ear *into his mouth* and happily laved each cum-slicked nook and cranny. Over and around, then back into that canal, working it so intently, Alec yowled. Couldn't help it, goddamnit. And now his dick was hard.

Thankfully, Zercy relented with a laugh not long after. "Nira, so sensitive." He lifted his weight. "I must remember to clean your little ears more often."

Alec shot him a glower, all but panting again. "Let's not and say we did, how 'bout that?"

Zercy smiled one of the biggest smiles Alec had seen from him yet. He didn't reply, though. Just got back to cleaning, dragging his tongue along Alec's jaw and under his chin. Alec's eyes slid closed, his irritation receding fast. Because, truth be told, that felt amazing.

Zercy made it to his cheek. Licked it softly. Slowly. Then his lips brushed feather-lightly over Alec's. Alec froze, lids still shut. Oh, God. What was Zercy doing? Surely, he wasn't trying to—Another graze. Shit. He was. Alec's heart took off racing. They could *not* kiss again. Not here. Not in this state. Alec was *sober*, for crying out loud. Not mindlessly drunk on desire.

"*Alick*... Open your eyes," Zercy murmured in his lilt.

Alec swallowed and lifted his lashes.

Zercy met his gaze. "There was something else you did while I was fucking your ass."

Alec cringed at his bluntness.

"You put your lips on mine. Aggressively. It was strange..." He paused, his eyes thoughtful. Tilting his head, he furrowed his brow. "And then you shoved your little tongue inside my mouth."

He seemed so perplexed.

Alec coughed out a laugh. "Right. Yeah. I remember."

Zercy regarded him. "Why did you do that?"

Loaded question if ever there was one.

Alec sobered and averted his gaze. "I was just... Shit, I dunno... It's a human thing, I guess."

"Does this human thing have a name?"

Alec fought the urge to smile. "Yeah. It's called kissing."

Zercy quieted, then seemed to try the word on for size. "Kissing," he rumbled. "A peculiar act, indeed. But I liked it... It was pleasing. Kiss me again."

Alec's eyes shot back to his. "Uh... *No*."

"Tah."

"*No*."

"Why not?"

"*Because*," Alec scrambled to explain. Kríe were so dense. "That kind of thing's intimate."

"Intimate."

"Yeah."

"As in, reserved for someone to whom you are attracted."

"*Yes. Exactly*. Not just any—" Alec froze.

Son of a bitch.

Zercy grinned, fangs flashing. "That is right. You are attracted to *me, Alick*. So, we kiss." His lips engulfed Alec's.

Alec stiffened, eyes wide, even as Zercy's thick lashes slid closed. This was all wrong. They weren't lovers in bed. He turned his head slightly, hoping to give Zercy the hint, but damn it, the king just growled and followed his mouth.

Alec stilled, heart pounding. He didn't know what to do. Because clearly, Zercy was just trying to exchange more affection, no doubt believing that Alec inwardly wanted the same. Something, in Zercy's defense, he was well in his boundaries to assume. For shit's sake, Alec just gave the Kríe free rein over his body, specifically to prove he *was* attracted to the guy.

But still. Their dynamic wasn't simple black and white. It was complicated and this would only make things worse. Problem was, as Alec lay beneath the king's body deliberating, Zercy had started doing that adorable thing again. Awkwardly trying to mimic Alec's kiss from earlier but failing—rather endearingly—despite his efforts. He needed better instruction. Probably just one more lesson, when he was focused and paying attention, not blind with lust.

Alec's heart thumped faster. He shouldn't encourage him. But for some reason, he wanted to help him out. Not because he'd enjoy it more if Zercy was practiced—quite honestly, he really liked his clumsy kisses. But because it would make the king happy on several fronts. And for some messed up reason, despite everything he should be pissed at him for, Alec still enjoyed making Zercy smile.

Fine. Just this once, Alec thought. He'd lead the king.

After, that is, Zercy concluded his current endeavor; cleaning Alec's teeth with his tongue while eating his face.

Alec laughed before he could stop himself. Zercy's kiss just felt so ridiculous.

The king paused, their noses mashed together, and opened his eyes. "*Alick*, this is not how it felt before."

"No," Alec laughed even harder, "it's not. Let go of my wrists, and I'll show you."

Zercy eyed him. "Your hands were not involved the last time."

"Just do it."

Zercy did.

Alec palmed his pointed ears—God, his head was big. He forgot sometimes how huge these Kríe were—then tilted his face just so and fused their mouths. Instantly, Zercy moved his eager lips against Alec's.

"Stop, Kríe," Alec murmured. "Just relax for a minute and learn."

Zercy quieted with a rumble. Alec exhaled and closed his eyes. He couldn't believe he was doing this. His motto tonight, it seemed. He pressed their lips together. Once, then twice. From this angle, then that. Parting his mouth for each connect, loosely closing it for each withdraw.

Zercy nodded, his dreads gently grazing Alec's chest. "Tah…" He absently gripped Alec's biceps. Hot current rushed up his arms.

Alec canted his head the other way and slid his tongue between Zercy's lips. The king's fingers tightened. That move clearly excited him. Which, in turn, excited Alec a little bit, too. He delved inside deeper but didn't have to go far. Zercy's tongue was easy to find—and surprisingly well mannered. Staying put instead of attacking like a shark.

Alec's insides lit brighter with every languid stroke he gave it. Back and forth along the top, slowly circling around its sides, each warm rub drawing growls from Zercy's chest. Alec loosed a silent moan. He fucking loved those heady sounds...

Abruptly, the king pulled back. Alec peeled open his eyes.

Zercy met his gaze and grinned. "Now I try."

Alec smiled, lids hooded. "Alright, big guy. Let's see how well you follow—*ungmfph.*"

The king seized his mouth before he could finish. And holy hell, he'd paid attention. Talk about a quick study. His lips were moving like pros. What's more, he wasn't merely simulating Alec's kiss, but embellishing it with hot little accents. Like teasing Alec's tongue with just the firm tip of his own, or tickling Alec's lower lip with his fangs.

The king was being frisky. Not trying to seduce. Behaving with innocent intent. Kind of ironic, considering it was times such as these that he seduced Alec's sensibilities the fastest.

Alec's pulse kicked up speed. His dick hardened. His body heated. He did *not*, however, have the strength for round two. Which was a good thing. Too many lines had been crossed already.

A moment later, Zercy severed their kiss.

Alec lifted his lids.

Zercy met his eyes and smiled. "I like kissing."

Alec blinked, feeling flushed—and pleasantly dazed. "Don't be expecting that on the reg, Kríe. I ain't your ho."

Zercy's eyes glittered. His smile widened. But he didn't reply. Just got back to his initial task at hand. Cleaning Alec up with his big warm tongue, laving it slowly in repeated upward strokes. His soft pumping purr rose back two seconds later, filling the quiet again with soothing cadence.

Alec closed his eyes as the king worked his way back down his throat. On the other side this time. Fortunately, that ear had dodged all cum. Then he leisurely lapped the whole of Alec's chest. His pecs, their nipples—Alec moaned in euphoria. His abdomen, licking every sticky smear. Clearing every puddle, swiping every glistening drop.

Alec exhaled, utterly relaxed. Zercy's ministrations were paradise, melting him mind and body into the furs. So much so that when the king reached his groin, Alec didn't bother resisting, just went with the flow. Wasn't like he needed to worry about getting an erection. He'd been hard the whole time, and Zercy knew it.

Zercy lapped along each crease between his hips and his thighs, then detoured lower while pushing up Alec's knees. Warm wet muscle delved between his cheeks and got busy caressing Alec's hole with cleansing swipes. Warning bells sounded, but Alec's brain shut them down. Because, again, the king wasn't trying to seduce. He was clearly just tending to his bedmate. Cleaning the mess they'd made. Properly. Thoroughly. Which, while unorthodox to cultures like Alec's, was still a gesture worthy of appreciation.

Besides, it felt... God, absolutely incredible. He'd only had a tongue lick his ass one time before. Miros', but it'd been brief, and felt self-serving. Hungry and rushed as he prepared Alec for the taking. Not like Zercy's in this moment, all unhurried and meticulous. Teasing it with his purring's swift vibrations. Alec's hole clenched in bliss with each pass.

Zercy moved to his taint. Alec's prostate stirred. Then the king was up and tonguing Alec's sac. Alec's jaw slackened. His nuts firmed. He never wanted this grooming to end. Zercy could lick his balls forever and he'd be happy.

But soon the king rose higher to his dick. Alec muffled a groan as Zercy got to work, dragging slow long swipes up its underbelly. Those strokes turned shorter though, when he reached the top. Swifter too, as he laved around its glans. Alec's lashes fluttered, his brain hazing in sensual serenity. Zercy angled his cock downward and cleaned its front as well, but never once drew it into his mouth. Because this wasn't a blowjob, no matter how good it felt. More like a *scrubjob* of repeated scrupulous laps.

Thing was, with his mind in such a state of drunken tranquility, so relaxed and at peace with what Zercy was doing, his body was left free to respond as it pleased. Which it did. At a rate Alec hadn't expected.

Pleasure mounting, his breaths shallowed as every muscle drew taut. And as Zercy quickened his strokes, his big tongue steadily lapping, pressure mushroomed without warning in Alec's crotch. His sac balled tight, his lower back arched. Then with a ragged gasp, he shot a second round.

Zercy chuckled through a thumping purr and licked up that mess, too. Next thing Alec knew, he was floating back to earth as the king laid down beside him and pulled him close. Zercy nuzzled Alec's neck and draped his arm over Alec's chest. Then his big thigh settled over Alec's leg. Affectionately—albeit effectively—pinning his body.

Something, truth be told, Alec was totally fine with. Why? Because the king was clearly readying for sleep, and Alec wasn't leashed with wrists restrained. Like Zercy was finally bestowing a gesture of good faith. A gesture that, going by the warmth in Alec's belly, meant more to him than just a comfortable night's rest.

But as he started to drift, his mind preparing for sleep, Alec stirred back to awareness at Zercy's voice.

"You soothe me," the king murmured, sounding reflective. Somber. "The light in my black night. You are mine." He pulled Alec closer. Pressed his nose against his ear. "My *Alick*," he mumbled. He was falling asleep. "I hope those humans you wait for never come."

Alec's drowsy eyes peeled open. His heart thumped uneasily.

Because while on the surface Zercy's words were of obvious endearment—something he probably wouldn't've confessed had he been coherent—all Alec could focus on as he replayed them in his head, was how sad Zercy had sounded when he said them.

CHAPTER TWENTY-ONE

* * *

"Finally. Some privacy," Noah muttered, climbing into his wall nest. Good God. Craziest night ever. Like of his entire life.

He settled onto the furs, wearing a freshly-donned loinstrap—the name the team had coined their loincloth jockstraps. It felt good to have some alone time. The last few hours had been exhausting, both mentally and physically, in that throne room. After Zercy had lost his shit and stalked out with Alec, things hadn't come to a stop. They'd resumed.

The leader of ceremonies was forced to tweak things, though. To make the tournament last longer, he had the two new teams continue wrestling in their oily pits for a good half hour. Then, when Bailey and Jamis finally yielded, pinned beneath their much stronger Niran opponents, Noah and Zaden were paired up against Chet. An interesting twist Noah hadn't expected. If they lost against their teammate, Chet would end the night as victor. But if they won, they'd go on to wrestle each other.

They won. Just barely, though. Chet was in a zone. Then, to give them a breather before the final round, Bailey and Jamis went at it again with their Nirans.

Noah smiled a little, remembering. With all the stress of winning gone, his friends had started to have fun, both clearly pretty comfortable with who they were grappling. Which wasn't a huge surprise really, where Jamis was concerned. He'd taken a liking to Ryze right off the bat. Back when the Kríe had first started giving lessons. The admiration in Jamis' eyes had been blatant.

Bailey's situation, however, was a little more intriguing, the way he and that Nen prince had hit it off. Noah supposed it helped a lot that the Niran wasn't huge, he was closer to Bailey's size than most of the others. He also seemed younger than a lot of those present, with a noticeably less intimidating air. Not that he looked like he couldn't do damage if he wanted. He had perceptive eyes and plenty of lean muscle.

Thing was, at least with Bailey, he just never threw that vibe. And Bailey had taken advantage of his good fortune.

Hell, Bailey had looked like he'd *wanted* to be out there. Like he was having the time of his life. No joke, when his second round with Nen came to a close, the scientist's painted shoulders had visibly drooped.

More curious still was how the two opponents parted. When Ryze left, he'd given a playful knuckle rub to Jamis' nape, with Jamis returning the gesture with a good-hearted shove. Bailey and Nen, however, just kind of stared at each other, as if neither one wanted to stand and walk away. Setch had had to come and physically get the two moving, personally escorting Prince Nen off the stage.

At which point, it was time for the final round. Long story short, Zaden took the belt, but Noah definitely gave him a run for his money.

Noah frowned and rubbed his temples as he thought back to the bouts. God, they'd been bizarre in every sense of the word. Pretending to be animals fighting feverishly in the wild? Doing so doused in oil in front of spectators? But one of the most peculiar things about the whole affair? How that kulaí crap they wrestled in fucked with his head. Which, in turn, wound up messing with his dick.

It hadn't taken him long to figure out what was happening, but unfortunately, that did nothing to stop the effects. Goddamn, it'd made him horny. Hornier than hell. Ultimately, it even made him imagine shit. No lie, at one point, he'd actually thought Jamis was Gesh, despite the drastic difference in color and size.

Once the bout concluded though, and he was perched up on those rocks? His brain had cleared up quickly. He'd been pissed at that point. He'd been more or less drugged. But as he watched Ryze, and then Nen, as they got physical in the pits too, it was clear that the Niran's weren't being affected. Meaning, the stuff didn't screw with them, and Lotis probably hadn't realized. Hadn't known the stuff would mess with humans differently.

So, Noah had let it slide and dealt with it for round number two. And just like before, he wound up imagining Zaden was Gesh. Was pretty sure Zaden thought him someone else, too. Naydo, maybe? Noah doubted it'd been a girl. Zaden was scrapping way too roughly to make that feasible.

Either way, it was weird. The whole event. Especially when Gesh kept invading his freaking mind. Noah sure as hell hadn't wanted him there. That asshole wasn't welcome. In fact, all Noah could think of to explain the strange phenomenon was the fact that they'd wrestled recently, too. In Gesh's cubby nest back at the fort. After they'd gone at it repeatedly in that spring. Three times to be exact. Noah's ass had been aching. But he'd never felt so exhilarated in all his life.

He sighed, chin in hand, elbow propped on the window ledge, as he remembered what transpired after that. Gesh, the big lug, had thrown Noah over his shoulder and taken him to his pack's large sleeping structure. One-handed, he'd climbed up its ladder to his nest, then without warning, tossed Noah onto a huge stretch of furs.

Noah smiled, recalling the way Gesh had laughed so robustly when Noah shouted as he soared through the air. He'd pounced on Noah not two freaking seconds later, barely giving him time to gather his bearings.

But that was okay. Yeah, Noah had initially been alarmed, what with a purple giant with flashing fangs tackling his ass—not hard, though. And after that, Noah had quickly figured things out. When Gesh said he wanted to play before the show, that's literally what the big Kríe meant. He wanted to get physical. To let loose and have fun. And while Noah hadn't rough-and-tumbled just for kicks since he was a kid, he'd been totally freaking game to give it a go.

Which is exactly what he did with the Kríe for the next twenty minutes, wrestling like rowdy tiger cubs in their cave. And with his brutal need to come gone and off his mind, he'd actually had one hell of a time. More than once, Gesh had him laughing his butt-naked ass off.

All too soon, however, Gesh dialed it down when he heard bongos thumping. Said it was time for the show, and Noah should join him on the furs to watch. Noah did, naively assuming that *the show* would be, well, different. Had been shocked when he saw Chet and Roni.

What he witnessed after that had been provocative as hell. It'd also been inexplicably arousing. Talk about erotic. He'd never seen such a spectacle—and he'd definitely watched his share of freaky porn. By the time his other teammates made their way onto the scene, Noah's dick was damn near ready to go again. Unfortunately, his energy was quickly winding down. He could feel the drop coming, like a sugar crash or something, and knew he'd soon be out like a light.

So, when Gesh pulled him back from the ledge, Noah happily complied, welcoming the calm precursor to sleep. Legs bent and ankles crossed, they'd sat facing each other, their bodies so close their knees were literally touching.

Noah's thoughts wandered, remembering the conversation that followed…

"Gesh?"

"Tah."

"Down on those furs, what Roni did to Chet. Licking his whole body. Every inch. You did that to me, too, back at the spring. Does that gesture hold meaning, or is it just for casual fun?"

Gesh ran his fingers idly through the locks of Noah's hair—along his neck, then around back to stroke his nape. "Brief licks are for fun. Or to sample someone's flavor. Extensive periods, however, are very much different."

Noah peered up into his eyes. This was an answer he wanted to hear. "Different how?"

Gesh grunted softly and added his other hand to the mix, sinking it into Noah's mane to caress his skull. "Those are one of a Krie's highest forms of affection. I suspect Roni is more endeared to Chet than he realizes."

Noah's eyelashes fluttered. He muffled a moan. Those claws grazing his scalp felt divine. He reached up and touched Gesh's ear, then slowly ran his fingers over its piercings. "And what about you?" His gaze settled on Gesh's face. "Does that mean you're *endeared to* me, too*?"*

Gesh met his eyes. The Krie's warm expression sobered. "Perhaps," he murmured. "Or maybe I just like your flavor."

Noah laughed a little. "Uh huh."

Gesh's lips twitched ever so slightly. Pulling his fingers from Noah's hair, he wrapped his big arms around him and flopped down onto his back. Noah landed with a grunt square atop of his chest.

"No more talking," Gesh ordered. "I have sated you. Go to sleep."
Noah couldn't argue with that. The Kríe had definitely sated him—
three times over, then licked his body clean. And truth be told, sleep had
sounded freaking amazing. He could feel the ache setting into his
bones...

Exhaling, Noah closed his eyes, reluctantly savoring the memory.
Of how, atop Gesh's warmth, he'd relaxed so profoundly that it'd felt
like he was one with the pack leader's chest. The other thing he
remembered as he'd drifted off to sleep? Gesh's breath as he nuzzled his
face in Noah's hair, then his warm tongue as he lapped at Noah's neck.

Gesh *was* endeared to him.

Noah knew he was.

What he *didn't* get though, was how the Kríe could sell him.

* * *

"You are outfitted in proper attire and instructed on your objective."
Kellim pointed to a location at the top of the closest mountain. "The first
of your team to reach that flag without capture," his lips curved into a
grin, "will win the prize."

"Capture?" Alec asked, as they stood in the back field. None of his
men had gotten much sleep the night before, their part in the previous
evening's festivities still fresh in their minds.

"Tah. You will be competing against more than just each other. You
also will be evading your pursuers."

Alec swapped looks with Zaden. They were going to be chased?

"Awesome," Chet muttered, irritably tugging at his getup—flaps of
hide protecting his man-skirt, pecs, and shoulders. "And what kind of
prize? It better be good."

Kellim looked his way. "He who lasts longest shall—"

"Wait. Lasts longest?" Chet glowered at him testily. "You just said
it was who got to the flag first without being captured."

Kellim smirked. "True, but why not be realistic from the start?
None will reach the flag. We will take down every one of you."

Chet opened his mouth, but then shut it. "What's the fucking prize?" he grated.

"He who lasts longest shall be granted a request."

Chet eyed him skeptically. "For real?"

"Tah."

"Whatever we ask for, you'll give?"

Kellim inclined his head.

"And Zercy's cool with that?" Alec asked, surprised.

"Tah. King Zercy decided on the prize himself. As long as your wish is reasonable, it will be honored."

"Ah. *Reasonable*," Chet drawled. "The tiny print."

Kellim pointed toward the mountainside to the left of the lake, where an opening in the trees could be seen. "You will enter through there and immediately disperse. None shall stick together. This is a challenge of individual skill."

The trio looked anxious.

Alec frowned and crossed his arms. "So, just to be clear: we're being hunted for sport."

"Tah." Kellim's smile turned into a full-fledged wolfish grin.

Alec scowled.

Unbelievable.

Bailey shifted his weight. "Hunted by *what*?"

Kellim chuffed. "Kríe, of course."

"Oh, thank fuck," Jamis exhaled, shoulders slumping in relief. "I had visions of velociraptors sicced on our asses."

Kellim regarded him curiously. His pointy ear twitched. "There is nothing Kríe relish more than hunting worthy prey. To relinquish such fun to another would be foolish."

"Whatever." Chet rolled his shoulders. Clenched his fists at his sides. "I got my jungle game on. Let's do this."

Kellim nodded and again gestured in the direction of the trees. "One Kríe has been assigned to every member of your team." His grin turned wry. "May your shrewdness prevail."

Alec clenched his jaw. This was going to be one interesting afternoon. Looking at his teammates, he tipped his head toward the mountain. "Shall we, gentlemen?" he sighed.

Chet stared in said direction. A dark smirk formed. "Yeah." His eyes glinted. "We shall."

They breached the forest's opening a few minutes later. "Alright, guys. Good luck." Alec scanned the wooded vicinity. "Stay low. Move quietly. Avoid leaving a trail. And mask your scent as soon as humanly possible."

Chet glanced up into the tree cover. "And when they're nearly on you, juke fast. Let's make these lumbering boners work for it."

The team dispersed, their varying expressions the last thing Alec noted as they disappeared in different directions up the side of the mountain. The trio's? Openly anxious. Zaden and Chet's? Utterly determined. Which matched Alec's state of mind to a tee.

First thing he did was look for stretches of dry ground. The harder the soil, the less his footprints would show up. Then he looked for plants with exceptionally large foliage. It didn't take him long to find a bush that fit the bill. Snapping off two oversized leaves, he quickly wrapped them around his sandals. He wanted to cover their soles and mask the shape of his feet. He may be walking on hard soil now, but there was a rainforest on the other side of the ridge. Meaning, eventually he'd be forced to traverse soft ground, so the more he obscured his footprints, the better.

Crouched low, he made sure the leaves were securely tucked in place, then glanced around, searching—and now sniffing—for fragrant flowers. None in the immediate area, so he slowly got a move on, trying like hell not to make noise as he went.

He didn't know when the Kríe would be set loose on their asses, how much time he and his team had to create distance. With their luck, their trackers were already in position, waiting for some green light to let them begin.

Soon he came to damper terrain. Not great where leaving tracks were concerned, but at least he could cover his skin with mud. That took him a few minutes as he squatted low to the ground. Before he resumed, he covered the soil he'd dug into with some leaves.

For the moment, everything felt good. Enough sunlight was spearing its way through the canopies to see. Even the wildlife didn't seem freaked out by his presence. Looked like his efforts were working as he moved at a snail's pace, trying not to stir up any commotion.

He scanned his surroundings, listening for tell tail sounds—not that his tracker would be anything but silent. Hearing a whole lot of nada, Alec rose to his feet and quietly made his way toward a well-trodden animal path he'd spotted up ahead. Being packed down by countless paws, hooves—whatever creatures there walked on—he hoped it'd serve to camouflage his footprints, too. It'd also keep him out of thick stretches of shrubbery where it'd be impossible not to leave a broken-twig or displaced-leaf trail.

High above, air creatures flew about, barking ardently. Tree critters squealed and squawked and brayed their asses off, too. Down where Alec walked, under groundcover or in the brush, even more wildlife chattered and skittered about.

Alec swept another keen glance to his left and right, drawing in big long lungfuls through his nose. Finally. Some kind of super-aromatic plant was nearby. He sniffed more intently and peered around. It was coming from somewhere to his left. Quietly, he exited the path to seek it out. The ground rustled beneath his feet, the leaves moving as if alive, leaning this way or that to dodge his steps. Alec frowned at the things but kept on going.

Sniff—sniff—sniff—

There. By that big ole downed tree. That cluster, with each flower the size of his hand. Alec reached the log and eased down onto his haunches to investigate. The deep yellow blossoms looked like orchids, but larger. And glossy, as if coated with lots of honey. Which was exactly what they smelled like, warm wild honey on steroids. Potent, with a strange gamey bite.

Whatever. It'd do. He plucked one carefully from its vine and smeared its petals all over his attire. Didn't want to disturb the coat of mud on his skin. Which, incidentally, was starting to dry. Not the best sensation. So, yeah, not going to add to it. No need to make his crusty ass all sticky, too.

He stood and glanced around again, ready to get serious about his mission, reaching that waving purple flag atop this mountain. Of course, that was the easy part, acquiring the flag. The trickier shit was what he had to *avoid*. AKA a highly skilled, ruthless Kríe tracker who was currently hunting his ass like prey.

Alec peered over his shoulder, wondering how long he had left until one of those big purple predators locked onto his position. Because once that happened, it was pretty much game over. No way he could outrun the guy, not with half the stride and leg muscles. Couldn't climb a tree to evade the fucker either. Alec's only chance to ever make it to his destination was to never give up his position. Which would be much easier said than done.

Exhaling silently, he listened one last time before heading up the side of the mountain. With each calculated step, his busy mind started to drift. Back to last night. But not to the tournament. To the time he spent in that bed of furs with Zercy. God, even now he couldn't believe he'd done those things.

Well, okay, yeah, he could. He'd been hornier than hell and wanting to get his freak on for too long. With Zercy. The unstable, arrogant Kríe king. It'd been exhausting him mentally. He'd needed the reprieve. A way to release the pressure and finally relax.

Problem was, that little freebie he'd allowed himself didn't work. Didn't cool his jets for the king one single bit. In fact, he now feared it may have just made things worse. Why else would he be struggling so hard to keep Zercy off his mind, to stop thinking about all the crazy things they'd done?

His mind wandered in remembrance. Fuck, it'd been amazing. And reckless. And euphoric. And irresponsible. And the best fuck of his life.

Alec muffled a groan, pausing to scrub his muddy face. What kind of mess had he gotten himself into? To just dive in and damn the repercussions? Now he was laying in the bed he'd made. Because sure enough, this very morning, when the king had woken up, he'd tried to get all frisky again. Fortunately, Zercy's aide had arrived a heartbeat later and pulled the king away in the nick of time. Alec had never been so relieved. They couldn't go down that road. Last night was a wild-hair, one-time deal. That was it. No more.

Abruptly, a flock of fowl took off out of the trees. Fast. As if in a hurry to get gone.

Alec froze, then dropped to his haunches.

Shit.

That couldn't be good. Hell, even the chatter from nearby branches had quieted down.

His heart shot into a gallop. Son of a bitch. His tracker was close. He could feel it in his bones. His time of peaceful wandering was officially over.

Still as a statue, Alec listened intently, trying to get a bead on the Kríe's location. For the longest time he heard nothing. What's more, the forest had gone silent. As if the woodland animals were watching Alec's pursuer with bated breath. Witnessing the *stalk* before the *pounce*.

Out of nowhere, a heavy *thud* sounded from somewhere behind him, just like the one Gesh made when dropping from the trees.

Alec whipped his head around. Scanned the vicinity. Nothing. He didn't see a goddamn fucking thing.

A low, sultry chuff flittered past his ears, again coming from somewhere behind him. And fuck him sideways, it sounded smugger than hell. An arrogant Kríe-style *I gotchu* if ever he'd heard one.

His heart slammed his ribs. He'd been spotted. He had to run. Maybe if he managed to juke and dodge for long enough, he could make it to the top without…

God, who was he kidding?

But he didn't have a choice. It was try or fucking surrender. And Alec never ever went down without a fight.

Launching himself off his haunches, he took off at a dead run, sprinting through the forest as fast as he could.

Creatures scattered out of his way, back to screeching and squawking, while behind Alec, loud-ass footfalls started pounding. Friggin' hell, they sounded like a bass drum. Kríe were heavy motherfuckers. And fast.

Way faster than Alec had expected, even. And he was no slow Joe himself. But at this rate, no matter how fast he juked left or right, once the Kríe had gotten close enough, it wouldn't matter. He'd just dive and take Alec out. And that'd be all there was to it.

Alec vaulted over a prehistoric-size log on its side, glancing over his shoulder as he leapt. A dark blur darted behind a tree. He shot forward and resumed his dash, but the footsteps had ceased. Had he lost the Kríe? No way.

Branches snapped high above.

Aw, fuck.

He glanced upward as he tore through the brush.

Naturally, he saw nothing.

The bastard was in stealth mode.

Alec scowled, breathing fast, but kept sprinting.

Air sawed from his lungs. His thighs started to burn. He didn't typically go at full throttle for so long. At such a steep incline, no less.

He tripped over a thick gnarled root and went flailing. He caught himself, though, before he hit the ground.

Another chuff reverberated. It sounded amused, but also excited, with the hint of a happy growl.

The asshole was enjoying himself. Having a blast hunting him down. Alec's anger spiked, even as a jarring thrill washed through his system. The sensation, he realized, prey must feel when fleeing, when running for their lives from a predator. Which just vexed him even more. On the planet he came from, he was the top of the food chain. Holding dominion over all other creatures.

Unfortunately, Alec didn't have time to brood. The snapping twigs above were nearly on top of him.

Cutting a hard right, he took off toward a gully, then when his tracker caught back up again, he juked left. That tactic only bought a scant few minutes more total, though. Soon that weighty *thump* shook the hard ground behind him.

His heart shot up his throat as every hair stood on his nape. By the sound of things, his pursuer was barely two yards away. Alec didn't even have time to steal a glance. Adrenaline stormed his blood stream. His legs pumped even faster. But the footfalls at his back were closing in.

He was out of time.

With a shout, Alec dove toward a bush, but the reach of his tracker was too large. A thick purple arm snapped around his waist, then its owner's muscular body took him down.

Air punched from Alec's lungs as he hit the forest floor. "Fuck!" he grunted.

A deep laugh met his ears. One he recognized. Intimately.

"Goddamnit, Kríe!" he shouted, still reeling from the chase.

But his bellow only made the king laugh harder.

Glowering, Alec rolled onto his back in Zercy's hold, but in truth, his mood had already shifted. Yeah, he was still pissed that he'd been hunted—and taken out—but that it was Zercy somehow distracted his indignation. That and those happy sounds thrumming in Zercy's chest.

Not that Alec would ever admit it.

Barely winded, the king gazed down at him, snugly caging Alec in his arms. "Greetings, pet," he rumbled.

Still panting, Alec grated, "Hello."

Zercy's golden eyes flashed. "You are easier to catch than koosa."

Alec ground his molars.

Zercy chuckled. "But much more fun."

Another backward-ass compliment. But damn it to hell, it did the trick, somehow managing to light Alec up like a dolt. Didn't mean he wasn't still irked, though.

He met Zercy's gaze. "This activity is demeaning. A man's got pride, you know."

Zercy's bright smile ebbed. He tilted his head. "You are mad?"

Alec balked incredulously. "You just hunted me like an animal."

"Tah, but for fun. I did not harm you. I never would."

"Fun for *you*," Alec gritted. "How 'bout you ask if *I* had fun."

Zercy frowned. "Did you have fun?"

"*No!* Look at me! I'm covered in *mud!* Mud and sticky shit to hide my scent!"

Zercy opened his mouth, then shut it and studied Alec's appearance. His lips twitched. He stifled a chuff. "It did not work."

Alec bristled, clenching his teeth. "Yeah, I noticed."

Zercy rubbed their noses. "Do not be angry. I did not mean it to offend."

Alec exhaled and closed his eyes. "You never do." A frustrating truth.

Another frustrating truth was how, beneath the king's body, Alec was already struggling to stay mad. Zercy shifted atop him, then thumbed some mud from Alec's cheek. His voice softened. "Would you like me to clean away the dirt? I am king, but I would do this for you."

Alec stilled and peered up at him. His pounding heart stumbled. Zercy's expression... The Kríe was serious. He would lick Alec clean. A gesture of humility to make things right. It took Alec off guard, that Zercy would lay down his pride. It humbled him and doused his veins with fuzzy warmth.

"Thanks," Alec rasped, "but I think I'll survive."

Zercy's smile returned. "I want to kiss you."

Alec stiffened. "What?"

Zercy focused on his lips. A happy rumbled emerged. "All morning, all I could think of was your mouth against mine. How good your kisses felt. I want that now."

Oh, crap. That was Zercy's I'm-about-to-take-what-I-want tone.

But before Alec could dodge, the king dipped down and captured his lips.

Alec sucked in sharply, eyes wide, heart hammering.

Zercy growled soft and low and started kissing. Moving his mouth, lashes down, warm tongue emerging. Alec's resistance melted instantly. Zercy's lips made him drunk. Made him want to flat-out just give in.

Only that's what he'd said the night before in Zercy's bed; one more time, then never again. And yet, here he was.

Zercy's kisses turned hotter.

Alec groaned in surrender, returning the king's affections.

Just one more time.

CHAPTER TWENTY-TWO

* * *

Alec woke for the umpteenth time with morning wood the size of a tree trunk. Fitting, he supposed, what with the nickname and all. Not that he didn't wake with hard-ons pretty regularly as it was. Just never with ones as big, or ridiculously hard.

Moaning drowsily, he rolled over, writing it off as a Niran side effect. God knew, his body was changing in plenty of other ways, too. His digestive tract, for example, with his intestines no longer operating. Or the way his brain could decipher alien language. In truth, he suspected even his emotions were changing. Why else would he suddenly be having feelings for a male? Until Nira, he'd always considered himself heterosexual.

Languidly, he peeled his eyes open, expecting to see the object of his unbidden affections lying next to him. But Zercy wasn't. In fact, the Kríe wasn't in the bed with him at all. Alec frowned, brain churning to life inside his skull. Zercy was always there when he woke. Not a day had passed that he wasn't.

Hell, for the last week—ever since they'd gotten intimate after the wrestling matches, which ultimately led to kissing for the first time—the king had deliberately waited for Alec to wake before heading off to court with his aide. According to Zercy, there was little he delighted in more than starting each new day with Alec 'in hand.'

Unreal, really, how much the king enjoyed making him come. Which wasn't to say Alec gave it up every time. Because he didn't. A very big part of him was still struggling with their relationship—or maybe he should call it their conundrum. But with each passing sunrise, as Alec woke against Zercy's warmth, the king's morning timbre playfully tickling in his ear, he found himself succumbing more often than not.

God, a few times he'd even stroked Zercy off, too. Pumping the king's cock as the king pumped his. Morning brain fuzz must've been affecting his better judgement—that, and his stamina, because he always came first. Couldn't hold it, though. Not that Zercy ever seemed to mind. He'd just chuff and unload too, then 'clean up' their mess.

Sitting up in bed, Alec scrubbed his face with free hands. Their status, incidentally, since the hunting stint last week, where Chet held out the longest against his predator. True to the king's word, he granted the winner one request. What did Chet ask for? No more bound wrists—for the whole team. Before then, the only time they'd let the guys go unrestrained was during activities that required full motion. That, and at night when the team was locked in their room. Every other part of the day, though? Wrists tied.

Ultimately, the king had agreed to Chet's request—under the condition that all remain on good behavior. One sketchy move and wrist binds were back in business.

Alec looked at his hands, still reveling in their freedom. Since their very first day on Nira, the team had perpetually been bound. First by Gesh's pack, and then under order of the king. Even when he slept, as precaution for Zercy's safety. Although, ever since the night Zercy fucked him with that tail, he'd allowed Alec to sleep freely. No binds. No leash.

Which was progress in Alec's book.

The king liked him. Maybe a lot. Was even starting to trust him.

Alec's heart *thump-bumped* anxiously.

Nope. Not going to think about how that knowledge made him feel.

Redirecting his focus, he peered out into the chamber and soon spotted Zercy over by a window. Facing Alec's direction, he sat propped against his desk as he quietly looked at a big scroll of parchment. With it fully unrolled, Alec recognized it immediately. It was his star map. The one he'd picked up at the market. The same one he'd studied every day since.

Zercy lifted his gaze. "My pet has awoken. I was beginning to think you were dead."

Alec offered a groggy smirk. "My alarm didn't go off."

"You have an alarm?"

"Actually, yeah, I used to. A human gadget… Now it's just a figure of speech."

"Mm. Figure of speech." Zercy's lips curved slightly. "Meaning your body is reluctant to rouse without my touch."

Alec coughed a small laugh. "Uh, *no*. Not meaning that."

"Hm." Zercy dropped his gaze back to Alec's map. "And yet, it is true nevertheless."

Alec grinned a little and shook his head, but didn't bother to respond. Just shoved the furs aside and pulled his ass out of bed. Feet meeting the slate, he glanced toward the door. "If it's so freaking late, how come your aide hasn't come yet?"

"I instructed my guards to turn him away."

Alec looked back at Zercy. "Why?" That wasn't typical. In fact, not once had he done that since Alec had been there.

Zercy rolled up the star map and set it on his desk. "Because I am taking the day off."

Alec's brows rose. "You are?"

"I have decided I need a break."

Alec looked at him.

Zercy smiled, but it didn't reach his eyes. "My duties as king, they weigh heavily on me, *Alick*. Like poison to my spirit."

Alec frowned at his tone.

"Fortunately," the king went on, "I have discovered an effective remedy."

"Time off?"

Soft chuff. "You."

Alec's heart tripped. "What—*Me?*"

Zercy crossed his arms, biceps bulging. "Tah. You distract me. Counter the toxin." His gaze glinted. "So I shall spend the day with you."

Alec stared at him. Shifted his weight. This news should not make him happy. Zercy's time away was Alec's time with his team. But for some reason, it did. To hang out with Zercy during the day, outside of his chambers? Curiously, the prospect kind of psyched Alec out. What would normal interaction be like? Outside of bed—when Zercy wasn't 'hunting' him.

Zercy pushed off his writing desk and strode Alec's way. "It is either that or take you to court with me, but that is risky. You could die."

Alec tensed. "*Die?*"

"Tah. Of boredom. It is dreadful."

Alec fought a grin.

So did Zercy.

He stopped a foot away. Peering down, he met Alec's eyes. "Kiss your king," he rumbled softly.

"You're not my king," Alec murmured.

Zercy's lids lowered. "Kiss me anyway."

Alec's stomach clenched. He shook his head.

Zercy smiled. "Must I beg?"

Something squeezed inside Alec's chest. He cleared his throat and rasped, "Please don't."

The king cocked a brow, then smirked a little. "As you wish."

Alec frowned, watching Zercy tie his wrist cuffs together. "What are you doing?"

"Obliging my pet." Zercy lifted Alec's bound hands, then hooked them up and over his dark head.

Alec stiffened, suddenly flush against the king's big-ass body. "What the fuck, Kríe?" He tugged his arms and glared up at the king. The fucker just trapped Alec's hands behind his neck.

Zercy palmed the sides of Alec's head. Loosed another soft growl. "Behold, *Alick*. Your mighty king *not begging.*"

Gaze hooded, he claimed Alec's lips. Guess the opposite of begging was *taking*. A Kríe truth that, in this moment, Alec found himself appreciating. Grateful for, as he groaned and closed his eyes. Why? Because it'd handed him the guilty pleasure of Zercy's kiss without having to openly consent to it. Something that, deep down, Alec realized he liked. Zercy taking what he wanted from him. At least, in private.

Without warning, a hot little visual slammed Alec's brain. Of Zercy shoving him face-first against a wall. Grazing Alec's neck with his fangs as he growled. Rumbling wicked promises as he groped him...

Alec's morning wood bucked eagerly against the king's strong thigh.

Zercy grinned. "Your cock is hungry."

Alec played it off. "Just need to piss."

Zercy chuckled against his mouth. "My little liar."

* * *

"Chet. Ugh. No. I said *hold* it, not *shred* it. Great." Bailey scowled. "Now I gotta start all over."

Chet frowned and glanced down at the twig he was clutching. Bailey had asked him to hold it up so he could sketch it. Thing was, just a minute ago, the thing had little leaves. Now however, it was pretty much bare. "Oops. Must've absently plucked the fuckers off. Sorry," he muttered. "I'll get you another one."

"Nah. It's all right," Bailey grumbled, setting his journal down. "I wanna get a good one. Be right back."

Chet watched him get to his feet, then amble toward the tree line while the rest of them lounged atop a thick-weaved blanket. The rest of them, minus the captain, that is. He was off somewhere with the king. Had been all day. They'd only seen him once, at breakfast. Zercy had been there, too. Which was weird. The Kríe king never ate with them.

He did today though, explaining between mouthfuls of food that Alec wouldn't be going to Ryze's lessons. Or to lunch with the team after. He wouldn't be participating in Kellim's sessions, either. Said he was keeping our captain all to himself, and that he'd return him to us in one piece the following morning.

Freak.

Chet scowled and tossed the stripped twig into the grass. Or whatever the hell it was their blanket was spread over. He eyed the tiny frond-like blades, then glanced back over at Bailey. He'd made it to the dark purple trees and was intently inspecting a branch. Due to his persistence, they'd scored a 'nature walk' after Kellim's boot camp. Apparently, Bailey and his sidekicks, AKA Jamis and Noah, wanted to sketch a bunch of different Niran wildlife.

So, after Kellim finished running their asses into the ground, he and the rest of the team's chaperones took them hiking. Across the training field, then into the forest, tromping up and down the side of a mountain. By the end, the trio had acquired quite the collection of samples, so they ended their little romp by the lake. Right on its bank, in fact, between two big ole flat boulders, easily able to see right into the water.

Which is where they sat now, atop their big, colorful blanket, as the scientists diligently sketched their little hearts out. Chet glanced at the two of them, so content in their tasks. Noah, meticulously capturing the perfect likeness of some weird flower. Jamis, rendering the strange leaves of a weed he'd propped on his knee. Talk about engrossed. The guy was concentrating so hard, even the tip of his tongue was peeking out.

Chet exhaled. God, he was bored. Wanted to wander around some more. Get a more perfect lay of the land. But their 'escorts' wouldn't let him. Like they could somehow sense his motives. Chet shot them a glare where they stood just yards away. Kríe were annoyingly perceptive.

"Oh, my God! Did you see that?" Jamis jerked in surprise. "My specimen! I—I think it's alive!"

Zaden paused from skipping rocks to cast the guy a curious look. "It's a plant. Of course, it's alive."

Jamis stared at the weed on his knee. "No, I mean *alive*-alive. As in, aware of its surroundings."

That quieted their co-pilot.

Noah's face lit up. "Are you serious?"

"As a heart attack," Jamis laughed. "Look." He touched its blossom with his writing utensil. Its feather-light tendrils twitched, then curled around it, as if investigating its essence via touch.

Chet gawked, eyes widening, then grimaced. "That ain't right."

Noah grinned from ear to ear. "Oh, yes, it is."

Zaden stared in fascination. "Alec mentioned plants like that."

Chet looked at him. "He did?"

"Yeah." Zaden nodded. "After his visit to Sirus. Said there were plants here that were sentient. Called 'em dygons."

Jamis and Noah swapped looks.

Chet frowned, doing the math. Alec had gone to Sirus for an exam. Why would he suddenly be aware of sentient plant life after the fact? Disturbing images doused his brain, but Bailey's return quickly distracted him.

Plopping down with fresh twig in hand, he was brought up to speed as both Jamis and Noah excitedly showed him the weed.

Chet grunted and shook his head. No matter what, weeds weren't cool.

But then movement across the field snagged his attention. Glancing that way, he stilled in recognition; Alec and Zercy, emerging from the forest and headed for the castle's rear gate. "Well, well. Check it out. Bossman making a surprise appearance."

The trio stopped talking and followed Chet's gaze.

Zaden did, too. "Wonder what they're doing."

"Looks like they're taking a stroll to me." Jamis quirked a brow. "Wow. Cap looks pretty chill."

Chet studied them with intrigue. Neither had noticed the team. Were too engrossed in whatever they were talking about. Alec's posture looked relaxed as he strode by Zercy's side. The king looked contented too, periodically gesturing. And even though the two of them were still far away, Chet swore he spotted Alec actually *smiling*.

Like he was enjoying himself. Having a good time with their *captor*.

Chet furrowed his brows broodingly and clenched his jaw. That vibe the cap was throwing had better be a façade, driven by ulterior motives. Like schmoozing the king into letting the team go. There was no other legitimate reason to look so friendly.

Noah watched them quietly also, until they wandered through the gate, his brown eyes suddenly looking super somber.

Zaden seemed to notice the same and gently bumped Noah's shoulder. "You okay, man?" he murmured.

Noah nodded with a shrug.

Zaden frowned and bumped him again. "You're thinking about Gesh."

Noah exhaled, not denying it, and glanced down at his sketch, but then looked back up and met Zaden's eyes. "Be honest," he spoke quietly. "Would you want to see Naydo again?"

Zaden stilled at his question. Clearly, he hadn't expected it. Expression thoughtful, he averted his gaze and skipped another rock. "Maybe? I dunno. It'd be stupid. He helped sell us. And it's not like he's out there wanting to see me." He looked back at Noah. Offered a small smile. "Me and Naydo... We weren't like you and Gesh."

Noah chuckled and dropped his gaze. "'Me and Gesh' weren't what I thought."

"Yeah, you were. It was obvious. He's just a dick."

Noah smirked. "That he is. A big, *stupid* dick." His smile faded. "But by the end, man—and I know this sounds ridiculous—it felt like he was *my* stupid dick."

Chet glowered at the two of them, unable to stand another word. "Are you out of your friggin' minds? You'd *want* to see those pricks again? They'd just pull the same crap. Ass fuck us both literally and figuratively."

Jamis and Bailey paused mid-conversation and looked their way.

Chet just kept on going, resentment climbing. "Don't forget, if it wasn't for them, we wouldn't be in this mess. Sold off as pets to yet another bag of dicks. Making us do completely screwed up shit. God only knows what they'll make us do next. Hell, in truth, they aren't any better than Gesh's pack. They'll screw us over too, there ain't no question in my mind. Just as soon as Zercy gets bored of his shiny new toys. And what'll happen to us then? Huh? It's not like we have any control over the situation." Irritably, he pointed to the massive white-washed castle. "Our fate's in *their* hands! Those asshole Kríe! Thanks to *other* asshole Kríe! Their species *sucks!*"

His teammates nodded grimly. He was right, and they knew it.

Exhaling a curse, Chet frowned and rubbed his crew cut. "We gotta come up with a plan. Gotta get the hell outta here. Then get back to the beacon so this doesn't happen to the others."

Jamis offered a bleak smile. "Gotta rescue the rescue team."

"Something like that anyway," Chet muttered, dropping his hand.

Bailey scowled down at the leather-bound journal in his hand. "Still pissed they took my smart pad. Wouldn't need this if they hadn't. Could've taken a hundred high-res pictures by now."

Zaden nodded and chucked another stone. "Yeah, I miss my music. Had enough in my pad's library to last a decade."

Jamis groaned. "Aw, man. To hear some quality tunes. So freaking sick of drums and flutes."

"Right?" Zaden chuckled. The first Chet had heard from him in days. "Someone around here needs to invent a guitar. Hell, I'd take a ukulele at this point."

"Hey now," Jamis laughed. "Ukuleles are cool."

"I used to play the cello," Bailey piped in with a smile.

"The cello," Chet drawled flatly.

"Yeah, man. The thing was *huge*. Started when I was young, so it literally came up to my—Whoa!" Bailey stopped, eyes locking on something in the water. "Did you see that?" He pointed to a huge protruding boulder.

Chet peered in its direction. Shook his head. "I don't see shit."

"Me neither," Zaden concurred.

Jamis searched the shadowy depths. "What'd you see? An octo-fish?"

"A guy!" Bailey blurted. "I saw a *guy!* With long teal hair! In the water! Just his head and shoulders were showing."

Chet scoffed. "Give me a break."

"I swear it! He was right there! Just chilling by that rock freaking watching us!"

Noah and Jamis swapped looks, excitement glittering in their eyes.

Zaden warily scanned the spot. "He was *watching* us?"

"Yes!" Bailey scrambled to the ledge on hands and knees. Peering around, he nodded repeatedly. "His face was partially covered by his hair, but we made eye contact." He froze, as if something big had suddenly occurred to him. "Damn. What if..." He glanced over his shoulder at the team. "What if it's the dude from the river?"

Noah's brows rose. "You mean the guy that grabbed your ankle?"

"Yes!" Bailey beamed.

Jamis blinked, then cracked up laughing. "Oh, my God, Bay. It's official. You're obsessed with your lover-boy merman."

Bailey's bright smile morphed into an irritated scowl. "I didn't imagine it. I saw him. He was there."

"Right." Chet smirked. "Did he blow you bubble kisses?"

"Fuck off," Bailey grumbled. Moving back, he snatched up his journal. "Gonna draw the dude and show you. Mermen are real."

"I believe you. But technically, that's not their name." Zaden eyed the lake. "Naydo called them Oonmaiyos."

Bailey stilled, then shot him a look. "The guy I wrestled with last week. Prince Nen. He was Oonmaiyos. Holy shit."

"Damn," Noah murmured, scanning their slice of lake again. "You don't think—"

"That *that* was the prince?" Chet asked incredulously. "Lurking like a hoodlum in Kríe territory?"

"He *did* kinda look like him," Bailey murmured, expression thoughtful.

"You sure?" Chet contested. "You said his face was obscured."

"Both had teal hair..."

"Maybe all Oonmaiyos do. Every Kríe has the same long black dreads."

Bailey frowned and averted his gaze back to the lake. "Whatever. It doesn't matter. But I didn't imagine him. He was right there. I saw him."

Chet grunted, letting it go. Still, he didn't understand. Bailey wasn't even gay, so why all the hullabaloo about that merman? Not that his species really mattered all that much. *Any* of these sex-crazed Nirans represented trouble. Best not to fixate on their otherworldly allure and risk getting screwed over. Or worse, infatuated.

Chet shifted his gaze to the mountain. Somewhere on the other side of its huge ridge, asshole Roni was off gallivanting with Gesh's pack. Chet's chest slowly squeezed. Even now, he couldn't believe he let that purple dick use him. Or that he let himself *enjoy* it while it was happening.

What was wrong with him? He scrubbed his face. He needed to get Roni out of his head. But everywhere he looked there were big-ass arrogant Kríe. Incessant reminders, never letting him forget. About the male he'd had sex with. About their raw, flammable chemistry. About the way Roni ultimately betrayed him.

Chet ground his molars. He hated how easily he'd been deceived. How, despite all the crap Roni subjected him to, he still somehow made Chet feel his equal. The way he'd verbally sparred with him, even challenging Chet to skirmishes. Chet might not be Kríe, but he still was a male, and invitations like that were only offered to worthy rivals. Not to those one viewed as inferior.

In hindsight, Chet suspected it was all just an act. A way to lure him into all of Roni's traps. Shrewdly feeding Chet's ego as he openly toyed with him. It would certainly explain why it was so easy for Roni to dump Chet off like worthless trash.

Chet's jaw muscle ticked as he pinned their guards with a glower. Kríe were pricks. Every one of them. With no morals whatsoever. Ever taking what they wanted with no concern.

His glare landed on Mannix. He wasn't so different from Roni. All arrogant and overbearing. Definitely wanted to fuck Chet, like Roni. Probably would've by now, had the king not forbidden it. Didn't stop the guy from hounding him, though. Propositioning him left and right. Talk about annoying.

Chet eyed the huge guard. Hell, maybe he should say screw it and give the Kríe what he wanted. If Mannix was like Roni—and Chet was certain he was—he'd lose interest once they fucked and let Chet be. Then Chet wouldn't have to worry about his shit anymore. One less aggravation to have to deal with.

Sighing heavily, Chet averted his gaze. No. Awful idea. He didn't need another brain fuck. One was plenty, fuck you very much, Roni.

CHAPTER TWENTY-THREE

*** * ***

"That was, by far," Alec wiped at his tongue, "the most disgusting thing I have ever put in my mouth."

Zercy stifled a chuckle as they exited the kitchen. "My pet is so uncultured. That was a delicacy."

"Ah, *no*," Alec laughed. "That was cruel and unusual punishment."

Zercy grinned. "Next time we will find something you like."

Alec eyed him suspiciously. "I think I'll pass."

Although in fairness, most of the foods he'd just sampled were okay, each specifically picked out by Zercy himself. He'd seemed almost excited to introduce Alec to his favorite dishes. Most were seafood, but one had definitely reminded Alec of dark chocolate.

Honestly, it'd been a pretty enlightening session. Alec had to admit, he'd learned quite a bit. After all, at most meals he had no clue what he was eating. Which wasn't to say he hadn't ever asked. Because he had, as had pretty much everyone on his team, but the answers they were given clarified nothing. But realistically, why would they? They didn't know Kríe terminology. Ryze had only taught them the basics where food was concerned. Fortunately, most of the stuff was pretty tolerable.

Not the case just a few minutes ago, but eh, whatever. Aside from the thing he'd just put in his mouth—that looked like an olive but tasted like unholy pickled death—the day with Zercy so far had been good. The king had taken him on an excursion along the mountain range, with his convoy of guards keeping out of sight.

Alec had to admit, it was nice having it feel like just the two of them. Zercy seemed to like it, too, and stayed in good spirits. That they were engaging in his favorite pastime probably helped. Hunting. Not a surprise. Zercy's skills, however, had been a shocker. Just watching him in action had been incredible.

When Alec could keep up with him, that is. Not an easy feat. Mostly he just hung back in the branches above, watching the agile king take down his prey. And those creatures weren't little. They hadn't been out there for rabbits. Alec even got to witness Zercy hunting a koosa. Man, the way he'd moved like a wraith in the trees. That beast in the brush never knew what hit it.

Afterwards, Zercy had ordered his guards to haul his quarry back, specifically directing them to bring the koosa to Lotis. Alec hadn't asked the whys of that even though he was curious. Was Zercy giving it to the Kríe as some kind of gift? The question had lingered in Alec's mind ever since; on their hike back to the castle, as they cleaned up in the bath house. Even during their visit to the kitchen.

Alec didn't know why. He shouldn't care in the slightest. And yet for some reason, he did. But shit, knowing Zercy was giving that koosa to Lotis? His most relished trophy of the day while hunting with *Alec?* It just felt wrong. Made Alec's gut feel all sludgy. Made him want to punch Lotis in the face.

Unhurriedly, they made their way down the center corridor, passing countless nobles as they walked. To some, Zercy inclined his head. To others, he didn't. Alec wondered if those who made the cut were his friends. Maybe they were simply higher born.

What was Lotis to the king? a voice inside his head wondered. Why would Zercy gift *him* his prized catch instead of Alec?

Irritated that he was irritated, Alec eyed Zercy as they walked. *Just ask him and be done with it.* "I have a question."

Zercy slowed and peered down at him. "Tah? Let us hear it."

"Why did you give Lotis that koosa?"

"Because I—" Zercy paused, then promptly pulled to a stop. Turning to Alec, he canted his head. "Why do you ask?"

Alec shrugged, stopping too. "I dunno. Just thought it was weird."

Zercy's eyes flickered. "Weird how?"

Alec looked away. Chewed on his cheek. "Because he wasn't even there. Had no part in its capture."

He could feel Zercy's golden gaze studying his face.

"You feel I should have given it to you."

Alec's stomach clenched. He frowned. "No... I just... thought it was weird."

"*Alick*," Zercy rumbled. His timbre had softened.

Alec looked at him.

Zercy smiled a little, then curled a finger under Alec's chin. "Lotis is my friend, so yes, I like to give him gifts."

Alec's chest tightened. "Define friends."

Zercy thought for a moment. "One whom I care for."

That clarified nothing. Was he trying to dodge? Ugh. Why did Alec even care? He tried to look away, but Zercy firmly held his chin.

"He is not my lover," he murmured. "Only you are this to me."

Alec stilled at his words—God, they felt way too good—but searched Zercy's eyes for deception.

A small grin tugged on Zercy's lips. "I did not give that koosa to Lotis. I had it brought to him so he could make use of its hide."

Oh.

Well, now Alec felt like a moron.

His cheeks warmed. "Ah. Yeah. I guess that makes sense."

Zercy released his chin and fondled his lobe instead. "I have him making something. For you."

What? Alec's heart skipped a beat. "For me?"

"Of course." He smirked playfully. "You played a part. *You were there.*"

Brat. Alec fought really hard not to grin. Zercy was mocking him for his show of jealousy. Which Alec couldn't believe he'd exhibited. What in the flying fuck was wrong with him?

Chuffing, Zercy turned and resumed their stroll. Alec silently fell in beside him. But before long, he noticed they were nearing those double doors. That closed-off, guarded entrance to the courtyard.

He eyed the bronze panels, so painstakingly crafted, explicitly designed to capture one's attention. Capture it, then demand their full reverence as they entered. As they stepped into the mysterious space beyond.

His pulse spiked. What was in there? More than benches and grass, he was sure. A place of worship? Some sacrificial altar where things were slaughtered? He couldn't stand the not knowing. He needed to see!

291

Strides slowing, his brain churned as he debated another attempt. Another stab at trying to get Zercy to spill. A lot had happened since the last time he'd inquired about the place. They'd connected more. Zercy was even showing signs of real trust. Would he confide in Alec this time, if Alec asked?

Only one way to find out. And honestly, what'd he have to lose? The king would either say okay and let him in on the secret, or he wouldn't, and things would stay the way they were.

They readied to pass the entrance not five seconds later. Alec bit the bullet and pulled up on the brakes.

Zercy paused too and looked at him.

Alec glanced at the doors.

Zercy stiffened and narrowed his eyes. "Why have you stopped?"

Alec scratched his cheek. Shifted his feet. Tentatively gestured to the entrance. "'Cause I was hoping that maybe you'd show me inside?"

Zercy shook his head. "Mah."

"Why?"

"The courtyard is off limits."

Alec held his gaze, unwilling to give up so fast. "Please?"

Zercy crossed his arms, bicep cuffs gleaming, and growled tightly, "*Mah.*"

"Aw, *come on.*" Alec waved at the door in frustration. "Not knowing, not understanding what's behind there? It's stressing me out. All I'm asking for is a peek. We don't have to go inside." Imploring Zercy with his eyes, he murmured, "*Please?*"

The king didn't respond. God, his whole frame looked tense. But as he flicked a wary look at the huge elaborate panels, Alec swore he saw a glimpse of indecision. As if a part of Zercy wanted to give Alec what he wished for. And not just that but share with him his troubles.

Alec's chest squeezed at the prospect, that Zercy would want to confide in him, about something that obviously tormented him deeply. Because of one thing Alec was certain, what laid behind those doors was tragic. Tragic, but also still critically imperative.

Which, in turn, made Alec restless as shit.

Problem was, in order to evade any possible dangers, he had to know what the fuck he was dealing with. He had a responsibility to his team. He couldn't just ignore this. Besides, who knew? Maybe he could help Zercy fix it.

But right as Zercy looked like he was ready to consent, Alec noticed a torrent of movement in his periphery. He looked in its direction. Down at the far end of the corridor, several armed Kríe herded a line of disgruntled captives. Deeply-tanned males with long blond hair, bound at throat and wrist—like Alec's team had been.

Alec tensed in remembrance. "Who are they?"

Zercy looked their way and glowered. Even his ears twitched. "They are prisoners."

Alec watched as they stopped at the tower's stairwell door. The Kríe were taking them down to the dungeon. But why so many? And why just that particular species?

Alec stilled. The day his team first arrived, Zercy mentioned something that Alec had forgotten all about. His plans to use them for labor—before Gesh swayed him into making them pets.

He frowned, doing more math. All that clanking en route to Ryze's. The guards had said the noise was coming from prisoners. Had those prisoners been captured, just like these guys? Or for that matter, just like Alec's team?

Dread filled his gut. These males weren't dungeon-bound to do jail time. They were going to the tunnels. To work.

Turning, he glared at Zercy. "*Prisoners?* Are you sure you don't mean *slaves*?"

A shadow fell over Zercy's features. "They are that also."

One of the armed Kríe turned and briskly approached. "My lord." He stopped a few yards away. "The newest wave has arrived and is ready for inspection."

Zercy shifted his weight. He actually looked uncomfortable.

Good. He should. This shit was deplorable.

"Take them down. I will check each one later."

"Right away, my lord." The Kríe pivoted and headed back.

Alec stared at Zercy crossly. In truth though, he didn't know all the facts. God, let him be wrong. Let this not be what it seemed. So badly, he wanted to give him the benefit of a doubt.

"Are they guilty of *crimes*?" he prompted. He needed answers.

"In a manner of speaking."

"So, they're criminals. They broke the law."

Zercy clenched his jaw. Averted his gaze. "In accordance with their actions, I have ordered their capture. Now, to pay for their transgressions, they are my slaves."

Alec frowned. Zercy's explanation sounded dubious at best. His stomach fisted tight. Anxiety washed through his system. Was Zercy not the male Alec thought him to be? Did he have a malevolent side Alec didn't know about?

His heart thumped uneasily. "What did they do?"

Something flashed in Zercy's eyes, a fleeting glimpse of raw emotion. His jaw ticked. His ears twitched again. "Not your concern."

Alec shifted on his feet. The dread in his stomach was getting stronger. "That Kríe said 'the newest wave.' How many 'waves' are there gonna be?"

"Again, not your concern."

Alec's agitation spiked. "So many, you don't wanna say? What, are you rounding up a whole tribe?"

Zercy shot him a look, dark energy pulsing off his frame.

Alec frowned. "Why keep them as slaves? Why not just punish them in your torture chamber? Then let 'em go and be done with it?"

Zercy growled through gritted teeth. "Because I need them to—" He stopped. Breathing deeply, he resumed. "Because I need them."

"For what?"

"To mine."

Alec blinked, then balked. "As in, for gold and jewels and shit?"

Zercy chuckled sardonically. "Mah. What they mine is much more precious."

Alec stared at him, his reality of the king wholly upended. Zercy was using those males for his own gain. What's worse, they were all probably innocent. Falsely accused to justify Zercy's actions.

Alec couldn't believe it. Although why, he had no clue. Kríe had always proven themselves to be bastards. Why on earth would the *king* of Kríe be any better?

He wouldn't.

So, why then was Alec so dismayed? Because he'd *wanted* Zercy to be different. A male with decency. And morals. And heart. A male who was intrinsically *good*. But the atrocities taking place in the mines down below? That wasn't good.

That was inexcusable.

Fists clenched, Alec felt his blood starting to boil, reminded of his own damn predicament. "They're innocent," he muttered, glaring up at the king. "And you're holding them against their will. *Like my team*."

Zercy stiffened, as if stung by his words. He searched Alec's eyes. "You would think so little of me? They are far from innocent. And you... I want only to keep you safe."

"Right. Lucky me," Alec bit out. The subject still chafed. "But unlike me, they're gonna spend the rest of their lives under a mountain— slaving away just to make *you* fucking *rich!*" He shouted the last word.

Zercy bristled, then shook his head. "You are wrong, *Alick*. They are *guilty*. And their punishment is *just*." His eyes narrowed, looking not just uber-angry, but offended. "When have you *ever* seen me treat others unfairly?"

Alec couldn't think of anything off the top of his head, but Zercy's refusal to give details didn't sit well. It made *him* look like the guilty one, not those males. "Then what was their crime?" Alec demanded, getting frustrated.

Zercy clenched his jaw. "This is something I do not want to discuss."

Goddamnit. More dodging!

"Why? Because there *isn't* any crime? Or maybe you need more time to come up with a believable lie."

"Unlike you, I do not lie! I have been honest with you *always!*"

"Then just tell me! What'd they do that was so bad?"

"The unspeakable!"

"That tells me nothing!"

Zercy vibrated from head to toe. "I am not the villain in this."

"Maybe not. But you're the slave holder. Not quite sure which one is worse."

Seething, Zercy furiously pointed a claw toward the stairwell. "Those hell spawn, those Tohrí, they—" Stopping short, he bared his teeth. Then, abruptly, his fiery expression turned to stone. "You criticize me, judge me," he muttered, dropping his hand, "on matters you know nothing about."

God, he sounded pissed, in a detached sort of way. But underneath his chilly front, he also sounded hurt. Alec's insides shifted anxiously. Had he somehow read this wrong? But how? What could possibly justify slavery?

"Then explain it," he urged. "'Cause, damn it, none of this makes sense."

Zercy crossed his arms again, and this time his body language was clear. He'd just distanced himself. Proverbially stepped out of reach. "There is unrest in the kingdom. Something terrible has happened. An offence against my people that still continues."

"What offense? Zercy, tell me," Alec all but implored.

"Why? So, you can condemn me all over again? Denounce me when you have not borne my burden?"

Alec shook his head. "No. I'm just trying to under—"

"Mah," Zercy cut him off. "Your eyes have said it all already. To you, I am the monster. But I assure you of this; there are monsters far more heinous than me." Resentment darkened his features. He lifted his chin. "The things that I do, I do for my kingdom. If that means that I am evil, then I am evil."

Alec stared at him, at an utter and total loss for what to think. Zercy's tone held such conviction. And absolutely no apology. Whatever was happening, he believed his choices were valid.

Why wouldn't that stubborn Kríe just level with him?

Exhaling, Alec rubbed his brow, then gestured toward the stairwell. "Look, where I come from, forced servitude is wrong. In fact, in most places it's a crime. So, forgive me if I'm struggling to see the honor in what you're doing. If you'd just tell me what's—"

"I am *king!*" Zercy exploded. "I explain myself to no one!"

Alec quieted.

Zercy stared at him. Several moments ticked by. "You do not see me," he finally muttered, "though I stand right before you."

Alec frowned, his stomach twisting.

Zercy turned to one of his guards. "We are done here. Take him to his team."

* * *

This was bullshit. Total bullshit.

Alec scowled and made another lap. Sometime during the last twenty minutes, he'd begun to absently pace, growing more and more restless by the second. He'd hung with his men for the rest of the day, then was taken back to his room well over an hour ago. And still, Zercy had yet to return. Typically, he retired for the night soon after suns down. But it was pitch black out, meaning he was still pissed off at Alec.

Which, again, was total bullshit. Alec hadn't done anything wrong. Zercy was the one with the slaves.

Dragging a hand through his hair, he pivoted once more, wearing a track in the slate floor by the fireplace. Fucking hell. He hated Zercy's hot-and-cold behavior. It threw him off balance. Made him restless.

He eyed the room's wet bar. He could really use a drink. Preferably, one that'd put him on his ass. The last time he'd gotten drunk was back on Astrum Industries' space station, just a few nights before they disembarked. His team had been celebrating. They'd scored the coveted trip to Nira, with the adventure of a lifetime just days away. All the teams had wanted it, but it was his who'd won the jackpot.

If only he'd known then what he knew now.

Alec frowned and headed for the libations. In truth, it might not've made a difference since their quest's conclusion was still unknown. The outcome just might make it all worth it.

And honestly, he couldn't exactly say he *hated* it here.

At least not vehemently.

It had its positives.

Alec reached for a decanter of deep amethyst liquid. He'd never tried that one before. Please let it be potent. So far, the others had proven pretty tame. Which was fine, but tonight he wanted something that'd knock him sideways, so he could pass out and stop stressing over Zercy.

Pouring himself a gobletful, he took a hardy swig. A growl of approval climbed up his throat. Tasted like cherries and amaretto. He took a larger swallow, then chugged the rest and poured another. Maybe if he was lucky, he'd finally found a winner. The equivalent of hard liquor. Or Valium.

He brought the stuff back to his lips and got busy, but still Zercy stayed lodged in his mind. It was crazy, how he'd somehow managed to turn the tables, making Alec the one to feel guilty. But Alec wasn't the one with slaves, goddamnit. He shouldn't feel bad. He'd merely called Zercy out.

But he did feel bad. Because he'd clearly hurt the guy. Assuming the worst without hearing all the facts. But he had slaves! How many facts did one really need?

And yet, Alec sensed deep in the core of his being that there was so much more going on than he realized. Things that would explain Zercy's actions. His motives. The reason he'd embraced such brutish ways. Although, Alec *did* sense that Zercy didn't particularly relish it.

Pets, ironically, he seemed to like just fine.

Alec's heart thumped. His stomach clenched. Because, in fairness, he'd gotten the impression early on that Zercy didn't keep pets typically, either. That Alec was an exception. An impulsive indulgence. AKA a needed distraction.

To you, I am the monster. But I assure you of this; there are monsters far more heinous than me.

Alec stared at his goblet, contemplating the king's words. Who were these 'more heinous monsters'? Clearly, Zercy was in contention with them. Were they somehow connected to what he was dealing with?

Alec scrubbed his face. Maybe Zercy was just being metaphorical. Referring to that sickness as a monster. Was there a plague running rampant? Was it somehow inside the courtyard?

Possibly, but that didn't explain why Zercy felt the need for slaves. Specifically, of that one particular species. Tohrí, Zercy had called them. Hell, he'd practically spat their name. Were they tied to the sickness? Did he blame them for spreading it? No. No way. If that were the case, Zercy wouldn't want them anywhere near his castle. Or contaminating whatever it was they were mining.

Which, of course, gave way to yet another unanswered question— what in the hell Zercy was excavating.

Alec scowled and took another swig of his drink. All this not knowing was driving him crazy. He needed to stop thinking about it. Right freaking now.

And what do you know, perfect timing; his muscles had started to tingle. Surely a promising sign. And a godsend. He upturned his goblet and chugged the rest, then poured one more and glanced at the door.

Screw it. He was done waiting for that crab ass to show. He was going to go and sleep off this funk.

But as he turned with cup in hand and slowly ambled toward the bed, his insides turned all dejected and heavy. He hated that this day had ended on such a fucked-up note. Until those last minutes, his time with Zercy had been awesome. Easily one of the best days he'd had in ages. They'd had fun together and had been headed to the castle's history museum when everything had suddenly decided to detour south.

Alec grumbled as he climbed through the wall nest's opening, careful not to spill his ticket-to-oblivion. He'd really been looking forward to chilling out in there with Zercy. Would've learned so much more about him, simply by the things he naturally gravitated to in the museum. What interested him. What mattered to him. More priceless clues to Zercy's riddle.

Setting his drink down on the wrap-around headboard, Alec parked it on his ass and slowly sighed. Who was he kidding? He wouldn't be able to fall asleep. He chugged a few more gulps. Well, maybe he would. His tingly muscles were starting to loosen, too. Like happy noodles all hugging the frame of his body.

He noticed a dish of stones in arm's reach by the window. The smooth kind, that Zercy had all around his room. Their glossy finish was irresistible, so he scooped up a couple and treated himself to a bit of tactile fun. Stroking them with loose fingers as he peered out at the night, wondering yet again where Zercy was. In the company of others? Maybe his aide's? Maybe Lotis'? Or maybe he was by himself somewhere, like Alec. Was he thinking about Alec like Alec was thinking about him?

Doubtful. The guy was a king for crying out loud. Had way more important issues to think about. The most pertinent, undoubtedly was how to help his people.

Alec exhaled and returned the smooth stones to their dish. Deep down, he wanted to help, but that would never happen. Not with Zercy keeping him in the dark.

His gaze dipped down, settling absently on the headboard, noting again all its small, decorative pegs. Or were those levers?

He paused and studied them curiously. Did they turn something on? Serve a function?

Having nothing better to do, he tried to push one up, then down. Nothing. Didn't budge. He tried to press it like a button. Twist it like a knob. Nope, no luck.

Alec pursed his lips, "Hmm," then gave the thing a tentative pull. It gave without resistance, and out flicked the wall torches. Simultaneously, another light source flared to life from above. Alec peered up—and smiled.

No way.

Small white stones embedded flush with the ceiling, softly glowing like a spattering of distant stars. Alec stared at them. They felt familiar. And then he realized why. They were situated to mimic the Niran constellations. Exactly, in fact, like the ones on Alec's star map.

"Well, I'll be damned," he murmured, laying down to study them. How come Zercy hadn't shown him them before? Come to think of it, he hadn't demonstrated what *any* of those fancy pegs did. And now Alec was intrigued. Time to find out.

Remaining on his back, he slid one hand under his head, then blindly reached with the other to start investigating. His fingers found knob two. He gave it a pull. Instantly, the bed beneath him started to move. Like waves of thick muscles, slowly rolling back and forth. Alec froze, eyes wide, but nothing more happened. Just the subtle steady sensation of a massage.

Interesting.

And pretty cool.

In truth, it felt amazing.

Eyes trained on the ceiling, he felt around for the next one, then gave another small, sturdy tug. Peculiar music emerged, like none he'd ever heard before. Soft and fluid, yet fundamentally different. In melody, but most especially in essence. Alec couldn't explain it, but it sounded *organic*. As in, not made from instruments, but something *else*. He'd have to ask Zercy when he showed.

Soothed by its cadence, he slid his fingers to the next peg. Sweet plumes of fragrance puffed from flowers above. Red ones on scatterings of ivy adorning the walls. Alec inhaled deeply, feeling their faint mist on his face, then reached for the next knob down the line.

It felt fatter than the others. And notably more ornate. Did that signify something? Was its offering extra-special? Alec pulled, eager to know. Nothing happened. He tried again. Still no visible change.

But then he felt it.

Deep beneath the bedding.

A soundless awakening.

He stilled. What the hell? But before he could move, something slid up through the furs and circled his neck.

CHAPTER TWENTY-FOUR

* * *

"Shit!" Alec grasped at the entity around his throat. It didn't resist when he tossed it to the side.

Another emerged to do the same with his arm.

"What the—" Alec peeled that one off easily, too.

He frowned at the things. Great, they looked like tentacles. Memories of Mina crashed into his brain. He shuddered, but thankfully, these weren't nearly as creepy. Just two purple limbs with an iridescent sheen. Kind of looked like tails, actually, what with their velvety texture. All long and sleek, and barely thicker than a banana.

He eyed them, frozen in morbid fascination.

What were they? Plants? An animal? Some kind of mixture of both?

Three more appeared as the first two happily slithered back over, leisurely snaking their way around his arms.

Alec scowled and pulled them off again. Just like before, they didn't fight. Didn't constrict or turn aggressive. Didn't bite. Just let him pluck them off, emitting a soft little clicking, only to glide right back to his body the second he dropped them.

He grunted as one prodded a particularly ticklish part of his ribs. "What are you doing? Go away. Leave me alone." He pushed at it. "Scat."

It just chittered and curled loosely around his arm.

"Oh, for fuck's sake," he muttered, shaking it off. "You don't quit." At the same time, the others circled his chest and shoulder.

His heart pumped faster. There were five of them and one of him. If they wanted, they could immobilize him in seconds. Thing was, he realized, as he continued peeling them off, the vibe the things were throwing was hardly threatening. It was like they wanted to play. Or more specifically, cuddle. Like a feline pushing against him, trying to nuzzle.

Alec paused in his struggle to keep them at bay and simply watched them moving along his body. Around his bicep. Across his abdomen.

Over his knee, then down to his ankle. Nope, they definitely didn't feel dangerous. Maybe just curious.

But God, their movements, so fluid, like a snake...

Alec relaxed atop the furs, resolving to chill and wait it out. Logically speaking, Zercy would never keep dangerous entities in his bed. Whatever these were, they were clearly for the king's enjoyment. Truth be told, their soft little bellies felt kind of nice. Gently kneading as they moved, contracting and relaxing against his skin. Hell, they put the bed's massager to shame.

Besides, it wasn't like he had much of a choice. They seemed determined to stay no matter how many times he peeled them off.

More soft clicking emitted, the sound exuding a strange contentment. Alec exhaled and let his gaze rise back to the ceiling. This world was so bizarre, and not always in a bad way. At the moment, he was getting pampered by purple tentacles.

As he laid on a bed of furs.

Drinking a cocktail.

Without warning, more emerged, right at the nape of his neck, maybe half a dozen, feeling smaller and notably thinner. Alec tensed, but as they moved along his skull to knead his scalp, he slumped back down in bliss and closed his eyes.

Good God, that felt amazing. And now he totally got it. Why Zercy had his bed rigged up with these things. His personal masseuse, ready and waiting with ample arms. Alec may not get the workings, but at the moment, who cared. With the way he was feeling thanks to that drink, and now this? His brain was on hiatus; just like he'd wanted.

Two tentacles slid in opposite directions over his torso. Two others wound up his arms toward his neck. Bumping noses at his collarbone, they detoured down his chest, with one casually gliding into his tunic.

Alec tensed but didn't move. There wasn't anywhere for it to go. Any minute and it'd be slithering right back out. Sure enough, after a little bit of wandering around—his belt keeping it from going past his navel—it made a one-eighty and headed back up, sliding over his nipple along the way.

Oh.

That felt good.

He bit down on his lip, but kept his eyes closed as it exited. Which didn't happen quickly. The thing was long as freaking fuck, moving in a continuous glide over his nub. Said nub hardened fast, teasing his pec with licks of pleasure.

Alec swallowed the start of a moan. He refused to make a sound. But if that thing wanted back in his tunic, he wouldn't stop it. Oddly, not two seconds after thinking the thought, that long-ass velvety tentacle did a U-turn. Squirming its way back up under his wrap, this time returning directly to his nipple.

He stilled in surprise, but as its tip caressed his nub, he couldn't think of a reason to make it stop. Just some harmless, innocent nuzzling. The thing was probably just investigating. Intrigued about the bump it'd just discovered. It wasn't like it had latched on and was sucking.

The unbidden visual entered his mind before he could stop it, of the tentacle securing a seal around his nipple. Enveloping it with some secret little mouth. Next thing he knew, just like before, the second he envisioned it, that frisky purple fucker latched on tight. Not hard, or painfully, but Alec sucked in sharply anyway—alarmed, and quite frankly, confused. Because how was it doing that? It didn't have a mouth.

His bafflement died fast though, when the appendage started to suck.

"Oh, God," Alec breathed, lashes fluttering against his cheekbones. Tendrils of bliss zip-lined to his crotch. His dick thickened in reaction.

He should tug it off.

He should.

But he kind of didn't want to.

Besides, he still had no freaking clue how this was happening.

Warily, he opened his eyes and lifted his tunic's flap to see. But just as he did, a second tentacle slid inside. Air left him in a rush as it secured his other nipple. Sensation doubled. His dick shot harder. But all he could do was stare. In shock and bewilderment, but also in wonder. Because they *did* have mouths—or at least something similar—lining the last few inches of each limb. Little circular hollows along their silky underbellies, barely even noticeable to the eye. The openings, however, that were locked on his nubs were located right at the tip and looked larger.

Alec's pulse kicked up a notch as he debated what to do. Pluck the buggers off, knowing they'd immediately slither back, or just go with the flow and let them have their fun. His dick gave a nudge. Guess it wanted them to stay. They certainly weren't causing any pain.

Groaning at the fact that he was in this predicament to begin with, Alec dropped his head and stared back up at the ceiling. Maybe they'd get bored if he laid really still. Or decide to suck on something a lot less sensitive.

They didn't though, as the others weaved their way around his torso. Even those tendrils in his hair kept messaging. His nipples thrummed euphorically. They'd never gotten so much attention. And in turn, their surging pleasure fueled his dick. In less than five minutes it was ridiculously hard, diverting Alec's focus to his crotch.

His eyes slid closed as he shifted his hips. Absently, his hands gripped the fur. Next thing he knew, he was thinking crazy thoughts again, picturing those insistent tentacles sliding lower. Gliding under his balls. Rubbing against his groin. Coiling up and down his rigid shaft.

The images were shameless, he had no business conjuring them, but at the moment he just couldn't fucking stop. Blame it on that drink that had his brain all fuzzed and tingling. Or on his five new sinuous friends that wouldn't relent. All Alec knew was that the need to fuck was growing and, in turn, was seriously messing with his head.

No other reason he'd have tentacle hand jobs on the brain.

God. He was losing it.

But right as he reached to squeeze his dick, one of the meandering limbs slipped under his tunic below his belt. Alec froze, eyes snapping wide, suddenly fearing for his nuts. What if it tried to nuzzle his boys with too much pressure? His question was quickly answered, nearly before he'd finished wondering it, when the velvet tail abruptly turned gentle. Like it'd sensed his concern or some crazy shit and adjusted in an effort to try and please him.

Alec stifled another moan as it wound around his loinstrap, caressing his balls through the fabric while rubbing his cock. His boner bucked eagerly. His heart pumped faster. Dropping his hand back down to the furs, he rocked his hips.

So strange, the tentacle's touch. And yet it felt amazing...

His eyes slid closed again as his brain had another go. This time, imagining the contact was from Zercy. Or rather, from Zercy's cock as it moved against Alec's.

Fuck, yeah. All big and firm. And so damn long.

Alec breathed an anxious curse. His urge to come was getting stronger, his dick all but thrumming, his nipples singing. But God, he couldn't stop it. Those suckling mouths were making him crazy. His brain shifted gears and envisioned Zercy's mouth. His mouth, not those tentacles, latched onto Alec's nip, teasing it while his fingers worked the other.

Alec licked his lips and restlessly turned his head to the side, his eyes still closed, his eyebrows starting to scrunch. He imagined the king's body heat smoldering him from above, then pictured Zercy reaching for his dick. Curling his clawed fingers around its straining length, squeezing and relaxing his grip as he stroked.

The tail seemed to take heed, pausing to slip beneath his loincloth, spiraling around his cock before resuming. Shifting up and down, constricting and releasing, just like Alec had envisioned Zercy doing. Effectively solidifying his fantasy even more.

A moan finally escaped.

Alec wanted this so bad. The physical connect with Zercy, but also the mental. Because if Zercy was touching him, all intimate like this? Then that'd mean he wasn't angry, and they were good.

Problem was, in the corners of his lust-drunk mind, he knew it was only those tentacles touching his body. Only those tentacles that were making him need to come. And despite how incredibly good they felt, he couldn't just *let* them give him an orgasm. Making him feel good was one thing, yeah, but making him climax was another.

"Fuck," he groaned, reluctantly reaching to pull them off.

But before he could, one of the last two limbs stopped him. Winding around his wrist and easing it back down, its gentle grip felt strangely nonthreatening. Alec turned his head and watched it as he lifted his arm back up. It hung on but didn't stop him—at least not at first. The second his hand neared his dick again, though? It pulled it back and pinned his wrist down by his head.

"Shit," Alec moaned, as those other limbs kept teasing.

Again, he lifted his arm, and again it let him move, but his efforts always ended up the same. He tried his other hand. The final limb swiftly rose, mimicking its buddy's efforts to thwart Alec's plan.

Great. So that was the rub. He could move his hands freely, just as long as he kept them away from his crotch.

Body reeling, Alec scowled, but left his wrists pinned by his head. As irritating as this was, it was also kind of convenient. He still had to come, after all. This just handed him the guilt-free pass to let it happen.

Shivering as that pressure in his junk intensified, Alec swore an oath and squeezed his eyes shut. If he was going to do this, he was doing it with Zercy, not with weird-ass tentacles running the show.

He pictured the king's face again and focused on his gaze, all smoldering as he pumped Alec's cock. His lips moved, dark and full, showing glimpses of his fangs.

"*You like my touch, Alick,*" he imagined him saying. "*Tell me, do you want to feel it everywhere?*"

Alec nodded despite the pointlessness. But the truth was, he did. He wanted Zercy's fingers touching everything. Including a place he didn't want to admit. So instead he'd just secretly envision it. Hell, maybe the image of Zercy stroking his backdoor would speed up the process and make him come.

"*Bellah,*" Zercy rumbled in his mind. "*No lies. Your good behavior deserves a reward.*"

His fingers grazed Alec's nuts as they slid even lower. Then his big, clawed index slipped between Alec's cheeks. Alec imagined him touching his hole.

"Yes," Alec moaned in approval. "There."

A second later, two tails wound around his legs. More had arrived? All the others were currently occupied. Not that his brain really cared. Securing a hold, they drew his knees up toward his chest, then eased them apart and held them steady.

Alec's head spun. Whatever. He could work it into the fantasy. His dick throbbed in agreement. So did his nuts.

Zercy started a slow caress, circling the pad of his finger. Alec even imagined the king's claw grazing his skin.

Something firm touched his tailbone, then slid up his crack. Instinctively, Alec clenched at the sensation. It stopped at his entrance and gave some gentle nudges. He tensed and quickly imagined it Zercy's finger.

More soft chittering as it lazily nuzzled, but soon it paused directly atop his door. A low warble emitted, so quiet he almost didn't hear it, then the thing against his hole sort of quivered.

"Uh!" Alec clenched a second time—that shit tickled!—but curiously, now his ring felt cool and wet.

Don't wanna know—Don't wanna know—

He swiftly envisioned Zercy's tongue.

The stroking resumed.

Alec's lashes fluttered furiously. *"Unngh... Fuck, yes..."*

Before too long though, the sensation shifted, feeling less like slippery rubs and more like prods. Gentle at first, but gradually growing more insistent.

"Alick," he imagined Zercy's husky voice purring. *"Relax your little starflower. Let me in."*

Alec exhaled a restless curse, but let his body obey.

The tip of Zercy's tongue wedged just barely into his sphincter. Alec's heart hammered feverishly. His dick went wild. Balling his fists, he bared down and—

It pushed inside.

Alec grunted, then hissed, squeezing his eyes shut even tighter. Because, goddamn, that didn't feel like a tongue. It felt like a lubed-up mammoth dick. His asshole screamed in pain as his brain shifted gears again, changing the visual, swapping out Zercy's tongue for his cock. Just in time, too. Said cock just drove inside even deeper.

"Uh!—Zercy! Fuck!" Alec heard himself shout. His pulse went friggin' nuts, but not from the sting. From the mind-blowing thought of Zercy inside him.

He rocked his hips anxiously. Zercy's dick delved farther.

Alec gasped. It'd just glided past his prostate.

Pleasure flared inside his channel. The king's cock kept on going.

"*Ungh*..." Alec groaned, fumbling blindly to fist the furs.

He'd forgotten how freaking long a Kríe's huge cock was.

Deeper it pushed. He could feel it in his gut. Any farther and it'd be tunneling through his bowels.

"No," he rasped, shaking his head. "That's it. Can't take more."

He imagined Zercy chuffing. *"My pet is full."*

Soft clicking resounded.

Alec's heart pounded anxiously.

Then just like that, Zercy's boner was easing back.

Alec moaned, clenching absently as it slowly withdrew. "Shit," he rasped. "That shouldn't feel so freaking good."

But when it rubbed back over his prostate, *good* shot to *great*.

Alec shuddered on a curse. "*Ungh*—My *God*."

Zercy's cock stopped dead in its tracks.

Alec pinched his brows, all but panting. But then that cock gave a nudge—and started doing something really odd. Alec gasped and twitched at the strange sensation. It felt like Zercy's glans was nosing around. Investigating or something. It pushed on his prostate.

Alec jerked with a start as pleasure ignited.

"Fuck, Kríe," he croaked. "That's really—sensitive there—"

He imagined Zercy chuffing again, then leaning down to bite Alec's lip. *"You like it, though. Tah?"*

Alec nodded. "It's just... intense."

The king grinned, still clutching Alec's lips with his teeth. *"You want me to be gentle."*

God, that'd be awesome.

Alec didn't actually say that, but it didn't seem to matter. Zercy's cock got busy regardless, slowly easing back and forth, the firm tip of his crown right on the money. His prostate thrummed in bliss.

"Aw, God.... Holy—*Unnngh*..." If Alec's eyes were open, they would've crossed. "That's gonna make me come. Don't stop."

Instinctively, he reached for his dick to work it faster, but those tails held him secure and did the honors. His junk went berserk. His ass went crazy. Zercy's dick picked up speed, in and out.

"Oh, God—*Oh, God*—"

That heavenly pressure was spiking, branching out from his groin to every nerve. Alec panted, his body heating. Fumbling, he freed his belt and ripped open his tunic wrap, then quickly got back to gripping at those furs.

Zercy suckled his nipples harder. Worked his singing G. But then, frustratingly, slowed down on his cock. Which was maddening; the more he gave Alec, the more urgent Alec became, needing more, which Zercy provided, driving him wilder.

Close—So damn close—

He nuts were high and ready.

His breaths sped faster.

His heart stampeded.

His knees shifted restlessly against his chest.

"Gonna come—" he gasped. His hips bucked. He clenched his jaw. His lids squeezed tighter. "*Ungh*, God—*Fuck*—Please don't—"

"*Alick*." Zercy's stern voice cut him off, sounding gruffer.

Alec couldn't think. "Yeah?" he panted.

"Open your eyes."

Alec frowned. Why would he fantasize *that?* If he opened his eyes, he'd—

"Do it. *Now*."

Confused, he obeyed, then shot stiff as a board. Every tentacle froze in unison, too.

"Zercy," he rasped.

The king was standing there, watching him, his auric gaze smoldering, his jaw set tight.

Alec frantically glanced around. Oh, God. This wasn't part of his fantasy. Which meant this was really happening. His heart shot into his throat as he dropped his feet, all his 'buddies' retreating—minus the one in his ass. He grunted with a wince as it squirmed around inside him, as if trying to get out but wasn't able.

Alec's channel lit up like fireworks. He choked back a moan, then glanced between his bent knees down his body. What the hell was going on? He was mortified enough. Why was that tentacle still—

Shit.

That's why.

Zercy had caught it mid-withdraw and was keeping it where it was for whatever reason.

Alec anxiously met his gaze, fighting like hell to keep his eyes open. At the moment, they urgently wanted to roll back. "This isn't how it looks. I—They just came out of nowhere."

Zercy lifted a skeptical brow.

"They wouldn't stop," Alec blurted. "They held me down and—"

"Grab your cock."

Alec stilled, said cock reeling. "W-What?" he panted, delirious. That flailing tail in his ass was rocking his sanity.

"Grab your cock," Zercy repeated. "You need to spill. We talk after."

Oh, thank God.

Alec quickly freed his dick from his loincloth—but then paused and looked back up at the king.

"Tah, *Alick*. Stroke."

And fuck, did he ever, trapped in Zercy's gaze the whole time.

Pressure soared back to critical. Rapture roared in his crotch. And thanks to that tentacle doing a jig around back, he was this close to losing his mind.

"You gonna keep that—" he gasped, "in my ass—the whole time?"

"Tah."

"F-Fuck." He cranked his head back into the furs.

"*Alick.*"

"What?" he panted, his bent knees twitching as he pumped.

"Look at me."

Alec did.

Their gazes locked.

"Spill for me. *Now.*"

His words hit Alec's ears, then dive-bombed straight to his crotch. Alec's muscles shot rigid. His whole body twitched. Then his straining boner flat-out frickin' exploded.

"*Fuck!*" Alec belted.

Hot cum punched from his dick, arching high, then splatting his chest. Again and again, while Alec fought to hold Zercy's stare. His asshole clenched hard. He could feel his taint contracting. His prostate powerfully pulsing in bliss.

But it wasn't until his orgasm finally relented that Alec felt the potent churning in his chest. An urgent kind of warmth that he couldn't describe. Couldn't describe yet knew exactly what it was. A surge of strengthening feelings for the king.

Struggling for breath, he closed his eyes and rubbed his sternum.

"Bellah," Zercy murmured. The tentacle slipped free.

Alec's cheeks flushed. He draped an arm over his eyes. "Those things..." he muttered. "I didn't mean for that to happen."

The bedding subtly shifted. Zercy had climbed inside the nest. His hand grazed Alec's knee. His other grazed Alec's thigh. Then hot breath whispered past his soft, spent cock.

Alec stilled. What was he doing?

A long, warm tongue touched his belly.

"Tell me," Zercy rumbled as he started to lap. "What wickedness befell you? What did my playthings make you do? Tell me, *Alick*. Tell me all your lies."

Alec stilled. His heart clenched. Zercy's words cut like a knife. Frowning, he dropped his arm. "You think I'm a liar."

"Would I be wrong?" Zercy slowly tongued a patch of thick droplets. "Have you not confessed to lying in the past?"

"Well... Yeah, but—"

"And were you not about to tell me right now that my *centiclees* did things to your body you did not want?"

Alec hesitated. The king was trapping him. He could feel it in his bones. He scowled. "Are you saying you think I wanted that?"

Zercy peered up through his lashes. "Are you saying you did not?"

Alec swallowed and looked away. That wasn't an easy question to answer. Maybe at first? But by the end, though? Yeah, not exactly.

Zercy's chuckle held no humor. He lapped up the rest, then dropped onto the furs next to Alec. Peering up at the ceiling, he smiled darkly. "Centiclees are dygons with a very unique skill. They can decipher the very thoughts of those they touch."

Alec blinked. Blinked again. "Whoa, wait, *what?*" He rolled to his side. "You're telling me they're telepathic? Were reading my mind?"

"*It*. Not they. Beneath my nest lies only one. And no, not telepathic, but close. If centiclees were intelligent like us, then perhaps. But they are not. They are merely sentient plants. We consider them more like gifted empaths."

"Holy shit," Alec murmured, looking back on the encounter. No wonder their actions felt so responsive to his thoughts, reacting so perfectly to every desire. He frowned. "But how? You say they do it by touch?"

"Tah. The smaller tentacles you felt along your skull, its sensory receptors are there. They pick up electrical impulses emitted from the brain. They also taste the chemicals it releases that drive emotions. Sirus says that from there they line up the data and interpret it. I do not know more than that, though... And do not care."

"Damn." Alec's scientists would have a field day with that. He looked at Zercy. "Has your centiclees done weird stuff to you, too?"

Zercy shifted on his back. "It does whatever I desire. If I want a massage, it gives me a massage. If I want it to take my cock, it takes my cock."

Alec's lips parted. "Takes it how?"

"Sometimes a toothless mouth is nice."

Damn. It sucked dick, too. Alec's brain churned in awe. "Has your centiclees ever... you know."

Zercy slid him a harsh smirk. "Fucked my ass? Of course. It has done many things." He looked away again.

Wow.

Alec wondered what else it could do.

Zercy exhaled and stared at the ceiling. And that's when Alec finally smelled it. The distinct scent of 'alcohol'—or whatever its equivalent was on Nira.

Zercy had been drinking. Alec studied him closer. Didn't look like he'd been celebrating. In fact, he looked morose as hell. Was he drunk? Had he been boozing for the same reasons as Alec, to drown out all the relentless stuff eating at him?

Alec's insides clenched uncomfortably. Had *he* played a role in that? In driving Zercy to drinking because of their argument? When he sent Alec away, he'd looked pretty unhappy. Mostly pissed off, but also hurt. Especially considering the last thing Zercy said.

You do not see me, though I stand before you.

Those words had stuck with Alec. In fact, they'd really bothered him.

"I *do* see you," he heard himself murmur in the quiet.

Zercy's gaze dipped a little. "Do you?" His voice sounded guarded.

"Yes... I have for a while... And what I see is not a monster."

Zercy didn't reply at first.

"What do you see?" he finally muttered.

"A king who's dealing with a lot. Who's had to make some difficult choices. I jumped the gun before and... I'm sorry. It just... looked bad. But the more I think about it, the more I believe that all of this is happening because it has to."

Zercy's hardened features softened. But not in warmth. Looked more like grief.

Alec's chest tightened. "Why won't you talk about it? Why won't you tell me what's going on?"

"Because just thinking about it pains me. Like a blade in my chest. Lancing my heart. Is that your wish?"

Alec exhaled. "No, of course not. I just... want to help."

Total truth. Zercy's struggle somehow felt like his, too.

Zercy slid his gaze Alec's way, as if moved by his words. "Gratitude, *Alick*, but there is nothing you can do. My kingdom, my people... Our fate is sealed."

In other words, he wasn't talking.

God, he looked exhausted.

Alec should probably just let it go.

Fine. He'd leave him alone. Would let the Kríe get some sleep.

After, that is, he asked him one last question.

"Zercy?"

"Tah, *Alick*."

"Do you *like* having slaves?"

Zercy closed his eyes and shook his head. "Mah."

CHAPTER TWENTY-FIVE

* * *

"It will only take a moment. I am certain it will be fine."

"No." Alec shook his head in the doorway of Zercy's chambers. "I don't wanna go see Sirus. He's crazy."

Setch exhaled in frustration, swapping quick looks with Kellim. "But the *elevator*. You need to instruct him how to build it. My brother and I, we are getting old. And those stairs—they are going to kill us."

Alec folded his arms. "Yeah, whatever. You're both in better shape than anyone I know."

The siblings preened visibly.

Alec tamped down a smile. "And old, my ass. What are you, forty?"

"Fifty-six," Kellim offered. "Nine years older than our king."

Zercy was forty-seven? Alec lifted a brow. Damn. The Kríe barely looked thirty-five.

The pair eyed him expectantly. "So, you will come with us? To Sirus?"

"Sorry, I don't think so." Alec shifted his weight. "Last time you took me to him I wound up naked, strapped to a table."

The guards stifled chuffs.

Setch outstretched his hands. "That was not our fault. We were only following orders. Obeying the king to keep our heads. You understand."

Alec stared at him irritably. That'd been one seriously fucked-up visit. "Yeah, well, *the king* has ordered that I be here. Every night, remember? When he retires."

"We will send word to let him know. I am sure he will not mind. Besides, he does not come back early anymore anyway."

Kellim shot Setch a look that said, *Bro, you're a moron.*

Setch cleared his throat and smiled. "He has been busy."

Alec's stomach twisted anxiously. Even the guards knew something was up. Frowning, he shook his head again. "Some other time."

"But—"

He shut the door, then turned and eyed the empty room. For the past week it'd just been him and the fucking furniture. It was like the king had gone MIA—at least until after Alec hit the sack. Every night, Alec dozed off on his side of the neatly made nest, only to wake with Zercy's side all rumpled and messy.

He was returning after Alec fell asleep—no doubt to purposely avoid him.

Alec bit his cheek. It'd all started after their argument regarding the slaves. But Alec had thought he'd made things right again later that night. When Zercy had watched Alec bust his nut, then cleaned up Alec's mess with his tongue. It'd been kind and attentive. And after, Alec had apologized sincerely. Yeah, the king had seemed quiet, but Alec assumed he'd just been stressing.

That's what Zercy did. Day and night.

Alec had obviously been wrong though, because every morning since, Zercy was gone before Alec woke up, and pretty much stayed that way. Had Alec messed up worse than he thought? Done more damage than he realized?

Restless and agitated, he strode to the bar. But as he eyed the different decanters, none looked appealing. Maybe because he didn't really feel like drinking. Strange, considering he had plenty to numb his brain over. The most prominent: Zercy's friggin' MIA act.

Alec exhaled and scanned the bottles again, then eyed the dishes sitting in front of them. Finger foods of some sort. Balls of this. Cubes of that. There was even a jar of what looked like long, thin jerky sticks.

His dad used to love those things. Alec smiled in remembrance. They used to smuggle pocketfuls into baseball games.

Snagging one up, he tried to take a bite. Didn't work. The center was too solid with just a slightly softer exterior. Evidently, the things were meant to be gnawed on. Like a toothpick or something. Alec pulled it out and looked at it. Didn't taste like beef jerky. Its flavor reminded him more of black licorice.

Eh. Whatever. He liked black licorice. Shoving it back between his molars, he started to wander. Not long after, he pulled to a stop at Zercy's writing desk.

Alec studied the thing. Made of some sort of rich purple wood, it appeared to have been fashioned to mimic a tree. Two large pedestal legs carved like trunks, forked like roots at the bottom, and branches up top. Engraved leaves circled the desk's thick ledge, and at the center, a giant sunburst was artfully branded. A sunburst that looked a lot like Zercy's birthmark.

Interesting.

Alec sat on its tree-stump stool and scanned the several items lying about. A huge, leather-bound notebook. Some charcoal-type pencils. Tools akin to T-squares and compasses. To the right though, was something he'd checked out before. A big, black stone globe with the likeness of Nira, impaled upon its own wrought-iron pedestal.

Alec reached for the thing as he chewed on his stick, its taste slowly growing a little sweeter. He didn't bother spinning the orb. He'd long since discovered it didn't turn. It *did*, however, come off its sturdy little stand. He palmed the globe and carefully slid it up and off, then held the volley-ball sized planet in his hands.

Etched in gold, each continent was skillfully outlined, then labeled with Kríe symbols, as were the oceans. He studied the markings as he'd done before, absently working that stick between his teeth. It made his jaw feel funny, made him want to bite down harder, so he did, as he continued to eye the symbols.

Slowly, he rotated the heavy onyx sphere until he found a spot he'd located previously; what looked like the etchings of a circular mountain range with the inference of a rainforest to its right. Zercy's kingdom. He was sure of it. With the jungle they crashed in beside it.

Intrigued by a planet so similar to Earth, yet so different, he reexamined every land mass and body of water. A good distraction, incidentally, to what he'd otherwise be thinking about. The moody king who dropped off the grid.

A lick of irritation at the thought had him scowling. Which in turn, had his molars grinding harder. Don't think about the bastard, he told himself. Focus instead on the ocean just west of Zercy's realm.

He turned it counterclockwise and eyed a cluster of islands. But now that feeling in his jaw was creeping lower. A little crawling tickle down his neck. He scratched under his chin, then beneath his ear, then finally set the globe down and pulled out his stick.

Frowning, he scrutinized it. Maybe he'd chewed that end too long. He turned it around and shoved it back between his teeth. On the other side of his mouth though, just to be safe. He resumed pouring over every inch of the planet. Couldn't help it. It was just so cool.

Zercy's world in his hands. How 'bout them apples?

Thing was, before long that sensation moved lower, sinking into the muscles of his shoulders. He rolled them with a growl. Felt like a feather under his skin, incessantly teasing his sensitive flesh. The curious tickle spread farther, down his spine, then into his tailbone, lighting up every nerve ending in his pelvis.

Grumbling, Alec set the orb back on its mount and promptly started rubbing his back and pecs. The feeling had inundated his torso. Even his abs and groin were experiencing it.

"What the fuck," Alec groaned, pulling the stick from his mouth.

Was that stupid thing seriously the culprit? He scowled while rubbing his cheek with his shoulder, then chucked his suspect licorice out the window.

It was moving to his limbs now. Even his palms felt kind of tickly.

Breathing a curse, he rubbed his arms, then his thighs, and man, that felt good. He worked his chest again. Shit, his nipples were rock hard. He rolled his head on his shoulders and loosed a moan. What the hell was freaking happening? He needed friction *everywhere*. Like a cat strung-out on catnip.

Behind him, the door opened.

Alec tensed, then turned on the stool.

Zercy, in the doorway, looking grumpy.

Great.

Alec met his gaze. Rubbed his neck, then his shoulder, then forced his restless hands to stand down.

Zercy held his stare and stepped inside. Kellim shut the door behind him.

Alec stood and cleared his throat. "Hey. Wasn't expecting you."

"Why is that?" Zercy muttered. He strode to the bar and poured a drink. "Is this not my private quarters where I come to sleep?"

"Well, yeah, but you haven't retired this early all week."

Zercy slid him a look. "Would you like me to leave?"

Alec crossed his arms, discreetly rubbing the sides of his pecs. "No. It's cool. I wanted to talk."

"Hm," the king grunted. Turning with drink in hand, he made for his nest. "I do not think I am of a mind to talk tonight."

Alec frowned, watching him go. "Yeah, well, too bad. I haven't seen you in six fucking days."

"Ah. Did you miss me?" Zercy's smirk was sardonic.

What was his deal? "No." Alec glared. "Just want some answers."

"Of course, you do." Zercy climbed into the opening of his bed. "Ever wanting answers. That is my *Alick*."

Grrr. Alec scowled and awkwardly shuffled his way over, giving himself a quick rub while out of view.

He stopped in front of the wall nest. Zercy was propped against the headboard, peering out the window, arms resting on his knees. His expression, as always, was pensive. But he also seemed tired. Even his typically strong features looked notably drawn.

Zercy didn't look his way, though Alec knew he was in his periphery. Nor did he speak a single word as Alec stood there. God, the vibe he was throwing. It made Alec wary. Unsettled. But his own need to know what was happening was definitely stronger.

"You've been avoiding me. Why?"

"I have not been—"

"Yes, you have." Inconspicuously, Alec ground his shoulder against the opening.

Zercy stared straight ahead, not replying right away. "Things are coming to a head… over which I have no control… Believe me when I say that you would not want me around… As of late, I…" He dropped his gaze, "would make very poor company."

Alec watched him, brows furrowed. He rubbed his shoulder again. "You couldn't have touched base, though? Sent a message? Just once?"

Fuck. His body was *humming*. He needed some serious friction *now*. Dropping his arms, he clutched his hips, then rubbed his thighs, then fisted his hands.

Zercy muttered, "I felt it best to stay away."

"Yeah, well, that's bullshit. Not to mention rude. I was stressing out, goddamnit. And none of your guards would tell me anything. For all I knew, you caught that sickness and bit the dust."

Zercy stilled and slid him a look. "Bit the dust?"

"It's an expression." Alec scrubbed his face, then attacked his neck. "It means you died."

Zercy grunted, eyes diverting again. "The sickness does not work that way."

"And I would know this *how?*" Alec grated, kneading the length of his shoulder.

Zercy swigged his blood-red beverage, but then stilled and looked at Alec. His smile was barely discernible. "You were worried."

Alec glanced away. "Was not."

"And you missed me."

"I didn't say that." Wrapping his arms around his sides, he briskly squeezed.

"Ah, but you did. Just with different words." Zercy canted his head and watched him.

Alec fought not to squirm.

Zercy's brows dipped. He frowned. "What is wrong with you?"

"Nothing," Alec bit out. But then a whimper escaped, too. He broke down and rubbed at everything. "I just need *friction.*"

Zercy narrowed his eyes, openly studying him as Alec shifted and writhed. A second later, something glinted in his gaze. His lips curved infinitesimally. A soft chuff rose up his throat. "Truthfully, *Alick?* You ate the *zenki?*"

"The what?"

"Spice canes. The slender sticks on my bar."

Alec tensed. Oh, no. "Why? What's wrong with them? Are they poisonous?"

"Mah," Zercy chuckled. "But they are not meant to be *eaten.*"

Alec groaned and twisted his back, then rolled his shoulders again. "Then what're they for?"

"As a complement." Zercy's eyes hooded as he watched Alec fidget. "A brief stir in one's drink to add some fun."

Alec clenched his jaw. Rubbed his chest up and down the side of the opening. "What kind of fun?"

"A little strum just for the flesh."

"Son of a bitch," Alec groaned, doing the math. "Just one stir? I am so screwed. Just shoot me now."

Zercy stifled another chuff. "Come to me. I will help."

Alec knew his face looked pitiful. "How?" he ground out, clutching his hamstrings.

Zercy crooked his finger. "I will show you. Nenya." *Come.*

Whatever. Alec was desperate. He clambered through the opening.

Zercy set aside his drink and eased down onto his back. Hooking his finger in Alec's collar, he tugged him over.

Alec grunted as he landed, sprawled on his stomach atop Zercy's chest. "Really, Kríe?" he grated. Was this just another of Zercy's antics? "How in the hell is this supposed to help with anything?"

The king's dark lips quirked, his sullen mood visibly ebbing. Palming Alec's back with his huge hands, he started to knead.

Alec's moan was instantaneous. "Oh fuck, Kríe. That's... *Yeaaahhh.*"

The shot of pure relief sent him grinding against the king, rubbing from hips to pecs all over Zercy's torso. His dick swelled rock hard in the torrent of sensation. It needed friction too, like everything else. Something big and firm to scrub against.

Fortunately for him, Zercy hardened just as fast, providing what Alec needed. The perfect grinding post.

"Shit," Alec breathed, rocking his hips, rubbing their chests.

Zercy rumbled, kneading the muscles flanking Alec's spine. "Tah, tend to your front, *Alick.* I will work where you cannot reach."

"Yes." Alec nodded, shifting eagerly. "God, yes—Thank you."

And yet, inwardly, he knew this was all just weird as hell. Not that he cared at the moment. The physical contact felt incredible. Drunk on the friction, he wedged his face against Zercy's neck. Even his stupid flushed cheeks needed attention. Twisting his pelvis, he rubbed their legs, then eagerly tangled their arms.

Zercy purred.

Alec groaned, his mind spinning euphorically.

The sensation was exquisite, every nerve ending in his body rejoicing. How in the hell did he get himself into these predicaments?

Zercy's hands moved lower and squeezed his ass, then slid lower still, to work his hamstrings. He kneaded them roughly. Alec moaned in sweet bliss, gripping Zercy's biceps, then his shoulders. Zercy's muscles flexed in time, bunching and rolling beneath his hands.

Alec's heart pounded. His breath quickened. Though his mind was fully sober, every cell within his skin felt wholly intoxicated.

Zercy clutched behind his knees and pulled them down to his sides, causing Alec to straddle him, but who cared. The contact to his inner thighs felt fantastic, too. He scrubbed their torsos tighter and fisted Zercy's hair, the long, velvety ropes teasing his palms. He released them and tunneled deeper, then gripped two more handfuls.

Zercy growled and vigorously kneaded Alec's ass.

Jesus. The need for contact was overwhelming.

Alec groaned. "Shit, Kríe. When will it stop? It's too much."

"Soon." Zercy's timbre sounded gravelly as hell.

Alec cursed and rubbed their faces. "I'm losing my mind."

Zercy's hands worked up his back, leaving tingles in their wake. Alec shuddered and absently shifted up Zercy's torso.

Goddamn. So good.

His eyes rolled back, his jaw went slack, his parted lips pressed to Zercy's cheekbone as he panted. Zercy purred husky-low and palmed the back of his head. Sharp claws lightly grazed his sensitized scalp.

"*Fuuuck*," Alec moaned, riding another wave of shivers. But as he braced, his knuckles brushed something hard. Zercy's horns. All warm and smooth. His fingers suddenly itched to grip them. Without thinking, he let go of those velvety dreads and tightly clutched the two horns instead.

Zercy stiffened. Even his busy hands froze.

But Alec was too far gone to grasp the whys. Up and down Zercy's torso, he rubbed his body, using the horns for leverage.

Zercy growled and shifted beneath him. Then shifted again and clutched Alec's hips. "*Alick*," he grated. His jaw was clenched, his muscles taut. "Your hands. You must not—"

"*Don't stop*," Alec cut him off, brows pinched as he writhed. "Please. Keep going." To hammer home his need, he tightened his grip on those horns and urgently ground his hips against Zercy's stomach.

A snarl filled Zercy's throat, but to Alec's relief, the king recommenced with his task, feverishly squeezing every muscle on Alec's body. His own frame, however, never relaxed.

Unfortunate, but hey, welcome to Alec's world. He was currently wound up tighter than a cable. His heart pumped faster, his blood pulsing in his ears. And fuck, now that he'd shifted farther up Zercy's body, he could feel the king's cock prodding his ass. His own dick reeled. He rocked against Zercy's abs, squeezing those sleek black horns with each grind.

"*Alick*," Zercy growled again, his voice exuding warning. He grasped Alec's arms. "You must not—"

"Quit stopping!" Alec squirmed in frustration. His restless grip shifted closer to Zercy's skull.

Once more, the king stiffened, then his whole body shook, a feral snarl tearing heatedly up his throat. Next thing Alec knew, he'd been thrown onto his stomach.

"What the hell, Kríe. I—"

"*Mine!*"

Alec stilled at Zercy's snarl, then— "*UH!*"

Zercy struck, sinking his sharp, fat fangs deep.

Alec went rigid taut. Raw pain streaked through the crook of his neck. He clutched the bed's thick furs. "Shit, Kríe—*Fuck!*"

Zercy growled against his skin, caging him in with his big body. Instantly, that searing ache morphed to a throb, pulsing down his torso with each firm pull.

Alec's hips started urgently grinding. Raw need ripped through his pelvis. And in his frenzy, he understood—why Chet had looked so crazed when Roni bit him. Because he *had* been crazed, with the frantic urge to fuck. And to *be* fucked.

Feverishly, he writhed.

Holymotherfuckingshit.

Zercy's mouth. It felt tethered, tethered wickedly to Alec's crotch, every draw he took feeling like a stroke to Alec's dick. But not just there. He felt that tether everywhere. In his balls. Inside his ass. Along his G.

Alec's brows pinched. He started to pant.

His heart hammered anxiously.

Oh, God. That felt incredible.

Overwhelming, but still insane.

Zercy quickened his pulls—then gave an exceptionally hard suck.

Alec arched with a shout, gripping the furs harder, a furious need to come suddenly nailing him. His hips bucked, his ass reeling, his nuts like rocks. "Zercy—" he gasped. "Oh, my—Oh my fucking—*ungh!*— God—"

The huge Kríe just growled, then started grinding against his ass. Alec's brain went on lockdown. All rationale flew out the window. Mindless, he shoved a fumbling hand under his hips and grabbed his junk. Maybe if he could just—

Zercy grabbed Alec's wrist and pulled it out from under them.

"*Mine,*" he snarled again, the sound muffled against Alec's neck. Pinning Alec's hand out of commission, he shoved Alec's legs apart with his knees.

Oh, God. He wanted to fuck.

Alec's restless hips rocked faster. Because, goddamnit, he wanted to fuck, too. To be taken hard and fast by this Kríe.

"Yes—" he panted, not thinking, just needing.

Zercy rumbled and yanked up his hips. Next thing Alec knew, something hot and firm pushed against his hole.

Warning sirens roared to life. Alec tensed in realization. As much as he wanted to get down and dirty, he couldn't take Zercy's cock. It was too big. It'd wreck him. His ass would rip in two.

"Zercy—Zercy, wait—"

But the king wasn't hearing. Sounded too far gone himself. Snarling against Alec's neck, he tried to enter.

Alec cursed, heart hammering. "Zercy—*Wait*—"

"Mah. I take you *now,*" Zercy grated. He took another exceptionally powerful draw.

White-hot pleasure tore through Alec's body, exploding up his reeling crotch. "*Ugh!*" he cried out in ecstasy.

Zercy pushed harder against his door.

Pain. Raw and searing.

Alec stiffened. "*Ugh!* Shit—*Wait!—*"

Fuck, but he wanted this! To feel the whole experience. The exquisite pleasure from Zercy's fangs while getting drilled.

Just not at the expense of his ass.

Brain clearing fast, he squirmed. "Please, Zercy—*Stop—*"

Zercy froze. Like a statue.

Then, just as abruptly, lurched off of Alec's body. "Apologies—I—" he croaked, breathing hard. "I lost control... I did not mean to attack you... Are you hurt?"

Alec flopped back down and groaned. "No."

Zercy exhaled raggedly.

Alec rolled over, still panting, and eyed him. "What just happened?"

"I lost control."

"Yeah, you said that... But why?"

Zercy scowled, as if angry at himself.

Alec stilled. "Because I touched your horns?"

He nodded sharply.

Alec frowned and sat up. Rubbed his brow. "What made you stop?"

Zercy averted his gaze. His voice dipped. "I heard your fear."

Alec thought about that, then thought about Miros, and the things he'd said when Alec had gripped his horns, too.

You touch me in a way you do not understand. Your hands make me need to mark you.

Alec looked at Zercy. "Is that the only reason?"

Zercy glanced down at his cock. Chuffing darkly, he scrubbed his face. "Had we continued, your status would have elevated drastically. No longer just my pet. We would be—" He stopped.

Alec blinked. Blinked again. "We would be *what?*"

Zercy met his gaze. "Bonded."

Alec's eyebrows hiked. "Whoa, *what?*"

"We would be bonded," he repeated. "Able to bear young with only each other."

Alec shook his head, confused. "Just from touching your horns?"

"Mah. That is merely the catalyst to it all, what ignites the powerful urge to bite and fuck. If *those* things had happened, our essences would have fused."

Alec stared at him, lost.

Zercy forced a small smile. "The simultaneous transference of seed and blood. It triggers a kind of coding within both parties. Once this happens, they are irrevocably bonded—at least where procreation is concerned."

So, marking meant biting one's partner while fucking. Ergo, Chet's bite from Roni was different since they'd just been wrestling.

Alec digested Zercy's words. Niran biology was insane. "So, their bodies' chemistry, it literally *changes*?"

"Tah. Forever. It is Nira's way."

Silence lingered.

Alec glanced away in thought, then looked back. "If there was a way… for us to fuck just now… I would've let you."

"I know… I tasted your need… In your blood… On your flesh… But I am glad that I did not… I would have hurt you."

That wasn't the only reason he was glad, and Alec knew it. "Glad 'cause you would've hurt me, but also because of that bond."

Zercy frowned and looked at the ceiling. "Tah. Because of that, too."

Alec watched him for a minute, his own dick still hard. "You want kids, then? An heir?"

"Of course."

His tone gave Alec pause. As if the subject of kids made him sad.

"Do you have siblings?" Alec asked.

"Mah."

"Where are your parents?"

"With Nira."

Nira? Alec frowned, but understanding came fast. His insides went heavy. "Shit… I'm sorry."

Zercy smiled a little. "As am I. They were noble kings."

"So are you."

No reply.

Maybe it was time to change the subject.

Alec sighed and glanced around, his focus settling on Zercy's chalice. He'd been in quite the mood when he took that drink to bed. His brain got to thinking. He looked at the king. "Earlier, you said the reason you'd stayed away all week was to spare me from your poor company. Did something change?"

Zercy turned his head and looked at him. "Change?"

"Yeah. For the better."

"Ah... Regrettably, no."

"Then why did you come back early tonight? Why not spare me your company yet again?"

The king's lids lowered. Then he kind of sort of smiled. "Do you truly not know?"

"No. I truly do not."

"Because I missed you, *Alick*," he murmured.

Alec stilled. "You... did?"

Zercy sighed and laid on his side. Slid Alec a look through his lashes. "I could not stay away a moment longer."

Alec floundered, trapped in his gaze, then laid down and faced him. "Oh."

Zercy smirked and shifted closer so he could nuzzle Alec's face. "You missed me, too."

Alec sighed but didn't deny either—Zercy's claim, or his nuzzle. Briefly, he closed his eyes. "It's been quiet."

"Hmm," Zercy rumbled. He took Alec's hand.

Alec watched him turn it over, watched his fingers start to roam, their gold and gem-strewn rings all burnished and gleaming.

He traced Alec's lifeline with the tip of his claw. His touch was nice, his fingers warm. It made other parts of Alec warm, too. Like that place inside his chest, behind his ribs.

God, he felt so content now that Zercy was back. Guess he *had* missed the guy. Might as well admit it. Ugh. It was just so frustrating though because he shouldn't feel that way. It was wrong. *They* were wrong. Thing was, aside from his parents, he couldn't remember a single person whose absence had ever made him so unhappy.

Hell, even the girl in his last relationship paled in comparison.

Which, Jesus, had been ages ago.

As the king leisurely traced every line on his palm, Alec couldn't help wondering about Zercy's love life.

He lifted his gaze. "Do Nirans ever... date?"

Zercy met his eyes. "Date?"

"Yeah, like... have relationships. Exclusively and shit. With one person."

Zercy nodded and looked back down. "Those that Nira gifts with a mate."

"A mate?"

"Tah." Zercy absently thumbed Alec's fingertips. "Those whose souls align just as perfectly as their cocks. Who bond through seed and blood, and raise young. They are rare though, true mates," he mused as if to himself. "So, no, not much 'dating.' Most just fuck."

Alec pondered that as Zercy toyed, inwardly liking the contact. "What about you? You said you wanted an heir."

Zercy's next nod came slower. "Tah. I do."

"Would you have to get married? And have your kid with a noble?"

"Married?"

"Yeah, you know, to unite kingdoms... or whatever."

"Tah." Zercy muttered. "I would."

Alec's ribcage tightened. Why'd he ask that question? Zercy's answer made him restless. He stared at their hands. "Do you see that happening soon?"

"Mah. I see that happening never."

Alec looked at him. "*Never?* But... what about an heir?"

"I will not sire one."

"*What?* But you have to. You're the *king*."

Zercy's fingers stilled. He set Alec's hand down and shook his head. "Mah. My royal bloodline ends with me."

Alec frowned again. Heirs were important. And Zercy wanted one. So, what was his deal? It was like he had some aversion to getting hitched.

Alec stilled. Maybe he did.

"Do you have history or something? A pairing in the past that went bad?"

He felt the king bristle.

"Tah. I was betrothed."

Alec's brows shot high. "Seriously? You never mentioned it. When?"

Zercy clenched his jaw. "Nearly four moons ago."

"That recently?" Alec gaped. "What happened? Where's he now?"

"*Dead*," Zercy snarled. His hands balled into fists. Turning away, he said no more.

Alec stared at his back. Shit. So that was it. Zercy was jaded by loss and didn't want to chance it again. Which Alec could understand. Death was brutal. Even now, his parents' death still made him ache. And they'd died five years ago.

He frowned. Zercy's loss was still fresh and new, his mood swings no doubt a form of mourning.

Oh, God. What if that mystery sickness in the courtyard killed the guy? It'd certainly explain why the subject made Zercy so mental.

Heart heavy, Alec touched his shoulder. "I'm sorry. I didn't realize."

"Never speak of it again."

Alec opened his mouth—

"In fact, do not speak at all. Go to sleep."

Sigh. Alec rolled onto his back and stared at the ceiling. He was glad that Zercy showed up, but their encounters were exhausting. Which wasn't exactly new. They'd always been that way. All hot and cold, and up and down, like a rollercoaster off its tracks.

The only difference with that rollercoaster now… was that he no longer wanted to get off.

CHAPTER TWENTY-SIX

* * *

"Wow, Bailey," Jamis laughed, watching his friend finally catch up. "Your lack of speed never ceases to amaze me."

Bailey rested, out of breath, against the huge submerged boulder, only its craggy top sticking out above the water. "Bite me." He wiped his face. "I got a cramp in my leg."

Noah grinned, gripping the rock alongside the rest of the team. "Is this something that happens every time you go in the water?"

Bailey flipped him the bird.

Jamis laughed again. "He makes a good point. You're *always* the last one to come in."

Bailey scowled, his dripping curls trying to cling to his cheeks. "You know what? Fine. I suck at swimming. There. Happy? I said it."

"Like we didn't know already," Chet muttered, scanning the lake. They'd been tasked by Kellim to do laps today. From shore to boulder, and then back again, twenty times.

"Oh, blow me, Mr. Sunshine Pants. You're never first to finish, either. It's always either Z-man or the cap." Bailey looked at Zaden and Alec. "Which was it this time, by the way? I was practicing my breaststroke. Didn't see."

Chet snorted. "You mean your doggie paddle?"

"Oooh," Jamis piped in. "You should learn the butterfly. Bet your water boy's got that one down *pat*."

"Damn, no shit…" Bailey mused. His lips quirked. "That was always my favorite to watch in the Olympics."

"'Cause the guys moved like mermen?" Noah grinned.

Bailey flushed. Smiling boyishly, he nodded. "Pretty much."

"Oh, for fuck's sake," Chet grunted, shaking his head. "Who's next? Jamis, you gonna start pining after fairies?"

Jamis laughed. "Maybe one day. Although, I typically call 'em fae."

Chet rolled his eyes.

The trio laughed.

Zaden and Alec swapped smirks.

"Again!" Kellim bellowed from the shore. "Lazy moyos! Rest time is over! Back to laps!"

The team peered over their shoulders at the annoying Kríe, eyed him for a second, then resumed talking.

"Saw more captives brought in today," Zaden offered with a frown.

"*Slaves*," Chet corrected. "Cheap labor, 'cause Zercy's a douche."

Alec shot him a glower before he could stop himself. "We don't know what's going on with them, or why he's keeping them, or anything."

Which frustratingly, was the total truth. Alec didn't know jack because Zercy wouldn't spill. Last week, when Zercy showed up after going all incommunicado, Alec had hoped they'd reached some kind of milestone in Zercy trusting him. Sure, the night had ended kind of rough, discussing Zercy's loss, but the bottom line was, he'd confided in Alec. At least a little bit. So that was progress on some level, and it'd given Alec hope.

Unfortunately, not a goddamn iota changed afterward. Hell, since then, Zercy dropped back off the map again. Even now, he still had yet to surface. But Alec didn't understand why. They hadn't argued or anything. In fact, they'd done the absolute opposite. Gotten downright intimate. Which was *not* what Alec had planned.

Blame it on that stupid zenki.

But one thing had led to another, and next thing Alec knew, Zercy's fangs were making him lose his ever-loving mind. So why then, was Zercy avoiding him yet again? Had bringing up his betrothed triggered some aversion? Made him not want to be around Alec intimately? Or in any way at all, for that matter?

The thought made Alec anxious. And aggravatingly, a little sick. Maybe he needed to follow Zercy's lead and nip shit in the bud. Go cold turkey. Wipe the Kríe out of his thoughts, out of his system, just like Zercy was clearly doing with him.

Alec frowned and looked down as water lapped at his chest. Because, damn it, he didn't want to.

Fucking Kríe.

"Earth to Alec." Zaden's voice finally cut through his musing.

Alec blinked and looked his way. "Uh… What?"

His co-pilot chuckled. "Damn, man. Where'd you go?"

"We were *saying*," Chet cut in, "that it sounded like you were defending the guy."

"Who?"

"Zercy, who else? You know, for having slaves? Those poor schmoes breaking their backs to make him rich?"

Alec tensed. *Was* he defending him? Fuck, maybe he was. "I'm just pointing out the facts."

"You sure? Those marks on your neck imply different."

Alec stilled. His team eyed him. Him and Zercy's bite. Cheeks heating, he rubbed the spot and cut Chet a defensive look. "You of all people should know this doesn't mean anything. Or was there something going on with Roni that I'm not aware of?"

The Chet pursed his lips and looked away, but the others continued to watch him.

Alec exhaled and dropped his hand, not ready yet—or even able—to explain the marks. "Look," he muttered, directing things back to the subject at hand. "All I'm saying is we don't know what's going on. We're only seeing part of the picture. There's something big happening, though. That much I do know. The guy's stressed out all the time and—" He stopped and looked at their bodyguard. "Wait. How'd you know that he's got them mining? I'm pretty sure that's not public knowledge."

Chet shrugged. "'Cause I've seen them, digging away under the castle."

Zaden frowned and eyed him. "We've never been taken to the mines. We only go down to Ryze's and that's it."

"Yeah," Noah agreed. "The only time we've ever seen prisoners was that day we spotted them being brought in through the back gate."

Jamis nodded. "And they definitely hadn't been mining then."

Bailey's eyes widened. "Holy shit. You've been sneaking out."

Chet shrugged. "Of course, I have. How else are we ever going to escape? We need the lay of the place, a solid bead on castle routine, so we know which way to high-tail it, and when."

"Really? You've been doing recon?" Alec asked, brows high. Not that the revelation was surprising. That's just the way Chet rolled. Always plotting, planning, ever proactive.

Something gleamed in Chet's gray eyes. "For weeks now. Every night."

"How?" Zaden demanded. He looked kind of pissed. "And why didn't you take me with you?"

"Because as of late, you're just as much the captain as Cap." Chet shot Alec a look. "Sorry, Boss, but it's true. As soon as you leave each evening, it's Z in charge."

Alec frowned, but nodded. Chet was right and he knew it. But it was still a bitter pill to swallow. He hated being the team's part-time leader.

"So what?" Zaden grated. Yup, he was pissed. "You know the drill. You need someone to watch your back."

"No." Chet shook his head. "It's dangerous. You could get hurt. I literally scale the castle's exterior walls."

"Get out." Jamis gawked. "You've been climbing out your window?"

Chet shrugged again. "Yeah. Kinda sketchy at times, but I manage."

"Sketchy." Noah coughed an incredulous laugh. "Because we're easily a good seventy-five feet off the ground? Or because the ledge below our windows is non-existent?"

"Both." Chet chuckled. Rubbing his buzz cut, he looked at Alec. "But I've gathered some good intel. Tonight, I'm headed into the mines to map out the tunnels, see if I can find some secret passageways."

"I'm going," Zaden announced.

Again, Chet shook his head. "No, you're not."

"That's not your decision. I outrank you."

"Burn!" Bailey cackled.

Jamis and Noah snickered, too.

Alec, however, just exhaled with a frown. Not because he didn't want Zaden going, that part was fine. Zaden was more than capable of handling himself. Hell, he'd be an asset. The best wingman Chet ever had. Alec was irked because he wanted to go, too. To be useful. Actively working to help his team. And the fact that he couldn't because he was holed up in Zercy's chambers? Not knowing if Zercy would come back and find him missing? It chafed something fierce. He wasn't a pet to wait on its master. He was captain, first officer, of his own unit.

Chet shoved Bailey's head, then shot Alec a look. "It's up to you, Boss. You cool with this?"

Alec nodded. "Yeah. Just be careful. Neither one of you is expendable."

Zaden's dark eyes flashed. He was excited. Understandable. They hadn't experienced real freedom in fucking weeks. Locked in their room from dusk till dawn. Escorted everywhere else by overbearing guards. But as soon as Chet and Zaden slipped out of their windows? They'd be free, at least for a little while. Sweet—albeit small-scale—liberation.

It filled Alec with envy. But it also unsettled him.

Because bottom line, those recon missions were for one purpose only. To help them escape the very Kríe Alec was falling for.

"Shit!" Bailey yelped. Twisting around, he searched the water. "Something just gripped my freaking calf!"

The whole team tensed and quickly looked around, too.

"Goddamnit," Chet grated. "Kellim said all the *big* sea creatures stayed at the bottom."

Bailey shook his head, still glancing around. "No, it—It felt like a hand."

Everyone stopped and stared at him.

"A hand?" Alec repeated. "Like with *fingers*?"

Bailey nodded. "Yeah. Exactly."

Jamis barked out a laugh. "Shut the front door. It's your merman."

"I think it was."

Noah's mouth fell open.

Zaden and Alec traded looks.

Chet scowled and shook his head. "You guys are morons. No way. It was probably some sucker fish with a freaky mouth."

Bailey pursed his lips. "I know what fucking fingers feel like, Chet."

"Yeah? Then where's your lover boy now, huh? 'Cause I don't see—"

A football-size rock slammed the water right by their heads.

"MOVE!" Mannix boomed, standing by Kellim at the shore. He lobbed another. It hit even closer than the first.

"Jesus!" Zaden shouted. "That dick's gonna hit us!"

"NOW!" the Kríe bellowed. A third came flying their way.

The team dove in all directions, barely dodging.

KERSPLASH!!

"That motherfucker." Chet shot the asshole a glare. "Swear to God, I'm gonna rip his fucking arm off."

But right as Mannix sneered and readied to chuck an even bigger one, a wadded ball of seaweed pegged him in the head. Jarred, Mannix stumbled to the side, plowing into Kellim.

"Ha!" Jamis crowed. "Serves you right, ya big dick!" Grinning, he turned to the others. "Nice aim. Who threw that?"

Treading water, every teammate shook his head in quiet bafflement.

Alec cursed, glancing around. "If it wasn't us, then who?"

Right on cue, something big smacked the water to their right, creating a giant splash just yards away.

All six heads whipped around.

"Holy fuck!" Bailey gaped. "Did you see that? It was a tail! With two big ole flukes and everything!"

"Flukes? You mean, like a dolphin?" Noah asked.

"Kinda yeah, but different. Gah. I only caught a quick glimpse."

Jamis eyed the dispersing ripples, then shot Bailey a grin. "Sounds like a merman tail to me. Your boy must not've liked Mannix using you for target practice."

Bailey blinked at his friend. Brain churning, his eyes lit bright.

Alec laughed. He couldn't help it. Bailey's deal was just too funny. "Come on, guys." He gestured with his head toward shore. "Mannix looks pissed. We better get going before he chucks a boulder."

* * *

"You're not coming with us?" Zaden frowned. "Why not?"

Alec glanced away as he and the team dried off from their swim and got dressed. As of late, their guards had been taking them into town once a week. Normally, to the market. Sometimes to sightsee a little, too. Today, however, Alec wasn't in the mood.

"I um… wanted to hit the history museum library thingy." He scratched his cheek and gave a shrug. "Do some research and stuff. See if I can find anything useful."

His co-pilot eyed him. "You okay? You seem off."

"Yeah. Of course." Alec nodded. "I'm fine."

Although, in truth, he felt pretty much the opposite. Head all wound in tangles. Stomach all tied in knots. Zercy was making it hard to function.

"Alright, man." Zaden shrugged. "Guess we'll see you at dinner."

"Cool." Alec forced a small smile and saluted.

His friend saluted back, then headed off with the others.

Alec sighed, watching them go, feeling a little like he was ditching them. But truth be told, he'd spent more overall time with them this week than he had during any other since they'd gotten there. Why? Because every day since his last encounter with Zercy, the guards had allowed him to stay with his men till midnight. No doubt, Zercy's way of making up for his continued absence. During their last conversation, when Alec had said that things had been quiet, the king must've been listening.

At any rate, Alec just needed some time alone. Some time to think and hopefully get his head back on straight. Maybe find a way to flush Zercy out of his system.

"Nenya," Kellim grunted. "I will take you to the library." He loped toward the gates, leading the way. Alec followed.

They entered through the back doors not long after. Kellim didn't say much as they walked. He rarely did, though. Always did most of his talking during physical training. Not that Alec minded. He wasn't in the mood for chitchat anyway. Just wanted to get where he was going and submerge himself in books.

They passed Lotis' *bottega*, then the double doors of the bathhouse. When they reached the corridor's T-junction, they took a left.

Alec's gaze dropped down, absently eyeing the stone floor. Those slate slabs were becoming too familiar. They shouldn't feel so comfortable. Shouldn't bring him a sense of security. But they did, like some home away from home.

He groaned and scrubbed his face as he wandered down the hall. He was getting too attached. To Zercy. To this place. Exactly what he'd feared had started to happen.

Goddamnit. He should never have kissed that Kríe. Should never have touched him at all. 'Cause now when they escaped—and ultimately they would—it was going to fucking hurt. No way around it.

He dropped his hands and breathed a curse. Rubbed his neck and lifted his gaze.

Then frowned at the sight up ahead.

The doors to the courtyard, there weren't any Kríe guarding them.

"What the hell?" he murmured.

Kellim kept walking, still leading the way. Did he not find that strange? Worrisome that not a single Kríe was posted? Maybe it was common, a small interval between the switching of guards.

Or maybe, Alec speculated as they steadily approached, Kellim *did* find it strange, but was playing it cool, not wanting to draw Alec's attention where it wasn't wanted.

Alec frowned suspiciously. But right as they neared within a half dozen feet, he spotted something that halted him in his tracks. The doors weren't even closed. Someone had left them ajar. Enough so that he could probably steal a peek.

His pulse kicked up a notch. He glanced back at Kellim. The oblivious Kríe was still ambling along. Alec bit his lip and looked back at the parted double doors, then soundlessly moved closer and peered inside.

His heart stopped in his chest.

Zercy, with his back to Alec, standing in the center of the courtyard.

Staring at a gargantuan tree.

Alec's muscles went tight. What was he doing in there? He looked still as a statue. Was he okay?

An ominous current washed over him. Darkness, sickness, death.

Then Zercy's energy reached him. Staggering sorrow.

Alec's heart dropped to his feet. He anxiously gripped the door, the urge to go to Zercy overwhelming. But, fuck, he couldn't. Wasn't even supposed to be there, witnessing any of this. He wasn't welcome.

He stared at Zercy's back, wondering why the king was there. Even the *air* inside the place felt toxic. Alec's chest clenched restlessly. What if Zercy got sick? He wanted to march right in and drag him out.

"Alec!" Kellim bit out from the far end of the hall.

Alec glanced his way. Shit. The Kríe was stalking back fast. He'd better retreat before Zercy discovered him.

Reluctantly, he peeled his fingers from the door and quietly stepped away—

"*Alick...* Nenya." A soft entreaty coming from the courtyard.

Alec froze. Busted. He peered back inside.

Zercy eyed him over his shoulder. "Do not go."

Alec's heart shot into his throat. "I—I'm sorry. I—"

"It is all right." God, his voice, it sounded so somber. "It is time I told you the truth. Nenya." *Come.*

Kellim stopped at Alec's side, glared irritably, then opened the door. "The king awaits," he muttered. "Move with haste."

Alec slid him a look of apology and stepped through the door.

Ah, so the king wasn't alone after all. The courtyard guards were posted inside the entry.

Unsettled, Alec made his way over to Zercy, taking in that big tree as he went. Sitting atop a hill, it kind of looked like a hybrid. Like an old giant oak mixed with willow. Thick trunk, draping branches strewn with oddly curled leaves, it had an uncanny resemblance to Zercy's throne.

Alec cranked his face upward to get a glimpse of its height, spotting stars through the opening high above. The top of the castle, it was open to the courtyard. He wondered how he'd missed that from Zercy's roof.

Blame it on the stars. Always distracting.

Alec scanned the vast enclosure. Pole torches and wall sconces blazed everywhere. That fern-like Niran grass covered the ground. Two granite benches. Meandering stone paths. Large marbled rocks amidst the thick roots. Roots, incidentally, that didn't look right.

Alec frowned, tracing them back to the looming tree's trunk. It didn't look right, either. Or rather, it didn't look healthy. In truth, it looked more dead than alive. From a distance, he hadn't noticed its washed-out appearance, nor the way its leaves looked withered and discolored. Infused through every inch with a sickly shade of gray. He glanced down. Even the grass seemed way too limp.

He stopped next to Zercy. The king didn't turn to look at him. Just kept his sober gaze on the tree. "Bordi, Fek. Resume your posts outside the door."

The guards at the entrance promptly turned and headed out, closing the panels behind them as they left.

Silence lingered.

Alec shifted his weight. Rubbed his nape. "You've been avoiding me again," he finally murmured.

"Tah."

"Because you're still in bad sorts? Don't seem too grumpy to me."

Zercy's lips curved infinitesimally. "That is only half the reason."

Alec looked at him. "Oh. Well... what's the other?"

Zercy's tiny smile faltered. "I am getting too attached. No king should crave his pet so intensely."

Alec stilled, his heart thudding. He knew Zercy was fond of him, but that confession just shed some really important light. They were on the same page. Had the exact same concern. That their feelings for the other were growing too strong.

A strange kind of panic streaked unchecked through his ribs. Whether Alec wanted something between them or not, it wasn't his call. He'd have to keep Zercy's company no matter what. But if Zercy didn't want it, that was totally different. One rash decision while in a downhearted mood, and Zercy could ban Alec from his presence altogether.

Alec chewed on Zercy confession. What exactly was he implying? That he didn't want Alec around anymore? That he'd decided to stop interactions? Had Alec become to him just another source of stress?

Alec wanted to ask... but was afraid to hear the answer.

So, instead he drew in a breath and averted his gaze. Couldn't help it. Zercy's face was suddenly making him ache.

Frowning, he cleared his throat and gestured to the tree. "It's contracted the sickness." Seemed like a pretty safe guess.

Zercy nodded once.

Alec shifted his weight. "Looks pretty old."

"She is. As old as time."

"She?"

"Tah," Zercy murmured. His gaze fell to her roots. "This is Nira, *Alick*. Our mother… And she is dying."

Alec's mouth dropped open. "What? *This* is Nira? This tree?"

"In one of her physical forms, yes, through which all Kríe life is formed."

Alec stared at the thing, wrapping his brain around Zercy's words.

"All Kríe who've ever lived came from this tree?"

"Mah. This is the matriarch. She brings forth only kings. Extensions of her, linked by the roots you see before us, are scattered throughout the kingdom in various regions. Offshoots, smaller replicas. They bear the young for all the rest. The very wombs that populate our species."

Wow. Things on Nira kept getting more and more bizarre. Alec weighed the sight before him with the things Zercy said. "So, if they're all connected, and this one's dying…"

A moment ticked by.

Zercy's next nod was faint. "Tah," he rasped. "They all are dying."

Oh, God.

Oh, Jesus.

Alec quickly did the math. If they died, then so did Zercy's race.

His pulse spiked in horror. "Are you saying you can't heal her?"

"We are trying. Doing all that we possibly can. Sirus toils day and night, as do all of my scientists, experimenting with every element from every land. Manipulating them. Testing every conceivable combination. But no cure for our mother has been found."

Alec's mind spun, assessing the data. Something didn't add up. "But how can she be this vulnerable? Obviously, she's an entity of higher existence. She's immortal for fuck's sake. Creates intelligent, complex life. There's gotta be *something* she can do."

Zercy closed his eyes. "I do not know… I used to think that she was angry and would not heal as punishment to me. For being so naive. So complacent. I do not believe that anymore." He looked back up at the tree. "Now I fear the reason is because... she is not able."

That didn't make sense.

"But you said once that she was mystical. That she can move walls at will. Why is this problem any different?"

Zercy looked at him sadly. "She is not a god, *Alick*. She is our mother, the heart of our planet. Limited to the elements she is made of."

"Okay." Alec nodded, working it through in his brain. "But the sickness, it's made of your planet too, right?"

Zercy held his eyes. Shook his head.

Alec blinked, then furrowed his brows. Scratching his cheek, he crossed his arms. "It's extraterrestrial?"

"Tah." Zercy exhaled. "Or from a foreign unknown god."

"Wait, huh? A *god?*" Talk about left field.

"It is the only explanation why our own gods have not helped. It would also explain why Niran antidotes cannot defeat it."

"Jesus," Alec muttered, dragging a hand down his face.

"Dark magic has found my people." Zercy's timbre was bleak. "And no matter what I do, I cannot save them."

Alec's stomach turned at the thought—and he was merely a bystander. He couldn't imagine what this was doing to the king.

He looked back at the tree, noting its trunk's curious texture. Satiny smooth with vein-like cords, reminding him of a muscular man's arm. Curiously though, it didn't give a masculine vibe. It gave, quite appropriately, a slightly feminine one.

"How did this happen?" he heard himself ask. "How did she even get sick to begin with?"

An arctic blast nailed him as Zercy visibly stiffened.

"A traitorous viper poisoned her with his traitorous venom."

"Someone you *knew* did this? *Intentionally?*"

Zercy's growl sounded glacial. "I welcomed him into my home, but he conspired against me. Deceived me with his pleasantries. With his lies. Like a fool, I suspected nothing, nor did any in my court… But why would we? He looked like a gift from the gods." His lip curled back. "With the smile of an angel."

Alec's insides twisted anxiously. He swallowed. "Who was he? A noble? A visiting dignitary?"

"My betrothed."

Oh, shit.

Alec's brain did a tailspin. All this time, he'd thought that Zercy had been mourning him, his betrothed. Now he realized he'd wanted to rip his throat out.

"Jesus. Zercy..."

"He disappeared one night... I searched for him... Found him here... So, I went to him, saying, *'Talik, what are you doing? It is late.'* He looked at me over his shoulder... He was smiling, but not like an angel. Like the demon prince he was. All his gods-damned body markings lit up like hell fire."

"Fuck," Alec murmured.

A tremor shook Zercy's frame. "When I reached him, I discovered that he was holding a bowl, and that its contents had been poured on Nira's roots."

"*'Talik, what is this?'* I asked. *'What have you done?'* He sneered and said, *'What I was chosen to do. End your race. And now I have.'*"

Alec's heart thumped painfully. The king was reliving his nightmare.

"It was then that I realized the magnitude of Talik's crime. Rage consumed me, like fury descended from the gods. A vessel for Ságe and Krye to deliver their wrath."

Alec watched him as he spoke, Zercy's raw gaze locked on the tree.

"I roared and did not stop until his blood drenched my body... until I tore him limb from limb and crushed his bones."

Alec cursed, not wanting to envision Zercy that way. "Was he prince of the Tohrí? Is that why you hate them?"

Zercy gave a stiff nod. "They sent him under the pretense of uniting empires, solidifying peace, when all along they had plotted the very opposite. To sabotage my kingdom by infiltrating my castle, so they could deal a lethal blow straight to our heart."

The thought had Alec absently rubbing his sternum. "So that's why you enslave them? Those Tohrí? As retribution?"

Zercy tiredly rubbed his face. "Mah. My vengeance will come soon enough. I enslave them for the labor. They owe me that much."

"To mine," Alec murmured.

Zercy dropped his hands and sighed. "We discovered a mineral in the ground below the mountains. One that slightly slows the rate of Nira's deterioration."

Alec's brows rose. "Well, at least that's something."

Zercy nodded again, frowning. "It is not a cure, but yes, it has bought us precious time."

Alec looked at the tree. Mineral or not, she still looked awful. Like she was hanging on by a thread. "How long does she have?"

Despair tightened Zercy's face. "The rate of her decline... has started to accelerate. Sirus says she has perhaps... a quarter moon."

Which was roughly a week.

"Goddamn." Alec rubbed at his mouth. That wasn't long at all. No wonder Zercy was having issues coping. His world was crumbling down all around him, literally dying. The weight on his shoulders must be crushing.

"We give her the mineral continuously now, but supplies are quickly dwindling, and in truth it makes little difference. Her time, our time, is running out."

No. Bullshit. There had to be a way.

"What if you got your own people to mine the stuff, too? Increase production. Then maybe concentrate the doses?"

"My soldiers are busy training. Readying for war. We suspect an attack by the Tohrí is imminent. That they will take advantage of our distraction. If they do, we will be ready. If they do not, they are fools. Because when Nira dies we are coming to destroy them."

Alec's jaw went slack.

Fuck. He was going to retaliate.

"As for the public..." Zercy shook his head. His features pinched miserably. "Mah. I will not risk them finding out our true state. Those in mourning could not bear it. It is too soon. They still suffer."

"Mourning?" Alec frowned. "But Nira hasn't died yet."

Zercy met his gaze, and Jesus, his expression tore Alec's heart. "When Talik poisoned the matriarch, that poison spread to the others, to all the other Nira trees in the land. But *unlike* the matriarch..." He paused. Closed his eyes. "Those trees were laden with young."

Oh, God... Oh, no...

"Babes still forming in her womb. Not yet big enough… Still too small…" His somber voice cracked. "Even the young who still nursed were not spared."

"Jesus… Jesus God…" Alec breathed, unable to fathom it.

Zercy groaned and pressed the heels of his palms against his eyes. "The outcry that night..." He swallowed and shook his head. "It was so great… So loud… Like a crash through the land… A torrent of pure agony that would not stop."

Heartache distorted his speech. He sank to his knees. "It would not stop, *Alick*. It would not stop. Went on for days. The roars. The wailing. Like a blade in my heart, ever twisting." His shoulders started to shake. His breathing turned ragged. "It was all my fault. Because of me, their young were dying. And there was nothing I could do. I could not save them."

A fissure cracked Alec's chest. Zercy was breaking before his eyes. The proud Kríe king was falling to pieces. Next thing he knew, he was on his knees too, wrapping Zercy in his arms from behind.

A second shudder shook Zercy's frame. "I have tried to imagine what my fathers would do. How they would counsel one another. How they would fix it. But the answers do not come! I am not wise like they were! I cannot save my people, *Alick!* I cannot save them!"

Fuuuck. His torment. He wasn't just wrecking Alec's heart. He was wrecking his soul.

Alec shifted to Zercy's side, wanting to face him, needing to see him. But those big hands still covered his eyes. "Zercy. Listen to me." Alec gripped the king's bicep, its golden cuff reflecting the light of countless torches. "It's not over. Not yet. Which means there's still hope."

Zercy dropped his arms and gazed at him. His black lashes glistened. "I am tired, *Alick*. It feels like the world is on my shoulders… I cannot hold its weight much longer… My strength is fading."

Alec's heart thumped painfully. The need to comfort him was staggering. But what on earth could Alec possibly say? Nothing. There was nothing. No words to right all these wrongs. No promises that he could make that things would get better.

All he had was his body, his closeness, his touch. Those were all that he could give him.

So, he did.

CHAPTER TWENTY-SEVEN

* * *

Still on his knees, Alec moved to Zercy's front, placed his hands on Zercy's shoulders and gently pushed down. Zercy sat back on his heels. Alec held his eyes. "If you're tired, then let *me* carry the weight."

Zercy frowned and glanced away, but Alec cupped his face, his hands barely covering the Kríe's cheeks. "Listen to me," he commanded in his captain's voice, resuming eye contact. "*My* back is sturdy. *My* back is strong. *Lean on me.* Let *me* be your support."

"*Alick...*" Zercy groaned. "This is my burden to bear."

"Not alone. Not anymore." Alec straddled his lap, then stroked Zercy's cheekbones with his thumbs.

Zercy palmed Alec's sides. Slowly nuzzled his hand. A simple gesture that, nevertheless, made Alec melt.

Leaning forward, he touched their foreheads.

This time Zercy nuzzled his cheek. "*Alick...* My *Alick...* I have missed you."

Fuck. His words. Like a healing balm to Alec's soul. He closed his eyes and exhaled. "Then stop avoiding me."

Zercy's soft chuff brushed his skin. "My *Alick* missed me, too."

Alec nuzzled him back. "Yeah... It sucked."

The king went quiet. Then the next thing Alec knew, Zercy wrapped him in his arms and held him tight. Hot breath moistened Alec's neck. He hugged Zercy back, wanting so badly to ease his pain.

"Kiss me," Zercy rasped in his ear. "Kiss your king."

Alec found his mouth and slowly moved his lips against it.

Zercy returned the gesture, hands moving up to palm Alec's shoulder blades.

His tongue slid into Alec's mouth. Alec's sensuously greeted it, rubbing lazily, unhurriedly against it. The king loosed a soft growl. Alec palmed the sides of his neck, then slid his fingers into Zercy's dreads. Gently, he grazed his scalp with his short blunt nails.

The king shuddered and squeezed him closer. Alec deepened their kiss, tilted his head to claim Zercy's mouth from another angle. He moved his lips harder against the king's, unable to help it. Zercy just had that effect on him. Made him burn.

And maybe it was Zercy's raw emotions, or maybe Alec had the same effect, but two seconds later, the king ramped their smoldering kiss into a bonfire.

Mouths crushing, tongues sparring, they both took what they needed. Hands grasping, breaths quickening, dicks hardening. Two virile males reacting to the other's passion.

"Tah, *Alick*," Zercy rumbled. "You make me forget." He gripped Alec's hips and crushed them closer.

Alec groaned and rocked against him.

Zercy clutched Alec's ass, then rocked his pelvis. His foot-long boner wedged against Alec's crack.

"*Fuuuck*." Alec grasped Zercy's shoulders and started grinding, rubbing his own erection into Zercy's stomach.

Shit, yeah... Even through the fabric of their tunics, he could still feel Zercy's washboard abs. And man, did they feel incredible against his dick. Pleasure surged. He rocked faster. Kissed Zercy's lips even harder.

Zercy's squeezed his ass possessively. "Mine," he growled.

Alec smiled, lips curving against his mouth. Couldn't help it. He loved when Zercy went all dominant. And how that one four-letter word made him feel.

Wanted.

Desired.

Treasured.

Needed.

Feelings that, in that moment, were totally mutual. Every single one of them. Even the last.

Zercy's hands slid under Alec's tunic and gasped his bare ass, his warm palms on Alec's skin making him vibrate. Sometimes he hated his loinstrap's lack of coverage, but sometimes he really loved it.

Zercy rumbled deep in his throat as he kneaded Alec's flesh, still rocking his pelvis against Alec's ass. "Want this," he snarled.

Squeezing Alec's cheeks, he spread them apart, then crushed them tightly together. Again and again. Which, needless to say, drove Alec wild.

"Fuck. You gotta stop that," Alec moaned. "It's making me crazy."

"Crazy?"

"Yeah," he panted. "For your dick."

Zercy growled, all low and hungry, but stopped, nevertheless. Or rather, moved on to other activities. Things like pulling Alec's ass cheek aside so he could stroke his backdoor.

Alec sucked in at the contact, his sphincter twitching, instantly sensitive as hell.

"So soft here. So tender," Zercy mused against his mouth. He slowly traced Alec's ring. Chuffed when it clenched, then did it again. "I could pet your little starflower all night."

Alec's eyes rolled back in bliss. "Fuck, Kríe. That's worse. That's fucking worse."

Zercy roamed his mouth up his neck. "But I like to touch you, *Alick*. To make you shiver."

And he was definitely doing that. Goddamn it, that finger, all lazily circling. Not to mention, the king's claw that kept grazing him just right.

Alec restlessly shifted against him, eyes closed, lips parted. "But that's cruel," he weakly rasped. "Making me want what we both know I can't have."

"What can you not have?" Zercy murmured against his ear.

"You," Alec moaned. "Inside me."

Zercy growled. Stroked his entrance a little faster. "What if I told you that was false? That I could be inside your body right now?"

Alec's brain whirled to a stop. Leaning back, he looked at Zercy. "Is that a trick question?"

The king's lips twitched. "It is not."

Alec frowned. "I don't understand."

"Give me your answer."

"If it were true... I'd say let's do it."

Zercy's golden eyes hooded. Pulling his hand back, he retrieved a small vial from his belt.

Alec regarded the thing. "Um, okay. What's that?"

"Tachi venom."

Alec stilled. Blinked twice. "Are you shitting me?"

"I do not know what that means—"

"Are you lying?" Alec blurted.

"Mah. It is tachi."

Alec stared at it, heart pounding. The impossibility of sex had always been his safety net. But now that it was feasible, and Zercy could really truly take him? Aside from that tail, which was a fraction of Zercy's size, Alec had only had Kríe cock one other time. Weeks ago. With Miros. It'd been over-fucking-whelming. Could he manage another dick that freaking huge?

"The night I bit you," Zercy murmured. "You said you would have let me fuck you. Your words stayed in my mind. My *Alick* would let me take him. Would allow me into his body because he wanted me there..." Something glinted in his gaze. "I could not resist and went to Sirus. Told him to bring me this tachi venom. So, he did."

Alec grinned before he could stop himself. Rubbing his mouth, he chuckled. "Wow."

Zercy searched his eyes. "You do not have to."

Alec shook his head. "No... I want to."

Another rumble emitted from Zercy's throat, this one thick with emotion. As if Alec's open admission to wanting him had moved him deeply. "Then we will. But correctly." He set the vial down, then reached for Alec's belt and removed it.

Alec blinked in surprise.

The Kríe king was undressing him.

Zercy slid Alec's tunic off his shoulders.

Alec's dick bucked, excited for the loinstrap to go, too.

Zercy's lips curved as he unwound it. "Your cock is eager."

Alec's heart hammered. "You've got no fucking idea."

Zercy gripped his erection and stroked.

Alec moaned and clutched Zercy's shoulders. Rocked his hips into Zercy's hand.

"Tah," Zercy purred. "Now *you* undress your king."

No need to tell him twice. Alec attacked Zercy's belt, fumbling at first to get the thing unfastened. Not his fault. The king's fist on his dick was killing his focus.

It finally came undone. He tossed it aside, then sank his hands inside the front of Zercy's tunic. Palming his huge pecs, Alec forced himself to slow. He didn't want to rush this. This pivotal moment in his off-the-tracks life. For God's sake, he was about to have sex with a male. Not because his *body* needed it—desperate to come with whoever could make him—but because *Alec* needed it. With Zercy.

Breaths shallow, dick thrumming as Zercy stroked it up and down, Alec thumbed the king's pierced nipples, then gave some tugs. Zercy growled again, hungrily. Rocked his cock against Alec's ass. Alec grinned and shoved off Zercy's tunic. Over his broad shoulders, his dark muscles bunching, then down his bulging biceps to his elbows. Zercy let go of Alec's dick so the thing could slide down and off his hand.

Alec took him in. His sculpted chest. His abs. That captivating birthmark. King? Hell, no. This Kríe was a motherfucking *deity*.

"*Alick,*" Zercy murmured. "Your eyes on my body... It heats my blood. My loins. Makes me drunk."

Alec met his smoldering gaze. "I can't help it. You're beautiful. I could look at you forever." And that was no lie. Total truth from the start. He'd just always been so determined not to admit it.

Something flashed in Zercy's eyes. Unwinding his loinstrap, he pulled out his rigid gold-ringed cock. "I am burying this in your body. Let the gods try to stop me. I have never wanted anything so badly."

Alec breathed a curse, lust spiking as he gripped that majestic dick. Zercy, in turn, tugged Alec flush to his chest and swiped up that vial. Alec heard the cork top pop. Zercy must've used his teeth. His pulse sped up. His dick jerked. So, he gripped it alongside the king's and got busy stroking both.

Zercy growled in approval and pulled Alec's ass cheek to the side. Then something small and rounded touched Alec's door. Instinctively, he clenched and pumped their dicks a little faster.

"Push against it," Zercy rumbled.

Alec did.

It breached his hole barely an inch. He grunted. Although, it didn't feel big. Not any thicker than his finger. Was probably the vial stopper. Slight pain lanced through his sphincter, but thankfully, it ebbed just as fast.

Zercy pressed his palm over the plug, no doubt to steady it, then curled his big fingers and stroked Alec's taint.

Alec twitched, his lashes fluttering. "So sensitive there."

Zercy grazed it with his claws.

"Uh!" Alec jerked.

Zercy nuzzled his cheek with a chuckle and grazed it again.

Alec twitched, then started undulating. "Ah, God. You're killing me."

"Mmm..." Zercy rumbled, releasing his butt cheek to palm Alec's nape instead. He fused their mouths. "Mine," he breathed. "You are *mine*."

Second time he'd said that—not that Alec was counting. And like the first, it lit his insides way too bright.

Alec moaned and kissed him back, his hand still pumping their cocks, his other hand tunneling deep into Zercy's dreads. He could already feel the venom doing its thing. Could feel his sphincter starting to ease. The muscle relaxing. Damn. It worked faster than the stuff at Gesh's camp. Knowing Sirus, he probably doubled its potency.

Alec panted against Zercy's mouth. Zercy rumbled, still teasing his taint. But this time, when Alec jerked in reaction, it bumped that vial stopper against Zercy's palm. With his backdoor loosening fast, barely able to grip at all, the plug shoved in deeper with no resistance.

Breath left him in a rush. He still felt absolutely everything.

Zercy chuffed in amusement and slid his tongue from Alec's mouth. "I think you are ready." He slid the plug free.

Cool air kissed Alec's opening. Zercy bit off the tips of his claws and effortlessly slid a finger through. An impressed rumble emitted from his chest. "Ságe and Krye... It *does* work."

Alec groaned, eyes closed, lips parted against Zercy's cheek, as the king slid his index in and out. The sensation was incredible, his ring's nerve endings alight. Fervently, the muscle tried to clench. Its efforts were futile, his backdoor offering nothing but utter passage.

351

A growl crawled up Zercy's throat as he added another finger, stretching Alec's opening wider. "So smooth. So hot. Want to feel this around my cock."

Instinctively, Alec's hips rocked against his digits. His fist, too, picked up speed around their shafts. Not that his fingers could wrap around them completely. Just barely enough to keep them together. It did the trick though, without problem, building that intensity in his nuts, suffusing his package in turbulent pleasure while Zercy readied him.

"*Fuuuuuck*," Alec rasped. The king just added another. That was three now. Three huge fingers up his ass.

"Does this hurt you?" Zercy murmured, his breath tickling Alec's ear.

Alec quickly shook his head. "No. Just *tight*."

"Bellah kai." The king pushed deeper, then pulled out and inserted an even four.

"*Unnnnngh*—" Alec's eyes popped wide. So did his mouth, his lips still drunkenly pressed to Zercy's cheek. His body locked up tight, his hand constricting around their dicks, the other urgently fisting Zercy's dreads.

He may not feel pain, but he sure as hell felt pressure. And there was a lot, stretching his asshole, filling his rectum.

Zercy paused. "This brings discomfort?"

Alec swallowed, panting. "No."

"Mmm...Your little starflower is just full."

Alec nodded, coughing a laugh. "Yeah. Just a bit."

Zercy chuffed too, then did a few slow in-and-outs. Carefully, steadily, preparing Alec even more. Although, with as snug as things now felt, Alec suspected he was as stretched as he could get.

Zercy seemed to think the same. His husky breath brushed Alec's ear. "You are ready for me, *Alick*. It is time."

Alec's heart went berserk. Zercy slid his fingers free. A waft of cool air swept inside. The king had truly *opened* him.

Zercy reclaimed his lips. As he kissed him, he pried his dick from Alec's grip. "I need this," he murmured.

Alec grinned. "So do I."

Zercy smiled against his mouth. "You will have it."

"Long time coming."

Low growl. "Indeed." Zercy stroked his gold-ringed cock as Alec rose to his feet, then tightly pulled his fist up the length of his shaft. A huge bead of precum emerged, all fat and glistening.

To Alec's surprise, he suddenly wanted to taste it.

What the hell? What was wrong with him?

That kind of thing shouldn't entice him. Yet, for some unknown reason... it did.

He averted his gaze to Zercy's face, but it quickly dipped lower. To the king's stunning—and utterly bare—body.

His heart pounded.

They were both naked. And just inches apart.

In the very freaking heart of Zercy's castle.

Zercy reached around with his free hand and palmed Alec's hamstring, prompting him to return. To mount his cock.

Alec couldn't believe he was doing this. It felt so surreal. And God, like so much more than just sex.

Dick clutched in one hand, his other gripping Zercy's shoulder, he bent his knees and tentatively eased back down.

Zercy watched him through hooded lashes. His gaze was downright blistering. An inferno bearing witness to his need. He slid his hand higher, up the back of Alec's thigh, and grasped a firm hold of his cheek.

His fingers were scorching. Alec could feel the tips of his claws. The next thing he felt though, was Zercy's dick. Right at his door. All broad and covered in lube, ready to push through like it owned the place.

Alec slowed, muscles tensing.

Zercy squeezed his ass. "Do not stop."

He felt it enter.

Holy shit. It was big.

He glanced down between their bodies. Zercy's crown was completely buried. Its golden regal band disappeared next.

Zercy groaned and closed his eyes, then slowly lifted his hips, as if dying to meet Alec halfway. "So tight... even with tachi..." He growled and inched higher. "My little pet with his little virgin ass."

At least he hadn't said his 'little cock.'

Alec bit his lip, inwardly grinning as he steadily sank lower—

He sucked in breath. Zercy's dick just ground against his prostate.

Holy hell.

His brows pinched tight. His heart sped faster, his mind starting to whirl inside his head. It was still hard to conceive that he was doing this. Willingly welcoming Zercy into his body. But not just his dick. The rest of him, too. Into Alec's heart. Into his soul.

Higher Zercy burrowed, overwhelming his channel.

"*Fuuuck—*" Alec strained, eyelids clamped.

His breathing sped faster. *So full, so fucking full*—and his knees weren't even close to touching the ground. He pumped his dick urgently. Pleasure delved into his junk, while inside, Zercy's girth kept pushing past his G.

Something wet engulfed his nipple. Zercy's mouth. Oh, God. The king latched on, then used his tongue to suckle. Hot firm strokes to Alec's nub, zip-lining bliss straight to his crotch. His nipple pebbled instantly, his hips feverishly rocked, which in turn, drove his ass farther down Zercy's shaft.

Zercy growled and switched to the other. Must've liked the results. More flicks of ecstasy teased Alec's junk.

"*Ungh—Aw, shiiit—*" His hips moved faster, sinking him lower.

Zercy groaned against his nipple. Grasped Alec's ass with both hands. "Tah, *Alick*..." He kneaded Alec's cheeks, then spread them wide. "So proud of my pet..." He eased him even lower. "You have taken so much of your king's cock."

Alec panted. "How much could possibly be left?"

"Half," Zercy rumbled. "Perhaps less."

"*Half?*" Alec balked.

His heart hammered in panic. He couldn't handle much more. No way Miros' dick was this big. He clutched Zercy's shoulders and started to shake his head, but the king's salacious smile quickly distracted him. Zercy actually looked amused that his size was freaking Alec out, yet in the same respect, he also looked turned on.

"Kerra, *Alick*." *Relax.* "I am not going to hurt you." He peered into Alec's eyes. "Hold my gaze."

Anxious and flushed, Alec did as he was told, watching as Zercy returned to his nipple. Holding Alec's stare, he latched on and sucked, his auric eyes blazing up through his lashes.

Fresh pleasure ignited with his tongue's first hot swipe. Alec's dick bucked. His mind swam, drunk on the king's gaze. And that's when he felt it. His insides adjusting. Yielding. Giving way.

Zercy growled against Alec's skin, as if feeling it, too. Clutching Alec's hips, he drew him lower.

Alec moaned, brows pinching. Yeah, his body just made room, but that cock still felt ginormous.

Zercy suckled a little harder. Alec's pelvis got back to rocking. A moment later, his ass cheeks met Zercy's lap. He groaned in sweet relief. The hard part was over. He'd taken the king's dick. Every inch.

And then reality hit. Zercy was inside him, their bodies connected. In the most intimate of ways, they were one.

His heart thumped. Warmth flooded him.

Palming Zercy's head, he claimed his lips. "You," he panted, "are one massive son of a bitch."

Zercy chuffed and rolled his hips. Alec grunted against his mouth. That cock felt like it took up half his abdomen. Zercy's hands moved back to his ass. Again, he kneaded and spread them wide, withdrawing his dick just a smidge before slowly reentering.

Alec's insides flared bright—from that stroke to his prostate, sure, but especially because Zercy was being so careful. Trying hard not to hurt him despite his desperate need to thrust. The urgency was written all over his face. The way his eyes churned, the way his nostrils flared, the way his jaw muscle ticked. Even his pointed ears kept flicking. Zercy needed to fuck badly. Like the sexual beast he was. Hard and fast and furious, with maybe some teeth.

Alec's dick kicked at the thought of Zercy's fangs in his flesh, driving him wild as Alec gave him what he needed. His pulse raced. His body thrummed. He kissed Zercy harder, gripping his shoulders as he gingerly started to move.

Up... and down... up... and down...

Syncing with Zercy's rhythm.

Zercy growled and lengthened his thrusts, then gradually accelerated his speed.

Alec's prostate responded first, pumping rapture through his ass. Then his tailbone and package lit up, too. "Oh, fuck…" He shuddered and clutched Zercy tighter.

Primal rumbles resounded. Zercy extended his thrusts more, each time pulling nearly halfway out.

Alec moaned, his eyes rolling back. Those slow-driving delves were sublime.

Zercy pulled his lips from Alec's and bit down on his lobe. Not hard, but all that hot and husky breathing in his ear? Instant shivers up his spine.

Zercy slid his hands lower and palmed the base of Alec's ass. Lifting him, he withdrew even farther, then sank back home, repeating the action again and again. Alec's heart hammered wildly. His prostate sang in bliss. Zercy moving inside his body was indescribable.

Before long, though, the king slowed. "*Alick*," he rasped. "I need more. Wrap your arms and legs around me and hold on."

More? Alec nodded, too overcome to even ask. Grasping Zercy's shoulder blades, he locked his ankles at the base of Zercy's spine. Zercy thrummed and leaned forward on all fours.

Alec moaned, holding on, feeling the shift in his ass. Zercy wrapped an arm around him and held him close. Bracing with his other hand, he spread his knees for leverage, then pulled out almost completely from Alec's body.

Alec groaned at the sensation, the sensation of Zercy retreating. Of the emptiness his huge cock left in its wake. In one fluid drive, it was back to the hilt.

"*Ugh!*"

Zercy pulled back and did it again.

Alec tightened his hold as pleasure rushed his channel.

Zercy rumbled. "Move against me. I have got you. You will not fall."

He withdrew a third time. Again, the move stroked Alec's G. Alec shuddered and angled his hips. Zercy held him secure, then drove all twelve inches nice and deep.

"*Shit*—" Alec ground out, losing focus of his grip. But sure enough, Zercy didn't let him fall. In fact, with the way his one arm braced Alec's weight, Alec really didn't need to hold on much at all.

Zercy repeated the motion. Alec did, too. But this time, when Zercy slid back into his body, Alec rocked his hips directly into his thrust. White rapture tore through his rectum.

Alec gasped.

Zercy groaned against his temple. "Tah, *Alick,* tah… Move your body against mine."

Alec shuddered, mind reeling, but hungrily obliged. He wanted, *needed*, to feel that again. Zercy loosed a growl of approval, then steadily accelerated his speed, encouraging Alec to dance to a headier pace.

Alec moaned, but kept up. Couldn't stop, even if he wanted to. Somehow his hips felt utterly tethered to Zercy's cock. Locked in some sensual, magnetic wave, pleasure building with each heated thrust.

Alec curled his fingers tighter around the king's massive shoulder blades, locked his lips on Zercy's neck, right at the base.

Zercy rumbled, raw and gravelly. "Gods, your mouth… It drives me mad." Snagging the shell of Alec's ear with his teeth, he held it as he feverishly fucked.

Alec groaned at the sensation. His pulse raced as he writhed.

Zercy snarled and thrust faster, an unspoken challenge for Alec to come with, to push his boundaries.

Current blitzed Alec's channel, then mushroomed hard through his junk. "Shit—" he panted. Every nerve lit up bright. If faster meant more of *that*, then *challenge accepted*. Breaths ragged, he hastened to nearly twice the pace, his body brutally stretched, yet yielding smoothly.

Zercy groaned around his ear, his teeth still clutching it tight. "*Alick*—" Thrust. "Your heat—" *Thrust*. "It unravels me like no other."

With the arm that supported them, he sank down to his elbow and rested Alec's shoulders on the ground. He didn't lower their hips, though. He kept those raised, his other hand moving to support the small of Alec's back.

The change-up was unexpected, but felt incredible just the same. Not only did it have Zercy plunging *downward* into his body, but allowed the king to fuck at a faster pace.

Curses flew up Alec's throat as his prostate went nuts, igniting his lower body with jarring bliss. His brows pinched. His legs tightened around Zercy's waist. His dick throbbed. His nuts firmed. He needed a freaking anchor.

As if reading his mind, the king growled and seized his mouth, crushing their lips together as he thrust. His hot tongue found Alec's, then proceeded to dominate. Which, in that moment, was exactly what Alec needed.

"*Ungh!*—Fuck!—*Yes!*" he gasped. His mind was unraveling. That cock wasn't merely plowing his channel a new one, but rocketing the rest of his being into outer space.

Breathing raggedly, Zercy grasped Alec's ass and straightened upright, with Alec's shoulders still on the ground. Eyes flashing, skin flushed, he peered down at him. "Can you feel it?" He slowly withdrew, and pushed back in. "How perfectly we fit?"

Alec's chest clenched.

He wasn't merely talking about their bodies.

"So many reasons," Zercy rasped, "why you and I should be incompatible. But we *are* compatible, *Alick*. I see this now. I feel it. Like the brightest stars of the cosmos, we align."

Alec's heart stumbled. "Please," he breathed. *Don't say things like that. It'll make me want to stay, and I can't.*

But Zercy misinterpreted his plea to mean something else.

Lids hooding, he held Alec's gaze and smiled, then steadily sped up his thrusts.

Pleasure rushed through Alec's body, reigniting every inch.

"*Shiiit*—" he strained out, gripping the grass at his sides.

His ass sang. His eyes rolled back. Pressure surged in his crotch, flicking wicked bliss straight up his cock. Goddamn, Zercy's boner, it felt bigger than ever, delving even deeper than before. His channel clenched, his prostate reeling.

"Tah," Zercy snarled, staring down at him as he fucked. "I can feel your little ass milking me—wanting my seed—"

Alec nodded before he could stop himself. Although, *why* he nodded, he didn't know. Having his ass filled with cum was never something he'd wanted in the past. But God, just the thought of Zercy unloading into his body...

He reached for his dick, needing the contact, his prostate on the verge of detonation. Not that he understood how, but he was definitely about to climax in his ass.

Zercy gripped his wrist, intercepting. "Mah. I will do this for you." He thrust to the hilt, then clutched Alec's cock. Only the tip of its crown remained visible in his grasp.

Big fucking hand.

Zercy stroked.

Pleasure spiked.

Alec arched with a curse, squeezing the king's waist with his legs. "Oh, God— Oh, shit—" Just like that, he teetered on the edge. "Gonna come—"

Zercy chuffed and shook his head. "Too soon."

Alec fisted the grass. "Oh, no, it's not."

A throaty rumble sounded. Zercy stroked him some more, but stopped when Alec tensed and started shaking.

"No—" Alec choked out. "Don't stop. One more pump."

Zercy chuckled and pulled out of his body. "You must wait for me to spill." Turning Alec over, he set him on all fours.

Alec shivered, mind whirling.

He was readying to mount him. To fuck him from behind.

Zercy clutched his hips.

Oh, God. Alec tensed. Would he fuck him fast and furious, or take things slow? A heartbeat later, all twelve inches were back with one swift, fluid thrust.

"Uh!" he grunted, barely bracing himself not to fall.

Zercy growled and held him steady. Then slowly, sensually, he rotated his pelvis. "I cannot see my cock, *Alick.* You have taken it completely. Hidden it inside your beautiful body."

Alec smiled, still finding his bearings. The tone in Zercy's voice felt genuine, adoring, laced with that streak of lustful need. Like he couldn't decide whether to fuck Alec's brains out or worship him under the tree.

Zercy's hips started moving. Guess he'd decided to stick with fucking. Excellent choice. Alec moaned as pleasure welled.

"Tah," the king rumbled, gripping Alec's sides. "So smooth under my hands. So tight around my cock. Even the scent of your tender flesh excites me."

Rapture pumped through Alec's body, inebriating his brain. Eyes heavy, he groaned and panted. "What do I—smell like?"

"Like *genza* wood in a glade—smoky sweet—warmed by the sun." Zercy's claws bit into his hips. "It stirs my instincts to hunt—To chase you down as prey—" *Deep thrust.* "And ravish you."

Alec's jaw went slack. His eyes rolled back. Just the thought was way too hot. "Wish you'd sink—your teeth—into me now."

Whoa. Did he just say that?

The king snarled.

Yup. He did.

Zercy gripped Alec's neck from behind and moved faster, dishing out hard, singular thrusts. "Do not tempt me, wicked pet—My will is weak—My hunger strong—"

Alec shook from head to toe. The current pumping through his body, it robbed his clarity, so potent and strong. His dick bucked urgently. His prostate threatened to blow again. Even his knees were seriously considering giving out.

Fingers fumbling, he clutched a root with his left hand and a patch of grass with his right. "Would it—*ugh*—be so bad? If you don't wanna bond, just—*ugh*—come on the ground."

Zercy growled. "I have waited far too long to spill inside you."

Leaning forward, he draped his huge body over Alec's. Hot lips locked on Alec's nape. Shivers raced down Alec's spine. Then the tips of Zercy's incisors grazed his skin. Right overtop the two dark fang marks that still remained.

His heart rate sped faster. Was Zercy actually going to bite him? Even though he planned to come in Alec's body? What about the kid thing? Alec wouldn't be there forever. Couldn't be Zercy's mate if they bonded.

Motherfuckingshit. He shouldn't have provoked him. It was selfish and insensitive. And wrong.

But right as he opened his mouth to change tunes, Zercy got back to feverishly thrusting. Stars littered Alec's vision. His ass went wild, his prostate leveling his sanity. But as he grappled to stay grounded, Zercy never broke skin with his teeth, just restlessly clamped and released at that spot on his neck. Like he was desperate to bite down, to obey his carnal instincts, but was just as fiercely desperate to resist.

Either way, those fangs were making Alec mental, as that dick in his ass rocked his world. Pressure surged through his junk, up his shaft, inside his balls. A firestorm of hot fantastical pleasure. His dick needed contact so bad!

But he couldn't grab hold. He needed both hands to brace. To brace against the king's pounding hips. Each time they slammed home, Alec nearly flew forward. Already, his shoulders were shaking from the exertion.

"Zercy—" he panted. His lungs sawed for breath. "Please—I need to—*Ugh!*—I need to come—"

Zercy growled against his nape. The heady vibrations tickled his flesh. Then big warm fingers wrapped around his cock.

Alec moaned in gratitude.

Zercy pumped the length of his shaft.

White hot pleasure ignited.

"Yes—" Alec gasped. He tried to thrust. He could feel his release descending. Just a couple more strokes.

Anxious rumbles resounded. Zercy was getting close, too.

His delves turned erratic. His pants scorched Alec's skin.

Alec trembled. "*Ungh!*— Zercy!—*Fuck!*—" His prostate ignited deep in his ass. Raw pleasure exploded, instantly triggering his nuts. "Shit! *Gonna come!*"

Zercy snarled and slammed to the hilt. "Tah, *Alick*—Spill *now*—" His dick bucked against Alec's G. "Take my seed—" He furiously unloaded.

And just like that, Alec's climax nailed him, too. He shattered, pelting the roots, the grass, the ground with his cum. It felt like a dream. His blinding orgasm. This world. The huge male surrounding his body from behind. Alec surrendered into his embrace, his heart thumping drunkenly in pure elation. He couldn't explain it. It didn't make sense.

But as he rode out his release, caged tight in the king's arms, Zercy suddenly felt like Alec's stars.

Like Alec's home.

Catching his breath, he slumped to the ground, his arms finally giving out beneath him. The king's huge cock, however, still fully buried, kept his lower half raised.

Zercy tiredly squeezed his hips. "I do not want to leave your body. Its heat warms me everywhere. Like a balm."

Alec groaned and closed his eyes. He felt like a noodle. A *really sated* noodle in post-fuck bliss. "How 'bout we compromise. You can stay until morning."

Zercy chuffed, his voice winded. "You would let me?"

"I would."

"My generous pet." Nevertheless, he palmed Alec's ass and started withdrawing.

Alec moaned.

Zercy growled, his timbre replete. "Nira, the sight of you relinquishing my cock..." His searing gaze was palpable as he watched his shaft emerge. "Mmm... Del`ahtchay." *Delicious.*

Alec exhaled at the sensation of emptiness filling him, of the warmth of Zercy's dick slowly receding. He didn't like it. Wanted it back. But before he could protest, Zercy dragged his hot tongue over his entrance.

Alec's lashes fluttered. "*Unnngh*... My *God....*"

Zercy rumbled and kept going, gently tending to Alec's ring, lapping carefully, languidly, in upward strokes.

Alec's mouth fell open. That tongue. Not only was it soothing his tender hole, but somehow was also prompting restoration. He could feel his sphincter firming, cinching tighter with every lick. Gradually returning to its original state.

When it finally clamped closed, Zercy nuzzled Alec's crack. "Bellah," he growled softly. "Racha." *Stay.*

Alec's lids peeled open. "Stay?"

"Tah. My seed. Let none escape." He brushed Alec's door with his lips. Once, then twice. "Do this for me. I want your little ass to drink it. To suck it into your handsome little body."

Fuuuck...

The eroticism that spouted from that Kríe's mouth. Just a couple words and Alec wanted to romp all over again.

Clenching, he shifted his hips and chuckled. "Won't make any promises, but I'll try."

Zercy's low thrum sounded happy. Holding Alec's hips, he slumped to the ground, then pulled Alec close until they spooned. His big arm wound around him. His nose nuzzled Alec's nape. A heartbeat later, he mumbled quietly, "Twice I was right."

Alec's lips curved. "About what this time?"

"You were worth every moment of the wait."

Alec's heart straight-up thudded. Then his stomach twisted tight. He'd rejected the king so many times. "I... Our situation... It's just... God, it's so complicated..."

"Indeed," Zercy murmured. "I wish it was not."

"Yeah... So do I." Alec sighed. "It's kinda funny."

"Funny?"

"Well, not *funny*. I guess more like ironic." Absently, he rested his hand on Zercy's arm. "You said it was worth the wait, and—"

"I said *you* were worth the wait."

Alec smiled. "Okay. But on my end? *I* hadn't been waiting. That hadn't been the case for me at all. You were just this big frustrating magnet I couldn't escape. But now? In the aftermath of what we just did?" He shook his head, perplexed. "I dunno, it's hard to explain, but it suddenly feels like I'd been waiting for this *all my life*."

The king didn't reply. At least not at first. But then his soft rumble brushed Alec's neck. Clutching Alec's shoulder, he eased him onto his back. Lashes hooded, he met Alec's gaze. "We align."

Alec stared into his eyes. Could that be true? His heart thumped anxiously. "Maybe." He cleared his throat and forced a tiny grin. "If nothing else, we have out-of-this-world sex."

The king's lips curved. His gaze dipped to Alec's mouth. "Tah. With your hard little cock and virgin ass. There is truly nothing sweeter in all of Nira."

Alec laughed. "You did *not* just call my dick li—"

Zercy silenced him with a kiss that went straight to Alec's toes.

Derailed, he moaned, insides warming like the sun. He cupped Zercy's neck, then slid his hands into his mane, all those thick velvety dreads caressing his fingers.

Zercy thrummed and kissed him deeper, tenderly dominating Alec's mouth. All too soon though, he pulled back and touched their foreheads. "*Alick*…"

Alec opened his eyes and met his gaze.

"Stay," the king murmured.

Alec frowned. "What do you mean?"

"When your people finally come for you. I will let them all go. All of them…. If you stay."

Alec's ribcage squeezed tight. "Zercy… I… I'm responsible for my team."

Zercy nuzzled his cheek. "Let them go, *Alick*. Choose me."

"But—"

The king reclaimed his lips. "I command you," he teased sternly.

Alec grinned against his mouth. "You're not my boss."

"I am your *king*." Zercy bit Alec's lip. "You must obey."

Alec chuckled. "I'll think about it, but you gotta do something for me first."

"Anything," Zercy rumbled.

Alec's playful smile ebbed. "Stop avoiding me, damn it. It pisses me off."

CHAPTER TWENTY-EIGHT

* * *

"I will see you at sundown."

Alec crossed his arms as they stood in the dining hall entryway. "Will you?" He eyed Zercy dubiously.

The king inclined his head.

"No more dodging me?"

"No more dodging."

Alec gave a little nod.

Zercy forced a small smile. "Until then." Turning, he made his way down the corridor with his aide, heading for a meeting he'd mentioned earlier.

Evidently, several scientists from neighboring regions had arrived, bringing with them every remedy in their arsenal. According to Zercy, these visits were common, allies traveling from far and wide to offer help. Unfortunately, every effort so far had fallen short. But Zercy hadn't given up. Not yet.

Alec frowned from the doorway, watching him go. They hadn't had much time to talk that morning. They'd slept late unintentionally. But he'd really wanted to discuss things with the king. Like letting his science trio help find a cure. The guys might have their goofy moments, but they were still brilliant. They had to at least *try* to help save Nira.

Sighing, he turned and ambled into the room where his team sat warily poking at their breakfast.

"S'up, Cap," Jamis greeted.

Chet lifted his cup. "Boss."

Alec nodded and grabbed a stool next to Zaden.

His co-pilot looked at him. "What happened to you last night? Thought we were gonna see you at dinner."

"Yeah," Bailey chimed in around a mouthful of bread. "You normally hang out with us. What happened?"

Alec shrugged and grabbed a pitcher from the center of their table. "I ran into Zercy. We ended up… um… talking."

"All night long?" Noah set down the tidbit he'd been sniffing and regarded Alec. "About what?"

Alec poured himself a cupful of what looked a lot like grape juice. In truth, after everything that went down in the courtyard, he and Zercy had retired to their room for the evening. Even had dinner delivered and everything. They'd just been too exhausted, both emotionally and physically, and hadn't wanted to engage with anyone but each other.

"State of affairs. Problems he's facing. Stuff like that." It didn't feel like his place to give specifics.

His teammates stared at him.

"You his confidant now?" Chet asked.

Good question. Alec would like to think he was, but one night of sharing—and crazy-hot fucking—didn't necessarily guarantee that.

Shrugging again, he grabbed a biscuit thingy and cleared his throat. "I dunno. I think he just really needed to vent."

"About what?" Jamis asked.

Alec's stomach turned. "Awful shit… If I told you, you'd lose your appetite." He dropped the baked ball on his plate and rubbed his brow. If Zercy was cool with it, he'd give a full briefing later. Until then though, he needed to change the subject. He looked at Chet and Zaden. "How'd it go last night, in the mines?"

The two men traded looks.

Chet grinned. "We found some."

Alec eyed them both. "Really?"

Zaden nodded proudly. "Yeah. At least a dozen inconspicuous tunnels."

The trio's eyes widened.

"Are you serious?" Bailey asked.

"Just like medieval castles on Earth." Noah's brown eyes gleamed behind his swath of blond bangs. "Everyone knows about the secret passages inside their walls, but they also had hidden tunnels underground. Some were pretty extensive too, leading to undisclosed locations, in case they got invaded and had to flee."

"Yup." Chet glanced over his shoulder at the guards, all yapping away by the wall. "We snuck down there, watched those slaves doing their thing for a while, then slipped into a vacant sector and poked around. I'm tellin' ya, those passageways were so obscured, we nearly missed a couple just inches from our face." He dunked a piece of bread into a dish of oily stuff. "I'm betting most of the guards don't even know those puppies are there."

Alec frowned and clutched his goblet. "So, where'd they lead, these tunnels?"

"Some into town," Zaden relayed. "Some to the forest, this side of the mountain."

Chet took a bite and slowly grinned. "But a couple definitely led to the jungle."

Alec's insides went tight. There it was. Their path to freedom. All they needed now was to get prepared, and then wait for their window of opportunity.

He cleared his throat. "Good job, guys. That's excellent news."

Chet nodded. "I've already started stockpiling provisions. I've been making some weapons, too."

"Seriously?" Bailey's expression looked both wary and surprised. "What the hell kind of weapons did you make?"

"Mostly blades, but also a sweet pair of brass knuckles."

Noah gawked. "Out of *what?*"

"You know all those times we've gone into town?"

Noah nodded.

Chet smirked. "While you've all been picking out notebooks and shit, I've been stocking up metal bicep cuffs."

Zaden lifted a brow and eyed Chet's arms.

Chet chuckled. "Yeah, haven't seen me wearing them, have you?"

"Damn." Jamis tucked a chocolate lock behind his ear. "Not once, come to think of it. You sneaky fox."

Alec frowned all over again. The whole concept made him tense, for all kinds of unsettling reasons. Putting the trio into a predicament where they'd have to scrap with knives was not a prospect he felt comfortable with at all.

Because while fighting predators in the wild was one thing, and most likely unavoidable, there was also a chance they'd have to face off with some Kríe. Possibly even their bodyguards. The males they'd been saddled to for weeks on end, some of whom they actually kind of liked. Kríe like Setch and Kellim had never been cruel to Alec's team, just overbearing in their annoying-yet-harmless way.

They'd protected them, taught them, both intellectually and physically. Had given them advice, answered questions, made them laugh. That his team might inflict fatal injuries on these males? It didn't sit well with Alec. Not at all.

Inwardly cursing, he dragged a hand down his face. "Great. How 'bout we focus on food and necessities. Then an escape plan that doesn't involve bloodshed."

* * *

Ryze stepped to the table in his underground quarters and set his writing slate in front of Jamis. "Read what I have written, then tell me what it means."

Alec watched Jamis peer down at the block of Kríe text, his dark blue eyes locked intently on each character. Reading Kríe wasn't easy. In fact, it was hard as hell. Because unlike with verbal discourse, his brain—now altered by Niran food—couldn't bridge language barriers via text. There were no sound waves for his brain to decipher, no spoken transmission for it to decrypt. It didn't help that their writing system was fundamentally different, either. The closest thing Alec could compare it to was hieroglyphics.

"Em…" Jamis murmured, absently chewing on his lip. "T'tegmai bibbéhn… kü tin'turro bibbéhn'tine."

"Bellah," Ryze rumbled. "And what does it mean?"

Jamis stared at the symbols, his brain palpably churning. "The tegmai is fast, but his teacher is faster?"

Ryze's lips curved wide. "Tah. Bellah kai. And very true as well, do you not think?"

Jamis blinked and looked up. Alec shook his head, amused. Ryze was referencing their wrestling match back in Zercy's throne room. Was teasing Jamis for losing to him in the pits.

Jamis smirked and leaned back, clearly connecting the dots, too. "I dunno…" He crossed his arms. "Theories typically need to be tested more than once. To know for sure, the tegmai and his teacher should compete again."

Bailey barked out a laugh.

Alec raised a brow, surprised. Did Jamis seriously just challenge Ryze to more wrestling?

Ryze's auric eyes flashed. "Perhaps you are right. Jumping to rash assumptions is never wise."

Jamis' grin morphed into a smile. Something glinted in his gaze.

Alec glanced between the two of them. What the hell? Before he could ask, a robust knock derailed his thoughts.

Ryze looked toward the door as the thing pushed open.

Setch stepped inside. "King Zercy desires to speak with his pet."

Alec stilled, both irritated—must they still call him that?—and surprised. Zercy never interrupted their sessions.

His team shot him looks.

Ryze merely inclined his head.

Setch grunted and gestured for Alec to get going.

Alec stood from his stool, equally agitated and worried. Was something wrong? What could the king possibly want that couldn't wait?

Setch stepped back as Alec exited, and there in the tunnel stood Zercy, looking stoic as ever.

"Greetings, *Alick*." He smiled a little. "Apologies for the—"

"What's wrong? Did something happen?"

Zercy paused, then shook his head.

"Then why are you here? You never visit me during the day."

Zercy frowned and stepped close. Cupping Alec's cheeks, he touched their brows. "I had a moment to spare…"

Bullshit. He was upset. Alec could feel it down to his bones. He gripped the king's wrists. "How'd the meeting go? Any luck?"

369

Zercy didn't reply, just slowly nuzzled their faces. Which was an answer in itself, and not a good one.

"Fuck..." Alec breathed. "Let my guys try to help. Please. They're scientists, like Sirus."

Zercy shook his head against Alec's. "There is not enough time."

"But Zercy," Alec pulled back and met his eyes. "They're smart. *Crazy* smart. Let them try. What could it hurt?"

Zercy smiled at him sadly, still cupping his cheeks. "It *would* hurt, *Alick*. Unfortunately, it would."

"How?"

Zercy exhaled. "They would slow my Kríe down. Things are different here. Our world is alien. My team would have to explain everything. But they cannot afford that. Every moment is a race against time."

"But—"

"*Alick*," Zercy stopped him. "Think logically in this. All of my teams' research, all that they have gleaned, every sentiment has been detailed in complex records. Information, as you know, that your men would need to reference. And yet, amid this whirlwind of vast foreign concepts... your team is only now learning to *read*."

Alec's heart sank. Goddamnit. Zercy made his point well. At the moment, the trio was out of their league. "If only there was more time... I know they could help... Cancel our lessons with Ryze and let *him* read them the notes."

Zercy forced another smile. Gave Alec's face a second nuzzle. "My little pet's heart... so very big..."

Alec frowned and closed his eyes, but before he could reply, the sound of thundering footsteps stole his focus. He glanced down the tunnel, in the direction of the stairwell. Zercy dropped his hands and looked that way, too.

The noise grew louder. Zercy's guards moved in front of him, taking up a protective stance. Two seconds later, Sirus tore around the bend, eyes ablaze as he headed straight for them.

"Sire!" He skidded to a stop. "You must come see!" A huge smile spanned his face. "Something has happened!"

Zercy frowned at him. "Tell me."

Sirus shook his head. "You must see." His whole body vibrated. "Come to the courtyard."

Zercy stiffened, then quickly swapped looks with Alec.

Alec's heart took off racing. "Let's go."

Nodding once, Zercy grasped his wrist and turned back to Sirus.

Sirus beamed and led the way. "Tacha!" *Hurry!*

They made it up the stairwell and into the courtyard in seconds flat, the guards standing post opening the way. Sirus rushed through the entry and bee-lined for the tree, stopping several yards from Nira's trunk.

Alec glanced around as he and Zercy came to a stop beside him. The place looked different during the day, engulfed in sunlight. Beautiful even, despite the ominous sickness.

"Denza!" *Look!* Sirus pointed to the ground at his feet. To a thick root and a patch of grass beside it. "Do you see these areas? Unlike everything around them, they did not deteriorate through the night. But even more promising is their *color!* It is returning!" He looked at Zercy. "It is a sign! A sign of hope!"

Zercy stared at the spot, no doubt thinking the same thing as Alec. That the ground on which they stood was the same ground on which they'd fucked. And the patches Sirus gestured to? Where Alec came. Where his cum hit the ground as he feverishly climaxed, while at the same time, Zercy unloaded inside of him.

The memory had Alec tingling. Had his heart rate spiking higher. He looked at Zercy.

Zercy met his gaze, dumbfounded, his gold eyes full of wonder. Swallowing, he turned to Sirus. "The humans," he rasped. "The humans... They are the key."

Sirus stilled and glanced at Alec.

Zercy pointed to the evidence. "Alec spilled on that very spot. Last night when we fucked."

Alec cringed. Must these Kríe always be so blunt?

Sirus' eyes shot wide. "Of course! He is not of this world!"

Both males looked at Alec, stares intense, brains visibly churning.

"Gather his team immediately." Zercy's voice sounded tight. "I want samples taken of everything. Their blood, their seed, their urine..."

"Of course, Sire."

"And since we already know their seed is effective, give them kirah nectar, too."

"Tah. Right away." Sirus bowed and turned on his heel, but not before shooting Alec a smile.

Alec watched him hustle off, his own emotions a warring jumble. Above all, he was elated by the pivotal breakthrough, and that he, inadvertently, had played a part. But in doing the math, he quickly realized what this discovery would mean for his team. The demands they'd undoubtedly have forced upon them, whether they wanted to have a hand in this or not.

Restless, he turned back and looked at Zercy.

The king met his gaze, his handsome expression vulnerable. "I am afraid to hope." His whisper wobbled. He grinned and gripped Alec's shoulders. God, his hands were trembling. "Could you really be the answer that I have prayed for?"

Alec smiled, too. Zercy's barely tamped joy was infectious. "I dunno. That'd be insane. But we should probably wait for more conclusive evidence."

"Tah, but your seed… Its effects are undeniable." Zercy's grin spread wider. "You are a gift from the gods." With shaky fingers, he gripped Alec's hand and pressed it flat against his chest. "Can you feel my heart racing? Racing for joy?"

God, yes. It was hammering like he'd just sprinted a mile.

"Yeah," Alec rasped. "I… I can feel it."

Zercy inhaled deeply, smiling, then tenderly fused their mouths. "I feel as though I can finally breathe… for the first time in ages. I have never been so happy in all my life."

Alec's insides straight-up liquefied. Didn't care that the guards were watching. Zercy's agony had been his, and now his joy was as well. Heart soaring, he smiled against Zercy's lips and tugged him closer.

Zercy growled, slowly, possessively dominating the whole of Alec's mouth, but soon pulled back and shook his head. "We must go."

"Go?" Alec mumbled, half dazed from their kiss.

"Tah. To Sirus' laboratory. You must give him samples, too." Zercy rumbled soft and huskily. "And drink your kirah."

Alec tensed at the mention. Not for himself, though. For his men. "Kirah. Right. Because it speeds up—"

"Seed production."

Alec stepped back and warily rubbed at his neck. "But we'll have already given a sample. Why even have us drink it at all?" Not that he didn't know the answer already, but deep down he hoped he was wrong.

"For the next collection, naturally. Then more kirah after that. A very simple regimen to ensure large donations—of which we will unquestionably need many."

Alec's stomach twisted. Fuck. Exactly what he feared. Pinching the bridge of his nose, he cleared his throat. "Exactly how many is 'many'?"

"As many as it takes. Every morning and night. Our mother is not small." Zercy gestured to where Alec came. "Your little cock's gifts, however, are."

Alec didn't bother defending the size of his dick. He was stressing too much over their brand-new predicament. How would his team react to this? Would they be cool with it? Appalled? Especially if Alec condoned it? Or hell, encouraged it?

Groaning, he scrubbed his face. "Zercy... I don't know about this."

Zercy grunted. "What is there to know? That is the logical course of action."

Alec dropped his hand and looked at him. "Listen, giving a couple 'donations' up front is fine. But requiring them indefinitely? A couple times a day? Fuck, Kríe. My guys... They aren't cattle."

Zercy stiffened incredulously. "Are you... *opposing* me in this?"

"No, of course not ..." Alec shifted his weight. "But what you're suggesting... Come on... You wanna milk them like cows."

Zercy clenched his broad jaw. His expression turned dark. "I cannot believe you are unable to see the larger picture here."

"I do," Alec insisted. "I do, Zercy. I swear it. There's just gotta be another way."

Zercy's eyes hooded coolly. His big ears slowly flicked. "Perhaps there is, but until it reveals itself, I will use you and your team as I see fit."

Alec blinked. "But you can't just—"

"*Silence,*" Zercy barked. "I *can*. And I *will*. Do not forget your place, *Alick*." He was teetering. Alec could hear it. "You are neither my counsel nor my consort. You are my *pet*."

Low blow. Alec fought to keep his cool. Zercy was just upset. Wasn't getting it. "Look," Alec rubbed his brow, "I'm all in, okay? I'll give you whatever you need, but my guys, you need to ask them, not just force them."

Zercy eyed him, then curtly shook his head. "If I ask, that gives them the option to say no."

"But Zercy, you can't just demand that kind of thing."

The king lifted his chin defiantly. "You are their leader. You give them orders. They must obey you in all things, tah?"

"Well yeah, but—"

"So, command them to do this, too."

Alec bit back a curse. "I'm not *that* kind of leader."

Zercy frowned. "I cannot believe you will not do this for me. That you are unable to see that this is bigger than you. So much bigger than your fragile sensitivities."

Alec shook his head. "I do see it, Zercy. I do. I want to help you more than anything in the world."

Zercy stared at him, sadness flickering in his big golden eyes. "I cannot choose your wishes over the survival of my race. They will always come before you, *Alick*. Always." He gestured half-heartedly for one of his guards to approach. "If you can find a viable alternative, I will gladly consider it. In the meantime, you are my property to use as I wish. And I *wish* to use you to save us from extinction."

Alec's heart sank. Zercy's words stung, even though he knew they weren't true. Zercy didn't think of him as property, Alec knew he didn't. The king was hurt, and angry, and lashing out. And Alec didn't blame him one bit. He'd said all the wrong things. Had come across as callous. But before he could open his mouth to apologize, Setch lumbered over and stopped at Zercy side.

Zercy averted his gaze, breaking their eye contact. "We are finished talking," he muttered. "Take him to Sirus."

* * *

Alec met up with the others a few minutes later in Sirus' lab, his men still flushed and breathless from the climb.

Setch walked him through the door, a little winded himself. "You. Tell. Sirus," he muttered, "about that *gods-damned elevator.*"

Alec slid him a look, then shook his head as he pulled up beside Zaden and his team. They barely noticed his arrival though; all eyes scrutinizing the huge room. Understandable. They'd never been to Sirus' workshop before, and the place had a lot of weird shit.

He cleared his throat. "S'up, guys."

"You tell us." Chet frowned, still peering around. "What is this place and why are we here?"

"They didn't say what's going on?"

Zaden shook his head. "Nope. They wouldn't tell us anything."

"Just that class was over early." Bailey warily eyed the ceiling. Ah. He'd spotted Mina. "Made us leave our journals behind and everything."

Jamis nodded, regarding the partitions off to their left. "Hustled us out of there like the place was on fire."

"But it wasn't." Noah met Alec's gaze and frowned. "You look uneasy. You know what's going on, don't you?"

Alec rubbed the back of his neck. Nodded a little and sighed. "Yeah... Um... This is Sirus' workshop and—"

"Sirus?" Bailey cut in. "The king's creepy scientist?"

"Yeah... Him."

"Oh, God. Is this where he gave you that exam?"

Alec awkwardly shifted his weight. "Yeah." He cleared his throat. "That was... here."

Everyone suddenly looked apprehensive.

Noah frowned and looked around. "How come Sirus isn't here now?"

"He probably is," Alec murmured, peering around.

Jamis glanced at the guards. "We're uh... not here for exams too though, right?"

"No."

"Then why *are* we here?" Chet ground out irritably.

Alec drew in a breath and slowly let it out. "Because this morning they—"

"Bellah!" Sirus emerged from a door at the back of the room. "You are all here, and I am ready. Let us begin."

The team watched him warily as the Kríe hustled over, then all five pairs of eyes shot to Alec.

"Begin *what* exactly?" Chet demanded.

Alec exhaled and shook his head. "Nothing extensive. They just want—"

"Samples," Sirus finished for him, beaming as he arrived. He whipped open five consecutive partitions, one after the other, revealing his aides inside, ready and waiting. "You, in here." He motioned for Jamis to enter the first, then ushered the rest of Alec's team into the others.

Chet cut Alec a look as Sirus guided him into the last one. "I assume from your silence that you're okay with this?"

Alec nodded reluctantly. "Yeah... It's cool."

"Yes, yes. All is *fine.*" Sirus steered him farther inside.

Chet glared at the male. "Get your paws off me, Doc. What d'ya want? My piss?"

"Tah. Your urine. And then some blood."

"You're not getting my blood."

"Moyo ochay." *Funny creature.* "Then after that, you will give me your seed."

"Whoa. Wait. *What*?"

"Your seed. From your little human cock."

"I know what fucking seed is," Chet grated through clenched teeth. Shoving his head back out the opening, he shot Alec a look. "I gotta give this freak my *cum*, Boss? Are you kidding me?"

Alec groaned and dragged a hand down his face. "Just do it. I'll explain everything after. I promise."

Chet scowled, jaw ticking, and looked back at Sirus. "I don't like you."

Sirus chuffed, beaming wide. "I think you do."

"No." Chat stalked back in. "I seriously don't."

Alec sighed and looked at the ceiling.

Sirus emerged, still talking to Chet. "Then I will like you enough for the both of us."

"Oh, Jesus," Chet muttered, out of view. "Please don't."

Sirus flashed his fangs, "Too late," and shut the curtain.

Alec looked at the Kríe.

Sirus grinned and came over, then stared at Alec thoughtfully. "Zercy's pet..." he rumbled. "So impossibly special in your own little way..." His big auric eyes roamed the length of Alec's body. "Will you be able to save her?" he mused to himself. His gaze rose back up. "To save *us*?"

Alec didn't bother answering. Sirus wasn't really asking. Besides, Sirus' guess was better than his.

Sirus' smile faded a little. He touched Alec's cheek. "Tah. You will... I believe this to my soul."

God, Alec hoped so. The last thing he wanted was to get Zercy's hopes up only to crush them all over again.

Sirus dropped his hand and gestured to the door he'd first emerged from. "You will go in there while your team gives blood and urine."

Alec eyed the opening dubiously. "Why? What's in there?"

"The receptacle in which you will leave your seed."

Alec frowned. "Receptacle? Don't I just use a little cup?"

Sirus frowned and tilted his head. "Where is the pleasure in that?"

"The *pleasure*? In giving a sample?" Alec stared at him, confused.

Sirus stared back at him, looking just as perplexed.

"Ugh. Never mind." Alec headed for the room. God only knew what he'd find inside those walls.

CHAPTER TWENTY-NINE

* * *

Five disgruntled faces stared back at Alec from their lunch table.

"So," Chet prompted, his voice laden with irritation, "you gonna tell us why we've got *cages* on our *dicks?*"

Alec exhaled and gave a nod. After Sirus had procured all his samples and had them drink kirah, he'd insisted they put on strange metal devices. Sheaths, worn in place of their typical loinstraps, that enclosed their cock, with only a small hole at the end for them to pee through.

At first, and understandably, the guys had been hesitant, staring at the things with looks of dread. Hell, even Alec hadn't wanted them anywhere near him. The whole concept was unnerving.

"What the hell are those?" he'd asked Sirus warily.

Sirus had answered like the flippant fucker he was. "Protection for your cocks, of course. Little suits of armor."

"But *why?*" Chet had bit out. "Why do we need to fucking wear them?"

"Because your cocks bring forth seed, and your seed is very sacred." His smile had been sly. "It must be kept safe at all times."

The team had swapped looks, brows pinched in confusion. By the expression on Sirus' face, and how the guards had quietly stepped forward, Alec knew that to resist would've been pointless. They wouldn't be leaving Sirus' workshop without their 'armor.'

Which meant his team could either agree and retain their dignity by giving consent, or they could have the things forced upon them like animals. Something Chet definitely wouldn't allow without a fight.

Ultimately, with the endgame ever at the forefront of his mind, Alec resolved to not only encourage his men to comply, but also be the first to have one put on. Whatever. So, the whack job wanted to keep their dicks protected. Not entirely unfathomable. After all, Alec could see why Sirus would want their cum guarded. It could potentially mean the survival of their race.

Unfortunately, what Alec—and his men, who'd reluctantly followed his lead—hadn't realized until after the things had been secured, was *who* Sirus wanted their dicks protected *from*. That became quite evident though, when mechanisms like mini padlocks were snapped closed at the small of their backs.

"What the fuck," Chet had barked. "Why're you *locking* these motherfuckers?"

"I told you," Sirus had replied, most matter-of-factly. "To keep your seed safe at all times."

"From us," Alec muttered in understanding. "To keep our fucking cum safe from *us*."

The team glanced back and forth between Alec and Sirus, then peered down aghast at their caged dicks.

"But why?" Bailey had rasped. "I don't understand. Why do you suddenly need our cum so bad?"

At that point, Sirus had slid his golden gaze to Alec. "I will leave that to your captain to explain."

And here they sat, after all was said and done, in the dining hall at a table loaded with food. Not that any of them had much of an appetite.

Rubbing his brow, Alec endeavored to shed some light. "Last night... the stuff I said Zercy confided in me about? It had to do with his people, or actually, his *species*, and how they're in some serious trouble."

"What kind of trouble?" Chet straightened. "Impending war? Someone attacking?"

"Uh, no. Well, not yet anyway. It isn't war related. It's got to do with their race's... survival."

"Whoa." Jamis perked up. "What's wrong? Is famine coming?"

"No." Alec shook his head. "Not famine. *Sickness*. But it's not *coming*." He frowned at them. "It's *here*."

Noah paled a little. "What kind of sickness?"

"The kind that can snuff out a whole species."

"Fuck..." Noah glanced at their guards. "Is it contagious?"

"No." Alec rubbed his face. "It's exclusive to Kríe. But they're running out of time and can't stop it."

For the next several minutes, he explained the sickness as much as he understood it, as well as how it all started with Zercy's betrothed. Needless to say, his team bombarded him with questions. The last one though, was the most uncomfortable to answer, but one Alec had definitely been bracing for.

Chet cleared his throat. "Shit... That's... That's horrible. But... what's that got to do with our junk?"

Bailey nodded, shifting uncomfortably. "And our 'super-special' jizz."

Alec scratched his cheek. "Right. Um... Well, this morning, a discovery was made. One that might be the break that they've been waiting for."

His team stared at him expectantly.

Alec awkwardly forced a smile. "Human semen. It's come to their attention that it may hold promising properties."

Every set of eyebrows raised.

A smile tugged at Jamis' lips. "Get the fuck out."

Noah blinked. "*Cum's* the cure?"

Alec coughed a humorless laugh and dragged a hand through his hair. "I don't know if it's a cure, but it seems to at least be helping. It stopped deterioration last night, where it made contact with one of Nira's roots."

Zaden stilled. "They put sperm on their sacred tree?"

"Um... Not exactly."

The team eyed Alec, perplexed.

He held their gazes. They needed to know. Time to fill them in one hundred percent.

Glancing down at the goblet held clutched in his hands, he relayed the truth. "*I* put it there. It was mine."

Chet reared back, grimacing. "What the hell? You rubbed one off all over the Kríe's holy mother? Jesus, man. God. That's just wrong."

Jamis barked out a laugh. "No, you idiot. He was with Zercy last night, remember? They were obviously fucking."

"*What?*" Chet pinned Alec with a look of disbelief. "You're fucking the enemy?"

"He's not the enemy."

"Like hell, he's not," Chet bit out. "He's keeping us here against our will."

Alec met his glare and held it. "We're safe here, and you know it. Out in that jungle? We'd be dead."

"Bullshit," Chet snapped. "We're not incompetent. Jesus, Alec. What are you doing? Didn't we learn our lesson the first time? These fuckers may be a bunch of big lumbering dolts, but they're still holding us captive. Treating us like property. Just like Gesh and his asshole pack. They sold us. Zercy bought us. How's that any better? These Kríe are *not* our friends. And that *king*," he spat, "doesn't care about you. They don't know what love is. All they care about is themselves. Zercy's not keeping you to ensure your safety. He's keeping you 'cause he wants you for his fucking *boy toy*. His fun little human *novelty*. Can't you see that?"

"No." Alec shook his head. "You don't understand. I've gotten to know him. He's not a bad guy. He's not. He truly believes he's helping us. When things calm down, he'll see clearly and let us go. I'm sure of it. He's just dealing with a lot of stuff right now."

"Yeah, we know," Chet sad flatly. "His people got themselves into trouble. But that's not our fault. And it's certainly not our problem. So, don't use that shit as an excuse to justify his actions."

Alec stared at Chet coolly, not appreciating his tone. "It's complicated. Just like everything on this goddamn trip. So, don't throw that black and white crap in my face. I'm not interested in your outside opinion of my personal affairs. You don't know Zercy. Not like I do. And if you're so quick to assume I'd just dive into this blindly, then you obviously don't know *me* much, either."

Chet opened his mouth, but Alec shut him back down. "I've told you what's going on. I've chosen not to hide it. But know this, soldier, right here and now. I don't care what you think about my deal with Zercy, and I'm sure as hell not asking for your approval."

Chet clenched his jaw and looked away.

Silent moments ticked by.

"What *is* it exactly?" Zaden finally asked. "This thing... Your deal with Zercy?"

Alec exhaled and rubbed his brow. "I dunno, Z. Honestly, this place we're at... It's pretty new."

"Do you care about him?" Noah asked, his voice soft. "Do you love him?"

Alec looked at him and frowned. "I dunno that, either. But I do know he's important to me. When he's stressed, I want to comfort him. When he's sad, I am, too. And when I make him laugh, it's like, my whole chest lights up." He smiled a little, but then frowned again at the severity of the situation. "I want to help him, because if Nira dies, it's going to destroy him. And I can't..." He shook his head and looked back at his cup. "I can't bear the thought of that. I just can't."

Jamis whistled low. "Damn. You've got it bad."

Alec's lips curved tiredly. "Yeah. Not the greatest timing. But it is what it is, and that's why the discovery was made."

Bailey rested his chin on his hand and shrugged. "Not really that surprised."

Alec blinked at him. "You're not?"

"Nah. You've been giving the guy low-key googly eyes for a while now."

Alec stiffened. He had?

Bailey grinned and waved it away. "But not just because of that. I mean, think about it, guys." He looked at the team. "Haven't you noticed how women, the very concept of *females*, is barely on our radar anymore? It's like, the longer we're here, on this one-gender planet, the more obscure the whole concept of them becomes. Hell, I have a hard time even picturing them these days. And yet I still have a sex drive, so what does that say?"

Jamis nodded thoughtfully. "Yeah... Now that you mention it, you're right. I know what you mean."

Zaden's expression said he felt a similar way as well. He looked at Alec. "Is that how you feel, too?"

Alec contemplated Bailey's words, but ultimately had to agree. "Yeah. I guess I do. How strange is that."

Chet scoffed. "I don't feel that way. You all are off your rockers." But his tone wasn't convincing. Way too defensive.

Bailey chuckled. "Whatever, macho man. For the record, I say you're full of shit."

Chet shot him a glower. "Just 'cause you fantasize about a merman doesn't mean *I'm* into guys."

"No," Noah corrected. "You're into Roni specifically."

Jamis snorted. "Wait. Wasn't it the other way around? Pretty sure it was *Roni* who was balls-deep into *Chet*."

Chet shot up, knocking his stool out from under him. "Shut your ass." Incensed, he raked everyone at the table with a glare. "He's a dick just like the rest of them. Tossed us away like used condoms. If I see him again, he's dead."

Zaden grunted. "Like you could take him, Chet. Get over it and sit down."

Chet scowled, then swiped up his stool and took a seat.

Alec sighed and shook his head. "Getting back on track to our current predicament, now you know the problem and how we fit in the equation. I suggest you take some time to look inside yourselves and make a decision."

"Right," Chet muttered. "Because our choices are so many. Voluntarily agree to be our asshole captives' cum cows or stand our ground until they bend us to their will." He chuckled sardonically and rubbed his nape. "Either way they'll get what they want. They always do."

* * *

Physical activities with Kellim were even less fun than usual. Not to mention, exceptionally awkward.

After all, for each session, they had to strip down to their loinstraps, but their loinstraps had been swapped out for chastity belts. Fucking ridiculous. Ambling around with their dicks decked in 'armor.' Alec had felt like a gladiator in some B-rated porn flick. His teammates hadn't looked any happier.

Their guards, however, had seemed downright entertained.

Thankfully, Sirus had had mercy and instructed Kellim to tailor their activities accordingly, choosing exercises that didn't require vigorous movement. Clearly, he'd known just how heavy their metal sheaths were, and how the family jewels could get injured should they smack into them.

When their lessons were finally over, they'd hit the bath house for a soak, then hung out for a while before dinner. As soon as the suns went down though, they were herded back up the tower, where Sirus eagerly awaited their arrival.

Alec headed inside with his men, nice and winded from the climb. A climb that'd been unpleasant for another reason, too. Throughout the day, he'd felt his nuts growing heavier. Fuller. More recently, even his prostate had started to swell. He knew this because it'd suddenly gotten super sensitive. He could literally feel its presence with every step. Needless to say, climbing the tower had been grueling when even the slightest movement set it off.

Sirus smiled from ear to ear. Wow. He certainly looked happy. "Beesha, little moyos. Welcome back."

"Uh huh," Chet grumbled, trying futilely to adjust his junk. "Would rather be anywhere else."

Sirus chuffed. "So cheerful." He gestured to one of his workstations. "Nenya. I have more kirah for you to drink."

Alec glanced at the table where six vials sat waiting. He frowned at the stuff, knowing exactly what it equated to. More super-engorged nuts and another swollen prostate by the time he woke up in the morning.

The team headed over.

Bailey picked up a vial and studied it. "I'm assuming this is the culprit that's making my balls feel like grapefruits."

"Tah," Sirus chuckled again, handing out the rest. "Amazing, is it not? How very well the nectar works?"

Chet glared at his portion. "Is this stuff related to senna`sohnsay? 'Cause it sure as hell feels awfully similar."

"Mah." Sirus shook his head. "Totally different fruit. Although, both *do* target reproductive organs specifically, enhancing seed production exponentially."

"Yeah, no shit," Jamis muttered. "Feels like my junk's about to pop."

Noah nodded, looking tentative. He frowned at his vial. "Not sure I wanna drink anymore."

"Do not worry," Sirus assured. "Once you spill you will feel fine."

Chet leveled him with a glower. "We don't appreciate you forcing our hands like this, you know." He set down his kirah and mulishly crossed his arms. "Makes me feel like you don't deserve our fucking cum."

Sirus' cheery air faded. "You will not donate your seed?"

"No."

The Kríe's eyes flared angrily. "Fine. That is your choice. But you will get no reprieve. Your protection will remain, and you will only grow fuller."

Chet bristled.

Sirus turned to the others just the same. "That goes for everyone, just so we are clear. I do not know why spilling seed is such an issue for your kind, but I am a very busy Kríe, with many important things to do. If you do not drink your kirah, nor spill your seed for me, your cages will stay locked, inaccessible. At which point, you will have to wait for the next collection appointment to have another chance at finding release. You will not waste my time. I do not have one moment to spare. So do as I have instructed or leave me be."

Clearly, the Kríe knew they'd eventually cave. And by the feel of things, probably really soon.

Alec exhaled and downed his shot. He wasn't interested in games. He just hoped his men would show compassion and follow his lead.

Bailey sighed and drank his, too. "Guess it's no different to trips to the sperm bank."

"True." Jamis nodded and swallowed his as well.

"And it's for a good cause." Noah did the same.

Zaden brushed his black bangs away and downed his, too. "Don't say we never did anything for you fucks."

Sirus' broody front diminished as he watched them comply, a happy glint returning to his eyes. "You did not resist..." He stared at each man. "You will do this voluntarily? For Nira?"

The trio shrugged a little. Zaden nodded reluctantly. But it was Chet's response that took Alec by surprise.

"If we do," he grumbled, "can we lose these cages?"

Wow. He was actually considering it.

"Of course," Sirus vowed. "As long as you agree to drink the kirah and refrain from spilling seed between visits." Smirking, he handed the last vial to Chet. "I will be able to tell if you do, you know. So do not try, or your cock goes back in its cage."

Chet scowled. "Relax. Geez, I'm not a *total* bastard. Just wanna be treated with a little respect."

"I understand." Sirus turned to face the others and beamed. "You are gifts from the gods. Every one of you. Gratitude. Nira will not forget your selflessness."

The team swapped looks. And what do you know, they all—even Chet—looked content. Like they knew what they were doing meant the world to these Kríe. A sacrifice they could feel good about, which made Alec proud. They'd chosen to look past their differences and 'be the bigger man,' despite all the shit these Kríe had put them through.

Sirus smiled and gestured to a door at the back of the room. "Shall we begin then?"

Alec frowned. He knew where that led. To the receptacles in which they deposited their cum. Small private stalls with bizarre erotic murals of Kríe fucking in every imaginable position. And yet, what was even crazier were the life-size Kríe statues, fashioned with an orifice to unload in.

That morning, when Alec had met his 'personal receptacle' for the first time, he'd admittedly been taken aback. In fact, he'd opted to jack himself to the brink before even going near that statue's ass. Eventually, he'd had to, though. It was where the damn catch was. Once he was in, he'd still had to thrust a bit to blow, and fuck, the way it'd constricted around his dick? Yeah, that'd been really fucking weird. So, he'd closed his eyes and... envisioned it was Zercy. Then, bam, just like that, he'd detonated.

Hesitating, he looked at Sirus, then gestured toward the partitions. "Don't you uh... need to get some of the other stuff first?"

Sirus shook his head. "Mah. Only seed from now on. I tested every sample that we collected from you earlier. Neither the blood nor urine had any effect. Only the seed."

The trio looked surprised. Even Alec had expected different.

Sirus must've picked up on their bewilderment, offering up his personal conclusion. "I do not know why for sure, but in a way, it does make plausible sense."

"How so?" Alec asked. He'd been sure blood would've been helpful, too.

Sirus led the way. "Nira's physical form is solely that of a reproductive entity. Likewise, so is your seed. Your blood, however, cannot make that claim. Nor, for that matter, can your urine."

Interesting, Alec thought as they followed Sirus back.

Sirus stopped at the door and motioned Alec closer, then turned him around and quickly unlocked his junk.

Alec tamped down a moan of pure rapturous relief. His dick had been hard for a good couple of hours and being crammed into those confines had not been awesome. Reaching under his tunic, he gave his goods a rub, then peered through the door at the first stall.

"Every drop," Sirus reminded. "Do not try to withdraw prematurely. Kirah works incredibly well, so compared to this morning, your yield should be twenty times as great. And since your receptacles are designed to milk you dry at the end, they will not let go." He smirked. "So do not hurt yourselves."

"Jesus," Jamis muttered. "That's not scary as fuck."

Bailey, however, was already doing the math. "Damn. So, if the average guy's cum dump's one teaspoon, then that means we're getting ready to kick out *twenty*."

"Holy fuck," Noah laughed. "That's a half a cup."

Alec stilled. Good god. No wonder his nuts felt so heavy.

"Wow." Jamis chuckled. "Think about last time. We didn't unload for a whole day after eating that senna`sohnsay. That's twice as long as this time." He grinned at Bailey and Noah. "We must've orgasmed a whole damn cup's worth."

"Yeah," Bailey snorted. "Right down those pervy twins' throats."

The rest of the team, as Alec recalled—although, who knew about Noah—dumped their mega-loads into tankards. Then, as soon as they'd caught their breath and gathered their bearings, they watched their handlers slurp it down like eggnog.

Uttering a curse, Alec headed for his stall as, behind him, Sirus got busy unlocking the others. He couldn't believe they'd be doing this indefinitely. For an arrogant species he barely even liked.

No, he corrected himself as he entered the small enclosure. There was one among the Kríe he liked a lot. Maybe too much, even. But at least he'd finally admitted it. He'd somehow fallen for the king. Who, come to think of it, was still pissed off at him. Because Alec had hurt him, cut him down when they should've been celebrating.

God, he was such a tool. Next time he saw Zercy, he'd make it right.

Next time he saw him, he'd make it clear how much he cared.

* * *

After they'd finished doing their thing in Sirus' workshop, Alec opted to head back to his room. Technically, he could've stayed with the guys a few more hours, but he'd wanted some time alone to think. And plan. Strategize a way to get back into Zercy's good graces, so they could revel together in the good fortune of Sirus' discovery.

Pacing the length of Zercy's chambers, he rubbed at his mouth, contemplating the best course of action. He'd apologize first, naturally, but then what? What could he do? A gesture of some sort, actions instead of words, to show Zercy the magnitude of his feelings. That he'd meant what he'd said in the courtyard last night. That he was there for Zercy when he needed him. Wouldn't go running when problems arose. Yeah, the whole situation with his team had definitely jarred him, but in the scheme of things, it'd be worth it to save an entire species. That his men were willingly cooperating certainly helped.

He pivoted on his heel at the far end of the room, readying to lap it back toward the foyer. But before he could take more than a couple of steps, the double doors pushed open, and there Zercy stood.

Alec stopped in his tracks as their eyes instantly locked.

Zercy's expression looked intense, but other than that, Alec couldn't read him.

He cleared his throat. "Hey."

Zercy didn't respond at first. When Setch and Kellim closed the doors though, he finally spoke.

"Nenya, *Alick*," he rumbled in his sexy-as-sin lilt. A lilt that only strengthened when he was emotional.

Alec's heart went nuts. Was he pissed? He couldn't tell.

Nodding, he headed over and stopped in front of the king.

Zercy peered down at him. "I spoke with Sirus. He told me what transpired during your visits."

Alec quickly wracked his brain for any behavior that could've been misconstrued. Besides Chet's typical, everyday ornery disposition, they'd all ultimately cooperated both times. "Not sure what you're referring to," he finally replied. "We did what Sirus asked. We all complied."

"Mah." Zercy shook his head. "More happened than that."

Alec shifted his weight. "What do you mean?"

Something glinted in the king's eyes. A potent little light. "Sirus told me," he murmured, "that you always came forward first and gave of your body without question." A small, tender smile slowly curved his lips. "And that because of this, your men followed your example."

Alec exhaled, gazing up at him, his heart pounding in relief. Zercy wasn't mad. He was grateful for Alec's help.

The king's smile spread wider. "I just left your team's quarters. I wanted to thank them personally. To show my gratitude."

Alec stilled, his brows lifting. He smiled, too. "No shit?"

Zercy chuffed. "Tah. 'No shit'." He slid his hands under Alec's armpits and hoisted him to eye level. "I brought them gifts."

"What?" Alec laughed, clutching Zercy's shoulders. "Are you serious?"

"Tah." Zercy turned and pushed Alec's back against the door, leaving his feet dangling above the ground. "But I had no idea what your teammates like, so I brought a little of everything I could think of." He leaned in and happily nuzzled Alec cheek. "Books, trinkets, plants, food, drink... Even pets."

"Pets?" Alec laughed again, Zercy's affections straight-up melting him. Drawing his knees up, he braced his feet against the door, which instantly had Zercy pushing between his thighs.

"Tah. Pets for my pets," he rumbled, biting Alec's ear.

A shiver raced up Alec's spine. He smiled and closed his eyes. "I can only imagine their reactions."

Zercy's soft pumping purr tickled the skin on his neck. "The little ones with dark hair were elated, to say the least. Gesh's pet, the golden-haired human, just smiled. Your co-pilot stayed stoic…" Zercy pressed closer, nuzzled harder, "but eventually smiled too, and said thank you."

Alec moaned and squeezed Zercy's waist with his thighs. "And Chet?"

Zercy leaned back and grinned. "The grumpy one with tiny hairs?"

"Yeah. That's him," Alec laughed. "What'd he say?"

"At first he just glared at me," Zercy slowly rocked his hips, "but was quickly distracted by my gifts' adamant squeaks."

"*Really?*" More laughter spilled unchecked from Alec's mouth.

"Tah." Zercy chuffed. "He let one crawl up his arm. A moment later, two sat chittering on his shoulder."

Alec shook his head, grinning. Chet had a soft spot for critters? Seriously, who would've thought?

Zercy friskily bit at Alec's chin, then continued down his jaw. "I offered them nonmaterial things, as well."

"Oh?" Alec murmured, insides thrumming in bliss.

Zercy smiled against his cheek. "In appreciation of their kindness, from this day forward, I am relieving them, and you, of your escorts."

Alec stilled, lips parting. "You're… giving us free rein?"

"I am." More purring as Zercy reclaimed Alec's lobe. "Within reason, of course. Anywhere you desire, you may go. As long as you remain inside the castle's walls."

Alec couldn't believe it. Zercy wasn't just showing his heartfelt gratitude. He was extending to Alec his utter trust. And not just with anything, but his most precious possession. Alec's team. AKA his only hope for Nira.

The gesture was enormous. Because in giving this gift, Zercy in turn made Alec's men a much larger flight risk. Chet wouldn't ignore that fact. It made escape ten times easier. And yet, Alec sensed that Zercy wasn't lost to this, but was choosing to trust Alec in spite of it.

Alec's heart throbbed in his chest. "Wow... That's... huge. Thank you."

"You are welcome." Zercy nuzzled his ear. "But there is more. Something I am certain you will like."

Alec shifted, snuggly sandwiched between the door and Zercy's body. "More?"

"Tah, more." Zercy leaned back and grinned. "I have decided to let your scientists work with Sirus."

Alec's eyes shot wide. "Holy shit. That's awesome!"

Zercy chuffed and rocked his hips again, sending bliss to Alec's junk. "According to Sirus, your seed is keeping Nira stabilized."

Alec's heart pounded. "So... she's cured?"

"It is too early to say. All we know at the moment is that, thanks to your team, she has been frozen in suspended animation. No longer does she deteriorate. In fact, she already grows stronger. Whether or not human seed can restore her to her original state? We do not know. Only time will tell."

Alec nodded in understanding. The not knowing was never a fun place to be, but in this case, it was far better than the alternative.

Smiling, he slid his hands from Zercy's shoulders to his cheeks. "She's going to survive this. My men will make sure of it. With them working alongside Sirus, anything's possible."

Zercy nuzzled Alec's palm. "I pray that you are right." One by one, he moved his hands to clutch Alec's ass, then claimed Alec's lips and pressed against him. "Apologies," he rumbled, "for being curt with you this morning. I was overwhelmed and emotional and—"

"I know. So was I." Alec sank his hands into Zercy's dreads. "I'm sorry for the way I acted, too."

Zercy eased back and met his gaze. For long moments they didn't speak. Then a huge, magnificent smile lit his face. "I want to celebrate. Right now. With you, upon the roof."

"Okay," Alec chuckled. "I'd say celebration's definitely in order."

The king growled happily and set him down, then pulled open the doors and called to his guards. "Send word to the chef to prepare a special meal. I will be dining under the stars tonight with my *Alick*."

"Right away, my lord." Kellim inclined his head and turned on his heel.

Setch remained to stand watch. A smile curved his lips. "It is a very good day, Sire."

"It is indeed."

CHAPTER THIRTY

* * *

Zercy strode to the wet bar and grabbed two chalices and a decanter, one filled with a ruby-red liquid. Beaming, he turned to Alec. "Crimson Night. You must try it. My favorite out of all of Nira's nectars."

Alec grinned, unable to help it. He'd never seen Zercy in such a mood. Sure, the king would smile at times, but most looked forced, and yeah, sometimes he'd laugh, but not that often. Now though? The way his big golden eyes were lit up? He looked almost boyish, and it was downright adorable. The king of Kríe looking adorable. Go figure.

Zercy went next to their wall nest and tugged out a fur, one of the largest on the bed, and draped it over his shoulder. Peering back at Alec, he gestured to his 'jungle maze.' "Nenya. We go to the roof now. You lead."

"Me?" Alec chuckled, heading to meet him at the opening.

"Tah." Zercy motioned for him to enter first. "I want to witness your gods in action, showing you the way."

Alec smiled and stepped inside. "They're not gods, they're just stars."

"*Esh.* If they call to you, they are *gods*."

Alec smirked, "Fair enough," then closed his eyes and drew in a breath. Truth be told, they *did* call to him, the stars in the sky. Had the last time he was in the maze and were doing so now.

Left. Something told him that he needed to go left.

Zercy rumbled at his back, a soft approval.

Alec took a right next, then another left, then a right…

Within a few minutes, they'd emerged on the other side, stepping onto the long stone terrace.

Alec grinned and looked at Zercy. "How'd I do?"

"Bellah kai." Zercy smiled warmly. "Your gods must long to see your face."

"They're my home." Alec held his gaze. "Maybe I'm theirs, too. Maybe they miss me... like I miss them."

Something dimmed in Zercy's eyes. "I would like to be your home. If you left me, I would miss you more than they."

Alec's heart thumped at his words. At his tone. At his expression. Averting his gaze, he cleared his throat, then noticed the oddest thing in Zercy's grip.

"Why are you holding the end of a rope in your hand?" The rest of it was on the ground, inside the maze.

Zercy glanced at the thing. A small smile curved his lips. "The other end is attached to the opening inside my chambers. If I do not leave a trail for those delivering our food, it will be cold before they ever find their way."

Alec stifled a laugh. "Breadcrumbs. Wise king."

Zercy cast him a playful grin. "Mah. Just hungry." Hooking the rope to a small wall hook, he headed up the stone stairs to their right. Alec followed behind him, and some two-dozen tall steps later, they reached the lush oasis atop Zercy's bedroom.

Alec scanned the incredible span of space, one of his very favorite places in the castle. Huge plants everywhere, extending more of that jungle feel, with overstuffed two-person lounge seats in the center.

Zercy took Alec's wrist and led him over to settle in. He picked the middle chaise with granite stands on each end and what looked like a rustic sofa table across the back. Alec eyed the reclined lounge, with its plush, deep-emerald padding, noting its mini-columns at each corner. Like some modified four-poster bed or something, exuding a rugged outdoor elegance.

Zercy set down the chalices and decanter and lit a few small torch stands for minimal light. When done, he snapped open the fur he'd brought atop the lounge and gestured for Alec to sit down.

Alec climbed aboard and instantly spotted that cool, retractable telescope. The steampunk one he'd discovered weeks ago. Back when he'd stumbled upon the rooftop haven by accident—then felt Zercy's wrath for the first time. He'd been bugging the king to tell him about the sickness, demanding to know what was in the castle's courtyard. Zercy had straight-up snapped, barking morbid cryptic words about things that made no sense to Alec at the time.

"What's behind those fucking doors!"

"Death! For my *people, not yours!"*

It definitely made sense to Alec now.

Zercy poured them each a drink, then joined Alec on the chaise.

Alec took a swig and licked his lips. "Tastes like Chambord."

"Chambord?" Zercy asked, his gaze dropping to Alec's mouth.

"Yeah... It's a... type of liquor..." The king's stare was distracting. "Raspberry... A kind of fruit back on... Earth."

"Mmm," Zercy rumbled. He swallowed some, too. "I do not know of this raspberry, but if it tastes like Crimson Night, I think I should like it very much."

Alec smiled and took another swig. "You would, but you couldn't drink too much. It'd get you drunk."

Zercy's mouth quirked up on one side. "As will this."

"Ah. Good to know," Alec chuckled. Although, in truth, for the first time, the idea sounded fun. Getting wasted with the king? The male he'd grown so hopelessly fond of? Out there under the stars, just the two of them? A chance to just let go for a while.

Zercy downed a larger swallow, then set his chalice off to the side. "Do not worry," he assured, reclining onto his back, "I will not let you drink too much."

"Gee, thanks," Alec drawled. "Pretty sure I can handle my own."

Zercy looked him up and down with an amused expression. "A moyo your size? No more than two cups at the most."

"Oh really? And how many glasses could you handle?"

Zercy slid his hands behind his head and stared at the sky. "Eight... Perhaps ten, if I have food in my belly."

Alec barked out a laugh. "Bite me. I'm not *that* much smaller than you."

Zercy slid him a side glance, then slowly licked his fangs. "I would love nothing more than to bite you, *Alick*. Come closer and I will sink my teeth in deep."

Alec's dick bucked in its loinstrap. His pulse kicked up a notch.

Smirking, he shook it off. "So frickin' literal."

"Join me," Zercy commanded. "I wish to stargaze with you."

Alec's smirk morphed into a smile. The king wanted to stargaze. One of Alec's all-time favorite distractions. He took his biggest swig yet and set his chalice aside too, then settled down beside Zercy on his back. Linking his fingers behind his head, he stared at the heavens. "Such a clear night... So beautiful."

Zercy raised his arm and traced five stars with the tip of his claw. "That constellation is called the Western Gate of Nasua. The star in the middle is the shield maiden, Asteria, tasked to guard the entrance for all eternity."

Alec eyed the formation. "I see it... Yeah, it does look like a gate."

Zercy pointed to another batch. "That is the constellation, Perileos' Sword. Perileos once walked upon Nira's soil like you and I. But he was captured by traffickers and sold into slavery where he was forced to fight for sport all his days. None could ever kill him. So impressive were his skills that the gods came and stole him, wanting him to fight in *their* arenas."

"Typical gods," Alec mumbled.

Zercy gestured to a third. "That is called the Tiny Hammer. And that," he pointed to the right, "The Eastern Claw."

Alec relaxed into the fur, contentedly listening to Zercy's timbre. Warm and soft, and most of all, at ease. He was surprisingly well-versed too, on not just stars and constellations, but also all the folklore and legends behind them. Next thing Alec knew, he was totally fucking rapt as Zercy told him about the fabled Northern Heart. Like Earth's North Star, it stayed put in one spot high above while all other stars circled around it. Alec smiled, the story inspirational—a warrior's heart gilded in gold—but what he loved just as much was the message it conveyed. How the cosmos, despite all its vastness and violent wonder, still ultimately revolved around a heart.

"And you?" Zercy murmured, when his tale was finally told. "You have constellations where you come from, as well?"

Alec nodded. "We do. Some, most likely, are parts of yours. Hard to tell though, when I'm viewing them from a completely different star system, at a completely different angle than I'm used to."

"What are their names?" Zercy rumbled. "Which is your favorite?"

"Orion."

Zercy turned his head and looked at him. "What is his tale?"

"He was a hunter."

Zercy stilled, then flashed a handsome grin. "Like me."

"Yeah," Alec laughed. "Just as arrogant, too."

"I like him already. Tell me more."

Alec looked back at the sky. "Greek mythology has it that he was the son of the sea-god, Poseidon. Could walk on water and everything. One day he walked to the island of Chios where he got drunk and attacked some chick. Of course, of all people, her dad was the *king*, who retaliated by blinding Orion. Orion fled to another island where he met the god of blacksmiths, who had his servant take Orion to Helios. AKA the sun, who lo and behold, healed Orion's eyes.

"Naturally, Orion went back to give that chick's dad an ass-whooping, but never found him 'cause the king was hiding. So, Orion headed to Crete and ended up hunting with Artemis, goddess of the hunt. Orion got so good, he started running his mouth, bragging he was gonna kill every beast on the planet. Understandably, Mother Earth wasn't too happy about that and—"

"Your planet has a mother, too?" Zercy's auric eyes flared wide. "Why have you not told me of this before?"

"No." Alec shook his head. "That's just part of the mythology. These days Mother Earth is... well, more like an expression... referring to like the weather and shit. On Earth there's no mystical presence."

Zercy's gaze dimmed. "That is sad. No mother for your people."

"Well, no, we do have mothers. Physical mothers, remember? The females?"

"Ah." Zercy nodded. "That is right. I had forgotten." His expression turned thoughtful. "It is a hard concept to imagine."

"Physical moms?"

"Flesh and blood females... that males mate with instead of each other. Who grow young inside their bodies... It boggles my mind."

Alec chuckled. "I could say the same about your Nira."

Zercy met his eyes. Smiled warmly. "Had you not come, she would have died."

"Funny how fate works sometimes," Alec murmured.

"Indeed," Zercy quietly agreed. He looked back at the sky. "What became of Orion?"

Alec shrugged a little. "A scorpion was sent to kill him. After that, all the goddesses petitioned the king of the gods, Zeus, to put Orion among the constellations."

"Hmm," Zercy mused. Thoughtful silence stretched on. "Tell me more," he finally rumbled. "What are some others?"

"Um." Alec scratched his cheek. "Let's see. There's the big and little dipper. The little dipper's tip is our north star. There's Cassiopeia and her daughter Andromeda. There's Scorpio who killed Orion. There's Centaurus the centaur, and—"

"My lord?" Kellim's baritone derailed Alec's train of thought.

Alec and Zercy looked his way. The guard stood at the top of the steps. Beside him, a handful of servants held trays of food.

Zercy waved them over. "Set them down. Tacha." *Hurry.* "Then be gone."

Kellim stayed put as the others hustled over and dropped off the dishes. Then just like that, they were heading back down the staircase.

Zercy rolled onto his side and propped himself on his elbow, then reached for a platter of various fruits. True to noble form, he offered the first piece to Alec. "Open your mouth," he murmured. "I should like to feed my pet."

Alec did as he was commanded, rolling to his side, too. But Zercy didn't feed him food at first, he fed him his finger. At least initially, giving Alec's tongue a sensual stroke, his short claw grazing a line right down the center.

"So warm," he rumbled softly. "And supple. And wet. I should like to feel this wrapped around my cock."

Alec's dick bucked again. Closing his lips, he gave a suck.

Zercy growled. "Gods, tah. Just like that."

Alec all but moaned at his tone, inadvertently biting down.

Zercy grinned and finally fed him the chunk of fruit.

Alec chewed, holding his gaze. Tasted like cantaloupe, but grilled, with some incredible savory glaze. "Damn, that's good."

Zercy's eyes glittered happily. He reached for another.

Alec stopped him. "My turn." He grabbed something comparable in size to a grape and brought it to Zercy's lips. "Open up."

Zercy smirked, clutched Alec's wrist, then did as Alec asked, drawing in Alec's fingers along with the fruit. Wet firm heat instantly tightened around them as the king began seductively suckling.

Alec's boner went nuts, his eyelids growing heavy.

Zercy grinned, holding his gaze. "Del'ahtchay." *Delicious.*

Fuuuck...

Alec's belly fluttered. His pulse started to race.

Zercy retrieved another piece and fed Alec more. They ate like that for the next twenty minutes or so, only eating what the other person fed them. Talking, joking, teasing, grinning. Drinking more of that sweet wine.

Alec's everything felt happy. He couldn't stop smiling.

Eventually, when their bellies were full and the nectar nearly gone, they laid back down to gaze once more at the sky.

"That one," Alec pointed to an arrangement of nine stars, "kinda looks like the constellation Leo."

"Leo?" Zercy asked.

"Yeah. Latin for lion." Alec turned to him and grinned. "A great nickname for you, actually."

Zercy's brows rose. "For me? Why, what is a lion?"

"King of all predators. With a brave, ferocious heart."

Zercy's eyes returned to thoughtful. Then he gave a little nod. "I should like to be this for you. *Your* lion heart."

Alec stilled. "*Mine?*"

"Tah. I will be fierce for you."

Alec's heart leapt into his throat. He looked back up at the sky. "Shit, Leo," he murmured, shaking his head with a smile. "That's the nicest thing anyone's ever said to me."

Zercy chuffed and turned his gaze back to the stars as well. "Leo... Not as regal as King Zercy, but it will do."

Alec grinned, insides happy. Peaceful quiet filled the air.

A moment later though, Zercy loosed a sober sigh.

Alec looked at him. "What's wrong?"

Zercy suddenly seemed unsettled. "You love the stars."

"Yeah."

"You said earlier that you missed them."

Where was he going with this? Alec nodded a little. "Yes. I do."

Zercy's eyes turned troubled as he looked at the sky. "You blame me for keeping you from your home."

What? Alec frowned and shook his head. "No. Of course not. You didn't wreck our craft. We'd still be here regardless, waiting for the search and rescue team."

Zercy kept his eyes diverted. "But if they arrived... and I kept you here... You would surely blame me then."

Alec's chest squeezed uncomfortably. Was Zercy giving him fair warning? That he didn't plan to ever let him go? A spark of anger flared in his suddenly heavy heart. "*Would* you?" he rasped. "Keep me here against my will? Even if I wanted to go home?"

Zercy frowned, going silent, as if saddened by Alec's question. Long moments later, he finally answered. "I would not want to. You would resent me, and that I could not bear... But for Nira, yes, I would... I would keep you."

Alec exhaled, strangely relieved. As long as Zercy wouldn't keep him selfishly... "Then no," he shook his head, "I wouldn't blame you."

Zercy looked at him.

Alec's lips curved. He wanted to keep things light. "Who knows," he shrugged, "for your mom, maybe I'd stay."

Zercy's golden eyes glinted. He smirked. "But not for *me*?"

"Hmm... For you?" Alec scrunched up his nose. "I don't think so, Leo baby. You're way too bossy."

Zercy blinked, brows rising, then barked a robust laugh. "You think me bossy? I go easy on you, *pet*."

Alec narrowed his eyes and smirked. "My case in point. Keep calling me that and see where it gets you."

Zercy quieted, smiling. "You like being my pet."

Alec laughed. "See? You just decided that without me."

Zercy chuffed, then quieted again, his golden gaze hooding. "I gave your men gifts. I want to give you one as well."

Alec paused and eyed him curiously. "You mean like a book or trinket?"

"Mah. Those are things I gave specifically to them, material things that you can have any time. What I wish to give to you now is much more personal."

Alec lifted a brow. "Personal?"

"Tah. I wish to give you me." His big eyes glittered. His sexy lips curved. "For the rest of this night I will be *your* pet, *Alick*. And you, in return, will be *my* king."

Alec blinked. Blinked again. Then shifted to face him. "Come again?"

Zercy chuckled and slowly unfastened his own belt. "I am yours to command in any way you see fit." He slid it off, then opened his tunic. "I am your property."

Holy what the fuck?

Alec stared at him, like a dolt.

Zercy smirked and rubbed his chest, grazing his pierced, pebbled nipples. "Would you decline the opportunity to do with me as you wish?"

Alec's dick went berserk right alongside his heart. "Are you serious?" he rasped.

Zercy's eyes smoldered. "Very."

Alec licked his lips, unable to believe it. Zercy was always in control. The unspoken understood in every encounter. But now? Now the king was relinquishing it all. Subjugating himself to Alec's will.

Alec awkwardly sat up and stared at Zercy's torso, the king's loinstrap all that remained to cover his junk. He rubbed his mouth. Shook his head. "I don't know what to say."

Zercy chuffed. "Do not *say* anything."

Alec met his gaze—and flushed. In truth, he didn't know where to begin. He'd never been in a situation like this. In total control over the indulging of another male. In fact, the only time he'd ever been in something similar, was after the wrestling match when Zercy had challenged him. Challenged Alec to prove that Zercy's body aroused him, but even then, the king had commanded his every move. Directed Alec where to touch him, for how long, and hell, how hard. Alec had merely been following orders the whole time.

Zercy gazed at him, his expression looking more than a little amused. "You do not know where to start."

Alec chuckled and shook his head. Dragging a hand through his hair, he confessed, "I really don't."

"Hmm," the king rumbled, all low and husky. Sliding his arms from his tunic, he tossed it aside, then rolled onto his stomach, baring his backside. He peered at Alec over his shoulder. "Would you like to begin like this?"

Alec bit his lip and nodded.

Zercy's hungry eyes darkened. "Bellah. Now remember, I am *Krie*."

"Meaning?" Alec chuckled.

Zercy donned a salacious grin. "The more debauched my king behaves, the happier his pet."

CHAPTER THIRTY-ONE

* * *

Alec's body lit up like a furnace, his mindset instantly shifting gears. The king wanted kinky. Wanted Alec to get freaky. "I'll keep that in mind." His voice sounded husky.

Zercy eyed him through heavy lashes, then looked forward again, resting his arms on the cushion's top ledge, his chin on his hands.

Alec gazed down his body. So big and packed with muscle. He wanted to touch every inch. Where should he start? His eyes roamed back up and settled on Zercy's shoulders. All dark and broad and beefy. Yeah, he'd start there.

Moving with purpose—and a barely tamped smile—he straddled the king's waist and palmed his massive shoulder blades. Good freaking lord. Even with his fingers fully splayed, his hands still didn't span the powerful slabs. He slid his palms upward and began to knead, something he'd wanted to do for some time. Massage Zercy's shoulders whenever he'd looked exceptionally stressed. Which, for the most part, was pretty much always.

Zercy's muscles eased. "Krye…" he rumbled. "You have the hands of a god."

"Hmm." Alec ground slow, deep circles with his thumbs. "I take it Krye's a god… along with Ságe."

Another soft rumble. "You have been listening to your king." He was smiling, Alec could hear it. "Paying attention."

"Don't you mean my *pet?*"

"Tah," Zercy chuffed. "My mistake."

Alec smiled as he continued. "You'll have to tell me their story sometime."

"I would love that," he murmured. "And you can tell me of your Sol."

Alec chuckled. "Sol's not a god. He's just my star system's sun."

"But every sun is a god. Do those on Earth not acknowledge this?"

"Em…" Alec slowly kneaded down Zercy's back. "Not really, no. I mean, ages ago, they did. Helios, who healed Orion's eyes? He was the sun god. Hell, back then, they even considered the *planets* gods. Although, they thought they were stars too, 'wandering stars,' so yeah."

Zercy scoffed. "Planets are merely the byproduct of two sun gods' love."

"*Two sun gods' love?* What, like some kind of cosmic offspring?"

"In a way."

"But what if there's only one sun? What are the planets in that star system? They can't be 'offspring'."

Zercy thought about that as Alec made his way lower, kneading the thick muscles along his spine. "I do not know," he finally admitted. "Perhaps the byproduct of your god's loneliness."

Alec frowned. "Well, that's depressing."

Zercy chuffed in amusement. "Have you truly not noticed? Life is tragic."

Alec smirked at his tone and worked the small of Zercy's back.

"Except for moments such as this," the king rumbled.

Alec grinned. Evidently someone was enjoying his massage. But while those husky noises emerging were undeniably hot, he'd love to somehow get the king to moan.

An idea quickly came to him. Something he knew the Kríe liked. Returning to Zercy's shoulders, he added his blunt nails and, applying pressure, dragged them slowly downward.

Zercy hissed, muscles tightening as he sensuously arched. A devious smile tugged at Alec's lips. He did it again, watching dark magenta lines form in his fingers' wake.

Then, hell fucking yeah, Zercy *moaned.*

"*Alick…* You excite me far too quickly that way. But your faithful pet relishes it. Do not stop."

Alec chuckled low in his throat. Zercy loved that bite of pain.

Another idea came to him. And then another.

Tunneling his hand into the king's velvet dreads, he fisted tight, then leaned down nice and close. "I'm sensing you like it rough," he murmured, lips grazing Zercy's shoulder.

He remembered Gesh and Roni's rowdy romp in the jungle. The way they'd clawed and bit and snarled the whole damn time.

Zercy growled. "I am Kríe."

Yup, enough said.

And all Alec needed to proceed.

Picking a nice meaty target on Zercy's shoulder, he opened his mouth—and bit down.

Zercy's whole frame went rigid. "Tah," he snarled. "Wicked moyo." His hips ground into the padding—once, then twice.

Alec grinned, but didn't let go, merely fisted his fingers tighter and cranked Zercy's head back, baring his throat.

Zercy's next growl sounded menacing—but in a purely sexual way, launching Alec's dick to rock-hard status. He released Zercy's shoulder and bit the side of his neck instead, neither time hard enough to break skin.

Zercy shifted beneath him, clutching the top of the cushion's ledge. "Your little teeth…" Restless snarl. "So exquisitely sharp…" Again, he rocked his junk into the chaise.

Alec's body thrummed. Zercy's reactions were intoxicating as hell. But Alec wasn't done. Wanted to try something else.

With teeth still clamped tight, he relinquished Zercy's dreads and curled his fingers around the king's horn.

Zercy's huge body shuddered like an earthquake under Alec's ass. His short black claws dug into the cushion. "*Alick…*" His voice had gone noticeably deeper.

Alec grinned against his neck and slowly started to stroke, pumping the king's horn like a cock.

Zercy moaned, harsh and ragged, and again, arched his spine, his chiseled ass decadently rising as a result.

Fuck. Yeah.

Alec gripped harder. Stroked faster. Teeth still locked.

A low growl crawled up Zercy's throat. "*Alick*," he grated in dark, drunken bliss. "If you continue—to do that—I cannot be blamed—for my actions—"

Alec chuckled against his neck, but relented, nevertheless. After all, he didn't want this playtime to end. He was having fun and wanted the king to stay put. Letting go of his horn, then his tasty flesh too, he sat back up and rubbed Zercy's back to calm him. The male's chest was heaving, every muscle taut. His claws had all but shredded the padding.

Alec shook his head, amused, and eyed the king's body, watching as he gradually relaxed. God, his reaction had been so charged. Like his horns were just as sensitive as his dick.

Alec slid his hands downward, reveling in how they contrasted with Zercy's skin. Lean tan fingers against deep midnight purple. He didn't know why, couldn't explain it at all, but the stark difference turned him on so bad.

Short moments later, said fingers ran out of space. He rose onto his knees and shifted backward, then settled atop Zercy's thick calves instead.

Lips curving, he palmed the king's glutes and gave the things a tentative squeeze. Zercy peered over his shoulder, his eyes like glowing embers.

Alec met his gaze. Smiled boyishly. "Nice ass."

Zercy loosed a husky chuff. "Truly? How would you know? You are only just now touching it for the first time."

Alec eased his grip. "Just going by observation."

The king's lashes hooded. "Go by more." He lifted his hips in invitation. "Taste me. Feel inside me. Use your cock."

Alec's dick bucked. He glanced down, his gaze heatedly locking on Zercy's ass. Absently, he squeezed again, then the next thing he knew, he'd pulled those strong, dark, muscular glutes apart.

Ah, fuck…

Zercy's entrance. So little and tight.

His heart kicked up a notch. His dick growled.

How? How was it possible? To find a backdoor so appealing. So enticing. He wanted to touch it and tease it. Lick it and *fuck* it. Freaking hell. What was wrong with him? Was he nuts?

Swallowing, eyes locked on that hot little star, he dragged the pad of his finger down it slowly. It clenched on contact, all tightening up. Damn, so warm and tender and soft.

Zercy purred, still watching him over his shoulder. "Bellah, *Alick*. Explore me more."

But he didn't say how. He was letting Alec drive. Encouraging him to dive into his fantasies. To throw all inhibitions to the wind.

Alec's dick throbbed as his fingers itched to play. Hell, even his mouth had started to water. Heart all but racing, he stroked Zercy's hole again, then leaned down and gave it a tentative lick.

Son of a bitch...

He tasted like he smelled. Lightly charred marshmallows over a fire.

Alec moaned and licked him again.

Zercy muffled a snarl and raised his ass higher.

The king wanted more. Alec lapped in earnest. A part of him couldn't believe that he was doing this. But Goddamn, was he ever. And he fucking loved it.

Reaching around, he blindly unfasted Zercy's loinstrap. The king's heavy cock thumped to the cushion. Alec paused at the sound, unable to resist stealing a peek.

Good god almighty. With Zercy's ass propped up and his knees partly spread, he could see the huge Kríe's everything on full display.

Alec took a second to admire his erection, all long and thick with those gorgeous veins. And those gold bands, all snug beneath his crown and around his base. It amazed him how a cock could look so exotic.

He eyed Zercy's sac, so smooth, round, and heavy. That taint above it, that tantalizing star. Every inch of him looked savory as hell. Alec had lost his mind. And didn't care.

Zercy thrummed. "Your expression hides nothing. So captivated by my body. You make me eager."

Alec met his gaze. A grin tugged at his lips. Dipping two fingers into his wine, he used them to trace Zercy's crack. Up and down... Just breaching his entrance with each lazy pass...

Zercy rumbled deep in his chest. "Stop tormenting, *Alick*. Give me more."

Alec's boner went wild. He stopped with the teasing and gently pushed his index finger inside. Fuck, so warm.

Zercy clenched around him. "Such a tiny little finger."

Alec smirked. The king was goading him. He sank it deeper, then added another.

Zercy squeezed them, eyes hooding.

Alec slowly pumped. Fuck, that muscle, so firm yet so pliant. Enraptured, he sank in a third.

"*More*." Zercy rocked his hips and spread his thighs. The action forced Alec to resituate between his knees.

He eyed his buried fingers. The king wanted *four*? But wouldn't that hurt?

A memory surfaced in his brain. Of that night at Gesh's compound, when Roni had mounted Chet's cock. It hadn't been enough, so he'd let a packmate add his fist. And then later, Roni had buried his own fist inside Chet. Granted, Chet had been prepped with tachi, but the fundamental action was the same. Evidently, for Kríe, shoving hands up other's asses was completely acceptable. And not just completely acceptable, but common practice.

Alec's dick twitched at the thought. Was that what Zercy wanted? Would that turn him on? Drive him wild? He supposed there was only one way to find out.

Heart pounding as he sat on his heels, he removed his wrist cuff, then grasped Zercy's left ass cheek. Pulling it aside, he fed his four fingers through. Slowly, and as carefully as he could. When those were secure, he gingerly added his thumb. Zercy clutched the cushion but didn't tell him to stop. Alec eased in up to his knuckles. To his surprise, he didn't need any lube. By the look of things, Kríe not only produced precum in their dicks, but a similar substance in their channel. All clear and glistening, making his task at hand delectably easy.

Still clutching Zercy's ass cheek, he pushed in farther. Zercy shifted against him. Alec breathed an intoxicated curse. A heartbeat later, his hand sank completely out of sight.

Zercy grunted as his sphincter gripped Alec's wrist.

Alec paused. "You okay?"

"*Gods, yes*," the king rasped. "You feel incredible inside my body. Go deeper, *Alick*, deeper, until you reach my end."

Alec's dick reeled. Nope, still couldn't believe he was doing this.

Steadily, he sank in his forearm. Zercy's channel engulfed it like a slick, heated glove. Deeper... till that glove reached his elbow. Then he finally bottomed out.

Zercy groaned and canted his ass.

"Still okay?"

"Tah…" His voice sounded gravelly and thick. "Now make a fist and fuck me, *Alick. Hard.*"

Oh, God.

Alec's junk went crazy. "Okay," he rapsed.

He seriously, *seriously* couldn't believe he was doing this.

Balling his fingers, he withdrew to his wrist, then started a deep, steady, in-and-out rhythm.

Zercy growled, pressing his forehead to the cushion. His strong hips got rocking to Alec's pace.

"Fuck," Alec breathed. "This is insane. But I love it. Love your hot insides hugging my arm."

A restless snarl curled in Zercy's throat. "Your little knuckles, *Alick…* How they tease my jewel…" His dark claws gripped the cushions.

His jewel? Alec was riling up his G?

A grin curved his lips. Things just got a lot more fun. Withdrawing to his wrist, he gave a searching pump. Sure enough, he found a bulge that hadn't been there before. It'd swollen up just now, in the time that he'd been playing. Guess the king *really* liked Alec's hand up his ass. Which instantly shot Alec's lust levels through the roof. Body thrumming, he got back to business. But this time, as he worked Zercy's body, he made sure his knuckles hit the Kríe's sweet spot with every delve.

Zercy sucked in a breath, body tensing, shoulders flexing. "Tah— Do not stop—"

Alec's mind spun. He felt drunk. Drunk on the rush of filling this mighty king with pleasure. Within seconds, he had his Kríe so wound so tight that it looked like Zercy's muscles might start snapping.

"Tah— *Alick*— Tah—" His choppy snarls were intoxicating. As was the way the male kept writhing.

Alec's dick went wild. It wanted action, too. To shove hard and fast into Zercy's heat. Thing was, at the moment, Alec was having too much fun. His boner's needs would just have to wait.

Pulse racing, he relinquished Zercy's ass cheek and reached between his growling pet's thighs instead. His fingers met instantly with a rock-hard cock. He grabbed on and started to pump.

Zercy loosed a oath and arched his ass higher. Shoved his knees even farther apart. Next thing Alec knew, the king's body was quaking from head to toe. "*Alick*—" His timbre turned ragged. "You are going to— you are going to make me— spill—"

No. Not yet.

Alec stopped and looked down. Sure enough, Zercy's balls were up hugging his cock. He frowned, not wanting the fun to end, and glanced around for a solution.

Nothing.

No, wait.

He eyed his discarded wrist cuff. That would work.

Withdrawing his hand from Zercy's body, he eased the king's balls slowly back down. God, they felt good in his hands. He paused for a moment to fondle them, then swiped up his wrist cuff and tightly bound their base.

No one would be spilling now.

Zercy peered over his shoulder, eyes drunk with passion. "You tie my sac?"

Alec's cheeks warmed. "Don't want you to come."

"Before you fuck me with your cock?"

"Yeah… Before that."

Thing was, once Alec buried his dick in Zercy's ass, it wouldn't be long before his own orgasm ignited. He'd be too excited. Too insanely turned on to last more than a couple of minutes tops.

So, he'd have to hold off if he wanted this to last.

With a smack to Zercy's ass, he prompted him to face forward again, then clutched Zercy's dick and pushed his other hand back inside.

Rapidly, he pumped that massive boner.

Repeatedly, he stroked that swollen G.

In seconds, the king was back to feral writhing. His claws tore at the cushion, his strong hips thrusting, every muscle bunching tight. The sight was inebriating. If Alec wasn't careful, it might actually make him come.

Letting go of Zercy's member, he gave his own dick a squeeze, his other hand still working Zercy's ass. Before long, the king's balls tried to climb again. *"Ah, Alick— Must spill!—"*

His shout was like a drug to Alec's brain. Zercy's hips bucked. His taint contracted. His entrance squeezed Alec's arm. And deep inside, his prostate pulsed against Alec's hand. He was climaxing. Alec could hear it in his broken snarls and gasps. But not a single drop of cum shot from his dick. His powerful body shook, his fangs urgently buried in the lounge chair's cushion.

Exquisite. The Kríe was exquisite.

Alec's dick all but roared in response. It needed *in.*

A moment later, Zercy's orgasm started to ebb. Not a moment too soon. Alec pulled free and ripped off his clothes. Then he grabbed his boner and rose to his knees. His heart hammered. His shaft throbbed. Heatedly, he eyed Zercy's star, then leaned in and nestled his dick into position.

Breath left him in shallow bursts. He was readying to fuck a *male.* An *alien* male. A *king.*

"Zercy," he rasped, grasping his hip. "I can't wait." His only warning before he shoved to the hilt.

Zercy shuddered and clutched the chaise, his back muscles twitching. No doubt, his prostate was still reeling.

Alec moaned and started to move, hands gripping Zercy's sides as he tentatively thrust.

Goddamn, so hot in there. So silky and slick.

Zercy growled, sounding as hungry as ever, and reached back to palm Alec's hamstring. "Tah... I feel you..." His voice sounded abraded. "Feel you feeding me your body. Your cock."

Alec clenched his teeth and moved his hips faster, burying his dick again and again, as deep as it'd go. Pleasure swelled in his balls and streaked up his shaft. Already, he could feel his climax swiftly approaching.

And yet, as his groans came more steadily, his muscles tightening, he realized something disheartening about his partner. Zercy wasn't blissing out like he'd been just moments earlier. His grip had eased, his ragged breaths stabilizing. Even his rumbles were less intense.

Alec frowned and thrust faster. Zercy clenched around his cock, clearly trying to grip him as hard as he could. All the while, his body's reactions remained controlled.

Like Alec's dick wasn't doing it for him.

Oh, God.

The memory of Roni quickly looped back around. Back at the compound when he'd mounted Chet's cock. Its size had only frustrated him. Teased him—but not in a *good* way—making him anxious to be filled to satisfaction. Which Chet's dick couldn't do, hence why that other Kríe stepped in. He was the one who'd ultimately given Roni pleasure.

Stomach sinking, Alec slowed in realization. Tachi was one thing, allowing their bodies to physically fit, but Alec's dick could never satisfy a Kríe. Could never bring this amazing male before him to rapture.

His hips drew to a stop.

Zercy peered at him over his shoulder. And there it was. That look in his eyes that said it all. He'd been thinking the same thing. How could he not have? It was painfully obvious. And utterly mortifying. But also heartbreaking. They truly weren't compatible in the way that mattered most. Not that Alec foresaw them being life mates or anything, but just knowing that wasn't even an option was strangely… crushing.

"*Alick…*" Zercy murmured.

Alec shook his head and pulled out. Cleared his throat and averted his gaze. "Whatever. It's fine." Reluctantly, he looked down at his hand. "I'll just go back to using this and—"

"Mah." The king's voice cut through the quiet like an axe. "I am done with your hand. I want *you.*"

Alec groaned. "But Zercy, I—"

"Do not say it. You are wrong." Zercy turned around to face him. "You are plenty. *More* than plenty."

Alec sat back on his heels. "Bullshit. We both know that's not true."

Zercy's gaze was rock solid. "Do not limit your worth. You are more than just the *size* of your cock."

Alec scowled and looked away. That did *not* make him feel better.

"Listen to me, *Alick*. No other soul on this planet has ever filled me with even half of what you do. The pleasure you give me transcends the mere physical. Touches me deeper than any mighty cock ever could."

Okay, that was kind of a nice sentiment.

Alec's heavy heart thudded, but still, the situation sucked.

Face downcast, he looked back at Zercy. "You asked me to fuck you *hard*."

Zercy grinned. "And you did."

"With my hand," Alec grated.

The king's eyes glittered. His smirk subtly warmed. "You want to fuck me hard with your cock."

"Yes!" Alec all but threw up his hands.

"Then we will make it so you can."

Alec stilled. "Wait, what?"

Zercy chuffed. "If it is so very important to you, we shall make it so you can. Hand me my belt."

Confused, Alec gave him what he asked for. "I don't follow."

The king's grin quirked as he located a pouch sewn discreetly into the strap's inner lining. The very pouch in which he'd kept that vial of tachi. Sure enough, another small container emerged.

Zercy pulled out its stopper and dumped its contents into his hand. Or rather, its one singular item. Alec eyed what resembled an extra-long paper clip, made from a material that was thin and green.

Zercy unwound it into a long straight line. Now it looked like an eight-inch stretch of soldering wire.

Zercy held it up and smiled. "Do you remember the tachi?"

Alec shifted warily. "Of course."

No way that thing was going inside his dick.

"This is ruka vine. It does the opposite."

"The opposite?"

"Tah." Zercy handed it over. "Rather than make lax what it touches, it constricts it. Sirus uses it often for medical purposes."

Alec frowned, still not sure he completely understood. "Uh huh. And you're giving this to *me*, why?"

"I want you to insert it into my body."

Alec's jaw went slack, finally grasping. "Into…"

413

"My ass."

His junk went nuts again. "Are you serious?"

"I am." Zercy smiled. "My Sirus is brilliant. Within moments, I should absorb the vine completely."

Which Alec deduced meant that, once absorbed, it'd shrink the king's channel to super-snug.

"Damn." He rubbed his mouth and glanced down Zercy's body. "Remind me to give your scientist a kiss."

Zercy stilled, his smile fading. "I do not like that idea."

Alec coughed a laugh. "Figure of speech."

The king eased.

Alec's grin ebbed. "You think it'll work?"

"Tah," Zercy rumbled. "I truly do... But Sirus gave us another option if it fails."

"He... did?" Alec eyed him. "And what option's that?"

Zercy's grin reemerged as he picked his belt back up. From another pouch he pulled another vial. That one was fatter though, with a wider top. Zercy opened it, shoved his index in and slid something out. Alec gaped as it unfolded to its natural shape. No way. It looked like a black, rolled-up condom.

"Sirus fashioned this to fit human erections."

"What... What is it?" Never safe to assume.

"A sheath for your cock, made of enyid skin." Alec remembered that stuff well. Lotis had used it the night of the tournament. A skintight wrap to cover his art pieces' dicks. "This skin, however, is much thinner than usual... and lined with a special night flower oil."

Alec regarded it. "What does special night flower oil do?"

"It makes things swell. Engorges tissue with blood. Sirus uses this substance for medical practices, too."

Alec grinned, unable to help it. What an insanely awesome concept. That is, as long as it didn't have side effects.

His brain churned curiously. "When the tissue expands... does it hurt?"

"Mah. No pain. But one's skin does grow taut. And, naturally, sensitive too, from all the swelling." Zercy folded it and brought it to its vial to put it away, but Alec gripped his wrist and stopped him.

"Let's use both."

Zercy lifted a brow. "Both?" His big ears twitched.

Alec fought back a smile. "Yeah. Why not?" After all, twice the options meant twice the effects. And he wanted to rock Zercy's world.

The king's dark lips curved, revealing his short, fat fangs. "Alright. We use both." Reclining back, he propped his feet atop the cushions and spread his thighs. "Insert the ruka, and then I shall sheath your cock."

Heart kicking, Alec nodded and reached for Zercy's ass. Pulling one cheek to the side, he inserted the vine, intentionally leaving the very exposed. Not so he could extract it—in minutes, it'd be totally dissolved—but to ensure that Zercy's star was cinched-tight, too.

Zercy growled, then sat up and gripped Alec's dick. Alec sucked in a breath, current surging through his junk. Zercy rolled the condom down his boner. A subtle, but noticeable tingle instantly engulfed it. In seconds, the tingle morphed into a burn. Fortunately, not a painful one, but it definitely got Alec's attention—and swiftly raised his heart rate a couple notches.

Shifting on his heels, he eyed his dick warily.

Zercy smiled, leaned in, and kissed his mouth. "Kerra... Móonday... Reesha et," he murmured against his lips. *Relax... Do not fear... It will not harm you.*

Alec exhaled and nodded, then clutched Zercy's dreads and crushed their mouths closer to distract himself.

The king rumbled heatedly. A moment later, though, he pulled back. Alec opened his eyes. Zercy grinned and met his gaze, then eased back onto the chaise and clutched his huge cock.

Alec watched him seductively stroke it.

"Distract yourself with this, *Alick*, while your body adjusts. I want to feel your tongue. Your tender lips."

Oh, fuuuck...

Alec's eyes locked on Zercy's shaft. All thick and long and rigid with those protruding veins. And God, that broad crown, so perfectly sculpted and round. Alec's mouth may be too small to accommodate Zercy's length, but that head should definitely fit.

Absently clutching his own ramped-up dick, he chewed his lip and smiled. "Another first."

Zercy's gaze hooded. He parted his knees.

Alec's pulse raced. Tentatively, he curled his fingers around Zercy's shaft, then leaned down and licked its warm crown. Shit, so smooth and firm. He licked again.

Zercy growled low in his throat. Alec peered up through his lashes. Wow, those auric eyes were blazing.

"Draw me into your warmth," Zercy purred.

Alec did. And sure enough, it filled his whole freaking mouth. Zercy's cockhead, that is, and nothing more. Alec laughed before he could stop himself, and pulled back. "Jesus, Kríe. Honest to God, you're *ridiculously* huge."

The king beamed.

Alec shook his head and resumed, attempting to actually suck. Wasn't easy, but he managed. Not too slow, not too fast, just the right pace to tantalize. All while stroking that notch on its underside with his tongue.

Another growl emerged. Claw-tipped fingers sank into Alec's hair. "Tah, bellah kai," the king praised through clenched teeth. "Such a sweet little mouth worshipping my cock."

Alec's whole body thrummed. He could feel his dick swelling, its skin stretching impossibly taut. Raw sensation engorged his junk, from his balls to his crown. Without thinking, he gave it a stroke—and sucked in sharply. Oh, God. So sensitive. Just one rub had damn near ignited him. He groaned around Zercy's glans and pulled back.

"Gotta take this thing off," he rasped. "It's making my dick crazy."

"Very well. It is probably ready now anyway."

Straightening, Alec looked down at his dick—and froze. Whoa. It *was* bigger. Like, a *lot* bigger. Not Kríe size by any means, but damn near two inches longer, and definitely thicker.

Grinning in disbelief, he peeled the enyid off, the simple action sending his whole package reeling. How in the *hell* was he going to last when the simplest graze nearly undid him?

"Beautiful," Zercy rumbled. "Rise to your knees. I want to taste."

Alec's heart pounded anxiously. Zercy's mouth on his dick? When it was feeling like this? What if he climaxed? Before he could voice a single word of concern, Zercy tugged him up and gripped his turgid shaft.

Alec gasped.

Zercy peered into his eyes, then parted his lips and slid his tapered tongue out to play. From the base of Alec's dick, up to its underbelly, then to his glans. A glans that, incidentally, had started leaking.

Alec shuddered, breathing a curse. "Aw, God. Too sensitive."

Zercy laved his seeping hole and growled. "Del'ahtchay."

Current tore down Alec's length. He inhaled sharply, body tensing as he clutched Zercy's dreads. The king snarled and took him fully, right to his base, lips wrapped around him tight.

Alec fought not to buck as pleasure bombarded his crotch. He clenched his fists. Hot suction engulfed his dick.

"Sh-Shit—" he hitched, fingers squeezing even tighter, which quickly created a wicked snowball effect. The fiercer he gripped Zercy's dreads, the faster the king worked his cock.

Pressure spiked to critical. His nuts balled like rocks.

"Fuck—Gonna come!" Abs starting to dance, he tried to push Zercy off. But instead of relenting, Zercy wrapped him in his arms, holding him nice and steady as he sucked.

Alec's orgasm was nearly on him. He could feel it barreling down.

"Zercy—Damn it—" He grappled to get free. "No—*Ungh fuck*— Don't make me come!"

Zercy chuffed around his mouthful and yielded at the last second, sliding his wet lips off Alec's cock.

Alec dropped onto his heels, body twitching, face flushed. "You can't be trusted," he panted, grinning.

Zercy reclined back on the cushions. "Mah," he smirked, "I cannot."

Alec stifled a laugh and shook his head. "You're such a brat."

The king's next chuckle sent a shiver up his spine.

Alec moaned and squeezed his dick. "Fine. So be it."

Once again, he glanced around searching for a solution. Something, anything, to guarantee his security. He alone would control when he came. He scanned the small tables. Drink and food were no use, nor was the telescope or standing torches. But then his gaze paused on their lounge's corner pillars, the ones that resembled a four-poster bed.

Hmm...

He peered down at his unwound, discarded loinstrap, then shifted his focus to Zercy's wrist. His lips curved slowly. He met the king's eyes. "Looks like I'm gonna have to tie you up."

Zercy's surprise was almost comical. The way he stilled, brows rising high. "You wish to restrain me?"

"Yes. Yes, I do." Alec moved to the corner post. "Give me your hand."

Zercy regarded him for a moment, but eventually smirked. "Wicked king," he rumbled, extending his arm.

Alec's oversized dick twitched excitedly against his thigh. He bound Zercy's wrist, then grabbed the king's loinstrap and made quick work of binding his other wrist, too.

Once he was finished, Alec settled back on his heels between Zercy's knees. Gazing at the king's gloriously naked, restrained body, he met Zercy's gaze and smiled. "Hot."

The king's eyes hooded. "Hot?" he murmured. His big ears flicked.

"Yeah." Alec leaned forward and braced his hands by Zercy's hips. "Means you're making me crazy to get back in you." He dipped his head and dragged his tongue up Zercy's cock.

Zercy growled, abs clenching. "Then do not wait."

"You think you're ready?"

Zercy nodded once. "My ass feels very tight."

Alec choked on a laugh. "Maybe I should check."

Drawing some spit, he lubed two fingers, then gently pressed their tips to Zercy's star. Zercy rumbled. The second Alec entered him, a small grunt pushed past the king's lips.

Zercy's eyes flared in surprise. "Ságe and Krye," he muttered softly.

Alec sank his fingers deeper. That stuff had definitely worked. Zercy's ass felt *super* narrow now. Slowly, he pumped his digits, relishing the snugness, then pulled out and added a third. Another grunt graced his ears, making his eager dick sing.

Zercy rocked his hips. "Your fingers feel as big as a Kríe's."

Alec chuckled. "Funny you say that, 'cause my dick kinda does, too."

Zercy cuffed. "As if that were possible."

"Hey." Alec coughed out a laugh. "You know what? Bite me."

"Come closer, little king, and I shall."

Alec narrowed his eyes, lips twitching, and reached for Zercy's shaft. Tightly, he gripped its base and pulled up. Zercy growled as a huge bead of precum emerged. Alec swiped it up, slicked his own dick, then Zercy's star.

The king's lashes hooded.

Alec met his heated gaze. Palming the crooks of Zercy's knees, he pushed them forward. When they met Zercy's chest, Alec grabbed his newly enhanced boner and pressed its head to Zercy's hole. God, how he wanted to just slam that fucker home. But the king wasn't pliant like he'd been just moments before, and Alec didn't want to hurt him.

"You ready?" he rasped. "'Cause, fuck, I need back in bad."

Zercy rumbled and nodded once.

Alec's pounding pulse spiked. He pushed his hips forward—slowly, steadily—until his cockhead breached the king's constricted ring.

Zercy hissed and bared his fangs.

Alec's eyes all but crossed. "Oh, Jesus. You're so tight now. Oh, my God…"

Zercy canted his ass. "Do not stop, *Alick*. Keep going."

Alec did, but fuck, those super-snug confines—they were going to set his dick off, and if he came now, he'd hate himself forever.

Zercy growled. Alec panted.

When he'd buried himself to the hilt, his dick was all but roaring for release. Goddamnit. No way could he fuck like this. He'd last for maybe eight point six five seconds. Groaning in cruel bliss, he gave some shallow thrusts, then paused with a shudder. "I need a sec."

Zercy grinned. "Your cock likes my tight ass too much."

Alec chuckled and nodded. "*Waaay* too much."

The king's smile faltered, as if something just occurred. "Spill too soon," he muttered darkly, "and I will whip you."

"Wow." Alec laughed. "Your pillow talk is seriously lacking."

"My what?"

"Never mind." Alec had something more important to focus on—like how he was going to keep himself from coming. His eyes dropped to Zercy's package, or more specifically, to his balls. The ones Alec had bound just moments earlier. Looks like their nuts' fates were one and the same. Removing his second wrist cuff, he shifted awkwardly, then carefully cinched his sac while his dick was still buried.

Zercy rumbled in amusement.

Alec smirked in response. "Quiet, pet," he murmured, then dipped down and snagged Zercy's nipple with his teeth. He gave it a playful tug.

Zercy snarled, muscles tensing. "Tah, *Alick*. Reeka moonsah." *Give me more of that.* He rocked his hips.

Alec groaned. That simple movement just slayed his dick. Nuts firming, he squeezed his eyes closed and bit down harder.

Zercy barked a heated oath. Balled his tightly-bound fists.

Alec tugged again, but this time with more oomph.

Zercy arched on a shout.

Alec's dick howled from the jarring. "Fuck, yeah," he grated, eagerly moving to nip the other.

Tug—twist—tug— as he pinned Zercy's knees.

Zercy growled for each one, shifting restlessly.

So hot.

Alec couldn't resist and dealt a salvo of short fast thrusts.

Zercy writhed beneath him, huge chest heaving, nipples swollen. Which only spurred Alec on to keep it going. More wicked yanks, more vigorous hip action, effectively getting his 'pet' all riled up.

Zercy's clipped, strangled roars rent the night like thunderclaps. Like heroin bullets straight to Alec's brain. Ramping his lust levels. Making him mindless. Crazy to delve even harder, faster, deeper.

Soon, though, his junk howled so fiercely for mercy, he had no choice but to slow his urgent thrusts. Panting, he migrated his teeth and lips northward, leaving a trail of sharp nips up Zercy's pec.

Zercy bared his fangs, lungs sawing. "Move too close and you are mine."

Alec grinned and bit Zercy's shoulder. At the same time, he surged his hips. Their bodies smacked together. Alec's abs hit Zercy's nuts. He loved the feeling, instantly addicted.

His balls firmed fast again, on the verge. Grabbing Zercy's cock, he pumped his huge shaft and bit down harder.

Zercy loosed another roar. Yeah, he loved that rowdy shit. And damn if his reactions didn't drive Alec wild. He'd never been so turned on. He could fuck like this forever. But only with Zercy. No one else.

Faster, he pumped Zercy's massive, straining cock, drunk on his scent, his heated growls. More, Alec needed more. Stretching, he reached for Zercy's lobe, inadvertently snagging its piercings with his teeth. Zercy snarled, jerking his head, and made a go for Alec's neck. Zercy snarled, jerking his head, and made a go for Alec's neck. Alec dodged, barely evading, Zercy's fat fangs glistening. The Kríe tugged feverishly on his binds.

God, he was magnificent.

Alec's whole body vibrated, the sight heating his blood to lava. Panting, he grinned and bit down harder on Zercy's ear. "You're so helpless. I love it."

Zercy's giant frame quaked. "You like me—" he rasped, "at your whim."

Damn. His timbre, all breathless and ragged, the sound was intoxicating as hell. Alec tightened his grip on Zercy's cock as he pumped, then tugged hard on Zercy's ear. "Do I ever."

The mighty king bucked on a stifled roar.

Alec groaned and fell back to fucking, unable to resist. With one hand gripping Zercy's shin and the other one jacking his cock, Alec rose up and thrust his hips like a piston. A crazy-train piston. Barreling off the tracks. As his hungry gaze stayed rapt on the king.

He could watch him lost in pleasure like this for hours. Back arched, fists clenched, eyes blazing, cheeks flushed. Lips parted, chest heaving as he snarled.

Alec's mind started to tailspin. Inebriated. Overwhelmed. His nuts just as rock hard as his dick. And still, even as his package fought to ignite, he needed *more*.

Pulling back, he slammed home extra hard with a shout, then let go of Zercy's cock and reached for his horns. It happened before he realized it, but as soon as his fingers made contact, the king's gigantic body went ramrod stiff.

"*Alick*," he gritted roughly, eyes urgent. "You play with fire—You must let go—When I am like this—I could hurt you—"

Thing was, at the moment, Alec's logic was nonexistent, and his dick in full control of the reins. Meaning, no letting go and absolutely no backing down. Besides, the king was tied. How much harm could he do?

With all the strength he could muster not to come right then and there, Alec tugged Zercy's head forward and fused their lips. Zercy's growls filled his mouth as he returned Alec's kiss, their fiery exchange raw, aggressive.

Alec launched back into thrusting. Zercy savagely snarled. No surprise. Alec was using his horns for leverage. Restlessly squeezing and gripping them as he fucked. Couldn't help it, though. He was struggling not to blow.

Soon, their kiss morphed into what felt more like a battle. Swollen lips, lashing tongues, feverish teeth.

"Need to bite you—" Zercy ground out, abruptly diving for Alec's neck. "Need to mark you— Sink my fangs into your flesh—" His voice had turned guttural. He pulled at his binds. But just as Alec suspected, he couldn't get free.

Nevertheless, Alec pulled back out of reach just in case, putting a nice safe distance between them as he thrust. The king wasn't having it though and lurched for his throat. Alec tightened his grip, barely holding him back by his horns.

"Release me!" Zercy bellowed. His massive frame quaked.

Fuck. That carnal shout. Like a stroke to Alec's crotch. Like a heady lick right up his cock. High on the rush, he moaned and pumped Zercy's horns.

Zercy roared and lunged again.

Again, Alec barely dodged. "Fuck," he laughed breathlessly. "You're hot when you get wild."

Zercy shuddered, chest heaving. "Come closer," he snarled.

Alec laughed again, heart pounding. "No way. You're gonna bite me." His nerve endings sang at the thought.

"You will like it."

Alec's dick bucked, buried deep in Zercy's ass. Because truth be told, *no*, he'd probably *love* it. But that'd mean conceding. Giving in.

Relenting. Which he wasn't going to do. He wasn't wired that way. "Maybe," he panted, "but I'm not done making you crazy."

Zercy grinned and bared his fangs. Gave his bindings another yank. "You think you are in control?"

Alec stifled a moan and thrust. "I'm not the one tied—so yeah, I do—" He stroked Zercy's horns with his thumbs, then gave a squeeze.

Zercy quaked again. "You are not—" Breath heaved from his lungs. "Now come closer, or I will make you."

Alec grinned and kept fucking. His nuts were going to pop. "Make me?" he rasped. "Uh-huh, whatever you say—*whoa!*"

Zercy snapped his legs around him in the blink of an eye and yanked him fast and furious against his body.

Alec grunted, crashing into him, but before he could scramble free, the king's sharp fangs pierced the crook of his shoulder.

"Ah!" Alec belted, every muscle going taut.

Oh, God. *So good!*

Zercy's legs pinned him close.

Then Alec's not-so-subservient pet snarled and started sucking.

Current shot through Alec's torso, instantly lighting him up like fireworks. His hips shot into crazy mode, his dick pistoning in a frenzy. White hot pleasure flared fast, then exploded through his groin.

Holy shit. He needed to come. If he didn't, something would rupture. Pitching and thrusting out of control in Zercy's hold, Alec shoved a hand between their bodies and blindly fumbled to unbind his nuts. The second he did, blood punched through his crotch in a hurry, wrenching free an urgent shout.

Lungs sawing, he scrambled to free Zercy's, too.

Another snarl met his ear, as if the king was wholly grateful. But Zercy's sucking never slowed, not one bit. His mouth was swiftly stealing Alec's sanity.

Alec's hips thrust wildly, his climax on the brink, every inch of him shuddering like an earthquake. Pleasure surged, hot and fast, then that telltale pressure spiked.

Bracing, Alec restlessly clutched Zercy's shoulders, then arched with a ragged shout. "*ZERCY!!—FFFUUUCK!!*"

His nut sac unloaded with a fiery vengeance, punching hot cum deep inside the king. A heartbeat later, as if triggered by Alec's deluge, Zercy roared against Alec's neck and slammed home, too. Bucking and shuddering and squeezing Alec's body, his huge frame like a massive quaking cage.

Alec struggled to breathe as thick heat pelted his torso, but his climax just kept coming, wouldn't stop. As if Zercy's fangs, those powerful draws, were somehow fueling it on. But even as *his* body kept on rapturously reeling, he could feel his lover's body doing the same. Unceasingly, relentlessly, clenching Alec's dick like a fist, as if wholly bound and determined to wring free every drop.

Alec shuddered, gasping and twitching. Long moments later, the tempest receded.

Zercy groaned and went limp, his rigid body deflating, his strong legs languidly releasing Alec from their hold. Sliding his fangs free, he lapped at the wounds. "I told you," his breathless pants kissed Alec's skin, "but you did not believe me. When will you learn?"

Alec chuckled, feeling drunk. "You totally cheated."

"Hardly. I even warned you in advance."

Alec's grin spread wider. Sliding his arms around Zercy's sides, he hugged him close and nuzzled his chest.

Zercy's rumble sounded happy. And really sated. "Untie me, *Alick*. I wish to hold you, too."

Alec's heart thumped at his words. Zercy wanted a post-fuck cuddle. And if Alec was honest, he wanted that, too. Fucking hell. He was falling way too fast for this guy. A male he was eventually going to have to leave.

Pushing the thought from his brain, he pulled out and reached for Zercy's wrist. One hand freed. He quickly untied the other. Then just like that, Zercy's strong arms were holding him.

Alec melted atop his chest, cheek pressed to his shoulder, eyelids closed. "Just for the record?" he mumbled. "Sirus rocks."

Zercy chuffed. "Tah. I told you, he is brilliant."

"Fuck yeah, he is. He needs a statue or some shit. My dick has never been so frickin' happy."

Zercy's next laugh was hardier. "Nor has my ass. I shall bring him a gift."

"Bring him twenty."

The king's big chest shook. "I am glad you enjoyed this. I enjoyed it, too. This has been the best of days."

Alec smiled at his tone. It was honest. Sincere. And Alec had played a prominent role. Hell, it hadn't been too shabby a day for Alec, either. He'd gotten to fuck the mighty king of the Kríe while scoring another mind-blowing bite.

He froze as something occurred to him. Lifting his head, he met the king's eyes. "You bit me while we were... What about *the bond*?"

Zercy shook his head. "It was only one-sided."

"One-sided? How? You bit me. I came in you."

"Tah, but there needs to be an exchange of essence, where both members receive a part of the other. That was not the case just now. *I* received both blood and seed." He frowned a little. "You only *gave* tonight. You did not take."

"Oh." Alec exhaled. "Yeah, okay. That makes sense." Not that the idea of being bonded was so terrible. He'd just never want it to happen accidentally. From the impression he'd gotten, it wasn't something Zercy wanted. Clearly a stance that Alec should take as well.

Rising up onto his arms, he gazed down at the king, but then frowned and glanced at their bodies. "Good god, Kríe. We're covered. Looks like you haven't come in years. Have you been dipping into that kirah nectar, too?"

Zercy chuckled, beaming proudly. "A Kríe's yield is always abundant." His lids hooded. "It is also always delicious."

Alec met his gaze, then peered at Zercy's cum-spattered chest. Was Zercy challenging him to taste? Alec absently licked his lips, then heard himself murmur, "Kinda feels like something I should decide for myself."

Fuck it. He'd gone this far. What was one little lick? Besides, with as often as Kríe claimed to love 'sacred seed,' he was starting to get kind of curious.

Bending his elbows, he lowered himself back down to tentatively taste one of Zercy's glistening nipples. But right as his tongue came just millimeters from its target, Zercy growled and quickly palmed his head to stop him.

"Mah, *Alick*. As much as I yearn for you to do this, you cannot take my seed into your mouth." Alec frowned and looked at him. Zercy frowned just as deeply. "The bond," he reiterated. "Technically, it does not matter how essence is transferred—orally, or through sex. Just so long as there is an exchange."

Well, shit.

Alec nodded. "I understand."

Zercy's golden eyes flashed. Another rumble emitted. "I, however, can indulge as much as I like."

Alec stilled. Zercy grinned. Next thing Alec knew, he was flat on his back. Flat on his back with Zercy's head between his thighs. Evidently, the king was starting with his dick. And man, was he methodical, licking clean every crevice, before moving on to see to the rest of him.

Zercy paused, though, when he finally reached Alec's throat, to slowly, tenderly lave at his wounds again. "I was not lying before," he murmured. "I could have hurt you. Injured you gravely. You had me mindless, *Alick*, and that is extremely dangerous."

Alec sighed, straight-up blissing from the feel of Zercy's tongue. From the soothing velvety timbre of his voice. "I'm fine. You didn't hurt me," he mumbled, his body a puddle.

"You are missing my point." A restless growl resounded. "You are so fragile compared to Kríe. I could have killed you."

Alec frowned and opened his eyes. Met the king's troubled stare. "Okay. I won't do that again."

Zercy exhaled and forced a smile, "Gratitude," then nuzzled the shit out of Alec's cheek and got back to his task.

When Alec was thoroughly cleaned, and Zercy wiped off, they settled back into lying together on the chaise. Staring at the stars, bodies sated, minds calm, their steady, thumping heartbeats nearly synced.

"This is strange," Zercy finally murmured.

Alec looked at him. "What's strange?"

"To just lie here and gaze at the sky."

Alec frowned. "You never stargaze?"

"Never."

"But why? You've got this amazing private rooftop all to yourself."

Zercy kept his eyes cast upward. Quietly, he exhaled. "Because lying alone like this would allow me time to think. But for so long, there has been nothing pleasant to think about. The death of my fathers. The betrothal to a stranger. Then the poisoning of Nira. The death of our youth..." He shook his head. "Mah. To have an idle mind is to think. So, I stay ever busy until I drop from pure exhaustion. It is the only way to keep what is left of my sanity."

Alec's chest squeezed. "But how is tonight any different?"

Zercy turned his head and smiled a little. "Because you are here, distracting me, allowing me to enjoy a bit of peace. Tonight, when I gaze at the stars in the sky, I think not of my troubles, but of you."

Alec's insides warmed like sunshine. Didn't matter that it was night.

Zercy eased onto his side and cupped the back of Alec's head, then pressed his lips to Alec's and murmured softly, "You have always been this to me. My shelter inside the storm. That quiet melodic music that soothes my beast."

Alec exhaled and shook his head. "I don't understand why, but... for whatever the reason, I'm glad." He rested his hand on Zercy's hip and inched closer. Gave the king a second kiss and nudged their noses. "'Cause while you haven't exactly calmed any inner beast of mine, you *have* managed to fill some pretty empty spaces."

Zercy met his gaze, eyes thoughtful, but didn't say a word. Just smiled a little and rejoined their mouths. A slow, wordless exchange between two star-crossed souls who couldn't be more different—but fit perfectly.

Unhurried moments later, they returned their focus to the sky. Alec stared up at the night, the lingering quiet between them serene. Without all the light pollution so common on Earth, the stars above were nothing short of breathtaking. Like a black-velvet tapestry pulled taut across the sky, dotted with a million glittering diamonds.

It was beautiful. Surreal.

Alec pretended he was among them. Finally, back in the heavens, where he belonged. Thing was, in that moment, it didn't feel the way it used to. A black-abyss embrace amidst the cosmos. Yeah, he still felt that quiet comfort deep inside, but now it seemed to come from somewhere else. Not high above, but rather, firmly on the ground.

Alec's chest tightened. He turned his head and gazed at the king. Studied every nuance of his face. His heart sank in realization. When he finally left this planet, he wouldn't be *going* home. He'd be *leaving* it.

CHAPTER THIRTY-TWO

* * *

"Stop! No! Gah!" Chet angrily shouted. "You just scored for the other team, you big purple lout!"

Alec glanced across the field as he and the team lounged by the lake, to see what had Chet so fired up. For the last few hours, the guy had been teaching the guards how to play football, but by the look of things, they still needed a bit of practice.

Some fifteen yards away, Chet ripped off his shoulder guards and threw them on the ground with a scowl. "You don't listen, you know that? What's wrong with your ears? They're big as fuck, how come they don't work?"

Mannix squared his shoulders and glared at him from the other team's end zone. "You said to catch the ball and run very, very fast!"

"Right!" Chet hollered, pointing to the opposite end of the field. "*That* way, you brainless dildo! Now we're losing!"

Setch and Kellim swapped looks, then erupted into laughter.

"What is a dildo?" Kellim chortled.

"I do not know!" Setch guffawed. "But it is brainless, so it certainly sounds like Mannix!"

Alec's lips twitched as he shook his head. Beside him, Bailey snickered. Even Zaden loosed an openly amused chuckle. Surprisingly, however, Jamis didn't seem as entertained. Instead, he pensively frowned down at his notebook.

Alec wasn't the only one to notice, either.

Bailey nudged his friend. "Hey, what's wrong?"

Jamis looked up, then shook his head and sighed. "This thing with Sirus. I keep going over the formula, the newest one we've come up with. So fucking close and still not right. Ugh. It's driving me *nuts* that we can't crack it."

Noah nodded to his right, his blond hair back in a ponytail. "Yeah, I'm getting frustrated myself. How long have we been at this now? A month?"

Alec looked at Noah and frowned, because yup, it'd been a month. A whole month since they'd started working with Sirus. Since the team unanimously volunteered to be a sperm bank while the science trio helped find a cure.

Something they'd yet to do, unfortunately.

Not that they hadn't made other advancements in all these weeks, because they had, strides that were definitely important. Like discovering a way to enhance their semen's strength. A huge step, of which everyone was very excited. From what Alec heard, all the trees in the kingdom had finally stabilized, thanks to transfusions received via the matriarch's roots.

More encouraging was how Sirus soon planned to send 'medicinal donations' to each tree personally. To date, none of the offshoots had successfully conceived yet, which wasn't to say the populace wasn't trying. Even at the castle, Sirus had been striving to impregnate the matriarch. Alec hadn't witnessed the process himself, but according to Zercy, Sirus was determined. Had tried every combination of every Kríe in the castle. He'd even tried Zercy's seed—which inwardly made Alec anxious—but in the end, even the king's had turned up fruitless.

Needless to say, Zercy was growing more disheartened by the day, having hoped that they'd have found a cure by now. After all, it'd been a month, like Noah had said. So many brilliant minds working ceaselessly with no results.

God, the look in Zercy's eyes when he didn't know Alec was watching... So fucking grim, like he'd started losing hope. Like he'd begun accepting the fact that no cure existed. That their path to extinction was written in the stars.

Jamis groaned and tossed his pad aside, then rubbed at his face. "Yeah, a fucking month, with no answers in sight. Which sucks because I'm starting to feel like a goddamn dairy cow."

"I know," Zaden muttered. "Thought we'd be done with this by now."

And honestly, who could blame the guys for feeling discouraged? Not to mention, a whole lot exhausted. This whole bizarre business had proven surprisingly draining. Not only were the guys required to 'fuck' twice a day, but also endure the relentless 'urge' twenty-four-seven.

No joke, that kirah nectar didn't mess around. As soon as they downed it and it entered their system, they immediately started feeling the effects. First to set in: tender nuts and sensitized dicks. Within the hour, they all had full-blown erections. Their heart rates stayed elevated. Their focus ever distracted. By two hours in, their nuts were swollen and twice as heavy. By four, even their prostates felt like balloons.

It made them cranky and twitchy, even the happy-go-lucky trio, turning Chet into an even bigger bear than he already was. And while technically they could go to Sirus and release the pressure early, in exchange they had to drink more kirah. Not overly worth it—although in the beginning, they'd all succumbed—since all it did was drop them back in the same boat.

Alec sighed. "Just hang in there. You're close. You said it yourselves. I'm betting you'll figure it out in the next couple of days."

Zaden rubbed his eyes and nodded. "True. You're Astrum Industries' finest. If anyone can figure it out, it's the three of you."

The trio swapped looks, looking tired but determined.

"They're right," Noah agreed. "We can do this."

Bailey lifted his chin. "Damn straight. And we will."

Jamis forced a tight smile, but then scowled and squeezed his junk. "My dick just wants a freaking day off."

Alec exhaled and glanced back at Chet, watching him irritably gesture at the Kríe. Not that the Kríe seemed deterred by his attitude. In truth, his disposition was a lot like theirs. Bossy and overbearing with an ornery short fuse. Yup, Chet was Kríe to a tee.

The other thing they had in common? A primal need to compete. To dominate. The reason, no doubt, that Kellim let Chet run the training session. So he could teach all the guards a new rough-and-rowdy sport where they could charge and slam and throw each other around.

Alec smirked as he watched them, two huge lines of big dark Kríe. Facing off in battle gear as offense and defense, while Chet took the famed role of quarterback. Unfortunately, just like nearly every single time before, the second he hiked the ball, both lines morphed into a mosh pit.

Alec grinned, watching his teammate barely escape the fray, then spike his makeshift ball in exasperation.

"No, goddamnit! This is not a wrestling match!" He glowered and quickly jabbed a finger at Setch. "Hey! What'd I say about using teeth!"

Zaden chuckled again, observing the same sad fiasco. "Our boy's lucky he didn't get pulled into that pile. Those guys easily weigh three hundred each."

"Yeah," Noah mused. "Next to them, Chet looks little."

Alec shook his head, smirking, and scratched his cheek, then overheard Bailey murmuring to Jamis.

"Chin up, man. Just keep telling yourself it's for a really good cause. What we're doing's gonna save an entire species."

"I know, I know," Jamis grumbled quietly. "I just can't fucking think straight. It's making me crazy."

"Right? Like we're going through puberty all over again." Bailey muffled a laugh. "God, back in high school? Stiff breeze and I got hard."

Jamis groaned. "Don't remind me. Honestly, Bay, this feels worse."

Bailey's voice sobered. "I know. It's definitely worse..." He paused, then cleared his throat. "When I'm in there, in that stall, wanting to be anywhere *but*, I pretend I'm fucking someone I've got it bad for."

Alec lifted a brow and glanced their way.

Jamis was eyeing his dark-haired friend curiously. "And who, might I ask, do you have it bad for?"

Bailey shrugged and chewed on his lip. Rubbed the back of his head. "No one in particular. I'm just saying."

"Uh huh." Jamis studied him. Even Noah was watching Bailey now. "I'm gonna guess it's that mer-dude from the river."

"Oonmaiyos," Bailey corrected. Exhaling, he frowned at his friend. "He's stuck in my head."

Jamis' expression looked almost surprised. "Damn. You're serious."

Bailey turned toward the water. "Believe me, I know it's weird. I honestly don't understand it." He searched the glassy surface, his hazel eyes thoughtful. "It's like we were saying before, the concept of women's just kinda fading. And in their place, it's like he's somehow filling the void."

"Yeah, but come on, Bay. I know we tease you, but you've never even seen him."

"I know," Bailey agreed, scratching his head. "It makes no sense. It's just… I dunno… Sometimes I *do* feel like I see him. Here at the lake. Or down in the aquarium. Just glimpses though, nothing solid, which of course, makes me wonder if I'm imagining things. But then I feel it. Feel *him*. Like he's somewhere close… watching me. And *that's* a whole lot harder to dismiss."

"Jesus, Bay," Jamis muttered. "That sounds stalkerish to me."

Bailey tamped down a laugh. "Yeah, I guess it kind of does. But it never skeeves me out. If anything, he just feels kind of curious."

Alec traded looks with Zaden. Should he be worried about this? What if Bailey just up and vanished one day while swimming?

Jamis brooded for a minute. A moment later, he cracked a smile. "Alright. Fair enough. But answer me this: Up in Sirus' workshop, when you're imagining this guy… If he's a fish, where the hell do you put your dick?"

Bailey stiffened… then muttered, "Under the dorsal fin, if you must know." A grin tugged at his lips. "It feels fantastic."

Noah choked back a laugh.

Jamis flat-out cracked up.

A heartbeat later, the trio tumbled over holding their sides. At which point, Alec laughed too, swept up in the hilarity. Couldn't help it, though. The images inside his brain—water splashing… Bailey grunting… His lover braying like a seal…

Problem was, in all the laughter, Alec was swiftly reminded of his current situation below the belt. Wincing, he quieted down and resituated atop the blanket, his mind detouring to the events of earlier that day. Specifically, when Zercy had snuck in unannounced to surprise Alec while he was 'donating' in one of Sirus' stalls.

Alec's dick stirred at the memory.

God, it'd been erotic. Why? Because no one knew the king was even there, and Zercy evidently had wanted to keep it that way. Meaning he forbade Alec to make a single sound. Which was a whole lot effing easier said than done. Not while Zercy sat atop the bent-over statue's ass, nipping up Alec's neck while Alec 'worked.' God, his strong legs, wrapped around Alec's waist, holding Alec close as he teased him. At one point he'd even clamped his hand over Alec's mouth, then slipped his wicked tongue in Alec's ear. Alec had gasped and thrust faster. Zercy had bit back husky laughs.

Not long after though, when Zercy had had his fun, he slid his hands under Alec's tunic and spread his cheeks. Next thing Alec knew, as he'd continued fucking that statue, a big claw-tipped finger pushed inside him. All toying and playing and moving in and out, as the king latched his lips onto Alec's neck.

Alec had muffled so many moans in Zercy's shoulder, he'd lost count. And when that finger homed in on his sweet spot and made him come, Zercy fastened his mouth over Alec's to smother his shout.

Fuck, he'd seen stars. Had released for *so long*.

When his O finally ended, Zercy slid off the statue and moved to stand all snug at Alec's back. At first, Alec had thought the king was going to take a turn, and worried his ass wasn't ready for another round. After all, Zercy had already fucked him good before breakfast, just like he tended to do every morning. Ever since he'd given himself as a gift to Alec a month ago, they'd been insatiable, messing around every chance they got. Using ruka when the king was feeling generous and let Alec top, tachi for every other time in between.

And in those times in between, Zercy tried to be gentle, something Alec could tell wasn't easy. Nevertheless, when those strong hips got pumping fast and furious, even with tachi, Alec still wound up sore.

To his surprise though, in Sirus' stall, Zercy hadn't shoved his cock in. He'd shoved something else in instead. A butt plug, which honestly, Alec should've seen coming. They'd been using them pretty regularly in an effort to train Alec's body. According to Noah, if given enough time, it'd allow Alec to handle Zercy naturally, without tachi. He'd pulled Alec aside one day, when the others were occupied, and given him the unexpected advice…

"So, this thing with you and Zercy," Noah had asked him point blank. "It's serious? As in, the two of you are active?"

"Um…" His question had taken Alec off guard. "I guess kinda? We've only *been together* a couple times."

Noah had nodded and glanced over his shoulder, then turned back and lowered his voice. "Bailey and Jamis, they said at Gesh's compound… the pack had used some kind of venom."

"Yeah." Alec eyed him. "Tachi venom. Didn't Gesh?"

Noah's lips curved. He shook his head. "No. I didn't need it."

Alec's brows had shot high. "How the—? But that's impossible."

"No," Noah chuckled. "It's actually not, and the reason I'm talking to you about it now."

"What do you mean?"

Noah had shrugged. "I just thought you might like some tips, from a guy who's pretty versed on the subject."

Alec frowned, not really following. "On the subject of mammoth dicks?"

"Well, that," Noah had laughed. "Or *anything* large lodged in that region." His gaze glinted. "Without the need of any help."

Alec's ears finally perked. "Okay... I'm listening." Who knew having a gay teammate could be so helpful.

"It's simple really. You just gotta train your body. Well, your ass. Like a gymnast gradually learning to do the splits."

The *splits?* Alec had suddenly felt a wee bit apprehensive. "How exactly are you proposing I... train my ass?"

Noah's cheeks had gone pink. "Gotta stretch yourself out. People, guys, they typically use butt plugs."

Alec tensed at that. "Like those tails."

"Yeah. Something like that. Anything, really, that you can keep, um, inserted, for a while."

"A while? What's a while? Like fifteen minutes?"

"Uh, no." Noah had chuckled. "I'd say at least a couple hours."

"*Hours?*" Alec balked.

Noah laughed. "It's not so bad. Teaches the muscles to stretch more than they're used to."

"Huh..." The thought of something big stuffed up his ass—all day long—definitely hadn't been what Alec expected.

Noah had shrugged again. "Anyway. Just thought you might wanna know. It works. I speak from experience. Love me some big toys..."

Alec flat-out started coughing. "Jesus, Noah. TMI."

The blond scientist grinned.

Which made Alec smile, too. "Thanks. Maybe I'll uh... give it a try."

Noah nodded and turned to go, but then stopped and looked back. "If you ever have questions... You know, about anything..."

"Thank you. I appreciate it. This is all so... so different."

Noah chuckled. "Not *that* different." But then he paused, his smile fading. "Just be careful. These Kríe... They'll rip your heart out... before you even knew that they had it."

Alec had frowned as Noah walked away. His words had resonated too quickly. Not because Alec believed Zercy would treat him like Gesh had Noah. Alec's situation with Zercy couldn't be more different. Nevertheless, he worried the outcomes would still end up the same. Their paths diverging, separation imminent. Someone somehow breaking the other's heart.

Because when the rescue team arrived, and it was time for Alec's team to go...

Alec exhaled quietly and closed his eyes, rubbing his sternum as he sat atop the blanket. Yes, it could very well be him who did the ditching. Who left Zercy behind like Gesh did Noah. Deep down, however, he wasn't so certain. By then, he might be too attached to ever leave.

But that was just his side. Zercy posed his own threat, too. Because alongside Alec's ever-strengthening feelings for the king, was a deep-seated fear in his gut. That ultimately, Zercy treasured Alec's value to Nira more than he treasured Alec himself.

After all, Zercy had bitten him countless times in the past month, but never while he came in Alec's body. His actions spoke volumes. His position was clear. To form a bond with Alec was simply out of the question.

It made Alec wonder if Zercy would ever want to mark him irrevocably. Or was the thought of kids with Alec somehow dishonorable? What if, while Alec grew increasingly more attached, Zercy continued to think of him as just his pet?

Alec swallowed and looked down. He knew that Zercy was fond of him, but what if Chet was actually right? What if Kríe really *didn't* know how to love? If their species just weren't wired that way? They weren't human.

His stomach twisted anxiously. All those times that Zercy had held him close and told him he was priceless... what if he'd really meant priceless *because of Nira?* After all, how many times, when feeling exceptionally disheartened, had Zercy confessed that Alec and his team were his only solace? His only source of comfort should they fail to find a cure? What if that's all Alec would ultimately become? A means to save Zercy's people? As much as he hated to admit it, it'd make sense. Hell, how could any rational mind *not* see him that way?

If this were Earth, they'd have him locked up in a lab.

Unsettled, he peered over his shoulder at the castle. Home of Zercy, the Krie he'd fought like hell not to want. Who took Alec captive, then stole his heart.

CHAPTER THIRTY-THREE

* * *

— PRESENT DAY —
Astrum Industries Search & Rescue Team
Location: Heart of the Niran rainforests

"What species are you? From what territory do you come? Why were Kríe holding you captive? Where were they taking you?"

Airis' interrogation hadn't stopped since he put his bow away. It was starting to make Garret's head spin. "Okay. Hold up." He closed his eyes to focus. "So… you just want answers? You're not taking us prisoner?"

Airis frowned, as if affronted by his very words. "Leí." *Yes.* "We are not like the Kríe. They are savages. We are civilized. Now answer my questions."

Garret flicked his team a look.

Still bound—and visibly roughed up from their scuffle with the Kríe—none looked especially happy. His gaze shifted to the dekdónni perched on their haunches a few yards away. Eyeing the men's cuts, they licked their beaks' chops, like they'd love nothing more than to clean up the blood.

Garret grimaced and looked back at Airis. "Fine. We'll tell you what you wanna know. But first you gotta cut us free." Because at the rate their luck was going, once they answered the Nirans' questions, the fuckers would take off and leave his team still tied.

Airis regarded Garret's wrists, and the purple vine that bound them, then eyed how it led down between his thighs. A cruel little rig job, pulled taut against his nuts, tethered to Garret's collar from behind.

Airis' handsome features tightened. "Boors," he muttered, disgusted.

Pulling a dagger free, he motioned to his buddies, then looked back at Garret and stepped closer. Garret tensed at his proximity. Airis may not be Kríe-size but was still a big fucker, no doubt about it. And that was coming from Garret, who wasn't exactly small. Six-foot-one. Six-foot-two with hiking boots.

Airis clutched his bound wrists, inadvertently touching his skin. Current surged up Garret's forearms from the contact. He sucked in a breath. Airis stilled and stared down at him, as if maybe he'd felt it, too.

Garret shifted his weight.

Airis chuffed low in his throat, then returned his attention to Garret's binds. "You are injured," he noted, eyeing the gash on Garett's shoulder.

Garret glanced at it and frowned. His team's brawl with the Kríe would've ended way worse if these Tohrí hadn't shown up and crashed the party.

Nodding, he cleared his throat. "Yeah. Kríe claws are sharp."

"Indeed," Airis murmured, slicing the vines.

Garret regarded the male's strong hands. Airis had short claws too, but not as sharp, and unlike a Kríe, his were pale. Like his hair, Garret realized, just as the Kríe's claws matched their dreads. He wondered if the species were really so different.

Several moments passed. Finally, his team was free.

Happy moans resounded as each member rubbed his wrists.

Garret stepped back and nodded. "Thanks, Airis. Much appreciated."

Airis smiled and stepped forward. "You are welcome."

Garret stilled. Then frowned. Airis was back in his personal space.

Again, he stepped backward.

Again, Airis advanced. Impishly, he peered down. "I am waiting."

"Waiting?" Garret asked, low-key flustered by his behavior.

"Leí." *Yes.* Airis grinned. "You promised me answers."

"Oh. Shit. Right." Garret gripped his hips and nodded. Awkwardly cleared his throat again. "Almost forgot."

"Mm." Airis clutched his hands behind his back and waited.

Garret eyed his new stance. Would he stay put this time if Garret stepped back? He tried again—and braced.

Airis smirked in amusement. "What species are you?" he prompted. "And from what territory?"

Garret eased. He'd stayed put. "We're humans, but not from this planet. We came here via a spacecraft. Our home is Earth."

Airis stilled, staring at him. His ear twitched. "Not from Nira?"

Garret shook his head. "No."

Airis frowned. Then closed in again. Leaning forward, he sniffed Garret's neck. "You *do* smell different."

Garret leaned back. "'Cause I am."

Airis glanced over at Kato. He too looked visibly dumbfounded. As did the others in his group. Airis straightened and stepped back. "Why did you come?"

"We're a rescue team, sent here to search for others of our kind. They came here a year ago, on an exploration mission, but we lost communication and think they got stranded."

"How many moons is a year?"

"On Nira... Around six." He knew as much thanks to Astrum Industries' full-stats report. Hell, he and his team were totally versed on the planet before they even left the AI's space station.

Airis furrowed his eyebrows. Unlike his mane, the things were dark. "Your people have been in this region for so long?" Again, he looked at Kato. "We have not seen them, but we should have. We patrol this terrain all the time. In fact, I believe we have even seen their craft. A half day's journey east of here. By River Dydum."

"They've seen their craft but not them? Not even once? That's not encouraging." Paris, their tracker, frowned and glanced around. "What if they've never seen them because they're dead?"

Sasha cursed and raked a hand through his light blond hair. "Don't say that. They're alive. They're smart. They'd survive."

Eli and Helix traded looks, both marines full-fledged realists.

"I dunno, Doc," Eli shook his head. "Sometimes smart ain't enough. We're smart too, but those tachi still almost ate us. And brains don't explain why they've vanished."

Helix nodded. "He's right. They would've stayed close to their beacon, which means these guys would've eventually run into them."

"Jaysus. Something got 'em," Kegan groaned, looking at Garret. "We're searching for ghosts. Got here too late."

Garret breathed an oath and slowly dragged a hand down his face.

"Nún." *No.* Kato spoke up. "There is another explanation. Another reason why they are no longer here." He turned to Airis, his dark eyes glinting. "Several moons ago, do you remember? There was talk within our clan. About a species not of this world seen at Múnrahki."

Airis glanced at the team. "Leí." *Yes.* "I remember."

Garret cocked a brow. "*Moonrocky?*"

"The Kríe king's castle."

Helix frowned at Kato skeptically. "Did your clan say what they looked like? How do we know it was even them?"

Kato turned to him, then slowly roamed his gaze down Helix's body, taking in every inch of his dark frame. "They said there were six. Described them as captivating. Intelligent eyes. Pleasing physiques. Covered in flesh so enticing and tender, it made their mouths water."

Helix blinked.

Kato impishly grinned and held his stare.

"Uh…" Kegan scratched his ginger scruff and eyed the two. "That still doesn't really tell us what they looked like."

Kato cut his gaze to the co-pilot and gestured to his duds. "Your clothing is odd. Very distinctive. And from the way my people described it, the same as the others."

Garret glanced down at his get-up: tank top, cargo shorts, hiking boots. Yup. Not similar at all to what they'd seen so far of Niran attire.

Sasha smiled. "That's them. It's gotta be."

"Maybe. But if it is…" Garret turned back to Kato. "What were our guys even doing there?"

Kato sobered and looked at Airis. Airis gave a tiny nod.

"From what we understand, they were captured and sold to the king. He keeps them now as pets inside his castle."

Paris gawked. "Holy shit."

"Let me guess," Garret grated. "Captured and sold by *Kríe.*"

Kato inclined his head. "Leí." *Yes.* "That is correct."

"Gesh," Helix ground out.

Garret scowled too, but then stilled. "Wait. Gesh talked about taking us to a castle." He glanced at Kegan. "Remember? To trade for his meesha?"

"That's right. He did." The ginger pilot's eyes widened. "Oh, fuck. I remember something else now, too. When he first saw Sasha and mistook him for Noah?"

Garret stilled. "He called him meesha. *Noah* is *meesha*."

"So, it *is* them." Sasha grinned. "Absolutely, one hundred percent."

"*That* is why they took you?" Airis asked, his voice intent. "And that is where they were taking you? Múnrahki castle?"

Garret nodded.

"Wait. Back up." Paris suddenly shook his head. "If Gesh *did* sell our guys to the king, like we're thinking, then why's he so hard-pressed to get one back? If Noah's so important, why sell him to begin with?"

"Maybe it *wasn't* Gesh that sold 'em," Kegan speculated, shrugging. "Maybe all Kríe are kidnappers and one *took* his 'meesha'."

"That's assuming Noah was *his* to begin with," Sasha pointed out. "Which would mean either he and Noah had gotten cozy super-fast, or he'd already been holding Noah captive and considered him his property."

Airis slid his friend Kato an uneasy look.

"What." Garret eyed him. "What aren't you saying?"

Airis frowned and folded his arms. Spread his stance and peered west. "My band and I are patrolling because we are looking for missing brethren. Countless have vanished within the past several moons. So many, we now believe they are being abducted."

"Shit," Garret muttered. "You mean, by Kríe?"

"We do not know. There are many factions that could easily be to blame, but…" He glanced down at the discarded vines they'd cut from Garret's team. "…after witnessing what they were doing with you, and then what transpired after…"

"After?" Kegan piped up. "You mean, when you were chasing them?"

Airis inclined his head. "Leí. As they fled, they shouted things. Disturbing things. Not the usual sentiments when our two paths sometimes cross. Encounters like today are not uncommon."

He glanced at his friend again. "Their strong words this time, however, we had not been expecting. That we are enemies of their nation. A declaration of their king. Which I do not understand. We just recently established an alliance. Our prince betrothed to their sovereign to solidify peace."

His troubled eyes slid back to Garret. "But now that we are aware of this contention toward our people... I cannot help but to believe more is going on. Too many have gone missing. Far too many, realistically, for this one rogue group to ever take credit for."

"Fuuuck," Eli murmured. "That's some messed up shit."

Garret couldn't agree more. To have so many kidnapped? Their families must be wrecked. He regarded each Tohrí. Did any of them have loved ones missing? He looked back at Airis. "I hope you find them."

Airis studied him. After a moment, he tipped his head. "Gratitude. I hope you find your people, too."

Garret nodded. "Oh, and thank you... for helping us back there."

Airis grinned and leaned forward. "You are welcome."

Garret leaned back to compensate, fighting a smile. Guess he'd gotten used to Airis' antics. It didn't last long though, because as Airis turned to go, reality slammed Garret in the chest. When these Tohrí left, Garret's team was on their own. With no weapons. Or supplies. Or anything at all. Just the sweaty, dirty clothes on their backs.

Airis gestured to the males in his band to head out, then called to his dekdónni. "Kotchka, come."

The big beast padded over. Airis checked its paws and wings. Garret cursed under his breath and glanced at his co-pilot. Kegan looked anxious. Garret regarded the rest of his team. Similar expressions of dread.

Fuck. The perks of being a captain. Time to throw his ass out on a limb.

He exhaled and looked at Airis, then nodded to his men—a wordless *wish me luck*—and headed over. Stopping beside the Tohrí, he cleared his throat. "Um, Airis? I kinda have to ask you a favor."

Airis paused and peered at him. So did Kotchka. "A favor?"

"Yeah." Garret pocketed his thumbs and frowned. "My team. We need your help. We lost all our gear. And this place, we don't know it, and earlier, we almost got eaten. We've got no way to protect ourselves, and it's getting dark, and—"

"Etay." *Stop.* Airis stared at him. "You… were almost *eaten?*"

"Yeah… By tachi… Fuckin' *sucked.*"

"Nira…" Airis muttered. "How did you evade them?"

"We didn't. Those Kríe showed up and saved us."

Airis stilled. His ears flicked. "You owe them a debt."

"*What?* They took us prisoner. No, we *don't.*"

Airis smirked and eyed Garret's men. "What kind of help?"

"Get us to our people's craft in one piece? You said you've seen it. Know where it is. If these rumors are wrong, they might still be there waiting for us. If they're not, we'll pack up any supplies they might've left and try that Múnrahki place next."

"The castle is far away. A half-day's journey west even from here."

Garret exhaled and rubbed his nape. "Yeah, well, we're kinda low on options. Our objective's to find our guys and if they're not at the beacon…" He held Airis' gaze. "Any protection you're willing to give, we'd really appreciate."

Airis folded his arms and regarded him. A moment ticked by. Finally, he tipped his head. "We will escort you."

Garret's brows shot up. "Seriously?"

"Leí… Because I find you pleasing to look at."

Garret paused. Blinked double-time. "I… You *what?*"

Airis grinned and leaned close again. "Find you pleasing."

Paris stifled a chuckle. Figured. He was bi.

Garret leaned back, cheeks heating. "Okay… Whatever works."

"Oh, thank God," Kegan exhaled on a groan. "Garret, give the guy a hug or something. I'm so relieved."

Garret shot him a glower, still awkwardly leaned over.

Airis straightened. "What is a hug?"

"*Nothing,*" Garret blurted, straightening, too. "We're just grateful." He gripped his hips and nodded. "So. Yeah. Thank you."

"You are welcome." Airis smiled, but then glanced at his companions. "First, however, we must return to our home."

"Your home?" Helix frowned, walking over.

Airis nodded. "Our people, we must warn them. The jungle is not safe. Nor is Kríe territory. They are dangerous."

Garret nodded again, apprehensive, but beggars couldn't be choosers. Besides, he totally got where Airis was coming from. "Okay. Your home. Not a problem. How far is that?"

"Many hours east."

"Awesome. So's our beacon."

Airis inclined his head. "Pellay." *Good.* "We will leave momentarily."

"Um, Chief?"

Garret glanced over his shoulder at Sasha.

"Can I get a sec to patch people up before we go?" He'd already begun cleaning and dressing Paris' wounds, but in truth, they all could use a bit of tending to.

Garret looked back at Airis. "This'll only take a minute." Their mini first-aid kits didn't have that much to offer.

"Of course." Airis regarded Garret's bleeding shoulder again. His lips curved. "So long as you let me help as well."

Garret frowned. "Help?" He followed Airis' gaze to his arm. "Uh…" He glanced at Sasha.

Sasha chuckled and shook his head. "It's okay. I'll keep an eye on him."

Not exactly the response he'd been hoping for.

Turning back, Garret forced a smile and gave the male a nod. "Yeah, okay… Sure."

Airis' grin spread wider. "Do not worry, little oddling. I will be gentle."

* * *

It didn't take Airis long to bandage Garret up, even despite the several other injuries he'd discovered. Two gashes on Garret's back and one on his elbow. So high on adrenaline, his brain never registered the pain.

Not that Airis had seemed to mind, what with those big chocolate eyes exploring Garret's first-aid kit. Garret had handed it over once they sat down on a log, thinking the Tohrí would want to use its contents. And while Airis certainly took pleasure in investigating each item, he'd ultimately resolved to do things his own way.

Garret realized this when Airis leaned in to inspect his cut—or at least that's what he *thought* the Tohrí was doing. Airis wasn't, though. Wasn't trying to study it at all. Instead, the crazy fucker flat-out licked it.

"What the—" Garret had jerked so hard he'd nearly fallen off the log.

Airis, however, just chuffed and held him steady. "Nira. Stay still. I am trying to clean your wound."

"*Clean* it?" he'd rasped, watching him take another swipe.

"Leí." A third lick.

"But—" Garret couldn't stop fidgeting.

Airis had paused and sat back. Eyed Garret curiously. "What is wrong with you?"

Garret flicked a look at Sasha. He was gawking. "You're licking me."

Airis glanced between the two of them and frowned. "Does human saliva not have healing agents?"

Garret shook his head and quickly dug an item from his first-aid kit. "Antiseptic spray." He'd shoved the tiny cylinder at Airis. "How 'bout we use that instead."

Airis had reluctantly agreed, but when it came time to dress Garret's wound, he'd once again reverted to Niran ways. Specifically, by using stuff he procured from their surroundings. Leaves and moss and flower petals—Garret wasn't delighted. He'd frowned, watching Airis grind the ingredients in his palm, pulverizing them with the butt of his knife. After, he'd mixed them into a paste with his spit, then scraped some up with his blade and reached for Garret's shoulder.

"Whoa—" Garret had caught his wrist and chuckled. "Yeah, *no*."

"But it will help your wound to—"

"You *spit* in it."

"It has *healing agents*."

"I don't care. It's fucking gross."

Frowning, Airis had stared at him for a good several moments, but eventually let it go and ditched the stuff. Sixty seconds later, Garret's wounds were covered in ointment—the stuff from a tube—and bandaged up.

Sasha had finished with the others at that point too, and soon after, both human and Tohrí were on the move. For the next several hours, they traipsed through the jungle, heading back in the direction they'd just come.

Along the way, two of the Tohrí chose to joyride on their 'griffins.' Garret watched them as they romped about, hurdling bushes and dashing through trees, exposing their naturally playful dispositions. More than once, he'd smiled at the Tohrí's yips and barks, the sounds reminding him of lively Native Americans.

They never went far, either. Always stayed in the vicinity, while Airis and Kato walked with Garret's team. Eventually they did seem to tire, however, circling back around to dismount and bring up the rear.

Walking beside Kegan, Garret glanced at Airis and Kato. Maybe Airis felt his eyes on him, or maybe he didn't, but he peered over his shoulder and met Garret's gaze.

Garret cleared his throat and nodded, then tipped his head toward Kotchka—who appeared to be chasing a rodent off in the brush. "Would you be riding her right now... flying instead of walking... if you didn't have us tagging along?"

"Leí, but not for the entire trip. Our weight fatigues them after a while."

Garret supposed that wasn't surprising. Tohrí were lean but still big. At six and a half feet, they easily weighed two-twenty-five.

"Do you ride them on the ground?" Sasha asked, to Garret's right.

Airis looked at the medic. "Sometimes." His brown eyes glittered. "Would you care to take a ride? She will not bite if I command it."

Sasha's brows shot up. He swapped looks with Paris. "I'd love to. That'd be amazing."

Airis grinned and turned to Garret. "This is okay with you as well?"

Garret shook his head and chuckled. "Yeah, it's cool."

Next thing he knew, Sasha was mounted and trotting about, with Paris and Kegan enviously looking on.

Airis fell in step with Garret. "You may have a ride, too."

"Thanks. I'm good." Garret glanced up through the treetops. "It's getting dark so fair warning, I'm gonna be tripping over shit soon."

Airis regarded him oddly. "You cannot see in the dark?"

"Not well, no." He looked at Airis. "Why? Can you?"

"All Nirans can." He frowned and eyed Garret's team. "You would not survive one night here. Blind, with no weapons." He looked back at Garret. Smiled from ear to ear. "Me and mine, we are saving you and yours from death. We are not your protectors. We are your *saviors*."

Garret fought back a laugh and peered straight ahead. "I suppose. In a roundabout way."

The blond Tohrí chuffed, then just like that, his body markings flared bright and lit their path.

Garret's heart sped up as he looked at him. Such a captivating sight. The way those sleek shapes along his arms and chest—as well as his abs—cast his face into a mix of light and shadow.

The other Tohrí followed suit and got their glow on too, illuminating the darkness around them like it was nothing.

Behind Garret, Eli laughed. "So wild."

The other teammates offered similar sentiments.

Garret met Airis' gaze and grinned. "How do you do that?"

Airis smirked and leaned close, his mouth just inches from Garret's ear. "I close my eyes and pretend I am a tree sprite."

Garret coughed another laugh and shook his head. "Whatever. Smartass."

"What's a tree sprite?" Paris asked.

"You do not know? Let me show you." Airis detoured off the path, then delved his hand into a bush and shook its branch.

Instantly, a swarm of oversized fireflies flared bright. Or at least that's what they appeared to be at first. But as they scattered in every direction, some flittering Garret's way, he realized they weren't insects at all. Rather, teeny tiny glowing fairy-like entities with two arms and two legs—and gossamer wings.

Airis grinned and swiftly caught one in between his large palms, then brought it over to Garret's team who'd stopped to watch.

"Tree sprite," he murmured, slowly parting his hands.

A pixie peered up at them, blinked its big sapphire eyes, then loosed a barely-audibly bark.

"Damn... Look at that," Eli marveled.

Helix chuckled. Actually, *chuckled*. Albeit quietly, but still.

Paris stared at it, rapt. "I want one."

But then, just like that, it darted away.

Garret smiled and looked at Airis, strangely charmed. "Very cool."

Airis grinned and resumed walking. "My light is better."

"Definitely brighter, I'll give you that." Garret hustled to keep pace. "But you don't need it to see in the dark. So, what's its purpose?"

"There are several, depending on the way we choose to wield it. Full strength works well to unnerve large predators, blinding them momentarily and confusing them. Low strength, on the other hand, helps soothe those in distress…" He stepped over a downed log and slid Garret a look. "Soft pulses seduce prey and lure them in."

His timbre eased under Garret's skin. Garret tensed, then quickly glanced away. "Huh…" He scratched his chin. Cleared his throat. Gave a nod. "Yeah… Guess that would be… kinda handy."

Airis chuckled. Kotchka trotted back over with Sasha. For the next several hours just more of the same. Lots of walking. A couple breaks to piss and replenish with fruit. Or maybe they were vegetables, Garret didn't know. Airis introduced each by name but not by category. Not that it mattered as long as it sustained them. Which it did. Most of it tasted pretty decent, too. Then back to the trail they'd promptly returned.

In time, Garret noticed a change in the terrain. Still lots of trees but no longer a jungle, with a whole lot less lush vegetation. Guess they were headed toward drier ground.

"So, uh, how much longer?" Kegan asked, to Garret's left.

"Not long," Airis answered. He pointed straight ahead. "Do you see that elevation in the distance? Through the trees?"

"Uh, no." Kegan shook his head. "I can't see much of anything. Just the five feet around us you've got lit up."

Airis dropped his hand and sighed. "Defenseless… Injured… Blind…" He glanced and Kato and chuffed. "They might as well be younglings tottering around."

Garret stiffened at the jab.

Kato and the other two Tohrí chuckled.

A few steps behind, Helix ground out, "I'll show you younglings."

Airis flicked him a look. "Will you?"

"Yeah, I fuckin'—"

"Helix," Garret shut him down. They couldn't lose their only ally.

Helix glowered but stopped talking.

Airis smirked at him over his shoulder, then gestured forward again. "We are nearly there. Look. Do you see?"

Garret stared into the darkness. The forest had thinned fast. "I see the shape of something big... and *really tall.*"

"That plateau is our beacon. The heart of our home."

They exited the tree line onto dry, dusty ground. Ahead, Garret made out a ravine, all wide and rocky. Behind that, a massive elevation loomed. He lifted his gaze and peered up its cliff side. "So, you're saying we're here?"

"Leí." Airis nodded with a smile. "Welcome to The Land of the Tohrí."

CHAPTER THIRTY-FOUR

* * *

"Damn," Kegan muttered. "That's a mighty big drop when you can't even see the bottom."

Garret peered over the edge of the bridge they were on—a stretch of rock spanning the gully's sixty-foot width. Kegan was right. The gorge was deep and, according to Airis, circled their territory just like a moat.

Up ahead, torch flames flickered and danced atop poles, flanking either side of the homeland's entrance. The dekdónni winged it over as Airis and Kato led the way. When they reached the other side, Airis gestured to the guards. The tall blond males eyed Garret's team with intrigue but didn't stop them as Airis and Kato took a left.

More trees emerged as they made their way around the base of the plateau. Not dense like the jungle, but still nicely wooded, leaving a generous berth for the path.

Garret peered into the distance. They were headed toward a village. He could see its countless homes, each lit by torches. Blocky yet aesthetically pleasing as they lined the settlement's main strip, an open unwooded thoroughfare right down the center. There were other homes, too. He spotted them through the trees, ones built into the side of the plateau. Several stories high, they reminded him of pueblos, connected to one another by steep cliff stairs.

As they drew closer, Garret noticed Tohrí everywhere. Males of every age, but no females. He frowned and glanced around as they finally reached the village. It was late, so not many children. Plenty of adolescents though, as well as varying ages of older Tohrí. No one, however, looked more than maybe fifty. And every single one of them was toned and fit.

He scanned the different gatherings. Long-haired towheads left and right. Perched around fires. Ambling out of homes. Interacting with more of those dekdónni griffin look-alikes.

But again, just males.

No females.

How bizarre.

Whatever. Maybe the ladies liked to hit the sack early. Something that sounded really nice right now, actually. He was exhausted. All-day hiking had his whole body aching. He'd give anything for a hot shower and comfy bed.

Airis gestured to a building at the far end of the strip. A structure ten times bigger than all the houses. A temple, maybe? Because it kind of had the shape of a pyramid, but with big block tiers and an entrance halfway up. "I must talk to the chieftain. He is head of our clan. He will see that our message reaches our people and our sovereign."

The aroma of roasting food from a campfire wafted their way.

Eli groaned. "Then can we eat?"

"Yeah, I'm starving," Helix grunted.

"And tired," Kegan muttered. "I wanna sit."

"It will not take long." Airis led the way. "And then we will fill your rumbling bellies."

Garret lifted a brow, following after him with his team. "You can hear our stomachs?"

All four Tohrí chuffed.

"How could we not? They have been growling at us all night. Ever since I showed you the little tree sprites."

Paris laughed, tucking a black lock of hair behind his ear. "He's right. Mine totally has been."

Sasha nodded, but wasn't smiling as he scanned their surroundings.

Garret frowned at the medic's expression, then glanced around, too. Ah. No wonder the guy looked so uneasy. Every Tohrí in the village was staring. Had straight-up stopped whatever they were currently doing to give Garret's team their full attention.

Garret supposed he shouldn't be surprised. To these people, he and his men were aliens. Strangelings, just like Airis said. The part of the picture that didn't belong. Truth be told, on the flip side, if Garret saw Tohrí sauntering through his hometown, he'd be staring just as hard without question.

"Do not mind them," Airis assured. "We are curious by nature. And in fairness," he smirked, "your species is very intriguing."

A moment later, they arrived at the temple. Airis stopped and turned to Garret's men. "Our chieftain waits inside." He gestured for them to follow. "Súsa." *Come.* "He will definitely want to meet you."

* * *

After introductions, Airis and Kato talked with their chieftain in private while Garret and his men waited outside. The other two Tohrí, Jori and Lark, hung out with them. Airis instructed them to do so to 'keep the oddlings company,' but Garret suspected that really meant 'keep them safe.'

Why? Because a lot of the Nirans cavorting about were rowdy young bucks. Garret watched them closely as they engaged with one another. Laughing one minute, then in the blink of an eye, diving into rambunctious, wide-grinned scuffles.

Which in itself wasn't an issue. What made Garret uneasy were the other teens nearby who were staring at his team rather intensely. No doubt, they had similar dispositions as their brethren, meaning if Jori and Lark weren't there standing guard, they might very well try to tackle Garret's men, too.

And make no mistake, despite their youthful faces, their size definitely didn't reflect their age. Most were as tall as Garret with slightly more muscle. And currently with a hell of a lot more energy.

Garret met one of their gazes. The male flashed a boyish grin. But his eyes? Yeah, his eyes looked a whole lot less innocent. Like he'd love to do far more with him than wrestle.

Unsettled, Garret looked away as Airis and Kato finally returned.

"We are finished. We can eat now," Airis announced, sounding lighter. Smiling, he motioned toward a fire pit. A big one incidentally, clearly communal, as a dozen or so Tohrí were already there.

"Oh, thank fuck," Eli exhaled, gratefully following him over. The rest of the team eagerly fell into step.

"Sit." Airis pointed to one of five logs circling the pit. The empty one, not too close to other Tohrí. Garret eyed them. They weren't like the downed logs in the forest. They were covered in what looked like thick hide—with padded cut-out indentions for one to sit in. Garret took a seat with his men.

Airis grinned, then gestured to his comrades for assistance and headed to a spread of prepared foods.

The four males returned swiftly, carrying several serving dishes— slabs of wood carved into beautifully-shaped plates. The one handed to Garret looked like a large jungle leaf, piled high with both raw and cooked items. He took the offering and regarded it. Its aroma filled his nose. Good freaking god, it smelled delicious.

Still, out of habit, he and his teammates hesitated for that first bite.

Kegan eyed his meal longingly. "Who wants to be the food taster this time?"

Paris coughed a small laugh. "Go for it, flyboy. I took my turn."

Eli held up a finger. "I did, too."

"So did I." Sasha nodded. He looked at Kegan and chuckled. "Bon appetit."

Kegan grunted, but then all too quickly took an enthusiastic bite. Just shoved what looked like a sausage link into his mouth. "Aw, man. Oh, yeah. This is *good*."

Garret warily watched him chewing. Sure, they hadn't had issues so far, but all it took was one time.

Airis sat down beside him, clearly having seen his face. "If I wanted to kill you, I would not waste good food doing it. I would simply drop you back off in the jungle."

Garret turned to him. A small, amused grin tugged on his lips. "That's not a guaranteed kill. We'd manage. One way or another. It'd just... really, *really* suck."

Airis chuffed and took a bite of what looked like a plum. "Tell yourself that if you must, little oddling. But you know."

"My name's Garret."

"Leí. You told me."

"So why do you keep calling me oddling?"

Airis smiled, his eyes merry, and leaned in conspiratorially. "Because you *are* an oddling, Garret. It is why I like you."

Garret stilled. His name on Airis' tongue sounded way too sultry. Maybe he should stick with the nickname.

Averting his gaze, he took a bite of something that looked like a garlic wedge. Didn't taste like it, though. It tasted like coconut. He glanced down the way. His men were wolfing down their food. Evidently, they approved of the stuff, too.

Thoughtfully, Garret watched them. They'd been lucky, really lucky, that these Tohrí had come along when they had. He didn't like admitting it, but the big blond was right. Out in that jungle, Garret's team would've been toast. Yet by some streak of good fortune amidst their run of bad luck, they instead sat contentedly resting in front of this fire. Eating food, *good* food, inside a well-protected community that they'd been brought to by a seemingly decent race.

Yeah, their craft had crashed and, yeah, they'd nearly been eaten by monsters. And okay, yeah, they'd also been captured by a pack of thugs. But right now, where it counted, they were safe with food in their bellies. In Garret's book, that was a win for day one.

Across the way, two dekdónni wrestled like oversized cubs. Playfully pouncing, then rolling and tumbling, pummeling each other with their hind legs while yipping and barking.

Kegan chuckled, mouth full. "Check them out. Just like my nephews."

Eli grinned. "Nah. Like my last girlfriend in bed."

Helix choked on whatever he was chewing. "The one that looked like Xena the warrior princess? From that ancient-ass TV show?"

"Yeah…" Eli growled, eyes glazing in remembrance. "Wild one, that girl. And a screamer."

Helix grunted. "You sure that wasn't you screaming, E? She was scary as shit. With crazy eyes."

Eli laughed, not denying it. "She *was* a bit of a psycho. But when I finally pinned her down with bare ass up and face in a pillow?" He shrugged. "It was all just spankin' and fuckin' from that point on."

Helix shuddered.

Kegan laughed.

Paris waggled his brows at Sasha.

Sasha smirked and shoved Paris' shoulder. "Not in this lifetime."

And that pretty much said it all for Garret's teammates.

Shaking his head, Garret turned back to Airis, returning conversation to the cubs. "I must've counted two dozen dekdónni just on the way to your chieftain. How'd your village end up with so many? Feed a stray and it invited all its friends?"

Airis grinned, watching them play. "They have always been with us."

"They have?"

"Leí." He nodded. "From the beginning of time. Which is why we believe they are gifts."

"Gifts. What do you mean?"

"Guardians Nira created especially for us. To be our companions. To help us in times of need." He smiled broadly. "To watch over her favorite children."

Garret blinked, then coughed a laugh. "And obviously her most modest."

"Admittedly," Airis chuckled, "that we are her favorite is not part of lore, but *clearly* it is safe to assume."

Garret laughed even harder.

His teammates turned and eyed him.

Quickly, he cleared his throat and resumed eating.

His men traded looks, then got back to their meals, Paris and Sasha watching the dekdónni as they grappled. Eli, Helix, and Kegan, however, were more interested in the teens, keenly taking note of their sparring tactics.

Not Garret, though. Not this time at least. Instead he continued talking with Airis, swapping questions and answers for pertinent intel. Like how far Tohrí territory reached beyond the plateau, and how many villages made up their species' province. According to Airis, there were over thirty clans, whom together stretched over roughly eighty miles.

Airis mostly asked about human technology, and by the end of the conversation seemed pretty eager to see their craft.

They finished their food not long after. Airis took Garret's plate and set it on the ground with his. "Turn." He gestured for Garret to face away. "I will check your bandages now."

"You don't need to do that. I'm sure they're—"

"*Turn.*"

Garret stared at him.

Airis stared back.

Garret sighed and shifted to his left, his new line of sight more pueblo houses. Although unlike true mud pueblos, these were constructed by large stone blocks, with slender purple saplings nestled beside them. Small flora cascaded from some of the windows. Around the entryways, he spotted strange etched designs. Over all, the homes were humble, yet strangely exotic. He suddenly wished he could take a couple pictures.

Behind him, Airis lifted up his tank top to have a look, hooking the fabric over Garret's shoulders. Gently, he peeled back the corner of one bandage. "Pellay," he murmured. *Good.* He checked the ones on his arm.

Garret's muscles tensed with each brush of his fingers. Because just like before, every time they made contact, warm current whispered over his skin. It made him want to dodge Airis' touch altogether. Another male shouldn't make him feel that way.

Luckily, Airis' checkup only took a couple of minutes.

"I am finished."

Garret turned back around and glanced at his men. They hadn't been watching. They were still preoccupied. Which wasn't really surprising. There was a lot of shit to look at, and a lot of activity going on.

Airis smiled, peering down at him. "You feel good now. Fed and rested." The tall flawless male looked pleased with himself.

Garret fought a grin and nodded. "Yeah, man. Very much so."

Airis smirked, then leaned close, as if to share some special secret. "I am not a *man*, little oddling. I am Tohrí."

His breath tickled Garret's neck.

Garret covered the spot with his hand. "Right... Yeah, I know... Just a figure of spee—"

Airis' fingers were around his wrist before he'd even finished speaking. Pulling it close, the Tohrí studied his palm, tracing its different creases with his thumbs.

Garret's first instinct was to extricate his hand from his hold, but the look on Airis' face gave him pause. Innocent curiosity and nothing more. And it wasn't like the long-haired male was hurting him.

"Little hands," Airis murmured. A new smile curved his lips. He toyed with Garret's pinky. "And little fingers."

Garret shook his head, smirking. "They're not much smaller than yours."

"Are they not?" His question sounded skeptical, but also amused. He pressed their palms together and compared. "Hmm..." His tone turned smug. So did his smile.

Garret chuckled in spite of himself. How could he not? Airis' claw-tipped digits reached past his by more than an inch. He tried to pull his hand away. "Small is subjective."

But Airis didn't let go. Instead, he got back to studying. Specifically, Garret's fingers. Or rather, the ends of them.

"No claws? What are these?" He touched Garret's blunt nails, then met his gaze. "Nira... Your species is so *tame*."

Garret shrugged. "We do all right. Fight a lot with our fists."

Airis regarded him dubiously. "Show me your fangs."

Garret laughed. "Fangs? Yeah, I don't have those, either."

Airis eyes flared wider, watching Garret's mouth as he spoke. "You truly do not. Not even small ones."

Garret shook his head. "Nope."

Airis suddenly appeared concerned. "All you have are your fists?" He looked back down at Garret's hand.

Garret balled his fingers tight. "Behold, my wrecking ball."

Airis grinned, amused, until something stole his attention—the fat, white-gold band on Garret's finger. "What is this?" he asked. Raptly, he traced its shiny surface, then studied its engravings and big ole stone.

Garret uncurled his hand and eyed it, too. "My college ring."

"What is college?"

Garret scratched his chin. "Where humans go to learn a trade... so they can get a decent job and pay the bills."

"Bills?" Airis looked at him. His pointed ear twitched.

"Yeah," Garret grunted. "We got 'em for everything. Water, housing, clothing, food. You name it, it's got a price. And never a cheap one, lemme tell ya."

Airis tilted his head, his gold-ringed eyes drifting in thought. Finally, he looked back at Garret. "What trade did *you* learn?"

"Aviation." Garret smiled a little. "I've always wanted to fly."

Airis' lips quirked. "Like dekdónni. But you were not meant to fly. You are a land walker. That is why your spacecraft crashed."

"Uh, *no*," Garret chuckled humorlessly. "We crashed 'cause big-ass dragons attacked us."

Airis' brows pinched. "Dragons?"

"Yeah, three of 'em. And they were *mean*."

The male's brain churned palpably. A second later, he grinned. "Flyers. Flyers pulled you from the sky."

"Whatever," Garret muttered, looking back at his hand—the one still clutched in Airis' grip. "I'm kinda bitter."

"Bitter but *alive*," Airis pointed out. Touché. He peered at Garret's ring again. "Let us trade."

Garret cocked a brow. "*Trade*?"

"Leí. Your college ring for…" Airis glanced down at his person. His gaze slid to his belt. "…my knife. Our finest bladesmiths fashioned it. But I like your ring very much, so in exchange, I will give you my favorite knife."

Garret made a face, hardly interested, until Airis pulled out said dagger. Damn. It was gorgeous, the craftsmanship exquisite on both handle and blade. And by exquisite, he meant badass. A dekdónni head on its grip, its beak open as if loosing a battle cry, its fierce eyes set with big gleaming gems.

He stared at it, wholly tempted, but ultimately declined. His ring, after all, represented the most pivotal time in his life. When the gateway he'd worked so hard for finally opened, allowing him to embark on adventures such as this. "Thanks, but I think I'm gonna hold onto my ring. It's got… you know, sentimental value."

Disappointment flickered in Airis eyes, but before he could respond, his friend Kato sat down beside him. Airis glanced at his buddy.

Kato looked at Garret's hand, specifically the one still clutched in Airis' grasp. "It is late," he muttered. "We must get an early start."

Airis loosened his grip. Garret pulled back his hand.

Not only did Kato's tone sound disapproving as hell, but also suspiciously possessive.

Airis leveled his friend with a look that Garret couldn't quite read, then turned back to Garret and his men. "It is too dangerous to travel anymore tonight. You will sleep here. In the morning we will take you to your beacon. If your friends are not there, we will escort you to the castle, as we will be heading there ourselves to find out more."

"You're going to Múnrahki?" Garret asked, surprised. After all, that was enemy territory.

Airis and Kato stood. "We must find answers to our missing brothers' whereabouts. For now, it will only be reconnaissance."

Garret and his men rose, too. "Alright then." Garret nodded. "We'll head out in the morning. Hopefully our guys will be waiting for us at their beacon."

"Leí." Airis faced him, his big brown eyes serious. "Because if the king *does* have your people, getting them back will not be easy. He will not just hand them over at your request."

Garret cursed under his breath.

Airis offered him a smile. "Do not worry over it now, oddling. The time for that will come." Turning, he gestured for the team to follow. "Súsa." *Come.* "I will show you to your lodgings."

CHAPTER THIRTY-FIVE

***

They were up bright and early the following day, having slept in several pueblos not far from the campfire. Airis fed them more odd foods that weren't so bad, then gathered additional Tohrí and got packed up. Packed up, meaning pretty much just more arrows to fill their quivers. That and a couple extra daggers.

Talk about traveling light. They didn't even bring water. Guess they didn't want to be weighed down. Which made Garret laugh, imagining Airis' face were he ever to get a look at the team's rucksacks. No doubt, he'd balk aghast—then laugh his big, blond, forest-elf ass off.

Departing with four more Tohrí than before, the convoy set off, each Niran bringing along his own dekdónni. Garret eyed the beasts as they made their way toward the bridge, some soaring with wings spread wide, some carrying riders. Did the Tohrí keep them like horses? Have stables for them and shit?

They crossed the huge stone catwalk and cut back into the forest, backtracking a bit northwest, according to Paris. Sure enough, after a good hour or two of hiking, the terrain turned wetter, denser. They were back in the jungle.

Garret scanned their surroundings. Every direction looked the same. He turned to Airis. "You sure you remember where you saw our people's ship? It's been a year, what if it's covered in vegetation?"

Airis and Kato exchanged looks as they moved through thick undergrowth, their steps damn near soundless, like all the Tohrí.

Airis smiled. "Leí, oddling. We remember it well. Nothing else on Nira looks anything like it." He pointed up ahead as several dekdónni padded nearby. "Not far from here, but we must first cross over a river."

Paris nodded. "Yeah, the river. Their beacon was on the other side."

"Oh yeah," Eli grunted. "Definitely remember the river. Almost got eaten by tachi along its bank."

Garret tamped back a shudder.

Kegan cursed and scrubbed his face. "Let's not ever bring that up again. Okay? Okay."

Airis chuffed, the sound soft, so much softer than a Kríe's. "I vow to Nira that we will not let you get eaten."

He was teasing, Garret could hear it clear as day in his tone, but his promise still eased Garret's nerves.

He flicked Airis a smirk. "I'm gonna hold you to that, Tohrí. We humans frown pretty heavily on being chow."

Airis cocked a brow, then glanced down the length of Garret's body. "Pleasant thought, I admit…" He grinned and looked away. "But you are far too small to hold me for long against anything."

Paris choked on a laugh.

Eli and Kegan snorted, too.

Garret rolled his eyes and fought a smile. Tohrí humor was wrong. Hell, if Airis wasn't male, he'd almost think the guy was flirting. Garret paused in thought, considering their tracker. Paris was male—but also bi. Maybe some Tohrí were bisexual, too? Figuring he'd never know, he brushed it off and just kept on walking.

They reached the large river roughly ten minutes later. It looked pretty deep and had a steady current going, with sheltered coves randomly nestled along the bank.

Garret glanced around. "Uh, Airis? I'm not seeing a crossing."

"And that's a pretty sizable drop," Eli added. He peered over the edge. "Yeah, man. Fifty feet easy."

"Fuuuck." Kegan ruefully eyed his dry clothes. "Please tell me we ain't swimming. Soggy sucks."

"Yeah." Paris nodded, regarding the water. "And since this here is an alien jungle, there's probably alien leeches all up in there."

The team groaned in unison.

Airis laughed and shook his head. "Nún. No swimming."

Helix crossed his arms. "Then what's the plan?"

Airis' eyes flashed. Peering upward, he loosed a low yip. Kotchka dropped down from a tree. "We fly."

Garret's brows shot up fast.

Paris punched the air. "Yes!"

Airis grinned and gave his companion a quiet command.

Next thing Garret knew, his black-haired tracker was flying, while rowdy Tohrí dove off the cliff with arms wide.

"Holy shite." Kegan gaped, watching dekdónni dive off too, barking and cawing as they swooped down to catch the daredevils.

"Fuck," Eli laughed.

Sasha smiled with a nod.

Even Helix's dark eyes betrayed his excitement.

Ten minutes later, they all were across—some wind-blown and grinning more than others. Another half hour longer, and they closed in on the site. Garret's heart kicked up a notch.

"There. Just to the right of all those tall broken trees." Airis pointed to a large metal structure in the distance. Damn near half of it was covered in vines and foliage.

"Jaysus," Kegan muttered. "They've been slackin' on the upkeep."

Garret frowned. The sight didn't bode well. His teammates wore similar expressions. The scientists weren't there and hadn't been for a while. From the look of things, maybe not since they first crashed.

Exhaling, Garret raked a hand through his dark blond hair, then gestured to the spacecraft. "Go on ahead and open her up. There's gotta be something inside we can use."

Kegan slid Garret a pessimistic look. "Gonna go check out the cockpit."

Garret nodded, watching his team jog ahead, the ship still a good sixty yards away. He glanced around, wondering where their own downed bird was. Paris had said that only a couple of miles separated them. Not that they had time to go searching for it now. *Two* detours hadn't been part of Airis' agreement. Besides, they'd probably never find it without their tracking gear.

Eli and Helix reached the spacecraft first and got busy clearing off vines. Sasha and Paris arrived soon after to help. Once they cleared the vessel's side plug door, Eli opened up the hatch and dropped the ramp.

Garret watched them climb inside, disappointed but not surprised by their findings. Tough break. Maybe their streak of better luck had come to an end. Next stop: Múnrahki castle.

Sighing, he traipsed forward with the remainder of the convoy, until he noticed that every Tohrí had pulled up short.

Garret paused too and looked at Airis. "What's wrong? Why'd you stop?" Even the dekdónni had gone stock still.

Stance braced, Airis scanned the trees intently, ears twitching. "We are not alone here," he murmured. "There are others." He sniffed the air.

Garret tensed and peered around again. The forest had gone quiet. "You mean, besides the usuals? 'Cause I don't see—"

Abruptly, he stopped, spotting something in his periphery. Movement up in the branches. Then a big dark blur dropped from a tree. It landed with a thump less than ten yards away. Garret gaped. The blur was one of Gesh's pack.

"Kríe!" Airis barked, quickly grabbing his bow.

His clansmen did the same, nocking their arrows.

Another Kríe descended, same distance away. This time to the left. Then one to their right.

The dekdónni lunged forward.

"Nún!" Airis barked. "Dekdónni, climb!"

The beasts snarled, but obediently darted up the trees out of sight, their angry caws echoing through the canopy. Garret glanced up after them, frowning. Guess there wasn't enough room to spread their wings, but fuck, couldn't they have stayed to help out?

More Kríe touched down behind them, then a few straight ahead, caught in Tohrí crosshairs the instant they landed. Garret recognized some of them. Miros. Roni. Naydo. Beng. Even the twins. Who, with the others, now surrounded—and outnumbered—them.

Garret's heart pounded anxiously. He glanced to their craft. His men had no weapons. Were utterly defenseless. Fortunately, he saw no Kríe around the ship. Maybe the pack didn't know the guys were there. As long as they stayed hidden, good and far from the action, they'd be safe until—Out of nowhere, Gesh dropped onto the spacecraft's large roof, the heavy impact resounding through the forest. Metal buckled beneath his weight. Still crouched from his landing, he loosed a thunderous roar that shook the trees.

Garret tensed from head to toe.

Airis growled.

Then right on cue, Helix and Eli tore out the door. Eyes darting to Garret's group, they braked in alarm, their gazes quickly registering all the Kríe.

Paris and Sasha emerged next, then Kegan did too, all three freezing in their tracks atop the ramp.

Shit, shit, shit.

Garret glanced up at Gesh. None of the team had even spotted him yet. Gesh grinned and stepped to the ledge, a big fat knife clutched in his hand.

Oh, God. What was he doing?

And still the other Kríe didn't budge, just held their position surrounding Garret's group. Garret's eyes darted restlessly between his men and the pack, while beside him, Airis aimed for one of their chests. Why were they just standing there? He didn't understand.

But then he saw them, more Kríe emerging from the brush, small sticks in hand as they headed for Garret's men.

Oh, fuck.

Garret finally understood.

These Kríe surrounding them were there to keep them at bay while the rest swooped in and captured Garret's team. The humans Gesh had wanted so desperately from the start—and clearly was still determined to get.

Air lodged in Garret's chest. The Kríe had been waiting for them. He eyed the strange implements in their hands. Were they weapons of some sort? Did they plan to stab his team? Weapons aside, not even his ex-marines stood a chance against so many.

The guys tensed, spotting them.

Eli and Helix braced to engage.

Kegan cursed and shielded Paris and Sasha.

"Secure them," Gesh snarled. "Incapacitate if you must. As long as they draw breath, they will suffice."

Jesus. Garret tamped down an anxious oath. Gesh just gave his pack the green light to do damage.

The Kríe readied to pounce.

"*NO!*" Garret bellowed, sprinting forward. "Get back inside! Get back inside the ship!"

His men glanced his way, clearly registering his words, but before they could take a single step to retreat, Kríe lunged, knocking the marines off their feet. They flew off the ramp and crashed hard to the ground. Kegan spun around to shove Paris and Sasha back inside. But more Kríe blitzed, bringing those instruments to their mouths. Tiny projectiles shot out and nailed the men still standing. They staggered, then stumbled, hands fumbling to pull out the darts, only to topple over the edge into Kríe arms.

"NO!" Garret hollered again, but before he could reach them, was tackled by one of the pack surrounding their group.

"Now!" Airis shouted.

Arrows whizzed overhead, a furious barrage in every conceivable direction. The Kríe atop Garret roared. Guess the bastard got hit. But then he yanked Garret up and dragged him, limping, toward the spacecraft. The reason was clear. Once they had all of Garret's team, the Kríe were going to up and split.

Garret fought to get free. "Get your fucking hands off me!"

"Quiet!" the Kríe grated. The one called Miros.

But Garret wouldn't be quiet. Wouldn't be cowed. Wrenching around, he grabbed the arrow in Miro's side and gave the thing a big ole hardy yank.

Miros howled and loosened his hold.

"Garret!" someone shouted.

Garret glanced over his shoulder as he grappled to escape.

Airis, racing his way, dodging countless Kríe. Juking as they dove at him. Hurdling obstacles while firing his bow—three arrows at a time, Garret noticed. But as the blond male closed in, he didn't slow down, just leapt up and plowed Miros over with both feet. The Kríe slammed into the dirt.

Airis yanked Garret off the ground. "Do not ever leave my side again!"

"But my men!"

"They will not take them! I vow to you, we will not let them!"

Arrows tore by their heads. Roars and shouts resounded. Garret glanced back. Both sides were fully engaged. Kríe on top of Tohrí. Tohrí ducking and dodging, ever unloading their bows into the enemy.

Garret gaped, eyeing the Kríe. They had arrows freaking everywhere. In their arms and shoulders. In their backs and thighs. Some had even taken them in their glutes. And yet, somehow the brutes barely seemed fazed. Their adrenaline must be like high-test octane.

Airis pulled him along, running and leaping over foliage. A handful of other Tohrí kept up pace. They advanced toward the ship. Garret couldn't see his men—until he did.

"Oh, God." His heart plummeted.

Piled haphazardly against the craft, his men lay unconscious. Even Eli and Helix had been tranq'ed.

They pulled to a stop at the foot of the ramp.

Garret vibrated, furious. "You bastard."

Gesh merely grinned and dropped down from the roof. "You are just angry because I won."

Garret glanced back at the battle still waging—or maybe it wasn't. Now that Gesh's pack saw that he and the others had gotten past them, they no longer seemed interested in fighting. Snarling, the Kríe turned and lumbered toward the ship, only pausing to bare their fangs at the Tohrí who kept shooting them.

Garret turned back and glared. "You haven't won. Not yet. Still got one more human to bag."

Gesh chuffed. "But to bag *you* is unnecessary, moyo. You will come with us voluntarily to watch over your men."

Airis drew his bow and aimed dual arrows at Gesh's face. "Release them to us or I will not be so kind with my aim. I have one notched for each of your eyes."

Gesh chuckled as the rest of Airis' band joined the gathering. "As if you would do such. You are rodents. You do not kill."

Airis narrowed his eyes. His chocolate irises flashed. "True. We try not to unless a life is in danger. Our dekdónni, however, are less rigid in their stance."

Gesh's grin faded fast.

Airis smirked and eyed the trees, then fired three deep yips up into the canopy. Instantly, all eight beasts dropped like lightning out of nowhere, plowing Kríe to the ground with fiery squawks.

The downed pack mates roared, but before they could shake it off, Airis shouted, "Dekdónni, seize!" and, yup, game over. The winged beasts had their victims pinned beneath their big paws, with their razor-sharp beaks clutching their necks.

The other Kríe went rigid, then turned to attack, but the Tohrí already had arrows trained on their chests. Notched and ready, the blonds' expressions unmistakable. This was no longer a game. The stakes had been laid. If they fired their bows this time, it'd be to kill.

Airis lifted a brow. "Well, savage? What say you? One word and your riffraff lose their throats."

Gesh's eyes shot to one pack member in particular who'd been pinned. His right-hand man. The one they called Roni. The leader's face wrenched into a mask of pure rage. He hadn't won after all. In fact, he'd epically failed. And by that murderous look in his eyes, he knew it.

His huge body bristled.

Then a roar ripped past his lips.

Garret stiffened, his ears screaming. The Tohrí just looked on, waiting for the leader to finish his tantrum.

"They are *mine!*" Gesh exploded, throwing his blade to the ground. "I had them first! But you stole them like rotten thieves!"

Airis scoffed, lowering his bow. "We have stolen nothing, *boor*. We do not claim a single one of these strange oddlings."

Garret fought not to roll his eyes. Could Airis *not* just call them humans?

"Bellah," Gesh snarled. "Then I will take them all back, and you and yours can be on your way."

"Hmm." Airis shook his head. "Tragically, we cannot. I made them a pledge and cannot honor it if you take them."

"What pledge?" Gesh ground out.

"To escort them to Múnrahki."

Gesh's lips curved into a sneer. "We are headed there right now." He slid his gaze to Garret. "*We* can escort them."

Airis smirked. "Where is the decency in passing my debt to another? I am a noble creature, savage. That means I have *honor*—"

"I know what it means!" Gesh snapped. He glanced at Garret's men. "If you do not claim them, if they are not yours, then it is up to them whether they come with us or stay."

Garret barked an incredulous laugh. "You think we'd *choose* to go with you? The assholes who took us prisoner? Who planned to trade us like goddamn cattle?"

Gesh leveled him with harsh eyes. "You wish to find your people, tah? I know where they are *right now*. I can take you to them directly. These rats cannot."

Garret clenched his jaw. "You said you didn't know where they were."

Gesh met him glare for glare. "I might have lied."

Airis looked at Garret. "No might. He did. I am certain. His kind lie all the time." He mouthed, *"No honor."*

"Silence, tree rodent!" Gesh boomed, shooting Airis a scathing glower. "I have waited too long for this. Have no time for your antics. These *hewmens*, they mean nothing to you, but they mean *everything* to me. So, return to your treacherous spawn and never come back."

Airis' smirk faded fast. "Why do you call us traitors?"

"Because according to our king, that is exactly what you are. Have betrayed us in ways that can never be forgiven."

Airis stilled and glanced at Kato who stood to his right, then looked back at Gesh. "Nún. You lie."

Gesh bared his teeth, ear twitching. "Why would I lie about that?"

"I do not know, but we are honorable. In what ways have we betrayed you?"

"Why not ask the king yourself?" Gesh countered, jaw clenched. "Your people's dark deeds, he keeps them close to his chest. Refuses to loose their stench upon his kingdom."

Every inch of Airis went rigid, his expression quickly troubled. The other Tohrí looked equally disturbed. "I do not know what has happened, but I assure you, we are innocent. Clearly, there has been a misunderstanding."

Gesh laughed. "Why is that? Because your people have *honor*? Because your precious Tohrí race can do no wrong?" The Kríe's grin vanished. He glared at Airis coldly. "In truth, yours is the worst race of them all."

Airis shook his head. "You are wrong. Your king is lying—"

"*Enough*, rodent!" Gesh cut him off. "Understand, *I do not care*. All I want is what is mine." He pointed at Garret's men. "And they are the only way to get it."

Airis frowned, then returned his bow to his back and irritably crossed his arms. "Then it appears we have come to an impasse."

Oh, thank God. Garret exhaled. Airis wasn't going to let Gesh take them.

"Look," he interjected, raking a hand through his hair. "Maybe there's a way we *all* can win. A way Gesh can get this thing he wants so badly and we can finally grab our guys and split."

No one responded. They all were too busy glowering at each other.

Garret cursed in frustration. "Come on. What's the alternative? Gesh and his pack will continue stalking our asses, and God knows *that's* no fun.

"And what if we find our scientists but the king won't let them go? Not to mention *your* guys." He looked at Airis. "What if the king *does* have them? What'll you do then? Your leaders have no leverage. The king hates you all too much. So how will you ever negotiate your people's release?"

Still holding Airis' gaze, he pointed to Gesh. "He's your only ticket. The only one you've got. If we somehow help him get this thing he's losing his friggin' mind over, maybe he'd be willing to talk to the king on your behalf."

Gesh furrowed his brows. "Talk to the king? Negotiate a release?" He turned his gaze to Airis. "He has your kin?"

"We suspect that he might. Many have gone missing. But until now, we did not know of his contempt."

Gesh rubbed his jaw and nodded.

Airis watched him expectantly. "Do you know of any such dealings? Heard of any talk?"

"Mah, not specifically. But he does have labor slaves."

Airis stiffened and glanced at Kato. His jaw ticked. "That is them."

"Sure looks that way," Garret muttered. He peered back at Gesh. "So? You gonna do this, talk to your king for them, or not?"

Gesh crossed his arms and brooded. Tense moments later, he finally nodded. "If I cannot trade you *hewmens* then there is only one option left. Steal meesha and his team from the castle."

"His team?" Garret prompted. It was time for Gesh to fess up— even though Garret and his men already knew.

"Tah." The pack leader nodded again. "Meesha is one of the *hewmens* you seek."

Garret stared at him crossly.

Gesh growled and looked away. "I sold them to the king. It is not my proudest moment. But I should have kept my meesha. I was a fool."

"If you knew they were at the castle," Garret shook his head, aggravated, "why not just tell us that before?"

"*Because*," Gesh complained, "you would have asked me more questions. Questions about things I could not reveal. 'How did they get there?' 'Why do they linger there still?'... I can only lie so much. It bothers my stomach."

Garret threw up his hands.

Tohrí muttered in disgust.

Gesh just grunted and waved them all off. "What is important is that I am willing to work with these betrayers. I have scouted the area and know of several hidden paths. But meesha, I know he will not leave his people behind, and my pack is just too small to handle them all. More will be needed. The castle grounds have many guards."

He paused to count all present. "Twenty-eight including my pack..." His expression looked uneasy. "That should be enough..."

Garret nodded, not really seeing an alternative at the moment. If they asked this Kríe king for their friends and he refused, no doubt he'd up his security as a precaution. They couldn't show their hand. The king could never know they were coming.

As if reading his mind, Gesh muttered, "We cannot fail. We will only get one chance. We must succeed."

Garret eyed him dryly. "You know what would've helped us out with that? If my team had our gear and the weapons you took from us."

Gesh met his gaze, slowly smiled, then gave his pack mates a nod. Just like that, they were loping off through the trees. Gesh looked back at Garret. His auric eyes gleamed. "Nira smiles on us. We have those very things right now."

Garret blinked. "You do?" He peered around. "Where?"

"Stashed nearby for safe keeping. After my pack and yours were *separated*, we came back to this craft, suspecting you would eventually show up. While we waited, and tended to our injuries—" He shot the Tohrí a glare, "—we combed the area until we found each of your packs."

Garret fought a burgeoning smile. When his team woke, they'd be ecstatic.

"So, to clarify," Airis crossed his arms, regarding Gesh skeptically. "You will go and negotiate with the king on our behalf, and in return, we will help liberate the humans?"

Gesh nodded once. "Tah. But if the mission fails, no more talks."

Garret looked at Airis. "You cool with that?"

Airis eyed his band of brothers. Their gazes said everything. They were anxious to find their kin. He inclined his head, "Leí," then called out, "Dekdónni, yield."

Garret exhaled. "Good. Let's go make ourselves a plan."

CHAPTER THIRTY-SIX

* * *

"Are you certain," Zercy rumbled, his lips a hair's breadth away from Alec's, "that I cannot talk you into coming along?"

Alec groaned as raw pleasure pulsed steadily through his body. Zercy had him pressed against a wall in their chambers, impaled on his huge cock beside a window. With his one hand, he'd pinned Alec's wrists above his head. With his other he slowly stroked Alec's dick.

Alec's thighs squeezed around his waist, his heels digging into Zercy's ass.

"I want to—I'd love to—" he rasped. "You know I would, but—" A moan shoved past his lips as Zercy rocked his hips upward. "—But my men—I can't leave 'em—I'm their captain—"

The king's shaft bucked inside him. Huskily, Zercy growled. "We will not be gone long—Five days, six at the most—" He pumped just Alec's crown. Alec's whole body stiffened. Zercy chuffed and got back to jacking his full length.

White bliss licked down Alec's shaft, firming his balls, tickling his hole. He needed to come so bad. They'd been going at it like this for an hour already, with Zercy repeatedly bringing him to the brink.

He was trying to get Alec to fold. To give in and agree. But a week away from his men? They were his obligation. He couldn't, even though he wanted to really bad.

"Maybe one day," Alec panted. Although, he wasn't holding his breath. This castle he'd lived in for a year now may feel like home, but he knew deep down that he wouldn't be there forever.

Another rumble curled in Zercy's throat. Letting go of Alec's dick, he gripped Alec's jaw and turned his head. "Denza, *Alick*." *Look*. "Out the window. Do you see? Past the mountain ridge and steppes? Those tall, faint cliffs that touch the sky?"

Alec nodded, trying to focus. Zercy's foot-long was making it hard.

"That is where they are holding the council meeting I must attend. The journey would be an adventure. A chance to experience more of Nira." Alec took in the sight. Zercy thrummed and resumed stroking him. "Surely you are due for a vacation."

Alec moaned, back arching. "Almost forgot those things existed."

Zercy growled and thrust his hips. "Time to remember."

Alec gasped. Pleasure surged. Through his ass. Into his junk. "Zercy—No more playin'—I gotta come."

"Agree and I will make you."

"I can't."

"Tah, you can. But that is fine. I can fuck my little pet like this all day." Zercy latched his mouth to Alec's neck and hungrily sucked on his flesh. Hand still teasing Alec's cock, he started to thrust.

Alec groaned, brows pinching, eyes sliding back into his head.

So, it was going to be like that? War of the wills? Whatever. Looked like Alec was going to have to *make* Zercy make him come.

Cursing through gasps as pressure mushroomed in his groin, Alec vised his thighs tighter around Zercy's waist. Zercy chuffed against his neck and stopped all movement—such a punk. Not that it would do any good.

Digging his heels in deeper, Alec pushed against Zercy's glutes and urgently started riding the fucker's cock. Up and down, up and down. Ecstasy welled, Zercy's hard swollen cockhead rubbing his G.

"Yeah—*Unnngh*—Fuck yeah—" Alec ground out, starting to quake. His orgasm was so close he could taste it.

Zercy laughed and let go of Alec's dick to still his ass. So, Alec switched things up and ground his dick against Zercy's abs. Pleasure lashed along his length. Into his package.

"Yeah!" he panted. "*Ungh—Shit!*"

Zercy growled and stepped back, trying to put space between their hips. All that did though, was spur Alec back to riding his cock. Up and down, up and down, his ass gripping that huge rod.

"*Uh!*" Alec cried out. His trapped hands fisted tight.

Harder tremors shook his frame from head to toe.

Then Zercy shuddered, too. Snarling, he shoved Alec back down his cock, trying once more to keep his ass from moving. But of course, that just sent Alec back into grinding. Urgently. Frantically. Against ribbed, rock-hard abs.

Oh, God—His orgasm—Barreling closer by the—

"FUUUCK!!" Alec detonated on a loud, strangled cry, his spine arching, his asshole clamping brutally.

And what do you know, that tight, frenzied hug triggered the king a heartbeat later. Releasing Alec's wrists, Zercy roared and clutched Alec's ass, then vigorously started thrusting into his heat. Alec's climax spiked higher. Digging his fingers into Zercy's shoulders, he held on till Zercy slammed home and violently came.

Long moments after, Alec rebooted to the feel of Zercy's body, his huge chest heaving for breath against Alec's own. Panting, eyes still closed, he grinned. "Wow, Leo... Thanks... That was great."

"Do not thank me, you little deviant," Zercy grunted against his neck. "You know I did not give you that. You *took* it."

Alec chuckled and nuzzled his ear. "I'll go on the next trip."

"I do not believe you. Next time I am abducting you, just so you know."

Alec laughed. "For what it's worth... I'm gonna miss you when you're gone."

Zercy eased back and eyed him with a warm sated smile. "You will be here when I return? Eagerly waiting for your king?"

Alec grinned and rubbed their noses. "Yeah... I'll be here."

Zercy thrummed a low, thumping purr. "I will miss you, too."

"Boss. Yo, Alec. Ground control to Major Tom."

Alec blinked from his reverie, thinking about earlier with the king. A morning not unlike most, as of late. In the past couple of months, since he'd embraced this thing with Zercy, their connection had only gotten stronger.

Unfortunately, such progress couldn't be said for other things. Notably, the Nira tree in Zercy's courtyard. Not that she hadn't recovered, because she had, as had all of her offshoots in the realm. But for some reason, she still wasn't able to conceive, nor sustain herself without Alec's team. Which, truth be told, was taking its toll on the nation. No young born since that tragic night. The people's morale was slipping every day.

Alec looked at Chet and shook his head. "I'm sorry. Guess I drifted. What were you saying?"

Chet regarded him as the team made their way toward the lake. "I asked you where Zercy was going."

"Oh, um, right. To some council meeting in Lendum. A kingdom south of here, past the plains."

"Long trip?" Zaden plucked a lime-tipped frond from the ground.

"A couple days each way."

Chet frowned. "So when's he comin' back?"

"About a week."

"Fuuuck," the marine muttered, rubbing the top of his crew-cut head.

Alec eyed him. "Why? What's wrong?"

Chet exhaled and glanced over his shoulder. Specifically, to where Mannix lingered by the gate. "You ever heard the expression, 'When the cat's away, the mice will play'?"

Alec followed his line of sight, not quite sure where he was going with that. "Yeah. What about it?"

Chet turned back around, pulling to a stop as they reached the water. "Because whenever Zercy goes away on his little trips, asshole Mannix always forgets his manners."

Alec stared at him, not liking the sound of that. "His manners."

Chet leveled him with a look. "You know, like keeping his hands to himself. And his pervy-ass thoughts. Not to mention his dick in his pants."

"Holy shit." Bailey gaped. "He's back to coming on to you?"

"*Please*. He never stopped."

Alec clenched his jaw. "Stay away from him. I'll talk to Zercy when he gets back. He'll deal with him."

Chet shook his head. "Fuck that. I'm not a snitch. I can handle him. *Have* been handling him since the day we got here. It just gets annoying when he kicks it up a notch." He scowled and clutched his crotch.

Irritably rearranged his goods. "And with my dick always hard from that fucking kirah shit…"

The others nodded absently in understanding. Hell, even Alec got what the guy was trying to say—and Alec was getting some regularly, unlike his team. Which was exactly what was making things extra difficult for Chet. A year without sex—sperm banks aside—was hard enough. But no sex for a year with a big sexual being constantly pushing Chet's ramped-up sexual buttons? Alec frowned and rubbed his neck. That'd make anyone crazy.

Noah glanced back at the gate. "Damn. He's watching you even now."

"When's he *not?*" Chet muttered.

Bailey scratched his curly-haired head. "So, what're you gonna do? Just deal with it?"

Chet turned around and eyed the Kríe, clutching his hips as he brooded. "Honestly? At this point I'm halfway tempted to humor the fucker. Just give him what he wants so he'll cool his jets. Screw it. I'd get something out of it, too."

"You *would?*" Jamis asked, dark brows hiking behind his bangs.

Chet cut him a sardonic look. "Yeah. You know, an orgasm *outside* of Sirus' cum dump for once?"

"Ah," Jamis nodded.

The others nodded, too.

Because for months now, since they first started 'donating,' they'd all had to give it up to Sirus twice a day. And even though it'd recently been reduced to once daily—thanks to the synthetic compound the trio developed that made samples stretch twice as far—after coming so often for so fucking long, none of them ever even whacked off anymore.

In fact, with the act always so damn clinical all the time, it'd made them crave physical contact more than ever. Intimacy with another virile hot-blooded being. Only Alec, however, was in a position to actually get it. Not that the Kríe wouldn't be happy to oblige his teammates, or hell, the Súrah nymphs for that matter. But in terms of being with someone they actually wanted to be with? Yeah, his guys were outta luck.

"I dunno," Chet muttered, tetchily glaring at the Kríe. "You think he'd bottom? 'Cause right now I'd be game for some angry sex… Trade a few punches... Take the guy down." He ground his molars and shook his head. "Then I'd pound his big Kríe ass *so fucking hard*."

Alec swapped surprised looks with Zaden.

Noah stared at Chet, jaw slack.

Jamis and Bailey, on the other hand, couldn't hold back their laughs.

"Holy shit. And to think I was worried about you." Jamis snorted. "Now I see I should be worried about Mannix."

Bailey rubbed his mouth and grinned. "Damn, man. Maybe you should. Just pretend you're banging Roni and maybe you'll bust twice."

Chet stilled and eyed him sharply, but then frowned and looked back at Mannix. "Roni *did* know how to fuck," he grumbled. "I'll definitely give him that."

"He must've," Noah chuckled, giving the marine a curious once-over. "Evidently, he fucked the hetero right out of you."

Chet grunted, but didn't deny it.

Bailey watched him, then eyed the water. Like he was suddenly contemplating his own orientation. Or that Oonmaiyo he swore he still kept catching glimpses of.

Hell, one day Alec found him down below, camped out in front of that big aquarium window. Just sitting on the floor, idly drawing in his notebook. Sketches of different entities beyond the glass.

Alec hadn't asked, and Bailey hadn't volunteered the information, but he suspected the scientist was hoping to spot the 'merman.'

Zaden looked to the east, his dark eyes thoughtful. "It's been a year now. A year since we fired up our distress beacon. You think search and rescue's gotten here yet?"

The team instantly sobered, no doubt all thinking the same thing: what if the others *had* arrived but got captured by Gesh's pack? They could be marching the men toward the castle right now. To hand over to Zercy in exchange for Noah.

Alec frowned, growing restless. What if Zercy let Gesh have him? He didn't think Zercy would separate Alec's team. But what if he was wrong? What if he would?

"Well, if they have," Jamis sighed, "I hope they're good dodgers. First, from those flyers, so they don't crash like we did. And then of course..." He stalled out, but that was okay. It was a given: The Kríe who'd bagged, tagged, and sold them to the king. Although in truth, *'snagged'* and *'shagged'* seemed much more fitting.

"I'm sure they're fine," Noah murmured, staring eastward like Zaden. He didn't sound very convinced, though. Was probably trying to battle his guilt. After all, if the rescue team *did* get captured, it'd be because of him, and he knew it.

"Yeah," Bailey agreed. "No way Gesh's pack is still waiting for them. I bet they lost interest *ages* ago."

Noah forced a smile and nodded. Picked up a stone and half-heartedly skipped it.

Alec wasn't so sure though, that those Kríe had given up. He didn't want to freak out his men—or get Noah's hopes up—but a few days ago Gesh had requested a meeting with Zercy. What about, Alec didn't know. The king wouldn't say.

Zercy *had* come out of the visit looking pretty angry, however. Why was anyone's guess. Had Gesh given up on the humans and tried to barter with something else? A crappy offer, maybe, that Zercy found insulting? Or maybe Gesh *did* have the rescue team after all, but Zercy had backed out and they'd verbally fought. Either way, it was proof to Alec that Gesh hadn't given up, regardless if he had the humans or not.

Still, the timing *was* suspicious. Exactly a year...

On the other hand, what if the rescue team somehow managed to dodge capture and came for Alec's team on their own, finding some way, some leverage, to convince the king to let them go? Alec didn't want to leave. He'd grown to love Zercy on some level and believed Zercy felt the same. Neither had ever actually come out and said it, but despite the king still calling him 'pet,' he'd privately elevated Alec to consort not too long ago. Alec was sure that meant something. A show of devotion. And a clear sign that Zercy considered Alec more than a plaything.

He still had yet to try and bond with Alec, though. Not that he didn't bite him regularly. Because he did. Whenever possible. As if inside he was fighting the urge to bond and biting maybe helped take the edge off.

Alec suspected that if he messed with Zercy's horns hard enough, it could get the guy to cave. But that felt low-handed, like he was cheating. He didn't want Zercy to bond with him unless he *wanted* to.

Besides, Alec wasn't sure he wanted to bond with Zercy, either. That was a pretty huge, not to mention irrevocable, plunge to take. Ironically, something he *had* been wanting to do as of late was to bite Zercy too, right on the neck. He wondered if it'd leave a mark like the king's always did. For some reason, he loved wearing Zercy's signature on his skin. Too bad it never lasted for more than a week.

Although the other night, after sinking his fangs in Alec's neck, Zercy revealed something that Alec found pretty interesting. The fact that, while regular bites didn't leave lasting marks, bites that triggered bondings left marks that lasted forever. The sign that a Niran was claimed, but more so than that, a symbol of unending devotion.

Which, of course, had Alec contemplating his feelings for Zercy—and the prospect of ever procreating together. He wondered if they could. If it was biologically even possible. The concept was definitely fascinating. And what they'd done a few nights earlier in the Kríe castle's courtyard? It only had him riveted that much more.

It'd all started when he came right out and asked Zercy how Niran babies were made. He'd only heard bits and pieces until then. Zercy had smiled, seeming pleased that Alec would want to know such things, but he'd also looked a little bit sad. No doubt, because it reminded him of his people's predicament, and how it seemed no future offspring would ever be had.

Because again, it'd been a year. A year with no promising signs. After all, the mother tree had been totally restored—aside from her ongoing need for medication—but still no offspring anywhere had been conceived. If Nira, happy and healthy, wasn't doing the trick, then what the fuck else logically would?

Ultimately, Zercy had decided to *show* Alec rather than tell him, taking him first for an impromptu snack in the kitchen. A snack, incidentally, that included senna`sohnsay.

Needless to say, Alec had been a little hesitant. His introduction to said fruit hadn't been the greatest. Sure, it'd ended with one cosmically mind-blowing orgasm, but via an exchange with someone he didn't know well or have feelings for. And Alec just wasn't the kind of guy who took sex casually.

Zercy talked him into eating it pretty easily, though. Seemed Alec would do almost anything for the guy. Besides, what'd been unpleasant about his last experience with senna`sohnsay was that he'd resisted having sex for so long afterward. There'd definitely be no resisting this time around.

Once Zercy had fed him every piece of the fruit by hand, they'd left the kitchen and headed to the courtyard. Zercy instructed the guards not to allow any interruptions, then led Alec over to the tree. Under the light of dancing torch flames, they removed each other's clothes, staring into each other's eyes the whole time.

With their garments at their feet, Zercy had smiled and drawn Alec against him, then dipped his head and claimed Alec's mouth. His tongue had been sweet, Alec remembered it well, as his fat little fangs grazed Alec's lip.

Unhurried moments later, Zercy severed their kiss and reached up to a branch above their heads. "This," he'd plucked a leaf from one of the closest twigs, "is where life once started. Where Kríe young used to grow." He handed it to Alec.

Alec had taken the thing and studied it. It'd reminded him of a sugar snap pea pod, but a little bit larger and rounder. It wasn't green either, but a deep shade of purple—Kríe purple, incidentally—and veined like marble. Didn't feel like marble, though. Wasn't hard at all. In fact, it had the texture of a delicate flower petal. Either that, or super-supple *skin*.

Eyes intense, Zercy had laid Alec in the grass beneath the tree and kissed him until he was fully aroused. Alec could feel the senna`sohnsay, in his blood, in his loins. Stirring his tender prostate, making it swell.

Zercy's hands and mouth had been everywhere, covering him with Kríe affection, preparing Alec's body to accept him. God, how Alec loved not needing tachi anymore. Hadn't used it in months, thanks to Noah.

Zercy entered him not long after—Alec had felt so impossibly full—driving into him again and again. Slowly at first, then steadily faster, restlessly ravaging Alec's neck with his mouth. He'd wanted to bite him, it was obvious, Alec could tell, but like always, managed to hold himself back. Which, be what it may, still kind of stung.

A good while later, Zercy growled, "Need to spill," pausing to enclose Alec's cock inside that leaf. Panting, Alec had peered down at the pod around his dick. Had watched as Zercy held it firm and resumed fucking. But when the king finally climaxed, his cum igniting Alec too, all Alec had seen were stars.

Goddamn, it'd been intense. The sensation of Zercy's seed. Not just it pumping into his depths, all thick and hot, but the tingle it evoked as it penetrated his prostate. As it passed through its membrane that senna`sohnsay had made permeable, allowing their two loads to literally merge. It'd driven Alec wild until he detonated as well and unloaded their combined cum into that pod.

When they'd both caught their breath, Zercy dug into the soil until he reached a complex network of tiny capillaries. Or at least that's what they looked like to Alec, more so than roots. Rounder. Smoother. Just like, well… just like blood vessels. Which curiously, made Alec smile.

Zercy nestled their delicate pod into the nest of exposed roots. "At this point," he murmured, covering it up with loose soil, "a couple would wait to see if Nira accepted their offering. If she agreed to fashion their young inside her womb."

"How would they know if she did?" Alec asked, watching him work.

"Within a week, tiny flowers sprout where they buried their seed. Each couple's blossoms are unique, distinguishable from all others, and remain until the young is full term." Zercy smiled but it looked sad. "The ground, it would swell, the flowers hugging its mound like a blanket."

Alec thought about that. So bizarre, yet oddly beautiful. "Do parents stay there the whole time? Take turns standing watch to keep it safe?"

"If they wish to, they can, but most just visit regularly. Each site is well guarded, day and night." Zercy gazed down at the soil. His timbre turned soft. "Maybe one day we will bond and have young of our own. An heir to the throne." He looked at Alec. "How does that sound?"

Alec hadn't seen that coming. Had been taken off-guard. Always thought that Zercy didn't want to bond. Heart thumping, he'd blurted restlessly, "I don't know," which was true, even though a part of him loved the way it sounded.

After all, bonding and childrearing equated to residing with Zercy permanently, something he couldn't impose on his team. And to shuck his duties, his responsibilities to them, just because he'd fallen for the king? It didn't feel right. It felt wrong.

But God, just the thought of living the rest of his days with Zercy? It made his heart hammer. Made his insides straight-up smile. Meaning, yup, he'd officially crossed the line of no return. When he finally left the king, it'd fucking kill him.

Exhaling, Alec peered over his shoulder at the castle. Ironic, how his teammates vigilantly plotted for ways to escape, while deep down he'd been looking for ways to stay.

Chet grunted and shook his head. "Well, if they did forget about us, like Bailey thinks and I highly suspect, then all the more reason for us to blow this joint ASAP. If we don't bust ourselves out, nobody will. It's not like the rescue team would ever be able to find us here."

The trio frowned.

Zaden lifted his chin to Chet. "We're almost ready though, yeah? Got supplies stashed in the tunnels. Got the tunnels all mapped out."

Chet nodded. "Yup, now we're just waiting for the right opportunity."

"What constitutes the right opportunity?" Bailey asked.

Chet shrugged. "Those numbskulls may not play chaperone anymore, but they still keep an eye on us, and definitely still guard our door every night. So, the way I see it, we're gonna have to bail through our windows. Just need a night where Alec can bail through his, too."

The team looked at Alec. Alec crossed his arms. Scratched his neck.

"Which would be now," Jamis established. "Since Zercy's away, right? He was the obstacle."

Chet nodded. "Yeah. I mean, I was gonna check out a few more passages I discovered last night. Gather a few more supplies, but you know what, screw it. Who knows when we'll get an opportunity like this again."

Zaden and the others nodded, looking anxious but also excited.

Alec frowned, stomach clenching. "I dunno. What about Nira? She still kinda needs us, doesn't she?"

"Yes and no," Noah answered. "Sirus has been stockpiling our semen for a while. Couple that with the synthetic we created, and they have enough to last for months."

"Months," Alec muttered. "But what about after that?"

Chet scowled. "So, what're you saying, Boss? That we should just stay here forever? Let some tree dictate our futures? Our *lives?*"

Alec exhaled and shook his head. "No. Of course not. But maybe if we just waited until an actual cure was found." He looked at the trio, searching each one's face. "You're close, right? That formula you've been working on, it's almost done?"

The three guys swapped looks.

Jamis sighed. "In theory. But we've been on the brink for ages. So close for so long, and yet we just can't seem to get there."

Bailey grunted. "Frustrating as hell. No way we can promise a definitive time frame."

Alec frowned, heart clenching. He couldn't just bolt. Couldn't leave Zercy so heartlessly. It'd wreck him. What's worse, Zercy would think that Alec abandoned him. Betrayed him. Which Alec supposed in a way would be correct.

Cursing, he rubbed his forehead. "Let's just wait a little longer. Give the rescue team a chance to find us. I can talk Zercy into letting us go if they come. He just wants to keep us safe. If they can prove they've got our backs, then he'll let us leave. He will. And in the meantime, Sirus can do more stockpiling and—"

"But what if search and rescue never comes?" Chet demanded, cutting him off. "Or they do and there's still no cure? You think Zercy's just gonna let us walk if the fate of his race still hangs in the balance? No way." He gestured to the castle. "He's *gone.* This is our chance. One we might never get again. We're ready, Boss. I know you like the guy but *come on.* He's a fantasy. We don't belong here. We need to keep some perspective."

Zaden met Alec's eyes, his expression sympathetic. "He's right, Alec. We have to go."

Alec held his friend's gaze. He knew what he said was true. That it'd be stupid to ignore this opportunity. That they couldn't possibly stay there forever. But he wanted to. God, he wanted to. So bad. To leave without saying goodbye just felt so—

"For real?" Chet bit out, clearly aggravated by Alec's reluctance. "We've waited and prepared for this for a whole fucking year and now you're suddenly dragging your feet?" Body tense, he rubbed his crew cut, then shook his head and looked around. "I can't hear this shit right now. I'm takin' a walk." Turning, he stalked his grumpy ass toward the trees.

Alec clenched his jaw. "Chet—"

"Just let him go," Zaden muttered. "He's been wound tight all day. Just needs some space."

Alec frowned, watching him go—until something moved in his periphery. He turned to look. Mannix, sauntering after their marine.

Alec's frown deepened. "What's he doing?"

Zaden eyed the Kríe, too. "Probably just keeping tabs on him… from closer range."

"That's gonna piss Chet off," Jamis chuckled. "Seek cover now."

Sure enough, as Chet reached the opening in the trees at the base of the mountain, he noticed Mannix approaching and pulled to a stop. Alec couldn't tell what he was saying, but his tone carried well enough. A slew of angry griping fired at the Kríe.

Alec exhaled and looked away. Chet was not a happy camper.

God, this situation seriously sucked.

His eyes settled on the castle, his brain churning intently. Maybe if he convinced Zercy to change the status of his team… No longer pets but guests. Truly guests of the castle. Able to come and go as they pleased. Then they wouldn't feel like prisoners anymore. Just live-in residents. Staying in a really nice place. For free. Would they want to leave so quickly then? After all, where else would they go? There was no place safer than the castle for miles around.

Heart thumping, he turned to voice the idea to his men, but was cut off before he'd even opened his mouth.

"Holy crap." Bailey gaped. "What is Chet doing?"

Jamis grimaced. "Death wish boy."

Noah groaned. "I can't watch."

Alec frowned and turned toward their bodyguard, then bit out a curse. Chet, all up in Mannix's big purple grill. Poking his chest, shoving his shoulders, as if trying to pick a fight with the guy.

Zaden exhaled. "That man is gonna get his ass kicked."

Sure enough, not long after, Mannix bared his fangs and leered, then grabbed Chet's bicep and yanked him close. Right smack into his chest. Chet face-planted his collarbone, only to yell something else and try to pull away.

Wasn't happening, though. Instead, Mannix wrangled him into a headlock, Chet's back to his front, Mannix's arm around his throat.

"Maybe we should head over before this escalates," Alec muttered.

"That'll only make things worse. Chet's pride is very sensitive." Zaden sighed and shook his head. "Let's give him a second."

Alec cursed and crossed his arms.

Gave Chet a second. And then another.

Low and behold, Chet grappled his way free. Or maybe Mannix just got bored and let him go. Either way, it didn't really improve the situation. Because instead of doing his usual—chuffing as Chet angrily stomped away—Mannix grabbed Chet's elbow and yanked him close again, then leaned in and told him something at close range. Chet visibly froze, then urgently tried to get free, but Mannix just grinned and dragged him into the woods. Specifically, out of view where no one could see.

Alec stiffened. What the hell did that Kríe think he was doing? Jaw clenched, adrenaline spiking, he looked back at Zaden. "Fuck his goddamn pride. *Let's go.*"

CHAPTER THIRTY-SEVEN

* * *

Alec sprinted for the trees with Zaden hot on his heels. To their left, several guards hustled over, too. The Kríe had less distance to travel though, and tore into the forest first, but Alec and Zaden joined them just seconds later. Joined them, but then slammed on the breaks in alarm at the fucked-up sight that greeted them straight ahead.

Chet, pinned to a boulder against the side of the mountain, with Mannix's fangs buried securely in his neck. Not that Alec could see said fangs, or them actually piercing Chet's flesh. Didn't have to, though. He could see Chet's face. And the way his body was behaving. The telltale reaction to a feverish Kríe bite. Bites that, as of late, Alec was very familiar with.

The frantic grinding. The gasps and mindless cries. Hands fumbling, body quaking. That grimace of ecstasy…

Thing was, where Alec would clutch Zercy's shoulders and yank him closer, Chet was palming Mannix's chest and *pushing away.*

Cursing, Alec and Zaden broke back into a dash, but the guards that arrived before them blocked the way.

"What are you doing?" Alec shouted. "He's attacking my guy!"

"Mah." The Kríe in front of him shook his head. "He must have consented."

"Like hell, he consented!" Alec tried to push around him.

The large guard grabbed his shoulders and held him. "Stay back. To sever a bite prematurely could cause injury."

Which was true. Zercy had told Alec as much in the past.

"So letting Mannix drain him dry is better?" Zaden shoved against his own lineman.

"He will relent," the first Kríe grunted, trying to hold Alec at bay. "He will not kill your friend. This is for pleasure."

"But Chet doesn't want it!" Alec shouted, pushing back hard. Just enough to get another glimpse of his hired gun.

Oh, God.

Mannix *was* sucking him dry! Maybe not to the point that he'd actually kill him, but enough to render Chet too weak to fight. Not that Chet ever stood a chance against the guy anyway. He overpowered Chet by a good hundred pounds.

Chet's shouts dropped to groans, his shoves now feeble, sloppy pushes. His hips were still grinding though, albeit not as vigorously as before, but he definitely appeared to be slumping against the rock.

Alec's heart hammered furiously as he fought with his obstructer. "Let go of me, goddamnit! And get that bastard off my guy!"

The trio raced in. Then more guards jogged onto the scene, led by none other than Kellim and Setch. Frowning, they eyed Alec and Zaden first, then cut their sharp gazes to Mannix and Chet.

"What is happening?" Setch barked.

But before anyone could answer, a furious bellow ripped through the forest. Every male froze in place, their wide eyes darting toward the sound. Even asshole Mannix paused what he was doing.

Alec heard the crashing flurry only seconds before he saw him.

Roni. Charging their way along the base of the mountain, like some huge, unhinged rhino on a rampage. To attack. To destroy. His murderous gold eyes like heat-seeking missiles locked on Mannix.

Mannix stiffened, then stepped back, bracing as he bared his bloody fangs. Roni roared with a lunge and the two went down in a tangle, their vicious snarls slicing past Alec's ears.

And, yup, that was pretty much all she wrote as the rest of Roni's pack stormed in behind him. Faces Alec recognized all too well. Naydo, Miros, Filli, Fin, and of course, dickhead Gesh—who, even from a distance, instantly locked eyes with Noah.

Noah stilled in surprise but kept his emotions in check. Was he happy? Not happy? Alec honestly couldn't tell. Didn't have time to contemplate it though, 'cause the next thing he knew, every Kríe had engaged, with one of the guards managing to sound his horn for aid.

Jesus. Alec glanced around as the two factions fought. What the fuck was Gesh's pack even doing there?

Wait.

Oh, hell.

There was only one reason. One purpose. They'd come on a mission to grab Noah.

Cursing, Alec anxiously glanced over toward Chet, a heap on the ground diligently trying to sit up. Alec pointed Zaden his way, "Help him!" then dashed toward the scientists, but Gesh was already gunning for them, too.

Unfortunately, before either of them could reach their mutual target, more guards flooded in and seized the trio. Not that that deterred Gesh in the slightest. He kept charging for his meesha, so Alec did as well, unwilling to risk Gesh somehow managing to snag him.

To his aggravation, however, the second Alec arrived, the guards grabbed and detained his ass, too. Gesh, on the other hand, didn't give them the chance, just plowed right into the Kríe restraining Noah. Snarling, guards lunged at the pack leader and took him down.

"Gesh!" Noah shouted. But he was quickly seized again and dragged with Alec and the others toward the castle.

"No! Stop! Wait!" Alec dug his heels in. He couldn't leave Zaden and Chet in all that chaos. They could get injured in the crosshairs. Stabbed by knives, slashed by claws.

But when he glanced back over his shoulder to seek them out, he gaped in utter shock at what he saw. Not the overpowering of Gesh's pack like he'd expected, that was for sure—what with all the guards now rushing in.

Instead, what he witnessed was another species completely, swooping down from the trees with bows and arrows. Unloading repeatedly into the guards as they landed, their blond hair down their backs like sleek white capes. They looked familiar. He couldn't place them. And yet, these creatures were only half of it.

His gaze darted past them to a whole other regiment rushing forward through the brush with fiery purpose. They had weapons, too, some gripping pistols, some wielding big badass rifles. Mowing down all in their path with invisible bullets.

Alec's heart tripped as he stared. This species he knew well.
Human.

It was the rescue team.
Holy hell.

Momentarily dumbfounded, he watched the cavalries descend, offering much needed backup to Gesh's pack. And yeah, they definitely needed it, already grossly outmanned. Although honestly, at the rate the castle guards kept flooding in, they'd *all* be outnumbered within minutes.

Behind Alec, Kellim barked, "Get them back to the castle!" as members of Gesh's crew bounded over.

In seconds, the pack mates had Gesh up off the ground and the guards who'd held him, knocked out of commission. Their blazing gazes locked on Alec and the scientists next. Setch and Kellim rushed forward to block their advance. Right as they clashed, an arrow nailed Setch's shoulder just as a pack member drove his blade through Kellim's gut.

"NOOO!!" Setch roared, watching his brother go down.

Face twisted in rage, he lunged at the assailant, but a barrage of bullet pulses dropped him like lead. He crashed to the ground at Kellim's side.

Gesh and the others stormed past and engaged the remaining guards, but only managed to grab Alec and Noah before more attacked.

Alec stumbled haphazardly as they dragged him along, staring back in horror at Setch and Kellim. They were his friends. He'd grown to care about them. He glanced at all the other Nirans down. Oh, God. They were everywhere. Pierced with arrows. Stabbed with blades. So much blood on his team's hands. This was wrong!

Fury exploded. Using combat tactics he'd learned as a soldier, he grappled with his handler to get free. "Let go of me! This is bullshit! What the fuck are you assholes doing?"

"Liberating you," Gesh snarled, tightly gripping Noah's arm. "So keep moving and I will let you thank me later."

Alec looked at Noah, who also looked distraught by what just happened, then glanced back over his shoulder at Jamis and Bailey. The guards had them nearly to the mouth of the forest, the scientists' gazes urgent as they struggled against their hold. They didn't want to be left behind, to be separated from the team, but were no match for the big Kríe ushering them forward.

The sight only made Alec angrier. He turned back and fought harder. "Get off of me, goddamnit!" He swung at the Kríe gripping him, landing punches, elbows, and kicks before the male stopped him.

"What is wrong with you?" the huge male grated. "We are helping you *escape*."

Alec glared up at him, meeting his eyes for the first time.

Naydo.

It was Naydo.

Alec glowered. "Let. Me. Go."

Naydo eyed him uneasily as they hustled along, clearly confused by his behavior. "You do not want to be free?"

"No, goddamnit! Now let me go!" He *didn't* want to leave. Not like this. It was too harsh of a severance. Zercy wouldn't understand. He'd be furious.

But just as much, Alec wasn't ready to say goodbye. He loved Zercy. Intensely. The Kríe was his home. For all he knew, the rescue team's ship was parked on the other side of this mountain, waiting to spirit his men back into space.

His chest constricted. No. He wasn't ready to live without him.

Heart pounding riotously, he steeled his resolve and upped his urgent efforts to get free.

Naydo held his bicep tight, but Alec's struggles still slowed them down.

"Deal with him!" Gesh snapped, ducking as an arrow tore by. "We do not have time for his madness. We must get out of here *now*."

Naydo growled, then gave a nod and frowned down at Alec. "I am sorry, moyo. But you have given me no choice."

Alec stilled at his tone.

Naydo drew back his fist.

"No!" Noah shouted.

Alec cursed, then—

WHAM!

Lights out.

* * *

491

Garret had never been in battle before. He hadn't been a soldier like Eli and Helix, or even the other team's captain. But as he glanced around, his back to Kegan's as they feverishly discharged their pistols, he was certain this was exactly what battle looked like.

All around him, huge males bellowed and shouted as they engaged, ducking and lunging as they attacked their opponents. Arrows flew non-stop in a horizontal shower. So did the rapid-fire spray of Eli and Helix's rifles.

Garret and the rest of his team kept unloading, too, both arms raised with guns blazing in each hand. Impressively, some Kríe managed to block the bolts with their arm guards, but with his men's fierce aim and a couple solid shots, most just crashed like dead weight to the ground.

Not that they *were* dead.

Unlike the bullets of Garret's forefathers, modern slugs were pure energy. Condensed current that incapacitated but didn't kill.

He glanced to his right as he *blam-blam-blam-blammed!* spotting one of the guys from the science team. The big one who Roni had deviated from their plans to save. Why the Kríe had snapped like that, Garret had no clue, but as they'd lain in wait earlier, he'd noticed Roni growing tenser. Fangs bared, snarls rumbling as he stared at something in the distance. Then just like that, he'd roared and took off running.

Garret had cursed, but quickly spotted what had set the Kríe off. A castle guard assaulting one of the science team's men. Needless to say, Garret was pretty surprised that a Kríe would give two shits about a human. Maybe Gesh, since he seemed to care so much about Noah, but Roni? No, Garret definitely hadn't seen that coming. And it definitely hadn't been Noah he'd been gunning for.

Going by the file, it was Chet, the military escort. The one, Garret remembered now, that Roni mentioned sparring with. The one he called *bitch* with a smile and open fondness. The one he stayed protectively close to even now.

Garret's mag ran dry. He swapped the thing out, watching as Chet and another guy tag-teamed a guard. The marine looked off balance, ready to topple over any second. Luckily, his buddy seemed competent enough for both of them.

Garret got back to firing, stealing glimpses of said buddy. Dark tan, jet black hair, onyx eyes. Must be Zaden. The co-pilot. Second in command to Captain Hamlin. Zaden, who currently was doing all the heavy lifting. In the time it took Chet to land one drunken punch, Zaden had already delivered at least three.

In Chet's defense though, the marine *was* a few pints too low. Garret hadn't realized until after Roni had gone ballistic that Chet's attacker had been draining the poor guy. But once hell broke loose and Garret got his first real look at him, Chet's slumped body and pasty face had said it all.

A bellow in Garret's ear had him whirling to the left. A castle guard, charging him at full throttle.

"Shit!" Garret barked.

Both he and Kegan turned to blast him, but the Kríe had gotten too close too fast. He plowed them over, the three crashing hard to the ground, Garret's co-pilot beneath him, that big unruly beast on top of Garret.

The male shoved to his knees, then roared and raised his paw, readying to take a vicious swipe. Garret's eyes went wide as those sharp claws came barreling down. A split second before contact though, the huge Kríe went flying, tumbling across the underbrush to Garret's right.

Garret gasped and whipped his head around, gaze locking on Airis' face. He'd just landed another of his badass two-footed kicks.

Yanking Garret to his feet, the Tohrí briefly pulled him close. "I saved you, oddling." He grinned. "You owe me a debt."

Garret blinked. Airis smirked, then tugged his co-pilot up, too.

But before Garret could formulate even a single response, a shout up ahead stole his full attention. Gesh and some others quickly headed their way. Others being his pack mates, a blond who must be Noah, and another human Garret couldn't make out. Not because the guy was looking the other way or something, but because he'd been slung over Naydo's big-ass freaking shoulder.

"Shit," Garret muttered. The dude looked out cold. Garret quickly ran the science team's file through his brain to figure out who he was. Wasn't Chet, Zaden, or Noah. Garret glanced past the stranger's group, spotting two more of the science team in castle guard possession. They were younger, like Noah. Must be the other two astrobiologists. Which made the unconscious guy over Naydo's shoulder their frickin' captain.

"Goddamnit," he grated. Had he been injured in the fight?

"Cover them!" Eli shouted, redirecting his huge pulse rifle. A spray of pure current tore into the guards in hot pursuit, those who'd been gaining on Gesh and Noah's retreating posse. The castle Kríe roared, then toppled down like bricks. But a fresh wave of guards just stormed forward behind them.

Another horn sounded in the distance, the cacophony of battle getting louder. More guards were coming. Garret could see them barreling across the field. Their little three-fold task force was about to get overrun. They needed to get out of there fuckin-A pronto. Meaning they had to grab the scientists *right fucking now*.

Heart racing, he glanced back at Chet and Zaden. Then Roni just off to their right. All three were outnumbered now, countless guards on the brink of apprehending them.

"Fuck," he bit out, then shouted over his shoulder, "Kegan, two o'clock!" He pointed in Chet's direction.

"Roger that!" Kegan tore off to help, pistols blasting.

He looked back at the youngest two still in Kríe guard custody, then turned to Airis, but he'd already delved back into battle. Still nearby, but busy unloading arrow after arrow, only breaking to whirl around and crack an adversary upside the head with his bow. That or kick the big-ass bastards' feet out from under them whenever they got too close for comfort. In other words, he was indisposed, completely swamped like everyone else.

Without question, they'd pissed on the goddamn hornet's nest.

Garret spun toward his teammates. "Paris, Sasha!" he shouted "Cover us!" Then he turned to his marines and pointed to Jamis and Bailey. "We can't leave without those scientists! Blaze a trail!"

They nodded and instantly directed their firepower forward, charging straight ahead as they unloaded. Garret took off after them, then low and behold, he heard Airis' voice from close behind.

"Tohrí!" the male shouted. "Nennáy!" *Assist!*

Next thing Garret knew, arrows volleyed past his head, adding to Paris and Sasha's staccato of current. Advancing Kríe went down in droves, but just as many ducked and dodged. Moments later, Airis fell in step running at Garret's side.

"You are very optimistic, oddling. Or very, very foolish." He gestured ahead with his arrow. "There are too many."

Garret ground his teeth, locking his sights on his two sole objectives. The pair of young scientists getting hauled back to the castle. Already, they were halfway across the field. Completely out of tree cover and to Garret's dismay, surrounded by more guards stampeding past them.

Son of a bitch. Had the king's whole army been unleashed?

On the heels of his thought, they neared the mouth of the forest, where just ahead Helix and Eli ground to a halt. The bottleneck's concentrated flow of guards was just too heavy, forcing his marines to stop in order to contain them. Garret and Airis slammed on the brakes too, and bolstered their defense, but their added efforts just weren't enough.

"Not happening!" Helix bellowed above his rifle's rapid fire.

"Gotta pull back, Chief!" Eli shouted over his shoulder.

"Fuck!" Garret barked. Without thinking, he looked at Airis. "This is our only shot! We gotta get them!"

Airis held his gaze, his big brown eyes anxious, intense, then gave a brisk nod. "I will see it done."

Garret blinked in surprise. He hadn't expected that response. But before he could say more, Airis tipped back his head and cupped the sides of his mouth. "Dekdónni, retrieve!"

Instantly, booming battle squawks ripped through the canopy above, thick branches jostling as the winged beasts all took flight.

"Shit," Garret breathed, eyes darting back to the field, where the formidable flock descended, all but two dive-bombing the guards. Swooping down and snatching them up off their feet, only to toss them into their counterparts like bowling balls.

The castle Krié roared, turning their attention from the forest to go after the dekdónni with fiery fury.

"Tohrí, assist!" Airis barked again.

With the guards momentarily distracted, the team could afford the drop-in support as the blond warriors rained arrows down on the dekdónni's attackers.

The scene was chaotic.

But then Garret saw the reason behind it—the two dekdónni now gunning for the scientists. Swooping down, they slammed their huge wings into their handlers, swords piercing their feathered appendages as Kríe went tumbling.

The beasts cried out but didn't relent.

Beside Garret, Airis stumbled.

Garret grabbed his arm and steadied him, confused by his display, but quickly returned his attention to the mayhem. Just in time, incidentally, to watch the dekdónni clutch both men, then launch with powerful hind legs back into the sky.

The Kríe roared, irate, lunging and swiping with their claws, but the foursome had already risen well out of reach.

Behind Garret, the science team's other members cheered. He glanced over his shoulder, catching the blond, Noah, grinning ecstatically. Clearly, those were his friends who'd just been rescued. Garret smiled and looked at Airis—then instantly tensed.

The Tohrí was grimacing.

"Whoa. Are you okay?"

Airis nodded once, then jogged ahead and, again, cupped the sides of his mouth. "Dekdónni, climb!" he shouted. "High! Dekdónni, *high!*"

Garret frowned, hustling forward to rejoined him. "Why'd you command that? Those guards don't have guns or even arrows that I saw. It's not like they can shoot 'em once they're airborne."

"The *guards* cannot shoot them." Airis watched the dekdónni retreating. "But the sentries on the mountaintops *can.*"

"Sentries?"

Airis nodded, eyes glued to the dekdónni with cargo. "Nún…" he murmured warily to himself. "Their injuries… The weight is too much… They will not make it…"

Garret turned his gaze to the beasts. They were fleeing toward the waterfall, their huge wings powering valiantly, men clutched in their forelegs. But Airis was right. With their injured wings, despite how impressively high they'd already climbed, they didn't seem able to increase their altitude farther.

His chest clenched. "They're in danger?"

Airis opened his mouth, but before he could speak, streaks of blue shot from the mountaintop straight toward the pair. "Nún!" Airis gasped, gripping his bow as he watched.

The dekdónni squawked, barely dodging the brutal blasts.

Garret cursed, following the discharge back to its source, and sure enough, he spotted what looked like an inconspicuous watchtower. Another blast ripped from said spot across the sky, again barely missing its two targets.

"Faster!" Airis barked, as if to no one but himself, his attention locked solely on the beasts.

They were nearly at the waterfall. More missiles of current tore straight for them. The dekdónni carting Jamis dipped to the right just in time, but the one carrying Bailey wasn't so lucky.

The shot nailed it right in the shoulder. It screeched in pain, its body going rigid, then instantly started to plummet.

Airis sucked in sharply, his knees buckling beneath him.

Garret caught him a second time. "Damn, man. What the—"

The dekdónni's cry in the distance instantly ripped his focus away. Glancing back, he watched the falling beast, with Bailey still in its grasp, snap out of it just yards from crashing into the water. Barking and squawking, it furiously started flapping, then attempted again to make the daunting climb.

Immediately, it came under another slew of fire, but seemed more determined than ever not to get hit. As if it'd made some mental notes during its paralyzed nose-dive and was trying out a few new maneuvering techniques. Twisting, arching, ducking, juking. Missing each hit by the skin of its teeth. Tense moments later, with the other dekdónny safely gone, it finally reached the precipice of the waterfall.

Garret's heart pounded, watching. It was on the home stretch, still dodging like a champ. Just a little farther. But right as it cleared the highest treetops of the mountain, a shot streaked forward that it just couldn't avoid. Not that the dekdónni didn't try with all the energy it had left. In fact, it probably would have if not for the added weight. Because as the blast made contact, it only grazed its foreleg.

Bailey, however, got nailed square in the chest.

Instantly he went limp, no doubt knocked unconscious, while the dekdónni flapped wildly, fighting to maintain its hold. But the hit to its arm made his weight just too much, and in seconds he was plummeting toward the water. He hit with a splash just feet before the waterfall, then visibly washed right over the edge.

"NO!!" Noah howled, racing forward, eyes wild. "Oh, Jesus! We gotta go get him! He's gonna drown!"

Gesh caught him with a snarl. "He is gone. We cannot save him."

Noah fought his hold frantically. "Bullshit! We gotta try!"

All around though, the majority seemed to share Gesh's opinion. After all, that waterfall was over a half mile away. Even without guards to contend with, they'd never make it in time.

Zaden went to Noah, looking just as freshly floored and distraught. "He's right." His voice was thick with emotion. "There's nothing…Fuck, there's nothing we can do."

Noah shook his head, his face crumbling. "Oh, God… No… Not Bailey."

"Guuuys!" Eli shouted. "Break time's motherfuckin' over! The guards are gunning this way again—with a vengeance!"

Helix fell back into blasting a non-stop torrent of charged bullets. "Gotta go! Ain't no reason left to stay!"

Too true.

"Fall back!" Garret bellowed. "Fall back!"

All three races took off running, the enemies they'd been combatting taken out, as on the front line, Eli yanked something from his belt and lobbed it forward. Garret watched it hit the ground, ever awed by the sight as an energy barrier exploded across the forest. A sizzling, impenetrable wall that stretched a mile in each direction, separating everything in front of it from everything behind.

"Party wall's up," Eli shouted, whirling around. "We got five minutes! Move! Move! Move!"

But as they dashed through the forest, hurtling bushes and logs, Garret heard the pack leader snarling up ahead.

"We do not have enough time. The escape route is too far. They will catch us. You *hewmens* move too slow."

"How 'bout you shut the fuck up," Noah snapped as he ran. "*None* of us would be in this mess if it wasn't for you." His features darkened. "And *Bailey* would still be here."

"But I rescued you. I have redeemed myself."

"The fuck you have," Noah laughed, the sound like ice-cold acid. "Now I have *two* things to hate you for."

They approached a mammoth downed log. Gesh clutched Noah from behind, then hefted him atop it like he weighed nothing.

Noah turned and glared down at him, his brown eyes raw with grief. "Don't touch me again. Do you understand me? I can get over a goddamn log without your help."

Gesh frowned up at him. "But meesha—"

"Do not *meesha* me, Gesh. You dicked me over hard. I'm done with you."

Garret's eyebrows shot high at Noah's words.

Had he and Gesh hooked up or something? Gotten *romantic?*

Gesh scowled as Noah turned and jumped down to the other side. "But I rescued you," he grumbled under his breath, climbing over. "Took three arrows in my ass to make this happen."

Garret smirked.

Two seconds later, pale-faced Chet called to the group. "I know another way outta here. A tunnel below the mountain. Will bet my nuts those pricks don't know it exists."

The science team's co-pilot Zaden nodded. "Yeah, up ahead." He pointed into the distance. "Behind that cluster of bushes and huge boulders."

Garret nodded. "Let's do it." If what Gesh said was true, they didn't really have much of a choice.

He glanced at Airis. The Tohrí moved silently to his right, his expression masked, but at least he no longer looked pained. What happened before was weird. Garret would have to ask Airis about it. Preferably when they weren't running for their lives.

They reached the hidden tunnel a few seconds later. The opening wasn't that big. Maybe five feet tall and three feet wide, max. Garret waited for everyone to squeeze in ahead of him, holding the branches aside that concealed it. Kegan, Airis, and Kato waited with him. By the time all had entered and only the four of them remained, Garret could hear the guards in the distance stampeding their way.

"After you," he muttered, shoving Kegan through the hole.

Kato went next.

Airis, however, paused to flick a glance toward the sky.

Garret frowned, understanding. "The dekdónni that rescued our guys. One of them was yours. One was Kotchka."

"Leí." Airis smiled a little. "She has always been one of the strongest."

Garret nodded, reflecting. "Where're they taking the scientist who made it?"

Airis took the branch Garret was holding and gestured for him to enter. "A secret rendezvous not far from here."

CHAPTER THIRTY-EIGHT

***

Alec roused to the sound of two deep-timbred males arguing. Unfortunately, he recognized both of their voices.

"I should flay you for what you have done!" Gesh snarled, his words echoing. They must be in a tunnel, or some kind of cave. "That was not the plan we agreed on! Those castle guards should have never seen our faces!"

"So they saw us!" Roni snapped back. "At least we are still alive."

"Not for long!" Gesh shouted. "Because now we are fugitives! Traitors who are working with the enemy! The king is going to hunt us down. Hunt us all down and kill us! Because *you* could not follow the gods-damned plan!"

"I had my reasons," Roni growled.

"Your reasons were not good enough!"

Alec grimaced and peeled his eyes open just as Roni stepped forward angrily. "So it is okay to champion your meesha, but I cannot champion my bitch?"

"I'm not your bitch!" Chet barked from somewhere nearby.

Alec groaned and sat up straighter, then looked to his right. Specifically, at the person he'd been propped against. Sad brown eyes met his, dimly lit by nearby torches.

"Noah," he rasped.

"Hey, Cap," the scientist murmured. God, what was wrong with him? He sounded like someone died.

Alec winced and palmed his cheek—why'd his face hurt so bad?—then gingerly turned and checked out their surroundings. It was dark. Really dark. But from the light of the torches, he could tell that he'd been right to guess a cave. No tunnel could accommodate all the silhouetted bodies standing around.

Memories began returning.

Mannix assaulting Chet… Gesh's pack showing up… Then others, too. Another species. Then the rescue team…

Alec frowned and squeezed his eyes shut. More memories filtered back.

All three factions fighting together against a throng of castle guards... People shouting... Bodies down... Gesh and his pack mates grabbing him and Noah...

His pulse spiked anxiously.

He hadn't wanted to leave... Had been fighting to stay... Naydo's apologetic face... Noah shouting, then—

Alec's eyes snapped wide.

That asshole had knocked him out.

So he could take Alec without struggle.

From Zercy's castle.

Oh, God.

Alec scrambled to his feet, heart suddenly racing, as Gesh and Roni continued to bicker. "Shut the fuck up!" The two Kríe stopped, looking his way in stunned silence. "Where are we? What have you done?" Alec restlessly looked around.

Zaden stepped from the darkness. "You're awake."

"Zaden," Alec exhaled. "What's going on? Where are we?"

"Beneath the mountain," his friend explained, his voice subdued just like Noah's. "We escaped the battle using the tunnels Chet and I found. The guards don't know about 'em or else they'd've found us by now. We stopped for a sec to pick up the supplies Chet stashed but are getting ready to move again. We're tight on time."

Naydo lumbered over and peered down at him. "My apologies for hitting you."

Alec glared up at him. "You're a dick."

Naydo frowned and turned to Zaden. "Gesh ordered me to do it. I could not refuse. He is alpha. I must obey."

Zaden eyed him coldly. "Why are you pleading your case to me? I'm not the one you decked." Just the one he *fucked.*

"Because I care if *you* are angry with me," Naydo admitted matter-of-factly. "Him? Not so much. Only a little."

Alec rolled his eyes and shook his head.

Zaden blinked, then scowled. "Go away."

Naydo exhaled and ambled off just as Chet headed over.

"Boss," he muttered. Even in the dim light, the bite on his neck was visible.

Alec frowned. "How're you feeling?"

"Probably better than you." His gray gaze studied Alec's face. "You're lucky he didn't break your jaw."

Alec sighed and rubbed his cheek again. More men came over and joined them. Men Alec had yet to officially meet.

"Captain Hamlin," the dark blond greeted. He extended his hand. "I'm Captain Garret Scott of the search and rescue team. Good to finally meet you. Glad you're okay."

Alec clasped the guy's palm. Nodded slightly. "Thanks for coming."

Garret grinned a little and shrugged. "Only took us a year."

He and his swapped introductions with Alec and his team. The ones that were present at least. Two were missing.

Alec glanced around. "Where's Bailey and Jamis?"

Chet and Zaden fell silent. Noah's whole demeanor wilted. Alec tensed. Oh, God. What happened? Ice doused his veins. Clenching his jaw, he muttered, "Where. Are. They?"

"Alec..." Zaden slowly dragged a hand down his face. "During the battle, the guards took them and—"

"Yeah, I saw that. Before Naydo punched me."

Zaden nodded. "Right, they'd been separated from the rest our team. Were fighting for all they were worth to get back to us. We tried to get them, literally the entire contingent at one point, but there were too many guards and—"

"So, they're at the castle." Alec eased. He'd been thinking of way worse scenarios.

"No," Noah blurted, his voice cracking. "They're not at the castle. Jamis got carted away by a dekdónni and Bailey... Bailey's dead."

Alec's heart stopped as all blood drained from his face. "What?" he rasped. He'd heard him wrong. He had to have heard him wrong.

"He's gone," Zaden murmured. "While trying to escape, he... he drowned."

Alec shook his head. Shook it again. Swallowed repeatedly. He'd been responsible for him. And he'd failed him. He'd let Bailey die.

Anger welled in his chest. Furious at himself. And everyone else. "You're telling me in the ten minutes I was out, we lost a fucking teammate? We lost Bailey?!"

"He is not lost."

Alec stilled at the unfamiliar voice. Turning toward the sound, he met a tall blond's gaze. A male from the other faction who'd helped whisk them away. So familiar looking, yet Alec had never met him before.

"What did you say?"

The male stepped forward. "He is not lost. He is not dead."

"What do you mean?" Noah stared at him. He looked scared to even hope.

The blond turned to him. Studied his drawn, distraught features. "Do not worry about your friend. The Oonmaiyos will take care of him."

Noah's mouth fell open. So did Zaden and Chet's.

"The Oonmaiyos?" Alec repeated. "Are you serious?"

He inclined his head.

"But how could you possibly know that?"

"Because the Oonmaiyos oversee *all* waterways in these parts. Their aquatic realm is vast and heavily patrolled."

"They could get to him in minutes?" Noah asked, eyes widening. "'Cause that's all the time it takes for a human to drown."

The male smirked a little. "We were making quite a commotion. I suspect they saw him coming before he ever hit the water."

Noah exhaled and dragged a hand through his golden locks, his brown eyes darting around in visible thought. He looked back at the tall blond. "What will they do with him? Where will they take him?"

"If he is injured, they will tend to him, then return him, as he is not theirs."

Alec frowned. "Return him to where?"

"The waterfall flows into Múnrahki lake. Múnrahki lake is castle territory. So, they will take him back to the castle. Back to the king."

Alec stared at him. Then nodded. "We're going back to get him."

"What?" Chet barked.

Gesh chuffed darkly. "I do not think so."

"Yeah," Garret muttered, crossing his arms. "That's not a good idea." His team grunted in unison, the two marines looking downright disgruntled.

"We can't just leave him," Alec argued. And if they went back, he could do damage control with Zercy.

"Look," Garret reasoned. "If we go back there, those guards will apprehend the whole lot of us. We're not exactly their favorite people right now."

"Then I'll go back myself."

"No. No way." Garret's voice turned sharp. "Listen, man. Ever since we got here, we've been risking our necks to find you. And that battle back there? That was no joke. We put our lives on the line to get your team outta that prison. Hell, so did every male in this cave. If you go back, that makes everything we did for nothing. Do not disrespect us like that. We'll figure something else out."

The tall blond male concurred. "I will send word to the Oonmaiyos and tell them to hold on to your friend. He will be safe."

Alec rubbed his forehead anxiously. He needed to get back. Preferably before Zercy returned from his trip. "I... I dunno..."

"They would punish you if you returned," Roni piped up. "Severely. Assume you knew of the plan all along."

"No." Alec shook his head. "Zercy wouldn't... He wouldn't order that."

"Not really feeling the urge to test that theory," Chet muttered. He met Alec's eyes. "We didn't just wander off without his permission. We put a hurtin' on his guards. Some might have even died."

Alec's heart clenched in his chest, remembering Kellim. He groaned. "Kellim was one of his royal guard."

Gesh snarled and glared at his pack mate. "Did you hear that, Beng? You killed a royal guard. That is punishable by death, and he will probably want *my* head."

Beng grunted from the shadows. "You told me to stop him."

"Ságe's cock," Gesh snapped. "I said stop him, not *gut* him." He turned to Alec, eyes grim. "The king is going to be very, *very* angry."

"Yeah, no way I'm going back there," Chet repeated.

Zaden shook his head and looked at Alec. "Me neither, man. The king's not stable. You know this deep down. He could snap and that'd be it. Are you really willing to take that kind of chance?"

With himself, yes, Alec thought. But with his team? The other team?

No.

Zaden was right and he knew it. Zercy *wasn't* completely stable. Hadn't been since the very first day Alec met him. Not that Alec didn't love him anyway despite his whiplash mood swings. But because of them, he couldn't guarantee the others' safety. And if he couldn't do that, then he couldn't make them go back, and since they were a team and he was their captain, they were still his responsibility. So, he couldn't go back without them. He had to stay.

His heart tore in his chest. Rubbing his brow again, he rasped, "Okay. We'll grab Bailey from the Oonmaiyos. Now tell me about Jamis."

"He is safe with our dekdónni," the blond reassured.

"Your what?"

"They're, uh, their friends," Zaden offered, "for lack of a better word. By the way, this is Airis. I was just talking to him a minute ago. He played a big part in search and rescue finding us."

Alec peered back up at the blond. So familiar looking... "Thanks. I'm Alec. Captain of the science team."

Airis inclined his head. "We will reunite with your Jamis soon."

"Actually," Garret prompted, "we should probably get a move on. Airis has offered us refuge, but his place isn't close, and this whole region's gonna be crawling with Kríe before too long."

"Mah." Gesh crossed his arms. "We will not go with the Tohrí. The agreement was to work with them until I retrieved my meesha, and I have. I will associate with them no more. They are enemies of my people."

Alec frowned at Gesh—then froze. *Tohrí.* He knew that name. Cutting his gaze back to Airis, he studied him fixedly. Tan, lean, muscular, with long white-blond hair. The same race he'd caught a brief glimpse of in the castle, enslaved for plotting to kill the Kríe's Niran tree.

His whole body vibrated. "You're one of *them*," he gritted.

Airis stilled. "One of whom?"

"The race who conspired to eradicate all Kríe."

All the air sucked from the enclosure as every Niran looked their way.

Airis eyed him intently, his features instantly tight. "You are mistaken. All my people have ever done is try to find common ground with the Kríe. That is why we offered our prince to wed their king, so our two kingdoms would finally be in accord."

Alec ground his teeth. "Don't you mean, so you could get him inside their castle so he could poison and kill their mother tree?"

Airis paled, lips parting. In his defense, he *did* look shocked. Glancing to his equally shocked looking band members, he shook his head. "Nún. We would *never* try to exterminate a species, let alone poison Mother Nira."

Gesh and Roni stepped closer, baring their fangs.

Airis stiffened, then pointed at them furiously as another Tohrí joined him. "Do not even *think* to challenge me, boors. I will end you." He looked back at Alec. "What you believe is wrong," he growled low. "I vow it on my life. Whoever has told you these things spews lies."

Alec stepped close, just as pissed. He was speaking on Zercy's behalf. "The king told me himself. Said he witnessed your prince *in the act*. Hell, I saw their tree nearly dead with my own eyes. My team's been helping keep her alive for months."

"Shit," Chet muttered. "You don't know the half of it."

Tension thickened in the air. Airis' band swapped devastated looks. All the while, even Garret's team eyed them guardedly.

Finally, Airis shook his head. "We... I swear, we had no idea. And I am certain that our king had none as well." His jaw went tight, his brown eyes distraught. "Prince Talik must have been acting on personal motives."

Likely story.

Although in truth, as Alec stared at the male, he had to admit, Airis *did* look genuinely leveled.

"We must return home *now*," Airis' friend prompted, his voice tense. "Warn our people. Surely an attack is imminent. All in our province are in danger."

Alec frowned and turned to Garret. "I won't go with them. I refuse to. I can't do that to Zercy. He's been good to us. It'd feel like a betrayal."

Garret scowled. "With all due respect, we don't really have a lot of options."

"They can come with us," Gesh offered. He stepped next to Noah.

Noah frowned but didn't move away.

Option two sucked but it was better than the alternative. Stiffly, Alec nodded.

Garret gaped in disbelief. "You realize he doesn't have any place to go either. He's a fugitive. Wherever he lives is as good as torched now."

Gesh growled and crossed his bulky arms. "We are friendly with a tribe to the north of here. The fire horde. Their keep is heavily fortified. We will stay with them."

Garret looked at Airis.

Airis inclined his head. "I am familiar with this tribe. They dwell in the mountains of Titus. You can see their realm from the cliffs of my own land."

"Perfect," Alec concluded, looking at Garret. "Your friends'll be close."

Garret coughed an incredulous laugh, then pointed at Gesh. "My team's not going with him. We don't trust him as far as we could throw 'em."

Alec scowled and glanced between them. "But you just ran a mission together."

"Because we *had* to. Otherwise, he'd've kept on hunting us."

"Hunting you?" Alec's brows hiked.

"Yeah, to trade us for your boy Noah." Garret cut Gesh a glare. "On our very first meeting, his pack abducted our asses." He glanced at Airis. "If it wasn't for the Tohrí, we'd be stuck at the king's castle right now with you."

Alec frowned, eyeing the three factions who'd come together on his team's behalf. They'd clearly all had completely different agendas.

"Look," Garret grated. "We don't have time to get into the specifics. Bottom line? My team ain't going with those conniving bastards and your team shouldn't be either."

Alec shook his head. "Until someone can prove that these Tohrí are innocent, I won't be associated with them. End of discussion."

"And we'll be staying with our captain," Zaden added.

Garret clenched his jaw, his expression that of pure agitation. "I can't believe you all would rather go with the assholes that *captured and sold* you, over your own goddamn people who came to rescue you."

"It's not about them over you," Chet piped in gruffly. "It's about our team sticking together. So, if Alec won't go with these guys, then neither will the rest of us."

"Maybe it's better this way, Chief," Eli, the marine, pointed out. "It's probably not a good idea to put all our eggs in one basket anyway. We spread out, disperse, until more help arrives to get us. More eyes on the ground is a good thing, yeah? We'll be privy to a lot more of what's going on in different regions. God knows if a war breaks out, that'll be worth its weight in gold. And our telecommunication gear'll keep us in touch with them at a second's notice."

"Uh, yeah. About that," Chet ground out, glaring at Roni. "We don't have our gear. These dildos we'll be traveling with took it."

Roni smirked and held his gaze. "Would you like it back, my bitch? Because we have it stashed and waiting for you at your ship."

Chet stilled, then just like that, his whole face lit up, his irritation evaporating fast into thin air. Even Alec couldn't hold his smile back. To have their gear again, all their tech? Shit, yeah. It suddenly felt like Christmas.

"Then disregard," Chet chuckled, rubbing the top of his head. "Communications will not be a problem."

Garret brooded for a long, angry, aggravated moment. Finally, he nodded. "Okay. Whatever. But we seriously gotta go. We'll discuss this more on the way. Let's move."

* * *

509

With no time to stop at Gesh's compound for additional supplies, the three parties agreed to travel together until their two paths ultimately diverged. Which Alec was grateful for. Their two teams needed time to get better acquainted. They hadn't exactly started off on the right foot.

By the time Chet and Zaden led them to the tunnels' outermost exit, their men were all at ease and talking freely. Lots of catching up, lots of filling each other in, on all the pertinent stuff both groups needed to know about.

They traveled north for hours, briefly pausing for breaks and, at one point, stopping to grab some more supplies. Garret's team's gear. Evidently, en route to the castle, they'd stashed their stuff, intending to snag them again later on their way back. Which was very fcool, because when it came time to finally make camp, they offered up half of their tents to Alec's team.

Not that Alec would ever actually be able to sleep. His chest hurt too much, the ache inside only strengthening. All he could think about, all he wanted more than anything, was to turn around and go back. But no one would allow it. They'd already been down that road.

He sighed, quietly sitting atop a log in front of the fire—a tiny fire, so as not to give their location away. At this point, his only hope was that Zercy came and found him. Tracked him down somehow and took him back home. Problem was, if Zercy *did* come, it wouldn't be pretty, possibly costing yet more lives on his arrival. Because he wouldn't be calm. Nor collected. Nor eager to *talk*. He'd be on a rampage. Unleashing his wrath. And that… Yeah, that wouldn't end well at all.

Frown deepening, Alec stared at the crackling flames, at the tiny embers sparking up into the night. He needed to get it together. His men were counting on their captain.

Honestly, it wasn't like this turn of events was unexpected. All along, his team suspected others would eventually come. And once they did—considering the extenuating circumstances—one of two things would've transpired to recover Alec's guys. An exchange of words with Zercy convincing him to relinquish the team, or a tactical effort to retrieve them on their own.

Looked like they didn't have much faith in diplomacy. And honestly, why would they? Considering the way Gesh's pack had treated them, and the knowledge that Zercy had *bought* Alec's team for pets? It was no wonder Garret had chosen to go the route he had. To him, all Kríe must seem like raging unethical savages.

Which, in fairness, most were. Savages, at least. And their principles? Yeah, pretty subjective, too.

To his right, Alec noticed someone approaching in his periphery. He glanced up just as Miros sat down to join him.

Miros.

Alec stilled at the sight of him. With so many in their group, and their entire trip made in darkness, he hadn't even spotted the male until now.

"Alec." Miros smiled, his friendly demeanor strangely comforting. Familiar, even though they hadn't seen each other in ages. Sure, he still carried himself like a typical arrogant Kríe, but he also still exuded his likability. Which wasn't to be confused with any other kind of feelings. Free of senna`sohnsay, Alec wasn't attracted to him at all.

He lifted his chin in greeting. "Hey. Long time no see."

Miros nodded, his black dreads swaying. God, he was big. "How have you been? Sometimes I think of you. Wonder how you are faring."

Alec looked at him. A dry smile tugged at his lips. "Wow. How good of you. To casually contemplate my wellbeing. The guy you fucked and then sold into captivity."

Miros' amicable expression ebbed. He turned his gaze to the fire. "Did he treat you well?" he murmured. "King Zercy? Was he kind?" His big eyes looked remorseful. So did his frown.

Alec sighed. Deep down, he knew that Miros felt bad. Even that fateful day at the castle, he'd looked contrite. "Yeah," he muttered quietly. "He was good to me. Really good."

Maybe there was something in his tone that tipped Miros off, but he returned his gaze to Alec's face and keenly searched it. "Back in the cave, I heard the way you spoke of the king. Unwilling to betray him. Fiercely loyal."

Alec scratched his cheek and glanced away. "I've grown fond of him. We've gotten close."

Miros canted his head. "Close?" He studied Alec curiously. Suddenly, his black brows rose high. "You like him," he rumbled, smirking. "You like the king and his big cock."

Alec coughed, cheeks heating, and opened his mouth to deny it. But as he met Miros' gaze he couldn't. And didn't want to. "Yeah," he nodded, chest tightening. "I like him a lot." His lips twitched. He muffled a chuckle. "Him and his cock."

Miros chuffed. "Not surprising. All Kríe cocks are impressive. But a *royal* Kríe cock?" He grinned thoughtfully. "I can only imagine."

Alec fought a smile and shook his head. Miros continued to regard him. "I am glad," he finally offered, "that I resisted and did not mark you. You were not mine. You are his. Nira makes this clear now. You are Zercy's to bond with. Zercy's. And he is yours."

Alec blinked at him, smile fading, the Kríe's words unexpected. They touched him—and made his heart hurt even worse.

Absently, he rubbed his sternum, then cleared his throat and looked away. "Yeah well, that's nice, but kinda irrelevant now. I'm headed with you guys to Titus, remember? Who knows if I'll ever see him again. Besides…" he frowned and shook his head as he stared at the flames, "he doesn't want to bond with me. Avoids marking me at all costs. I may be his, but he doesn't want me that way."

Miros grunted. "I do not believe that. You clearly mean very much to him. Why else would his whole army come to fight for—"

A howl in the distance had him stopping mid-sentence. Hell, *every* male in their convoy froze at the sound. A deep anguished roar, or maybe a cry, of some large injured animal miles away. Twenty at least, considering its faintness. And yet it still shot a chill up Alec's spine.

Pulse quickening, he looked at Miros. "What the holy fuck was that?"

Miros' wary expression instantly set him on guard. Kríe weren't afraid of *any* predators, big or small. *They* were the kings of the jungle and all creatures knew it. So why then, did some wounded beast so far away make him nervous?

"Miros?" Alec persisted. "Should we be worried about something? Are there animals out there that'll attack large numbers of your kind?"

Again, Miros didn't reply, just kept staring toward the howl. Not that any more had followed. Just that one gut-wrenching cry. The one that chilled Alec's blood and shot straight through his soul.

Ears twisting like radar receivers, Miros finally loosed a grunt. "It was nothing. No beast in this jungle would ever challenge a Kríe." His tone wasn't convincing. Alec stared at him, disconcerted.

Miros' lips finally twitched. He chuffed in amusement. "Do not worry, moyo. They are setting up perimeter traps as we speak. If any approach we will know it."

Alec glanced around. "Really?"

Miros nodded. "Tah. My pack has added another safeguard as well."

"Nice. What kind of safeguard?"

"We pissed a circle around the campsite. Its scent will deter predators."

Alec coughed a laugh and looked at him.

Miros beamed an arrogant Kríe grin. "Our mighty cocks are good for many things."

CHAPTER THIRTY-NINE

* * *

Just as Alec suspected, he couldn't sleep. His head was a maelstrom. His chest was caving in. And his gut felt like it was going to implode. Knotted so tight, it was making it hard to breathe, as his heart pounded anxiously in overdrive.

Lying on his back beside his co-pilot in their tent, he stared into space, seeing only Zercy's face. He needed to get back to him. It was the one thing he knew for sure. It was also the one thing he couldn't do.

Scrubbing his face, he sat up and looked down at Zaden. Fast asleep. Understandable. It'd been a long day. Alec regarded him in the quiet. His friend was the best right-hand man ever. And a damn good second-in-command. God knew, he'd picked up the slack during their stay at the castle when Alec was holed away in Zercy's quarters.

In many ways, Zaden had been the team's surrogate captain for a big portion of the last year. And he'd been amazing at it. The team took to him. It was a natural fit. Even now, they sometimes turned to Zaden before Alec out of habit, having grown so accustomed to looking to him for leadership.

Alec was lucky—they all were lucky—to have Zaden as part of their team.

Exhaling, he got up and quietly headed out of the tent, the construct a dark green, seven-foot-high energy dome. He needed some fresh air to try and clear his head. He also needed to take a leak.

He glanced around their campsite. It was quiet. All were sleeping, minus the few he spotted designated to stand watch. A couple of Kríe, a handful of Tohrí, Garret's military escort, Eli.

Eli glanced his way. Alec gestured to his crotch, letting the guy know he had to piss. The marine nodded and got back to scanning the darkness, his pulse rifle clutched in both hands.

The Nirans eyed him too, but didn't say a word, so Alec made his way into the trees. He'd stay within the perimeter, though. Miros had shown him the invisible line. Or more specifically, where he and his pack mates had drawn the border in yellow.

Although in truth, Kríe piss was closer to chartreuse.

Quietly stepping through the jungle's lush groundcover, Alec stopped beside a thick glossy trunk. He peered up its length to the diamond-speckled sky. Through an opening in the canopy, he spotted a formation of stars. He recognized them. The constellation Tiny Hammer. Zercy had pointed it out to him on the rooftop of his castle. The night he'd let Alec take him for the first time...

Alec's heart squeezed painfully. He frowned down to his soul. The roaring urge to turn around and run back to his king had risen to a deafening pitch. He sucked in a ragged breath and closed his eyes. Pinched the bridge of his nose and tried to calm his mind.

But he couldn't. His insides were a storm of churning turmoil, relentlessly demanding he go back. Because this wasn't right. None of it. Leaving Zercy had been wrong. He could feel it in the marrow of his bones. Instinct and fate, the goddamn universe, shouting that he'd severely veered off course.

Lungs accelerating to accommodate his rapid heartbeat, he opened his eyes and stared into the darkness.

Maybe he should.

Head back.

While the others were sleeping.

Would he be able to find his way? Could he even survive the trip, with so many nocturnal predators lurking about? Even Gesh's 'feared pack' avoided night ventures when possible. Alec chewed his cheek anxiously, eyes drifting to the ground. Maybe if he was able to get far enough from the others, he could bunker down somewhere until morning and make the trip then.

He groaned and dragged a hand down his face. Who the hell was he kidding? He wouldn't make it one hour without getting eaten. Besides, he couldn't do that to his team. Just up and bail. Split without saying a freaking word. Because that's what he'd have to do. No one would let him leave otherwise. They weren't idiots. Even the humans knew traveling at night was straight-up suicide.

Goddamnit. This sucked.

Angry and frustrated, he bit out a curse and reached for the bottom of his tunic. Not that he couldn't be wearing cargo shorts right now. When they made camp, Garret's team had donated changes of clothing as well, but Alec had opted to don his in the morning.

He made quick work of watering the tree, then shoved his dick back in place and straightened his garb. But right as he readied to turn back toward camp, a low menacing growl met his ears. Alec froze on the spot, the threatening rumble way too close. Easily just a few yards behind him.

His heart shot into his throat. A predator had found him.

It came again, the sound. Rough and ragged under its breath, as if the beast wasn't right, maybe rabid.

Shit. What if it was starving and now utterly desperate? Enough so to take chances in lethal territory.

The next growl was closer. Alec could feel its eyes on his back. And it didn't sound hungry. It sounded furious. The dark ominous kind though, held at bay by just a thread. Ready to snap at any given moment.

Alec swallowed, trying to focus. If he called for help, the beast might attack, triggered by his shout. But if he ran, that could trigger it into action, too. And in the game of chase, he didn't stand a chance. His only option? To face the thing. If nothing else, he could punch and block, warding off its jaws with arms and fists.

Pulse hammering in his ears, he whirled around and—

The beast lunged and slammed him against a tree by his throat. Alec's head hit hard. His skull howled in pain. He gasped but couldn't breathe, then gaped in shock. Shock, as he stared into the feral gaze of his king.

Zercy.

He'd come for him.

And yet he wasn't really there. Not the Zercy Alec knew.

This male was madness.

Clothes in disarray. Breaths irregular. Leaves in his dreads. A sheen of sweat covering his skin. Jesus. He'd lost it. Was in full-fledged predator mode, his mind focused on nothing but the hunt. And going by that crazed, volcanic look in his eyes, he planned on tearing his prey to pieces.

Alec's heart went ballistic. He clawed at Zercy's grip, his feet too far off the ground to do any good.

The king quaked, every inch of him, his fingers trembling against Alec's throat. Shoving his face close, he bared his fangs and snarled. "I found you, *Alick*. I will always find you. Your blood runs hot in my veins."

Alec choked, trying to shake his head.

Zercy tightened his grip.

But then his murderous expression morphed into despair. "Why have you forsaken me, *Alick?* Why would you leave me? You are my heart."

I didn't! I didn't leave you! Alec urgently tried to shout. But all he managed to do was gag and cough.

Zercy's face snapped back to fury, his golden eyes manic. "You betrayed me!" he barked brokenly. "I have found you with my enemy! How could you do this to me, *Alick?* How? They tried to end my people!"

No! Alec thought frantically. *I would never!* He struggled against him, desperate to breathe.

Zercy's anger wavered again, his gaze back to desolated. "You promised you would be there," he groaned. His brows pinched. His jaw clenched. "But you lied. You were not waiting! You deserted me to go with *them!*"

No! I fought to stay! I didn't want to go! I told them no!

Zercy vibrated harder, like a warhead about to detonate. He pressed closer. Ground his face against Alec's cheek like an animal. "I would have cherished you forever…" His words were ragged, his breaths choppy. "But you drove a blade through my chest, *Alick*…" His deep timbre cracked. "My heart is bleeding… I can feel it… I want to die…"

Features warring, he touched their foreheads, then pressed his parted lips to Alec's—but it wasn't a kiss. No sign of affection whatsoever. Just another raw display of abject misery.

Tears sprang to Alec's eyes. Zercy was ripping him to shreds, crushing him under the weight of his broken heart. Alec needed to make him see, needed to make him understand.

Vision starting to spot, he upped his efforts, trying to pry Zercy's fingers off his throat. But all that did was snap the king back into a fury.

Rearing back, fire surging even hotter in his eyes, he leveled Alec with a look that seared. "You wish to flee from me again? There is nowhere you can run! I will always find you, *Alick!* You are mine!"

Which Alec had no qualms with at all. In fact, he loved the idea. As long as he didn't die from asphyxiation first.

Lungs on fire, strength ebbing, he pleaded with his eyes. For Zercy to see the truth. That Alec loved him and wouldn't leave him. Not now, not ever. But the king was too far gone. All rationale a thing of the past. Alec's abandonment had stolen the last shred of his sanity.

Alec choked on a sob as his sight began to tunnel, his pulse faltering as the darkness rose up to greet him. He should've told Zercy how he felt months ago, so he'd have known. But Alec hadn't. Hadn't said those three simple words.

Thump-bump… Thump… Bump…

He felt himself go limp. Black snuffed out his vision, his hearing receding.

"*Alick,*" Zercy snarled in the recesses of his mind.

"*Alick, answer me. Why do you——Alick!*"

His tone turned anxious fast.

"*Alick!—Alick, open your eyes!—Alick!—Mah, Nira!—ALICK!!*"

But Alec couldn't open his eyes, and as consciousness called it a night, the last he registered was the mad king's devastated roar.

* * *

"Alec… Alec… Hey, bud… You okay?"

Alec lurched with a start, then sucked in a breath, eyes instantly locking on his co-pilot's face.

"Zaden," he rasped hoarsely. Ow. He winced and touched his throat.

His friend forced a smile. "You gotta quit nappin' on us like this."

Alec glanced at the others looming over him with frowns. Chet and Noah. Garret and his co-pilot. Their medic was there too, crouched down on his haunches next to Zaden.

Sasha shined a small light into each of Alec's eyes, then held up his index. "Follow my finger." He moved it left and right.

Alec tracked it for a second, but quickly lost interest, fumbling to sit up and look around instead. "Where is he?" he asked anxiously. His pulse spiked. "Where's Zercy?"

Sasha gave Zaden a nod, then rose and stepped out of the way, giving Alec a clear view of straight ahead. His heart clenched in his chest. On the other side of their campsite, partially illuminated by the small fire, was Zercy. Unconscious and tied to a tree.

Alec lurched to his feet and staggered toward him. Fuck, his head felt dizzy. "What happened? Why isn't he awake?"

"We had to sedate him," Gesh grunted.

Alec glanced to his right. The pack leader stood glowering with arms folded.

"So you didn't have to fight him?"

A darker grunt. "I did not say *that*."

Alec frowned but kept going until he reached his tranquilized Kríe. Slowly sinking to his knees, he looked Zercy over. He'd been secured in the same fashion that Alec had been secured when, a year ago, Gesh had tied *him* to a tree. Rope around the chest and throat. Bound ankles tied to bound wrists. Bent knees lying open atop the ground.

Alec sighed at the sight of him. He looked like he'd been through hell. His tunic was tattered. Scrapes and dirt marred his skin. One of his horns had a nick and a large bruise darkened his jaw.

Alec stilled at the injury, then angrily ground his molars. "What the fuck happened to his face?"

"I told you," Gesh growled. "We had to sedate him... But it did not take effect right away."

Alec cut the Kríe a glare.

Gesh glared right back.

"It is true," Roni spoke up. His tone held a hint a wonder. "We have never seen anything like it. How long it took him to go down. There must have been more adrenaline in his veins than blood."

Miros nodded with a frown. "We did not want to hurt him. Zercy is our king. But when we saw him hunched over your body and darted him as precaution, he came at us like some crazed cornered beast..." He paused, eyes thoughtful. His big shoulders slumped. "Or a desperate Kríe protecting his mate."

Alec's heart clenched painfully. Exhaling, he gazed at his sleeping giant, insides crumbling as he noticed Zercy's glistening lashes. That and a tiny dried streak down his cheek. A proud king's tears. Even in sleep, the Kríe looked heartbroken.

Not caring who saw, Alec reached out and palmed the side of Zercy's face. "Leo…" he whispered. "I'm so sorry."

God's honest truth. He felt terrible about what happened. But a part of him also felt glad. Or rather, relieved, that the king had actually come for him. That Zercy was there now, just inches away.

Quiet murmurs rose up behind him from what sounded like all three species, their tones exuding a very distinct, *Well, what do you know…* His show of affection had allowed them to do the math. Had shown them the situation in its entirety.

Zercy had gone postal because they'd taken his mate. And despite their efforts, Alec had never wanted to leave.

"So, what in Nira's black night are we going to do with him?" Roni muttered a moment later, presumably to Gesh.

"Well, we cannot just leave him here," Gesh grumbled, "tied to that tree. He needs to be able to defend himself from predators."

"But if we untie him, he will come after us again when he wakes."

"Leí," Airis chimed in, "but being untied will not matter anyway if a predator finds him here *before* he wakes."

"Well, we cannot take him with us," Gesh snapped. "We would have to keep him bound. And that would make us abductors on top of all else."

"Newsflash," Chet laughed darkly. "You're already abductors. What the fuck do you think you did to us?"

"Esh. Hardly the same. You are creatures not even of Nira. He is Mighty King of the Kríe."

Chet muttered something under his breath.

Alec stood and turned to face them. "It's okay. I'll stay behind with him."

"*What?* The hell you will," Chet objected.

"We don't have any other options. Besides, this makes sense if you think about it. I watch over him until he wakes up, then I try to talk some sense into him. Talk him down. He knows I won't hurt him. That I'm not a threat. And if he's tied up, he can't hurt me, either."

His men didn't look sold. Wary frowns etched their faces.

Alec sighed and glanced down at Zercy. "Look, if I explain to him what happened, make him understand, then I can potentially defuse a very volatile situation. I can act as a mediator, convince him not to do anything rash."

"But where does that leave you?" Zaden asked, his voice tense.

"With Zercy... I'd go back to the castle with Zercy."

"Then we all go with you," Zaden insisted. "We're a team. We stick together. We don't split up. No matter what."

Alec frowned and held Zaden's gaze. "We do this time, Z."

"No." Zaden crossed his arms and shook his head. "We don't separate. That's the rule and you don't get to break it."

Alec's small smirk was sad. "Yeah, I do. I'm the captain."

Zaden clenched his jaw. Pursed his lips.

Alec's gut went all tight. They were friends, best friends, so he felt that shit, too. The bitter taste of goodbye.

Garret finally chimed in, but not with what Alec wanted to hear. "I'm with your men, Alec. Splitting up's a bad idea. As it is, we're doing too much of it already."

His marines nodded behind him.

But then, out of nowhere, Miros spoke up. "Let him go. His path is his own."

Chet coughed a humorless laugh. "Oh, that's rich coming from you, the guy who took him captive then *sold* him."

"Mah. That is *precisely* why it is coming from me. It was wrong what we did, holding your team against your will. Even Gesh can admit we did not think it through. But if we plan to be allies in the moons ahead, then we must make amends and try to right our wrongs against you."

"And you think by sending our captain back to a castle of angry wolves, you'll be doing the guy a favor?" Chet sounded incredulous.

Miros folded his thick arms and lifted his chin. "I do not know what wolves are, but I do know this. He is his own. His choices should be his own. Let him return to what makes him happy."

"Makes him happy? You think captivity makes him happy?"

"I am willing to bet he is no unwilling captive."

All eyes slid back to Alec.

Awkward.

He shifted his weight.

"Look at him," Miros went on. "Are you truly that blind? He *yearns* to be with one of ours, just as Gesh yearns to be with one of yours."

Alec chuckled uncomfortably. Scratched his neck, his cheeks heating. "Yearns... That's uh... kind of a strong word there, Miros..."

"I'll go with you," Noah announced. "In case Bailey shows up."

Alec sobered. "Noah, no." He gestured to Zercy. "He's not stable. As much as I'd like to defend his honor and deny it, I can't, not if it means risking your safety."

Zaden and Chet opened their mouths, but Alec stopped them before they could start. "That goes for you two as well. I can't guarantee the safety of any of you right now. So you gotta stay away. And you gotta stick together. You'll need each other, now more than ever. Jamis and Bailey will need you guys, too."

"How do we know *you'll* be safe?" Chet asked, ever the protector.

Alec glanced at Zercy and smiled a little. "I won't untie him 'til he promises to be nice."

Chet grunted and rolled his eyes.

Alec turned his gaze to Zaden. "You'll assume the role of captain, Z. Hell, you've been doing it part-time now for months."

Zaden nodded tightly, frowning. "When will we see you again?"

Good question.

"Um..." Alec scratched his cheek, not really sure what to tell him.

"Yeah, I doubt anytime soon," Garret offered. A definite realist. "But you can *talk* to him any time you want."

Alec and Zaden stilled and looked at him. So did Noah and Chet.

Garret smiled a little, then shrugged and tossed his telecom device to Alec. "So you can chat with your boys. We've got five others. I'll grab yours when Gesh's pack hands over your gear."

Alec eyed the portable gadget.

Technology. It'd been so long.

God, it felt like heaven in his hand.

He grinned, idly thumbing it, its silver body a sleek flat trapezoid, then looked back at Garret. "Thanks, man."

"You bet."

Alec's teammates visibly eased, no doubt feeling much better about the situation.

Gesh walked over and eyed the king. "We should go. He will wake soon, and we do not want to be here when he does."

Everyone ambled off to pack up. When they were ready to roll, Alec clasped palms with each of his men. "Be safe. Let me know the minute you meet up with Jamis."

"Will do." Zaden tugged him into a hug. "See you soon."

Funny, how his parting words sounded more like a demand.

Alec nodded and squeezed him tight. "Yeah. Very soon." He was going to miss them all, but especially Zaden.

Eli and Helix sauntered over. Each one handed him a pistol. "Locked and loaded, captain."

Alec happily accepted them. "Aw, fuck. Thank you. It's been ages." He handled the things for a second, savoring their flawless engineering, then tucked them around back in his belt.

Eli smiled, as if pleased by Alec's show of appreciation. Understandable. Those guns were probably like his babies.

"Oh, and these…" The marine dug into one of his cargo shorts' countless pockets. "Some boom dogs and scat cats. To scare away the beasties." He dropped a handful of pulse grenades and silver disks into Alec's palm, then clapped him on the shoulder. "Godspeed. Don't die."

Alec chuckled. "I'll do my best."

Helix gave him a nod. Then just like that, all three species headed out.

Alec watched them intently until the darkness enveloped them whole, then turned and looked at Zercy. Still unconscious.

Alec sighed and glanced at the fire. Shit. It was nearly dead. Just wisps of flame atop a bed of glowing embers. He should probably get more wood. Revive the thing while Zercy slept.

Glancing around, he set his sights and traipsed off.

Not five minutes later though, is when he first heard it. The distant sounds of Zercy finally rousing.

A soft groan… Some groggy grunts…… A *very* uneasy rumble…

Alec peered in his direction, too many trees in the way to see.

Then, like a crash of thunder, Zercy's howl ripped through the jungle.

CHAPTER FORTY

* * *

Alec dropped the wood he was carrying and took off at a run, weaving through the dense foliage back to Zercy. But when he cleared the last trees, he skidded to a halt, the sight hitting him square in the chest.

Zercy, eyes frantic, face wrenched up toward the sky, roaring in anguish to only God knew who. Nira? The cosmos? Those deity dudes, Ságe and Krye? All Alec knew was that his bellows were unceasing; tortured, broken pleas, again and again.

"Mah! Please, I beg you! It was not my intention to hurt him! I have been your faithful servant! Please do not take him!"

A lump welled fast in Alec's throat. His king was distraught. With blatant desperation. But also grief. He thought Alec was dead. Probably thought that he killed him. And now he was pleading to get him back.

Chest threatening to crack open, Alec shoved back into gear and made his way over, albeit cautiously. Not that Zercy noticed him as he approached from the left. When his eyes weren't squeezed shut, they were locked on the heavens, as hot tears streamed in rivulets down his cheeks.

Alec arrived just as he arched back and loosed another howl.

"Zercy." His voice cracked as he dropped to one knee.

Zercy jumped.

Then his big wild eyes locked on Alec's face.

Alec stared into his gaze, a gaze still very far from right, but somewhat less deranged than before. Until, that is, his expression started to war—relief, betrayal, confusion, rage. A tumultuous firestorm reignited by Alec's presence.

Instantly he fell into grappling with his binds, baring his fangs even as his brows pinched up miserably. Alec's heart split in two. He needed to reach his Kríe. But how? Zercy wasn't in any condition to rationally converse.

At a loss for what else to do, he eased into the space between Zercy's knees, then tentatively cupped his cheeks and nuzzled his face. The way Zercy always did with him. When he couldn't find the words, or didn't feel the need to speak, but still wanted to show Alec affection.

Zercy snarled, the sound choppy, his chest heaving, his mind still raw.

Alec pressed his lips to his cheek and lingered. "Leo…"

Zercy shuddered, then quieted slightly. Alec could hear his lungs fighting to regulate.

"*Alick*—" he hitched. "*Alick*—"

Alec closed his eyes. "Yeah."

"You—" He struggled to speak, his breaths erratic. "Thought—you were—"

Alec eased back. "I'm okay."

Zercy stared at his face, his body still quaking, his auric gaze frazzled—and wary. As if he knew all too well that his sanity had left him and feared his mind was playing vicious tricks.

God, he looked broken.

Alec thumbed away his tears.

Zercy shook his head restlessly. Something flashed in his eyes. Then his savage face crumbled. "*Alick*—" he rasped. "W-Why—" His struggling lungs jarred his words.

Alec's soul splintered. He knew what Zercy was asking. "I didn't. I didn't leave you."

"Tah—Tah, you did—"

"Not willingly. I told them no. I fought them, Zercy. But they didn't understand. And with the chaos all around us, I got knocked out and next thing I knew, I was waking up in some cave beneath a mountain."

Zercy stared at him, lashes wet, his hitching lungs slowly calming. "You… fought to stay?"

Alec held his gaze. Nodded.

The king's features softened. But then he stiffened right back up again. "Where are they?" He glanced around. "Your men. Gesh's pack." His lip curled back menacingly. "Those Tohrí traitors."

Shit.

"They're gone."

Zercy bristled from head to toe. "Untie me," he ground out. "I will hunt them down and slaughter them for what they have done."

"Zercy... Just calm down."

"Untie me!" he roared.

"No!" Alec belted back. "I won't! Ain't happening!"

Zercy froze, chest heaving again, and balked at him incredulously. "I am your *king!* You *must* comply!"

"You're not my king where *orders* count!"

"Esh!" he barked, exasperated. "In what other way does it count to be king?"

"King of my *heart,* you fucking oaf."

Zercy stilled and stared at him.

Alec exhaled and closed his eyes. "Look. They left. They don't want any trouble. They came with one objective, to free us from captivity." He lifted his gaze. Met Zercy's eyes again. "They thought that's what we wanted. They're not happy with how things turned out. They hadn't meant for anyone to get hurt."

"They betrayed me. Stole what was mine. And those Tohrí still must pay."

Alec shook his head, then dragged a weary hand down his face. "I talked to them, the Tohrí—"

Zercy growled.

"—told them I wouldn't go with them. They asked why. I explained that what they did was unforgivable. They didn't know what I was talking about. And when I spelled it out, they looked horrified."

"They are deceivers!"

"I dunno, Leo..." Alec shook his head again. "It didn't feel like it. And I'm not just makin' some half-assed assessment. Their vibe, their disposition and overall conduct, their reaction to the news. It doesn't add up. They're not insidious by nature. Not hungry for dominance. They don't even have a real motive. I think that prince was either psychotic, or under the influence of some outside force. A faction maybe, that has a reason to want Kríe dead."

Zercy's jaw ticked. "You defend them."

"I'm not defending them. I'm just calling it how I see it."

But the king wasn't hearing him. Was still too frayed at the edges. "Pick a side, *Alick*," he grated. "My enemies or—"

"You," Alec blurted. "I will *always* pick you."

Zercy eyed him. Intently. Another shudder shook his body. But this one felt different, not like the others. Not fueled by anger, but another flammable emotion. One that burned hottest both in the chest and below the belt.

Alec stilled, pulse spiking.

Zercy rumbled, all dark and possessive, the sound sliding sensuously under Alec's skin.

Alec shifted between his legs. That shit was going to make him hard.

Two seconds later, the king's thick cock firmed underneath him. "Need to claim you, *Alick*," he growled. "Need to make you truly mine."

Alec's lips parted. *Damn.* Zercy's gaze was suddenly scorching.

Blood coursed through his veins, heady and hot like a drug, then pooled like molten lava in his crotch.

Zercy wanted to fuck, and so did Alec.

But Zercy also wanted to bond. Wholly commit.

Which in itself wasn't a bad thing. The timing, however, gave Alec pause.

Sliding his fingers into Zercy's dreads, he leaned in close and touched their brows. "You don't have to do that, Leo. I'll stay with you anyway. I won't ever leave you. Not ever."

Alec knew this now. For certain. From the moment he told his men that he was going back with Zercy to the castle. He was retiring. For good. Would never be their captain again. He suspected on some level they realized the same.

Zaden's eyes had certainly said as much. Deep down, he'd known. Just hadn't wanted to voice it, as if afraid that doing so would somehow cement the future.

It wouldn't have though, because Alec's path was already laid. Maybe before they'd even touched Niran soil. He was meant to be there. With Zercy. It was fate. Felt *right*. More so than anything ever had in all his life.

Lashes heavy, Zercy gazed at Alec's mouth and shook his head. "Mah, *Alick*," he murmured, his hunger laced with emotion. "I do not want this, for us to bond, to ensure that you stay... I want it because now I know with absolute certainty that you would stay with me *even if we did not.*"

The lump in Alec's throat swelled. *That* was why Zercy had waited. Because he didn't know for sure if Alec would leave. And in the king's defense, it made sense. He'd only been reading Alec's vibes, who until tonight hadn't known if he'd leave, either. But he knew now, and clearly, Zercy had felt the change.

Alec smiled, not bothering to ask if Nira had anything to do with it. On his end, he knew she didn't. Yes, she was important. Yes, he'd never let her die. But this thing happening now, this choice he was making? It was between him and Zercy and nobody else. And in his heart, he believed that Zercy felt the same.

Which Alec knew sounded naïve, or if nothing else, self-absorbed. But reflecting back, when Zercy came for him, all out of his mind that Alec had left, never once did he accuse him of abandoning Nira. Her name never came up. She was off his scope completely.

No, even for Zercy, this was only about them.

Not his mother tree. Not the kingdom.

Just the need to be together. The realization—on both of their parts—that life was no life at all if they had to live in a world without the other.

Heart welling, along with the need to have Zercy's body inside his, Alec claimed his king's mouth and kissed him hard.

Zercy growled against his lips. Palmed Alec's ass with his bound hands. Then rocked his hips to the rhythm of their quickening breaths. "Untie me," he ordered heatedly.

This time, Alec complied. Well, sort of, anyway.

Without breaking their kiss, he reached for Zercy's belt and pulled his dagger free from its sheath. Zercy thrummed in anticipation. Squeezed Alec's ass. Then stilled as Alec leaned back to slice the rope. Just the one at Zercy's neck, though. He kept his chest bound to the tree. And his hands bound to his ankles—'cause, truth be told, that shit was hot.

"Wicked moyo," Zercy snarled, craning his head forward to kiss him deeper.

Alec's lips curved. Tossing the knife aside, he shoved his hands in Zercy's tunic. "You're Kríe. You *like* wicked," he murmured against his mouth, kneading Zercy's pecs before moving to work his nipples. Thumbing and rolling those rock-hard nubs, twisting and tugging their metal piercings.

Zercy growled in erotic response, blatantly loving the way Alec toyed, but clearly just as anxious to finally impale him. Alec moaned, envisioning it, and snagged Zercy's lip with his teeth, then dropped his hands to fumble with Zercy's belt.

The strap fell away. Alec shoved open Zercy's tunic wrap and delved his eager fingers inside his loinstrap. One hand gripped Zercy's boner and pulled the huge erection free, its golden bands glinting regally in the firelight. The other slid lower and cupped his heavy balls, his whole hand barely big enough to hold them.

"*Tah*...." Zercy rumbled, thrusting his cock through Alec's fist. "Get me ready for your tender little star."

Alec's dick bucked at the thought. He kissed Zercy deeper, his blood pumping faster through his veins. Stroking Zercy's shaft, he paused to squeeze its base, then pulled his clenched fist up the king's hard length. Warm, thick precum emerged. A big, fat bead. Alec swiped it up with his fingertips and switched his hands. The one massaging Zercy's balls relocated to grip his cock, while the one sporting warm, fresh lube dropped to his sac. Not to knead it like before, though. This time his fingers had other business, slipping under and behind them to slick Zercy's star.

Not that he'd be fucking Zercy tonight. He just loved playing with his backdoor. In truth, he did it every chance he got. So firm and hot, but what he loved about it most was how, over time, it'd grown tighter and tighter.

Turned out, all this time that they'd been sexually active, they hadn't been training Alec's ass exclusively. They'd been training Zercy's, too. Not to stretch and yield like Alec's, but in essence to do the opposite. They hadn't realized it at first, but every time Alec topped—which to his great pleasure amounted to pretty often—they'd been teaching Zercy's ass to constrict by way of that ruka vine. Constrict, and *stay* constricted, for hours and hours. Eventually, it just sort of adopted that as its natural state.

In the same respect, the same thing happened to Alec's dick. After using that enyid skin maybe a dozen or so times, his cock had just stayed visibly larger. Lately, he didn't even need the enyid skin. His dick would grow twice its size all on its own.

Zercy loosed a thrumming snarl as Alec stroked his tight hole, then a hot little grunt as Alec pushed his digits through. Just his index and middle finger, but again, that was enough. He moaned just from the feel of Zercy's tightness.

Slowly, he sank things deeper. Zercy's kiss turned more aggressive. When Alec started his in-and-outs, Zercy added teeth. Biting at Alec's lip, Alec's tongue as Alec repeatedly delved deep, hitting the bound king's sweet spot every time.

Zercy shuddered and growled, digging his claws into Alec's ass. "Those fiendish fingers," he grated. "I adore them."

Alec's chuckle came out husky. He could do this all night. And damn, Zercy's cock, the way it bucked in his grip? Two words, raging bull. If only Alec's own dick wasn't howling so bad, and his backdoor reeling so hard for penetration.

But they were, something fierce, so he settled for a compromise. Tease his wanton king for just a little while longer, then get down to business on Zercy's cock. Decadent moments later, when Alec finally slid things free, his big proud king was writhing, about to burst. Leaking from both his mammoth dick and his ass.

Cool little fact: work a Kríe's G just right and he'll get juicy.

Breathless from their kiss, Alec eased back and met Zercy's gaze, then grinned and slid his fingers into his mouth, sucking them slowly as Zercy watched with captivated eyes.

"Depraved little pet," he growled. "You are perfect."

Alec laughed. He didn't know about perfect, but he'd definitely come a long way since first arriving on the planet. A heterosexual man now sitting happily in an alien jungle, sucking his male lover's honey off his fucking fingers.

Crazy universe. But he'd take it.

Standing up in the space between his bound king's bent knees, Alec shucked his belt and tunic, and then his loinstrap. But as he maneuvered to straddle Zercy's hips, he noticed Zercy hungrily eyeing his dick.

Alec's insides straight-up smoldered. That primal look in Zercy's gaze. His Kríe wanted to devour him. His pulse sped faster. He gripped his erection. "You want this?" His lips curved.

Zercy's scorching eyes slid up to his. "Give it to me," he commanded.

Goddamn, his timbre. All thick and husky. Like some rich, dark drug that entered through the ears.

Alec shuddered and absently squeezed, then moaned as pleasure surged up his shaft.

Zercy grinned and licked his lips. Opened his mouth in invitation, his big black pupils dilating up at Alec. Alec breathed a curse, gaze dipping to Zercy's fangs. Short and fat, but still sharp. Not that they had ever cut his dick. But those tantalizing grazes they delivered with each pull? Those teasing scores along each side of Alec's length? Yeah, he loved when Zercy sucked his cock. Forget king of the Kríe. He was king of blowjobs.

Eyes rapt on Zercy's face, Alec slid his swollen crown between his lips. Zercy instantly engulfed it and pulled Alec's dick halfway in.

Alec moaned, knees going weak, eyes rolling back in his head. "Leo, fuck…"

Zercy growled and suckled deeply, then roughly drew in the rest—which still wasn't difficult, despite Alec's new and improved dick, for a species designed to accommodate twelve-inch cocks.

Alec inhaled sharply and grasped for something to steady him. Zercy's horns. The perfect handles.

Now Zercy moaned. Alec stared down at him, drunk on lust, as Zercy held his gaze, his blazing auric eyes ramping his even hotter. The king sucked faster, tugging aggressively with his mouth, those fangs, those fucking fangs, frying Alec's brain.

Pleasure licked up his length. Teased his tailbone. His backdoor. Making his abs and everything lower tense up tight. Alec groaned, jaw clenched, and gripped Zercy's horns tighter, then ground out a curse and started using them for leverage. Leverage as he endeavored to fuck Zercy's face.

The king snarled excitedly, the vibrations driving Alec nuts, sending licks of wicked bliss into his balls. He shoved his boner deeper, till his glans plugged Zercy's throat, hoping it'd earn him a tiny reprieve. But all that did was spur the king into swallowing. Snuggly and steadily around Alec's sensitized crown.

"Fuck—" he gasped, gripping Zercy's horns.

Zercy quaked, eyes turning wild again from Alec's touch. Alec loved that transparency in his gaze. How visibly crazy he was making him to mark. To bond. Every shift of Alec's grip making him shudder.

And while a stronger man might be able to hold off and enjoy it longer, drinking down the sight of Zercy's state, Alec evidently was not a stronger man because Zercy's urgency only made him urgent, too. With the need to bury Zercy's rigid length inside him and connect in the most fundamental of ways.

Breaths ragged, Alec pulled out and gripped his dick. Squeezed it hard to calm it down. Groaned a curse.

Zercy was panting as well. His cheeks flushed, his lips wet. His big eyes filled with emotion. Anticipation. "Take me inside you," he grated anxiously. "I cannot wait a moment longer. I must have you, *Alick*. Must mark you." He looked restless. "The need to bond has turned to an ache."

Alec breathed another curse. Absently stroked his dick. Gave a nod.

This was it. Once the king was buried inside him, there'd be no turning back. The bond would happen, mating them irrevocably. Aligning them, mind and body, for all eternity.

A monumental moment. A choice they could never unmake. And what do you fucking know; Alec couldn't wait.

Reaching between their bodies, he gripped Zercy's boner, then eased down until he felt it. The king's broad crown pressed snugly against his door, wholly at Alec's mercy as to if it would enter. He met Zercy's gaze. The king's dark features were tight with need. So ruggedly handsome, and yet so savage. Alec's head spun, ever awed by such a creature.

Reeling with desire and overwhelmed by devotion, he captured Zercy's mouth and sank lower. Zercy's crown breached his ring. Both males moaned and sucked in breaths. Alec fisted Zercy's dreads and continued his slow descent.

"Fuuuck," he ground out. Still so snug. His ass may be able to accommodate Zercy now, but it still wasn't easy.

Zercy growled against his mouth. Kissed his lips with raw urgency, as if needing Alec fully seated, lest he die.

Lower Alec sank onto his rod, its ridges and veins so hard he could feel physically them, rubbing against his prostate as he drove the Kríe king higher into his depths.

Zercy snarled.

Alec could feel the huge male trembling, struggling with all his strength not to thrust. Dutifully waiting till he'd opened Alec up. Properly, fully, on that first slow drive home. After that, though, all bets were off. King Zercy was going to let loose.

And Alec was going to love every vigorous second of it.

He settled onto Zercy's crotch. Zercy's bound hands clutched his ass. His claws bit into Alec's flesh, sending shivers through his body.

Zercy growled again, then nuzzled Alec's face. "You are my heaven, *Alick*," he rasped. "Not up in the sky amidst the stars. Not with Nira, nor with the gods ... Mah. Buried in your heat, sharing your breath, your chest to mine... *This*," he stated intently, *"this* is my heaven."

Alec's heart did a somersault. Then every cell in his body melted. Tunneling his fingers into the dreads at Zercy's nape, he claimed his mouth.

Zercy groaned as their tongues tangled. Then his hips began to move. Thrusting upward, at first in short pumps, starting slowly, then moving faster. Each plunge longer than the last, punching higher into Alec's gut, as his huge hands held Alec's ass firmly in place.

Goddamn. Even strapped down to a mother-effing tree, he still managed to rock Alec's world.

"Shit, Kríe—*Ungh, shit*—" Alec moaned through hard grunts, fumbling to clutch tighter to Zercy's dreads. The king was stoking his fire fast, getting that pressure surging higher, driving pleasure like living current through his channel.

Zercy snarled, growing rougher with his teeth at Alec's mouth. Snagging his bottom lip, nipping his tongue, even his chin, before severing their kiss completely to go for Alec's neck. Below the ear at first, then urgently suckling his way down its length until he finally latched on right at the base.

Alec's pulse tore sky high. This was it. He closed his eyes. But those devilish fangs never broke skin. As if yet again, Zercy was holding off, resisting the urge to bite. But why? What was wrong? Alec thought Zercy wanted this.

Panting wildly as Zercy fucked him toward the brink of oblivion, he cupped Zercy's jaw with both hands and gasped out, "Do it."

Zercy met his gaze, eyes flashing. "I cannot," he bit, teeth clenching. "Not in this state. Not while tied. I must have full control."

Alec blinked, half mindless. Then Zercy's words slammed his brain, igniting him in flames with just the visual. Of Zercy taking over. Complete domination.

Not able to move fast enough, he scrambled to grab Zercy's dagger, then fumbled to carefully cut the last few ropes. Easier said than done while still impaled on Zercy's cock. Not so much with the ropes around the king's big broad chest, but reaching his wrists and ankles? Alec moaned, twisting around, Zercy's huge rod shifting inside him at awkward angles.

Zercy growled, mouth latched anxiously on Alec's shoulder as he worked, as if the urge to use his teeth was just too powerful. And maybe it was, because the second that last rope dropped, Zercy lunged forward, still fully buried in Alec's body.

"Fuck!" Alec yelled, half laughing, half terrified, as Zercy took him to the ground, flat on his back. Air punched from his lungs. Zercy's hips wedged between his thighs.

But instead of dashing back into a frenzied ravenous fuck, Zercy stilled, breathing heavily, and peered down at him. Alec met his hooded gaze, two orbs of smoldering liquid gold, and just like that, was instantly entranced.

Zercy's eyes dipped to Alec's mouth, then slid back up to Alec's stare. "You are everything to me," he rumbled. "I want you to know this. That I put you above all I hold dear. Nothing means more to me. Not my kingdom. Not my crown..." His hips started to move. His black lashes fluttered. "Not even life, or Nira herself. I live for you."

Alec moaned, holding his gaze. Fuck, the things Zercy was saying. Velvet fingers across his heartstrings, serenading his soul, while Zercy's rigid heat moved deep inside.

Pleasure coursed through Alec's channel with each stroke, then delved with heady pulses into his junk. He shuddered, fighting to focus, and palmed the back of Zercy's head. Because as good as it felt, as much as he'd love to just let go, he wanted—no, he *needed*—to reply. To tell Zercy the things he should've said before.

With Zercy's hips still rocking slowly, Alec groaned, then fisted Zercy's mane and pulled him closer. So their lips were nearly touching. So Zercy's dreads brushed his chest as he spoke the words he never thought he'd say.

"You're my whole world too, Leo." He smiled and shook his head. "You drive me crazy... But I love it... It makes me happy like nothing else... No one in all my life has felt so right."

Zercy's hips slowed to a stop. A soft thrum curled in his throat. "I am your home," he murmured roughly. "Just as you have become mine."

Alec nodded a little. "Hadn't realized I'd been without one all this time. Always thought home was the stars. But even the stars can't hold a candle to you."

Zercy blinked. Blinked again. Then a grin lit his face. "I am your home *and* your lion heart."

Alec chuckled. "You were certainly fierce for me tonight."

Zercy loosed a spicy growl.

Alec laughed and pulled him closer. "I love you, Kríe. Do you hear me?" Their lips brushed as he spoke. "On a level that is ludicrous. Looks like I've lost it."

Zercy chuffed, sounding equal parts flattered and perplexed. "I have never heard it used that way. *Love*... But I like it." Hooking Alec's leg over his big beefy shoulder, he grinned. "I should like to do the same."

Alec grunted, bent in half. "Do the same?"

"Tah," Zercy growled. "Love you." *Thrust.* "To a level that is ludicrous."

Rapture tore through Alec's body. He arched on a moan, then grasped Zercy's biceps and held on. Held on, as Zercy's hips started pistoning steadily, and his mouth latched back onto Alec's throat. No teeth, though. Just feverish sucking, the tips of his fangs pressed to Alec's flesh.

Pressure surged in Alec's junk. His prostate sang. Zercy's smooth, yet forceful plunges were stealing his sanity. A heartbeat later, he was totally consumed. Ecstasy had flooded his mind, his body. A maelstrom inside his ass, igniting his junk. All awareness homed in on his swiftly approaching orgasm. That and all things Zercy. His taste, his scent, his weight, as his heat suffused Alec wholly, inside and out.

He moaned and gasped, writhing mindlessly beneath him. His massive male was too much. Too powerful, his thrusts too strong. Yet, Alec couldn't get enough. Needed more.

With Zercy's lips latched to his neck, Alec clasped his horns and started grinding. Instantly, Zercy snarled and slammed his hips against Alec harder, punching his cock even deeper with violent shudders.

White hot bliss tore through Alec's body, wrenching shouts from his throat. His fingers clenched, squeezing tighter. Zercy arched with a bellow, his hot flesh pressing against Alec's, his huge hands anxiously gripping Alec's hips.

Drunk. Utterly wasted. Alec's mind was in shambles, overwhelmed by this hurricane of sensation. Such vehement passion, so ferociously physical. This kind of fire, this intimate aggression, could be found from no other species in existence. It was unique only to Kríe. Of this, he was certain.

Zercy growled with a shudder, then rasped raggedly, "Instinct rides me to mount you from behind. It is the way of Kríe. I cannot hold back any longer."

Zercy's erotic warning tumbled through Alec's brain. Two seconds later, the king withdrew from his body. No. Come back. Emptiness engulfed him. He reached for Zercy, only to find himself abruptly on his stomach.

"Tahhh..." Zercy snarled in his ear from behind, his timbre straight-up dripping with primal need.

Alec's blood thrummed. Then just like that, his ass was yanked up and stuffed to capacity.

"Uh!" he cried out, the new angle jarring.

Zercy rumbled, then enfolded him in his warmth, his chest to Alec's back, his muscular arms around him tight.

Alec's heart went wild. Zercy started to thrust, then gradually lifted Alec's upper half off the ground. So that he straddled Zercy's thighs as Zercy sat on his heels, their bodies back to vertical as they fucked.

Pressure burgeoned in a blink to critical. His nuts hugged the base of his dick. Zercy's cock relentlessly grinding against his prostate was making him mental.

"Fuck—Leo, fuck—" he panted. "Gotta come."

He reached for his dick, but Zercy clutched it before he could. "We spill together," he grated raggedly, curling his free hand around Alec's throat.

Alec swallowed against his palm. Groaned an oath. Turned his head —then reached back and gripped those horns with all his strength.

Zercy's whole body stiffened. "You are mine," he snarled hoarsely. "Mine. And I am yours."

His only warning.

He sank his fangs into the crook of Alec's neck.

Alec arched with a shout, eyes slamming shut. *"Ungh—FUCK!!"*

White-hot pleasure exploded through his body. Zercy growled and started to suck, each eager draw like jolts of current lashing Alec's junk.

Alec gasped and cursed, writhing, the potent onslaught spreading fast. Into his ass, wreaking havoc on his reeling G. Down his thighs, making every muscle tremble. In his toes, in his fingertips. Erotic tingles rocking his spine. A tempest in his gut, igniting his chest.

Zercy's growl sounded like gravel. And God, his cock felt like steel, delving in and out of Alec's body. Alec's nuts balled like rocks. He was on the absolute brink, with Zercy's fangs making him downright delirious.

"Fuck—" he panted. "Shit—" Pressure mushroomed without warning. He gasped, gripping Zercy tighter. *"Shit!—Gonna come!"*

Zercy inhaled sharply. His massive frame quaked. Then, just as his muffled roar tore past Alec's ear, Alec's orgasm barreled home and detonated.

"UHHH!!—UNNNGHFUUUH!!" he belted, sphincter clenching, nuts unloading, as Zercy's cock slammed to the hilt.

Alec could feel it, as his own dick fired; Zercy's pulsing shaft pumping seed up into his gut. So hot and thick. Filling his recesses. So sensuously carnal. The sensation turned him on so much. To the point that it kept powering his own climax on. And considering how much his body was trained to produce, he ended up orgasming nearly as long as Zercy.

Long moments later, Zercy groaned against his neck and wrapped him even tighter in his arms. Alec could feel the king's exhaustion as his huge body slumped, then felt his sharp fangs gently sliding free. A warm tongue took their place, tender laps along the wounds.

Alec's eyes closed in bliss. Still panting, but replete, wholly content. And then he noticed it, Zercy's heartbeat against his back. Strong and steady, yes, but what garnered his attention was how it'd somehow synced up perfectly with his own.

He stilled in pure wonderment. Then he felt something else. A wave of warm awareness slowly washing through his system, filling his empty spaces, blanketing his soul with new-found joy. He couldn't explain it. Had never experienced anything like it before, but nevertheless knew intrinsically what it was.

Pulse quickening, he turned his head. "You feel that?" he murmured breathlessly.

Zercy's rumble sounded sated. It also sounded awed. "Tah... I feel it... Did not think the myth was true..."

"Myth?"

"Of the song."

".... Yeah, I still don't understand."

Zercy chuffed and nuzzled Alec's cheek. "During the mating. It is said that, when two souls embrace for the very first time, they can actually feel their bonded spirits singing."

Alec contemplated that for a moment. A small smile formed. Myth or not, it was a cool explanation. Although, truth be told, this warm thrum did feel strangely transcendent, as if a fundamental part of him had somehow *changed*.

Zercy's soft thumping purr tickled his ear. Alec grinned and lifted his shoulder, then twisted slightly and met Zercy's gaze. God, those gorgeous eyes. His heart thumped with emotion. "Thank you," he murmured.

Zercy regarded him tenderly. Cupped his cheek. "For what?"

"Coming for me. Not letting me go… For entrusting me with your heart." His voice grew thick. He shook his head. "No one's ever loved me the way you do."

Zercy smiled, then lifted Alec's chin with his finger and claimed his mouth with a soft, gentle growl. Alec's eyes slid closed. He kissed Zercy deeper, absently shifting to try to face him more fully. But the king was still buried to the hilt inside his body, and the movement instantly elicited a moan.

Zercy leaned back with a smirk, his golden eyes hooded. "Noisy moyo. You are making my cock hard again."

Alec fought back a laugh. "My bad."

Zercy grinned and eased him back on all fours. Pressing Alec's chest to the ground, he pulled out, then true to form, got busy licking. Alec moaned, eyes rolling back as Zercy cleaned his tender flesh. Warm cum seeped free. Zercy lapped it away, then coaxed Alec's ring to close with teasing flicks. Alec shivered, instinctively clenching until his sphincter cinched tight. Which was clearly what Zercy wanted, so that his huge load stayed put.

"Bellah," the king praised. "Such an obedient little starflower." He nuzzled Alec's crack. "Let none escape."

Alec grinned, inwardly shaking his head at Zercy's antics. Two seconds later, though, the king was helping him to his feet. Alec tensed, squeezing his butt cheeks as gravity fought him for Zercy's cum.

Zercy grinned like a punkass.

Alec smirked and took his hand. "Come on," he chuckled, leading him over to where they'd be sleeping. There were still a few hours left before the suns came up, and Alec was bound and determined to get some sleep.

Zercy paused in front of the energy dome and regarded the thing oddly. "You sleep inside this spectacle? Its walls are strange... Not even real."

Alec grinned, eyeing the tent that Garret had so graciously left him. "Real enough to keep the predators out."

He tapped on its control panel, a hologram of illuminated icons, and an opening instantly formed. Alec gestured for Zercy to enter, adding a playful little bow. "After you, my king."

Zercy chuffed, then ducked his head inside to peek.

Alec laughed, "Go on," and shoved him through with his foot.

Zercy stumbled out of view. Alec grinned and followed him in, closing things back up again behind him. Unfortunately, there wasn't much to see on the inside, just a couple of one-way windows and a sleep pad.

To Zercy, however, even one-way windows were captivating. He studied them raptly. Alec smirked and flopped on the mattress. Not long after, Zercy joined him on the bed.

And just like that, the world around them melted out of existence as the Kríe king's full attention fell back to his mate.

His mate.

Alec smiled as Zercy set in to pampering him, dragging that huge warm tongue all over his body. Lapping and laving every imaginable nook and cranny while his softly thumping purr soothed Alec toward sleep.

Muscles loosening, he idly weaved his fingers through Zercy's dreads. Traced the shell of his pointed ears. Stroked his cheek.

"Leo?" he murmured drowsily.

Zercy settled in beside him. "Tah, *Alick?*" he rumbled.

Alec nestled into his warmth. "You missed a spot."

Soft chuff. "Did I?"

Alec grinned and pointed to his mouth.

Zercy chuckled, licked there too, then kissed him soundly.

CHAPTER FORTY-ONE

* * *

Alec woke the next morning to the sound of Kríe talking, their deep timbres seeping in from outside the tent. He peeled open his eyes. Rolled onto his back. Groggily glanced around. No Zercy. Must be part of the powwow.

Alec got up and donned some clothes, then headed out to see what was happening. Stepping through the opening of their big, dark energy dome, he instantly spotted Zercy and several Kríe. Not his castle guards, though. These males were dressed like tactical hunters. Like some special band of soldiers, going by their garb. Still armor, but sleeker. And darker. More maneuverable. Quieter. Made from thick hide instead of steel.

The Kríe turned and eyed him. So did the king, his gaze immediately taking in Alec's attire. Black tank top, tan cargo shorts, big ole black hiking boots. Clothing Garret had given him the night before.

Zercy lifted a brow, then grinned at Alec wryly. "Strange. I thought I had had those things burned."

Alec smirked and crossed his arms. Gestured his chin toward Zercy's visitors. "Who are they?"

"My trackers. Those I originally set out with to find you."

"Originally? What does that mean? You guys get separated or some shit?"

"Tah… *or some shit*," Zercy muttered, glancing away. His lilt made human curse words sound amusing.

Alec's lips twitched. But then something in his periphery made him freeze. Something really big amidst the trees. A monstrous predator, ready to pounce on their asses?

Quickly, he turned his head—then groaned in relief. Not maneaters, just *zahka* from the castle's royal stables. Three-toed hooved beasts that Kríe would oftentimes ride. Big, black, and beefy, and generally pretty friendly. Always reminded Alec of buffalo—but way less furry.

He regarded them as they munched on leaves, secured to nearby trees. "Are we taking those back?" He wouldn't mind the lift.

"Tah." Zercy nodded. "We will be leaving here soon." He signaled to several of his Kríe. "Roz, fetch us clothing from my satchel. Mundo, Fel, accompany us to the river." Zercy turned back to Alec and extended his hand. "Come, my prince. I should first like to bathe."

Alec stilled. Blinked once, then twice at Zercy's words. The other males, however, didn't even seem fazed. Zercy must've told them earlier while Alec was sleeping. His heart thumped happily. Zercy thought of him as his prince.

Insides warming, Alec headed over and took his hand.

Zercy led the way as his Kríe fell in behind them. "I hope you do not mind." He smiled sheepishly at Alec. "I could not keep it to myself. I had to tell them."

Alec chuckled and shook his head. "Nope. I'm all about transparency."

"Bellah," Zercy exhaled, then squeezed his hand. "When we return to the castle, I will make an announcement. All will know of our mating. The whole kingdom."

For the first time in ages, Alec got butterflies.

They arrived a few minutes later. Alec regarded the river. Looked like the same one he'd cooled off in with his men. A year ago, while Gesh's prisoners, when their bodies had been reeling. Reeling from the effects of senna`sohnsay.

God, he'd been dying, so desperate for relief. He'd actually tried fingering himself in the water. Just a few feet away, Zaden had nearly scored some dick, had he not been interrupted by *the incident*. Namely, when a merman grabbed Bailey's ankle.

Alec's chest tightened, thinking about his teammate. Was he truly okay, like Airis said? He glanced around, wondering if Oonmaiyos were nearby now, silently watching. Ugh. Who knew. Hopefully, he'd hear some news soon. *Good* news about Bailey and Jamis. That they were alive and well. Please let his teammates be okay.

Zercy stripped and got in. Alec did the same. Their escorts took up post along the bank. Guess Zercy's trackers were also impromptu bodyguards. They had a strange look in their eyes though, as if disgruntled.

"What's with them?" Alec asked.

Zercy eased to a stop. Gentle waves lapped at his abs. "They are irritated with me. Not happy that I broke from them last night. Searched for me 'til dawn. Have yet to sleep."

"You broke from them? Why?"

Zercy glanced toward the bank. Fel had just joined the others. He dug something from the satchel and tossed it to Zercy. A small bag of soaps Kríe used to bathe.

Zercy caught it and turned back. His eyes looked thoughtful. Sad. "Because they could not keep up... Were slowing me down."

"Wow," Alec murmured. "You must've been moving pretty fast. How'd you even know which way to go?"

Zercy's smile was bittersweet. He met Alec's gaze. "Your blood, it called to me. I could feel it in my veins. Beckoning me to come for you. To find you."

Alec remembered him saying something similar last night. He frowned. "But how? How is that possible?"

Zercy's pensive gaze dropped as he lathered his stomach, rich suds clinging to his birthmark and washboard abs. "I do not know. I have never experienced anything like it. But the moment I felt it, I knew what it was." He paused and looked back up. "You. Inside of me. Telling me to run. As fast as my legs would carry me, before it was too late."

Alec's heart squeezed in his chest.

Zercy frowned and held his gaze. "So that is what I did... I ran as fast as I could... I did not stop. I did not rest. Not when fire burned my lungs. I just... kept running. Toward you."

Alec stared at him, speechless. Moved beyond words.

Zercy's lips curved a little. He boyishly looked away. "The reason, I suppose, why my trackers could not keep up."

And how.

Alec smiled. Down to his very soul. This male standing before him, so arrogant and exasperating, was the most amazing individual he'd ever met. And he was Alec's. All Alec's. And Alec was forever his. He felt like the luckiest astronaut in the universe.

Reaching for Zercy's soap sack, Alec took it from his hand and proceeded to finish washing Zercy's chest. "I'm glad," he murmured roughly. Peering up, he met Zercy's eyes. "So glad you didn't stop running."

Zercy gazed at him tenderly. His rugged features softened. "I could do no other, handsome prince. You are my beating heart." Hefting Alec up like he always loved to do, Zercy nuzzled his face affectionately, then captured his lips.

Alec grinned against his mouth. Wrapped both legs around his waist. Then started a frisky grind against his stomach.

Zercy chuffed through a growl. "Impish little water pup."

His only warning.

Alec hit the water.

SPLASH!!

He sputtered to the surface.

That bastard had tossed him!

Zercy laughed. Like big time. Threw his head back and everything.

Alec fought a laugh of his own but the mirth in Zercy's robust timbre made it really hard to stay straight-faced. He cursed and dove at the guy, but instead of taking him down, just jostled the shit out of his own damn self when they connected.

Brick fucking wall.

Zercy laughed even harder, then palmed the top of Alec's head and dunked him under.

Alec launched right back out, wholly laughing through a battle cry, and snapped both arms securely around Zercy's head. Jerking all his weight, he fought to tip the giant over, but only managed to muss up Zercy's dreads.

"Goddamnit!" he barked, still laughing as he grappled. "What are you made of?" *Grunt.* "Titanium?" *Grunt.* "You're not natural!"

Zercy cracked up harder. His boisterous chuffs drugged Alec's soul. When he quieted, he pulled Alec down his big wet body. Face to face— with Alec still panting from exertion—Zercy grinned and hugged him close. "Funny moyo."

Alec chuckled. "Feeling kinda *ineffectual* at the moment."

Zercy snickered and claimed his mouth. Slowly sank them beneath the surface. Then continued to kiss Alec senseless under the water.

* * *

Sometime later they finally finished, with both males thoroughly washing the other. Not that Zercy hadn't already done as much just hours earlier, meticulously tongue-bathing Alec's body from head to toe, but dirt still clung to Zercy everywhere, giving testament to his mad dash through the jungle: dried mud and gashes all over his midnight purple body, tiny twigs and leaves tangled in his dreads. So Alec made sure to clean him to the best of his ability.

After drying off and getting dressed, then packing up their scant gear, they climbed aboard one of the zahka and headed out. It was nice, not having to walk for once. And those big beasts were comfortable. Or maybe Alec just liked Zercy nestled against his back.

They traveled with Zercy's trackers, some traveling in front of them, some behind. None too close though, which was cool. It gave them privacy. To talk mostly, but also to fool around. With only a half dozen hours behind them, Zercy had already given Alec two secretive hand jobs and even taken him once from behind.

God, it'd been hot, having to be all covert, so as not to give away what they were doing. No wonder Zercy had insisted Alec wear one of his tunics instead of the cargo shorts. Easy access around back. Just some fabric draped over a loinstrap. To any wondering eyes, Alec would've looked like he was napping, lying forward against the huge nape of their zahka. And Zercy, sitting upright, crotch snugly pressed to Alec's ass, probably looked to be riding along normally.

Alec shivered, reminiscing as they rounded a mammoth bush, the day already half gone with much ground left to cover. Not that they were in a hurry, or even moving at a rushed pace at all. In fact, for the most part, they'd been taking it easy, chilling on the back of their lumbering beast.

Nevertheless, it still felt like they'd been traveling for ages, which made Alec wonder about something. Turning his head, he peered over his shoulder. Before he could speak though, Zercy growled and bit his ear.

Alec grinned and tugged it free. "Tell me something, Krie. This is a pretty long trek. And now that I think about it, running nonstop or not, you still caught up to us crazy fast last night. I mean, it's not like you were starting at the castle. You'd been en route since morning for that council meeting you had to attend. So how'd you do it? Hell, how'd you even find out to begin with? It's not like Krie have long-range communication technology."

Zercy nuzzled the back of Alec's head. Pulled him closer against his body. "When the enemy arrived, and my guards ascertained all that had happened, they immediately dispatched messengers on our fastest zahka."

"And when they found you?"

"They told me what had happened, that many had fallen. Kellim... Mannix... Even one of your scientists... And that the rest of you had managed to escape."

Alec's chest tightened at the memory. It'd all been so chaotic. "How—" He cleared his throat, afraid to ask but needing to know. "How is Kellim? Is he... okay?"

Zercy's exhale sounded worried. "Sirus is doing all that he can."

Alec's heart sank. Oh, God. That did not sound very promising. Sirus may be a genius, but he only had so much to work with. It wasn't like Krie had kickass medical equipment. Even Sasha's travel gear was far superior.

"And Mannix?" he muttered brusquely.

Zercy loosed a low growl. "I believe he is stable. When he recovers, he will be dealt with. As will the guard that abetted him. Setch told me what happened. I vow to you, *Alick...* I vow to you they will not go unpunished."

Alec eased, not realizing his muscles had gone tense. Deep down, he'd known Zercy would exact proper justice. He was a stand-up guy like that and always had been. But to hear him actually say it, that they would pay for their crimes? Yeah, that was definitely reassuring.

He exhaled quietly. "So you turned around? Went back to the castle?"

"Tah. I needed to see for myself... Because a part of me could not believe it. They were wrong. About you. You would never have left. You promised me you would be there when I returned... But when I got there... and saw with my own eyes that you were gone..."

Alec's gut clenched at his tone.

Zercy's lips brushed the back of his head. "My heart... It broke in two..." A low rumble arose. "The beast within broke free... And all turned to madness."

Alec swallowed back a groan. That distant howl he'd heard... It'd been Zercy. Somehow, he knew with utter certainty. He nodded a little. Cleared his throat again. "So, you left. Grabbed your trackers and came after us."

"Tah." The king's arms tightened like steel bands around his torso.

"I'm sorry," Alec murmured. "I didn't mean to make you think about that again."

Zercy chuckled, his timbre dark. "It has yet to leave my mind. I have calmed but I have not forgotten. I am King of the gods damned Krie. Their crimes against me are punishable by death. Until I have my retribution, *I will never forget.*"

Alec's blood chilled at his words. Zercy wanted his revenge. Which meant countless Nirans were going to pay for helping Alec's team.

"Wait. No. Listen to me." He twisted in Zercy's arms. "What happened back there? That was a *rescue* mission."

Zercy barked a laugh. "That was Gesh being the unethical scavenger he is. *Stealing* his little pet back after *selling* him for *profit.*"

Alec scowled. "Fuck Gesh. That was about so much more than him. That was males who had no ties, no obligations to each other whatsoever, banding together to do *the right thing.*"

Zercy grunted tersely. "How is coming onto my land, attacking my guards, then stealing what is mine *the right thing?*"

Alec pursed his lips. "Have you forgotten that you were technically holding us prisoner? Because that right there plays a very big role in your answer."

Zercy scoffed. "I was holding no one prisoner. I bought you. Which makes you rightfully my possessions. Possessions whom, by the way, I treated like royals."

"You were keeping us against our will."

Zercy eyed him, looking hurt. "You did not want to be with me?"

Alec clenched his jaw in frustration. "Fine. Not me, but my teammates."

Zercy's expression eased. Still, he glanced away and frowned. "I would have let them go. You know this. I told you such before. Once your people came and could provide them proper protection, I would release them."

Alec reflected back to the events of the last couple of days. "So what you're saying is... if our rescue team had come and asked you personally to let us go, you would've said yes? Just like that?"

"Tah."

Alec narrowed his eyes, remembering how Gesh had come to speak with Zercy recently. Their talk hadn't gone well, and Zercy never said what Gesh had wanted. But low and behold, just a few days later, Gesh showed back up again with Garret's team. Risking his life, his whole pack, to help free not just Noah, but *all* of Alec's men. Clearly, Gesh had been speaking to Zercy on the rescue team's behalf. Asking for him to let their people go. Made sense. If Garret knew the king was holding humans captive, then going to speak to Zercy himself was too big a risk. He could easily have taken Garret and his men prisoner, too.

Alec shook his head. "But isn't that why Gesh came here, to talk to you for the rescue team? Asking on their behalf to let us go?"

"Mah," Zercy grunted. "He spoke nothing of humans. Wanted only to discuss matters of the Tohrí." Typically, he'd growl that last word with venom, but this time, curiously, he'd merely muttered it.

Either way, Alec was surprised. Hadn't seen that coming at all. He turned and met Zercy's eyes. "He came to talk about the *Tohrí*?"

"Tah. Those in my dungeon. Said he suspected they might be innocent. That he wanted to discuss the possibility of their release."

Alec's mouth dropped open. Gesh hadn't been speaking on behalf of Garret. He'd been speaking on behalf of freaking *Airis*. But why? He didn't like the guy at all. Considered them traitors just like Zercy did.

And then it dawned. It was the only way to get them to help. Gesh desperately wanted his meesha back but hadn't been able to bag Garret's team. And in order for the only other alternative to work—the physical extraction of Alec's team—they needed more numbers. Which Airis had. And conveniently, he'd needed Gesh's help, too. To get his own people back. So, he'd agreed to offer his men's help in exchange for a mediator.

Finally, the motives of all three factions were clear.

And all objectives were ultimately met—minus the Tohrí's.

Which disconcerted Alec since he suspected the race wasn't to blame after all. He didn't want to go back to a castle where, far beneath his feet, innocent males were being kept as slaves.

Alec frowned and met Zercy's eyes. "You can't keep them. Not if they're innocent."

Zercy exhaled and dropped his gaze. Shook his head in agitation. "Their prince poisoned our lifeline. They are guilty by association."

"Leo…" Alec murmured. Zercy was better than that and they both knew it.

Zercy scowled and furrowed his brows. Looked back up at Alec and growled. "If not them, then who? Whom do I hold accountable?"

Alec could feel his raw anxiousness. He didn't want to punish innocent people, either.

"For now, how 'bout Talik." Alec gripped Zercy's hand. "The asshole who committed the actual crime."

Zercy glanced at Alec's fingers settled soothingly over his own, then peered back into Alec's eyes. "But what of Nira?" he rasped. "The mineral…"

Alec squared his shoulders. Held his gaze. "I'll sustain her. All by myself. It's possible now, with the advancements. Even without my help, she's good for months."

Zercy turned his hand under Alec's and gripped it tightly. Clenched his jaw and peered into the distance. "I will think on it, *Alick*. Right now I am still too raw. Still too angry with the Tohrí's latest transgression."

Fair enough, Alec supposed. For now.

Nodding, he faced forward again and nestled himself back into Zercy's chest.

Zercy held him but didn't speak again for a long unsettled moment. His restless, churning mind was almost palpable.

Finally, he nuzzled Alec's neck. Rumbled softly against his skin. "You have a good soul, *Alick*. Will make a very fine prince."

A smile curved Alec's lips. Reaching back, he stroked Zercy' ear. "Hope so, 'cause currently all I'm trained in is 'very fine captain'."

Zercy chuffed and nuzzled him more. "Funny moyo."

* * *

Their convoy finally reached its destination early evening, pausing before the gates of Castle Múnrahki. The market they'd just passed through had been bustling, but quickly quieted the instant Zercy and company had been spotted. All creatures big and small dropping down to one knee, rapt eyes drinking in the king, then lingering on Alec.

They'd been curious. It was written all over their faces. Why this creature not of their world—the team's origins had traveled—sat so snugly between their king's thighs, held so possessively in their king's arms after, no doubt, a very unsettling evening prior. If Alec had heard Zercy's pained roar, they most certainly had, too. And yet, there Zercy sat, calm and collected with his Alec, riding atop a zahka down the thoroughfare.

Several guards pushed open the castle's gates, and just like that, they were headed into the courtyard. Alec eyed the huge front doors, unable to keep his smile at bay. He was home. Truly home. Where he belonged.

Again, they came to a stop, this time at the castle's large stone steps. Alec dismounted first, with a guard helping him down. Those zahka were big motherfuckers. Zercy dropped down next, gave the guards a brisk nod, then took Alec's hand and headed up the stairs.

They'd only made it a couple of steps before the huge doors started to part. Without warning, Sirus tore through the opening.

"Sire!" his shouted, charging toward them with his aides.

Alec tensed. His tone sounded urgent. His eyes too big.

Zercy stilled on the stairs, visibly bracing as Sirus neared, as if concerned the Kríe might plow right freaking into them. He was definitely moving fast enough. Alec gripped Zercy's hand and braced, too.

Luckily, Sirus managed to slam on the brakes in time. Barely though, wobbling to stop just two steps shy.

"Sire!" he panted. Jesus. Had he sprinted there from his workshop? "You must—" He gestured wildly. "You must come *now!*"

"What is it?" Zercy snapped. The ardent greeting had clearly agitated him.

"I—I cannot—" he stammered, shaking his head. "Please—Please hurry—You must come!"

Alec stiffened, spotting tears in the frantic Kríe's eyes. Oh, God. What had happened? Was Kellim dying? On his last breaths? Was Setch coming unhinged? Going postal inside the castle?

Heart rate spiking, he clutched Zercy's hand. "*Come on!* Let's go!"

Zercy snarled but complied, quickly passing Alec on the steps, his powerful legs impossible to compete with. Sirus loosed a sound of relief and easily dashed past Alec too, leading the way with his aides toward the huge entrance.

They tore into the grand foyer and veered to the right, then hauled ass down the castle's eastside corridor. Specifically, the one that led directly to the infirmary, where injured and dying Kríe were presumably kept. Alec's chest squeezed anxiously. Please let Kellim be okay.

But as they neared the halfway point, Sirus cut into the central corridor instead of continuing on farther toward the clinic. Alec swapped looks with Zercy as they ran past the kitchen, heading toward only God knew fucking where. And then he spotted them, Fek and Bordi, the courtyard guards, moving out of Sirus' way and opening the doors.

Wait, what? They were going to the—Alec's heart locked up tight. All blood drained from his head.

Nira.

Oh, God.

What was wrong with Nira?

Zercy shot him a look of pure dread, his grip on Alec's hand vising anxiously.

Sirus dashed inside with his aides. Alec and Zercy followed suit.

Instantly, Alec's eyes shot to Nira. From what he could tell, she looked okay. Wasn't withering. Or graying. In fact, he detected a subtle glow. Some delicate ethereal aura he'd never noticed before.

They pulled to stop. Alec looked at his mate, but Zercy was wholly focused on the tree. He'd sensed her new air too and looked pretty baffled.

"Denza!" Sirus crowed. *Look!* He dropped to his knees. In front of him, tiny blossoms peeked through the grass. "Life! Flowers *of life*, Sire!" He turned to his king. Tears trickled from the corners of his eyes. "She has conceived," he laughed, voice wobbling. "She is with child."

Alec's mouth dropped open, noting the spot where the flowers were growing. Zercy's jaw went slack as well. Because, yeah, that's where they'd planted their little pea pod.

Zercy's wide eyes slid to Alec's. Alec gaped right back at him.

"It is yours! I am certain!" Sirus leapt back up to his feet. He grinned from ear to ear. "Ask how I know!"

Zercy blinked, still half in a stupor, and turned back to Sirus. "How?" he rasped hoarsely. "How... How do you know?"

"Besides the obvious, that no other couple is permitted to mate in this sanctum..." He gazed up at Nira, gold eyes bright with elation. "When I first came to medicate her... Before I ever noticed the flowers... I was taken by her appearance... This new gentle radiance... It is faint," he looked at Zercy, "but surely you see it."

Zercy nodded, already back to staring raptly at the tree. "Tah, I see it," he murmured. "Celestial... like the heavens... Like she is communing with the stars..."

"Tah!" Sirus beamed. "Such a beautiful sign! So, I went to her, admittedly afraid to hope, and took a sample from one of her roots. Alec's scientists developed the method many moons ago, a way to ascertain if sickness still remains. I check often, but always the poison lingers." He shook his head, grinning widely. "Not this day though, Sire. Not this day. It is gone!" He threw up his hands. "She is healed!"

Again, Zercy and Alec swapped wide-eyed glances.

Alec couldn't believe it.

"I was ecstatic! But also confused! We had done nothing different. Why had she suddenly been purged? What had changed? I gazed at her, mystified. And then I saw it!" Sirus dropped back to his knees and gestured to an exposed root on the ground, winding elegantly past the tiny batch of flowers. "Denza!" *Look!* He pointed to its smooth, graceful cords. "Her veins have always been purple, the color of Kríe, but now one is different..." He slid his gaze to Alec. "Now one is the very distinct color of *human*."

Alec's mouth fell back open.

Zercy rumbled soft and low, then pulled Alec with him for a closer look. Sure enough, there it was. They stared at it, bewildered. A sleek, slender floral vein in the shade of Alec's flesh, weaving harmoniously up the root toward Nira's trunk.

"Ságe and Krye," Zercy breathed.

Sirus barked a jubilant laugh. "Indeed, Sire! No greater proof! The young she carries is yours and Alec's! The kingdom's first conception in over a year! A child of both Nira and the stars!"

Alec's heart pounded like a drum. A delirious drum on drugs. Nira was pregnant? With their baby?

Holy shit.

As much as he'd romanticized the idea of such a thing, he'd never actually thought that it was possible. And not just because of the obstacle of Nira's sickness. He and Zercy were different everything; different genera, different species, with undoubtedly different chromosomes. Which meant, according to basic biology, procreation was impossible.

Evidently, the big bad cosmos begged to differ.

"*Alick*," Zercy rasped, his voice unsteady. "*Alick*, denza..."

Alec followed the king's gaze as Zercy drew his eyes upward, tracking the light-beige vine up Nira's trunk. It disappeared into the canopy, but then to Alec's utter wonderment, he discovered something incredible amidst the branches. Brand-new, light-beige leaves sprouting to life beside the purple ones.

Air rushed from his lungs.

Zercy choked on a chuff. Then loosed a hardier chuckle. Then out of nowhere, just started laughing. All deep and hearty, the sound coursing straight to Alec's soul.

"*Alick!*" He beamed radiantly. "She bears our child!"

"And your child," Sirus added, "has saved her from death."

Both Alec and Zercy looked at him.

Sirus' golden eyes gleamed. "The entirety of Alec's essence, not just his seed, has been the answer. Once it infused with that of Nira's, they became as one the antidote. The very cure we have been seeking all these moons. They have destroyed it, the black poison. It is no more."

Zercy looked back at Alec. Alec met his gaze, floored.

There were no words in existence for this emotion.

Tears welled in Zercy's eyes. He swallowed and shook his head. "We have done it," he murmured roughly. "We have beaten cruel fate. I do not know how to process this kind of happiness."

Neither did Alec. It was too powerful.

His stupid chin trembled. Wiping his lashes, Alec nodded, then shoved into Zercy's arms and closed his eyes. Zercy growled and hugged him tight, lifting Alec up to nuzzle his neck. Alec laughed and buried his face in Zercy's dreads. Even now, he could feel it, their bond going strong as their two hearts thumped as one in perfect time.

Alec smiled and opened his eyes, absently peering over Zercy's shoulder, then stilled in sheer surprise at what he saw. Kellim, leaning heavily against his brother in the doorway, wrapped in bandages and looking weak, but grinning wide.

Alec's insides did a backflip.

Kellim was okay.

Closing his eyes again, he melted back into the moment, his heart and mind still spinning from Sirus' news. It felt so surreal. So hard to believe. That such an amazing gift could be his.

Smiling, he kissed Zercy's ear. "Looks like you got your heir after all."

"*Our* heir," Zercy rumbled. "Yours and mine, *Alick*. Ours." He eased back and met Alec's gaze, his eyes bright. "All is right now. All is perfect. I can feel it. Can you feel it?"

"Yeah," Alec chuckled, touching their brows. "I can feel it."

Nothing had ever felt so perfect in all his life.

THE NIRA CHRONICLES GLOSSARY

NIRA [**neer**-*uh*] 4th planet of the binary star system, Siri. Smaller than Earth, rotating at half the speed.

CHARACTERS

- HUMAN -

SCIENCE & EXPLORATION TEAM
Alec Hamlin – Pilot and first captain. Light brown hair, blue-green eyes.
Zaden – Co-pilot. Black hair. Dark brown eyes.
Chet – Military escort. Buff, covered in ink. Brown crewcut. Gray eyes.
Noah – Astrobiologist. Shoulder-length sandy blond hair, brown eyes.
Bailey – Astrobiologist. Curly, dark brown hair. Hazel eyes.
Jamis – Astrobiologist. Shaggy, dark brown hair. Green-gray eyes.

SEARCH & RESCUE TEAM
Garret Scott – Pilot and first captain. Dark blond, blue-gray eyes.
Kegan – Co-pilot. Ginger hair, scruffy five o'clock shadow. Green-gold eyes.
Eli – Military escort. Buff. Brown, spikey crewcut, brown eyes. Covered in tattoos.
Helix – Military escort. Buff. Black, spikey crewcut, dark brown eyes. Covered in tattoos.
Paris – Expert tracker. Shoulder-length black hair, blue eyes.
Sasha – Medic. Shoulder-length light blond hair, blue eyes.

- KRÍE -

MÚNRAHKI CASTLE [moon-**rah**-kee]

Zercy [**zur**-cee] King of the Kríe
Sirus [**seer**-*uh* s] Head scientist, physician
Kellim [**kel**-*uh* m] Royal guard
Setch [sech] Royal guard
Mannix [**man**-iks] Royal guard
Lotis [**loh**-t*uh* s] Castle artisan
Ryze [rahyz] Castle pedagogue
Bordi [**bohrd**-ee], Fek [fek] Courtyard guards
Roz [rawz], Mundo [**moon**-doh], Fel [fel] Battle trackers

JUNGLE PACK MATES

Gesh [gesh] Pack leader. Noah's lover.
Roni [**roh**-nee] Pack mate, Gesh's 'right-hand.' Chet's sensuous adversary.
Miros [**mir**-dohs] Pack mate. Alec's first-time male lover.
Naydo [**ney**-toh] Pack mate. Zaden's first-time male lover.
Filli & Fin [**fil**-ee] [fin] Twin pack mates. Bailey and Jamis' first-time male lovers.
Beng – Pack mate

- TOHRÍ -
Airis [**air**-is] Band leader
Kato [**key**-toh] Band mate and Airis' best friend
Jori, Lark [**johr**-ee] [lahrk] Band mates
Talik [**tal**-ik] Malevolent Tohrí prince

NIRAN SPECIES

- INTELLIGENT -

Kríe [kree] Muscle-packed, 7+ ft. midnight-purple indigenes, weighing roughly 350 lbs. with golden eyes, black dreads, pointed ears, black horns, small black claws, and short fat fangs. Arrogant and domineering, originating from the Mighty Realm of the Kríe inside the Múnrahki Mountains.

Tohrí [**tohr**-ee] Lean, muscular, 6½+ ft. deeply-tanned indigenes, weighing roughly 275 lbs. with large brown/gold eyes, long, sleek white-blond hair, pointed ears, short, pale claws, small fangs, and glowing body marks. Frisky and lithe, originating from the plateau plains of the Land of the Tohrí.

Oonmaiyos [oon-**mahy**-*oh* s] Lean, athletic 6+ ft. pale, luminescent-skinned water indigenes, weighing roughly 225 lbs. with long sapphire/teal hair, fin-tipped ears, and big dark purple eyes. Playful and curious, originating from the aquatic realm of the Oonmaiyos.

Súrah [**soo**-rah] Lean, youthful-looking 6 ft. nymphs weighing roughly 200 lbs. with mulberry skin and jaguar spots along their arms and legs. Short, dark-gold, spiraled-nub horns, pointed ears, mohawk and tail of dark-gold dreads, and two sets of nipples. Impish and sensual, a syndicate of Súrah run a sex lair in Múnrahki castle.

- ANIMAL -

Bellacoy [**bell**-uh-coy] Flyers/ dragons

Dekdónni [dek-**dawn**-ee] Griffin/lynx-type flying creature.
Guardian/companions of the Tohrí. Kotchka: Airis' dekdónni.

Zahka [**zok**-ah] Big, black, beefy, and generally pretty friendly three-
toed hooved beasts ridden by the Kríe. Similar to buffalo in
appearance, but not as furry.

Tachi [**tah**-chee] Large, black, cobra/jaguar-type predators that hunt the
rainforest in packs. Contain venom that reduce their quarry to
flaccid prey.

Koosa [**koos**-*uh*] Large predator with spots similar to a jaguar. Zercy's
favorite prey. Alec's animal façade for the wrestling
tournament.

Dembra [**demb**-*ruh*] Large predator with stripes like a primordial tiger.
Chet's animal façade for the wrestling tournament.

Kygo [**kahy**-goh] Large predator with leopard spots in wicked patterns.
Zaden's animal façade for the wrestling tournament.

Tegmai [**teg**-mahy] Large predator with mean zebra stripes. Jamis'
animal façade for the wrestling tournament.

Belshay [**bel**-shey] Large sea creature predator with blazing scales.
Bailey's animal façade for the wrestling tournament.

Fekni [**fek**-nee] Large predator with ferocious angular blotches similar to
a giraffe. Noah's animal façade for the wrestling tournament.

KRÍE LANGUAGE COMPILATION

Aussa – To go
Bahka root – Thin sucking root reed
Bayo – Pet
Beesha – Greetings
Bellacoy – Flyers/ dragons
Bellah – Good
Besh – Bad
Bibéhn – Fast
Botch – Wait
Bukah – Pleasing
Centiclees – Multi-tentacle dygon that lie dormant until activated. One
    of these is kept as a pet beneath Zercy's bed.
Chay – Lot/ bunch
Dedók – Kill/ death/ die
Del`ahtchay – Delicious
Deletta – To see
Denza – Look
D'ish – Now
Dóonda – Fight
Dydum – Large river that leads from The Mighty Realm of the Kríe
    realm to The Land of the Tohrí.
Dygon genus – Plant species with a comparable sentience to insects
Eenta – Smart
Eetay – Soon
En – And
Enday – Pleasure
Enyids – Aquatic plants of the *dygon* genus whose silky-soft, flexible,
    waterproof skin detains their prey.
Esh – Kríe sound of disapproval
Et – That
Feyah - Cold
Gai – Fruit
Genji – Glad

Genza – Tree in the jungle whose scent reminds Zercy of Alec's. Smoky-warm and sweet.

Gonja – Take them.

Kahtcha – Warm beverage

Kai – Very

Keensay – Alright/ okay

Kensa – Warrior

Kerra – Relax

Key'kai – Very, very

Kirah nectar – Promotes virility, accelerates seed production

Kü – But

Kulaí – A slippery blend of oil and nectar. Used for oil wrestling.

Kuntah – Entertaining

Reesa – Water

Mah – No

Mahn – Not

Mahneenta – Stupid

May – Me

Meesha – Precious one

Móonday – Do not fear

Moonsah – More

Móotah – Do not like

Moyos – Creatures

Myah – My

Nenya – Come

Ocha – Other

Ochay – Funny

Óondah – To release/ To spill

Otah – One

Otahtah – One at a time

Racha – Stay

Reckay – I need

Reesa – Water

Reeka – Give

Reesha – Will not harm

Rhya – To fuck

Ruka – Plant whose vine constricts things it makes contact with

Senna`sohnsay – Fruit of unrelenting fire

Shawní – Trees/ forest

Shay – Us

Suki – Plant that channels electrical current through its vines

T'– The

Tacha – Quickly/ hurry

Tah – Yes

Tai – Now

Tay – You

Teag – The unit of weight equal to three pounds.

Terah – The unit of length equal to slightly smaller than an inch.

Tibbi – Chittering, energetic critters the size of gerbils that look like tiny, blue, wingless bats.

Tin `– His

`tine – more so (bibéhn vs bibéhn`tine = fast vs faster)

Titus – Rocky mountain region where Gesh's pack and Alec's team decide to take refuge.

Tukah – Hungry

Tuga – To get

Turro – Teacher

Vai – View

Way – All of you

Zenki – Spice canes to stir in beverages to give the flesh a little happy tickle

"T`tegmai bibéhn… kü tin`turro bibéhn`tine." – "The tegmai is fast, but his teacher is faster."

TOHRÍ LANGUAGE TIDBITS

Etay – Stop

Leí – Yes

Nennáy – Assist

Nún – No

Pellay – Good

Seekesáy – Greetings

Súsa – Come

KORA KNIGHT

Born and raised in the Northern Virginia, Kora has always loved to read, but it wasn't until her preteen years that she discovered her deep-seated love for writing. With published literary teachers and play writers in the family tree, that probably shouldn't have come as a surprise. Starting with her involvement in social book forums, she then tried her hand at literary role playing which, in turn, led to her becoming a fervent online independent writer. Since then, she's endeavored to share with the world her impassioned stories of love, adventure and sensual wonderment, her current and most prominent delight being that of m/m erotic romance.

* * *

For fun insights into her stories and characters, including visual and audio muses, as well as glossaries and deleted scenes, visit her website at:

http://www.koraknight.com

You can also find Kora interacting regularly with readers at these social media sites:

https://www.facebook.com/authorkoraknight/
https://www.instagram.com/koraknight/
https://twitter.com/KoraKnight_Auth
https://koraknight.tumblr.com/

Printed in Great Britain
by Amazon

72582082R00322